Mark Billingham has twice won the Theakston's Old Peculier Award for Best Novel of the Year, most recently for *Death Message*, as well as the 2003 Sherlock Award as the creator of the Best Detective created by a British writer. Each of the novels featuring Detective Inspector Tom Thorne have been a *Sunday Times* bestseller, and *Sleepyhead* and *Scaredy Cat* were made into a hit series on Sky 1 starring David Morrissey as Thorne. Mark lives in north London with his wife and two children.

Also by Mark Billingham

MARK BILLINGHAM
OMNIBUS

Lazybones
The Burning Girl

sphere

SPHERE

This omnibus edition first published in Great Britain in 2010 by Sphere
Reprinted 2011

Copyright © Mark Billingham 2010

Previously published separately:
Lazybones first published in Great Britain in 2003 by Little, Brown
Paperback edition published by Time Warner Paperbacks in 2004
Reprinted by Time Warner Books in 2005, 2006
Reprinted by Sphere in 2007, 2008 (twice), 2009
Copyright © Mark Billingham 2003
The Burning Girl first published in Great Britain in 2004 by Little, Brown
Paperback edition published by Time Warner Paperbacks in 2005
Reprinted 2005 (twice), 2006
Reprinted by Sphere in 2007, 2008 (twice), 2009
Copyright © Mark Billingham 2004

'Lyrics from 'Bigmouth Strikes Again' (*The Burning Girl*) reproduced
by kind permission of Morrissey and Sanctuary Records.

The moral right of the author has been asserted.

A CIP catalogue record for this book
is available from the British Library.

ISBN 978-0-7515-4451-0

Printed and bound in Great Britain by
Clays Ltd, St Ives plc

Sphere
An imprint of
Little, Brown Book Group
100 Victoria Embankment
London EC4Y 0DY

An Hachette UK Company
www.hachette.co.uk

www.littlebrown.co.uk

LAZYBONES

For
Pat and Tony Thompson
&
Jeff and Pam Billingham

ACKNOWLEDGEMENTS

Thanks are due to those people who helped this particular Lazybones get this one done . . .

DI Neil Hibberd of the Serious Crime Group (again) for his insight, for fighting off the desire to sleep and for providing the usual invaluable advice.

Victoria Jones, for answering a thousand stupid questions, and, ironically, opening the right doors.

The Governor, staff and inmates of HMP Birmingham.

Sarah Kennedy, for kind words, very early, where the pictures are best.

Wendy Burns – Supervising Social Worker (Fostering) – and Louise Spanner – Family Placement Panel Administrator, at Essex Social Services.

And of course . . . Hilary Hale, Sarah Lutyens, Susannah Godman, Mike and Alice Gunn, Paul Thorne, Wendy Lee and Peter Cocks.

And my wife, Claire. I still demand a recount . . .

*For one night or the other night, will come the Gardener
in white, and gathered flowers are dead . . .*

James Elroy Flecker, *Golden Journey to Samarkand*

PROLOGUE

13 March

Dearest Dougie,

I'm sorry about this being another typed letter, but as I explained before, it's difficult for me to write to you from home, so I do it at work when the boss isn't looking, or in my lunch hour (like today!) or whatever. So, sorry if it seems a bit formal. Trust me, when I'm writing to you, the last thing I'm feeling is formal!

I hope things with you are OK and even if they're not brilliant, I hope that my letters are making you feel a bit better. I like to dream that you look forward to them and that you think of me sitting here, thinking about you. At least you have the pictures now (did you like them?), so you don't have to use your imagination too much ... (wicked grin!)

I know that it's really horrible in there but you must believe that things will get better. One day you will be out, with a bright future. Is it silly of me to hope that perhaps I can play a part in that future? I know that you are in there when you should not be. I know that you being in that place is unjust!!

I should sign off now, because I want to get this in the post before the lunch hour is over and I haven't had anything to eat yet. Writing to you, feeling near to you, is more important than a cheese sarnie anyway (she sighs!).

I will write again soon, Dougie, maybe with another picture. Do you put them on the wall? I don't even know if you have a cell all to yourself or not. If not, I hope whoever you are sharing with is nice. They are very lucky!!

It will all be over soon and when you are out of there, who knows, perhaps we can finally get together. I'm sure the wait will have been worth it.

Please look after yourself, Dougie. Hope you're thinking about me.

Yours, VERY frustrated ...

PART ONE

BIRTHS, MARRIAGES AND DEATHS

10 AUGUST, 1976

He inched himself towards the edge, each tightening of the sphincter muscle moving him a little further across the narrow breadth of the banister's polished surface. He twisted his wrists, wrapping the towel once more tightly around them. Not giving himself the get-out, knowing his body would look for it. Knowing he would instinctively try to free himself.

His heels bounced rhythmically against the banister spindles below him. The blue tow rope that he'd found at the back of the garage was itchy against his neck. He smiled to himself. Scratching it, even if he could, would have been stupid. Like dabbing at the skin with disinfectant before slipping in the needle to administer a lethal injection.

He closed his eyes, bowed his head, and let his weight tip him forward and over and down.

It felt as if the jolt might take his head off, but it was not even enough to break a bone. There hadn't been time to do the maths, to set weight against height. Even if there had been, he wasn't sure he'd have known what the relationship between them was. He remembered reading somewhere that the proper hangmen, the Pierrepoints or whoever, could do the calculation, could figure out the necessary drop, based on nothing more than shaking the condemned man's hand.

Pleased to meet you – about twelve feet, I reckon . . .

He clenched his teeth against the pain in his back. The skin had been taken off his spine by the edge of the stair rail as he'd dropped. He could feel warm blood trickling down his chin and he realised that he'd bitten through his tongue. He could smell the motor oil on the rope.

He thought about the woman, in bed, not ten feet away.

It would have been lovely to have seen her face when she found him. Her liar's mouth falling open as she reached up to stop his body swinging. That would have been perfect, but of course he would never see it. And she would never find him.

Somebody else would find both of them.

He couldn't help but wonder what the authorities would make of it all. What the newspapers would say. Their names would be spoken, would be whispered again in certain offices and living rooms. His name, the one he'd given her, would echo around a courtroom as it had done so often before, dragged through the mud and the filth that she'd spread before her like an oil slick. This time they themselves would be mercifully absent as others talked about them, about the tragedy, about the balance of their minds being disturbed. It was hard to argue with that, now, this very moment. Him waiting to die, and her upstairs, thirty minutes ahead of him, the blood already soaking deep into their mushroom-coloured bedroom carpet.

She had disturbed both their minds. She had asked for everything she'd got.

Half an hour before, her hands reaching to protect herself.

Eight months before that, her hands reaching, her legs spread, on the floor of that stockroom.

She'd asked for everything . . .

He gagged, spluttering blood, sensing a shadow preparing to descend, feeling his life beginning, thankfully, to slip away. How long had it been now? Two minutes? Five? He pushed his feet down towards the floor, willing his weight to do its work quickly.

He heard a noise like a creak and then a small hum of amazement. He opened his eyes.

He was facing away from the front door, looking back at the staircase. He shifted his shoulders violently, trying to create enough momentum to make himself turn. As he spun slowly around, seconds from death, he found himself staring down, through bloodied and bulging retinas, into the flawless brown eyes of a child.

ONE

The look was slightly spoiled by the training shoes.

The man with the mullet haircut and the sweaty top lip was wearing a smart blue suit, doubtless acquired for the occasion, but he'd let himself down with the bright white Nike Airs. They squeaked on the gymnasium floor as his feet shifted nervously underneath the table.

'I'm sorry,' he said. 'I'm really, really, sorry.'

An elderly couple sat at the table opposite him. The man's back was ramrod straight, his milky-blue eyes never leaving those of the man in the suit. The old woman next to the old man clutched at his hand. Her eyes, unlike those of her husband, looked anywhere but at those of the young man who, the last time he'd been this close to them, had been tying them up in their own home.

The trembling was starting around the centre of Darren Ellis's meticulously shaved chin. His voice wobbled a little. 'If there was anything I could do to make it up to you, I would,' he said.

'There isn't,' the old man said.

'I can't take back what I did, but I do know how wrong it was. I know what I put you through.'

The old woman began to cry.

'How can you?' her husband said.

10

Darren Ellis began to cry.

On the last row of seats, his back against the gym wall-bars, sat a solid-looking man in a black leather jacket, forty or so, with dark eyes and hair that was greyer on one side than the other. He looked uncomfortable and a little confused. He turned to the man sitting next to him.

'This. Is. Bollocks,' Thorne said.

DCI Russell Brigstocke glared at him. There was a *shush* from a red-haired squaddie type a couple of rows in front. One of Ellis's supporters, by the look of him.

'Bollocks,' Thorne repeated.

The gymnasium at the Peel Centre would normally be full of eager recruits at this unearthly time on a Monday morning. It was, however, the largest space available for this 'Restorative Justice Conference', so the raw young constables were doing their press-ups and star jumps elsewhere. The floor of the gym had been covered with a green tarpaulin and fifty or so seats had been laid out. They were filled with supporters of both offender and victims, together with invited officers who, it was thought, would appreciate the opportunity to be brought up to speed with this latest initiative.

Becke House, where Thorne and Brigstocke were based, was part of the same complex. Half an hour earlier, on the five-minute walk across to the gym, Thorne had moaned without drawing breath.

'If it's an invitation, how come I'm not allowed to turn it down?'

'Shut up,' Brigstocke said. They were late and he was walking quickly, trying not to spill hot coffee from a polystyrene cup that was all but melting. Thorne lagged a step or two behind.

'Shit, I've forgotten the bit of paper, maybe they won't let me in.'

Brigstocke scowled, unamused.

'What if I'm not smart enough? There might be a dress code . . .'

'I'm not listening, Tom . . .'

Thorne shook his head, flicked out his foot at a stone like a sulky schoolboy. 'I'm just trying to get it straight. This piece of pondlife ties an old couple up with electrical flex, gives the old man a kick or two for good measure, breaking . . . how many ribs?'

'Three . . .'

'Three. Thanks. He pisses on their carpet, fucks off with their life savings, and now we're rushing across to see how sorry he is?'

'It's just a trial. They've been using RJCs in Australia and the results have been pretty bloody good. Re-offending rates have gone right down . . .'

'So, basically, they sit everybody down pre-sentence, and if they all agree that the guilty party is really *feeling* guilty, he gets to do a bit less time. That it?'

Brigstocke took a last, scalding slurp and dumped the half-full cup in a bin. 'It's not quite that simple.'

A week and a bit into a steaming June, but the day was still too new to have warmed up yet. Thorne shoved his hands deeper into the pockets of his leather jacket.

'No, but whoever thought it up is.'

In the gym, the audience watched as Darren Ellis moved balled-up fists from in front of his face to reveal moist, red eyes. Thorne looked around at those watching. Some looked sad and shook their heads. One or two were taking

12

notes. On the front row, members of Ellis's legal team passed pieces of paper between them.

'If I said that *I* felt like a victim, would you laugh?' Darren asked.

The old man looked calmly at him for fifteen seconds or more before answering flatly. 'I'd want to knock your teeth out.'

'Things aren't always that clear-cut,' Darren said.

The old man leaned across the table. The skin was tight around his mouth. 'I'll tell you what's clear-cut.' His eyes flicked towards his wife as he spoke. 'She hasn't slept since the night you came into our house. She wets the bed most of the time.' His voice dropped to a whisper. 'She's got so bloody thin . . .'

Something between a gulp and a gasp echoed around the gymnasium as Darren dropped his head into his hands and gave full vent to his emotions. A lawyer got to his feet. A senior detective stood up and started walking towards the table. It was time to take a break.

Thorne leaned across and whispered loudly to Brigstocke. 'He's very good. Where did he train? RADA?' This time, several of the faces that turned to look daggers at him belonged to senior officers . . .

Ten minutes later, and everybody was mingling in the foyer outside. There was a lot of nodding and hushed conversation. There was mineral water and biscuits.

'I'm supposed to write a report on this,' Brigstocke mumbled.

Thorne waved across the foyer to a couple of lads he knew from Team 6. 'Rather you than me.'

'I'm trying to decide on the right word to use, to describe the attitude of certain attending officers on my team. Obstructive? Insolent? You got any thoughts . . .?'

'I *think* that was one of the stupidest things I've ever seen. I can't believe people sat there and took it seriously and I don't care *what* the results were in sodding Australia. Actually, no, *not* stupid. It was obscene. All those silly bastards studying every expression on that little prick's face. How many tears? How big were they? How much shame?' Thorne took a swig of water, held it in his mouth for a few seconds, swallowed. 'Did you see *her* face? Did you look at the old woman's face?'

Brigstocke's mobile rang. He answered it quickly, but Thorne kept on talking anyway. 'Restorative Justice? For who? For that old man and his skeletal wife?'

Brigstocke shook his head angrily, turned away.

Thorne put his glass down on a window sill. He moved suddenly, pushing past several people as he walked quickly towards where he'd seen a group emerging from a door on the other side of the foyer.

Darren Ellis had taken his jacket and tie off. He was handcuffed, a detective on either side of him, their hands on his shoulders.

'Good show, Darren,' Thorne said. He raised his hands and started to clap.

Ellis stared, his mouth opening and closing, an uneasy expression that had definitely *not* been rehearsed. He looked for help to the officers on either side of him.

Thorne smiled. 'What do you do for an encore? Always best to finish on a song, I reckon . . .'

The officer to Ellis's left, a stick-thin article with dandruff on his brown polyester jacket, tried his best to look casually intimidating. 'Piss off, Thorne.'

Before Thorne had a chance to respond, his attention was caught by the figure of Russell Brigstocke marching purposefully across the room towards him. Thorne was hardly aware of the two detectives leading Ellis away in the other direction. The look on the DCI's face caused something to clench in his stomach.

'You want to restore some justice?' Brigstocke said. 'Now's your chance.' He pointed at Thorne with his mobile phone. 'This sounds like a good one . . .'

It was called a hotel. They also called MPs 'right', 'honourable' and 'gentlemen' . . .

The sign outside *said* 'Hotel', but Thorne knew full well that certain signs, in less salubrious parts of London, were not to be taken too literally. If they all meant exactly what they said, there would be a lot of frustrated businessmen sitting in saunas, waiting for hand-jobs they were never going to get.

The sign outside should have read 'Shithole'.

It was as basic as they came. The maroon carpet, once the finest offcut the warehouse had to offer, was now worn through in a number of places. The green of the rotting rubber underlay beneath matched the mould which snaked up the off-white Anaglypta below the window. A long-dead spider plant stood on the window ledge, caked in dust. Thorne pushed aside the grubby orange curtains, leaned against the ledge, and took in the breathtaking view of the traffic inching slowly past Paddington Station towards the Marylebone Road. Nearly eleven o'clock and still solid.

Thorne turned round and sucked in a breath. Opposite him in the doorway, DC Dave Holland stood chatting to a uniform – waiting, like Thorne, for the signal to step in and start. To sink both feet deep into the mire.

In different parts of the room, three Scene Of Crime Officers crouched and crawled – bagging and tagging and searching for the fibre, the grain that might convict. The life sentence hidden in a dustball. The truth lurking in detritus.

The pathologist, Phil Hendricks, leaned against a wall, muttering into the new, digital voice recorder he was so proud of. He glanced up at Thorne. A look that asked the usual questions. Are we up and running again? When is this going to get any easier? Why don't the two of us chuck in this shit and sit in a doorway for the rest of our lives drinking aftershave? Thorne, unable to provide any answers, looked away. In the corner nearest him, a fourth SOCO, whose bald head and bodysuit gave him the look of a giant baby, dusted the taps of the brown plastic sink with fingerprint powder.

It was, at least, a shithole with en suite facilities.

Altogether, seven of them in the room. Eight, if you counted the corpse.

Thorne's gaze was dragged reluctantly across to the chalk-white figure of the man on the bed. The body was nude and lay on the bare mattress, the spots of blood joining stains of less obvious origin on the threadbare and faded ticking. The hands were tied with a brown leather belt and pushed out in front of him as he lay, prostrate, his knees pulled up beneath him, his backside in the air. His head, which was covered in a black hood, was pressed down into the sagging mattress.

16

Thorne watched as Phil Hendricks moved along the bed, lifted the head and turned it. He slowly removed the hood. From behind, Thorne saw his friend's shoulders stiffen for an instant, heard the small, sharp intake of breath before he laid the head back down. As a SOCO moved across to take the hood and drop it into an exhibits bag, Thorne took a step forward so that he could see the face of the dead man clearly.

His eyes were closed, his nose small and slightly upturned. The side of the face was dotted with pinprick-size bloodspots. The mouth was a mask of dried gore, the lips ragged, the whole hideous mess criss-crossed with spittle strings. The stained, uneven teeth were bared and had gnawed through the bottom lip as the ligature had tightened around the neck.

Thorne guessed that the man was somewhere in his late thirties. It was just a guess.

From somewhere above them, Thorne became aware of a rumble suddenly dying – a boiler switching itself off. Stifling a yawn, he looked up, watched cobwebs dancing gracefully around the plaster ceiling rose. He wondered if the other residents would care too much about their morning hot water when they found out what had happened in Room Six.

Thorne took a pace towards the bed. Hendricks spoke without looking round.

'Bar the fact that he's dead, I know bugger all, so don't even ask. All right?'

'I'm fine. Thanks for asking, Phil, and how are you?'

'Right, I see. Like you only came over here for a fucking chinwag . . .?'

'You are *such* a miserable sod. What's wrong with exchanging a few pleasantries? Trying to make all this a bit easier?'

Hendricks said nothing.

Thorne leaned over to scratch at his ankle through the bodysuit. 'Phil . . .'

'I told you, I don't know. Look for yourself. It seems pretty obvious how he died, but it's not that simple. There's . . . other stuff gone on.'

'Right. Thanks . . .'

Hendricks moved back a little and nodded towards one of the SOCOs, who moved quickly towards the bed, picking up a small toolbox as he went. The officer knelt down and opened the box, revealing a display of dainty, shining instruments. He took out a small scalpel and leaned across, reaching towards the victim's neck.

Thorne watched as the SOCO pushed a plastic-covered finger down between the ligature and the neck, struggling to get any purchase. From where Thorne was standing, it looked like washing line, the sort of stuff you can get in any hardware shop. Smooth, blue plastic. He could see just how tightly it was biting into the dead man's neck. The officer took his scalpel and carefully cut away the line in such a way as to preserve the knot that was gathered at the back of the neck. This was, of course, basic procedure. Sensible and chilling.

They'd need it to compare with any others they might find.

Thorne glanced across at Dave Holland who raised his eyebrows and turned up his palms. *What's happening? How long?* Thorne shrugged. He'd been there more than an hour already. He and Holland had been over the room, taking notes, bagging a few things up, getting a feel of the scene. Now it was the technicians' turn and Thorne hated the wait. It might have made him feel better, were he able to put his impatience down to a desire to get stuck in. He wished he could say, honestly, that he was itching to begin doing his job, to kick off the process that might one day bring this man's killer to justice. As it was, he just wanted to do what had to be done quickly, and get out of that room.

He wanted to strip off the plastic suit, get in his car and drive away.

Actually, if he were being *really* honest with himself, he would have had to admit that only *part* of him wanted that. The other part was buzzing. The part that knew the difference between some murder scenes and others; that was able to *measure* these things. Thorne had seen the victims of enraged spouses and jealous lovers. He had stared at the bodies of business rivals and gangland grasses. He knew when he was looking at something out of the ordinary.

This was a significant murder scene. This was the work of a killer driven by something special, something spectacular.

The room stank of hatred and of rage. It also stank of pride.

Hendricks, as if reading Thorne's mind, turned to him, half smiling. 'Just another five minutes, OK? I'm not going to get anything else here . . .'

Thorne nodded. He looked at the dead man on the bed – the position of him, as if he were paying homage. Had it not been for the belt, for the livid red furrow that circled his neck, for the thin lines of blood that ran down the backs of his pale thighs, he might have been praying.

Thorne guessed that at the end, he probably had been.

The room was hot. Thorne raised an arm to rub a sore eye and felt the tickle as a drop of sweat slid down his ribs then took a sudden, sharp turn across his belly.

Down below, a frustrated driver leaned on his horn . . .

Thorne was not even aware that he'd closed his eyes and when he heard a phone ring, he snapped them open, convinced for a few wonderful moments that he'd woken suddenly from a bad dream.

He turned, a little disorientated, and saw Holland standing next to the bedside table. The phone was an off-white seventies model, the dial cracked, the grimy handset visibly jumping in its cradle. Thorne was now fully alert but he was still somewhat confused. Was this a call for them? Was it police business? Or was it possible that whoever was down at what passed for a reception desk had not been told what was happening and had put a caller through from the outside? Having met one or two of the staff, Thorne could well believe that even knowing exactly what had happened, they might still be dim enough to put a call through to the occupant of Room Six. If that was the case, it would certainly be a stroke of luck . . .

Thorne moved towards the ringing phone. The rest of the team stood frozen, watching him.

The victim's clothes – it had to be presumed they *were* the victim's – lay strewn about the floor nearby. Trousers – minus their belt – and underpants were next to the chair. Shirt, crumpled into a ball. One shoe under the bed, up near the headboard. The brown corduroy jacket, slung across the back of a chair next to the bed, had contained no personal items. No wallet, no bus tickets, no crinkled photographs. Nothing that might help identify the dead man . . .

Thorne did not know if the phone had already been dusted for fingerprints, and he had no time to check. He reached out to grab a plastic evidence bag from the fat, babyish SOCO and wrapped it around his hand. He held the hand up, wanting silence. He didn't need to ask.

He took a breath and picked up the receiver. 'Hello . . .?'

'Oh . . . hi.' A woman's voice.

Thorne locked eyes with Holland. 'Who did you want to speak to?' He was holding the phone an inch or so away from his ear and didn't hear the answer properly. 'Sorry, it's not a very good line, could you shout up?'

'Is that any good?'

'That's great.' Thorne tried to sound casual. 'Who do you want to speak to?'

'Oh . . . I'm not really sure, actually . . .'

Thorne looked at Holland again and shook his head. *Fuck.* It wasn't going to be that easy. 'Who am I talking to?'

'Sorry?'

'Who are you?'

There was a short pause before she spoke. The voice was suddenly a little tighter. Confident though, and refined. 'Listen, I don't want to sound rude, but it was somebody there who called *me*. I don't particularly want to give out . . .'

'This is Detective Inspector Thorne from the Serious Crime Group . . .'

A pause. Then: 'I thought I was calling a hotel . . .'

'You *have* called a hotel. Could you please give me your

name?' He looked across at Holland, puffed out his cheeks. Holland was poised, notebook in hand, looking utterly confused.

'You could be anybody,' the woman said.

'Listen, if it makes you happier, I can call you back. Better still, let me give you a number to call so you can check. Ask for DCI Russell Brigstocke. And I'll give you my mobile number . . .'

'Why do I need your mobile number if you're calling me back?'

The conversation was starting to get faintly ridiculous. Thorne thought he could detect a note of amusement, perhaps even flirtation, creeping into this woman's voice. Pleasing as this was on an otherwise grim morning, he wasn't really in the mood.

'Madam, the phone I'm speaking on, the phone you've called, is located at a crime scene and I need to know why you're calling.'

He got the message across. The woman, though suddenly sounding a little panicky, did as she was asked.

'It was on my answering machine. I got here, I got into work this morning, and checked my messages. This one was the first. The man who called left the name of the hotel and the room number for delivery . . .'

The man who called. Was that the man on the bed, or . . .?

'What was the message?'

'He was placing an order. Bloody funny time to be doing it, though. That was why I was a bit . . . cautious about calling. I thought it might be a joke, you know, kids messing about, but kids wouldn't give you the right address, would they?'

'Did he leave a name?'

'No, which is one of the reasons I'm calling. And to get a credit card number. I don't do cash on delivery . . .'

'What do you mean, *bloody funny time*?'

'The message was left at ten past three this morning. I bought one of those flashy machines that tells you the time, you know?'

Thorne pressed the mouthpiece to his chest, looked across at Hendricks. 'I know the time of death. A tenner says you don't get within half an hour either side . . .'

'Hello?'

Thorne put the phone back to his ear. 'Sorry, I was conferring with a colleague. Can I ask you to keep the tape from the machine, Miss . . .?'

'Eve Bloom.'

'You said something about placing an order?'

'Oh sorry, didn't I say? I'm a florist. He was ordering some flowers. That's why I was slightly freaked out, I suppose . . .'

'I don't understand. Freaked . . .?'

'Well, to be ordering what he was ordering in the middle of the night . . .'

'What exactly did the message say?'

'Hang on a minute . . .'

'No, just . . .'

She'd already gone. After a few seconds, Thorne heard the click of the button being hit and the noise of the tape rewinding. There was a pause and then a bang as she put the receiver down next to the machine.

'It's coming up,' she shouted.

Then a hiss as the tape began to play.

There was no discernible accent, no real emotion of any sort, in the voice. To Thorne, it sounded as if someone was trying hard to *sound* characterless, but there was a hint of something like amusement in the voice somewhere. In the voice of the man Thorne had to assume was responsible for the bound and bloodied corpse not three feet away from him.

The message began simply enough.

'I'd like to order a wreath . . .'

3 DECEMBER, 1975

He inched the Maxi forward until the bumper was almost touching the garage door before yanking up the handbrake and turning off the ignition.

He reached across for his briefcase, climbed out of the car, and nudged the door shut with his backside.

Not six o'clock yet and already dark. Cold, as well. He was going to have to start putting his vest on in the mornings.

As he walked towards the front door he began whistling it again, that bloody song he couldn't get out of his head. It was on the radio every minute of every day. What the hell was a 'silhouetto' anyway? Do the bloody fandango? The thing went on for hours as well. Weren't pop songs supposed to be short?

He shut the front door behind him and stood on the mat for a second, waiting for the smell of his dinner to hit him. He liked this moment every day, the one where he could pretend he was a character in one of those programmes on the TV. He stood and imagined that he was in the midwest of America somewhere and not stuck in a shitty little estuary suburb. He imagined that he was a rangy executive with a perfectly presented wife who would have a pot-roast in the oven and a cocktail waiting for him. Highballs or something they called them, didn't they?

It wasn't just his little joke, it was theirs. Their silly ritual. He would shout out and she would shout back, then they would sit down and eat the frozen crispy pancakes or maybe one of those curries out of a packet with too many raisins in.

'Honey, I'm home . . .'

There was no reply. He couldn't smell anything.

He dropped his briefcase by the hall table and walked towards the lounge. She probably hadn't had time today. Wouldn't have finished work until gone three and then she would have had shopping to do. There was only a fortnight until Christmas and there was loads of stuff still to get . . .

The look on her face stopped him dead.

She was sitting on the settee, wearing a powder-blue house-coat. Her legs were curled underneath her. Her hair was wet.

'You all right, love?'

She said nothing. As he took a step towards her, his shoe got tangled in something and he looked down and saw the dress.

'What's this doing . . .?'

He flicked it up and caught it, laughing, looking for a reaction. Then, letting the length of it drop from his fingers he saw the rip, waggled his fingers through the rent in the rayon.

'Christ, what have you done to this? Bloody hell, this was fifteen quid's worth . . .'

She looked up suddenly and stared at him as if he was mad. Trying not to make it obvious, he began looking around for an empty bottle, making an effort to keep a smile on his face.

'Have you been to work today, love?'

She moaned softly.

'What about school? You did pick up . . .?'

She nodded violently, her hair tumbling damp across her face. He heard the noise then from upstairs, the crash of a toy car or a pile of bricks coming from the loft they'd turned into a playroom.

He nodded, puffed out his cheeks, relieved.

'Listen, let's get you . . .'

He had to stop himself taking a step back as she stood up suddenly, her eyes wide and wet, folding herself over slowly, as if she were taking a bow.

He said her name then.

And his wife gathered up the hem of the powder-blue house-coat and raised it above her waist to show him the redness, the rawness and the darker blue of the bruising at the top of her legs . . .

TWO

Thorne lost his bet with Phil Hendricks.

He answered the phone barely four hours after they'd found the body and within a few seconds he was lobbing his half-eaten sandwich across the office, missing the bin by several feet. He chewed what was left in his mouth quickly, knowing that his appetite was about to disappear.

Hendricks was calling from Westminster mortuary. 'Pretty quick,' he said. He sounded extremely chipper. 'You've got to bloody admit . . .'

'Why do you always manage to do this when I'm eating lunch? Couldn't you have left it another hour?'

'Sod that, mate, there's money at stake. Right, you ready? I'm going for time of death at somewhere around quarter to three in the morning.'

'Bollocks.' Thorne stared out of the window at a row of low, grey buildings on the other side of the M1. He didn't know if the window was dirty or if that was just Hendon. 'This had better be worth a tenner. Go on . . .'

'Right, how d'you want it? Medical jargon, layman's terms, or pathology-made-easy for thick-as-shit coppers?'

'That's cost you half the tenner. Get on with it . . .'

Hendricks spoke about death and its intimacies with considerably less passion than he demonstrated for Arsenal FC. Being a Mancunian who didn't support the dreaded Man United was far from being the only V-sign he stuck up at convention. There were the clothes in varying shades of black, the shaved head, the ludicrous number of earrings. There were the mysterious piercings, one for each new boyfriend . . .

He might have *spoken* dispassionately, almost matter-of-factly, but Thorne knew how much Phil Hendricks cared about the dead. How hard he listened to their bodies when they spoke to him. When they gave up their secrets.

'Asphyxia due to ligature strangulation,' Hendricks said. 'Plus, I think it happened on the floor. He had carpet burns on both knees. I think the killer put the body on the bed afterwards. Posed it.'

'Right . . .'

'Unfortunately, I still can't tell for sure whether or not he was strangled before, after or during the sodomy.'

'So, you're not perfect, then?'

'I know one thing. Whoever did it has a big future in gay porn. Our killer's hung like a donkey. He did quite a bit of damage up there . . .'

Thorne knew he'd been right to get rid of the sandwich. He'd lost count of the conversations like this he'd had with Hendricks over the years. His head was used to them, but his stomach still found them tricky.

Thorne called it the H-plan diet . . .

'What about secretions?'

'Sorry, mate, bugger all. Only thing up there that shouldn't have been was a trace of spermicidal lubricant from the condom he was wearing. He was careful, in every sense . . .'

Thorne sighed. 'Where's Holland? He still with you?'

'No chance, mate. He shot away first chance he had. Why did you send him down anyway? Actually, I'm hurt you didn't want to watch me work . . .'

These conversations, the ones that followed bodies, always ended on something light-hearted. Football, piss-takes, anything . . .

'DC Holland hasn't seen you work nearly *enough* though, Phil,' Thorne said. 'It still gives him the heebies. I'm doing him a favour, toughening him up . . .'

Hendricks laughed. 'Right . . .'

Right, Thorne thought. He knew very well that when it came to slabs and scalpels you never toughened up. You just pretended you had . . .

Standing in the Incident Room, preparing to brief the team, Thorne felt, as he often did on these occasions, like a teacher who was feared but not particularly liked. The slightly psychotic PE teacher. These thirty or so people in front of him – detectives, uniformed officers, civilian and auxiliary staff – might just as well have been children. There were as many different types as could be found sitting in any draughty school hall in London, even as Thorne was speaking.

There were those who appeared to be listening intently but would have to check with colleagues later to find out exactly what they were supposed to be doing. Some, on the other hand, would be over-keen, asking questions and nodding eagerly, with every intention of doing as little as possible when the time came. There were the bullies and the picked-upon. The swots and the morons.

The Metropolitan Police Service. *Service*, note, with the emphasis on caring and efficiency. Thorne knew very well that most of the people in the room, himself on some occasions included, were happier back when they were a force.

One to be reckoned with.

It was four days since that first post-mortem conversation with Hendricks and if the pathologist had been quick, the team at Forensic Science Services had outdone him. Seventy-two hours for DNA results was really going some, especially when the crime scene was as much of a DNA nightmare as that hotel room had been. One notch up from a doss-house, it had yielded hair and skin samples from upwards of a dozen individuals, male and female. Then there were the cats and dogs and at least two other animal species as yet unidentified.

And yet, incredibly, they'd found a match.

They were no nearer finding the killer, of course, but now they were at least certain who his victim had been. The dead man's DNA had been on file, for a very good reason.

Thorne cleared his throat, got a bit of hush. 'Douglas Andrew Remfry, thirty-six years of age, was released from Derby prison ten days ago, having served seven years of a twelve-year sentence for the rapes of three young women. We're putting together an accurate picture of his movements since then, but so far it looks like a pretty consistent shuttle between pub, betting shop and the house in New Cross where he was living with his mother and her . . .?' Thorne looked across at Russell Brigstocke who held up three fingers. He turned back to the room. 'Her *third* husband. We'll hopefully have a lot more in terms of Remfry's movements and so on later today. DCs Holland and Stone are there at the moment with a search warrant. Mrs Remfry was somewhat less than co-operative . . .'

An acnefied trainee detective near the front shook his head, his face screwed up in distaste for this woman he'd never met. Thorne gave him a good, hard stare. 'She's just lost a son,' he said. Thorne let his words hang there for a few seconds before continuing. 'If the landlady is to be believed, Remfry, unless his killer happens also to be his double, booked the room himself. He didn't feel the need to give a name, but he was happy enough to hand over the cash. We need to find out why. Why was he so keen to go to that hotel? Who was he meeting . . .?'

Thorne, in spite of himself, was smiling slightly as he recalled the interview with the hotel's formidable owner – a bottle-blonde with a face like Joe Bugner and a sixty-fags-a-day rasp.

'And who pays for the replacement of those sheets?' she'd asked. 'All them pillows and blankets that this nutter nicked? They were one hundred per cent cotton, none of 'em was cheap . . .' Thorne had nodded, pretended to write something down, wondering if her memory was as good as her capacity to talk utter shite with a straight face. 'And the stains on the mattress. Where do I get the money to get that lot cleaned?'

'I'll see if I can find you a form to fill in,' Thorne said, thinking, *Will I fuck, you hatchet-faced old mare . . .*

In the Incident Room, the trainee detective Thorne had stared at before poked a single finger up. Thorne nodded.

'Are we looking at the prison angle, sir? Someone Remfry was in Derby with, maybe. Someone he got on the wrong side of . . .'

'Someone he got up the *back*side of!' The comment came from a moustached DC sitting off to Thorne's left towards the back of the room. Thorne did not know the man. He'd been brought in, like many in the room, from different squads to make up the numbers. His 'backside' comment got a big laugh. Thorne manufactured a chuckle.

'We're looking at that. Remfry's sexual preference was certainly for women before he got put away . . .'

'Some of them develop a taste for it inside, though, don't they?' This time the laugh from his mates felt forced. Thorne allowed it to die away, let his voice drop a little to regain attention and control.

'Most of you lot are going to be tracing the most likely group of suspects we've got at the moment . . .'

The trainee nodded knowingly. One of the swots. He thought this was some kind of conversation. 'The male relatives of Remfry's rape victims.'

'Right,' Thorne said. 'Husbands, boyfriends, brothers. Sod it, fathers at a push. I want them all found, interviewed and eliminated. With a bit of luck we might eliminate all of them except one. DI Kitson has drawn up a list and will be doing the allocations.' Thorne dropped his notes on to a chair, pulled his jacket from the back of it, almost done. 'Right, that's it. Remfry's were particularly nasty offences. Maybe someone wasn't convinced he'd paid for them . . .'

The DC with the porno moustache smirked and muttered something to the uniform in front of him. Thorne pulled on his jacket and narrowed his eyes.

'What?'

Suddenly, he might just as well have been that teacher, holding out a hand, demanding to see whatever was being chewed.

The DC spat it out. 'Seems to me that whoever killed Remfry did everyone a favour. Fucker asked for everything he got.'

It was far from being the first such comment Thorne had heard since the DNA match had come back. He looked across at the DC. He knew that he should slap the cocky sod down. He knew that he should make a speech about their jobs as police officers, their need to be dispassionate, whatever the case, whoever the victim. He should talk about debts having been paid and maybe even drag out stuff about one man's life being worth no more and no less than any other.

He couldn't be arsed.

Dave Holland was always happiest deferring to rank or, if he got the chance, pulling it. When it was just himself and another DC, things were never clear-cut and it made him uncomfortable.

It was simple. As a DC, he deferred to a DS and above, while *he* was able to large it with trainee detectives and woodentops. Out and about with a fellow DC, and things *should* just settle into a natural pattern. It was down to personality, to clout.

With Andy Stone, Holland felt outranked. He didn't know why and it niggled him.

They'd got on well enough so far, but Stone could be a bit 'up himself'. He had a coolness, a *flashiness* Holland reckoned, that he turned on around women and superior officers. Stone was clearly fit and good-looking. He had very short dark hair and blue eyes and though Holland wasn't certain, when Stone walked around, it looked as though he knew the effect he was having. What Holland *was* sure of was that Stone's suits were cut that bit better, and that around him he felt like a ruddy-cheeked boy scout. Holland would probably still edge it as housewives' choice, but they all wanted to mother him. He doubted they wanted to mother Andy Stone.

Stone could also be over-cocky when it came to slagging off their superiors, and though Holland wasn't averse to the game himself, it got a bit tricky when it came to Tom Thorne. Holland knew the DI's faults well enough. He'd been on the receiving end of his temper, had been dragged down with him on more than one occasion . . .

Yet, for all that, having Thorne think well of him, consider that something *he'd* done was worthwhile, was, for Holland, pretty much as good as it could get.

He'd been on the team a lot longer than Andy Stone, and Holland thought that should have counted for something. It didn't appear to. It had been Stone who'd done most of the talking when they'd shown up bright and early on Mary Remfry's doorstep with a search warrant.

'Good morning, Mrs Remfry.' Stone's voice was surprisingly light for such a tall man. 'We have a warrant to enter and . . .'

She'd turned away then and, leaving the door open, had trudged away down the thickly carpeted hallway without a word. Somewhere inside a dog was barking.

Stone and Holland had entered and stood at the bottom

of the stairs deciding who should start where. Stone made for the living room where, through the partially opened door, they could see a silver-haired man slumped in an armchair, lost in *Kilroy*. As Stone leaned on the door he hissed to Holland, nodding towards the kitchen where Mrs Remfry had seemed to be heading.

'Cup of tea on the cards, you reckon?'

It wasn't.

It seemed odd to Holland, needing a warrant to search a victim's house. Still, like Stone had said, Remfry *was* a convicted rapist and the mother's attitude hadn't really given them a lot of choice. It wasn't just the grief at her son's death turning to anger. It was a genuine fury at what she saw as the implication in one particular line of questioning. Considering the manner and circumstances of her son's death, it was a necessary line to pursue, but she was having no truck with it at all.

'Dougie was a ladies' man, always. A proper ladies' man.'

She was saying it again, now, having suddenly appeared in the doorway of her son's bedroom where Holland was methodically going through drawers and cupboards. Mary Remfry, mid-fifties, tugging a cardigan tightly over her night-dress, watched, but did not really take in what Holland was doing. Her mind was concentrated on talking at him.

'Dougie loved women and women loved him right back. That's gospel, that is.'

Holland was considerate going through the room. He would have been whether Mrs Remfry had been watching or not, but he made the extra effort to be respectful as he sorted through drawers full of vests and pants and thrust a gloved hand into pillowcases and duvet covers. In the short time since his release, Remfry had obviously not acquired much in the way of new clothing or possessions, but there seemed to be a good deal still here from the time before he went to prison. There was plenty from before he ever left school . . .

'He never went short where birds was concerned,' Remfry's mother said. 'Even after he came out they was still sniffing round. Calling him up. You listening to me?'

Holland half turned, half nodded and, as if on cue, pulled out a decent-sized stash of porn magazines from beneath the single bed.

'See?' Mary Remfry pointed at the magazines. 'You won't find any men in *them*.' She sounded as proud as if Holland was dusting off a degree certificate or a Nobel Prize nomination. As it was, he squatted by the bed, flicking through the pile of yellowing *Razzles*, *Escorts* and *Fiestas*, feeling his face flush, turning away from the proud mother in the doorway. The magazines all dated from the mid- to late eighties, well before Dougie began his days at Her Majesty's pleasure, banged up with six hundred and fifty other men.

Holland pushed the dirty mags to one side, reached back under the bed, and pulled out a brown plastic bag, folded over on itself several times. He let the bag drop open and a bundle of envelopes, bound with a thick elastic band, fell on to the carpet.

As soon as he saw the address, neatly typed on the topmost envelope, Holland felt a tingle of excitement. Just a small one. What he was looking at would probably mean nothing, but it was almost certainly more significant than fifteen-year-old socks and ancient stroke mags.

'Andy . . .!'

Mary Remfry wrapped her cardigan a little tighter around herself and took a step into the room. 'What have you got there?'

Holland could hear Stone's feet on the stairs. He slipped off the elastic band, reached inside the first envelope and pulled out the letter.

'So we can definitely rule out auto-erotic asphyxiation, then?' DCI Russell Brigstocke, a little embarrassed, looked around the table at Thorne, at Phil Hendricks, at DI Yvonne Kitson.

'Well, I'm not sure we can rule *anything* out,' Thorne said. 'But I think the "auto" bit implies that you do it yourself.'

'You know what I mean, smartarse . . .'

'Nothing erotic went on in that room,' Hendricks said.

Brigstocke nodded. 'No chance it was an extreme sex game that went wrong?' Thorne smirked. Brigstocke caught the look. 'What?' Thorne said nothing. 'Look, I'm just asking the questions . . .'

'Asking the questions that Jesmond told you to ask,' Thorne said. He made no secret of his opinion that their Detective Chief Superintendent had sprung fully formed from some course that turned out politically astute, organisationally capable drones. Acceptable faces with a neat line in facile questions, a good grasp of economic realities and, as it happened, an aversion to anybody called Thorne.

'They're questions that need answering,' Brigstocke said. 'Could it have been some sort of sex game?'

Thorne found it hard to believe that the likes of Trevor Jesmond had ever done the things that he, Brigstocke or any other copper did, day in and day out. It was unimaginable that he had ever broken up a fist-fight at chucking-out time, or fiddled his expenses, or stood between a knife and the body it was intended for.

Or told a mother that her only son had been sodomised and strangled to death in a grotty hotel room.

'It wasn't a game,' Thorne said.

Brigstocke looked at Hendricks and Kitson. He sighed. 'I'll take your expressions of thinly disguised scorn as agreement with DI Thorne then, shall I?' He pushed his glasses up his nose with the crook of his first finger, then ran the hand through the thick black hair of which he was so proud. The quiff was less pronounced than usual, there was some grey creeping in. He could cut a vaguely absurd figure but Thorne knew that when he lost it, Brigstocke was as hard a man as he had ever worked with.

Thorne, Brigstocke, Kitson, Hendricks the civilian. These four, together with Holland and Stone, were the core of Team 3 at the Serious Crime Group (West). This was the group that made the decisions, formulated policy and guided the investigations with – and even on occasion *without* – the approval of those higher up.

Team 3 had been up and running a good while, handling the ordinary cases but specialising – though that was not a word Thorne would have used – in cases that were anything but ordinary . . .

'So,' Brigstocke said, 'we've got everybody out chasing down all the likely relatives of Remfry's victims. Still favourite with everybody?'

Nods around the table.

'A long way from odds-on, though,' Thorne said. There were things which bothered him, which didn't quite mesh with the vengeful relative scenario. He couldn't picture an anger carried around for that many years, fermenting into something lethal, corrosive, then manifesting itself in the way it had in that hotel room. There was something almost stage-managed about what he had seen on that filthy mattress. *Posed*, Hendricks had said.

And he was still troubled by the early morning call to the florist . . .

Thorne thought there was something odd about the message. He couldn't believe that it was simple carelessness, so the only conclusion was that the killer must have *wanted* the police to hear his voice on that answering machine. It was as if he were introducing himself.

'What came up at the briefing,' Kitson said, 'the stuff about Remfry turning queer inside? Worth looking into . . .?'

Thorne glanced towards Hendricks. A gay man who was choosing to ignore the word Kitson had used, or else genuinely didn't give a fuck.

'Yeah,' Thorne said. 'Whatever he might or might not have got up to when he was inside, he was definitely straight before he went in. Don't forget that he raped three women . . .'

'Rape's not about sex, it's about power,' Kitson said.

Yvonne Kitson, together with DC Andy Stone, had come into the team to replace an officer Thorne had lost, in circumstances he tried every day to forget. Of all the murderers he'd put away, Thorne was happy to remember that the man responsible was serving three life sentences in Belmarsh Prison.

Thorne looked at Phil Hendricks. 'Never mind Remfry, can we be certain the *killer*'s gay?'

Hendricks didn't hesitate. 'Absolutely not. Like Yvonne says, the rape's got nothing to do with sex, anyway. Maybe the killer wants us to *think* he's gay. He may well be, of course, but we have to consider other possibilities . . .'

'Whether it was a gay thing or not,' Kitson said, 'he could still have been set up by someone he did time with, someone with a major grudge . . .'

Brigstocke cleared his throat, at some level finding this all a bit embarrassing. 'But the buggery . . .?'

Hendricks snorted. 'Buggery?' He dropped his Mancunian accent and adopted the posh bluster of the gentleman's club. 'Buggery!!'

Brigstocke reddened. 'Sodomy, then. Anal intercourse, whatever. How could you do that if you weren't homosexual?'

Hendricks shrugged. 'Close your eyes and think of Claudia Schiffer . . .?'

'Kylie for me,' Thorne said.

Kitson shook her head, smiling. 'Dirty old man.'

Brigstocke was unconvinced. He stared hard at Thorne. 'Seriously, though, Tom. This might be important. Could *you*?'

'It would depend how much I wanted to kill somebody,' Thorne said.

There was a silence around the table for a while. Thorne decided to break it before it became too serious. 'Remfry went to that hotel willingly. He booked the room

41

himself. He knew, or thought he knew, what he was getting into.'

'And whatever it was,' Hendricks added, 'it looks as though he went along with it for a while.'

'Right,' Kitson said. She turned the photocopied pages of Hendricks's post-mortem report. 'No defence wounds, no tissue underneath the fingernails . . .'

The phone on the desk rang. Thorne was nearest.

'DI Thorne. Yes, Dave . . .'

The others watched for a few seconds as Thorne listened. Brigstocke hissed at Kitson. 'Why the fuck did Remfry go to that hotel?'

Thorne nodded, grunted, took the top off a pen with his teeth. He took it out of his mouth, put it back on the pen. He smiled, told Holland to get his arse in gear and ended the call.

Then he answered Brigstocke's question.

4 DECEMBER, 1975

They sat in the Maxi, outside the house.

She'd held it together all morning, through all the really hard parts, the personal stuff, the intrusion. Then, when it seemed the worst was over, she'd begun to wail as she'd stepped through the doors he'd held open for her. Out of the police station and running down the steps towards the street, her heels noisy on the concrete, her sobbing uncontrollable.

In the car on the way back, the crying had gradually given way to a seething fury which exploded in fitful bursts of abuse. He kept his hands clenched tightly around the steering wheel as she rained blows down on his shoulder and arm. His eyes never left the road as she screamed words at him that he'd never heard her utter before. He drove carefully, with the same caution he always showed, and as he manoeuvred the car through the lunchtime traffic on the icy streets, he absorbed as much of her pain and rage as he could take.

They sat in the car, both too shattered to open a door. Staring straight ahead, afraid to so much as look towards the house. The house, which was now simply the place where, the night before, she had told him what had happened. The collection of rooms through which they'd staggered and shouted and wept. The place where everything had changed.

The home they'd never feel comfortable in again.

Without turning her head, she spat words at him. 'Why didn't you make me go to the police station last night? Why did you let me wait?'

The engine was turned off, the car was still, but his hands would not leave the steering wheel. His leather driving gloves creaked as he grasped it even tighter. 'You wouldn't listen, you wouldn't listen to sense.'

'What do you expect? Christ, I didn't even know my own name. I had no idea what I was fucking doing. I would never have had the shower . . .'

She'd been too upset to think clearly, of course. He'd tried to explain all this to the WPC that morning, but she'd just shrugged and looked at her colleague and carried on taking the clothes and putting them into a plastic bag as they were taken off and handed over.

'You shouldn't have had a shower, love,' the WPC said. 'That was a bit silly. You should have come straight in, last night, as soon as it had happened . . .'

The engine had been off for no more than a minute, but already it was freezing inside the car. The tears felt warm as they inched slowly down his face, running into his moustache. 'You said you'd wanted to wash . . . to wash him off you. I said I understood but I told you you shouldn't have. That it wasn't a good idea. You weren't listening to me . . .'

Standing there in the lounge after she'd told him. The horrible minutes and hours after she'd described what had been done to her. She wouldn't let him do a lot of things. She wouldn't let him hold her. She wouldn't let him ring anybody. She wouldn't let him go round to the bastard's house to kick what little he had between his legs into a bloody mush and punch him into the middle of next week.

He looked at his watch. He wondered if the police would pick Franklin up at work or later on at his house . . .

He needed to call the office and tell them he wouldn't be in.

He needed to call the school to check that everything was OK, that the previous night's explanations for why Mummy was so upset had been believed . . .

'What did that woman mean?' she said, suddenly. 'That WPC? When she asked if I always wore a dress that nice to go to work?' She slid her hands beneath her legs and began to rock gently in her seat.

Snow was starting to fall quite heavily, building up quickly on the bonnet and windscreen. He didn't bother to turn on the wipers.

THREE

Later, when they talked about it, both Thorne and Holland admitted to fancying the Deputy Governor of Derby Prison. What neither of them *quite* got round to admitting was that, attractive as she undoubtedly was, they actually fancied her more *because* she was a prison governor.

They didn't really go into it all that much . . .

'He's certainly made a very good job of it.' Tracy Lenahan put down the letter, actually a photocopy of one of twenty-odd letters written to Douglas Remfry during his last three months inside, plus a couple to his home address after he'd been released. The letters that Holland had found under Remfry's bed.

Letters written by a killer, pretending to be a twenty-eight-year-old woman named Jane Foley.

Thorne and Holland had already been taken through the procedure for the sorting of prisoners' mail. The letters – five sackfuls a day on average – would have been taken by two, perhaps three, Operational Support Grade officers to the Censor's room for sorting. The X-ray machine had been done away with by the present Governor, but drug dogs might be used and each letter

46

would be slit open and searched for illegal enclosures. The OSGs did not *read* the letters, and providing there was no good reason, they would not usually be seen by anyone else.

'A good job of sounding like a woman, you mean?' Thorne asked. He thought the letters were pretty bloody convincing and so did Yvonne Kitson, but other opinions couldn't hurt.

'Oh yes, but I think he's been much cleverer than that. I've seen one or two letters like this before, genuine letters. You'd be amazed how much mail like this people like Remfry really get. This has that same, odd tone to it. It's something slightly crazed . . .'

'Something a bit needy,' Holland suggested.

Lenahan nodded. 'Right, that's it. She's claiming to be a bit of a catch, a sexy bit of stuff looking for fun . . .'

'A sexy *married* bit of stuff,' Thorne added. The fictitious Jane Foley was conveniently hitched to an equally fictitious and awfully jealous husband, so Remfry couldn't write back to her.

Lenahan read a few lines of the letter again, nodded. 'All the suggestive stuff in the letter is bang on, but there's still a kind of hopelessness. Something sad underneath . . .'

'Like she's a bit desperate,' Thorne said. 'A woman who's desperate enough to write these sorts of letters to a convicted rapist.'

Holland puffed out his cheeks. 'This is doing my head in. A bloke, pretending to be a woman, pretending to be a different kind of woman . . .'

Lenahan pushed the letter back across her desk. 'It's subtle, though. Like I said, he's bloody clever.' She didn't need to tell Thorne that. He'd studied every one of 'Jane Foley's' letters. He knew that the man who wrote them was very clever indeed. Clever, calculating and extremely patient.

Lenahan picked up the photograph. 'And this is the icing on the cake . . .'

Thorne was struck by her strange choice of phrase, but said nothing. On the wall behind the desk was the regulation portrait of the Queen, looking rather as if she could smell something unpleasant wafting up from the canteen. To Her Majesty's left were a series of framed aerial views of the prison and, hung next to these very modern images, a pair of large landscapes in oil. Thorne knew next to bugger all about it but they looked pretty old. Lenahan glanced up, followed Thorne's gaze.

'Those have been knocking around the place since it opened in 1853,' she said. 'Used to be gathering dust down in Visits. Then six months ago, we had an inmate in for receiving stolen antiques. He took one look at them and went pale. Worth about twelve thousand each, so they reckon . . .'

She smiled and her eyes dropped to the black and white photo in her hand. Thorne's went to the silver picture frame on her desk. From where he was sitting he couldn't see the photo inside, but he imagined a fit-looking husband – army perhaps, or maybe even a copper – and a smiling, olive-skinned child. He looked again at the woman behind the desk, her dark eyes wide as she stared at the picture. She was ridiculously young, probably not even thirty. Her black hair was shoulder length. She was tall and large-breasted. It would have been clear to a blind man that the

Deputy Governor would figure regularly in the fantasies of the men she locked up every night.

Thorne glanced across at Holland and was amused to see him struggling not to blush, as he waited for Tracy Lenahan to finish studying the photograph of 'Jane Foley'. The picture was of a woman kneeling, her head bowed and hooded, the artful lighting concealing much, but revealing tantalising glimpses of the full breasts, the neatly trimmed thatch of pubic hair. Of the leather belt around the wrists.

Holland had earlier expressed surprise that the photos had not been confiscated, especially as Remfry was a sex offender. Surely this kind of image was risky on 'Fraggle Rock' – the term used by many police officers for the Vulnerable Prisoners wing. Lenahan, bridling slightly at the slang, had explained what she called the Page Three rule. Stuff like this was discretionary. Obviously images of kids were not allowed on the VP wing, but if it was the sort of thing you might see on Page Three, then the OSGs would have a look, pass the odd comment and put it back in the envelope.

'Jesus,' Holland had said. 'Page Three must be going seriously fucking arty . . .'

Lenahan put the picture down, scraped at the edge of it with a long red fingernail.

'This is clever too. It's the ideal image to have chosen. Just what would be needed to hook an offender like Remfry, to tease him with the promise of something. This is a rapist's wet dream. Wherever your killer got it from, it's perfect.' She swallowed, cleared her throat. 'Remfry was a man who got off on submission . . .'

49

Thorne and Holland exchanged a glance. They hadn't told Tracy Lenahan, but they were pretty sure the picture wasn't one the killer had just gone out and bought. The naked woman was wearing a hood identical to the one that Phil Hendricks had taken off Douglas Remfry's body . . .

'There's half a dozen similar pictures,' Thorne said. 'They were sent with the most recent letters. They start to get more revealing the closer the letters get to his release date.'

Lenahan nodded. 'Increasing the excitement . . .'

'By the time he got out he must have been gagging for it,' Holland said.

She picked up the photograph again in her left hand and reached for the letter with her right. She brandished them both. 'Your killer is sensitive to the way this kind of woman might think, *and* to what will best stimulate the man she's writing to.'

Thorne said nothing. He was thinking that she sounded bizarrely impressed.

'Sensitive, like a gay man maybe,' Holland said.

Thorne shrugged non-committally. They were back to that. He had to agree it was possible, but he was growing irritated at the way the investigation was fixing on what they presumed the killer's sexuality to be. Yes, the violent sodomising of the victim was clearly significant. The rapist had been raped and Thorne was sure that this would prove to be crucial in finding out why he'd been murdered. Thorne was *less* sure that who the killer chose to sleep with was as important.

Holland slid forward in his chair, looked at Tracy Lenahan. 'This is an angle we obviously have to consider –

that Remfry was killed by someone he'd known in prison. Someone with whom he'd possibly had a non-consensual sexual relationship . . .'

Lenahan looked back at him, waiting for the question, not appearing terribly keen to do Holland any favours. 'Is that possible, do you think? Could Remfry have sexually assaulted another prisoner? Could he have been sexually assaulted himself?'

The Deputy Governor leaned back, something dark passing momentarily across her face. It vanished as she clasped her hands together and shook her head. Thorne thought that the laugh she produced sounded a little forced.

'I think you've been watching too many films set in American prisons, Detective Constable. There're some very nasty pieces of work in here, don't get me wrong, but very few of them are called Bubba, and if you're looking for bitches or puppies, you should look in a dogs' home. Prisoners form relationships, of course they do, but as far as I know, nobody's going to get gangbanged if they drop the soap in the shower.'

Thorne couldn't help but smile. Holland smiled too, but Thorne could see the skin tighten around his mouth and the reddening just above his collar. 'As far as you know?' Holland said. 'Meaning that it's possible.'

'The week before last, in the kitchens, a prisoner had his ear cut off with the lid from a tin of peaches. That was an argument over a game of table-tennis, I think.' She smiled, sexy and very cold. 'Anything's possible.'

Thorne stood and walked away from Lenahan's desk towards the door. 'Let's presume that the man we're looking

51

for is *not* an ex-con. The obvious question is how he got the information. How did he find Remfry? How could he find out where a convicted rapist was serving his sentence and when he was going to get released, in enough time to set all this up?'

Lenahan swivelled in her chair to face the computer screen on the corner of her desk. She hit a button on the keyboard. 'He would have had to have got it from a data-base somewhere.' She continued typing, watching the screen. 'This is a LIDS computer. Local Inmate Data System, which has everything on the prisoners in here. I can send stuff down the wire to other prisons if I need to, but I wouldn't have thought this would be enough . . .'

Thorne looked at the nearer of the two landscapes. The dark, thick swirls of the paint on the canvas. He thought it might be somewhere in the Lake District. 'What about national records?'

'IIS. The Inmate Information System. That's got every-thing – locations, offence details, home address, release date.' She looked up and across at Thorne. 'But you'd still need to type a name in.'

'Who has access to that?' Holland asked. 'Do you?'

'No . . .'

'The Governor? Police liaison officer?'

She smiled, shook her head firmly. 'It's headquarters-based only. The system's pretty well restricted, for obvious reasons . . .'

Thanks and goodbyes were brisk and Thorne would have had it no other way. Though he hadn't so much as glimpsed a blue prison sweatshirt the whole time they'd been there, he was aware of the prisoners all around him.

Beyond the walls of the Deputy Governor's office. Above, below and to all sides. A distant echo, a heaviness, the *heat* given off by over six hundred men, there thanks to the likes of him.

Whenever he entered a prison, moved around its green, or mustard or dirty-cream corridors, Thorne mentally left a trail of breadcrumbs behind him. He always needed to be sure of the quickest way out.

For most of the drive back down the M1, Holland had his nose buried in a pamphlet he'd picked up on his way out of the prison. Thorne preferred his own form of research.

He eased *Johnny Cash at San Quentin* into the cassette player.

Holland looked up as 'Wanted Man' kicked in. He listened for a few seconds, shook his head and went back to his facts and figures.

Thorne had tried, *once*, to tell him. To explain that *real* country music was fuck all to do with lost dogs and rhinestones. It had been a long night of pool and Guinness, and Phil Hendricks – with whichever boyfriend happened to be around at the time – heckling mercilessly. Thorne had tried to convey to Holland the beauty of George Jones's voice, the wickedness in Merle Haggard's and the awesome rumble of Cash, the dark daddy of them all. A few pints in, he was telling anybody who would listen that Hank Williams was a tortured genius who was undoubtedly the Kurt Cobain of his day and he may even have begun to sing 'Your Cheating Heart' around closing time. He couldn't recall every detail, but he *did* remember that Holland's eyes had begun to glaze over long before then . . .

'Fuck,' Holland said. 'It costs twenty-five grand a year to look after one prisoner. Does that sound like a lot to you?'

Thorne didn't really know. It was twice what a lot of people earned in a year, but once you took into account the salaries of prison staff and the maintenance of the buildings . . .

'I don't think they're spending that on carpets and caviar, somehow,' Thorne said.

'No, but still . . .'

It was roasting in the car. The Mondeo was far too old to have air-con, but Thorne was very pissed off at being completely unable to coax anything but warm air from a heating system he'd had fixed twice already. He opened a window but shut it after half a minute, the breeze not worth the noise.

Holland looked up from his pamphlet again. 'Do you think they should have luxuries in there? You know, TVs in their cells and whatever? PlayStations, some of them have got . . .'

Thorne turned the sound down a little and glanced up at the sign as the Mondeo roared past it. They were approaching the Milton Keynes turnoff. Still fifty miles from London.

Thorne realised, as he had many times before, that for all the time he spent putting people behind bars, he gave precious little thought to what happened when they got there. When he *did* think about it, weigh all the arguments up, he supposed that, all things considered, a loss of freedom was as bad as it could get. Above and beyond *that*, he wasn't sure exactly where he stood.

He feathered the brake, dropped down to just under

seventy and drifted across to the inside lane. They were in no great hurry . . .

Thorne knew, as much as he knew anything, that murderers, sex offenders, those that would harm children, had to be removed. He also knew that *putting these people away* was more than just a piece of argot. It was actually what they did. What *he* did. Once these offenders were . . . elsewhere, the debate as to where punishment ended and rehabilitation began was for others to have. He felt instinctively that prisons should never become . . . the phrase 'holiday camps' popped into his head. He chided himself for beginning to sound like a slavering Tory nutcase. Fuck it, a few TVs was neither here nor there. Let them watch the football or shout at Chris Tarrant if that was what they wanted . . .

Sadly, by the time Thorne had formulated his answer to the question, Holland had moved on to something else.

'Bloody hell.' Holland looked up from the pamphlet. 'Sixty per cent of goal nets in the English league are made by prisoners. I hope they've made the ones at White Hart Lane strong enough, the stick Spurs get from other teams . . .'

'Right . . .'

'Here's another one. Prison farms produce twenty million pints of milk every year. That's fucking amazing . . .'

Thorne was no longer listening. He was hearing nothing but the rush of the road under the wheels and thinking about the photograph. He pictured the hooded woman, the make-believe Jane Foley, feeling a stirring in his groin at the image in his head of her shadowy nakedness.

Wherever he got it from . . .

Suddenly, Thorne knew where he might go to find the answer, at least any answer there was to be found. The woman in that photo might not be Jane Foley, but she had to be somebody, and Thorne knew just the person to come up with a name.

When he started to listen again, Holland was in the middle of another question.

'. . . as bad as this? Do you think prisons are any better than they were back in . . .?' He pointed towards the cassette player.

'1969,' Thorne said. Johnny Cash was singing the song he'd written about San Quentin itself. Singing about hating every inch of the place they were all stood in. The prisoners whooping and cheering at every complaint, at each pugnacious insult, at every plea to raze the prison to the ground.

'So?' Holland waved his pamphlet. 'Are prisons any better now than they were then, do you think? Than they were thirty-odd years ago?'

Thorne pictured the face of a man in Belmarsh, and something inside hardened very quickly.

'I fucking hope not.'

At a little after six o'clock, Eve Bloom double-locked the shop, walked half a dozen paces to a bright red front door, and was home.

It was handy renting the flat above her shop. It wasn't expensive, but she'd have paid a good deal more for the pleasure of being able to tumble out of bed at the last possible minute, the coffee steaming in her own mug next to the till as she opened up. Every last second in bed was precious when you had to spend as many mornings as she did, up and dressed at half past stupid. Walking around the flower market at New Covent Garden, ordering stock, gassing with wholesalers, while every other bugger she could think of was still dead to the world.

She liked this time of year. The few precious weeks of summer, when she wasn't forced to choose between working in scarf and gloves or punishing her stock with central heating. She liked closing up when it was still light. It made the early starts less painful, gave that couple of hours between the end of the day and the start of the evening a scent of excitement, a tang of real possibility.

She closed the door behind her and climbed the stripped wooden stairs up to the flat. Denise had wielded the sander and done the whole place in a weekend, while Eve had taken responsibility for the decorating. Most domestic chores got split fairly equally between them, and though there were the sulks, the occasional frosty silences that followed a pilfered yoghurt or a dress borrowed without asking, the two of them got on pretty well. Eve knew that Denise could be quite controlling, but then she also knew there were occasions when she herself needed to be controlled. She tended to be more than a little disorganised and though Den could be Mother Hen-ish at times, it was nice to feel looked after. The endless list-making could get wearing but there *was* always food in the fridge and they never ran out of toilet roll!

She dropped her bag on the kitchen table and flicked on the kettle. 'Oi, Hollins, you old slapper, you want tea?' Almost before she'd finished shouting she remembered that Denise was going straight out from work, meeting Ben in the pub next to her office. Denise had called the shop at lunchtime, told her she wouldn't be home for dinner, asked her if she fancied joining them.

Eve walked through to her bedroom to put on a fresh T-shirt while she was waiting for the kettle to boil. No, she'd stay in, veg out in front of the TV with a bottle of very cold white wine. She couldn't be bothered to change and go out. It was sticky outside and uncomfortable. She'd feel dirty by the time she got there. The pub would be loud and smoky and she'd only feel like a gooseberry anyway. Denise and Ben were very touchy-feely . . .

She stared at herself in the mirror on the back of her bedroom door, striking a pose in bra and pants. She saw herself smiling as she thought again about the policeman who had answered the phone a week before. Impossible to picture from just the voice of course, but she'd tried anyway and was pretty keen on what she'd come up with. She was fairly sure that, crime scene or no crime scene, he'd been flirting with her on the phone, and she knew full well that she'd been flirting right back. Or had she been the one to start it?

She pulled on a white, FCUK T-shirt and went back into the kitchen to make her tea.

They'd sent a car round the day after she'd called, to collect the cassette from her answering machine. She told the two officers that she'd have been more than happy to bring it into the station, but, understandably, they seemed eager to take it with them.

Walking around the flat opening windows, she debated whether a week was quite long enough. She couldn't decide whether she should just turn up, or if it might be better to call. The last thing she wanted was to look pushy. She had every right of course, being involved, to see what was going on. It was only natural that she should be a bit curious after the business with the phone call, wasn't it? Surely, going along to enquire if there had been any progress in the case was no more than any other concerned citizen would do.

She suddenly realised that, wandering around the flat, she'd put her tea down and couldn't remember where. Sod it, the kitchen was close and she knew *exactly* where the fridge was.

Opening the wine, she wondered if Detective Inspector Thorne was one of those funny blokes who got put off by women who appeared a bit keen.

Maybe she'd leave it another day or two . . .

The evening was ridiculously warm.

Elvis, Thorne's emotionally disturbed cat, looked uncomfortable, following him from room to room, yowling like she was asking to be shaved. Thorne got sweaty, cooking and eating cheese on toast, wearing an open Hawaiian shirt and a pair of shorts he'd bought during a short-lived dalliance with a nearby gym.

Thorne lay on the sofa and watched a film. He turned the sound on the TV down and looked at the pictures with the radio on. He flicked through the music section in the previous week's edition of *Time Out*, trying to find the band with the most ridiculous name. Finally, just before midnight, his empties cleared away and nothing else to do that might put it off any longer, he reached for the phone.

It didn't matter that it was late. His father's body clock was only one of the systems that had broken down.

In some ways, the Alzheimer's diagnosis had come as something of a relief. The eccentricities were now called symptoms and, for Thorne, the vagaries of old age becoming certainties, however unpleasant, had at least provided a focus. Things had to be done, simple as that. Thorne still got irritated with the terrible jokes and the pointless trivia, but the guilt didn't last as long as it had before. Now, he just got on with it, and the shape of the guilt had changed. Hammered into something he could recognise as anger, at an illness which took father and son and forced them to swap places.

There was a financial burden now that wasn't always easy to meet, but he was getting used to it. Jim Thorne was, at least physically, in pretty good nick for seventy-one but still, a carer needed to visit daily and there was no way an old-age pension was going to cover it. His younger sister Eileen, to whom he had never been close, travelled up from Brighton once a week, taking care to keep Thorne well informed of his dad's condition.

Thorne was grateful, though it seemed like a terribly British thing to him. Families coming good when it was practically too late.

'Dad . . .'

'Oh, thank Christ, this is driving me mad. Who was the first Doctor Who? Come on, this is doing my head in . . .'

'Was it Patrick somebody? Dark hair . . .'

'Troughton was the second one, the one before Pertwee. Oh shit and bloody confusion, I thought you might know.'

'Look in the book. I bought you that TV encyclopaedia . . .'

'Fucking Eileen's tidied the bugger away somewhere. Who else might know . . .?'

Thorne started to relax. His father was fine.

'Dad, we need to start thinking about this wedding.'

'What wedding?'

'Trevor. Eileen's son. Your nephew . . .'

His dad took a deep breath. When he breathed out again, the rattle in his chest sounded like a low growl. 'He's an arsehole. He was an arsehole when he got married the first time. Don't see why I should have to go and watch the arsehole get married again.'

The language was unimaginative but Thorne had to admit that his father had a point.

'You told Eileen you were going.'

There was a heavy sigh, a phlegmy cough and then silence. After a few seconds, Thorne began to think his father had put the phone down and wandered away.

'Dad . . .'

'It's ages. It's ages away, isn't it?'

'It's a week on Saturday. Come on, Eileen must have talked to you about it. She talks to *me* about sod all else.'

'Do I have to wear a suit?'

'Wear your navy one. It's light and I think it's going to be warm.'

'That's wool, the navy one. I'll bloody roast in the navy.'

Thorne took a deep breath, thinking, *Please your bloody self*. 'Listen, I'm going to come and pick you up on the day and we're stopping the night down there . . .'

'I'm not going down there in that bloody death-trap you drive . . .'

'I'll hire a car, all right? It'll be a laugh, we'll have a good time. OK?'

Thorne could hear a clinking, the sound of something metallic being fiddled with. His dad had taken to buying cheap, second-hand radios, disassembling them and throwing the pieces away.

'Dad? Is that OK? We can talk about the details closer to the day if you want.'

'Tom?'

'Yeah?'

To Thorne, the silence that followed seemed like the sound of thoughts getting lost. Slipping down cracks, just beyond reach and then gone, flailing as they tumbled into darkness. Finally, there was an engagement, like a piece of film catching, regaining its proper speed. Holes locking on to ratchets.

'Sort that Doctor Who thing out for me, will you, Son?'

Thorne swallowed hard. 'I'll ask around and call you tomorrow. OK?'

'Thanks . . .'

'And listen, Dad, dig out that navy suit. I'm sure it's not wool.'

'Oh shit, you never said anything about a suit . . .'

22 DECEMBER, 1975

They were both in the kitchen. A few feet apart, and nowhere near each other.

Just a couple of days till Christmas, and from the radio on the window sill the traditional songs did a good job of filling the silences. Seasonal stuff from Sinatra or Elvis mixed in with the more recent Christmas hits from Slade and Wizzard. That awful Queen song looked like it was going to be the Christmas Number One. He didn't like it much anyway but he knew that he'd never be able to hear it again without thinking about her. About her body, before and after. Her face and how it must have looked, Franklin pushing her down among the cardboard boxes . . .

She stood with her back to him, washing up at the sink. He sat at the table and looked at the Daily Mirror. *The newsprint, the soapsuds, the absurdly cheery DJ – things to look at and listen to as, separately, they both went over and over it. Remembering what had happened at the station that morning.*

Thinking about the police officer, pacing around the Interview Room, winking at the WPC in the corner, leaning down on the desk and shouting.

He thought about the copper's face. The smile that felt like a slap.

She was thinking about the way he'd smelled.

'Right,' the officer had said. 'Let's go over it again.' And then, afterwards, he'd said it again. And again. Shaking his head indulgently when she'd finally broken down, beckoning the

WPC who strolled across, pulling a tissue from the sleeve of her uniform. A minute or two, a glass of water and then they were back into it. The detective sergeant marching around the place, as if in all his years of training he'd never learned the difference between victim and criminal.

He'd done nothing, said nothing. Wanted to, but thought better of it. Instead, he'd sat and watched and listened to his wife crying and thought stupid thoughts, like why, when it was so cold, when he was buttoned up in his heaviest coat, was the bastard detective sergeant in shirtsleeves? Rings of sweat beneath both beefy arms.

Now there was a choir singing on the radio . . .

He stood up and walked slowly towards the sink, stopping when he was within touching distance of her. He could see something stiffen around her shoulders as he drew close.

'You need to forget everything he said, OK? That sergeant. He was just going over it to get everything straight. Making sure. Doing his job. He knows it'll be worse than that on the day. He knows how hard the defence lawyer's going to be. I suppose he's just preparing us for it, you know? If we go through it now, maybe it won't be so hard in court.' He took another step and he was standing right behind her. Her head was perfectly still. He couldn't tell what she was looking at, but all the while her hands remained busy in the white plastic washing-up bowl . . .

'Tell you what,' he said. 'Let's just get through Christmas shall we, love? It's not just for us after all, is it? New year soon, and then we can just keep our heads down, and get on with it, and wait for the trial. We could go away for a bit. Try and get back on an even keel maybe . . .'

Her voice was a whisper. He couldn't make it out.

'Say again, love.'

'That policeman's aftershave,' she said. 'I thought at first it was the same as Franklin's. I thought I was going to be sick. It was so strong . . .'

She began to scream the second his hand touched the back of her neck and it grew louder as she spun around, the water flying everywhere, her arm moving hard and fast, striking out instinctively, the mug in her hand smashing across his nose.

Then she screamed at what she had done and she reached out for him and they sank down on to the linoleum, which quickly grew slippery with blood and suds.

While the voices of young boys filled the kitchen, singing about holly and ivy.

FOUR

Back when the Peel Centre had been a centre for cadet training, Becke House had been a dormitory block. To Thorne it still felt utilitarian, dead. He swore, on occasion, that rounding a corner, or pushing open an office door, he could catch a whiff of sweat and homesickness . . .

No surprise when, a month or so earlier, everyone on Team 3 had got very excited at news of improved facilities and extra working space. In reality, it amounted to little more than an increased stationery budget, a reconditioned coffee machine and one more airless cubby-hole which Brigstocke had immediately commandeered. There were now three offices in the narrow corridor that ran off the Major Incident Room. Brigstocke had the new one while Thorne shared his with Yvonne Kitson. Holland and Stone were left with the smallest of the lot, negotiating rights to the wastepaper basket and arguing about who got the chair with the cushion.

Thorne hated Becke House. Actually it *depressed* him, sapped his energy to the point where he hadn't enough left to hate it properly. He'd heard somebody once joking about Sick Building Syndrome, but to him the place wasn't so much sick as terminally ill.

66

He'd spent the morning catching up. Sitting at his gunmetal-grey desk, sweating like a pig and reading every scrap of paperwork there was on the case. He read the post-mortem report, the forensic report, his own report on the visit to Derby Prison. He read Holland's notes on the search of Remfry's house, the interviews with relatives of the women Remfry had raped and the statements from some of the men he'd shared cells with in three different prisons.

Inches thick already and only one promising lead. An ex-cellmate of Remfry's had mentioned a prisoner named Gribbin, whom Remfry had talked about falling out with, back when the pair of them were on remand in Brixton. Gribbin had been released from prison himself only four months before Remfry and had skipped parole. There was a warrant out . . .

When Thorne had finished reading, he spent some time fanning his face with an empty folder. He stared at the mysterious scorch marks on the polystyrene ceiling tiles. Then he read everything again.

When Yvonne Kitson came in, he looked up, dropped the notes down on to his desk and gazed towards the open window.

'I've been thinking about jumping,' he said. 'Suicide seems like quite an attractive option, and at least I'd get a breeze on the way down. What d'you reckon?'

She laughed. 'We're only on the third floor.' Thorne shrugged. 'Where's the fan?'

'Brigstocke's got it.'

'Typical . . .' She sat down on a chair against the wall and reached into a large handbag. Thorne laughed when she pulled out the familiar Tupperware container.

'Wednesday, so it must be tuna,' he said.

She peeled the lid off and took out a sandwich. 'Tuna *salad*, actually, smartarse. My old man went a bit mad this morning and stuck a slice of lettuce on . . .'

Thorne leaned back in his chair, tapped a plastic ruler along its arm. 'How do you do it, Yvonne?'

She looked up, her mouth full. 'What?'

Still holding the ruler, Thorne spread his arms wide, waved them around. 'This. All of it. As well as three young kids . . .'

'The DCI's got kids . . .'

'Yeah, and he's a fucking mess like the rest of us. You seem to manage it all without breaking a sweat. Work, home, kids, dogs *and* your sodding lunch in a box.' He held out the ruler towards her, as if it was a microphone. 'Tell us, DI Kitson, how do you manage it? What's your secret?'

She cleared her throat, playing along. Truth be known, they were both glad of a laugh. 'Natural talent, an old man who's a pushover and ruthless organisational skills. Plus, I never take the job home.'

Thorne blinked.

'Right, any more questions?'

Thorne shook his head, put the ruler down on his desk.

'Good. I'm going to get a cup of tea. Want one . . .?'

They walked along the corridor, past the other offices, towards the Major Incident Room.

'Seriously, though,' Thorne said, 'you do amaze me sometimes.' He meant it. Nobody on the team had known Yvonne Kitson for very long, but bar the odd comment from older, less efficient male colleagues, nobody had a bad word to say about her. At thirty-three, she would almost certainly have been furious about the fact that many of them, Thorne included, found her comfortingly mumsy. This was more to do with her personality and style than with her face or figure, both of which were more than attractive. Her clothes were never flashy, her ash-blond hair was always sensible. She had no sharp edges, she did her job and she never seemed to get rattled. Thorne found it easy to see why Kitson was already earmarked for bigger and better things.

At the coffee machine, Kitson leaned down to take Thorne's cup from the dispenser. She handed the tea to him. 'I meant it, about taking the job home.' She began to feed more coins into the machine. 'Couldn't if I wanted to, there's no bloody room . . .'

Every window in the Incident Room was open. Bits of paper were being blown from the tops of desks and filing cabinets. Thorne sipped his tea, listened to the flutter of paper, to the grunts of those bending to pick it up, and he thought how different he was from this woman. He took the job everywhere, home included, though there wasn't usually anybody there to bring it home *to*. He and his ex-wife Jan had divorced five years earlier, after she'd started getting distinctly extra-curricular with a Fine Arts lecturer. Thorne had had one or two 'adventures' since then, but there hadn't been anyone significant.

Kitson dropped the red-hot plastic cup into another empty one and blew across the top of her drink. 'By the way, the Remfry case?' she said. 'Is it just me, or are we getting seriously fucking nowhere?'

Thorne saw Russell Brigstocke appear on the far side of

the room. He beckoned, turned and headed back in the direction of his office. Thorne took a step in the same direction, and, without looking, he answered Kitson's question.

'No, it isn't just you . . .'

When Russell Brigstocke was really pissed off, he had a face that could curdle milk. When he was *trying* to look serious, there was a hint of the melodramatic, a cocking of the head and a pursing of the lips that always made Thorne smile, much as he tried not to.

'Right, where are we, Tom?'

Thorne tried and failed not to smile. He didn't bother to hide it, deciding that a more upbeat response than the one he'd just given Yvonne Kitson might not be a bad idea anyway. 'Nothing earth-shattering, but it's ticking along, sir.' It was always *sir* after one of Brigstocke's looks. 'We've traced most of the male relatives now. Nothing that hopeful, but we might get lucky. Spoken to most of Remfry's former cellmates and the Gribbin thing looks the most likely . . .'

Brigstocke nodded. 'I think it sounds promising. If someone bit half my nose off, I think *I'd* bear a fucking grudge.'

'Remfry *said* it was him that did it. Probably just larging it. Anyway, we can't find Gribbin . . .'

'What else?'

Thorne held up his hands. 'That's it. Apart from chasing up the computer side of it. We can start looking at the Inmate Information System as soon as Commander Jeffries reports back.'

'He has,' Brigstocke said. 'Don't get too excited . . .'

Stephen Jeffries was a high-ranking police officer who actually worked for HM Prison Service. As the official Police Adviser he was based at Prison Service Headquarters, in a grand-looking building off Millbank, from where he could stare directly into the offices of MI6 on the opposite side of the river.

Jeffries had been looking, *quietly*, into the feasibility of a leak from the Inmate Information System. If this was where the killer was getting his information from, an awful lot of people would be wanting to know how.

'Commander Jeffries has delivered an interim judgement, suggesting that as an avenue of inquiry, this would be unlikely to prove fruitful.'

'You'll have to help me,' Thorne said. 'I haven't got my "bullshit to English" dictionary handy at the minute . . .'

'Don't be a twat, Tom. All right? That would really help *me*.'

Thorne shrugged. It sounded as if Jeffries came from the same place that shat out Chief Superintendent Trevor Jesmond. 'I'm listening.'

Brigstocke glanced down at the piece of paper on his desk, speed-read a section out loud. '"Individuals with computer access to the system are based at the main HQ building as well as the twelve regional offices nationwide – London, Yorkshire, the Midlands etc. . . ."'

Thorne groaned. 'We're talking hundreds of people . . .'

'Thousands. Checking them all out would be a major drain on manpower, even if I had it.'

Thorne nodded. 'Right. So even if that *were* to prove fruitful, it wouldn't be proving very fruitful very bloody quickly.' He picked up his empty tea cup from Brigstocke's desk, spun round on his chair, and took aim at the waste-paper basket in the corner.

'No,' Brigstocke said.

The paper cup missed by more than a foot. Thorne spun around again. 'What about somebody hacking into the system?'

'Bloody hell, thousands of suspects is bad enough, now you want millions . . .'

'I don't *want* them, but if the system isn't secure . . .'

'If that system isn't secure, a lot of people are going to get their arses severely kicked. The IIS has information on the whereabouts of every prisoner in the country, terrorists included. There's all sorts of stuff on there. If it turns out that somebody's been able to break into it, for *whatever* reason . . . Jesus, they'll be talking about Douglas Remfry in Parliament.'

'They're looking into it though?' Thorne asked.

'As far as I know . . .'

'They've got things that tell them, haven't they? If they've been hacked. Like alarms. If somebody's been trying to break into the system?'

'Don't ask me,' Brigstocke said. 'I can barely send a fucking e-mail . . .'

Not long ago even doing *that* would have been beyond Thorne, but he'd made an effort and was starting to get to grips with the technology. He'd even bought a computer to use at home. He hadn't used it very much, yet.

'So, one thing's a drain on manpower, the other's polit-ically sensitive. Has Commander Jeffries got any suggestions as to what we *can* do?'

Brigstocke took off his glasses, wiped the sweat from the

frames with a handkerchief and put them back. 'No, but *I* have. I think there are other ways that the killer could have got the information he needed about Remfry.'

'Go on . . .'

'What about if he got it from the victim's family? Gets his mum's name out of the phone book, rings up and says he's an old friend who wants to visit . . .' Thorne nodded. It was possible. 'Once he finds out where Remfry is and when he's coming out, he starts sending the letters . . .'

'He gets everything from Remfry's mother?'

'Remfry's mother . . . maybe one of the prison staff. I just think there are other things we could be looking at . . .'

'What's the motive, Russell?' Still the big question. 'Why was Remfry killed?'

Brigstocke puffed out his cheeks, leaned back in his chair. 'Fucked if I know. Got to be worth talking to Mrs Remfry again though . . .'

Thorne couldn't see it, and yet there was something in what Brigstocke had said. *Something* that had caused Thorne's heart to beat faster, just for a second; but, like the face of someone in a dream, like an object he ought to recognise, glimpsed from an unfamiliar angle, it had faded away before he could see it for what it was.

He was still trying to work it out when he spoke. 'I'm chasing something else up. Something with the photos . . .'

Brigstocke leaned forward, raised an eyebrow.

'I'll tell you if it comes to anything,' Thorne said. He looked at his watch. 'Fuck, I'm going to be late . . .'

As he was standing up, the phone began to ring in his office next door . . .

★

Holland's mobile had rung just as he was heading across to the pub, for what was becoming something of a regular lunchtime pint. Andy Stone had given him that look. The one he'd been getting from a few of the lads, whenever the mobile rang, and they saw his face as *HOME* came up on caller ID.

'Shit,' Holland said.

Stone took a few steps towards the pub doorway and stopped. 'Shall I get you one in, Dave?'

Holland pressed a button on the phone and brought it to his ear. After a few seconds he caught Stone's eye and shook his head.

Sophie was still crying when he walked through the door twenty minutes later.

'What's the matter?' He wrapped his arms around her, knowing what the answer would be.

'Nothing,' she said. 'I'm sorry . . . I know I shouldn't call.' The words sputtered into his collar between sobs.

'It's OK. Look, I've only got about a quarter of an hour, but we can have a quick bit of lunch together. I'll go back when you're feeling calmer.'

The baby was three months away. It was easy enough to put these weekly collapses down to hormones, but he knew that there was much more going on. He knew how frightened she was. Frightened that he would make a choice between her and the job. That he would think she was *forcing* him to make a choice. That the baby would not be enough to make him choose her.

He understood because he was twice as scared.

They sat on the sofa and cuddled until she grew quiet. He whispered and squeezed, feeling the bump against his leg that was the child inside her, staring across the living room and watching the minutes go by on the video recorder display.

'Thorne.'

'This is Eve Bloom . . .'

It took him a second to place the name, the voice. To put the two of them together. 'Oh . . . hello. Sorry, I was miles away. Already thinking about lunch.'

'Is this not a good time? Because . . .'

'It's fine. What can I do for you?'

'Just being nosey, if I'm honest. Wondered how it was all going. Stupid really, when I haven't the faintest idea what *it* actually is. Just, you know, curious as to whether that tape you took away has helped you . . . solve . . . *it*!'

He remembered hearing the amusement in her voice before. The phone in that hotel room, pressed tight to his ear. Happy to hear it this time.

'Fine, but I have to be somewhere about ten minutes ago, so . . .'

'That's OK, I didn't really mean now anyway . . .'

'Sorry?'

'What about lunch on Saturday? You can ask me a few pointless questions about answering machines, claim that I'm still helping you with your inquiries and stick it all on expenses. Twelve-thirty any good . . .?'

He hung up a few minutes later, just as Yvonne Kitson strolled back into the office. 'What on earth are you grinning about?' she said.

'Forget it, Mr Thorne. No fucking way am I eating duck's feet.'

75

The fact that Dennis Bethell was built like a brick shit-house, and had a voice like a chorus girl on helium, made most things he said sound vaguely ludicrous, but this was up there with the best of them . . .

It had been Thorne's idea. The last time they'd met had been in a pub and the voice, as it often did, had caused something of a scene. A sedate lunch sounded like a better idea and Thorne was fond of this place. The New Moon in the heart of Chinatown served the best dim sum in town. Thorne loved the ritual every bit as much as the food. He enjoyed watching the grumpy-looking old women as they wheeled their trolleys around the place. He liked stopping them, asking them to lift the lids, making his selections.

Thorne had had to explain the system to Bethell, who'd been sitting in a corner looking very confused when he got there. He was twenty minutes late, but Bethell hadn't been difficult to find. He was six feet three with the build of a WWF wrestler, spiky peroxide hair and a great deal of gold jewellery. Spotting him in a restaurant where the clientele was almost entirely Chinese was not exactly taxing.

Today, Bethell was wearing camouflage combats and a bright blue T-shirt stretched across his enormous chest, bearing the slogan BITCH.

'Shark's fin soup and all that, fine. Duck's *feet*? That's horrible . . .'

'Relax, Kodak,' Thorne had said. He smiled at the old woman as she lifted another bamboo lid. 'I'll order for you . . .'

They'd chatted for a while, Thorne putting his man at ease but also enjoying the to and fro of it. He was comfortable in these places, around the likes of Dennis Bethell.

Thorne popped a wafer-wrapped prawn into his mouth

and slid the photograph of Jane Foley across the table. Bethell wiped soy sauce from his fingers with a napkin and picked it up.

'Nice,' he said. 'Very nice . . .'

Thorne knew that Bethell would be talking about the picture itself. The composition, the lighting. As a hardened pornographer, he was way past appreciation of the models themselves.

'I knew you'd like it,' Thorne said.

'I do. It's very tasty. Who took it?'

'Well, do you know what, Kodak? I said to myself that if anybody could find out for me, it would be you . . .'

A bit more chat. Business, Bethell said, was booming. Though the dotcom filth merchants had once threatened the likes of him, Bethell was delighted to report that his work was more in demand than ever. Thumbnails from his legendary 1983 'Barnyard' series of pictures were being eagerly downloaded, having acquired almost legendary status among smut surfers . . .

Dennis Bethell's high-quality wank-mag work had been getting men off for about as long as Thorne had been on the job. From slightly saucy to graphic glamour spreads, Bethell was a dab hand at anything that involved a lens and nipples. He was harmless enough and had been a reliable snout for a good many years. Thorne had come to regard him as one of the city's great eccentrics. A pumped-up East End vaudevillian with a hair-trigger temper, a talent for making girls take their clothes off and his own catch-phrase, '*Nothing with children!*'

'So, come on, then,' Thorne said. 'Is it professional or not?'

Bethell peered at the image, held it up to the light, sucked his teeth. 'Yeah, maybe . . .'

'Not good enough, Kodak.' Thorne raised a finger to attract the attention of the woman behind the small bar. He held up his empty bottle of Tsing Tao, ordering another.

'It's complicated,' Bethell said. 'These days there's a huge market for professionally taken stuff that's *made* to look like it was snapped by an amateur. Like it's a picture of someone's girlfriend. See what I mean? The whole readers' wives thing. Especially with this sort of stuff.'

'What sort of stuff?'

'This S & M stuff. Handcuffs and whips and chains. Fetishism.' Bethell held up the picture which Thorne had looked at a hundred and more times. He looked at it again. This one had been taken from above, the woman flat on her face, hands bound behind her back. The hood tied at the bottom this time, like a noose.

'You ever do this sort of thing?' Thorne asked.

By now Bethell had a mouthful of minced crab dumpling. He answered cautiously, as if he thought the question was meant to catch him out somehow. 'Yeah, I *have* done. Plenty of these pervy mags around. My stuff's better than this, though . . .'

'Naturally. Listen, if this *is* a professional job, can you find out who took it?'

'I could ask around, I suppose, but . . .'

'What about where the film was developed?'

'Waste of time. Unless the bloke's a moron, he'd have done it himself. Digital camera, straight to his PC. Piece of piss . . .'

'Find out what you can, then. I want to know who the model is and who paid for the shoot.'

Bethell looked pained. 'Oh be fair, Mr Thorne. A bit of info is all well and good, but that's like doing your job for you. Like being a bloody detective.'

The waitress delivering Thorne's beer sniggered at Bethell's despairing squeak and hurried away. Thankfully Bethell didn't catch it.

'Think of it as another string to your bow, Kodak. You might fancy a change of career. The force is always on the lookout for eager young lads like yourself . . .'

'You can be a right sod sometimes, Mr Thorne . . .'

Thorne leaned across the table and held a chopstick inches away from Bethell's face. 'Yes I can, and just to prove it, if you don't make a decent fist of this for me, I will come round to your dwelling slash business premises, take your zoomiest zoom lens and stick it so far up your arse, you'll be taking pictures of your large intestine with it. Pass the prawn crackers, will you . . .?'

Bethell sulked for a few minutes. Then he picked up the photograph and slid it into the pocket of his combat trousers.

'You really should try one of these duck's feet, Kodak,' Thorne said. 'Did you know, they can actually make you swim faster?'

Bethell's eyes widened. 'Are you winding me up, Mr Thorne . . .?'

Welch was standing, waiting in the doorway when Caldicott appeared at the other end of the landing with the mail trolley. As it got closer, agonisingly slowly, stopping at almost every door, it became clear that Caldicott's face still hadn't healed properly.

One side, from mouth to forehead, was shiny, like it was slick with sweat, and the colour of something that might have been skinned. Against the raw, weeping red, the lines of tiny white rings stood out clearly, the ones on what was left of his lips looking like a row of cold sores . . .

The mail trolley squeaked that little bit nearer. Caldicott grinning as best he could, the mail round a nice cushy number. A sweetener from the caring sharing screws on the VP wing, after the weeks spent in hospital.

A couple of morons from B-wing had caught him in the laundry room. They shouldn't have been anywhere near the place by rights, should have been banged up, but someone, somewhere, had turned a blind eye. Left a door open.

One of Caldicott's women had *actually* been a girl. A fourteen-year-old. Caldicott had told Welch, sworn to him that he thought she was older, that he wasn't into meat that tender. Surely, Caldicott pleaded, surely *he* must be able to understand. He must have been in a similar position. I mean, come on, some of the girls around these days! Welch had admitted that, yes, he knew what Caldicott meant and he *had* been there himself, several times, and he mentally thanked his lucky stars that the girl he'd been caught for had been over sixteen, if not by a great deal. Caldicott had probably told *them* as well, the animals down in the laundry room. He'd have pleaded, told them that he thought the girl was older, but they wouldn't have been interested in that kind of bollocks from a nonce. These were men who dealt in facts.

While one held Caldicott calmly by the cock and balls,

the other had emptied the dryer, dropping the laundry neatly into the red plastic bucket. Then, his screams unheard or ignored, they had bent Caldicott over and forced his head and shoulders into the massive steel drum, pressing his face down on to the red-hot metal . . .

Caldicott holding out a letter, a smile pulling the seared skin up and back across his yellowing incisors. Welch, thinking he looks like the phantom of the fucking opera, snatching the envelope and stepping quickly back behind the door . . .

The envelope has been opened, of course, but he's long past caring about privacy or any of that. He has a few precious minutes alone and the chance to read her letter, the last one he will be forced to read in a tiny room that stinks of his cellmate's shit.

There's another photo. It's the first thing he looks for and he almost shouts out loud when he feels it tucked down between the pages of the letter itself. He pulls it out and slaps it down flat on his chest without looking. Then slowly he lifts it up, little by little, moaning out loud as he catches his first glimpse of her. The hood has gone, but this time her back is to the camera, her head lowered. Just a glimpse of shortish hair, the face hidden. She is sitting on her heels, her wrists fastened securely behind her, the shadows falling across her shoulder blades and beautiful, round arse . . .

The door opens and he is not alone any more. He quickly draws his knees up to hide the erection and presses the picture flat against his chest again. As his cellmate drops with a grunt on to the bed opposite, Welch is already closing his eyes, every last detail of Jane's nakedness clearly recalled and perfectly visible on the back of his eyelids.

7 MAY, 1976

'Ladies and gentlemen, you may find this surprising, but I wish, for the next few minutes, to concentrate on the evidence of a witness called by the defence . . . I invite you to consider the evidence given here by Detective Sergeant Derek Turnbull. Sergeant Turnbull's record as a police officer is exemplary and I believe we should set great store by his testimony. We should take seriously the words we have heard him speak during this very disturbing case.

'I want you to remember these words . . .

'We should remember Sergeant Turnbull's words about the interviews he carried out with the woman who accuses my client of this serious offence. He spoke about the "confusion", about the "lack of focus", he conceded under cross-examination that this woman's thinking "seemed to be all over the place". I ask you, should an incident that was, allegedly, so distressing not be easy to recall accurately? Should it not be seared into the memory? Yes, of course. And yet this woman cannot be sure about exact times. There is no consistent description of what my client was wearing at the time of the supposed attack. Just a good deal of hot air and a lot of irrelevant nonsense about aftershave . . .

'We should remember Sergeant Turnbull's words when he described the results of the physical examination. Nothing was found beneath this woman's fingernails. Nothing was found to suggest any resistance whatsoever. Sergeant Turnbull repeated to the court what she said when questioned about this fact. "I couldn't fight back," she said.

'Could not? Or did not want to?

'We should remember too, the Sergeant's words when describing the circumstances of the first interview, the first physical examination. This examination was, in his words, "worse than useless", taking place as it did the morning after the alleged attack and after the so-called victim had showered. Remember his colleague's words when describing the dress which you have been shown as Exhibit A? "Too nice to wear to work." I put these things together, ladies and gentlemen, and I come up with an altogether different version of what happened in that stockroom in December of last year . . .

'Could not that dress have been torn during the frenzied, and consensual, bout of lovemaking to which my client freely admits? Could not the bruising be no more than the marks of excessive passion? Could not that shower have been taken, yes, to wash away the smell of my client, but only so as to hide the truth of her ongoing sexual relationship with him from her husband?

'I have asked you to remember the words of a police officer whose evidence was intended to damn the man I represent here today. Instead, unwittingly, I'm sure, he has done quite the opposite. I have asked you to consider these words and I can see that you are doing just that. I can see from your faces, ladies and gentlemen of the jury, that these words have caused you, quite rightly, to doubt. If you doubt, as you surely must, the truth of what this woman claims to have happened, then I know that your deliberations in the jury room will be very short.

'The law, of course, is quite clear about reasonable doubt. I feel sure that this being the case, doubting as you must, you will do the right thing. You will do the just thing. You will do as His Honour must instruct you so to do, and acquit my client . . .'

FIVE

Another hot, humid evening. The air outside heavy with the taste of a storm on the way. Tantalising snippets of conversation from people walking past drifted into the living room through the open windows.

Thorne had sat eating in T-shirt and shorts, listening to the noise from a party on the other side of the road. He didn't know what annoyed him more – the raised voices and the cranked-up sound system, or the good time that some people he didn't know were clearly having.

His plate licked clean by Elvis, Thorne had opened a can of cheap lager, tuned out the sounds of music and laughter and spent a couple of hours reading. A summer's evening absorbed in violent death.

These were the reports based on searches of CRIM-INT – the Criminal Intelligence database – looking for any cases whose parameters might overlap with the Remfry killing . . .

Holland and Stone had been thorough. It was largely about trial and error, about narrowing the search down and coming up with hits that might be significant. Keywords were entered. Matches were sifted and examined in relation to those from other searches. *Rape/murder* produced few cases where the victim was male, but the results were still cross-referenced with those that came up when other, more specific keywords were punched into the system.

Sodomy. Strangulation. Ligature. Washing line.

And up they'd come . . .

A series of unsolved murders going back five years. Eight young boys brutally abused and strangled, their bodies dumped in woods, gravel pits and recreation grounds. A paedophile ring that was too well organised or too well connected. Uncatchable.

A man attacked in his own home. Tied up with washing line while his home was ransacked, then kicked to death for no good reason. Thorne thought about Darren Ellis, the old couple he'd tied up and robbed . . .

A catalogue of vicious sexual assaults and murders, many still unsolved. The grim details now little more than entries in a uniquely disturbing reference library. A resource to be accessed, in the hope that a past horror might shed light on a present one.

Not this time.

Holland *had* actually pulled the files on two cold murder cases: a young man, thirty or so, found in the boot of a car in 2002. Raped and choked to death with an unidentified ligature. A man in his sixties, attacked in a multi-storey car park and strangled with washing line in 1996.

Thorne had agreed both with Holland's initial assessment and his final conclusion. Both files had been worth a closer look. Both had been put back.

Once he'd stuffed the report away in his briefcase,

Thorne went over and stood by the open window. For ten minutes or so he'd stared across at the house where the party was, trying and failing to identify a song from its annoyingly familiar bass-line. Trying and failing to stop thinking about bodies years dead and a body as yet unburied and the photograph he'd given Dennis Bethell . . .

Then he'd called his father.

After he'd hung up, twenty frustrating minutes later, Thorne stood, holding the phone, and tried to imagine the synapses in his father's brain misfiring, the thoughts exploding in a shower of tangential sparks . . .

The cascade of colour blackened. It became the dark hood that covered the head of a naked woman and masked the terror on the face of a pale, stiffening corpse. Life choked off and arse exposed and a thin line of brown blood on rusty bedsprings.

Thorne took off what few clothes he still had on, walked through to the bedroom and dropped down on to the mattress. He lay there in the semi-darkness, staring up at the outline of the lampshade that had cost a pound from IKEA, realising that it was cheap because it was also nasty.

The bed felt as if it were full of grit.

He could feel the dreadful, delicate weight of the case upon him. Like the dark tickle of something unwanted crawling across his body. The sharp, spindly legs of it picking their way across the sheen of sweat on his chest.

Thorne closed his eyes, remembering a moment of calm and contentment on a bracken-covered hillside.

Except that he was unsure it *was* a memory. If it had ever happened, the details had slipped away over time.

Perhaps it was the memory of a dream he'd once had, or a fantasy of some sort. Maybe it was a scene from a long-forgotten film or TV show he'd once watched and into which he'd projected himself . . .

Wherever it came from, two others were always there with him, lying on the hillside among the bracken. A man and a woman, or perhaps a girl and a boy. Their ages were as unclear as their relationship to him or each other, but all three of them were happy. Where they actually were never seemed to matter. The geography of the place was change-able. Sometimes he was sure there was a river down below them. At other times it was a road, the hum of insects becoming the distant drone of traffic.

The only constants were the bracken and the presence of the pair lying just a few feet away, the ground beneath and the sky above the three of them . . .

It seemed as if they'd eaten something, a picnic maybe. Thorne felt full, lying there, his arms spread out wide, six inches off the ground, moving lazily back and forth through the bracken. He had a smile on his face and his stomach still jumped and fluttered with the final bursts of laughter. He could never be sure who or what had caused them all to laugh such a lot. He could never be sure of much beyond the fine, unfamiliar feeling that surged through him as he remembered. As he imagined. As he *lay* on that hillside.

Blurred as the edges of Thorne's reality on that hillside were – the whys and whens and whos so indistinct as to be virtually non-existent – it still seemed, at moments such as these, ankle-deep in madness and butchery, a pretty good place to be.

With the first, fat raindrops beginning to fall outside, he pressed his head back into the pillow and imagined the fronds of bracken, feathery against his neck.

As the headlights from passing cars played across the bedroom window, Thorne felt only the sunlight on his face.

12 JUNE, 1976

They moved through the shopping centre, almost touching, their faces blank, each carrying a bag. A couple walking around the shops together. Seeing them, no one could ever have known.

The enormity of the space between them.

The pain that grew to fill it.

How little time they had left . . .

They touched things in shops, picked up items to get a closer look, occasionally made the same banal comments they might have made six months before. 'We could put that in the kitchen.' 'Do you think one of those would look nice in the bedroom?' 'That colour really suits you.'

They walked into a shop which sold ugly ornaments, useless knick-knacks, like two people in a dream . . .

Since the day the trial had ended, they had been going through the motions. Shopping, eating, tidying toys away. Sitting on the settee together and watching It's a Knockout *and* George and Mildred. *Getting through the days. The only obvious change being that she hadn't gone back to work. Unlike Franklin. He'd been welcomed back with apologies and open arms.*

Out of one shop and into another. They strolled through a department store, taking care, of course, to avoid the cosmetics department. The perfumes, and especially the aftershave. These days, the great smell of Brut was liable to make her throw up all over the place.

They were almost perfect, like the victims of bodysnatchers. They were a 'Spot the Difference' competition that was unwinnable. The 'before' and 'after' were, to all intents and purposes, identical, but what was in their heads and their hearts would never be seen, could never be imagined. Least of all by them.

She had retreated into herself and he had become unbearably buoyant. Around the house their bodies did the normal things, while her silence and his false cheer chased each other from room to room. While the mania and the suspicion festered and matured.

It was my fault . . .

Why didn't she struggle . . .?

He was looking at picture frames, remembering the face of the jury foreman. A few feet away, she stood, spinning a display of postcards, seeing only stubby fingers reaching into trousers, scrabbling at her crotch. He caught her eye but she looked away before he could smile.

The next second, Franklin's wife had stepped from behind a glass display case and was standing in front of her.

He took a step towards them, then stopped as his wife raised a hand, reached towards this woman who had looked down on her, at her, every day from the public gallery. He watched as Franklin's wife ignored the hand that reached out to her, pulled back her head and snapped it forward, releasing a thick gobbet of spittle into his wife's face.

There was a gasp from a woman nearby. Another stepped back, open-mouthed, and knocked a glass decanter crashing to the floor.

He stepped in front of his wife then, and guided her gently but firmly towards the exit. As they left she never took her eyes from the woman who had spat at her. She never made a move to wipe the spit away.

She didn't speak a word, as she was taken back to a house she would never leave again.

SIX

From Kentish Town, Thorne took every rat-run he knew, cutting through side streets until he reached Highbury Corner and then heading east along the Balls Pond Road towards Hackney.

Thorne took a quick glance at his *A–Z*. The florist's was tucked away somewhere behind Mare Street, a stone's throw from London Fields. This area of parkland stood alone in the midst of one of the most depressed areas in the city. It was once grazed by sheep, and prowled by highwaymen. Now, up-and-comers who directed videos or worked in advertising sat on benches sipping their skinny lattés, or walked their whippets across the green, doing their best to convince as geezers.

Thorne drove along streets bustling with Saturday-morning shoppers. Noisy with the cries of greeting, the shouts of traders in the markets. And every few hundred yards, a look on a face or a hand thrust into a pocket that Thorne recognised as the signs of an altogether different kind of business.

Here, as in a dozen other boroughs, street crime was out of control. Phone-jacking was virtually a form of social interaction and if you walked around with a personal stereo, you were a tourist who couldn't read a street map.

These days, the highwaymen prowled in gangs.

So the powers-that-be, in their infinite wisdom and desire for good press, were targeting areas like Hackney, piloting schemes that would involve the youth of an area. Thorne had read a report of one such scheme involving a couple of earnest young officers trading in the blue serge for hooded tops, and getting down with the kids in a local community centre. One had asked a thirteen-year-old gang member if he could think of ways he might avoid getting into trouble with the police.

The kid had answered without a trace of irony. 'Wear a balaclava.'

It was a small place, sitting between a minicab firm and a locksmith's. The shopfront was pleasingly old fashioned; the window display minimalist, the name painted in a green, creeping ivy design on a plain cream background.

BLOOMS.

Inside, the shop was lit by candles. There was classical music playing quietly in the background. There wasn't a single flower Thorne recognised . . .

'Are you looking for something in particular?' A man, thirty or so, with a paperback in his hand, stood behind a small wooden counter.

Thorne moved towards him, smiling. 'Do people not buy daffs any more? Roses, chrysanthemums . . .?'

A woman carrying an enormous assortment of flowers stepped through a door at the back of the shop. She looked to be in her mid-thirties. As soon as she spoke, Thorne recognised the voice – gabbling, confident, *amused*. It was clear that Eve Bloom had recognised him as well.

'Well, we can get that sort of specialised stuff in if you want, Mr Thorne, but it *will* be very expensive . . .'

He laughed, sizing her up in a few seconds. Though her hands stayed busy among the stems she was carrying, he could tell that she was doing the same.

She was short, maybe five feet two, with blond hair held up by a large wooden clip. She wore a brown apron over jeans and a sweatshirt. Her face was dotted with freckles, and the smile revealed a gap between her two top teeth.

Thorne fancied the pants off her on sight.

The man behind the counter had picked up a notepad. 'Shall I put in an order, Eve? For the roses and those other things . . .?'

She put down the arrangement, lifted the apron over her head, smiled gently at him. 'No, I don't think so, Keith.' She turned to Thorne. 'I thought we could go to this great little tea-room just around the corner. Cream teas to die for. What do you think? We've got the weather for it after all. We can pretend we're in Devon or somewhere . . .'

As they strolled, she talked virtually constantly. 'Keith helps me out on a Saturday morning. He's fantastic with flowers, and the customers are very fond of him. Rest of the week I can manage the place on my own, but Saturday, early, that's when I have to make up most of the wedding arrangements, get ahead on the paperwork, accounts and what have you. Anyway, sod it! Today, Keith can keep an eye on things for an hour or so while we pig out. He's not a genius, bless him, but he works his socks off for . . . well, for bugger all, if I'm honest.'

'What does Keith do the rest of the time?' Thorne said. 'When you're not exploiting him.'

Eve smiled and shrugged. 'Don't really know, to be honest. I think he has to look after his mother a lot. Maybe she's well off, because he never seems to be short. He's certainly not working in *my* shop for the money, not on what I can afford to pay him. God, I am *so* gasping for a cup of tea . . .'

The tea-room was kitsch beyond belief, with check tablecloths, art deco tea-sets and Bakelite radios dotted around on shelves and window ledges. The cream tea for two arrived almost instantly. Eve poured Earl Grey for herself, monkey tea for Thorne. She lathered jam and clotted cream on to her scone, grinned across the table.

'Listen, when I'm eating is probably the best chance you'll have to get a word in, so I should take your chance if I were you. I know I talk *way* too much . . .'

'The man who left the message on your answering machine, has he been in touch with you again?' She looked at him, confused. 'Follow-up question,' Thorne explained. 'Justify the expenses claim, like you suggested. Bit of a long shot, but it seemed as good a question as any . . .'

She cleared her throat. 'No, Detective Inspector, I'm afraid that I never heard from the man again.'

'Thank you. If you think of anything else you will get in touch, won't you? And I needn't tell you that we'd prefer it if you didn't leave the country . . .'

She laughed and pushed the last piece of a scone into her mouth. When she'd finished it she looked straight at him, raising a hand to shield her eyes against the sunlight that streamed in through the picture window. 'I take it you haven't caught him yet?' Thorne looked back at her, still eating. 'Did he kill somebody?'

Thorne swallowed. 'I'm sorry, I shouldn't . . .'

'I'm just putting two and two together, really.' She leaned back in her chair. 'I know it's a man, because I've heard his voice, and you told me you were with the Serious Crime Group, so I'm guessing that you're not after this bloke because he hasn't taken his library books back.'

Thorne poured himself another cup of tea. 'Yes, he did kill somebody. No, we haven't caught him yet.'

'Are you going to?'

Thorne poured *her* a cup . . .

'Why me?' she said. 'Why did he pick me to order the wreath from?'

'I think he picked a name at random,' Thorne said. They'd found a tattered Yellow Pages in the cupboard beneath the bedside table. It had been covered in finger-prints. Thorne doubted any belonged to the killer. 'He just let his fingers do the walking.'

She pulled a face. 'I knew I shouldn't have stumped up for that bloody box-ad . . .'

Though she talked twice as much, and ten times as quickly as he did, Thorne still talked more, and more easily, in the hour or so that followed than he could remember doing to almost anybody for a long time. To any woman, certainly . . .

'When's the wedding?' Eve asked, as their plates were cleared away.

Thorne was struck then by how much ground they'd covered and how quickly. 'A week today. God, I'd rather stick needles in my eyes . . .'

'Do you not get on with your cousin?'

Thorne smiled at the waitress as she popped the bill down on the table. 'I barely know him. Probably wouldn't recognise him if he walked in here. Just family dos, you know . . .'

'Right. You choose your friends, but you can't choose your relatives.'

'Yours as bad as mine, then?'

She brushed a few stray crumbs from the tabletop into her hand, emptied it on to the floor. 'Is he the same sort of age as you? Your cousin?'

'No, Eileen's a lot younger than my dad, and she had Trevor pretty late. He's still only early thirties, I think . . .'

'What are you?'

'How *old*, you mean?' She nodded. Thorne opened his wallet, dropped fifteen pounds on top of the bill. 'Forty-two. Forty-three in . . . fuck, in ten days.'

She clipped up a few stray hairs that had tumbled loose. 'I won't say that you don't look it, because that always sounds so false, but looking at you, I'd say that they were forty-three pretty interesting years.'

Thorne nodded. 'I'm not going to argue, but just so you know . . . I don't mind about the sounding-false thing.'

She smiled, put on a pair of small, almond-shaped sunglasses. 'Forty then. Late thirties at a push.'

Thorne stood up, pulling his leather jacket from the chair behind him. 'I'll settle for that . . .'

Back at the shop they swapped business cards, shook hands and stood together, a little awkwardly, in the doorway. Thorne looked around. 'Maybe I should get a plant or something . . .'

Eve bent down and picked up what looked like a miniature metal bucket. A cactus-like plant sprouted from a layer of smooth white pebbles. She handed it to him. 'Do you like this?'

Thorne was far from sure. 'What do I owe you?'

'Nothing. It's an early birthday present.'

He studied it from every angle. 'Right. Thanks . . .'

'It's an aloe vera plant.'

Thorne nodded. Over her shoulder, he could see Keith watching them closely from behind the counter. 'So I should be all right for shampoo . . .'

'There's a gel in the leaves, very good for cuts and scrapes.'

Thorne looked at the fierce-looking spikes growing along the edges of the plant's sword-shaped leaves. 'That'll come in handy.'

They stepped out on to the pavement, the slight awkwardness returning. Thorne noticed a silver scooter parked by the side of the shop – one of the latest Vespas, based on the classic design. He nodded towards it. 'Yours?'

She shook her head. 'God, no. That's Keith's.' She pointed to the other side of the road. 'That's me over there . . .'

Thorne looked across the road at the grubby white van behind which he'd parked the Mondeo. The name of the shop was painted on its side, in the same creeping-ivy design as was on the shopfront.

'The name certainly fits,' he said.

She laughed. 'Right. Like being an undertaker called De'Ath. What else could I do? Flowers are the only thing I can think of that bloom . . .'

Thorne could think of several other things, but he shook his head, not wanting to say anything that might spoil a nice afternoon. 'No, you're right,' he said.

Thinking . . .

Bruises. Tumours. Bloodstains . . .

For the fourth time in the last hour, Welch was answering the same stupid set of questions.

'Date of birth?'

Maybe the officers just passed the list between themselves. You'd have thought that at least one of them could have come up with something more interesting . . .

'Mother's maiden name?'

But no. Same tired old teasers designed to catch out the impostor. The process had gone unchanged for many years but these days they really weren't taking any chances. Not since the incident a couple of months earlier. A couple of Pakis in a prison up north had swapped places on release day and the silly bastards had let the wrong one out. Several screws had blown their pensions that day and, once the jungle drums had finished beating, given every con in the country a fucking good laugh . . .

'Do you have any tattoos?'

'Can I ask the audience?'

'You want to be a smartarse, Welch, we can start the whole thing over again . . .'

Welch smiled and answered the questions. He wasn't going to do anything silly at this stage of the game. Each door he walked through, each successfully completed series of questions, each tick on a chart took him one step further away from the centre of the place. One step closer to the final door.

Answering pointless questions and signing his name over and over. Taking receipt of his travel warrant and discharge grant. Taking back his property. The battered wallet, the wristwatch, the ring of yellow metal. Always 'yellow metal'. Never 'gold' in case the bastards lose it . . .

Then through another door and on to another screw, and all this one gets to say to him is 'goodbye'.

Welch walked away towards the gate. He moved slowly, savouring every step, seconds away from the moment when he would hear the clang of the heavy door behind him and feel the heat of the day on his face.

And look up at a sun the colour of yellow metal.

For Thorne and Hendricks, a Saturday night in front of the television with beer and a takeaway curry was a regular pleasure. For nine months of the year there was football to watch, to argue about. Tonight, the start of the new season still seven weeks away, they would probably watch a film. Or just sit through whatever was on until, a couple of cans in, they stopped really caring. Maybe they would just put some music on and talk.

It was nearly nine o'clock and the light was only just starting to fade. They walked down Kentish Town Road, away from the restaurant and back towards Thorne's place. Both wore jeans and a T-shirt though Thorne's were far and away the baggier and less eye-catching. Hendricks carried a plastic bag, heavy with cans of lager, while Thorne took responsibility for the curry. The Bengal Lancer delivered, but it was a nice evening for a walk and there was the added attraction of a cold pint of Kingfisher while they'd waited, the smell coming from the kitchens sharpening the edges of their appetites.

'Why the rape?' Thorne asked suddenly.

Hendricks nodded. 'Right. Good move. Let's get the shoptalk out the way – you know, the rape and murder stuff – then we can relax and enjoy *Casualty* . . .'

Thorne ignored the sarcasm. 'Everything else, so well planned, so meticulously done. He takes no chances. He strips the bed even after he's killed Remfry on the floor. Takes everything away to make sure he leaves nothing of himself behind . . .'

'Nothing strange about not wanting to get caught.'

'No, but it was all so careful. Ritualised almost. Whether it happened before or after the murder, I don't see the rape as part of that. Maybe he just snapped at some point, lost it . . .'

'I can't see it, myself. The killer didn't just go mental and do it without thinking. He knew what he was doing. He wore a condom, so he was still wary, still in control . . .'

There were dozens of people gathered outside the Grapevine pub. They spilled across the pavement, laughing and drinking, enjoying the weather. Hendricks was forced to drop behind Thorne as they stepped into the road to skirt round the crowd.

'You think the rape wasn't part of the plan?' Hendricks was abreast of Thorne again. 'You think he just decided to do it once he'd got there?'

'No, I think he planned the whole thing. The rape just seems . . .'

'It was more violent than most, I agree, but rape's hardly delicate, is it?'

An old man waiting at a zebra crossing to cross the road caught just enough of the conversation. He jerked his head around and, ignoring the signal to cross, watched them walk away. A frustrated driver waiting at the crossing glared at the old man and leaned on his horn . . .

'I'm not sure why it bothers me,' Thorne said. 'It's a murder investigation but it's the rape part that feels significant . . .'

'You think the killer was making a point?'

'Don't you?' Hendricks shrugged and nodded, heaved the bag up and slid a protective arm underneath. 'Right,' Thorne said. 'So why is the simple grudge scenario not playing out . . .?'

They walked on past the sandwich bar and the bank. Music was coming from behind open windows, drifting out of bars and down from roof terraces. Rap and blues and heavy metal. To Thorne, the atmosphere on the street seemed as relaxed as he could remember. Warm weather did strange things to Londoners. On sweaty, rush-hour tubes, tempers shortened as temperatures rose. Later, when it got a few degrees cooler and people had a drink in their hands, it was a different story . . .

Thorne smiled grimly. He knew it was only a small window of opportunity. Later still, when darkness fell and the booze began to kick in, the Saturday-night soundtrack would become a little more familiar.

Sirens and screaming and breaking glass . . .

As if on cue, as Hendricks and Thorne walked past the late-night grocers, two teenagers, standing outside, began to push each other. It might have been harmless, it might have been the start of something.

Thorne stopped, took a step back.

'Oi . . .'

The taller of the two turned and looked Thorne up and down, still clutching a fistful of the other's blue Hilfiger shirt. He was no more than fifteen. 'What's your fucking problem?'

'I don't have a problem,' Thorne said.

The shorter one shook himself free and turned square on to Thorne. 'You will have in a minute if you don't piss off . . .'

'Go home,' Thorne said. 'Your mum's probably worried.'

The taller one sniggered, but his mate was less amused. He looked quickly up and down the street. 'You want me to smack a couple of your teeth out?'

'Only if you want me to nick you,' Thorne said.

Now they both laughed. 'You a fucking copper, man? No way . . .'

'OK,' Thorne said. 'I'm not a copper. And you're just a couple of innocent young scallywags minding your own business, right? Nothing I should have to worry about, you know, if I *were* a police officer, in any of your pockets.' He saw the eyes of the taller boy flick towards those of his friend. 'Maybe I should check though, just to be on the safe side . . .'

Thorne leaned, smiling, towards them. Hendricks stepped forward and hissed in his ear. 'Come on, Tom, for fuck's sake . . .'

A girl, two or three years older, walked out of the shop. She handed each of the boys a can of Tennent's Extra, opened one herself. 'What's going on?'

The boy in the blue shirt pointed at Thorne. 'Reckons he's a copper, says he's going to arrest us.'

The girl took a noisy slug of beer. 'Nah . . . he's not going to arrest anybody.' She pointed with the can towards the bag Thorne was holding. 'Doesn't want to let his fucking dinner go cold . . .'

More laughter. Hendricks put a hand on Thorne's shoulder.

Thorne carefully put the bag on the ground. 'I'm not hungry any more. Now turn out your pockets . . .'

'You love this, don't you?' the girl said. 'Have you got a hard-on?'

'Turn out your pockets.'

The boys stared at him, cold. The girl had another swig of beer. Thorne took a step towards them and *then* they moved. The shorter boy stepped round his friends and away, running a step or two before slowing, regaining his composure. The girl moved away more slowly, dragging the taller of the boys by the sleeve. They stared at Thorne as they went, walking away backwards up the street.

The girl lobbed her empty can into the road and shouted back at Thorne.

'Poofs! Fucking queers . . .'

Thorne lurched forward to chase after them but Hendricks's hand, which had never left his shoulder, squeezed and held on. 'Just leave it.'

'No.'

'Forget it, calm down . . .'

He yanked his shoulder free. 'Little fuckers . . .'

Hendricks stepped in front of Thorne, picked up the bag and held it out to him.

'What are you more pissed off about, Tom? The fact that I was called a queer? Or that *you* were?'

Unable to answer the question, Thorne took the bag and they carried on walking. They veered almost immediately right on to Angler's Lane, a one-way street that would bring them out close to Thorne's flat. This narrow cut-through to Prince of Wales Road had once been a small tributary off the River Fleet, now one of London's 'lost' underground rivers. Here, when Victoria took the throne, local boys would fish for carp and trout, before the water became so stinking and polluted that no fish could survive, and it had to be diverted beneath the earth, confined and hidden away in a thick iron pipe.

Now, as Thorne walked home along the course of the lost river, it seemed to him that nearly two centuries later the stench was just as bad.

By a little after ten, Hendricks was fast asleep on the sofa, and likely to remain so well into Sunday morning. Thorne tidied up around him, switched off the TV and went into the bedroom.

He got no reply from the flat. She answered her mobile almost immediately.

'It's Thorne. I hope it's not too late. I remembered from the sign on the door of the shop that you weren't open on Sundays, so I thought you might . . .'

'It's fine. No problem . . .'

Thorne lay back on the bed. He thought that she sounded pretty pleased to hear from him.

'I wanted to say thanks,' he said. 'I enjoyed today.'

'Good. Me too. Want to do it again?'

During the short pause that followed, Thorne looked up at the cheap, crappy lampshade, listened to her laughing quietly. There was a noise he couldn't place in the background. 'Bloody hell,' he said. 'You don't waste a lot of time . . .'

'What's the point? We only saw each other a few hours ago and you're ringing up, so *you're* obviously pretty keen.'

'Obviously . . .'

'Right, well, tomorrow's for sleeping and I'm busy in the evening. So, how keen would you say you are, *really*? On a scale of one to ten . . .'

'Er . . . how does *seven* sound?'

'Seven's good. Any less and I'd've been insulted and more would have been borderline stalker. Right then, what about breakfast on Monday? I know a great caff . . .'

'Breakfast?'

'Why not? I'll meet you before work.'

'OK, I'll probably have to be at work about nine-ish, so . . .'

Eve laughed. 'I thought you were keen, Thorne! We're talking about when *I* start work. Half past five, New Covent Garden flower market . . .'

17 JULY, 1976

It was more than half an hour since he'd heard the noises. The grunting and the shouting and the sounds of glass shattering. He heard her footsteps as she moved around, from her bedroom across that creaky floorboard that he'd never got around to fixing, into the bathroom and back again.

He spent that half-hour willing himself to get up off the settee and see what had happened. Not moving. Needing to build up some strength, some control before he could venture upstairs . . .

Sitting in front of the television, wondering how much longer this was going to go on. The doctor had said that if she kept taking the tranquillisers, then things would settle down, but there was no sign of that happening. In the meantime, he was having to do all the stuff that needed doing. Everything. She was in no state to go to the shops or to the school. Christ, it had been over a week since she'd last come downstairs.

Walking across to the foot of the stairs, stiff and slow as a Golem . . .

Listening to it, watching it, feeling it all come apart. They'd given him the time off work, but the sick pay wasn't going to last for ever and she was contributing nothing and now the debts were growing as thick and fast as the suspicion. Mushrooming, like the doubts that sprouted in every damp, dark corner of their lives; had been, ever since that moment when the foreman of the jury had stood and cleared his throat.

He walked into the bedroom, feeling the carpet crunch beneath his feet. He glanced down at a dozen, distorted reflections of himself in the shards of broken mirror, then across to where she lay, no more than a lump beneath the blankets. He turned and walked back the way he'd come. Back across the creaky floor-board.

In the bathroom, he skidded in the puddles of ivory face-cream. He stepped across the piss-coloured slicks of perfume. He kicked away the broken bottles into every corner.

So much that was designed to smell alluring, desirable, mingled unnaturally on floor and walls, making him heave . . .

He moved across to the sink, afraid he would retch. He found it filled with the contents of the cabinet that stood empty above it.

Blusher and lipstick and eye-shadow ground into the porcelain.

Moisturiser clogging the plughole like poisonous waste.

Powder and shampoo and bath oil, thrown and poured and sprinkled.

The edges of her fancy soaps blunted against the walls. Dents in the plasterboard, pink as babies, blue as bruises. The mirror cracked, and spattered with nail varnish, red as arterial spray . . .

He ran a tap into the perfumed swamp, splashed water on to his face. He looked around at her handprints in talcum, the fingertrails dragged through brightly coloured body lotion. Hints of herself left behind in everything she was trying to discard.

She'd been fine until they'd found her out, hadn't she? Fine with the knowledge of what she'd done as long as it stayed just between her and Franklin. Now the guilt was eating at her, wasn't it? Sending her fucking mental or making her pretend that she was, it didn't really matter which.

Half a minute later he was walking back down the stairs, thinking, She lied, she lied, she lied, she lied . . .

She. Lied.

SEVEN

Thorne might well have gone right off Eve Bloom had she been a morning person – one of those deeply annoying types who is always bright-eyed and bushy-tailed whatever the ungodly hour. As it was, he was relieved to find her wedged into a quiet corner, clutching a polystyrene cup filled with seriously strong tea, and grimacing at nothing in particular. She clearly felt as much like a warmed-up bag of shit as he did . . .

Thorne cranked his face into action and forced a smile. 'And there I was, thinking that you'd be full of the joys of it.' She stared at him, said nothing..'Fired up by the noise and the colour, intoxicated by the sweet smell of a million flowers . . .'

She scowled. 'Bollocks.'

Thorne shivered slightly and rubbed his arms through the sleeves of his leather jacket. It might have been the hottest summer for a good few years, but at this time in the morning it was still distinctly bloody nippy.

'Like that then?' he said. 'Floristry losing its appeal, is it?'

She took a noisy slurp of tea. 'Some aspects get ever so slightly on my tits, yes . . .'

They stepped back as a trolley piled high with long, multicoloured boxes came past. The porter behind it winked at Eve, laughed when she gave him the finger.

'You know you want me, Evie,' he shouted, wheeling the trolley away.

She turned back to Thorne. 'So, you love *everything* about your job, do you?'

'No, not everything. I'm not big on post-mortems or armed sieges. Or team-building seminars . . .'

'There you go, then . . .'

'Most of the time though, I *think* I love it . . .'

There was the first hint of a smile. She was starting to enjoy their double act. 'Sounds to me like maybe you love it, but you're not *in* love with it . . .'

'Right.' Thorne nodded. 'Problems with commitment.'

She blew on to the tea, her pale face deadpan. 'Typical bloke,' she said. Then she laughed and Thorne got his first glimpse that day of the gap in her teeth that he liked so much . . .

They moved methodically through the vast, indoor market. Up and down the wide concrete aisles. He followed a few steps behind her, cradling his own cup of rust-coloured tea and feeling himself coming slowly to life, the creases cracking open. Taking it all in . . .

The shouts and whistles of traders and customers alike echoing through the gigantic warehouse. Twenty- and fifty-pound notes counted out and slapped into palms. Porters humping boxes or steering noisy forklifts in their green, fluorescent jackets. *All* the colours – the stock, the signs, the punters' fleecy tops and puffa jackets – all standing out against the dazzling white buzz of a thousand striplights, dangling from the girders forty feet above.

Eve Bloom clearly knew every inch of this space the size of two football pitches; where to find every wholesaler and specialist; where to get the pots, the bulbs, the sundries; the location of any plant, flower or tree among tens of thousands of others. Thorne watched as she ordered, as she haggled and as she connected with stallholders and market staff.

'All right, Evie darlin' . . .'

'How are you, sweetheart . . .?'

'Here she is! Where you been hiding yourself, love . . .?'

Despite her earlier stab at grumpiness, Thorne could see that she really enjoyed *this* part of the job. The smile was instant, the banter good natured and flirtatious. If her customers liked her half as much as those she was buying from, her shop was probably doing pretty well. For all this, it was clear that she drove a hard bargain and would take nothing unless the price was right. The wholesalers shook their heads as they tapped at their computer keyboards or scribbled in their pink order books. 'I'm cutting my throat selling at this price . . .' Within half an hour she was done and there was no shortage of porters volunteering to load up her boxes and take them out to where her small white van was parked.

Once business was out of the way, she took Thorne on one last circuit of the market. She showed him a bewildering selection of different flowers – the ones she liked or hated, the sweetest smelling and the oddest looking. She pointed out the red and yellow gerberas, lined up neatly in rows and stacked in small square boxes like fruit. The pink

peonies, the orange protea like pin cushions, and the phal-
lic anthuriums, their heads like something Dennis Bethell
might photograph. Thorne saw enough Jersey carnations to
fill every buttonhole at a century's worth of society weddings and enough lilies for a thousand good funerals. He
looked at daisies and delphiniums, the stuff of cheap and
cheerful bouquets for desperate men to buy from petrol
station forecourts in the early hours. Then there were gang-
ling, blue and orange birds of paradise at five pounds a
stem and fruiting lemon trees in vast pots, both surely destined for the dining tables and bespoke conservatories of
Hampstead and Highgate.

Thorne nodded, asked the occasional question, looked
keen. When she asked, he told her he was enjoying himself.
In truth, though he was impressed by her knowledge and
touched to a degree by her enthusiasm, he was dreaming of
bacon sandwiches . . .

Half an hour later, and Thorne's fantasy had become
greasy reality. Eve had kept him company, working her
way through sausage, egg and chips like a long-distance
lorry driver. It may or may not have been her breakfast of
choice, but the café was not the sort of place that offered
much in the way of a healthy alternative.

'How often do you do this?' Thorne asked.

'Harden my arteries or get up horribly early?'

'The market . . .'

'Just one day a week, thank God. Some people do it two
or three times a week, but I'm much too fond of my bed.'

Thorne swallowed another mouthful of tea. In the two
and something hours he'd been up, he'd already drunk

more tea than he'd normally consume in a week. He could feel it, sloshing about in his belly like dirty water at the bottom of a tank.

'So what you bought this morning's going to last you the week, then?'

'Well, if it does, the business is in big trouble. The rest of the stock I need comes over from Holland. This mad Dutchman drives a big van over on a Friday, goes round every small florist in East London. It's more expensive than coming down here but I get a lie-in, so sod it . . .'

She reached into a small leather rucksack, pulled out a packet of Silk Cut. She offered it to Thorne. 'Want one?'

'No, I don't, thanks.' This wasn't strictly true. Fifteen and more years he'd been off the fags, and he *still* wanted one . . .

She lit up, took a long drag. Drew the smoke down deep and let it out slowly with a low hum of contentment. 'It's your birthday a week today, isn't it?'

'You've got a good memory,' he said. He puffed out his cheeks. 'Mine's getting worse the older I get.' He pulled a mock-sulky face. 'Thanks for reminding me about *that*, by the way . . .'

A spark flared briefly inside his head then fizzled and died. There was something he was trying to remember, something he knew was important to the case. It was something he'd read. Or maybe something he hadn't *read . . .*

He brought his eyes back to Eve and saw that she was speaking. Saying something he couldn't hear. 'Sorry, what . . .?'

She leaned across the table. 'Be a nice birthday present to yourself if you solved your case, wouldn't it?'

112

Thorne nodded slowly, smiled. 'Well, I *had* promised myself some CDs . . .'

She flicked ash from her cigarette, rubbed the tip around the edge of the ashtray. 'You don't like talking about your job, do you?'

He looked at her for a few seconds before answering. 'There's things I *can't* talk about, especially with you being involved. The stuff I *can* talk about just isn't very exciting . . .'

'And you think I'd be as bored as *you* were when I showed you round the market . . .?'

'I wasn't bored.'

'Do the criminals you interview lie as badly as you do?'

Thorne laughed. 'I wish.'

She stubbed out her cigarette, leaned back in her chair and looked at him. 'I'm interested. In what you do.'

He remembered the way he'd felt talking to her in the tea-room. How it had seemed like a long time since he'd spoken to a woman like that. It was a hell of a lot longer since he'd talked about the job. 'Murder cases go cold very quickly . . .'

'So you need to catch the killer straight away?'

Thorne nodded. 'If you're going to get a result it tends to happen in the first few days. It's been a fortnight already . . .'

'You never know . . .'

'I do, unfortunately.'

She pushed her chair away from the table and stood up. 'I need to go and get rid of some of that tea . . .'

While she was in the toilet, Thorne stared out of the steamy window. The café was in a side street between

113

Wandsworth Road and Nine Elms Lane. From where he was sitting, Thorne could see the rush-hour traffic moving slowly across Vauxhall Bridge. Cars carrying their occupants north towards Victoria and Piccadilly, or south to Camberwell and Clapham. Towards shops and offices and warehouses where they would moan and joke about another bloody Monday and then not spend it failing to catch a killer.

It was a close call, but Thorne would not have swapped places with them.

Eve rejoined him. Above them, a train rumbled by on its way into Waterloo. She had to raise her voice. 'I forgot to ask,' she said, 'how's the plant?'

'Sorry?'

'The aloe vera plant . . .'

Thorne blinked, remembering the vision that had greeted him on stumbling bleary-eyed into the living room at five o'clock that morning. Elvis, squatting awkwardly atop the small metal bucket. Keeping his belly low to avoid the spikes. Looking Thorne straight in the eye as he pissed happily into the white pebbles . . .

'It's doing fine,' Thorne said.

Thorne's phone rang.

'Where are you?' Brigstocke said. 'We've got Gribbin . . .'

'I'm on my way in . . .'

'When I say "got him" I just mean we know where he is, all right? We've got to go and *get* him. Holland's waiting on your doorstep . . .'

'Tell him I'll be back home in half an hour . . .'

'Where the hell are you?'

Thorne looked across at Eve who smiled and shrugged. 'I've been jogging . . .'

What does a child-sex offender look like?

Thorne knew this to be a pointless question. Pointless because, truthfully, it was unanswerable. It was also extremely dangerous.

And yet, people had been taught to believe that they knew the answer. That they should stick their hands up and shout it out. It was always an answer that came too late though, wasn't it? After the damage had been done and the children had been hurt. After the man had been caught and that first, fuzzy photo had appeared on the front of the newspapers. Then, it was as though everything that people already knew had been confirmed. Of course! It was so bloody obvious, wasn't it? *That* was what one of those men looked like. Knew it all along . . .

If it was so obvious, if the evil that these men did was written clearly across their faces for all to see, then why did they live next door and go undetected? If you could see it in the bastards' eyes, then why did they pass by unnoticed on the streets? Why did they teach your kids? Why were you married to one?

Because, as Thorne knew all too well, you couldn't see it, no matter how much you wished that you could or how hard you looked. Nobody looked like a child-sex offender. *Everybody* did.

Thorne looked like one. And Russell Brigstocke. And Yvonne Kitson . . .

What Ray Gribbin did *not* look like was the *popular perception* of a child-sex offender. He was not your typical,

115

tabloid, kiddie-fiddler. He did not have bad skin or lank, greasy hair. He did not wear thick glasses, carry a bag of boiled sweets or wear a dirty anorak. As well as the misshapen nose that Douglas Remfry had claimed responsibility for, Gribbin had a shaved head, cold eyes and a smile that said 'fuck right off'. He was a child-sex offender who looked like an armed robber.

Whatever the hell an armed robber looked like . . .

Thorne put the photo together with the other paperwork he had been studying, and handed the lot across to where Stone and Holland were sitting in the back seat. Stone looked at the photo. 'Christ, he's not what I expected,' he said.

Thorne said nothing, stared out of the passenger window.

Brigstocke flashed the lights and put his foot down. The car in front of them pulled across to let the unmarked Volvo pass. 'I know what you mean,' he said. 'Looks like the sort who might bear a grudge, though, doesn't he?'

Thorne couldn't argue with that. He watched, slightly dizzy, as the fields of rape and wheat that bordered the M4 flew past at ninety miles an hour. He made himself belch; the reading had made him feel a little sick . . .

Brigstocke spoke up to get everybody's attention. 'Right, you should all have had a chance to look at the notes by the time we get there . . .' Thorne wound down his window an inch. Brigstocke glanced across at him, carried on. 'This is a bit of a kick-bollock scramble but we didn't have a lot of choice. We're doing this in a hurry but let's all make sure we do it right, shall we?' There were grunts from the two in the back. Thorne turned to look at him. 'Gribbin's got a history

116

of violence and if Remfry's story is to be believed, that's the *only* time Gribbin's come off worse. He's been picked up with knives on him before, so we're taking no chances . . .'

Stone leaned forward, an arm on each headrest, and his face pushed between the seats. 'How many going in?'

'Probably be the four of us, plus a couple of the local boys . . .'

Stone nodded, carried on speed-reading the notes.

'Watch out for the woman as well,' Brigstocke said. 'Sandra Cook's got plenty of form. Drug abuse, theft, prostitution. She did three months in Holloway for taking half a DC's face off with her nails . . .'

Holland shuffled forward. If Brigstocke had so much as touched the brakes, Holland would have smashed into the back of his head. '*Patricia* Cook's the woman who called up about Gribbin, right?'

Stone glanced at him. 'Sandra's sister . . .'

Thorne took a gulp of cold air and shut his window.

'So, why does she grass up her sister's boyfriend?' Holland asked.

Brigstocke tried to catch Holland's eye in the mirror. 'That's the other reason we're not fucking around this morning,' he said. 'Non-attendance is not Gribbin's only violation of his parole conditions.'

'Shit . . .' Stone had seen it. He held the notes out for Holland to take.

Thorne turned his head, looked at Holland. 'There's three people in the house, Dave. Gribbin, Cook and Cook's eleven-year-old daughter . . .'

Thorne swivelled round again, pulled his seat belt taut. Beneath it, he could feel his heart start to thump that little

117

bit faster and louder. Around the nape of his neck he could sense the smallest tingle beginning to build. He caught his breath as an insect hit the windscreen in a mess of blood and wings.

It was a horseshoe-shaped cul-de-sac on a modern housing estate, and the property they were interested in was at the far end . . .

Thorne looked at the houses as the van slowly made its way past them up the drive. Taking in the detail, the attempts to personalise and gentrify. The bright, differently coloured front doors; the hanging baskets overflowing with geraniums; the wooden signs for The Elms and The Thistles. Most of the houses and garages were empty, the occupants having left for work hours earlier, but still the occasional curtain twitched. This was probably as exciting as it would ever get.

It was one of those funny towns on the outskirts of the city that couldn't quite make its mind up if it was urban or rural. Twenty-odd miles to the west of central London, it lay uncomfortably between the M25 and the Chilterns. For its population of commuters, the proximity to rolling hills and quaintly named villages probably made the daily slog up the motorway worthwhile, but it was a different story for their teenage children. No amount of fresh air could make the place any less boring. Antique shops would not prevent them pissing it up the wall on a Friday night and cutting up rough in the centre of town . . .

Thorne saw a woman staring down at him from an upstairs window. He read the alarm on her face and watched her back away quickly, almost certainly heading for the phone. It was understandable. Those who peeped from behind curtains on one side of the drive saw a blue Transit van. Those like her, in houses on the *other* side, could see the four men in jackets, jeans and trainers, who crept slowly alongside it, moving at the same speed, the van's progress masking theirs.

When the van began a long, slow sweep around the curve of the horseshoe, the police officers behind it moved in a similar arc. As it slowed right down, they did the same, and when it stopped and the engine was switched off, the four men gathered into a tight huddle and waited.

Five hundred yards away, at the other end of the drive, two police vans had sealed off the entrance. Traffic police kept the vehicles moving as drivers slowed down to gawk. Half a dozen uniformed officers in shirtsleeves moved curious pedestrians along.

Behind the Transit, Thorne listened. He could hear the distant squawk of a two-way. The drone of traffic from the other side of the field behind the estate. Somewhere nearby there was a radio playing. He tuned the sounds out and tried to concentrate on what Brigstocke was saying . . .

'Are we clear?' Brigstocke asked. He looked hard at Thorne, Holland and Stone. Thorne knew he was looking for focus. Nods all round. This was probably going to be straightforward enough, but it only took a second for something run of the mill to go very tits up.

'Right . . .'

A beat, then Brigstocke hammered with his fist on the side of the van and two more officers jumped immediately from the front. The van doors still swinging, they began

119

sprinting towards the house, the biggest one lugging a heavy, metal door-ram.

Thorne and the others came around from the far side of the van, running. Brigstocke and Stone went immediately left towards the gate at the side, making for the back of the house. Thorne and Holland veered away from them, following in the wake of the two from the front of the van . . .

Grunts, and short breaths, and the pounding of rubber soles across tarmac and pavement and grass, and still the sound of the radio coming from somewhere . . .

Thorne came up next to the officers at the front door. He crouched down, ready to spring forward, and nodded. A couple of deep breaths. The big officer gritted his teeth and swung the battering-ram.

'Police . . .!'

Thorne could hear shouting from inside the house and from around the back. The door hadn't given. He began kicking at the lock, then moved quickly as the ram was swung into the door again. This time it crashed open and, leading with his forearm, Thorne rushed in.

'Police! Everybody in the property show themselves now . . .'

From behind him, Thorne heard the clang of the battering-ram as it was dropped on to the doorstep. From somewhere up ahead he could hear a thump and, upstairs, a woman screaming . . .

A woman, Thorne thought. *Not a child . . .*

'Anybody here, show yourself!'

He saw a long hallway ahead of him. Two, three doors off to his right . . .

'In there!'

He glanced left at the big officer coming past him, at the bulk of his wide back moving beneath his car coat as he charged up the stairs two at a time.

At the other end of the hall was a kitchen, and through it he could see Brigstocke and Stone outside the back door. Holland pushed past him, ran to open it.

The doors clattered open, smashed in ahead of him. In the first room, nothing . . . He stepped back out into the hall, turned to see Brigstocke and Stone running towards him.

From the second room, a shout . . .

'Here . . .'

Thorne shoved his way past the officer in the doorway and burst into the room. It was small – a sofa, an armchair, a widescreen TV still on. At the other end was an archway leading off right to another room, a dining room, Thorne guessed.

Gribbin stood next to the armchair, his hands above his head. His face showed nothing. His eyes moved from Thorne's to the doorway through which Sandra Cook was being propelled by one of the local CID boys. She pushed her way past Brigstocke and Stone, all but dragged Holland out of the way.

'What the fuck do you want?' she shouted.

Thorne ignored her, turned to look at Gribbin. 'Raymond Gribbin, I'm arresting you in connection with breach of parole conditions, which . . .'

He stopped and looked towards the archway in the right-hand corner as a figure stepped cautiously through it. One by one the heads of the other seven people crowded into the small room turned, until everyone was looking at the girl.

'Is everything going to be OK, Ray? I'm scared . . .'

Gribbin took his hands from above his head, opening his arms as he stepped towards her. 'It's all right, sweetheart . . .'

It all happened in a few seconds. It was a testament to Andy Stone's speed and strength that he was able to do so much before being dragged away by Thorne, Holland and a screaming Sandra Cook.

'Don't fucking touch her . . .'

As Gribbin's hands slid across the girl's shoulders, Stone was halfway across the room. He was on him by the time Gribbin was reaching to pull the small, blond head to his barrel chest, the girl squealing as he pushed her away and turned to defend himself . . .

Gribbin reached up and grabbed Stone around the collar, staggering back into the television which tipped against the wall. Stone brought both fists up fast into the thick, tattooed forearms and pulled them back down hard as he dropped his head into Gribbin's face. It was then that three pairs of hands grabbed Stone, around collar, belt and sleeve, yanking him backwards across the armchair as Gribbin dropped to his knees and the girl ran sobbing to her mother.

Stone tried to stand up, to tell those around him that he was calm, that they could get their bloody hands off him . . .

Thorne stepped across and knelt down next to Gribbin.

His head had fallen back against the television, one hand scrabbling at the carpet, balling itself into a fist. Blood

122

dripped through the fingers of the other hand. On the screen behind Gribbin's head, there was applause as a woman welcomed viewers to her show and invited the studio audience to share their holiday nightmares.

Twenty minutes later, with the inhabitants of the quiet cul-de-sac pressed against their windows, Gribbin was led out, a bloody handkerchief pressed to what was left of his nose.

By teatime, the initial interviews had been completed. Heads were starting to hang. Though there were still a few things to check out, it was pretty clear, to Thorne at least, that Gribbin had got nothing whatsoever to do with the murder of Douglas Remfry.

The phone rang just before eleven. The voice could have belonged to only one person.

'I think you might have had a bit of luck, Mr Thorne.'

'I'm listening, Kodak.'

'Well, don't get too excited, because whatever happens we've got to wait a few days, but it looks good. Remember me joking about doing your job for you . . .'

Thorne listened. It did sound very promising, but after the fiasco with Gribbin he found it difficult to get excited. It was hard to see anything as more than just another straw to be clutched at.

He went into the bedroom and lay down.

It was starting to get cooler.

Beneath him, the bracken felt sodden, and above, the sky was darkening.

3 AUGUST, 1976

'You smell. You smell like death. You fucking stink . . .'

Her eyes showed nothing. Not hurt at the accusation, not denial, not pain at the weight of him pressed down on to her arms, his face inches from her own.

He pushed himself off her, moved down to the end of the bed to where the tray had been left untouched.

'I'm fucking sick of this,' he said. *'You want to starve your-self that's up to you, but don't make me cook the shit for you, all right?'*

She raised herself up on the pillow, stared past him.

'What?' he said, shouted. *'What?'*

He looked at her for a minute or more. Her face was, as always, blank enough for him to imagine it changing, to create the expression that he knew should be there as large as life. To picture the eyes dropping, the tightness around the lips, and the clenching of the jaw. To see shame.

He grabbed the plate and hurled it against the wall above her head. She didn't flinch. She didn't blink.

He stopped in the doorway, turned and stared at her. Her eyes flat as glass. Beans running down the wall behind her.

'In court they tried to make out that if you had been raped it was like you were asking for it anyway. The dress, other things. They just meant the way you behaved, like you were flirting, coming on to him. They didn't know the half of it, did they? You did ask for it. I know what you did. You literally asked him for it. Took him, dragged him into that

124

fucking stockroom and asked him. Told him what you wanted . . .'

As he closed the bedroom door behind him, he could hear her, saying the word over and over again.

'If . . . if . . . if . . .'

She could not hear herself saying it. The sound of the screaming inside her head was all she'd been able to hear for a while.

EIGHT

Thorne turned right off the Charing Cross Road. Eleven o'clock in the morning or thereabouts and baking hot. He took off his jacket, threw it across his arm as he began walking up Old Compton Street.

Soho was a difficult area to categorise at the best of times, which had probably been its trouble down the years. Was it bohemian or squalid? Characterful or seedy? Thorne knew that today it was all these things and probably the better for it, but it had been a struggle. Four decades on and the villains that had run Soho in the fifties and sixties had become trendy. Thanks to the new wave of British gangster films, Billy Hill, Jack Spot and their boys, with their sharp suits and slicked-back hair, were now officially iconic. For all their new-found sexiness, it was these men and those who followed in the seventies who had driven the resident population of the area away, who had silenced the noisy heart of it.

It was thanks mainly to the gay population that Soho's heart had begun to beat again. Now it was one of the few areas in the centre of the city with a real sense of community; a sense that the horrific bombing of the Admiral

Duncan pub a few years earlier had only strengthened. Though Thorne had not felt *totally* comfortable on the few occasions Phil Hendricks had brought him down here drinking, he couldn't deny that there was a good atmosphere to the place.

Thorne walked past Greek Street, Frith Street. The Prince Edward Theatre and the awning of Ronnie Scott's off to his right. Young men sat outside cafés, enjoying the hot weather, the chance to show off well-developed bodies. Soho was still a great place to eat and drink, but for every Bar Italia there was a Starbucks or a Costa Coffee; for every family-run deli, two branches of Pret A Manger . . .

Thorne suddenly felt hungry and realised that he had a problem. He knew that he didn't have time to grab an early lunch, but he also knew that if he ate any later he would run the risk of spoiling dinner, and he was really looking forward to that . . .

'Well, we might as well,' Eve had said when he'd called. 'We've already had breakfast and lunch . . .'

On the corner of Dean Street was a shop selling fetish wear. Thorne stopped and looked at the garish window display. A dummy was clad in rubber. A spiked dog-collar around the neck and a gas mask obscuring the face. He thought about the photographs of Jane Foley; the reason he was here.

He looked at his watch. He was going to be late . . .

'Did you really look at this photo?' Bethell had asked on the phone.

'What?'

Bethell sounded cocky, pleased with himself. 'Study it, you know . . .'

Thorne was not in the best of humours. 'I'm tired and I've had a shit day, so get on with it, will you . . .?'

'I mean *really* look at it, Mr Thorne. In one of your labs or whatever. Get it on to some state-of-the-art magnifying equipment, break it down into pixels . . .'

'This is the Met, Kodak. I haven't even got a fan in my fucking office . . .'

'I've got some good gear indoors. I use it for airbrushing, you know? Stuck it on there and bingo!'

'What . . .?'

'The picture's shot against a plain white backdrop, all right? Sheet on a roller, usual kind of thing. Now, there's a small mark bottom right-hand corner, looks like a smudge, remember?'

'No, I don't . . .'

Thorne turned right, then immediately left into Brewer Street. This, more than anywhere in Soho, was where you could see the sleazy and the sophisticated cheek by jowl. The peep show next door to the sushi bar. A place that offered shiatsu massage opposite premises delivering an altogether more intimate type of service.

A bored blonde in a cubicle beckoned him, inviting him into a show that promised a 'live double act'. Thorne wondered if there were any shows that offered dead ones.

'Come on in, love,' the woman said. Thorne smiled and shook his head. She looked like she didn't give a toss. Of course, the sex industry had always been just that, had always been about the money, but Thorne had known hookers who did a better job of disguising it. He'd only ever *read* about his favourite hooker of all time, but he would have liked to have met her. A legendary whore called Miss

Corbett who'd worked these streets in the eighteenth century, and had surcharged her gentlemen an extra guinea for every inch that their 'maypole' fell below the nine inches she deemed satisfactory.

Two hundred and fifty years on and now it was the drugs squad, not vice, who worked these streets every night. The sniffer dogs did what they'd been trained to do but Thorne thought it was pretty much a waste of time and effort. A lot of hard work and resources to nail the odd casual user, the occasional tin-pot dealer if they had a bit of luck . . .

'You know you're always saying how you need a bit of luck sometimes?'

Thorne had stretched out on the sofa by now, the phone pressed to his ear, the other hand reaching down to rub Elvis's belly. 'Are you ever going to get to the point, Kodak?'

'Well, this is it. Your bit of good luck. I scanned the photo into my computer, blew it up big time, OK? You can do all sorts of stuff if the quality of the original's decent enough, yeah?' Thorne would have said it was impossible, but Bethell's voice was actually getting that little bit higher as he got more excited. 'So, I pixellated the bastard, zoomed in, and then I could suddenly see what that brown smudge was. I recognised it, see.'

'Recognised it?'

'It's a burn mark, like a scorch on the white backcloth. I recognised it 'cause I was there when it happened. I was shooting a threesome nine months back and some silly tart, done a couple of pills too many, knocks over a big lamp. Fucking whole lot could have gone up, but all it did

129

was leave this big burn mark up the roller. I remembered the shape of it. Tight fucker that runs the place never bothered to replace it . . .'

By now Thorne was sitting up. 'Tight fucker's name and address would be good.'

'Charles Dodd. Charlie, really, but he insists on Charles. Likes to pretend he's posh, even though the cunt comes from Canvey Island . . .'

'Kodak . . .'

'The place is above a fishmonger's on Brewer Street.'

Thorne knew the shop. 'Right, listen . . .'

'You'll have to wait a few days I'm afraid, Mr Thorne. He's in Europe. I checked.'

Thorne was thinking it through. Should he wait? Could he get a warrant and turn the place over while Dodd was away . . .?

'I think I did a pretty good job, Mr Thorne,' Bethell said. 'What d'you reckon?'

'I want to know the second he's back . . .'

Now, three days since that conversation, Thorne watched Dennis Bethell in the bookshop on the other side of the street. He was browsing through the remaindered art books, though some of his own, slightly racier stuff was almost certainly on sale downstairs.

Thorne moved to cross the road and was bumped roughly by a man coming fast, from his left. Thorne's response was typically British. 'Sorry,' he said. The other man grunted, raised a hand and carried on walking.

Bethell was waving at him now from inside the book-shop. Thorne nodded towards the other end of the street and began walking. Bethell put down a coffee-table book of nude freak-show photographs, squeezed out of the shop doorway, and followed.

Welch laughed as he strolled away up Wardour Street. He'd learned a few things during the years he'd spent in various institutions. Never say sorry was one. How to recognise a copper was another . . .

Since his release he'd spent a lot of the time just walking around. The hostel was depressing, and he'd really enjoyed being out and about. The weather was amazing; a couple of days out in the open and he'd already got a bit of colour back. If *he* looked better, less prison-pale, he thought that the women who were walking about, wearing next to nothing, looked *gorgeous*. Seriously horny. Fuck it, if this was global warming then who gave a toss about the ozone layer?

There were windows all along the street with adverts in each for a new film. Welch stopped and looked at a couple that he liked the sound of. Maybe when his dole money came through he might spend a couple of afternoons catching up. He'd enjoyed the cinema before he'd gone inside, tried to see most of the stuff that came out, providing it wasn't too arty.

He'd been to the pictures the night before he was arrested of course. *The Blair Witch Project*. She'd been all over him then, snuggling up in the scary bits, hand on his knee all the way through. Well up for it, she was. He could read the signals. It was only later that the bitch decided to change her mind. To fuck him around.

To this day, it amazed him that they could do that. Take a bloke all the way there, get him worked up, get him so as his bollocks felt like they'd explode and then just turn around and casually announce that they didn't feel like it. That it was too much too soon, or some such crap. He'd decided that it *was* crap, that she just didn't want him to think she was a slag. That all she needed was a little persuasion . . .

He'd been gobsmacked when the police had come knocking the next afternoon. Couldn't fucking believe it. He was still shaking his head while they were taking the swabs.

He could see that the male copper, the detective sergeant, thought it was rubbish, that they were all wasting their time. When he'd told them how randy the silly bitch had been in the cinema, he was *nodding*, for fuck's sake. He could see exactly what had been going on. The woman officer was different, though; she'd had it in for him straight away.

'Good at reading signals, are you?' she'd said. Her expression blank, the spools on the tape squeaking as they turned in the recorder. 'Tell me what I'm thinking right now . . .'

'That you'd fancy me if you weren't a dyke?'

Looking into the window, he saw himself smile, remembering her face when he'd said it. The smile faded a little when he recalled the look on the same face eight months later; the grin from the other side of the courtroom as he was taken down.

He moved on to the next window. There was a poster advertising the new Bruce Willis blockbuster. Some new missile and Bruce's cheeky smile and a tasty blonde with fake tits. Maybe next week, the week after, whenever he started getting the dole cheques, he might go and see it. He couldn't afford it just yet. The discharge grant wasn't going to stretch much further and besides, he'd need a fair bit tomorrow night, to pay for the hotel.

'You sure he's in there?'

'He's in there, Mr Thorne. Got back from Holland yesterday. Went over to pick up a few bits and pieces.'

Thorne nodded. Flowers weren't the only thing that came across from Holland in vans . . .

They were standing across the road from the fishmonger's, the flashing neon sign above Raymond's Revue Bar reflected in the shop window. The reds and blues dancing across the shiny heads of salmon, herring and turbot. Next to it, a narrow brown door.

Bethell forced his hands into the pockets of tight leather trousers. Shifted his weight from one expensive training shoe to the other. 'Right, I'll get out of your way then, shall I?'

Thorne reached for his wallet, wondering if the tightness of Bethell's trousers might have something to do with the height of his voice. He counted out fifty in tenners. Bethell took it and handed over an envelope in return.

'There's your photo back . . .'

Thorne took a step into the road, turned and held up the envelope. 'I'd better not see this popping up on the Internet, all right?'

Bethell laughed. A series of shrill peeps. 'I didn't know you visited those sorts of sites . . .' Thorne was already starting to cross. 'Listen, you won't mention my name, will you . . .?'

Thorne stopped to let a car pass, spoke without turning. 'Oh, so I can't say, "Dennis sent me", then?'

'Seriously . . .'

'Relax, Kodak. Your reputation will remain squeaky clean. No pun intended . . .'

Thorne pressed the button on the grimy, white intercom and stepped back. He glanced up at an unmoving grey curtain, and right, into the black eye of a large, ugly looking fish he couldn't put a name to. The shopfront was original, the tiling that edged the window ornate, but the prices and stock were firmly in line with the twenty-first-century trendiness of the location. Swordfish steaks at a fiver a pop, and not a whelk to be seen . . .

'Yes . . .?'

'Mr Dodd? I was wondering if I could talk to you about renting some studio time . . .?'

Thorne could hear suspicion in every crackle of the speaker. He looked back at the ugly fish, found himself raising his eyebrows. *What d'you reckon?*

He was buzzed up.

Charlie Dodd stood at the top of a narrow, carpetless stairway. He was in his fifties with thin lips and a comb-over. He smiled, barring the way and trying to make it look like a welcome.

By the time Thorne had reached the top of the stairs, warrant card in hand, the smile had become a grimace.

'Have you got a warrant?'

'I don't need one, you invited me up.'

'Listen, you obviously aren't one of DCI Davey's boys. Everything's been sorted . . .'

Plenty of things in Soho were still the same forty years

on. Thorne made a mental note of the name as he stepped past Dodd and pushed open an unpainted plywood door.

Dodd scuttled after him. 'What the fuck's your game . . .?'

The studio was no bigger than an average double bedroom and the main feature was indeed a double bed. *Unlike* the average bedroom, the walls were painted black, there were lights hung from a ceiling bar, and Thorne guessed that the array of sex toys and costumes on display was only likely to be replicated in the bedrooms of a few high-ranking Members of Parliament . . .

A man turned from the foot of the bed, lifted a large video camera down from his shoulder. Behind him, a foot or so away from the bedstead, Thorne could see the white backdrop with the burn mark in the bottom right-hand corner.

Two thin, pale girls lay on the bed. One pulled her arm from beneath the other and reached down to pick up a packet of cigarettes from the floor. The other stared at him, her face blank and white as new paper.

'What's this?' the man with the camera said.

Thorne smiled. 'Don't mind me . . .'

Dodd raised a placatory hand to the cameraman and turned to Thorne. 'Now listen, there's nothing illegal going on here, so why don't you sod off?'

'What about the stuff you've just brought back from Holland, Charlie?' Thorne stepped forward and steered Dodd into the corner of the room. 'Sorry, I know you prefer Charles . . .'

The watery, green eyes narrowed as Dodd's mind raced, trying to work out who had the big mouth. 'What do you want?'

Thorne took the picture from the envelope. 'This photo was taken here.' He handed it to Dodd. 'I just want to know who took it. Nothing too difficult . . .'

Dodd shook his head. 'Not here, mate.'

Thorne squeezed behind Dodd, stood close enough to smell the sweat and hair oil. He jabbed a finger over his shoulder at the smudge on the photo and then lifted up Dodd's head and pointed it at the scorch mark on the backcloth.

'Have another look, Charlie . . .'

Dodd turned back to the photo. The man with the camera had put it back on to his shoulder. He was mumbling something to the girls who were lazily shifting their position on the bed.

'If it was taken here, I wasn't around at the time,' Dodd said, handing the photo back to Thorne. He inclined his head towards the bed. 'Stuff like this today, run of the mill, I usually stick around, get on with other things . . .'

One of the girls began to moan theatrically. Thorne glanced across. The camera was trained on one girl's head as it busied itself in her friend's crotch. At the other end of the bed, the girl who was moaning stared at the ceiling, still smoking her cigarette.

'You saying you don't remember this picture being taken?'

'There's times, punters would rather I wasn't here. You understand what I'm saying? Maybe there's things being shot I'd prefer I didn't witness anyway and they're paying good money for the place, so . . .'

'Bollocks.' Thorne pushed the photo into Dodd's face. 'Do you see any animals? Underage boys?'

Dodd swatted Thorne's arm away, shook his head.

'This is top-shelf stuff, no stronger than that. There's a whole series of these and they're much the same, so start remembering, Charlie . . .'

Dodd was starting to get upset. He ran his hands back and forth through the oily strands of hair. As he spoke, Thorne watched a white fleck of dried spittle move from bottom lip to top and back again. 'I wasn't here. All right? I'd remember if I was, I can remember every fucking shot taken up here, ask anybody. Like you say, the picture's harmless enough, so what reason have I got to piss you about . . . ?'

On the bed, the girl who was being worked on leaned across to stub out her cigarette on a saucer. The cameraman moved in closer. 'Go on,' he said to the other girl. 'Get your tongue right up her arse . . .'

'All right,' Thorne said. 'Think about anybody who might have asked you to make yourself scarce while they were shooting. Last six months or so . . .'

'Jesus, d'you know how many people use this place?'

'Not a regular. Probably a one-off.'

'Yeah, but still . . .'

'Just one man and a girl. Think . . .'

The cameraman kicked the end of the bed in annoyance and spun round. 'For Christ's sake, can you two shut up? I'm recording sound here . . .'

The girl who had been going down on her friend raised her head and turned to look at Thorne. The lights washed out her face, exaggerating the job that the heroin had already done. Dodd opened his mouth to speak and Thorne was grateful for the chance to look away.

'There was one, four or five months ago. It was like you said, a one-off. He just wanted the place for a couple of hours. Normally, even if they want rid of me for the shoot I stick around to set the lights up, but this bloke said he was going to do all that himself. Said he knew what he was doing.'

'What about the girl?'

'I never saw a girl. It was just him . . .'

'Give me a name.'

Dodd snorted, looked at Thorne in disbelief. 'Right. I'll check the files, shall I? Maybe ask my secretary to look it up. For fuck's sake . . .'

Thorne took a step towards the doorway. 'Get your coat on, Charlie. I need a picture of this fucker and for your sake your memory for faces had better be as good as it is for tits and arse . . .'

'Sorry, mate, it's not going to happen. That's why I remembered him, as it goes. First I thought he was a dis-patch rider, you know, dropping off some negs or something. Head to foot in leather, with a dark visor on his helmet . . .'

Thorne knew straight away that Dodd was telling the truth. It felt like something starting to press heavily against the back of his head. His piece of good luck turning to shit.

'You must have seen him more than once. He didn't just turn up on the off-chance . . .'

'Once to make the booking, once on the day.' Dodd was starting to sound slightly smug. 'Never got a look at him, though. Both times he had the motorbike clobber on. I remember him standing out there on the stairs, in all the leather gear like a fucking hit-man, waiting for me to leave . . .'

On the other side of the room, a vibrator began to buzz. The camera was rolling again.

Thorne turned and yanked open the door. The statement could be taken later, for what it was worth. He'd run headlong into another wall, and right now it felt as real, as black, as the one that ran around the tatty fuck-parlour behind him.

He took the stairs down two at a time. The jolt that ran through his body at every step failed to dislodge the image that had fixed itself in his head. The face of the girl on the bed when she'd raised up her head and turned to look at him . . .

Her mouth and chin glistening, but the eyes as black and dead as those of the fish that lay on slabs in the window of the shop next door.

10 AUGUST, 1976

It was the first time in a long while that he'd seen anything at all register on her face. He wasn't expecting a reaction, but it tickled him nevertheless. To see her jaw drop a little, watch her eyes widen when she saw his hand tighten around the base of the lamp . . .

'Please,' she said. Please . . .

In the few seconds that he held the lamp high above his head, he thought about the different uses of that word. The meanings that it could take on. Its many, subtle varieties, conjured by the tiniest changes in emphasis.

He thought about the number of ways it could mislead.

Please don't.

Please do.

Please don't stop doing . . .

Please me. Pleasure me. Please . . .

Pleading for it.

As he brought the lamp down with every ounce of strength he had, he thought that, all in all, it was a pretty appropriate word. For her very last.

At least, the way she meant it now, it was honest.

With each successive blow he became more focused, his thinking becoming less cluttered until finally, when she was unrecognisable, he could remember where in the garage he'd last seen the tow rope.

NINE

That dreadful hiatus between arriving, and anything actually happening . . .

The cling-film, they were assured, would be coming off the buffet platters *very* shortly, and the DJ wouldn't be too long setting his gear up. Until then, there was a hundred and fifty quid behind the bar, so everybody could get a couple down them and toast the bride and groom one more time while they were waiting for the fun to start. Everyone could mingle . . .

Tragically, there weren't quite enough people in the rugby club bar for a significant hubbub to develop; there was no comforting blanket of noise for Thorne to hide under. He got a pint of bitter for his dad, half a Guinness for himself, and looked for the nearest corner. He sat sipping his beer and tried to summon up the necessary enthusiasm for Scotch eggs and pork pie and cold pasta salad. Raised his glass to anyone whose eye he caught and tried not to look too bored or miserable or, God forbid, in need of cheering up.

His father was *certainly* in no need of it. Jim Thorne sat on a chair at the bar holding court. Telling jokes to a couple of teenage boys who sniggered and sipped their shandies. Informing any woman who would listen that he had a memory like a goldfish, because he had that disease with the funny name. He'd forgotten, *what* was it called again? Asking with a twinkle to be forgiven if he'd slept with any of them and couldn't remember.

Thorne was delighted to see his dad on such good form. To see him enjoying himself. It was a huge relief after the phone call twenty-four hours earlier that had put paid to his evening with Eve Bloom . . .

The large, stripped-pine table in the kitchen had been set for four. Thorne had yet to encounter anybody else. Eve turned from the cooker.

'In case you're wondering, they're in her room.' She spoke at the level of a stage whisper. 'Denise and Ben. I think they've had a row . . .'

Thorne was pouring wine into two of the glasses. He whispered back. 'Right. Was it a big one? Should I start clearing away a couple of these place settings . . .?'

Eve moved over to the table and picked up her wine. 'No chance. Ben won't let an argument get in the way of his dinner. Cheers.' She took a sip and carried the glass back across to where several large copper pans sat on the halogen hob. She nodded towards the door at the sound of footsteps and raised voices coming from elsewhere in the flat. 'Those two enjoy a good row anyway. They're pretty violent, but usually short-lived . . .'

Thorne tried to sound casual. 'Violent?'

'I don't mean like that. Just a lot of shouting. Bit of throwing stuff, but never anything breakable . . .'

Thorne glanced across at her. She was busy at the cooker again, her back to him. He stared at the nape of her neck. At her shoulder blades, brown against the cream linen of her top.

'I'm more of a seether myself,' she said.

'I'll watch out for that.'

'Don't worry, you'll know it when it happens . . .'

Thorne looked around the kitchen. A couple of framed black and white film posters. Chrome kettle, toaster and blender. A big, expensive-looking fridge. It looked like the shop was doing pretty good business, though he couldn't be sure which things were Eve's and which belonged to her flatmate. He guessed that the vast array of herbs in terracotta pots were probably down to Eve, as were the scribbled Latin names of what Thorne presumed to be flowers on the enormous blackboard that dominated one wall. He was pleased to see his own name and mobile-phone number, scrawled in the bottom left-hand corner.

'So, what are they arguing about? Your friends. Nothing serious . . .?'

She turned, licking her fingers. 'Keith. Remember? The guy that helps me out on a Saturday. He was here when Ben arrived. Ben reckons he's got a bit of a thing for Denise, and Denise told him not to be such an idiot . . .'

Thorne remembered the way Keith had looked at him when he was talking to Eve in the shop. Maybe Denise wasn't the only one he had a bit of a thing for . . .

'What do you think?' he asked. 'About Keith and Denise . . .'

A door squeaked and slammed and a moment later the door to the kitchen was pushed open by a slim, fair-haired woman. She was barefoot, wearing baggy, combat-style shorts and a man's black vest. She marched up behind Eve and gave her backside a healthy tweak.

'That smells fucking gorgeous!'

She turned and beamed at Thorne. Her hair was a little shorter and a shade lighter than Eve's. Though she seemed slight, the vest she was wearing showed off well-defined arms and shoulders. Her delicate features sharpened as an enormous smile pushed up cheekbones you could slice bacon on.

'Hello, you're Tom, aren't you? I'm Denise.' She all but ran across the kitchen, grabbed his outstretched hand and flopped down in a chair on the other side of the table. 'So, Tom? Thomas? Which?' She reached for the wine bottle and began pouring herself a very large glass.

'Tom's fine . . .'

She leaned across the table and spoke as though they were old friends. 'Eve's been going on at *nauseating* length about you, do you know that?' Her voice was surprisingly deep and a little theatrical. Thorne couldn't think of anything to say. Took a sip of wine instead. 'Bloody *full of it*, she is. I'm guessing that the only reason she is resolutely refusing to turn around from the oven, *at this very moment*, is that she's gone bright red . . .'

'Shut your face,' Eve said, laughing and without turning round.

Denise swallowed a mouthful of wine, gave Thorne another massive smile. 'So, in the flesh,' she said. 'A man who catches murderers.'

Thorne needed to relax after the morning he'd spent in Soho. Now, he was starting to enjoy himself. This woman was clearly as mad as a hatter but likeable enough.

144

'Right at this very minute, I'm a man who *isn't* catching them . . .'

'We all have off days, Tom. Tomorrow you'll probably catch a bagful.'

'I'll settle for just the one . . .'

'Right.' She raised her glass as if in a toast. 'A really *good* one.'

Thorne leaned back on his chair and glanced across at Eve. As if she sensed him looking, she turned, caught his eye and smiled.

Thorne turned back to Denise. 'What about you? What do you do?' He stared at the tiny, glittering stud in her nose, thinking, *Actress, poet, performance artist* . . .

She rolled her eyes. 'God, IT. Sorry. Dull as fuck, I'm afraid.'

'Well . . .'

'Don't bother, I can see your eyes glazing over already. Bloody hell, how d'you think *I* feel? All day surrounded by *Lord of the Rings* readers, making jokes about floppy *this* and hard *that*. PCs going down on them . . .'

At the cooker, Eve laughed. Thorne knew straight away that she was thinking the same thing that he was. 'I know,' he said. 'Where *I* work, having a PC go down on you means a *very* different thing . . .'

When the man whom Thorne presumed to be Ben strolled into the kitchen, it was Denise who stopped laughing first. He walked over, leaned against the worktop next to where Eve was cooking and began chewing a fingernail. He tilted his chin towards Thorne. 'Hiya . . .'

Thorne nodded back. 'Hi. Are you Ben?'

Denise spoke pointedly over the noise of the wine

glugging into her glass. 'Oh yes, he's Ben.' Ben looked none too pleased at the horribly fake smile she gave him as she spat out his name.

Eve lobbed a tea-towel at her. 'All right you two, stop it.' She leaned across and kissed Ben on the cheek. 'This'll be ready in about five minutes . . .'

Ben moved across to the fridge, opened it and took out a can of lager. He turned to Thorne, held it up. 'Want one?'

Thorne lifted his glass of wine. 'No, thanks . . .'

Ben moved round behind his girlfriend and sat next to Thorne. He was tall and well built, with fair, wavy hair, a gingerish goatee beard and neatly trimmed, pointed side-burns. Although in his thirties, and clearly fifteen years too old for it, he was wearing what Thorne guessed was skate-boarding gear. He stuck out a hand, introduced himself. 'Ben Jameson . . .'

Thorne did the same, suddenly feeling a little awkward, and somewhat overdressed in his chinos and black M & S polo shirt . . .

'I'm starving,' Ben said.

Eve carried four plates across to the table. 'Good. There's loads . . .'

For half a minute there was only the sound of china and glassware clinking. Of cutlery scraping against dishes, and chairs against the quarry-tiled floor as the meal was dished up.

'This looks amazing,' Thorne said.

Nods and grunting from Denise and Ben, a smile from Eve and then silence. Thorne turned to his right. 'You in IT as well, Ben?'

'Sorry?'

'I wondered if the two of you had met up at work . . .?'

'God, no. I'm a film-maker.'

'Right. Anything I might have seen?'

'Only if you watch a lot of corporate training videos,' Denise said.

Thorne could feel his foot pressing against something underneath the table. He pushed, hoping it was Eve's foot. She looked up at him . . .

'Yeah, that's what I'm doing at the moment,' Ben said. He drummed his fork against the edge of his plate. 'But I've got some stuff of my own I'm trying to get off the ground as well.'

Denise reached across and laid a hand across Ben's, stilling the movement of the fork. Her tone was blatantly patronising. 'That's right, darling. Course you have . . .'

Ben pushed his pasta around a little, spoke without looking up from the plate. 'So, what's new at your place, then, Den? Any riveting system crashes? Any interesting computer viruses to tell us about . . .?'

Thorne took his first mouthful, caught Eve's eye. She smiled and gave a small shrug. He glanced across at Denise and Ben who were looking anywhere but at each other. The row might be officially over, but they were clearly intent on scoring a few points off each other.

'Right.' Eve folded her arms. 'If you two don't kiss and make up, you can fuck off next door and ring out for pizza. Fair enough?'

First Denise and then Ben raised their eyes to Eve, who was doing her best to look serious. The antipathy between the couple seemed to melt away in the face of her mock-annoyance, the two quickly shaking heads and nuzzling

147

necks and saying sorry for being stupid. Thorne watched all three clutching hands – apologising without embarrassment to him and to each other – and he was struck by the dynamic between these people who were clearly great friends, by the warmth and strength of it.

He smiled, waving away their apologies. Impressed by them, and envious . . .

When his phone rang, Denise leaned forward, seeming genuinely excited. 'This could be the first of those murderers, Tom . . .'

Something tightened inside Thorne when he saw the name come up on the phone's display. For a second he thought about leaving the room to take the call, maybe even pretending it *was* work. He decided he was being over-dramatic, mouthed 'sorry', and answered the phone.

'This is bad, Tom. Very bad. I've been getting my things ready for tomorrow. Ready for the trip. Laying it all out on the bed, trying to choose and there's a problem with this blue suit . . .'

Thorne listened, watching Eve and her friends pretending *not* to, as his father moved from panic to complete hysteria at frightening speed. When all he could hear down the phone was sobbing, Thorne pushed back his chair, dropped his eyes to the floor and stepped away from the table.

'Dad, listen, I'll be there first thing in the morning, like I said I would.' He moved across to the kitchen window, stared out across London Fields. The light at the top of Canary Wharf winked back at him as he stood, wondering if Eve and the others could hear the crying, and trying to decide what to do.

Eve stood and moved across to him. She put a hand on his arm.

'It's all right, Dad,' Thorne said. 'Look, I'll have to go home first, all right? To get my stuff and pick up the hire car. Calm down, OK? I'll be there as soon as I can . . .'

The snotty cow behind the reception desk looked at Welch like she thought he was going to nick something. Like he was a piece of shit that one of those businessmen laughing loudly in the bar had brought in on their shoes. It wasn't like it was the fucking Ritz either . . .

'I rang a couple of days ago to book,' Welch said.

The receptionist stared at her computer screen, plastered on a smile that was fake and frosty at the same time. 'So you did,' she said. 'Just the one night, is it?'

Welch felt like reaching across the desk and slapping her. He had half a mind to ask for the manager, to demand the level of service and fucking courtesy to which he was entitled. 'Yeah, one night. I get breakfast, don't I?'

The girl didn't look up. 'Yes, sir, breakfast is included in your room rate.'

Welch suddenly wondered what would happen if there were two of them coming down in the morning. He didn't know if she would want to stay for breakfast. He thought about asking, decided to leave it.

'I won't keep you a second, sir . . .'

While the receptionist punched her keypad, Welch stared around the lobby. The plants were plastic. The grey carpet looked like it would take your skin off if you fell on it. There was a sign next to the desk which said *The Greenwood Hotel, Slough, Welcomes Thompson Mouldings Ltd* . . .

'There we go, sir. If you could just fill that in.' She slid the booking form across to him. He had to think for a few seconds before he could remember the address of the hostel. 'I'll need an imprint of a credit card. Nothing will be charged to it, but . . .'

'No need. I'm paying cash.' He signed the form and reached into the pocket of his jacket for the roll of tenners.

'That's fine, sir . . .'

Welch took out the money. He had a card he could have used if he'd felt like it, but he wanted her to see the cash. He slipped off the elastic band, started counting it out. The hostel was fucking horrendous, but being released NFA – having No Fixed Abode – did have its advantages. The discharge grant was more than double what you'd get normally.

'No payment in advance, sir. You settle the bill when you check out.' She placed a key card on top of the pile of cash and pushed the lot back towards him. 'Room 313. Third floor.'

He grabbed his money, tried not to shout. 'I do bloody well know. I know what you're supposed to do, all right?'

The receptionist reddened and turned away from him.

Welch picked up the plastic bag that contained a toothbrush, condoms, clean pants and socks for the morning. He thought about joining the gang from Thompson Mouldings in the bar, having a quick one. On second thoughts, he'd go straight to the room, maybe have a shower, try to enjoy every single minute of it . . .

Grinning at nobody in particular, he walked towards the lift.

*

This was stuff that only went on at family weddings. That Thorne knew could never happen anywhere else: an old woman, seventy if she was a day, dancing awkwardly in the corner with a small boy; two women in their forties shouting at each other across the table, raising their voices so that their comments about the food/dress/service could be heard above the Madonna/Oasis/George Michael; small children sliding on their knees across the polished dance floor, while smaller ones screamed or struggled to stay awake in spite of the loud music.

Some related by blood, for ever, and some for only an hour or two. Eyeing each other up and staring each other out. A fuck or a fight not much more than a look or a lager away . . .

Twenty minutes since the happy couple had taken to the floor to dance the first dance to 'Lady in Red', and Thorne hadn't moved from his seat in the corner. From there he could watch what was happening in the main hall and keep an eye on his old man.

He looked across. His father was no longer sitting at the bar. Thorne got up, ordered himself another Guinness, and while he was waiting for it to settle, wandered through into the main hall.

He passed people he knew not well or not at all, their faces coloured by the DJ's piss-poor lighting rig – red then green then blue. At the far end of the hall, Thorne looked to his right and through the archway that led to another, smaller room, he could see his father shuffling along the buffet table, muttering to himself, piling food he would never eat on to a paper plate . . .

'Go easy, Dad. How many chicken legs can one man eat?'

'Mind your own fucking business . . .'

'It's too much . . . look, get your hand underneath it . . .'

'Shit . . .'

The flimsy cardboard folding, unable to sustain so much food. The plate collapsing in on itself. *The mattress sagging beneath the weight of the dead man . . .*

Thorne was suddenly angry with his father, at having to play nursemaid. Then angrier still at knowing that if he *were* at home there would be fuck all happening, the leads dried up, the new angles non-existent. There was no reason for him to be missed.

He bent to pick up the food that had spilled on to the floor, thought better of it, and kicked it under the table.

The room was absolutely fucking huge. Or perhaps it just *seemed* huge. He knew that his sense of perspective was still a little skewed. Christ, having a crap without company felt like luxury . . .

It was all Welch could do to stop himself running into the bathroom for a wank. That had been exactly what he'd done when Jane had got in touch with him at the hostel. Grabbed one of her photographs and thrown one off the wrist, hardly able to believe what she was suggesting.

He'd been gobsmacked, how had she known where he was? He didn't bloody care, mind you, he'd been fucking delighted. He hadn't thought he'd hear from her again. He'd presumed she was one of those silly tarts that got off on writing to cons while they were inside, but would run a mile once they got out. He'd been so sure that he'd actually chucked away the letters she'd sent him in prison when he got out. He kept the photos, obviously. No way was he getting rid of *them* . . .

He pulled out the one photo of Jane that he'd brought with him. God, she looked gorgeous. He dreamed that perhaps she would bring the hood with her, maybe even the handcuffs. He'd secretly brought the picture along in the hope that they could try to recreate it.

He'd spent such a long time imagining what she looked like underneath the hood, or with her face lifted up out of the shadow and now, when he was about to see her, the truth was that he didn't care. He knew what her body was like, that she would surrender it to him, allow him to take it. Besides, when it came to it, he'd always been a firm believer in not looking at the mantelpiece when you were poking the fire.

Welch let out a long, slow breath. Looked at his watch. He stroked himself through his trousers, unsure that he'd be able to contain himself if she didn't get a bloody shift on . . .

Somebody knocked at the door. Three times. Softly.

On the way back to the bar, his father out of harm's way, Thorne had been collared by his Auntie Eileen who asked if he was having a good time, and would he mind having a quick word with one of her nephews who was thinking of joining the police force? Thorne thought that he'd rather wash a corpse and said that yes, of course he would, and pushed his way back towards where he hoped his drink would still be waiting . . .

He downed a third of the pint in one and as it went down, he watched as hard glances were exchanged on the other side of the bar. Some cousin or other and the bride's mate, looking like they fancied it. Thorne decided that even if they started punching seven shades of shit out of each other right there and then, he wasn't going to raise a finger.

He realised that he was wrong about this stuff only happening at family weddings. With the possible exception of the disco, you could get it all at family funerals as well. The key word was *family*, that first syllable stretched out and said with a metaphorical jab of the finger, if you were a character on *EastEnders*, or a mockney TV celebrity, or from a particular part of South-east London.

Thorne looked across. He guessed that the trouble would kick off a little later. In the car park, maybe.

It was events like these, he thought, *births, marriages and deaths*, that saw the undercurrents rise to the surface and become unstable. Bubbling up and swirling in eddies of beer and Bacardi. Sentimentality, aggression, envy, suspicion, avarice.

History. The ties that bind, twisted . . .

This was the stuff that was reserved for those closest to us, that was hidden away from strangers, even when that was *exactly* what most of your family were.

Thorne saw a lad, sixteen or seventeen, walking across the bar towards him. This was probably the nephew in search of careers advice. On second thoughts, Thorne was in just the mood to give him some . . .

He might start with a few statistics. Such as the number of murders committed by persons unknown to the victim, and how tiny they were compared to those committed by persons to whom the victim was actually *related*. He would tell the boy that when it came to families, to the tensions within them and the acts carried out in their name, he should never, *ever* be surprised. He would tell the stupid, eager young sod that families were dangerous.

That they were capable of anything.

When the man had come through the door, Welch could see straight away that he was in trouble.

There was a look on the man's face that Welch recognised, that he'd spent years in prison trying to avoid. It was the look he'd seen often on the faces of ordinary, honest-to-goodness murderers and armed robbers. The same look of contempt, of threat, that Caldicott must have seen down in that laundry room before they flash-fried his face . . .

Welch thought that perhaps he should have struggled more, but there was little he could do. The man was far stronger than he was. The years inside had toughened him up mentally but his body had gone soft and flabby. Too much time reading and not nearly enough in the gym . . .

Welch spent his last moments thinking that pain was so much worse when you were unable to fight it, when you could not protest its presence . . .

The scream in his throat was stopped by whatever had been thrown around his neck and pressed back into a strangled, bubbling hiss. His body, too, could do nothing. It drew itself instinctively from the agony, but each jerk away from the tearing, from the stabbing, just tightened the grip of the line that was crushing the breath out of him.

Welch pushed his head down towards the carpet, feeling the line bite further into his neck, his teeth deeper into his tongue. He strained against the hands that dragged his neck back, contorting himself, his body foetal in the seconds before death.

I'm dying like a baby, Welch thought, his eyes wide but seeing nothing inside the hood, a softer, blacker darkness beginning finally to come over him . . .

Thorne had just put his father to bed. He was walking across the corridor to his own room when the phone rang. He let it ring until he was inside the room.

'You're up late . . .'

'Great, isn't it?' Eve said. 'Lie-in tomorrow. So, how was the wedding?'

'Perfect. Dull speeches, shit food and a fight.'

'What about the actual *wedding* . . .?'

'Oh *that*? Yeah, that was OK . . .'

She laughed. Thorne sat on the bed, wedged the phone between shoulder and chin and started to take his shoes off. 'Listen, I'm really sorry about last night . . .'

'Don't be silly. How's your dad?'

'You know, annoying. Mind you, he was annoying before . . .' Thorne thought he could hear the sound of traffic at the other end of the line. He guessed Eve was out somewhere, but thought better of asking where. 'Seriously though, sorry about rushing off. Did the food get eaten?'

'Don't worry, it will . . .'

'Sorry . . .'

'It's fine, there would have been tons left anyway. I'd made loads and Denise eats sod all, so I wouldn't worry about it.'

Thorne began to unbutton his shirt. 'Say thanks to her and Ben for the entertainment, by the way . . .'

'Good, wasn't it? I think I broke it up too early though. Another minute, and I'm sure we'd have seen a glass of wine thrown in someone's face . . .'

'Next time.'

She yawned loudly. 'God, sorry . . .'

'I'll let you get to bed,' he said. He was imagining her in the back of a cab, pulling up outside her flat.

'Sleep well, Tom.'

Thorne lay back down on his bed. 'Listen, you know that scale of one to ten? Can I move up to an eight . . .?'

Thorne's phone rang again eight hours later. Its insistent chirrup pulled him up from the depths of a deep sleep. Dragged him from a dream where he was trying to stop a man bleeding to death. Each time he put his finger over a hole, another would appear, as if he were Chaplin trying to plug a leak. Just when it seemed he had all the wounds covered, the blood began to spurt from a number of holes in *him* . . .

'You'd better get back, sir,' Holland said.

'Tell me . . .'

'The killer's ordered another wreath . . .'

PART TWO

LIKE LIGHT

27 NOVEMBER, 1996

Stooping to pick up the car keys he'd dropped, Alan Franklin winced in pain. A fortnight shy of retirement, and his body, like a precision alarm clock, was telling him that it was just the right time. The back pain and the talk of retirement cottages abroad had begun on almost exactly the same day . . .

He straightened up, his noisy exhalation echoing around the almost deserted car park. They'd probably talk about it again tonight, the two of them, over a bottle of wine. Sheila was leaning towards France while he fancied Spain. Either way, they would be off. There was nothing to keep them, after all. The three children he'd had with Celia were grown up with kids of their own. Not that he had any contact with his boys any more, and he'd never seen the grandchildren. There were friends, of course, and they'd be missed, but it wasn't like he and Sheila were going to be far away. They had no real ties . . .

He fumbled for the key to the Rover, pushed it towards the lock.

Sheila would probably get her way in the end of course, she usually did. It had to be said that more often than not she was right. She'd been right this morning, telling him that it was going to freeze, that he needed to wrap up warm.

He turned the key, popped up the central locking.

As he reached for the door handle, something passed in front of his eyes with a swish and bit back, hard into his neck, pulling him off his feet . . .

161

He hit the floor before his briefcase did, before he had a chance to cry out, one leg broken and bent behind, the other straight out in front of him, hands flying to his throat, fingers wedging themselves between line and neck.

Hands scrabbled at his own, tearing at his fingers, pulling them away. A fist crashed into the side of his head and as he rocked with the impact, he felt his fingers, numb and running with blood, slipping from beneath the line. And hot breath on the back of his neck . . .

He watched his leg shooting out, the foot kicking desperately against the Rover's dirty, grey hubcap.

He remembered suddenly the face of the woman underneath him. Smelt himself, the aftershave he used to love. Felt again that strength in his arms.

He saw her legs kicking out against the boxes piled high on either side of the stockroom. Heard the dull thud of her stockinged feet on the cardboard. He felt the movement beneath him die down and then stop, saw her eyes close tight.

It seemed to be getting dark very quickly. Perhaps the lights in the car park were on some sort of timer. Fading to save electricity. He could just make out his foot, the heel of his brogue still crashing into the hubcap, again and again. Cracking the cheap plastic.

Then, just black and the rushing of his blood, and the sound of his heartbeat which thumped inside his eyeballs as the line tightened.

He saw his wife, smiling at him from the garden, and the woman beneath him trying to turn her head away, and his wife, and then the woman, and finally the woman where his wife should have been, telling him how cold it was going to get.

Laughing, and reminding him not to forget his scarf . . .

TEN

Carol Chamberlain had always been an early riser, but by the time her husband shuffled, bleary-eyed, into the kitchen at a little after seven o'clock, she'd already been up a couple of hours. He flicked on the kettle, nodded to himself. He'd known very well she would have trouble sleeping after the phone call.

It had come the evening before, in the ad break between *Stars in their Eyes* and *Blind Date*. As soon as the caller had identified himself, begun to tell her what he wanted, Carol had understood the quizzical look on Jack's face when he'd handed her the receiver.

She'd listened to everything that the Commander had to say. From the audible exasperation in his voice it was clear that she'd asked a lot more questions than he'd been expecting. After fifteen minutes she had agreed to think about what she'd been asked.

The new team had been set up, she was told, to utilise some of the resources that had been – how had he put it? – *wasted* in previous years. The basic idea was that highly capable ex-officers could bring years of valuable experience to bear on re-examining old, dead cases. Would be able to cast a fresh eye across them . . .

For most of the time since she'd hung up, since they'd gone back to watching Saturday-night TV, Carol had been in two minds. She was certainly a 'wasted resource', but much as she was happy, no, *desperate*, to do something, she had also heard something dubious in the voice of the unspeakably young Commander. She knew immediately that he and many others would be picturing hordes of aged ex-coppers shuffling in from Eastbourne, on sticks and Zimmer frames, waving dog-eared warrant cards and shouting: 'I can still cut it. I'm eighty-two, you know . . .'

Jack put a mug of tea down in front of her. He spoke softly. 'You're going to do it, aren't you, love?'

She looked up at him. Her smile was nervous, but still wider than it had been in a while.

'I can still cut it,' she said.

While Thorne had been racing back from Hove, shagging the hired Corsa up three different motorways, Brigstocke had made the scene at the Greenwood Hotel secure. By the time Thorne arrived, it was nearly three hours since the body they would later identify as Ian Welch had been discovered, and more than twelve since he'd been killed. There was little else for Thorne to do but stare at him for a while.

'Well, it's a slightly nicer hotel anyway,' Hendricks said.

Holland nodded. 'They even sent us up some coffee . . .'

'There's a CCTV set-up in the lobby as well,' Brigstocke said. 'It's pretty basic, I think, but you never know.'

It was a classic businessman's hotel. Trouser presses, Teasmades and bog-standard soap in the bathroom. The simple, clean room couldn't have been more different from the pit they'd stood in three weeks earlier. Save of course for the one, gruesome feature they had in common.

As with the murder scene in Paddington, the bed had been stripped and the bedding taken away. The clothes lay scattered but the body itself had been precisely positioned. Dead centre with head towards the wall, belt around the wrists, white hands bloodless. The hood, the line around the neck, the dried, red-brown trails snaking down the thighs like gravy stains . . .

This one looked a little older than Remfry. Late forties maybe.

Brigstocke gave Thorne what little they had. Thorne took the information in, standing by the window, one eye on the fields beyond the main road. They were two minutes from the motorway, fifty yards from a major roundabout, but on this Sunday morning, Thorne could hear nothing but birdsong and the rustle of a bodybag.

This time the killer had ordered his floral tribute personally. The order had been placed with a twenty-four-hour florist at just after eight-thirty the evening before and paid for with the victim's debit card. Thanks to that, they already had a name for the dead man . . .

'He didn't fancy leaving a message this time,' Brigstocke said.

Thorne shrugged. Either the killer had learned from his mistake or had done what he needed to do in leaving his voice on Eve Bloom's machine.

'Twenty-four-hour florists?' Thorne shook his head. 'Who the hell needs flowers in the middle of the night?'

'They're not *actually* twenty-four hours,' Brigstocke said. 'But there's always somebody there until at least ten o'clock. They don't guarantee to get your flowers delivered by the next morning, but apparently they made a special effort in this case, due to the nature of the order . . .'

At 9 a.m., a delivery man had waltzed into hotel reception carrying the wreath. The receptionist, somewhat taken aback, had rung room 313 and, on getting no reply, had asked the delivery man to wait, and had gone up to the room. Five minutes later, her screams had woken most of the hotel.

'Sir . . .?'

Thorne turned from the window to see Andy Stone coming through the bedroom door. He was clutching a piece of paper, grinning, and moving quickly across to where Thorne and Brigstocke were standing.

'The victim checked in under his own name . . .' Stone said.

Brigstocke shrugged. 'No real reason for him not to, was there? He thought he was coming here to get fucked.'

'Looks well and truly fucked to me,' Holland said.

When Stone had finished laughing, Thorne caught his eye. 'Go on . . .'

Stone glanced down at the piece of paper. 'Ian Anthony Welch.' He half turned towards the body. 'Released eight days ago from Wandsworth. Three years of a five-stretch for rape.'

Thorne spoke to nobody in particular. 'I don't know why we never considered it. Remfry wasn't killed because of who he was. He and Welch were killed because of *what* they were. Christ, this is the sort of case we normally get brought *in* for . . .'

Brigstocke stretched, his plastic bodysuit rustling. 'Well, this time, we've got our very own.'

Now, things were going to change: in the previous week and a half, priorities had shifted. Older cases that had been downgraded in the immediate wake of the Remfry murder had, suddenly, three unsuccessful weeks on, been shunted forward again. Members of the team found themselves knee-deep in court preparations for a domestic, processing the arrest of a teenager who'd stabbed his friend for a computer game or gathering the papers on a drug-related shooting. This reallocation of resources was normal and now it would need to be done all over again. Now that the Remfry murder was the Remfry and Welch mur*ders*, the more straightforward cases would slide back on to the back-burner.

Now, Team 3 would be handling no other cases at all . . .

'One, two, three . . .'

Thorne watched as four officers heaved the body off the mattress and on to the black bodybag which had been stretched out on the floor next to the bed. The belt had been removed but the hands were still clenched tightly together behind the back, fingers entwined. Rigor mortis had set in hours ago and the body rolled awkwardly on to its side, knees drawn up to the chest. The officers looked at each other and, after a few moments, a DS stepped forward. He placed a hand on the chest and as he rolled the body on to its back, he pushed the legs downwards as far as they would go. Flattening the body just enough to zip the bag up.

'I forgot to ask,' Brigstocke said, 'how was the wedding?'

Thorne was still watching the sergeant, whose eyes

were closed the whole time his hands were on the naked body.

'Not a lot more fun than this,' Thorne said.

Fifteen minutes later, just after midday, the core of the team gathered in the lobby. They were about to go their separate ways. The post-mortem was being rushed through at two o'clock and while Thorne would be following Hendricks to Wexham Hospital, Brigstocke and the others would be heading back to the office.

While the DCI spoke on the phone to Jesmond and then to Yvonne Kitson back in the Incident Room, the others sat on mock-leather armchairs and shared a pot of coffee. Less animated than the small gaggle of hotel staff and guests, they stared out through the plate-glass windows in reception at the body being loaded into the mortuary van.

Brigstocke joined them, sliding his mobile back into the inside pocket of his jacket. 'Well, that's everybody up to speed, me included . . .'

'What words of wisdom from the all-knowing Detective Chief Superintendent?' Thorne asked. Outside, the mortuary van was moving away. Hendricks waved as he climbed into his car to follow it. Thorne raised a hand in return.

'Nothing I can argue with,' Brigstocke said. 'We'll have reporters here before they've put new sheets on the bed. So here it is. Officially, we can't confirm *or* deny a link with the Remfry murder.' He paused, making sure the message was sinking in. 'It makes sense. The tabloids would have a fucking field day with this one. Screaming about vigilantes, running polls. *Is the killer doing a good job? Yes or no?'*

'Is that a possibility, you think?' Stone asked. 'Could this be some sort of vigilante thing?'

Thorne reached for the coffee pot, poured himself another cup. 'This is something very personal. The man who's doing this isn't doing it for you or me . . .'

'Maybe,' Brigstocke said. 'But all the same, there *will* be people asking whether or not we should be grateful . . .'

The hotel manager walked through reception, talking quietly to a small group of guests in golfing gear. They stopped at the main doors and chatted some more. The manager shook their hands before watching the bemused golfers duck underneath the police tape and walk away, shaking their heads. It was a game Thorne had little time for, but he guessed they'd have something other than new cars and holidays to talk about on the first tee.

Brigstocke cleared his throat. 'Right. Forensics will be moving as quickly as they can, but while we're waiting, there's plenty we need to do . . .'

'We'll get nothing,' Thorne said. 'It's cleaner than the last place, but it's still a hotel room. They'll be gathering samples into next week.'

'We might get lucky,' Holland said.

'More chance of six numbers coming up Saturday night . . .'

Brigstocke tapped a spoon against his coffee cup. 'Let's cut the morale-building short for a minute, shall we? Talk about what we *can* do . . .'

Holland raised a hand. 'Sir. If I *do* get six numbers up on Saturday night, I'm officially requesting permission to resign from the case and fuck off to Rio de Janeiro with twin super-models.' The few seconds of laughter did everybody good.

'I want to know exactly what Ian Welch has been doing since he came out,' Brigstocke said. 'Where he's been staying, who he's been seeing . . .'

Stone cut in. 'He came out NFA. The prison gave me the address of a hostel . . .'

Brigstocke nodded. 'Good, and you're going to be calling a *lot* more governors before we're finished. We'll need to contact every prison in the country housing sex offenders, talk to anyone with an imminent release date. That's the easy bit. We're also going to trace every rapist, groper and flasher who's been released in the last six months. Check that none of them have received letters. Warn them in case they get any.'

'How many are we looking at?' Holland asked.

Brigstocke picked up a small pack of biscuits, sealed in plastic. He dangled it between two fingers. 'Based on the last set of Home Office stats, probably one serious sex offender is released somewhere in the country every day.' He tore open the packet with his teeth, spat out the plastic, looked at the faces of the other men around the table. 'I know. Frightening, isn't it? Just going back to the start of this year, we're going to be looking for something like a hundred and fifty offenders . . .'

Stone raised his eyebrows. 'Well, we should know where most of them are, in theory at least. Still might be a shitload of work, though.'

'Yes, it might be,' Brigstocke said.

'Are we going to be able to justify that? I mean, like you said, these aren't exactly innocent victims, are they?'

Brigstocke blinked, opened his mouth to shout. Thorne got in first. 'Not your worry, Andy.'

'I know. I was just saying . . .'

Thorne raised a hand. 'What we *can't* justify are bodies . . .'

They walked out to their cars. Brigstocke drifted away from the others towards his Volvo, took Thorne with him. He glanced towards Andy Stone.

'Have a word . . .'

Thorne nodded. 'Well, he *was* making the same sort of point you made yourself earlier. Remfry, Welch, doing what they did, being what they are. Some people might well think that . . .'

Brigstocke pressed the remote, deactivating the car alarm with a squawk. 'I'm not talking about what he said back there. I'm talking about the Gribbin business.'

Thorne had been waiting for this. He had known that Stone's behaviour during the raid was not just going to be forgotten. 'Right . . .'

'Don't worry, it's not going as far as the Funny Firm. All been put down to protecting the girl. Still, I want you to let him know he overstepped the mark.'

'Fair enough . . .'

Brigstocke got into the car, started the engine. He began to pull slowly away. 'Call me from the Wexham as soon as Phil's finished . . .'

Holland loped across the gravel as Thorne walked to the Corsa. 'You up for a drink later?'

'I'm likely to be up for several,' Thorne said.

Holland ran a hand along the front wing of the hire car. 'This is the sort of thing *you* ought to get.'

'Sort of thing I ought to get *when*?'

'Come on, your car is fucked. This is nice, though . . .'

'It's *white* . . . and my car is not fucked . . .'

'Name one thing that's good about it.'

Thorne opened the Corsa's door, hesitated before getting in. 'What? Straight off the top of my head?'

Holland laughed, leaned down as Thorne climbed in. 'If this was a woman we were talking about, you'd dump her.'

The electric window slid down. 'You've got a very strange mind, Holland.'

'How's it going with the florist, anyway?'

'Mind your own business.'

There was a rumble as an engine started up. Thorne looked across to see Stone watching them from behind the wheel of his own car, a silver Ford Cougar. He nodded towards it. 'What d'you think of Stone's motor?'

'It's a bit flash,' Holland said.

Thorne could see Stone slapping his palm off the steering wheel. 'Better get a move on. He looks keen to get back.'

Holland took a step away from the car, stopped. 'Did your dad have a good time at the wedding?'

'A good time? Yes. I think so . . .'

'I meant to tell you . . .' Stone sounded the horn. 'William Hartnell was the first Doctor Who. I looked it up on the Internet.'

'I'll tell him . . .'

Thorne turned the key in the ignition, watched as Holland ran across and climbed into Stone's car. He could hear the music being cranked up as the sports car roared past him, and out on to the main road with hardly a look from Andy Stone towards anything that might have been coming.

Thorne looked at his watch and turned the engine off again. Not quite one o'clock yet. The post-mortem wasn't until two and it was no more than a ten-minute drive to the hospital. He sat for a few minutes trying to decide between sleep and a Sunday paper and then he started to hear distant shouting, a cheer, a solitary handclap. The noise recognisable, tantalising. Carrying easily on the warm, afternoon air.

It took him twenty minutes to find the game, a quarter of a mile away up the main road in a small park. The season was still a month and a half away, but Sunday footballers cared as little for the calendar as they did for other trivialities like fitness and skill. A team in red and a team in yellow and a dozen or so lunatics watching, living every less than beautiful second of it.

Thorne could not have been more content. He stood on the touchline and lost himself in the game. In a little over an hour he would be watching organs meticulously excised, the flesh expertly sliced and laid aside . . .

For a while, he was happy to watch a team in red and a team in yellow, running and shouting and kicking lumps out of each other.

Thorne picked up his pint and turned from the bar. Except for Russell Brigstocke, one of whose kids was unwell, and Yvonne Kitson, most of the senior members of the team had come out. There was an unspoken need to loosen up, to enjoy a night out that they might not have the chance to repeat for a while, now that the case had moved up a gear. Now that there was a second body.

Thorne wasn't planning on staying long. He was wiped out. One drink, maybe two, and then home . . .

They were gathered around a couple of smallish tables. Holland and Hendricks were sitting at one end with Andy Stone and Sam Karim, a DS who worked as office manager. They were playing *Shag or Die*, a game that involved choosing between a pair of equally undesirable sexual partners, which had swept through the entire Serious Crime Group in the last few weeks. The choice between Ann Widdecombe and Camilla Parker-Bowles was prompting heated debate. Phil Hendricks was trying to make himself heard, claiming that as a gay man, he should not have to sleep with either of them. His point was eventually accepted as valid and he was given a choice between Jimmy Savile and Detective Chief Superintendent Trevor Jesmond to mull over . . .

If the Royal Oak had a theme other than drinking heavily, nobody had ever worked out what it was. Apart from being the *nearest* pub to Becke House, it had nothing whatsoever to recommend it. The fairly constant presence of police officers may have had something to do with it, but there was rarely anybody drinking in the pub who didn't have a warrant card.

Thorne looked around. Sunday night and the place was all but deserted: a couple at a table near the toilets, staring into their drinks like they'd had a row; the room quiet, save for his team's graphic deliberations and the tinny, musical stings from the unused quiz machine in the corner.

Hardly any more there than had gathered earlier in the

Dissecting Room: Phil Hendricks; a trio of mortuary atten-
dants; the exhibits officer; a stills photographer; a video
cameraman; the PC who had been first to arrive at the
Greenwood Hotel, there to confirm that the body was
indeed the same one he had seen on the bed in room 313.
And Thorne . . .

Nine of them, gathered in a cold room plumbed for
hoses, with easy-to-clean surfaces and drains in the floor.
The smallest murmur or the crunching of peppermints
magnified, bouncing off the cracked, cream tiles. A small
crowd, waiting for the body of Ian Welch to be uncovered
and taken apart.

Thorne had attended hundreds of post-mortems, and
though it was a process he had become resigned to, he had
found that lately it was a difficult one to leave behind, to
shed easily. The visceral onslaught disturbed him now far
less than the tiny details, the sensory minutiae which might
stay with him for days after each session . . .

Blinking awake in the early hours, as a brain plops
gently into a glass jar.

Dabbing at his freshly shaved face, the water spiralling
away, its momentary slurp like the sucking of the flesh at
the finger that presses into it.

A smell at work, the odour of something very raw, lurking somewhere deep within the medley of sweat and
institutional food . . .

Nine of them gathered. Waiting like embarrassed guests
at a bizarre party, strangers to each other. *That dreadful
hiatus between arriving, and anything actually happening* . . .

Finally, Hendricks drew back the white sheet and asked
the equally white PC to confirm it was the same body he'd

seen earlier. The constable looked as though the only thing he could confirm was rising rapidly up from his stomach. He swallowed hard.

'Yes,' he said, 'it is.'

And they were away . . .

Holland had moved across to the bar to get a round in and Thorne took his place next to Andy Stone. Karim leaned across, eager to involve Thorne in the game. Before he had a chance to speak, Thorne angled his body away, turned into the corner, towards Stone.

'Idiotic, bloody game,' Stone said. Thorne had only just got there, but Stone sounded like he was three or four drinks ahead of him. 'If it's shag or *die*, you'd shag anybody, wouldn't you? So what's the point?'

Thorne swallowed a mouthful of lager and leaned a little closer to Stone. 'I need to have a quick word about what happened when we picked Gribbin up.'

If Stone had been on the way to being drunk, he sobered up very quickly. 'I was protecting the kid. I didn't know what he was going to do . . .'

'Which is exactly what the DCI is going to say. Still, I'm here to tell you, off the record, that you overstepped the mark. That nobody wants to see it happen again, OK?' Stone stared forward, said nothing. 'Andy . . .?' Thorne took another drink. Half the pint had gone already. 'Nobody's very fond of blokes like Gribbin, but you were over the top.'

'There's just so bloody many of them. I don't understand how there can be so *many* of them walking about.'

'Listen . . .'

Stone turned. He spoke low and fast as if imparting dangerous information. 'I've got a mate on the Child

Protection Team over at Barnes. He told me about this time they were after a child-killer up in Scotland. This bloke had already killed three kids, they had a description, and some woman claimed she'd spotted him on a beach one bank holiday, right? So they appealed for people to come forward with their holiday snaps, see if anybody might have got a picture of this fucker accidentally . . .'

Thorne nodded. He remembered the case. He had no idea what Stone wanted to tell him.

'So, they get hundreds of films handed in. They develop them all and go through the pictures. Thousands of them.' Stone picked up his glass, stared into it for a moment. 'The woman couldn't pick out the man she'd seen, but the police identified thirty known child-sex offenders. In *one* fucking weekend, on *one* beach. Thirty . . .'

Stone drained his glass. 'Right. Toilet, I think . . .'

Thorne watched Stone go, and drained his. He decided to leave the Corsa in the car park at Becke House. It was easy enough to get the tube home . . .

The rest of the evening passed quickly and easily. Thorne had some success with a couple of his dad's jokes; Holland argued with Sophie on the phone, pulling faces for the lads, doing his best to laugh it off; nobody could choose between Vanessa Feltz and Esther Rantzen; Holland spoke to Sophie again, then turned his phone off; Thorne bet Hendricks ten pounds that Spurs were going to finish above Arsenal the following season; Hendricks had one Guinness too many and told Holland that several of his gay friends fancied him . . .

Stone grabbed Thorne's arm as they were all stepping out into the clear, warm night. Saying their goodbyes.

'Something else my mate told me. They arrested this one bloke who had all these pictures of kids off the Internet, you know? Downloaded them on to his computer, hundreds of them. He said that he was searching through all these pictures, looking at them all, at their faces, hoping that one day he might find the pictures of himself . . .'

Thorne tried gently to pull away. Stone was squeezing his arm tightly.

'That's rubbish, isn't it?' Stone said. 'That's bollocks. That's an excuse, don't you think? That's not really true, is it, sir . . .?'

Thorne stepped through the front door into the communal hall he shared with the couple in the flat upstairs. The breath he let out was long and noisy. He picked up the post, sorted the bills from the pizza delivery menus, fumbled for his flat key.

As soon as the door was open he knew. He could feel the breeze where there should be none. The scent of something carried on it . . .

He moved quickly into his own, small hallway. The cat was rubbing itself against his shin. He put down his bag, dropped the letters on to the table next to the phone and stepped around the corner into the living room.

He stared at the space where the video had been. Looked up at the dusty shelf he'd never bothered to paint, on which his sound system had sat. The leads were gone, which meant they'd obviously been in the place for a while. The ones who were in a hurry just ripped the spaghetti out of the back, left it still plugged in.

He reached to pick up the few scattered paperbacks that had previously been held upright by his BOSE speakers. Clearly, whoever now had his speakers wasn't a great reader. They *had* taken every single CD . . .

Fuckers would hand over his entire collection for a day's worth of smack.

Thorne walked through to the kitchen, stared at the small window they'd climbed through. The window he'd left open. In a hurry two nights earlier, throwing his stuff for the wedding together and not locking up properly because he was rushing across to calm his fucking stupid father down . . .

Aside from the obvious gaps, the place seemed pretty much as he'd left it. He guessed that there would be a suitcase or two missing from the wardrobe in the bedroom. Away out of the front door, casual as you like, as if they were taking something very heavy on their holidays.

The smell hit him the second he opened the bedroom door, and Thorne had a pretty good idea where it was coming from. He moved his hand to cover his mouth, needing to unclench the fist as he did so. His first thought when he threw back the duvet was that it must have taken a good deal of skill to have done the job so accurately, smack in the centre of the bed.

Thorne backed quickly out of the room, his guts bubbling. Elvis yowled at his feet; hungry, or keen to deny responsibility for the turd on the bed, one or the other. Thorne wondered if it was too late to ring his father and shout at him for a while.

He looked at his watch. It was ten past twelve . . .

He'd just turned forty-three.

All through Sunday, every time he was beginning to enjoy himself, he'd remembered the bloody message and become prickly, irritated. It had been there on his answering machine, waiting for him when he'd got back from Slough on Saturday night. He'd ignored it, collapsed exhausted into bed and played it back first thing the next morning. It was exactly what he did not need. It was spoiling things.

He needed to deal with it.

As he moved around his flat, dressing himself, he remembered the look on Welch's face when he'd walked into the hotel room. The face was the very best thing. Remfry's had been the same. It was the look that passes across the face of someone who thinks that they are about to get one thing, and then realises that they are in for an altogether different sort of experience.

He wondered if they saw that expression on the faces of the women they raped.

He didn't know the details of their particular offences, he didn't care. Rape was rape was rape. He did know that most attacks did not involve dark alleys and deserted bus stops. He knew that most rapists were known to their victims. Were trusted by them. Friends, colleagues, husbands . . .

They would have seen that terrible realisation on the faces of the women they attacked. The horror and surprise. The very last thing they were expecting.

The very last person they were expecting it from.

180

He'd enjoyed watching that same expression distort the smug, expectant features on the faces of these men. He'd savoured it for a few seconds before taking out the knife and the washing line . . .

Creating an entirely new expression.

He pulled on his jacket and picked up his keys. Checked himself in the mirror by the front door. He glanced down at the answering machine.

He would definitely sort the message business out later.

ELEVEN

It was no more than a ten-minute walk from the tube station, but Thorne had a healthy sweat on by the time he reached Becke House. A figure loitered by the main doors, wreathed in cigarette smoke. Thorne was amazed when it turned round and revealed itself to be Yvonne Kitson.

'Morning, Yvonne.'

She nodded, avoiding his eye and blushing like a fourth-former caught fagging it behind the bike sheds. 'Morning . . .'

Thorne pointed at the cigarette, almost burnt down to the butt. 'I didn't know you . . .'

'Well, you do now.' She tried her best to smile and took another drag. 'Not quite so perfect, I'm afraid . . .'

'Thank Christ for that,' Thorne said.

Kitson's smile got a little warmer. 'Oh, sorry. Was I starting to intimidate you?'

'Well, not *me*, obviously. But I think one or two of the younger ones were a bit scared.' Kitson laughed, and Thorne saw that she was still carrying her bag across one shoulder. 'Have you not even been *in* yet?' he asked. She shook her head, blowing out smoke from the side of her mouth. 'Bloody hell, how stressed out can you possibly be then?' Kitson raised her eyebrows, looked at him like he didn't know the half of it.

They stood for a few seconds, looking in different directions, saying nothing. Thorne decided to make a move before they were forced to start discussing the hot weather. He put one hand on the glass doors . . .

'I'll see you upstairs . . .' he said.

'Oh shit.' Like she'd just remembered. 'Sorry to hear about the burglary . . .'

Thorne nodded, shrugged and pushed through the doors. He trudged up the stairs, marvelling at the incredible speed and efficiency of the Met's jungle drum system.

A desk sergeant in Kentish Town, who knows a DC in Islington, who calls somebody at Colindale . . .

Throw a few Chinese whispers into the mix and you had a culturally diverse ensemble of rumour, gossip and bullshit that outperformed any of the systems they actually used to fight crime . . .

It took Thorne almost five minutes to get from one side of the Incident Room to the other. Running the gauntlet of digs and wisecracks. A cup of coffee from the reconditioned machine in the corner the prize that awaited him.

'Sorry, mate . . .'

'You look a bit rough, sir. Sleep on the sofa?'

'Never done a crime prevention seminar, then, Tom?'

'Many happy returns . . .' This was Holland.

Thorne had wanted to keep it quiet. He'd deliberately said nothing in the pub the night before. He must have mentioned the date to Holland some time. 'Thanks.'

'Not a very nice present to come home to. I mean the burglary, not . . .'

'No. It wasn't.'

'Somebody said they took your car . . .'

'Is that a smirk, Holland?'

'No, sir . . .'

The night before. Thorne, hauling the mattress out through the front door when he remembered that he hadn't seen the Mondeo outside when he'd arrived home. He didn't recall seeing his car keys on the table as he'd come in either. He *had* been worrying about other things at the time . . .

He dropped the mattress and stepped out into the street. Maybe he'd parked the car somewhere else.

He hadn't. Fuckers . . .

'Birthday drink in the Oak later, then?' Holland said.

Thorne stepped past him, almost within reach of the coffee machine now. He turned and spoke quietly, reaching into his pocket for change. 'Just a quiet one, all right?'

'Whatever . . .'

'Not like last night. Just you and Phil, maybe.'

'Fine . . .'

'I might ask Russell if he fancies it . . .'

'We can do it another day if you're not up for it.'

Thorne slammed his coins into the coffee machine. 'Listen, after dealing with the fallout from our second body, and spending fuck knows how long I'm going to have to spend on the phone to house insurance companies and car insurance companies and whichever council department is responsible for taking shitty mattresses away, I think I might need a drink . . .'

After Holland had gone, Thorne stood, sipping his

coffee and staring at the large, white write-on/wipe-off board that dominated one wall of the room. Crooked lines scrawled in black felt-tip, marking out the columns and rows. Arrows leading away to addresses and phone numbers. The *Actions* for the day, each team member's duties allocated by the office manager. The names of those peripheral to the investigation. The names of those central to it: REMFRY, GRIBBIN, DODD . . .

In a column all of its own: JANE FOLEY??

And now a second name added beneath Dougie Remfry's, with plenty of empty space for more names below that one. The heading at the top of the column hadn't been altered yet. Nobody had thought to add an S to VICTIM, but they would.

Thorne heard a sniff and turned to find Sam Karim at his shoulder.

'How's the head?'

Thorne glanced at him. 'What?'

'After last night. I feel like shit warmed up . . .'

'I'm fine,' Thorne said.

Samir Karim was a large, gregarious Indian with a shock of thick silver hair and a broad London accent that was delivered at a hundred miles per hour. He planted half of his sizeable backside on to the edge of a desk. 'Fuck all off those tapes, by the way . . .'

'Which tapes?'

'CCTV tapes from the Greenwood.'

Thorne shrugged, unsurprised.

'Couple of possibles,' Karim said. 'But only from the back. The cameras only really cover the bar and the area around the desk and the lifts. You can walk in and go straight up the stairs without being seen at all, if you know where the cameras are . . .'

'He knew where they were,' Thorne said.

They stared at the board together for a moment or two. 'That's the difference between our team and all the others, isn't it?' Karim said.

'What?'

'They have a victim. We have a list . . .'

There's a moment in film and TV shows, a particular shot, a cliché to signify that moment when the penny drops. For real people this means remembering where they've left their car keys, or the title of a song that's been annoying them. For the screen copper, it's usually a darker revelation. The instant that provides the break in the case. Then, when that pure and brilliant comprehension dawns, the camera zooms towards the face of the hero, crashing in quickly or sometimes creeping slowly up on them. Either way, it goes in close and it stays there, showing the light of realisation growing in the eyes . . .

Thorne was not an actor. There was no nod of steely determination, no enigmatic stare. He stood holding his coffee cup, his mouth gaping, like a half-wit.

A *list* . . .

The certainty hit him like a cricket ball. He felt a bead of sweat surface momentarily from every pore in his body before retreating again. Tingling; hot, then cold.

'Feeling OK, Tom?' Karim asked.

Zoom in close and hold . . .

Thorne didn't feel the hot coffee splashing across his wrist as he marched across the room, up the corridor and into Brigstocke's office.

186

Brigstocke looked up, saw the expression on Thorne's face, put down his pen.

'What . . .?'

'I know how he finds them,' Thorne said. 'How he finds out where the rapists are . . .'

'How?'

'This *could* all be very simple. Our man might work for the prison service, or hang about in pubs around Pentonville and the Scrubs, hoping to get matey with prison officers, but I doubt it. At the end of the day, finding out where rapists are banged up isn't that hard. Families, court records . . . he could just go to newspaper archives and sift through the local rags if he felt like it . . .'

'Tom . . .'

Thorne stepped quickly forward, put his coffee cup down on Brigstocke's desk and began to pace around the small office. 'It's about what happens *afterwards*. It's about release dates and addresses. I *had* thought that maybe there was some connection with the families, but Welch was NFA. His family disowned him and moved away years ago.' He glanced across at Brigstocke as if he were making everything very obvious. Brigstocke nodded, still waiting. 'Release details are fluid, right? Prisoners move around, parole dates change, extra days get tagged on to sentences. The killer has to have access to up-to-date, accurate information . . .'

'Do I have to phone a friend?' Brigstocke said. 'Or are you going to sodding well tell me? How does he find them?'

Thorne allowed himself the tiniest flicker of a smile. 'The same way we do.'

Behind his glasses Brigstocke blinked twice, slowly. The

confusion on his face became something that might have been regret. Or the anticipation of it. 'The Sex Offenders Register.'

Thorne nodded, picked up his coffee. 'Jesus, we need shooting 'cause it took us *this* long . . .'

Brigstocke took a deep breath. He began stepping slowly backwards and forwards in the space between the wall and the edge of the desk. Trying to take this vital, but daunting piece of new information on board. Trying to shape it into something he could handle. 'I don't need to say it, do I?' he said, finally.

'What?'

'About this not getting out . . .'

Thorne looked up, past Brigstocke. The sun was moving behind a cloud but it was still baking in the tiny office. He could feel the sweat gathering in the small of his back. 'You don't need to say it.'

'Not just because it's . . . sensitive. Although it *is*.'

Thorne knew that Brigstocke was right. The whole issue of the Register had been what the tabloids were fond of calling a 'political hot potato' for years. This was just the sort of thing to blow the whole 'naming and shaming' debate wide open again. When he looked back to Brigstocke, the DCI was smiling.

'This might be the way we get him, though, Tom.'

Thorne was counting on it . . .

Brigstocke came around his desk. 'Right, let's start with the bodies that are informed about an offender's registration requirements. The ones that get fed the notification details as a matter of course.' He started to count them off on his fingers. 'Social services, probation . . .'

'And us, of course,' Thorne said. 'We'd better not forget the most interesting one, had we, Russell?'

Macpherson House was located in a side street off Camden Parkway. In the course of a century, the building had been a theatre, cinema and bingo hall. Now it was little more than a shell, within which was situated temporary hostel accommodation.

'Fuck me gently,' Stone said. He was craning back his head, staring at the grimy, crumbling ceiling high above him.

Holland looked up. There were still traces of gilt on the mouldings. Decorative swirls of plaster leaves trailed across the ceiling and then down towards four ornate columns in each corner of the vast room. 'Must have been amazing . . .'

There was a week-old copy of the *Daily Star* on the floor. Stone pushed it aside with his foot. He sniffed at the stale air and pulled a face. 'It's a bloody shame . . .'

As they walked, Holland took Stone through the simple, ironic history of the place. The theatre that had become a cinema. The cinema done for in the seventies by the more popular entertainment of the bingo hall. The bingo hall itself made redundant thirty years later by the easy availability of scratchcards and the National Lottery.

'From music hall to the Stupid Tax,' Holland said.

Stone snorted. 'I take it those six numbers never came up, then?'

'I'm still here, aren't I?'

Their footsteps echoed off the scuffed, stone floors, else were muffled as they walked across the occasional threadbare rug, or curling square of carpet. 'Can't see what's going to replace the Lottery, can you?'

Holland shook his head. 'Not as long as there's a call for it.'

They were walking ten yards or so behind Brian, the hostel supervisor, a big man in his fifties with long, grey hair, a large hoop earring and a multicoloured waistcoat. Without turning round, he held out both arms. Taking in the place.

'Always be a call for *this*, though . . .'

Now, forty feet below the faded rococo grandeur, the space was taken up with cracked sinks and metal beds. A kitchen and a serving hatch. A pair of small televisions, each attached with a padlock and chain to nearby radiators. Behind the beds, along the walls, stood row upon row of scratched and dented lockers – some without locks, many without doors. All rusting and covered in graffiti.

'Council got them for a song,' Brian said. 'When the swimming pool down the road was knocked down. Same week they got this place off Mecca . . .'

Holland looked down at the floor as he walked. Shoes under many of the beds, trainers, mostly. The occasional tatty suitcase. Dozens of plastic bags.

Stone took off his jacket. 'Dossers by and large, is it?'

Brian looked back over his shoulder. Holland thought he looked powerful, like he could handle himself. He probably needed to on occasion. 'All sorts. Long-term homeless, runaways, addicts. The odd ex-con like Welch . . .'

'Where do they go during the day?' Holland asked.

The big man slowed, let Holland and Stone draw level

with him. 'Wandering about. Begging. Trying to find somewhere to sleep.' He smiled when Holland looked confused. 'This place is warm and they can get something to eat, but there's not a lot of sleeping goes on. Most of them are scared of getting stuff nicked. Even if they do want a kip, a hundred blokes coughing and shifting around on creaky bedsprings is worse than a neighbour with a drum kit . . .'

'My ex-girlfriend kept me awake half the night,' Stone said. 'Talking in her sleep, grinding her teeth . . .'

Brian smiled thinly. 'It's quiet enough in here now, but you won't be able to hear yourself think by dinnertime. They'll start drifting back as soon as it starts to get dark. Be rammed in here by nine o'clock.'

Holland looked at the lines of beds, three and four deep. Imagined it.

Eyes down for a full house.

The supervisor stopped. He tapped on the open door of a locker and immediately began moving away again. 'This was Mr Welch's. I'll be in the front office if you need anything . . .'

They both pulled on gloves. While Stone went through the locker, Holland got down on his hands and knees and, for the second time in a little over a fortnight, went rummaging under the bed of a recently murdered rapist.

It took less than two minutes to gather together Welch's worldly goods: a battered green holdall full of clothes which smelled of Oxfam; a plastic bag of dirty pants and socks; a radio spattered with white paint; an electric razor; a couple of tatty paperbacks . . .

At the back of the locker, between the pages of one of the books, the photographs of Jane Foley.

'Here she is,' Stone said, holding one of the pictures up between his fingertips. 'Lovelier than ever.'

Holland got to his feet, moved across to take a look. 'How many?'

'Half a dozen. Can't see any letters. Must have chucked them . . .'

Stone slid the photos into an evidence bag, popped it into an inside pocket. Holland shoved everything else into a black bin-liner. When he'd finished he picked the bag up. It wasn't heavy.

'Not a lot, is it?' he said.

Stone pushed the locker door closed and shrugged. 'That's what you get.'

It was nearly midday and starting to get really warm. Holland rubbed the sweat off the back of his neck. He thought about what he guessed was going through Stone's mind. 'Do you not give a shit because Welch was an ex-con?' he said. 'Or because he was an ex-con who was also a rapist? Honestly, I'm interested . . .'

Stone thought about it. Holland bounced the bin-bag against his knees.

'I suppose I'd give a bit *more* of a shit if he'd been a forger,' Stone said. 'Less if he'd murdered half a dozen schoolgirls . . .'

Holland looked at the expression on Stone's face. He couldn't help but laugh as they began to move away, back towards the entrance. 'I don't believe it. You've actually got a fucking sliding scale . . .'

They walked up Parkway towards the pay and display bay where Stone had parked the Cougar. At regular intervals, rubbish bags like the one Holland was carrying were piled high on the pavement. After Madame Tussaud's, Camden's Sunday market was now the second most popular tourist attraction in the city, and cleaning up after it was becoming a little like painting the Forth Bridge.

'So, what is it now? Couple of months till the baby?' Stone asked.

Holland swung the bin-bag from one hand to the other. 'Ten weeks.'

'Sophie must be the size of a house . . .'

Holland smiled, turned to look into the window of a Japanese restaurant. The plates of plastic sushi, red and yellow and pink. He promised himself that one of these days he'd try some.

They turned left and Stone unlocked the car with a remote. 'So? Excited then?'

'Yeah, she's very excited.'

Stone opened the car door. Looked at Holland across the roof. 'I meant *you* . . .'

'Get your arse up. Right up in the air, that's it. Now, let your fingers do the walking . . .'

Charlie Dodd was making himself useful. The place had been hired out for a web-cam session and he'd thrown in his services, gratis. He was cheerfully relaying on-screen instructions to the bored-looking girl on the bed when the phone rang.

'Just do some moaning for a minute, sweetheart . . .'

His hand was slippery against the receiver as he mumbled a greeting and waited.

'I got your message . . .'

Dodd recognised the voice straight away. Without looking round he used his hand to indicate to the girl on the bed that she should carry on, then brought it to his mouth and took out the cigarette.

'I was wondering when I was going to hear back from you.'

'I've had a busy weekend.'

Dodd reached for a plastic cup, flicked fag-ash into the inch of cold tea at the bottom. 'Anything interesting?'

For a few seconds there was nothing but the crackle of static. 'You said something about doing me a favour.'

'*Done* you a favour, mate,' Dodd said. 'Already did it. A big favour.'

'Go on . . .'

Dodd thought that the man on the other end of the phone sounded relaxed. He was probably putting it on, of course, trying to sound cool because he could guess what was coming. Because he knew he might have to part with some money and wanted to be in control in case there was haggling to do. It was a pretty convincing act though. Sounded like he knew what Dodd was going to say . . .

'The police were here with one of the photos you did. A photo of the girl with the hood on.' Dodd waited for a reaction. Didn't get it. 'I got asked a lot of questions . . .'

'And did you tell any lies, Mr Dodd?'

Dodd pinched the cigarette between thumb and forefinger, took a final drag. 'A couple of little white ones, yeah. And one dirty, big fucker.' He dropped the nub-end into the plastic cup, turned and watched the girl on the bed. 'I told them I never saw your face. Said you never took the crash helmet off . . .'

The girl's rear end bobbed and swayed. Dodd thought the moaning was a bit over the top – silly cow sounded like she had food poisoning. There were red blotches at the top of her legs. Finally, the man on the other end of the phone spoke . . .

'Come on, Mr Dodd, spit it out. Don't be shy.'

Dodd reached into the top pocket of his shirt for another cigarette. 'I'm not fucking shy, mate . . .'

'Good, because there's really no need to be . . .'

'Not about money, anyway.'

The man laughed. 'There we are. No point in going round the houses. Now, if I remember rightly, there's a cashpoint just round the corner from your studio, isn't there . . .?'

Thorne was somewhere between Brent Cross and Golders Green when he began finding it hard to stay awake . . .

He had been as good as the promise he'd made to himself and Holland that morning, having left the Royal Oak in time to make the last tube going south. He was tired and there was still plenty to sort out back at the flat, so it was no great wrench to walk out of the pub before closing time.

He'd left just as Phil Hendricks was starting to let rip. He'd made his feelings about the Sexual Offences Act clear plenty of times before. In the pub, once the subject of the Register had come up, there was no stopping him . . .

'Don't forget the gay men,' Hendricks had said. 'Those evil bastards who are twisted enough to enjoy loving, consensual sex with their seventeen-year-old boyfriends.' The words were spat out, the flat Mancunian vowels lending an edge of real anger to the irony.

Thorne knew that Hendricks had every right to be pissed off. It was ridiculous that men convicted of what was still termed 'gross indecency' should be lumped together with child abusers and rapists. Even when the age of consent for gay men was lowered to sixteen, as one day it would be, Thorne knew that those convicted prior to its equalisation would remain on the Register.

Thorne could only agree with his friend's pithy assessment, the last words he'd caught as he walked out of the pub.

'It's a queer-basher's charter,' Hendricks had said.

Eve had called to wish him a happy birthday as he was heading for the tube station at Colindale. As they talked, Thorne walked past the KFC, the chippy, more than one kebab shop. His stomach urged him to go in, then changed its mind as he told Eve about the burglary, and the little gift that had been left for him.

'Well, it's certainly original,' Eve had said.

Thorne laughed. 'Right, and a home-made present's *so* much more thoughtful, isn't it?'

Thorne was walking slowly, absorbed in the conversation but keenly aware, as always, of exactly where he was and what he was doing. Keeping track of any movement on the other side of the street, at the corners up ahead, behind parked cars. This wasn't Tottenham or Hackney, but still, there was no point in being stupid when people were getting shot for £9.99 handsets . . .

'So . . . when are you going to replace that bed?' Eve had asked.

'Oh, I suppose I'll get round to it eventually . . .'

'I sincerely hope so.'

They were joking, but suddenly Thorne sensed a real shift. A hint of impatience. Like she was making the running and wanted him to do some catching up.

'Well, we can always go to your place, can't we?' Thorne said.

There was a pause. Then: 'It's a bit tricky. Denise can be funny about that sort of thing . . .'

'About you having men over?'

'About men *staying* over . . .'

Thorne heard Eve sigh, as if this was a conversation she'd had before. With Denise herself, most probably. 'Hang on, she has Ben round, doesn't she?'

'I know, it's mad. But trust me, it isn't worth going into . . .'

Then, Thorne had arrived at the station and they'd wound it up. While he fed coins into the ticket machine they'd made a hasty arrangement to meet the following week. She'd said goodbye as he went down on the escalator and he lost the signal before he could say it back.

The train was all but deserted. A teenage couple sat at the far end of the carriage, the girl's head on her boyfriend's shoulder. He was stroking her hair and muttering things which made her smile.

Thorne took a deep breath. His brain felt fuzzed up. He'd only had a couple of pints but his head was thickening, getting heavier with every lurch and sway of the train. He needed to stay awake. Tempting as it was to close his eyes, to let his head drop back, the last thing he wanted to do was to nod off and wake up in Morden.

He thought about the conversation with Eve. When they'd arranged to meet, why hadn't he pushed to make it sooner? Was that panic he'd felt when she'd been talking about the bed? Maybe with the case and his old man and the burglary there was too much other stuff going on. Maybe he was just subconsciously prioritising. He was *definitely* feeling far too fucked to think straight about anything . . .

At Hampstead, a man got on through the doors to Thorne's right, and despite the availability of seats chose to stand at the end of the carriage, clutching on to the rail above his head. Thorne looked at the man. He was very tall and thin with chiselled features and a frenzy of greying hair and a battery of bizarre visual tics from which Thorne found it impossible to avert his gaze . . .

It quickly became clear that the tic, which Thorne guessed to be Tourette's syndrome, was in three parts. First the man would raise his eyebrows theatrically and his chin would jerk up. A second later the entire head would be wrenched round to the side, and finally, the jaws would snap noisily together, the teeth clacking like castanets. Thorne watched guilty and mesmerised as this three-part pattern repeated itself over and over, and he found himself assigning a word, a sound-effect, to each, distinct spasm. The eyebrows, the wrench of the neck, the snap of the jaws. Three movements that in rapid succession seemed to display surprise, interest and then ultimately, a bitter disappointment. Movements which sounded to Thorne like 'Ooh! Whay-hay! Clack!'

Oh really? Sounds interesting! Ah, fuck it . . .

After a minute or two the man seemed to be bringing the seizure under control and Thorne finally dragged his own head around and his eyes away. The young couple in the left-hand carriage had got off and had been replaced by a pair who were a good deal older and less tactile. The woman caught Thorne's eye and dropped her gaze to the carriage floor like a piece of litter.

When Thorne turned back and looked to his right, the man who was holding on to the rail was now still, and staring straight at him.

Thorne leaned back until he felt his head, big and wobbly as a baby's, hit the window. The glass was cool against his scalp.

He closed his eyes.

He was only a couple of stations away from where he'd need to change at Camden. He could afford to spend just a minute or two drifting, wide awake and counting the stops, and floating towards his hillside . . .

Almost as soon as Thorne had completed the thought, he was asleep.

He had plenty of stuff to do, a few more images to download from the camera and print, but he thought he deserved a quick break. Ten or fifteen minutes messing about on the Net wouldn't hurt and then he'd get back to business. Put all the pictures together and stick them in the post . . .

He enjoyed working at the computer, now that he felt like he'd mastered it. He'd needed to learn, so he'd learned. In just a couple of years he'd gone from being a novice to being more than comfortable with pretty much any machine.

He opened the bookmark, drummed his finger against the mouse as he waited for the page to appear . . .

Once you became skilled at something, it was easy to enjoy it. Like the work he did on those fuckers with the knife and the washing line. He was certainly enjoying that. It was funny, he thought, that the word 'skilled' had 'kill' sitting right there in the middle of it.

He'd first found the site when he was looking for inspiration, for help with the photos of Jane. Now he just popped back every now and then to keep abreast of it all. Just to see . . .

It had been a strange week, all in all. By rights he should have been doing other stuff, but he'd been forced to tweak the schedule, to rearrange things a bit in view of the hiccough with Dodd. That's all it had been. It was easily fixed.

There were several new links from the site since the last time he'd been here. One or two were begging to be checked out. He pointed and clicked, held his breath . . .

He was itching to get back to the serious work. Apart from anything else there was the challenge of a change in routine. Now that the prisons had been warned, there couldn't be any more letters.

'Jesus . . .'

The woman's head was shaved and she had been hog-tied. A chain ran from a ring in her collar down to the leather strap between her ankles. The buckled harness snaked across her face like a spider's web, her mouth at its centre, filled by a large, red ball-gag . . .

It was a shame. If he was going to use more pictures, this was just the sort of thing he might have gone for, but now it was academic. With Remfry and Welch it had been a lovely, long, slow tease. With the next one things would have to be simple and direct. A bit more 'in your face'.

He hoped it would be as much fun as wooing.

TWELVE

Carol Chamberlain felt twenty years younger. Every thought and sensation was coming that bit quicker, feeling that bit stronger. She felt hungrier, more awake. The night before in bed, she'd leaned across and 'helped herself', for heaven's sake, which had certainly surprised and delighted her old man. Maybe the battered green folder on her lap would prove to be the saving of both of them . . .

Jack was still smiling twelve hours later, as he brought a plate of toast through to her. She blew him a kiss. He took his anorak from the stand in the corner, off to pick up a paper.

Carol had been fifty-two, a DCI for a decade, when the Met's ludicrous policy of compulsory retirement after thirty years had pushed her out of the force. That had been three years ago. It had rankled, for each day of those three years, right up to the moment when that phone call had come out of the blue.

Carol had been amazed, and not a little relieved . . .

She knew how much she had to offer, *still* had to offer, but she also knew that this chance had come along at the very last moment. If she was being honest, she would have to admit that recently she'd felt herself slowly giving in, throwing in the towel in much the same way that her husband had.

She heard the gate creak shut. Turned to watch Jack walking away up the road. An old man at fifty-seven . . .

Carol picked up the folder from her knees. Her first cold case. A sticker on the top right-hand corner read 'AMRU'.

The Area Major Review Unit was what it said at the top of the notepaper. The Cold Case Team was how they thought of themselves. In the canteen they were just called the Crinkly Squad.

They could call her what they sodding-well liked, but she'd do the same bloody good job she'd always done . . .

The day before at Victoria, when she'd collected the file from the General Registry, she'd noticed straight away that it had been pulled only three weeks earlier by a DC from the Serious Crime Group. That was interesting. She'd scribbled down the officer's name, made a mental note to give him a call and find out what he'd been looking for . . .

Three years away from it. Three years of reading all those books she'd never got round to, and cooking, and gardening, and catching up with friends she'd lost touch with for perfectly good reasons, and feeling slightly sick when *Crimewatch* came on. Three years out of it, but the flutter in her stomach was still there. The butterflies that shook the dust from their wings and began to flap around as she opened the folder and started to read.

A man throttled to death in an empty car park, seven years earlier . . .

★

A week into his forty-fourth year. The discovery of his burnt-out car being far from the low point, Tom Thorne was already pretty sure that the year was not going to be a vintage one. Seven days since he'd rushed back from a wedding to attend a post-mortem. Seven days during which the only developments on the case had been about as welcome as the turd he'd found waiting for him in his bed.

Welch's movements between his release from prison and the discovery of his body, painstakingly reconstructed, had yielded nothing.

Forensically, the photos recovered from the locker in Macpherson House had been a black hole.

A hundred and more interviews with *anybody* who could feasibly have seen *anything*, and not a word said that might raise the blood pressure.

The ACTIONS outlined and ticked off on the white board. Allocated and diligently carried out. Contacting the sex offenders who had themselves been diligent about signing the Register at the right time. Tracking down those who were not *quite* so assiduous, who had perhaps forgotten, or mixed up the days in their diaries, or buggered off to another part of the country and gone underground. Checking and double-checking the statements of everyone from the traumatised receptionist at the Greenwood Hotel to the semi-pickled dosser who had been occupying the bed next to Ian Welch for the few days before he was killed . . .

This was what 99 per cent of police work really consisted of. It was procedure like this, together with a little bit of luck, that would provide pretty much the best chance, the *only* chance, of getting a result. And Thorne, of course, hated every tedious minute of it.

While he was waiting for that elusive bit of luck to arrive, even his one moment of genuine inspiration was proving to have been useless . . .

Sitting in Russell Brigstocke's office – Monday morning and feeling like it – Thorne listened as he was told *just* how useless it was. He had thought that the killer's access to the Sex Offenders Register might hold the key to catching him. Detective Chief Superintendent Trevor Jesmond was more than happy to disillusion him . . .

'Fact is,' Jesmond said, 'tabloids or no tabloids, the information's already public property. Every force has a community notification policy. Supposed to be on a case-by-case, need-to-know basis. Information gets released to schools, youth clubs and so on, but, as with anything else, we can't know for certain where that information goes later on.'

Brigstocke glanced at Thorne, raised his eyebrows. Jesmond was just getting warmed up . . .

'Yes, we *might* be looking for a prison officer. But we might also be looking for someone who's a friend of a friend of a teacher with a big mouth. Or someone who lives next door to an indiscreet social worker, who likes to natter while they're washing their cars on a Sunday morning . . .'

'Are you saying that we've been wasting our time for a week?' Thorne said.

The Detective Chief Superintendent shrugged, like he'd been asked if he'd lost weight, or caught the sun. 'Ask me that again when we've caught him . . .'

Jesmond seemed to relish moments like this. Thorne looked across at him and thought, *You really enjoy pissing on my chips, don't you?*

'I see what you're getting at, sir,' Thorne said. 'But it can't hurt, I mean, at least in the short term, to carry on assuming that the killer has a direct contact with one of the bodies we're talking about. Social services, the probation service . . .'

Jesmond cocked his head to one side, waiting to be unconvinced. Brigstocke tried to help out. 'It's a decent avenue of inquiry, sir,' he said.

Thorne sniffed. 'Our *only* decent avenue of inquiry . . .'

'Well, I think you'd better go out and find us another one,' Jesmond said. 'Don't you?'

Thorne said nothing. He watched the hand pushing back the wisps of sandy hair. The strange area on either side of the nose where webs of veins met spatters of freckles. He looked at the dry lips cracking themselves into a smile and it struck him, as it always did, that Jesmond smiled with his eyes closed.

Thorne smiled himself, remembering how he'd once described Jesmond's face to Dave Holland. 'You know the sort of face,' he'd said. 'If you hit it once, you couldn't stop.'

Jesmond leaned forward across the desk. 'Seriously, though, let's think about what you're saying. As an example, why don't we look at the possibility that the killer has a direct connection with the police service . . .'

'A police officer,' Thorne said.

Jesmond simply repeated himself and pressed on. 'A direct connection with the police service. Now, apart from the sheer numbers involved, the methods employed to access and utilise the Sex Offenders Register vary wildly from force to force. Some access it via the Police National Computer. Some graft Register information on to existing systems, or create dedicated databases . . .'

Brigstocke puffed out his cheeks. Thorne could already sense things going away from him, could feel himself starting to drift.

'Some are still using manual, paper-based systems, for heaven's sake,' Jesmond said. 'And we all know just how secure *they* are.'

Brigstocke nodded. 'How secure *anything* is!'

Thorne was tuning it out. Thinking about those jungle drums . . .

'The fact is, the whole system's a mess,' Jesmond said. 'There is no single strategy for managing and sharing sex-offender information, either with other agencies or with one another. Some believe that general access to local officers is vital to obtain the full intelligence benefit. Other areas, other stations, simply have a nominated officer who gets informed whenever the Register is updated . . .'

Thorne could smell another turd in his bed . . .

The way it was being laid out, the killer could have found his rapists almost anywhere. On the Internet or in a wastepaper basket. It was clear that if they had ten or a hundred times as many officers working on this, tracking down the man they were after the way he'd been hoping to was a non-starter.

'It isn't just us, either,' Brigstocke said. 'The courts are supposed to notify us when there's a need for an individual to register, and for how long, and it should be confirmed by the prison or the hospital or wherever when he gets released. Well, that's the bloody theory, anyway. Sometimes the first you hear about a sex offender on your patch is when they tell you *themselves*, for fuck's sake . . .'

Jesmond leaned back in his chair and smiled. Eyes closed. 'So, when I say you'd better find us another decent avenue of investigation, I'm simply being practical. I'm thinking of the best way, the fastest way to catch this man . . .'

Thorne nodded. Said it under his breath . . .

'Ooh! Whay-hay! Clack!'

In the Major Incident Room, business carried on as usual, but each officer was keenly aware that things might be about to change. Each man or woman on the end of a phone or hunched over their paperwork glanced across occasionally in the direction of Brigstocke's office, knowing that behind its closed door, decisions were being made which would affect them all.

Each casual conversation full of unspoken concerns. Some less to do with overtime than others. Some, at bottom, fuck all to do with work at all . . .

'Jesmond had a face like fourpence when he marched through here,' Kitson said.

Holland glanced up from his computer screen. 'Looked much the same as he always does, if you ask me . . .'

'I know what you mean,' Kitson said. 'He's a miserable sod. Still, I think we must be doing *something* wrong. They've been in there a while.' She looked across to where the Incident Room led out on to the corridor that housed the small suite of offices – Brigstocke's, the one she shared with Tom Thorne, Holland and Stone's . . .

Kitson sat down on the edge of the desk. She placed a hand on top of the computer Holland was working at. 'Can't you do this in your office?'

Holland peered at his screen. 'Andy's working in there . . .'

There was grime on the top of the computer. Kitson took out a tissue, spat on a corner, and began rubbing at the heel of her hand. 'Not a problem, is there?'

Now Holland looked up at her. 'No, it's fine. Just easier to concentrate in here sometimes . . .'

Kitson nodded, carried on rubbing, though her hand was clean. 'Sam Karim tells me you've been putting yourself up for quite a bit of overtime lately. Working all sorts of hours . . .'

Holland clicked furiously at his mouse. 'Shit!' He looked up, blinked. 'Sorry . . .?'

'It's a good idea. Trying to stash a bit of money away before the baby arrives.'

Holland's face darkened for a second. The smile he conjured didn't altogether chase the shadows from around his eyes.

'Right,' he said. 'I mean, they're expensive, aren't they?'

'You think nappies are a price, mate, wait until he wants CDs and the latest trainers. Is it a he or a she? Do you know . . .?'

Holland shook his head, his eyes meeting Kitson's for half a second and then sliding away to her chin. 'Sophie doesn't want to know.'

'*I* did.' Kitson's voice dropped down a tone. She opened up the tissue and began to tear it into small pieces. 'My other half wanted to wait and see, but I've never really liked surprises. I sent him out of the room after we'd had the scan so they could tell me. Did it with all the kids. Managed to keep it secret right up until the births . . .'

Holland smiled. Kitson crushed the pieces of tissue into her fist and stood up. 'Are you going to take any time off afterwards?'

'Afterwards?'

'All this overtime you're piling up now, you can probably afford a break, spend a bit of time at home with Sophie and the baby. Mind you, the Federation's still fighting to get paternity leave up from two days. Two days! It's a bloody disgrace . . .'

'We haven't really talked about it . . .'

'I bet she'd like you to though.' Kitson saw something in Holland's eyes, nodded sympathetically. 'She must hate all this extra work you're having to do . . .'

Holland shrugged. Let his head drop back to his computer screen. 'Oh, you know . . .'

Kitson took a step away from the desk. She opened her hand above a wastepaper bin and sprinkled the pieces of dirty tissue into it.

Holland watched her go, thinking, *Actually, you probably don't.*

Thorne stuck his head round the door of the Incident Room, tried not to gag on a breath of late-afternoon hot air and fermenting aftershave. He waved to Yvonne Kitson. She clocked him and walked quickly across.

'Get everyone together at the far end,' Thorne said. 'Briefing in fifteen minutes.'

Without waiting for a response, Thorne turned and moved away, back up the corridor towards his office . . .

Sensing that Jesmond was probably right. Knowing that *he* was right about the Register, but that even if the killer was a social worker or a probation officer or a copper, they were going to have to get him some other way.

He threw his jacket across the desk, dropped down into the chair. There was a small pile of mail he hadn't dealt with. He began to sort through it . . .

If he was a copper?

Thorne would not have bet on it. In all his years he'd known plenty of bad apples, worked with his fair share of shitbags, but never a killer. It was an interesting idea, a seductive one even, but beyond being convenient in TV shows, it was not much use to him.

He dropped a bunch of envelopes into the bin, those that obviously contained circulars or dreary internal memos going in unopened. He always saved the interesting-looking ones until last . . .

There were still aspects of the case that bothered him, that he'd flag up at the briefing. The bedding that had been removed for a kick-off. And the other thing. The thought he couldn't articulate, couldn't shape and snap up.

Something he'd read and something he hadn't . . .

It pretty much amounted to less than fuck all. Not a decent lead, not a bit of luck. He could only hope that some bright spark came up with something useful at the briefing.

When the photographs tumbled out of the white envelope, it took Thorne a few seconds to understand what he was looking at. Then he saw it. Then his heart lurched inside him and began to gallop.

As an athlete's heart rate recovers more and more

quickly as his fitness increases, so Thorne reacted less and less, physically at least, to images like those that would soon be scattered across his desk. The thumping in his chest was already slowing when he reached into a drawer, took out a pair of scissors and snipped away the elastic band that held the bundle of pictures together. The breaths were coming more easily as he used the tip of a pencil to separate them. By the time he'd decided that he wanted a closer look, remembered where he could find the gloves he needed, his heartbeat was slow and steady again.

There was no longer any visible movement, no judder of the flesh where his shirt stuck damp against his chest . . .

Thorne stood, moved out into the corridor and turned towards the Incident Room. As he walked, he felt amazingly calm and clear-headed. Coming to shocking conclusions and making trivial decisions.

The killer was even more cold-blooded than he had imagined . . .

He was supposed to be seeing Eve later on. Obviously, he would have to call and cancel. Perhaps she would be free tomorrow . . .

Into the Incident Room, and Kitson was moving across from the right of him, eager to talk about something. He held up a hand, waved her away. The box stood, a little incongruously, on a filing cabinet in the far corner of the room, exactly where he'd remembered seeing it. He pulled out the plastic gloves, like snatching tissues from a cardboard dispenser, revealing the transparent fingers of the next pair.

Holland was behind him, saying something he didn't catch as he turned to walk back . . .

The briefing, whenever they had it, would certainly be a bit more lively. Whatever Jesmond thought about the route the investigation was taking, it had definitely become heavy going. Those photos, what was in them, would get it started again.

Jump leads.

Not a bit of luck, exactly, but fuck it, close enough . . .

Thorne walked into his office and straight across to his desk. He knew even as he was doing it, even as he pulled on the gloves and delicately picked up a photo by its edge, that he was probably wasting his time. He had to go through the motions, of course, but the gloves were almost certainly unnecessary. Though he knew the surface of a photograph was as good as any at holding a fingerprint, he also knew that the man who had taken it was extremely cautious. Aside from the prints of postal workers and prison officers, or the hair and dead skin of the victims themselves, they'd got nothing from any of the photos or letters thus far. This was, after all, a killer who removed the bedding from his murder scenes.

Still, everybody made mistakes now and again . . .

Thorne flicked quickly through the photos. The close-ups of the battered and bloodied face, those thin lips thickened, then burst. The movement in the full-length pictures captured in a sickening blur. Pictures taken, unbelievably, while the victim was still alive. Thrashing . . .

He pushed aside the interior shots and lowered his head, checking to see if the killer had made one mistake in particular. He stared closely at the photo that had been very deliberately placed on the top of the pile. The first picture he had been intended to see. The window of the shop next door . . .

A killer's little joke.

Thorne was dimly aware of the figures of Holland and Kitson, watching him from the doorway as he squinted at the picture. Hoping to see a distorted image that would probably be worse than useless, but would show him that he was dealing with fallible flesh and blood. Searching in vain for a reflection of the cameraman in a tiny, black mirror.

Looking for the killer's face in the eye of a dead fish.

He was pretty sure he'd picked a good one.

The list had to be looked at carefully. He couldn't just print off a copy and stick a pin in. Not that there was that much time to look at it when he had the chance, but he was getting better at selecting the likely candidates quickly. With the previous two he'd chosen a couple of decent-looking ones and gone through the details more carefully later, when he could take his time. He'd done the same thing with this one, rejecting a couple of names for various practical reasons – location, domestic set-up and so on – and coming up with a winner.

Christ, though, there were plenty to choose from. The serious cases, the ones he was interested in, would be on the Register indefinitely, and those that did eventually come off the list, after five, or seven or ten years, had been replaced a hundredfold by the time their names were removed.

It was a growth industry . . .

This one would shape up very nicely, by the look of it. He lived alone in a nice, quiet street. Friends were an unknown quantity as yet, but it didn't look like there was any family around. It might even be possible to avoid using a hotel altogether . . .

He was ambivalent about that. Doing it in a house or flat would be simpler, but there was an unpredictability that made him uncomfortable. It would be tricky to get inside in advance and look at the layout of the place. He couldn't count on the place being as forensically friendly as the average hotel room.

An unexpected visit from a neighbour couldn't be prevented with a 'Do Not Disturb' sign on the door.

He hadn't had the choice with Remfry or Welch, but using hotels had worked out well so far and he was somewhat reluctant to change a winning formula. Hotels did mean a lot more possible witnesses and a security system to get around but that wasn't too much of a problem. He'd learned that people saw fuck all when they weren't really looking, and cameras saw even less if you knew how to avoid them.

He'd avoided being seen, being really seen, for a very long time.

THIRTEEN

'I was wondering how much it would cost to send a bouquet of flowers . . .'

'Well, we charge five pounds fifty for delivery, and the bouquets start at thirty pounds.'

'Christ, I don't want to spend *that* much. I haven't even snogged her yet . . .'

Eve laughed. 'Are you sure there's snogging on the cards?'

'Definitely,' Thorne said. 'She's *well* up for it . . .'

'Shit, I've got a customer. Better go . . .'

'Listen, I'm sorry about cancelling last night. I couldn't . . .'

'It's fine. Hold that thought, all right? The snogging, I mean. I'll see you later.'

'Yeah . . . I can't say what time, though.'

'Call me when you're about to leave. We can just grab a quick drink or something . . .'

'Right . . .'

'Seriously, if you *are* ever tempted, flowers wouldn't guarantee a snog. *Chocolates*, on the other hand, will get you just about anything . . .'

She hung up.

Smiling, Thorne reached inside the bodysuit, dropped the phone into his jacket pocket. He took a long swig from a bottle of mineral water and turned, to find himself confronted by a family of backpackers. Mum, Dad and two blonde children were all sporting rucksacks of decreasing size, and staring at him expectantly from the other side of the cordon. Thorne stared back at them until eventually, having decided that nothing much was going to happen, they wandered away.

Six hours earlier, when there *had* been something they might have been able to tell their friends back home about, the onlookers had been a little harder to dissuade. With the nightclubs emptying and the streets buzzing, a sizeable crowd had quickly gathered and gawped from behind the lines of police tape. A hundred yards back towards Wardour Street one way and Regent Street the other, they had stood and watched excitedly. The drunks heckled and the tourists took pictures, as the body of Charles Dodd was carried out.

Once the body had been loaded up and taken away, the cordon had been relaxed a little. Now there was just a square of blue tape running from the narrow doorway leading up to Dodd's studio, around to the furthest side of the fishmonger's shop next door. Fluttering ever so gently . . .

'What's going on in there, mate?'

Thorne looked up at a small, skinny individual with birdshit highlights and an improbable amount of jewellery, nodding at him from behind the tape. The man, who was wearing satin tracksuit bottoms and a sleeveless camouflage vest, took three drags of a cigarette in quick succession then flicked it into the gutter.

'It's a raid,' Thorne said. 'Fashion Police. I'd be on my way, if I were you . . .'

The man bounced twice on the balls of his feet, grimaced and jogged away. On the other side of the narrow street, a girl in a tiny leather skirt and crop top was leaning against the kiosk of a peep show, eating a bacon sandwich. She grinned over at Thorne, having clearly heard the exchange. Thorne smiled back at her. It was a little after nine in the morning but evidently not too early to try and get something going inside the shorts of the passing male trade. Already warm enough for the tables of a pavement café to be filled with customers downing cappuccino and scoffing pastries. Pretending they were somewhere more exotic.

Thorne watched them. Wishing *he* was somewhere else. Thinking of things that would put anybody off their breakfast . . .

When they'd battered down the door early the previous evening, Thorne had known exactly what they would find. The smell, thick against his face-mask, would have told him anyway, but as he'd climbed the narrow staircase, Thorne had been very well aware of what was waiting for him at the top. He'd already seen the pictures.

The real thing, several long, hot days after the event, was a whole lot worse.

The body had been strung up. The washing line had been tied in a makeshift noose around Dodd's neck and thrown over one of the lighting bars above the studio floor. It was tied off around the foot of the bed, the weight of the body lifting one end of the bed twelve inches off the ground. The pictures, taken while Dodd was still alive, had shown the spasms, the desperate clawing at the neck and

219

kicking of the legs. Several days dead, the corpse hung, stiff and still. It was only the rumble of the tube trains passing beneath them on the Bakerloo Line that caused the slightest tremor, that made the body start to swing just a little . . .

Each time, Thorne had fought a bizarre urge to stop the movement. To step across and grasp the legs that protruded from dirty shorts like bloated blood sausages. To clutch the feet, purple with lividity, straining against the straps of the plastic sandals.

Thorne had stood by the bed in the middle of the studio, remembering a pair of pale girls, writhing on nylon sheets.

He had watched a SOCO leaning across the mattress, scraping at whatever had dripped down from the body that dangled above it.

He had looked up at the tongue that stuck out from Dodd's mouth. Blue, and big as a man's hand. Telling him to fuck off.

Once it had been cut down and loaded up, Thorne had been only too grateful to do precisely as Dodd's corpse had seemed to be requesting. Home for a change of clothes, and food he couldn't finish. Four hours not sleeping, and then back to the murder scene.

Opposite him, the girl finished the last mouthful of her sandwich. She wiped the back of a hand across her mouth, reached down behind the kiosk for her handbag. She shrugged at Thorne and began to apply lipstick.

Thorne turned at the sound of the door opening. Holland stepped out. He moved across to join Thorne, unzipping his bodysuit and gulping down the fresh air as he walked.

'Fuck, it's hot in there.'

Thorne handed Holland the bottle of water. 'How much longer?'

'Almost done, I think.'

Holland stood next to Thorne, leaning back against the window of the fishmonger's shop. They stared across at the peep show and the pavement café. A waiter smiled across at them. They might just have been friends enjoying the good weather, their plastic outfits far from being the most outlandish on display.

'So he's probably just cleaning up after himself,' Holland said. 'He kills Dodd to make sure he can't say anything.'

'Maybe . . .'

Holland turned, pressed his hands against the window, already dusted for fingerprints. The fishmonger had been given very little time to get his stock into the freezer room and no time at all to clean up afterwards. Holland looked at the pink swirl of blood and fishguts, floating on top of the water in a metal tray. 'He knew you'd get it.' He nodded towards the window. Flies bumped against the glass, buzzing around the scattered flaps of puckered skin. 'He knew you'd understand what that photo meant.'

Thorne nodded. 'Oh, he knew I'd been here all right.' Holland looked sideways at him, raised an eyebrow. 'Don't get excited. Yeah, he might have followed me, or he *might* be Trevor Jesmond hearing voices from the devil, but I think there's probably a simpler explanation.' Holland turned, listening. 'I think you were right. I think Dodd was killed because of what he could tell us. And because he was threatening to.'

'Dodd tried to blackmail the killer?'

221

Thorne folded his arms. 'Only the daft twat didn't *know* he was a killer, did he? I can't prove any of it, obviously . . .'

'It sounds feasible,' Holland said.

'Dodd was lying, of course he was. That crap about the killer keeping his crash helmet on, about not having any records. I should have fucking pulled him on it . . .'

'You weren't to know.'

'Yes, I was. If wankers like Dodd are breathing, they're lying. He didn't know who we were after, or why, but that didn't matter. If he thought I was chasing someone who hadn't paid their TV licence, he'd have lied through his back teeth, as long as he could see a way to make money out of it.'

They watched as a middle-aged man handed over his money at the peep-show kiosk and hurried inside. The girl caught Thorne's eye, put her thumb to the tips of her fingers and made a wanking gesture. Thorne didn't know whether she was indicating what the man would be doing or what she thought of him. Or what she thought of *them* . . .

Holland cleared his throat and took a drink. 'So, after you come round and show him the photo of Jane Foley, he contacts the killer . . .'

Thorne stepped away from the window, turned and looked up towards the second floor where the studio was. 'I've been through the place and there's no sign of an address book or anything like that anywhere . . .'

'Maybe the killer took it,' Holland said.

'He might have done.' Thorne put his hand up to shield his eyes from the sun. 'Let's go over every inch again, anyway. If there's a scrap of paper with an address or phone number on it, I want it found.'

'What about phone records?'

Thorne nodded, pleased that Holland was thinking so fast, was so close behind him. 'I've got Andy Stone on to it. I want everything, landline and mobile, if Dodd had one. Every call he made since the day I was here . . .'

'He might have just gone round, if he had an address . . .'

'In which case we're stuffed.' Thorne reached across for the water bottle. He took a swig, held the now tepid water in his mouth for a while before swallowing. 'We're still none the wiser as to how the killer hooked up with Dodd in the first place. People like Dodd don't advertise. It's word of mouth, it's *contacts* . . .'

'We've already spoken to everybody we could find,' Holland said. 'Anybody who's ever taken so much as a snap of their wife's tits in that studio has made a statement.'

'So talk to them again. And find me some you haven't spoken to at all.' Holland groaned, let his head drop back against the glass. 'Just get on it, Dave,' Thorne said. 'Yvonne can work up a new list. I'll catch up with you later.'

While Holland climbed out of his bodysuit, Thorne watched as two young media types stood up from their table at the café opposite and shook hands. They were dressed casually in shorts and trainers, but their top-of-the-range mobiles and designer sunglasses gave them away. An advertising campaign agreed maybe, or a TV project given the green light.

He wondered if they knew that only a few hundred yards away, in an attic room over a coffee shop on Frith

Street, John Logie-Baird had given the first-ever public demonstration of television nearly eighty years before.

Thorne opened the door, took a second or two before heading back inside . . .

Christ, a commercial break *would* be nice. A catchable made-for-TV killer would be even nicer. He might just as well have *been* a TV cop. For the umpteenth time that morning, Thorne watched a passer-by clock him, the bodysuit, the police tape . . . and look around eagerly for the camera.

After the post-mortem at Westminster Mortuary, they walked over to a small Italian place near the Abbey. Talked about murder over pizzas and Peroni.

'I think Dodd was beaten until he was more or less unconscious,' Hendricks said. 'Then the killer tied the line around his neck, tossed it over the lighting bar and hauled him up.' Thorne nodded, took a swig of beer. 'Would have taken a fair bit of strength . . .'

'So we know he's not a nine-stone weakling. What else?'

'He's a nasty fucker . . .'

'We knew that already.'

Hendricks poured more chilli oil over what he had left of an American Hot. 'Dodd wakes up pretty bloody quickly when he works out what's going on but it's far too sodding late by then. The killer ties the line off, picks up his camera and starts taking pictures.'

'How long?' Thorne asked.

'He'd have blacked out in a couple of minutes.' Hendricks speared a slice of pepperoni, popped it into his mouth. 'Death through cerebral hypoxia pretty quickly afterwards . . .'

Thorne thought about it. Dodd had been a sleazy piece of shit, but he hadn't deserved that. Dancing at the end of a line, like something in the shop next door. Tearing at the flesh of his own neck. Staring through half-closed eyes at the maniac responsible, calmly snapping away, trying to capture his best side . . .

'When they talk about killers like this, they use words like "organised" and "disorganised",' Thorne said. 'Two basic categories. The ones who plan carefully, who follow an almost ritualised pattern of killing, of cleaning up after themselves. And those who just act on instinct, who don't have as much control over what they're doing . . .'

'So where does this nutter fit in?'

Thorne put down his knife and fork. There was half a pizza left but he'd had enough. 'That's what I was thinking. Part of him is organised. The letters to the men in prison. Dodd needs to be got rid of, so he gets rid of him. The washing line, the lack of forensics, the photos he sent to me . . .'

'He's getting off on *that*, definitely . . .'

'Why beat the bloke half to death though? Dodd's face looked like cheap mince. Why not just smash him across the back of the head then string him up?' A waitress was hovering, trying not to earwig. Thorne held up his plate. She took it gingerly and moved quickly away. 'At some level, they're always angry, you know? I haven't met a killer yet who wasn't pissed off somewhere about *something*.' Thorne downed the last of his beer. He swallowed, seeing the bodies of Welch and Remfry, the mess that had been made of their necks. Of their insides. 'This bloke, though? He's off the fucking scale . . .'

'You doing anything tonight?' Hendricks wiped his mouth. 'I could come over.'

'What?'

Hendricks glanced across to where the waitresses were gathered near the till. 'I'm changing the subject. Before they call the police.'

'They're staring because of what you look like, mate, not because of our interesting table conversation. And no, you can't come over. I'm meeting someone a lot better looking than you.'

'Surely not.'

'With no embarrassing piercings . . .'

Hendricks grinned. 'You never know. She might have them in special, secret places.'

The waitress was there again. She took the plate from in front of Hendricks. He'd left a perfect ring of pizza crust.

'You won't get curly hair,' Thorne said.

Hendricks ran a hand across his shaved head. 'With the look I'm cultivating, that's not really a problem . . .'

The afternoon had bled into the evening and by the time Thorne pushed through to where Eve was sitting, at a small table next to the cigarette machine, it was almost last orders. Plenty of time to get through a bottle of wine between them. For Thorne to apologise for messing her about, and for Eve to tell him he was being stupid. More than enough time for Thorne to tell her almost nothing about the sort of day he'd had.

It was a small, friendly pub near the Hackney Empire. They stepped out on to Mare Street and looked up and down the road. They fastened unnecessary buttons on jackets, studied parked cars, filling up a suddenly awkward moment.

Eve stepped over to him, put her hands on his shoulders. 'Now, about that snog . . .'

Thorne didn't need asking twice.

They kissed, his hands moving around her waist and hers to the back of his head and neck. She bit softly on his lower lip. He pushed the tip of his tongue into the gap between her teeth. Then his mouth widened into a grin and they leaned away from each other.

'I *knew* you were well up for it,' Thorne said.

She dropped her hand down, gave his backside a good hard squeeze. 'I'm well up for anything.'

They were a few minutes' walk from Eve's flat. A short bus or cab journey from Thorne's. This wasn't the reason for the uncertainty which Eve saw in Thorne's expression.

'You still haven't bought a new bed, have you?' she said.

Thorne tried his best to look like a guilty schoolboy. He imagined that it made him look endearing. 'I haven't had time . . .'

She grabbed his hand and they began to walk.

'I've only really had last Sunday and there was all manner of shit that needed doing.' Thorne decided not to elaborate. He didn't explain that the shit in question had involved replacing his stereo system and those twenty-five or so CDs that he *really* couldn't do without. Spending his nights curled up on the sofa as he was, some people might have questioned his priorities. With the prospect of a night curled up with Eve Bloom looking distinctly achievable, even *he* had to agree that they seemed completely bonkers.

They walked a little way up Mare Street and then turned left, crossing the railway line and cutting across London Fields. The night wasn't as muggy as some had been recently, but it was still warm. There were plenty of people around.

'You're not waiting for the insurance, are you?' Eve asked suddenly.

'What?'

'To pay for a new bed.'

Thorne laughed. 'I think I can run to a new bed. It's actually only a new mattress so it won't break the bank. I'll need the insurance to sort out a new car though. I'm getting pissed off with buses, and bangers from the car-pool . . .'

'What are you going to get?'

Thorne wasn't sure whether he'd spent more time the previous week on the phone chasing the insurance company or sitting at his kitchen table poring over car magazines. 'I'm not really bothered,' he said.

Eve leaned in close to Thorne to let a jogger go past. 'Do coppers fiddle their insurance like everybody else?'

'Well, fiddle is putting it a bit strong. I may have got the make and model of the stereo ever so slightly wrong. All right, *and* the price. I might have thrown the odd boxed set in when I was doing my CD inventory, but fuck 'em, I probably forgot stuff as well.'

They walked on in silence for a minute or so and then stopped at the edge of the park. They watched a group of lads having a kickabout, floodlighting courtesy of a couple of lamp-posts and a full moon.

Thorne remembered the game he'd watched just over a

week earlier. The park near the hotel in Slough. That one had been just *before* a post-mortem . . .

'There was another body today,' Thorne said. 'Well, last night and today. That's why I had to cancel.'

Eve squeezed his hand. 'Is it the same man? The one who left the message on my machine?'

They moved away from the game and out on to the road that ran parallel to the one where Eve lived and worked.

'He kills men who have assaulted women,' Thorne said. 'Who've raped them and been to prison for it. The one we found yesterday was slightly different, but that's basically what he does. Fucked if I know why he does it, or when he's going to do it again, and fucked if I know how I'm going to stop him.'

'So don't.'

Thorne laughed. Stared at the pavement. Stepped around the dogshit. 'I'm not the one who decides . . .'

'It's not like he's chopping up old ladies, is it?'

They turned on to a small side street, and walked slowly up the middle of the road.

Hand in hand, at arm's length.

'I'm always reading about how stretched police resources are,' Eve said. 'So why not use them on something a bit more worthwhile?'

'More worthwhile than a murderer?'

'Yeah, but look at who he's murdering . . .'

Thorne took a deep breath. He shouldn't have said anything. He did *not* want to get into this. 'Look, whatever you think about what those men had done, whatever any of us thinks, they'd been to prison for it. I haven't got a *lot* of respect for the legal system, but surely . . .'

'All right. Just think of this bloke as cutting re-offending rates then.'

Thorne looked at her. She was smiling, but there was something set around her eyes. She clearly felt strongly about what she was saying, and Thorne knew that it was tough to argue with. 'I can't think like that, Eve. I can't go down that road . . .'

'As a police officer, you mean? Or just . . . personally?'

They emerged from the side street. Eve's shop stood in darkness on the corner opposite. Thorne's change of gear was as grinding as the one he'd picked Hendricks up for at lunchtime.

'Listen, just how much of a problem would it really be with Denise? If I was to stay?'

Eve sighed heavily. 'I told you. She gets a bit weird . . .'

'Aren't there nights when she's not there? Doesn't she ever stay at Ben's?' Eve shook her head. 'Why not?'

'I don't know. He's just as batty as she is. Come on, you've seen them together . . .'

They walked past the shop, stopped at Eve's doorstep. Eve reached into her bag for the door keys.

'She's got no right to tell you who you can have staying,' Thorne said.

Eve pressed her palms against his chest. 'She doesn't exactly tell me. Listen, it's just not worth the hassle.' She grabbed the lapels of Thorne's leather jacket, pulled him towards her. 'Especially when you can just buy a mattress. I could do it for you, if you like . . .'

They stopped kissing when the front door of Eve's flat suddenly swung open from the inside. Denise stood in the doorway, looking surprised. A figure loomed behind her, and Thorne recognised the man he'd seen working in the florist's that first day he'd been in there.

'Hello, Eve,' he said.

Denise stepped out into the street. The man followed her. 'Keith just dropped round to say he won't be able to make it again on Saturday,' Denise said.

Eve moved forward, put a hand on Keith's shoulder. 'Everything OK, Keith?'

He shook his head, reddening. 'It's difficult . . .'

Eve turned to Thorne. 'Keith's mum hasn't been well . . .'

The four of them stood there a little awkwardly. Denise's arms were bare and she rubbed at them, shivering slightly as a breeze began to pick up.

Keith pulled on the denim jacket he'd been carrying. 'I'm going home.' He nodded to himself a couple of times, then turned and marched quickly away. The others watched him go.

'I'm going to bed, hon,' Denise said. 'I'm utterly fucked.' She bounded across and threw her arms around Eve's neck. 'See you in the morning . . .'

Thorne watched as she kissed Eve on both cheeks. He was slightly taken aback when she leaned over and kissed him too. Half on the cheek and half on the mouth.

''Night, Tom . . .' She turned and stepped smartly back inside the flat, pushing the door behind her until it was almost, but not quite, closed.

Thorne checked his watch. There was probably still time to make a late bus to Kentish Town or Camden.

'I'd better be getting off as well,' he said.

Eve gave him a cod leer. 'You won't be getting off with

231

anyone if you don't buy yourself a bed. I'll take you to IKEA at the weekend . . .'

'Oh please God, no,' Thorne said.

Thorne could see Keith striding along the street a hundred yards or so ahead of him. He hung back, trying not to catch up. Feeling awkward, the goodnights having been said, and not wanting to go through it again. Thorne was relieved when he saw Keith turn off on to a side street. Keith looked back and stared at him for a few seconds before he moved out of sight.

When Thorne reached the turning and looked, there was no sign of him.

As he hurried towards the bus stop on Dalston Lane, Thorne admitted something rather puzzling to himself. He'd asked Eve about staying the night at her place only because of what she'd already told him about Denise. Because he'd known very well that it wasn't going to happen. He actually felt comfortable that it hadn't . . .

There was a dodgy-looking burger van opposite the bus stop and Thorne was suddenly starving. The late-night bagel bakery was five minutes' walk away. It was a toss-up between food poisoning and the risk of missing the last bus.

Ten minutes later the bus rumbled into view and he was already wishing he hadn't had the burger. As he rummaged in his jacket for the exact change, Thorne wondered why on earth he should be feeling something like relief that he was on his way home alone.

The man on the machine next to him stopped pedalling and sat for a few moments, eyes closed, getting his breath back. The man climbed off and walked across to the water fountain. Still pedalling fast, he watched as the man gulped down water, flung his sweat-towel around his neck and walked through into the weights room.

When the song he was listening to had finished, he unplugged his headphones, got off the bike and followed him.

Howard Anthony Southern was a creature of habit and was serious about looking after himself. These two things meant that keeping an eye on him, getting to know him, was not only easy but fairly enjoyable. He worked out anyway, but a few extra hours a week couldn't hurt. It was easy enough to join the same gym and make sure he was here at the same time that Southern was as often as he could. That wasn't always straightforward, of course. Sometimes he couldn't get away, but he'd seen enough to know what he was dealing with.

He knew enough already. That Southern had done what he'd done, that his name was on the list, was more than enough. Still, it was good to find out a bit more. To know for certain how much stronger than Southern he was, how easy it would be to take him when the time came. To see his face contorted and running with sweat. To glimpse in advance what it would be like as he strained against the ligature . . .

He walked through into the weights room. Southern was on

the pec-fly. He took a seat next to him on the mid-row, began to work.

He could see instantly that Southern was eyeing up a woman on the other side of the room. She was bending and stretching, her flesh taut against the black lycra. Southern pressed his forearms towards each other, grunting with the effort, all the time watching the woman in the mirror that ran along one wall.

He knew this was why Howard Southern came here.

He wondered if Southern had offended again since his release. Was he more careful having been caught once? He might have been getting away with it for years. Was he watching the woman in the mirror and thinking about forcing himself on her? Working himself into a lather, his eyes like sweaty hands on her, convincing himself just how much she wanted it . . .

The weights dropped back with a clang as Southern released the handles. He turned and puffed out his cheeks.

'Why do we do it?'

This was a bonus. He'd been planning to talk to Southern today anyway. To strike up a casual conversation at the juice bar maybe, or in the locker room . . .

'It's bloody madness, isn't it?' Southern nodded towards the woman in the black leotard. 'Here I am killing myself for the likes of her.'

He smiled back at Southern, thinking that the idea was right, but that he had an altogether different reason.

FOURTEEN

Carol Chamberlain was three-quarters of a team of two.

She had been assigned a research officer, but ex-Detective Sergeant Graham McKee was, to use a favourite phrase of her husband's, about as useful as a chocolate teapot. When he wasn't in the pub, he made it perfectly clear that he thought Carol should have been the one making coffee and phone calls, while he was out doing the interviews.

A few years ago, she'd have had his undersized balls on a platter. Now she just got on with doing the job, his as well as her own. It might take a bit longer, but at least it would get done properly. She believed in that. She couldn't be sure yet, but if the case she was on now had been handled properly first time round, there might well have been no need for her to be doing anything at all.

The drive to Hastings hadn't taken her as long as she'd thought, but she'd left early to be on the safe side. Jack had got up with her, made her some breakfast while she got ready. She could see that he was unhappy that she was going out on a Sunday but he'd tried to make a joke of it.

'Bloody unsociable hours. Sunday gone for a burton. Now I *know* you're working for the police force again . . .'

She checked her make-up in the mirror before she got out of the car. Maybe she'd overdone the foundation a little but it was too late now. She was pleased with her hair, though; she'd run a rinse through it the night before to get rid of most of the grey.

Jack had told her she looked great.

She walked up to the front door and knocked, telling herself to calm down, that she'd done this a thousand times, that there was no need to grip on to the handle of her briefcase as though it were stopping her from falling . . .

'Sheila? I'm Carol Chamberlain from AMRU. We spoke on the phone . . .'

Carol could see that the woman who answered the door was clearly not expecting someone who looked like her, rinse or no rinse. She had gained a stone in weight for each year that she'd been out of the force, and at a little over five feet tall she knew very well how it looked. Her hair could be as fashionable and artificially auburn as she wanted, but – whatever lies Jack might tell her – she could do little about the rest of it. However sharp she *felt*, she knew that those thirty years on the job showed in her face. Some mornings she stared at herself in the bathroom mirror. She looked into her dark, disappearing eyes. Saw currants sinking into cake mix . . .

The woman opened the front door a little wider. However disappointed or confused she might be, Carol hoped that good old British reserve would prevent Sheila Franklin saying anything about it.

'I'll put the kettle on,' she said eventually.

In the kitchen, while tea was being made, they spoke about weather and traffic. Sheila Franklin wiped down surfaces and washed up teaspoons as she went. Settled a few minutes later in the small, simply furnished living room, her face crinkled into a frown of confusion.

'I'm sorry, but I thought you said that the case was being reopened . . .'

Carol had said no such thing. 'I'm sorry if you were misled. I'm re-*examining* the case, and if it's considered worthwhile, it might be reopened.'

'I see . . .'

'How long were you and Alan married?'

Alan Franklin's widow was a tall, very thin woman whom Carol would have put in her mid- to late fifties. Not a great deal older than she was herself. Her hair was pulled back from a face dominated by green eyes that did not stay fixed on any one spot for more than a few seconds. From behind the rim of her teacup, her gaze darted around like a meerkat's as she answered Carol's questions.

She'd met Franklin in 1983. He would have been in his late forties by then, ten years older than she was. He'd left his first wife and a job in Colchester a few years before that and moved to Hastings to start again. They'd met at work and married only a few months later.

'Alan was a fast worker,' she said, laughing. 'Very smooth, he was. Mind you, I didn't put up much of a struggle.'

As always, Carol had done her homework. She was up to speed with what very few background details there were. 'How did Alan's kids react? What would they have been then? Sixteen? Seventeen . . .?'

Sheila smiled, but there was something forced about it. 'Something like that. I'm not even sure how old they are now. In all the time we were married, I think I saw the boys once. Only one of them bothered to show his face at Alan's funeral . . .'

Carol nodded, like this was perfectly normal. 'What about the first wife?'

'I never met Celia. Never spoke to her on the phone. I'm not even sure that *Alan* ever did, to be honest, after they split up.'

'Right . . .'

Sheila leaned forward and put her cup and saucer down. 'I know it probably sounds odd, but that's just the way it was. It was Alan's *past* . . .'

Carol tried not to let any reaction, any *judgement* of these people's lives, show on her face, but it was hard. She and Jack had married relatively late, and there were times when relations with his ex-wife were a little strained, but they were civil. They acknowledged each other. And Jack's daughter had *always* been a part of their lives.

'I did make an effort with the children,' Sheila said. 'For a while I tried to persuade Alan that he should see them, that he should try and build bridges. He was always a bit funny about it.'

'Perhaps he thought his ex-wife had turned them against him.'

'He never said so. The kids were more or less grown up anyway, and we did try briefly to have our own.' She began piling the tea things back on to the tray she had brought them through on. She took hold of the tray and stood up. 'I was nearly forty by then, and it never happened . . .'

Carol followed Sheila as she walked back towards the kitchen. 'Did Alan never talk about why he and Celia had divorced?'

'Not really. I think it was unpleasant.'

From what Carol was hearing, that was probably an understatement. 'Presumably there was alimony though? They must have communicated through solicitors . . .?'

'For the last few years we didn't even know where they were living. The son who turned up at the funeral only knew Alan was dead because he saw it on the news.'

'I see . . .'

The cups and saucers were already being washed up. When Sheila turned from the sink, Carol saw her read something in her face. Maybe that judgement she'd been trying to hide . . .

'Look, it was always just Alan and me,' Sheila said. 'We were self-sufficient. Anything that happened before didn't seem to matter. And I was the same, honestly. I never bothered with old boyfriends or what have you, and we never saw much of my family. Alan had no contact with the family he had before, because he had me.' She took a step towards Carol, who was standing in the doorway, water dripping from a teacup on to the lino. Her face seemed to soften as she spoke. 'That's what he always used to say. That I was his life now. What he had before hadn't worked out and so he didn't want to think about it. Alan was trying to get away from his old life . . .'

Carol nodded. 'Could I use your loo . . .?'

She leaned against the sink, letting the water run a while.

She had never worked much on instinct, but in thirty

years Carol Chamberlain had learned to give it breathing space. Back in 1996, Alan Franklin's murder had gone unsolved. Unsolved, largely because it had been seemingly motiveless.

She smelt the soap, began to wash her hands . . .

It was at least possible that whatever Alan Franklin had been trying to escape from, here in this house with his new job and nice new wife, had finally caught up with him in that car park.

Sheila Franklin was waiting for her at the foot of the stairs.

'Do you have any of Alan's old things?' Carol asked. 'I don't mean clothes or . . .'

'There's a couple of boxes in the loft. Papers and what have you, I think. Alan put them up there when we moved in.'

'Would you mind if I had a look?'

'God, no, not at all. Actually, you could do me a favour and take them with you.' Sheila looked past Carol, back up the stairs. She blinked slowly and a film appeared over her eyes. 'I could do with getting things tidy . . .'

It wasn't exactly a photo-fit, but then there wouldn't have been a lot of point . . .

Thorne had taken the picture out of his bag while the train was pulling out of King's Cross, laid it out on the table in front of him, stared at it for ten minutes.

The waiter from the café opposite Dodd's studio had made his statement the day after the body had been found. He'd described a motorcycle courier who'd been hanging around a few days before. He hadn't actually seen the man in the dark crash helmet and leathers go in through the door, or even go up to it. It was a hot afternoon. He'd had a lot of tables to look after . . .

A Wednesday, nearly a fortnight ago. Five days before they'd broken down the narrow, brown door and smelt a murder scene.

So, Charlie Dodd had not been *completely* full of shit. The man to whom he had rented out his studio *had* worn a crash helmet. The lie, Thorne guessed, had been about not seeing the face underneath it. It was a lie that Charlie Dodd thought might make him a few quid and had ended up costing him a lot more.

At the noise of the buffet trolley squeaking down the carriage Thorne glanced up. Thameslink food would not be his Sunday-morning breakfast of choice, but he was hungry. He felt in his pocket for change.

Dodd had probably felt totally safe as the man in the motorbike gear had strolled up the stairs in the middle of the afternoon. As likely as not, he'd felt in control, ready to squeeze the mug for whatever he could get. He'd had no idea of the kind of man he was dealing with.

No witness from the Remfry or Welch killing had mentioned seeing anybody in a crash helmet, but all the same it needed to be checked out. On any given afternoon, Soho was thick with bikes, scooters and mopeds, delivering scripts and videos, sandwiches and sushi. It had taken the best part of two days to trace every courier who had been in the area on legitimate business and eliminate them. Two days dicking about to confirm what Thorne had known to be true from the moment the waiter had described what he'd seen.

The face behind that visor had belonged to the killer, and the black rucksack slung across his shoulder had contained a length of blue washing line.

'What can I get you, love?'

The trolley was at Thorne's table. He plumped for tea and a Kit-Kat. He took the top off the cardboard cup, mopped up the inevitable spillage with his napkin and began to dunk the tea bag.

He stared again at the picture he had begun to draw a few days earlier. A man in a crash helmet was too generic to have justified any kind of official image, but Thorne had begun scribbling at his kitchen table and added to it on subsequent days at his desk, or on the tube to and from Hendon. Thorne was about as competent an artist as he was a medieval dancer, but he could see *something* in his thick and clumsy shading. Something about the heavy, cross-hatched pencil lines suggested a darkness behind the visor. Blacker and harder than tinted plastic . . .

He looked up, and out at the scenery moving past. He watched it get greener, saw the houses get bigger, as the train moved into Hertfordshire.

Thorne drank his tea and ate his chocolate. Reflected in the window, he watched as the old boy sitting across from him dithered over what to order. One of the women working the trolley rolled her eyes at the other, and a teenager in a tracksuit sighed loudly, impatient to get past.

Eileen had rung him from Brighton a couple of nights before. His father's home-help had come down with shingles and there was a bit of a flap on. Eileen had sorted a neighbour who was coming over with a casserole on the Friday, and arranged for a temporary home-help to come

242

in, but *she* wouldn't be able to start until Monday, and with nobody there to make sure . . . the old man wouldn't eat a thing . . .

Thorne had felt guilty that she'd asked him like it was a favour. A few miles away from St Albans, a packet of his dad's favourite mints in his pocket, he felt guiltier still that he was wishing he was somewhere else. Thinking about a Sunday in a pub by the river with Eve.

The automatic door at the end of the carriage slid open. The two women manoeuvred the trolley past the teenager in the tracksuit, now enjoying a crafty fag by the toilets. He shrugged at them, turned and blew his smoke out of the window.

Thorne remembered Yvonne Kitson with her cigarette outside Becke House. He didn't really think of her as a friend, they had never socialised outside work, but something about that encounter pricked at him. Without thinking too much about it, Thorne reached into his bag for the contact sheet, looked up Kitson's home number and dialled. She was probably up to her elbows in getting Sunday lunch ready . . .

A man, presumably Kitson's husband, answered.

'Hi, could I speak to Yvonne, please?' Thorne said.

'She's not here.'

Thorne waited for a bit more information but none was forthcoming. 'It's not important. Could you just tell her that Tom Thorne rang? I'll maybe try later . . .'

'You can try, but I don't know when she'll be back. She said she'd only be a couple of hours . . .'

Thorne was still thinking about the conversation five minutes later, as he walked out of St Albans station looking for a taxi. Maybe Yvonne Kitson's husband was a naturally surly bugger. Maybe he had the hump because he'd got the kids to look after when he wanted to be out playing golf or reading the Sunday papers. Maybe it was something else altogether. Whatever the reason he was pissed off, he didn't seem bothered about letting a total stranger know about it.

'She *said* she'd only be a couple of hours . . .'

Ahead of him, Thorne watched a young couple climb into the only available cab. He thought about Eve again, the things they could be doing. What the hell, he'd managed to avoid a Sunday being dragged around IKEA . . .

In the living room, when Thorne had suggested cooking something, his father had reddened and called him a 'silly little bastard'. Half an hour later in the pub, his dad seemed an awful lot happier. A pint of bitter and a plate of sausage and chips could cause mood swings in the old man every bit as radical as those brought on by the changing chemistry of his brain.

'This is number three on my list of rules, you know?' his dad said.

They were sitting at a table in the corner: Thorne, his father and his father's friend Victor. There used to be quite a gang of them, regulars in this pub two or three nights a week. Since the Alzheimer's had been diagnosed, his dad's other old friends tended not to be around quite as much. Victor was the only one who didn't seem to think he could catch it . . .

'What is?' Thorne said.

His father held up his pint, pleased as punch. 'This. "*No beer*". Number three, coming after "no going in the kitchen" and "no going out alone". My list of stupid rules, you know?'

Thorne nodded. He knew . . .

'No booze.' Jim Thorne cleared his throat, lowered his voice, tried to sound like a DJ. 'Straight in at number three in the Alzheimer's Hit Parade . . .' Thorne and Victor laughed. Thorne's father began to hum the theme to *Top of the Pops*, then stopped suddenly and looked across at Victor, his face creasing with panic. 'Who are the top three chart acts of all time? In terms of weeks on the chart, I mean . . .'

Victor leaned forward, the mood suddenly urgent. 'Elvis . . . Cliff Richard . . .'

'Obviously, yeah,' Jim said, agitated. 'It's the third one I can't bloody think of. Christ, I know this . . .'

Thorne tried to help. 'The Beatles . . .?'

With the perfect timing of a music-hall double act, his dad and Victor looked at each other, then at Thorne, before answering simultaneously, 'No . . .'

Thorne could see his father beginning to sweat, to breathe heavily. The fact that he was wearing two sweaters was not helping. 'I can see his bloody face. You know, bloke who fancies other blokes.' He began to raise his voice. 'Christ, he plays the . . . the thing with keys on, black and white keys . . .'

'Piano,' Thorne said. His father often spoke like this, when the right word wouldn't come. *The thing you put in your mouth to clean your teeth with.* Bacon and . . . *those things that come out of a chicken.*

Victor thumped his fist on the table triumphantly. 'Elton John,' he said.

'I know,' Jim said. 'I fucking know . . .' He began stabbing at the chips on his plate, one after the other, looking as if he might weep at any moment.

'I'll get some more drinks in,' Thorne said quickly. 'If you're going to break one of your rules, you might as well really break the bugger . . .'

Victor drained his pint, handed Thorne the empty glass. 'Course, your dad might not have Alzheimer's at all . . .'

Thorne shot him a look. This kind of discussion was pointless, though Victor was, strictly speaking, correct. Alzheimer's could not be, could *never* be confirmed. They were 90 per cent sure, though, which was about as good . . . or bad, as it got.

'Same again, Victor . . .?'

'Are you listening, Jim?' Victor said. 'You can't be *certain* it's Alzheimer's . . .'

Thorne put a hand on Victor's arm. 'Victor . . .'

Then Victor shot *him* a look, and Thorne suddenly saw what was happening. He saw that he was trampling all over the feed to one of his dad's favourite lines. He felt sick with shame . . .

His father put down his knife and fork, picked up his cue. 'That's right, Vic. The consultant told me that the only way they can be sure is to perform a post-mortem. I said, "No, thank you very much. I don't think I'm too keen on one of those just yet!"'

Victor and his father were still laughing loudly as Thorne stood at the bar waiting to get served . . .

The 'middle stage' of the dementia was how it had been described to him. It all sounded a bit vague, but Thorne figured that as long as there was another stage to go, things would be all right for a while longer. As long as the bad jokes outnumbered the moments of terror and despair, he would try not to be too worried.

Just briefly, for a minute or two, Carol had wondered about what she was doing, had thought about swapping places with her husband. She was a middle-aged woman, for heaven's sake! She ought to be inside like Jack, curled up on the sofa in front of *Heartbeat* instead of wrapped up in an anorak, rummaging through filthy cardboard boxes in their freezing garage.

That had been before she'd got into it. As soon as she began to delve into all that was left of Alan Franklin's past – his *first* past – she'd stopped feeling the cold. She'd rediscovered that bizarre and exciting feeling of looking for something, *getting after it*, without having the foggiest bloody idea of exactly what 'it' was.

All around her, in front rooms and kitchens on her quiet little road in Worthing, women her age were doing crosswords, or losing themselves in crappy romances or pouring breakfast cereal into bowls ready for the morning . . .

Carol pulled a pile of dusty, blank paper out of one of the boxes, swept away the grime with the side of her hand. She wouldn't have swapped places with any one of those women . . .

There was lots of paper in both boxes; reams of the stuff in a variety of sizes, once presumably white, but now yellowed and slightly damp. There were envelopes too, and smaller packages of file cards, sticky labels and rusted staples. Franklin had met Sheila while working for an insurance firm in Hastings, but had clearly wanted to hold on to a few odd souvenirs of the working life he'd had before.

None of the other stuff would have caused pulses to quicken at the *Antiques Roadshow*: a couple of unused Letts diaries from 1975 and 1976; a bunch of keys on a Ford Escort keyring; plates and teacups wrapped up in old newspaper; a couple of Polaroids inside a manila envelope – two boys; one a baby, the other a toddler, and later the same two as a pair of gawky, unsmiling teenagers.

Carol unwrapped the dry newspaper from around what turned out to be a large silver tankard. She laid it to one side and smoothed out the crumpled page on the garage floor. It was from a local paper. She looked at the date – presumably the day Franklin had walked out on, or been thrown out by, his wife. Not a great deal seemed to have happened in Colchester that day: a small protest about a proposed ring road; a leisure centre reopening after a refit; a smash-and-grab at the jeweller's on the High Street . . .

Carol smiled at a phrase she hadn't heard for many years. *Smash-and-grab.* Not much more than twenty years ago and even the crimes seemed more innocent somehow . . .

She picked up the tankard which, after a closer look, she could see was silver-plated. In spite of the newspaper, it had blackened slightly on one side but she could make out an engraving. She held it up to the light from the bare bulb, and read:

> *From the boys at Baxters, May 1976.*
> *Welcome back.*
> *Have one to celebrate or <u>more</u> than one*
> *to forget the whole thing!*

Carol thought about ringing Sheila Franklin, but knew instinctively that she wouldn't be a great deal of help. Her husband had not shared his past with her. Maybe he went up into the loft once in a while and peered at it, or perhaps he was trying to forget it himself. Either way, Carol was pretty sure that she would have to work it out on her own. She'd start tomorrow. It couldn't be that hard. She'd get that lazy bastard McKee to make a few calls.

Wincing, Carol hauled herself up from where she'd been kneeling on the floor. She'd put a cushion down on the concrete but her knees still felt very sore. She switched off the garage light and stood for a few seconds in the darkness before going inside.

Wondering what Alan Franklin had cause to celebrate back in 1976. And what he might have wanted to forget . . .

On the twenty-five-minute train journey back from St Albans, Thorne had the entire carriage to himself.

He reached into his bag for his CD Walkman and a couple of discs. He opened up an album by a band called Lambchop – a birthday present from Phil Hendricks which, until he'd shelled out three hundred quid in Tower Records, had been the *only* CD he'd owned for a day or two after the burglary. It was 'alt. country', Hendricks had told him. Apparently, Thorne needed to move with the times a little . . .

Thorne pressed PLAY, let it come and thought about the curious goodbye he and the old man had shared.

Half an hour after Victor had left and whatever tea was still in the pot had gone stone cold, Thorne and his father had stood together on the doorstep. Both, for very different reasons, trying to find the right thing to say.

Jim Thorne had never been one for tactile displays of affection. Occasionally a handshake, but not today. Instead, with a twinkle in his eye, he had leaned in close and, as if imparting a great pearl of wisdom, told Thorne that 'Three Steps to Heaven' by Eddy Cochrane had been number one in the hit parade on the day he'd been born.

Thorne kicked off his shoes, put his feet up on the seat opposite. What his father had said, what he'd *remembered*, was, he supposed, touching in its own way . . .

The music in his headphones was slow, and lush and strange. Thorne couldn't make head or tail of the lyrics and there were horns, for crying out loud. Not *Ring of Fire*-style Tijuana trumpets, or mariachi, but proper *horns*, like you'd hear on a soul record . . .

Thorne ejected the Lambchop CD, put it back into its jewel case. Another time, perhaps. He put on Steve Earle's 'Train a Comin'' and closed his eyes.

Soul was all well and good, but there were times when guts sounded a whole lot better.

It was stupidly easy.

He never ceased to be amazed at how pathetic these animals were. How simple it was to lead them by the nose. By the nose between their legs . . .

It was less than a week since the first casual remarks had been exchanged and already he could start thinking specifically about when and where Southern was going to be killed. It had been such a piece of piss that he half regretted all that effort with the others. The months of planning, the build-up, the letters. It might have been just as easy to wait until after they'd been released and collar them in a bar somewhere. Just smile and say hello.

People like that, like Southern, didn't need subtlety. Fuckers didn't understand it, wouldn't recognise it. Using their cocks like blunt instruments . . .

He'd won Southern's trust quickly, and now that he had it, the rest was fairly straightforward. Times and places. Arrangements.

It was all about trust, about getting it and keeping it. The gaining of trust was something he was good at. People gave it to him all the time, like a gift, without him needing to ask for it.

By contrast, he never, ever gave it. Not any more. He knew very well what could happen if you did.

FIFTEEN

Carol lifted the handset and dialled, checking the number on her pad twice as she pressed each button carefully. She reached over to straighten a picture on the wall as the phone at the other end began to ring.

She had only been able to stand watching McKee tit about for so long before she'd taken over herself. Two and a half days spent on the phone, digging through records at Companies House, getting wound up. Reminding herself of how shit the job was most of the time.

'Nobody made you do it,' Jack had said. 'Nobody would think any the worse of you if you chucked it in.'

Nobody except her . . .

Tracking down Baxters, the company Alan Franklin had worked for in Colchester nearly thirty years before, had proved enormously frustrating. She'd discovered quickly that the company, a stationery wholesaler, had not only left the area in the early eighties, but had changed its name. She was pretty much starting from scratch. She had spoken to every company in the south of England able to provide so much as a plain brown envelope, and got precisely nowhere. Then, just at the point when Jack was starting to talk about divorce, she'd got lucky. The personnel manager of a firm in Northampton knew *everybody* in the stationery supply business, played golf with most of them, God help him! He was only too delighted to tell her *exactly* where to find the person she needed to talk to, and gave her the name of a company in King's Lynn . . .

'Hello, Bowyer-Shotton, may I help you?'

'Yes, please,' Carol said. 'I'd like to speak to Paul Baxter.'

'I'll put you through . . .'

Andy Stone sat, sweating through his white linen shirt, some small fraction of his mind on the report he was writing up . . .

He thought about the woman he'd woken up next to. He remembered the look on her face the night before, and the look she'd given him as she'd slipped out of his bed that morning without a word . . .

She'd been attending a tedious conference at the Greenwood Hotel a couple of weeks earlier, when Ian Welch had been killed. Stone had interviewed her, given her his number in case there was anything else she remembered. She'd remembered that she fancied him, rung and asked if he wanted to go for a drink.

He guessed that she was turned on by the fact that he was a copper. A lot of women seemed to find it exciting. The power, the handcuffs, the war stories. Whatever the reason, once the novelty wore off, most of them seemed to lose interest in him very quickly.

Meantime, the sex was usually pretty good . . .

He wanted to control things in bed. He liked to be on top, the woman's arms flung above her head, his hands around her skinny wrists, pushing himself up and away from her while he was doing it. He'd done weights, built up his chest and arms so that he could hold the position for as long as he needed to.

Last night had started really well. She'd looked up at him, her eyes wide, and said all the right things, *just* the sort of words he imagined hearing whenever he thought about it. She told him he was too big, that he might hurt her. He threw back his head, gritted his teeth, pushed harder . . .

Then she'd spoiled things. She'd begun to moan, to grab at his shoulders, to say that she liked it rough. Then, between ragged breaths, she'd told him that she *wanted* him to hurt her.

In seconds he had shrunk and slipped out of her. He dropped down and rolled on to his side, listening to her sigh, aware of her inching across to her own side of the bed, so that no part of their bodies were touching . . .

Stone looked up at the greeting of a colleague passing his desk. He smiled and continued to type. He remembered the warm feeling of his hand, cupped between his legs, and the sound of the woman's body sliding across the sheet as it edged away from him.

Carol had been put on hold . . .

She had probably been listening to Celine Dion for no more than a couple of minutes, but she could feel herself growing a hell of a lot older.

Moments like this, the empty minutes that made up so much of any case, made her glad she'd agreed to take the job on the clear understanding that she could work from home. She'd guessed that AMRU would not be given the swankiest office facilities, and working as they did (or were supposed to do) in teams of just two, she'd have been lucky to get a cupboard.

Jack had cleared a space for her in the spare room. They set up the old computer that his daughter had used, and shelled out twenty quid on an extra handset for the cordless phone. Her filing system consisted of yellow Post-It notes stuck around a picture frame, her husband doubled as a coffee machine, and when Carol glanced at the mirror above her desk, she saw dusty hat boxes, old lamps without plugs and a collection of china dogs that had seemed like a good idea a couple of years before.

It was cramped, but she liked her things around her.

The day she'd taken up residence in her new office, Jack had stood behind her and they'd both stared into the mirror. Carol sat at her desk and smiled at the rubbish they'd amassed together down the years, piled up on the single bed behind her. The reflection of her retired self.

'That'll stop you getting too carried away,' Jack said.

The muzak came to an abrupt and merciful halt. 'Can I help you?' a man asked.

'Yes. Paul Baxter, please . . .'

'Wrong department, love. You've come through to accounts. Let me try and transfer you . . .'

Ten seconds of clicking and then a familiar voice. Carol's heart was already sinking as she spoke.

'Paul Baxter, please . . .'

'Is that you again? Sorry dear, you've come back to the switchboard. I'll put you through . . .'

*

The sun, blazing through even the grimiest of the big windows, had turned the Major Incident Room into a sauna by midday. Yvonne Kitson didn't really need to reapply her lipstick, but did it all the same. Any excuse to spend a few minutes in the cool of the toilets was welcome.

She didn't usually wear a great deal of make-up. Just enough to feel good, but that was all. In this job more than most, people were quick to judge, to form instant opinions that would be passed around and set in stone before you'd so much as got your work-station organised.

She knew very well what people thought about her. She knew what the likes of Tom Thorne thought she *was*, thought she *did*. She knew just how wide of the mark they were.

Make-up – the colours, how much, when you wore it – gave off a signal. It said you were this, or that. Concealing, lying, *making it up* . . .

She stood for a few moments, looking at herself in the cracked mirror. She moved her head a few inches, until the crack ran right down the middle of her face. Until it looked about right.

She would give it one more minute . . .

She began to count down the time in her head. Fifty-five seconds more, then she would slam the phone down, make some tea and go and shout at her old man for a while. No, she would snatch the phone back up, call McKee and shout at *him* . . .

Carol began to swear repeatedly under her breath. *Fuck, fuck, fuck.* She'd turned her back on gardening, and old films in the afternoon, and the *Reader's Digest*, for *this* . . .

'Paul Baxter's phone . . .'

She almost cheered. 'Thank God. Is Mr Baxter there?'

The woman sounded unsure. 'Well, he was here a minute ago. He might have grabbed an early lunch. Let me see if I can find him for you . . .'

There was a clatter as the receiver was dropped, then silence. Thirty seconds later Carol heard voices, then muffled laughter which grew suddenly louder before the receiver was picked up and abruptly replaced. Then she just heard a dialling tone.

Carol took a deep breath and dialled again, jabbing at the buttons as if each were the eyeball of a Bowyer-Shotton employee.

'Hello, Bowyer-Shotton, can you hold for a moment . . .?'

Carol shouted. 'No!'

It was too late . . .

Dave Holland was in a reasonable mood until the little gobshite started to get cocky.

'Listen, I don't think I have to go into the details . . .'

'Well, that depends, doesn't it?' Holland said. 'On just how much of a pain in the arse you want me to be.'

'I did some modelling up there. Fair enough?'

'Right. Catalogue stuff, was it? The Debenham's autumn collection . . .?'

'You want to know my connection with Charlie Dodd, so I'm telling you. I was booked to do some filming, all right?'

'Did you ever mention it to anybody else?' Holland asked. 'Pass Dodd's name on? Maybe you told somebody about the studio?'

257

There was a hollow-sounding bark of laughter down the line. 'Yeah. I was so proud of the work, wasn't I? I mean, *London Cock Boys* and *Borstal Meat* are fucking classics. Maybe you've seen them . . .'

Holland hung up, put a line through another name on the list.

Charlie Dodd had known a lot of people. They'd worked their way through every number on his phone records and everyone appeared to have a valid, if occasionally sordid, reason for being a friend, or 'business associate'. Photographers, film developers and suppliers, video production companies, prostitutes. Each person was asked to give the name of anybody else they thought might have known Dodd and this, together with a few more contacts provided by Thorne's squeaky-voiced snout, had generated another, much bigger list to be worked through.

Holland stifled a yawn. At the end of the day, it would probably result in nothing more than a handy contact list to pass on to Vice. It was certainly unlikely to provide any link to the killer as, contrary to what Thorne had said, Dodd had discovered that it *did* pay to advertise. One of the first numbers on the list had turned out to be a specialist S & M magazine. They were suitably saddened at the news that a much-valued client would not be placing any further small ads to advertise his facilities . . .

Holland leaned back in his chair, thrust up his arms and stretched. Wasting his time, as he'd wasted it the night before at home. Making calls that could have waited, crossing names off the list. An excuse, an escape . . .

Sophie had come through in her dressing gown. One hand cradling her stomach and the other holding a mug of tea. She'd put it down in front of Holland and stood look-ing over his shoulder at the paperwork on the tabletop, her hand resting on the top of his head.

She'd laughed softly. 'Little sod's been kicking the shit out of me all day . . .'

When Holland had looked up half a minute later, she'd been standing in the doorway. He'd picked up his tea, smiled a thank-you at her.

'I know you think I want you to choose,' she'd said. 'And I really don't. Yes, I sometimes hate what you do, and I get pissed off at your pig-headed boss and the fact that you worship the ground he walks on, but you know all that. Yes, I would be happy if you took some time off and, no, I don't want you doing anything stupid. Not now. I wouldn't ask you to make a choice though, Dave.' Then she'd turned to stare out of the window for a moment. 'I'd be too scared . . .'

For a few seconds there had been only the sound of the traffic rumbling up the Old Kent Road, and a radio from the flat downstairs. Holland had picked up the phone from its cradle, reached for his pen. 'Can we talk about it later?' He'd looked down at the papers on the desk, at the point-less list of names. 'This is really important . . .'

Thorne watched his team going through the motions. Holland, Stone, Kitson . . .

He saw dozens of other officers and civilian staff talking and writing and thinking – the impetus running out. As if the heat had thickened the air, made it a little harder to move through.

Thorne stood watching from the doorway of the Incident

Room, thinking about the thrashing limbs of a body near to death . . .

It was always the same pattern. In the days that followed the discovery of a murder victim, the activity was frantic. An urgency seized the team, the knowledge that the hours, the days immediately following, would be when they had their best chance. After Dodd, they'd run around like blue-arsed flies, checking records and tracing contacts and taking statements and chasing couriers. Waiting for *anything*.

And, gradually, as always, the flurry of activity on the case had slowed, like the movements of the victim himself as death had approached. The frenzy became drudgery. The phone was picked up and the statement taken reflexively, the small spark of hope fizzling to nothing, until the body of the investigation itself began to stiffen and cool, to swing aimlessly . . .

Something would be needed. The case, and those working it, needed a jolt to kick some life back into them. An external force, like the passing train that had given movement to Charlie Dodd's corpse.

Thorne had no idea what it was, or where it might come from.

'Paul Baxter . . .'

'Am I *speaking* to Paul Baxter?'

'Yes, who's this?'

Carol felt a little of the tension in her back and neck begin to ease. 'My name's Carol Chamberlain, from the Metropolitan Police Area Major Review Unit. You would not believe the trouble I've had trying to get hold of you . . .'

'Get hold of *me* . . .?'

'You, your company . . .'

'We're in the phone book . . .'

'Right, but I was looking for *Baxters.*'

There was a pause. Carol could hear Baxter taking a drink of something, swallowing. 'Blimey, that was a long time ago. My dad got bought out in . . . '82, I think. I stayed on as head of sales when we moved up here, that was part of the deal . . .'

'Anyway . . .'

'So how can I help you?' Paul Baxter laughed. He had a low, sexy voice. Smooth, like a DJ. 'Does the Met need some new headed notepaper?'

'Do you remember an employee called Alan Franklin? He would have left in . . .'

Baxter cut her off. 'God, yes, of course I do. I was helping out in the warehouse when all that happened, working for my old man. Run-up to Christmas, I think . . .'

'When all *what* happened?'

She could hear confusion, suspicion even, in Baxter's voice as he answered. 'Well, I don't suppose we'll ever know for sure, but I remember the court case obviously. God, and all that dreadful stuff afterwards . . .'

Carol realised suddenly that she was on her feet, leaning on her desk. In the mirror she saw the face of a woman who, for the first time in three long years, was feeling the buzz. Feeling it across her chest like a heart attack. In her head like a hole that sucked away the breath in a second. Rushing through her blood and bone like light.

Like a lease of life.

'Hello . . .?'

She became dimly aware of Baxter's voice on the other end of the phone. She lowered herself into the chair, took just another second before moving on.

'OK, Mr Baxter, when can I come and see you?'

Done and dusted . . .

The suggestion had come from Southern himself. How brilliant was that?! An invitation back to Southern's small flat in Leytonstone had been politely declined. He'd already decided that he would be sticking with the hotel. Southern had gone for that idea straight away – same as the others had. There was something about a hotel that gave the rendezvous an excitement for them. It was the same for him as well, of course, but then he knew just how exciting it was really going to be . . .

The hotels he'd chosen, on each occasion so far, had suited the mood of the event, and the character of the individual concerned, perfectly. He always gave some thought to that, as well as to the necessary issues of security. Remfry, if he'd had the chance, would have done it up a back-alley, across a rusty oil drum. The place in Paddington had the seediness that got him off, the squalor that turned him on. Welch, on the other hand, had wanted somewhere a bit nicer. He was clearly a man with aspirations, ideas above his station. The Greenwood had fitted the bill nicely.

The place that he'd found for Howard Southern would be ideal. It was a small, country-house-type hotel in leafy Roehampton. On the outskirts of Richmond Park, there was a romantic, woodland view from some of the bedrooms.

He was sure that it would go down well. Howard Southern loved the countryside. Hadn't he brutally beaten and raped his first victim on a disused bridle path in Epping Forest?

Done and dusted.

263

SIXTEEN

Two Bs and a C. Two Bs and a C . . .

The results she needed to see when she opened that envelope at the end of August. The offer from the university she wanted. The grades that she had to get if she was going to take up her place on the drama course in Manchester. Two Bs and a C. It had become Fiona Meek's mantra in the weeks since her final paper.

Most of her friends were still celebrating the end of the exams. One or two of those with parents richer than her own were away travelling, and the rest were pissing it up the wall in one way or another. There were only a couple, like her, who had decided to put a bit of money away and take summer jobs. She knew she could be a bit too sensible sometimes, but she didn't mind missing out. She didn't care if her friends took the mickey. They wouldn't be laughing when their student loans ran out halfway through the first term.

It was the perfect job, and plenty of people wanted it. A friend of her dad's was the corporate hospitality manager and had put in a good word. Working the two shifts suited her. It was an early start, but she was finished mid-morning and not on again until teatime, so she had her days to herself.

Fiona waved as, further up the corridor, she saw one of the other girls coming out of a room, dumping dirty towels into the laundry hamper. She parked her own trolley, began loading soap and shampoo into a small basket. The smell was familiar from the mountain of stuff she now had in her own bathroom at home.

The seven-to-ten bedroom shift was the hardest. She'd been amazed these last couple of weeks to see just what pigs some people lived like when they weren't at home. She hadn't had any *really* bad ones yet – no used condoms, or what have you – but still, some people behaved like animals. Equally weird were the rooms that barely looked lived-in at all. Towels neatly folded and beds made. These were the sort of people, Fiona supposed, who tidied their houses before their cleaners came round.

Either way, as she moved around the bedrooms, replenishing toiletries and coffee sachets, smoothing sheets and checking mini bars, she tried to get inside the heads of these people whom she rarely ever met. She tried to flesh out lives she could only guess at by the labels on strangers' shoes, the smells in their bathrooms and the paperbacks by the sides of their beds.

It was all good practice, she reckoned, for being an actress. If she ever got the chance. Two Bs and a C. Two Bs and a C . . .

She slid the plastic pass-key into the lock and shoved open a bedroom door.

A lot of murders went unsolved, but compared to the clean-up rates for burglary, Thorne reckoned that he, and others like him, were doing pretty bloody well.

'For fuck's sake, Chris, it's been nearly three weeks. You must know *most* of the likely lads in the area . . .'

On the other end of the phone, Chris Barratt laughed like a drain. It sounded to Thorne as if this conversation was making the Kentish Town crime-desk sergeant's day.

'You're not a punter, Tom,' Barratt said. 'You know what it's like. This early on a Saturday morning, you want to count yourself lucky there was anybody here to answer the bleeding phone . . .'

Thorne knew how stretched things were in many areas. Violent street crime was, quite rightly, being targeted, and uniformed manpower was being taken away from such everyday London trivialities as common housebreaking. He was aware that because he was on the job, they were probably making twice the effort they would normally be making to lay hands on whoever had turned his flat over. He also knew that twice nothing was pretty much fuck all.

'Three weeks, though, Chris . . .'

'We found your car.'

'Yeah, and got nothing off it . . .'

'It was burnt out . . .'

'Only on the inside.'

The Mondeo had been found on an estate behind Euston Station. The inside had been torched, the wheels nicked and the words POLICE WANKERS spray-painted on the roof. Yet more cause for amusement around the Incident Room at Becke House . . .

'What about fences?' Thorne asked. 'The bastard should have got something for my CD system . . .'

'Duh! We never thought about that . . .'

Thorne sighed. He took the gum he'd been chewing out

of his mouth and lobbed it out of the open window. 'Sorry, Chris. Any kind of fucking result would be good at the minute, you know?'

'You're sorted with the insurance, aren't you?' Barratt said.

'Yeah, fine.' Thorne was still waiting for the money to come through, car and contents, but there was no reason why it shouldn't . . .

'So are you really that bothered?'

A clammy Saturday morning. Working up a sweat in slow motion. The arse-end of a week that felt like a tight space he was too big to squeeze through.

'Yes, I'm bothered,' Thorne said. 'So should you be. And when you eventually catch the little toe-rag who used my bedroom as a khazi, he's going to be *very* fucking bothered . . .'

A guest in a smart suit hurried past her towards the lift. Fiona said good morning and put the back of a rubber-gloved hand across her mouth to stifle a yawn. She moved up the corridor towards the next bedroom, thinking about what she might do later on.

The early evening shift was usually a bit of a doddle. A chance to flirt with her favourite waiter as she cleaned the tables in the bar, or to gossip with the girls in reception while she hoovered. A couple of times she'd managed to finish all her jobs double-quick and find a quiet corner, somewhere out of sight, where she could sit and open a book.

If she wasn't too knackered, she might go out for a couple of drinks, catch up with some of her mates. Maybe she could slip away from work a few minutes early . . .

No such luck the evening before. There was a dose of summer flu going around and the place was short-staffed. She'd had to do the whole of main reception herself and was just thinking she might finally be able to get away when she'd been roped into lending a hand up in the Conference Room, laying the table for a Saturday-morning business breakfast the following day.

She'd wheeled the trolley laden with cutlery and table linen into the lift and pressed the button for the top floor. Just as the doors were closing, a couple had stepped in. She was attractive, wearing a smart skirt and silk blouse. He was *very* attractive, and dressed a little more casually.

On the first floor, the woman got out. They hadn't been a couple after all. As the doors closed, the man turned to her and smiled. Feeling herself redden, Fiona looked down and began to count the knives and forks.

The bell rang as the lift reached the top floor and she straightened her wheels, nudged them towards the door. The man took a step forward to hold the door for her. He gave her another smile as she pushed the trolley out, the cutlery clattering noisily as she moved past him.

A few feet up the corridor, she'd turned and looked at him, a little confused that he hadn't stepped out of the lift himself. Just as the doors began to shut, the man in the leather biker's jacket had caught her looking at him. He turned his palms upwards and shook his head at his own stupidity.

'Miles away. Missed my floor . . .'

There were times when investigations seemed shrouded in darkness. When the light, no matter the season or time of day, seemed to have faded away in those rooms where a case was worked, where progress in catching a killer was discussed and evaluated. For those groping around in the dark, there was always the frustrating feeling that if someone could just point a torch in the right direction, something important would be revealed. Then the shadows would shorten and slip away, but nobody knew where to shine the light.

The day was getting off to a slow start, but Brigstocke seemed in no mood to crack the whip. It was fine with Thorne. He sensed that an extra ten minutes or so spent sitting around together, talking about nothing much for a while before they got down to it, might do everybody some good.

Might shorten a few shadows . . .

They sat on and around three different desks in the Incident Room. The coffees and teas were being eked out. Magazines and papers were being flicked through, space stared into, clocks glanced at.

'Anybody have a decent Friday night?' Thorne said. Nobody seemed awfully keen on answering one way or the other. Thorne laughed. 'Fuck me, what a bunch of party animals!' He turned to look at Stone. 'Come on, Andy, you're young and single . . .'

Stone looked up, but only for a second. 'Too knackered . . .'

Holland laughed. 'You big girl . . .'

'You won't be laughing once your missus sprogs,' Brigstocke said.

'Right.' Kitson walked across to the recently installed water cooler. 'You should be making the most of your Friday nights, Dave. Soon be a thing of the past . . .'

Holland grunted, turned his attention back to the sports page of the *Daily Mirror*. Thorne craned his head to look at the headline. The latest on a story that Spurs were about to sign some temperamental Italian midfielder.

'What about the rest of the weekend, then?' Thorne threw the question open to any of them. 'Any plans?'

The reaction – a lot of non-committal shrugging – was much the same as before. Thorne began to think that his own social life, such as it was, looked pretty bloody exciting by comparison. Mind you, it had picked up a lot lately . . .

'Sundays in the Brigstocke household are sacred and unchanging.' The DCI picked up his briefcase, moved away in the direction of his office. 'Dog-walking, laundry, the bloodbath of Sunday lunch with one set of parents or another. Oh, and a trip to the garden centre, or maybe B & Q if I'm *really* lucky . . .'

Thorne laughed, looking around, sharing it. He thought about the last Sunday *he'd* spent. Something Brigstocke had said sparked another memory and Thorne turned to watch Yvonne Kitson heading back across the room, drinking from a paper cone filled with cold water.

'Did you get my message last Sunday?' She swallowed, looked at him blankly. 'I called. Late morning, I think . . .'

Kitson dropped the empty cone into a wastepaper basket. 'Any particular reason?'

'Well, if there was, I'm buggered if I can remember it,' Thorne said.

Kitson looked at him for a second or two, her face showing nothing. 'I didn't get the message.'

Thorne shrugged. 'Doesn't matter.' He nodded towards where Brigstocke had been just a minute before. 'I'd thought it would be a good time to catch you, you know? Reckoned you'd be another one with a family routine on a Sunday.'

Kitson moved past him, picked up the magazine she'd been reading and dropped it into her bag. She took a step towards the toilets, then turned to Thorne, nodding as though she'd just remembered something. 'I was at the gym . . .'

The Incident Room was coming to life, starting to fill with noise and movement. Holland walked across it, evidently catching the tail-end of Thorne and Kitson's conversation.

'You should get together with Stoney,' he said. 'He's well into weights and all that.' Holland looked over to where Andy Stone was sitting on the edge of a desk, chatting to a trainee detective. 'He might be a lanky streak of piss, but he looks like a light-heavyweight with his shirt off . . .'

Kitson looked at Thorne and raised her eyebrows. Her face was open and relaxed again. Her tone, when she spoke to Holland, was matey and suggestive. 'Easy, tiger,' she said.

Holland started to say something else, but Thorne was already moving away from them. He knew that by the end of the day the heat and the frustrations of the case would combine to leave him as tightly wound as the E-string on a pedal-steel guitar. He wanted to get into his office, call Eve and organise something that would help lessen that tension just a little.

'Christ, you sound even more harassed than *I* am . . .'

'I told you, Saturdays are the busiest day.'

271

'Keith's mum still no better, then?'

'Sorry?'

'Keith not around to help out?'

'Oh. No . . .'

Thorne looked up as Kitson walked in and moved across to her desk. Her look told him that she knew exactly who he was talking to. Thorne lowered his voice . . .

'Fancy going to see a film tonight?'

'Yeah, why not. There's a copy of *Time Out* in the flat, I'll see what's on . . .'

From nowhere, and for no immediately obvious reason, the case burst its way into their conversation. Into Thorne's head. The image that would not focus. The thought that would not reveal itself.

Something he'd read and something he hadn't . . .

At the sound of Eve's voice, the phantom thought vanished as suddenly as it had arrived. 'Tom?'

'Yeah . . . that's fine. Maybe we could do a bit of shopping tomorrow.'

There was a pause. 'Anywhere in particular?'

Thorne dropped the volume even further, cupped his hand around the mouthpiece.

'The bed shop . . .'

Eve laughed, and when she spoke again, *her* voice was lowered. Thorne guessed from the noise that she had a shop full of customers. 'Thank fuck for that,' she said.

'I'm pleased you're pleased,' Thorne said.

'Yes, well, it's about bloody time. I'd decided I wasn't going to mention it again. I didn't want to sound desperate.'

Thorne glanced up. Kitson was hunched over some paperwork. 'Listen, I had a long look at myself in the mirror this morning. I'd say "desperate" is a pretty good word for it . . .'

Fiona only had a couple of rooms left.

The girls usually worked to a set pattern in terms of floors, corridors and so on, but the order in which individual rooms were cleaned varied from day to day. Rooms with a DO NOT DISTURB sign hung on the door would obviously get done later than those with used breakfast trays left outside, while some rooms would get knocked on to a later shift.

There were two rooms at the end of her corridor on the first floor that still needed doing. She looked at her watch. It was twenty to ten . . .

Fiona grabbed a bucket crammed with sponges, sprays and bottles, nudging the Hoover towards the bedroom door with her foot. She knocked on the door and counted to five, thinking about eggs and bacon and bed. It was the same most mornings. By this time, by the end of this corridor, she would be thinking about home, a late breakfast and a few more gorgeous hours wrapped up in her duvet.

Twenty minutes. She might get both rooms done before the end of her shift if she was lucky, though it would obviously depend on what sort of state they were in.

She reached down for the pass-key card hanging from a curly, plastic chain around her waist . . .

There was a tune going through her head. The song that had woken her on the clock-radio, a present from her nan when the exams had finished. The song was very old fashioned, just a singer and a guitar, but the tune had stayed with her all morning.

She eased the card into the lock and slid it out again. The light below the handle turned green. She pushed down and leaned against the door . . .

From the corner of her eye, she saw someone coming towards her along the corridor. It looked like one of the snotty old cows that ran housekeeping. She couldn't be sure because the woman's face was all but hidden behind an enormous arrangement of lilies.

Turning sideways, she eased open the door with her hip. The Hoover was kicked across the threshold, left to hold the door ajar while she turned back to the trolley to grab her other bits and pieces . . .

Two months later, Fiona would be offered her chance, her place on the drama course in Manchester, but she would not take it up. Not *that* September, at any rate. She would get her two Bs and a C but it would not mean a great deal to her. Two months later, her mother would remove the slip of paper from the envelope and read out the results and try to sound excited, but her daughter would still not be hearing very much. The scream that had torn through her body eight weeks earlier would still be echoing in her head and drowning out pretty much everything.

The sound of a scream and a picture of herself, of a young girl stepping through a doorway and turning. Faced with a peculiar kind of filth. Stains that she could never hope to remove with the bleaches and the waxes and the cloths which spill from a bucket, tumbling noisily to the bedroom floor.

It wasn't much past ten yet, but Thorne was already starting to wonder what the lunchtime special at the Royal Oak might be, when the middle-aged woman walked into his office.

'I'm looking for DC Holland,' she said.

She'd marched in without knocking, so Thorne wasn't keen from the kick-off, but he tried to be as nice as he could. The woman was short and dumpy, probably pushing sixty. She reminded him a bit of his Auntie Eileen, and he suddenly had a good idea who she was.

'Oh, right, are you Dave's . . .?'

The woman cut him off and, as she spoke, she dragged a chair from behind Kitson's desk, plonked it in front of Thorne's and sat herself down.

'No, I'm not. I'm Carol Chamberlain. Ex-DCI Chamberlain from AMRU . . .'

Thorne reached for a pen and paper to take notes, thinking, *Fucking Crinkly Squad, all I need.* He leaned across the desk and proffered a hand. 'DI Thorne . . .'

Ignoring the hand, Carol Chamberlain opened her briefcase and began to rummage inside. 'Right. *You'll* do even better. I only asked for Holland' – she pulled out a battered green folder covered in yellow Post-It notes, held it up – 'because his was the name . . . attached to *this.*' Emphasising the last word, she dropped the folder down on to Thorne's desk.

Thorne glanced at the file and held up his hands. He tried his best to sound pleasant as he spoke. 'Listen, is there any chance we can do this another time? We're up to our elbows in a very big case and . . .'

'I know *exactly* what case you're up to your elbows in,' she said. 'Which is why we should really do it now.'

Thorne stared at her. There was a steel in this woman's

voice that suggested it would not be worth his while to argue. With a sigh, he pulled the folder across the desk, began to leaf through it.

'Five weeks ago, DC Holland pulled the file on an unsolved murder from 1996.' Aside from the steel, her voice had the acquired refinement that often came with rank, however distant, but Thorne thought he detected the remnants of a Yorkshire accent beneath. 'The victim's name was Alan Franklin. He was killed in a car park. Strangled with washing line.'

'I remember,' Thorne said. He flicked a couple of pages over. It was one of the cases Holland had pulled off CRIM-INT. 'There were a couple of these that we looked at and then dismissed. Nothing suggested that . . .'

Chamberlain nodded, dropped her eyes to the folder. 'This was handed to me as a cold case. My *first* cold case, as it happens . . .'

'I read about the initiative. It's a good idea.'

'I've been looking at the Franklin murder again . . .'

'Right . . .' Thorne stopped, noticing the faintest trace of enjoyment then, another tiny line around her mouth that cracked open for just half a second and was gone. It was enough to prompt a reaction in *him*, a flutter of something that began, as always, at the nape of his neck . . .

'Alan Franklin should have been known to us, to those who were investigating his murder back in '96. His name should have come up on a routine check . . .'

Thorne knew there was no need to ask why. He knew she was about to tell him. He watched, and listened, and felt the tingle grow and spread around his body.

'In May 1976, Franklin stood trial at Colchester Crown Court. He was accused of rape. Accused and acquitted.'

Thorne caught a breath, let it out again slowly. 'Jesus . . .'

Like a beam of light in the right direction . . .

Later, when Thorne and the woman he'd thought was Dave Holland's mother knew and liked each other better, Carol Chamberlain would confess to him that *this* was one of those rare moments she'd missed more than anything. The seconds looking at Thorne, just before she revealed the most significant fact of all. When she'd had to fight very hard to stop herself grinning.

'Alan Franklin was accused of raping a woman named Jane Foley . . .'

PART THREE

HARM'S WAY

The grunting seemed to be coming from somewhere very deep down. A noise of effort and of immense satisfaction. Rising up from his guts and exploding, carried on hot breath from between dirty, misshapen teeth. Beneath these animal sounds – dog-noise, monkey-noise, pig-noise – the counterpoint provided by the dull slapping of hot flesh against cold as he pushes himself harder, again and again.

Refusing to speed up. Giving no sign that it might soon be over.

Taking his pleasure.

Inflicting his pain.

How was this allowed to happen? Naivety and trust had proved to be the perfect complements to frustration and hatred. It had happened in a moment. How long ago was that? Fifteen minutes? Thirty?

There seems little point in struggling. It will be over eventually, it must be. No point in thinking about what happens afterwards. Probably a shy smile, maybe an apology and a cigarette and a speech about signals and crossed wires.

Fucker. Fucker. Fucker.

Until then . . .

Eyes that cannot bear to stay open, shut tight and a new picture presents itself. Small at first, and far away. Posed, waiting in a distant circle of light at the end of a tunnel.

Now it is the grunting and the slapping that begin to recede into the distance as the picture gets closer, rushing up the tunnel, sucking up the darkness until it is fully formed and clearer than it has ever been.

Clearer even than it ever really was. The colours more vivid: the red wetness against the white shirt; the cobalt-blue of the rope's coils around the neck like an exotic snake at his throat. The sounds and smells of the body and the rope, deafening and pungent. Creaking and faecal.

The feeling: the unique horror of seeing it. Seeing the inde-scribable pain in those eyes at being seen.

Then, at the end, watching it. Sensing something struggle to escape, and finally float free, up and away from the body that twirls slowly at the end of a frayed and oily rope.

SEVENTEEN

It was as grim a story of broken bodies and bruised lives as Tom Thorne had ever heard . . .

A week since Carol Chamberlain had sat in Thorne's office and blown everything wide open. Holland was at the wheel of a car-pool Laguna as they drove into Essex, heading towards Braintree. The two men were comfortable enough with each other to let silences fall between them, but today's was particularly heavy. Thorne could only hope that what was in Holland's head was a sight less dark than what was in his own.

As grim a story . . .

Jane Foley was raped by Alan Franklin. Thorne was convinced of it, though if it had not been proved *then*, there was very little chance that the truth would emerge over twenty-five years on. What nobody doubted, then or now, were the bizarre and brutal actions taken by her husband, Dennis. What he had done to Jane, and then to himself, on the afternoon of 10 August, 1976.

Thorne would probably never know for certain *exactly* what had gone on in that house, what had passed between those two people and led to those last, intimate moments of horror. Thorne *did* know that he would spend a good deal of time imagining those moments: the terror of Jane Foley as her husband draws near to her; the guilt and the anguish and the fear of a man who has just committed murder; the blood not yet dry on his hands, the tow rope slippy with it as he fashions a makeshift noose.

Worst of all, the incomprehension of the two children, finding the bodies of their parents . . .

Thorne started slightly as Holland smacked his palms against the wheel. He opened his eyes to see that they'd run into a line of slow-moving traffic. Ever since they'd come off the M11 it had been snarled up. Mid-morning on a Saturday and no good reason for the jam, but it was there all the same.

'Shit,' Holland said. It was the first word either of them had spoken in nearly an hour.

If Thorne was going to spend time thinking about what had happened between Jane and Dennis Foley, he was also going to be dwelling on something equally as painful. Something that, God help him, might have been responsible for horrors all of its own.

Thorne had fucked up. He had fucked up as badly as he could remember and, for him, that was saying something . . .

Carol Chamberlain had presumed that the officers working on the Franklin murder in 1996 had also fucked up. It looked as if they'd failed to check Franklin's name against the General Registry at Victoria, which would have revealed his part in the Jane Foley rape case twenty years before that.

In fact, it was a matter of record that those officers *had* phoned the General Registry. What was *not* a matter of record, what would have to remain conjecture, was that the brain-dead pen-pusher on the other end of the phone – a man long-since retired and, Thorne hoped, long-since dead – had missed Franklin's name. One eye on his crossword as the other had simply skipped past it. It had been a costly mistake.

But Thorne's had been costlier.

Unlike the officers in 1996, Thorne had *not* checked. Jane Foley's name had never been run past the General Registry, had never been put through the system. Strictly speaking, it had not been Thorne's job to do it, but that didn't matter. As far as Thorne was concerned, he carried the can. He never made sure, and even if he *had* thought of it, it would not have struck him as important.

Why would they need to check out the name of a woman who didn't really exist? Jane Foley was the made-up name of a made-up person, wasn't it? Jane Foley was a fantasy . . .

Thorne knew very well that if they . . . he . . . *anyone* had checked, made one simple phone call after they'd found Remfry's letters, that Ian Welch might still be alive. As might Howard Anthony Southern . . .

The traffic had begun to move again. Holland yanked the gearstick down, took the car up into second. 'I wouldn't mind, but there's never a decent bloody pile-up at the end of it . . .'

The body of the third victim had been discovered, in a hotel in Roehampton, at around the same time as the woman from the Crinkly Squad had walked into Thorne's office and dropped her very welcome bombshell. She had still been there when the call came through and Thorne had invited her along to the murder scene. It had seemed the very least he could do.

In that hotel room, with SOCOs and pathologists and an honest-to-goodness body, Thorne had thought that, even standing in the background as she was, Carol Chamberlain had looked as happy as a kid in a sweet factory . . .

In the days that followed, the investigation had begun to move forward in two distinct directions. While the latest victim was being processed, and the change in the pattern of the killings was being looked at, Thorne and those closest to him had begun to work on a new front. They would be chasing the major new lead that Carol Chamberlain had given them.

Holland steered the car into an ordinary-looking road lined with drab sixties houses, and spindly trees which didn't help a great deal. They'd managed to snaffle one of the few team vehicles with air-conditioning and the street felt like a sauna as they stepped out of the car. They pulled on their jackets, grimacing.

As they walked towards Peter Foley's house, Thorne thought about leads. Why on earth did they talk about 'chasing' them? He wondered if it was because, no matter how inanimate they were, or how quick you thought *you* might be, some had a nasty habit of getting away from you.

Dennis Foley's younger brother, the only surviving relative of either Dennis *or* Jane they had yet been able to trace, was not the most gracious of hosts.

Thorne and Holland sat perched on the edge of stained velour armchairs, sweating inside jackets they had not been encouraged to take off. Opposite them on a matching sofa, Peter Foley sprawled in baggy shorts and a loud Hawaiian shirt, open to the waist. He clutched a can of cold lager which, when he wasn't drinking from it, he rolled back and forth across his skinny chest.

'You were, what, eleven years younger than Dennis?' Holland said.

Foley swallowed a mouthful of beer. 'Right, I was the mistake.'

'So when it happened you'd have still been a student?'

He shook his head. 'Nope. Least you could do is get your facts right. I was twenty-two in seventy-six. I'd left college the year before . . .' His accent was pure Essex, the voice high, and a little wheezy.

'And you were doing what?' Thorne asked.

'I was doing fuck all. Bumming around, being a punk. I did a bit of roadying for The Clash at one point . . .'

Thorne had been a punk as well, though he was six years younger than Foley, who was pushing fifty. The man sitting opposite him certainly didn't look like he listened to 'White Riot' much any more. He was skinny, though his arms were well muscled; worked on, Thorne guessed, to better display the Gothic tattoos. His greying hair was tied back in a ponytail and the wispy beard teased into a point. From the look of him, and the copies of *Kerrang!* tossed under the coffee table, Thorne figured that Peter Foley was something of an ageing heavy-metal fan.

'What do you think happened to Jane?' Thorne said.

Foley lifted himself up, pulled a pack of Marlboros from

his shorts pocket and sank back down again. 'What? You mean when Den . . .?'

'Before that. With Franklin.'

'Fucker raped her, didn't he.' It wasn't a question. He lit his cigarette. 'He'd have gone down for it as well if it wasn't for you fucking lot . . .'

Holland bridled a little, opened his mouth, but Thorne cut across him. 'What do you mean, Mr Foley?' Thorne knew *exactly* what Foley meant and he knew that he was right. The force, back then, was not exactly famed for the sensitivity with which it treated rape victims.

'You get the transcripts of that trial, mate. Have a look at some of the things they said about Jane in court. Made her sound like a total slag. Especially that copper, talking about what she was wearing . . .'

'It was handled badly,' Thorne said. 'Back then a lot of rapists got off, simple as that. I'm sure you're right about what happened to Jane, about Franklin.'

Foley took a drag, then a drink, and leaned back, nodding. He looked across at Thorne, like he was re-evaluating him.

Thorne glanced at Holland. Time to move on. As far as the interview went, they hadn't worked out a system – who would ask what, who was going to take the lead – they never did. Holland did the writing. That was about as far as it went.

'Did you know that Alan Franklin was dead?' Holland said. 'He died in 1996.'

Now it was Thorne's turn to do the evaluating. He studied Foley's face, trying to read the reaction. All he saw, or thought he saw, was momentary shock, and then delight.

'Fucking good,' Foley said. 'I hope it was painful.'

'It was. He was murdered.'

'Even better. Who do I send a thank-you letter to?'

Thorne stood up and began to wander about. Foley was getting altogether too comfortable. Thorne was not considering the man to be a suspect, not at the moment anyway, but he always preferred his interviewees on the back foot . . .

'Why do you think he did it, Peter?' Thorne said. 'Why did Dennis kill her?' Foley stared back at him, sucked his teeth. He emptied the last of the lager into his mouth and crushed the can in his hand.

Thorne repeated the question. 'Why did your brother kill his wife?'

'How should I know?'

'Did he believe what they said about Jane in court?'

'I don't . . .'

'He must have thought about it at least . . .'

'Den thought about a lot of things.'

'Did he think his wife was a slag?'

'Course he fucking didn't . . .'

'Maybe they had problems in bed afterwards . . .'

Foley leaned forward suddenly, dropped the empty can at his feet. 'Listen, Jane went weird afterwards, all right? She had a breakdown. She stopped going out, stopped talking to anyone, stopped doing anything at all. She was mates with this girl I was seeing at the time, you know, we all used to go out together, but after the trial, no . . . after the *rape*, she just wasn't there any more. Den pretended like everything was fine, but he was bottling it all up. He always did. So, when Franklin walked out of that court like Nelson fucking Mandela, like *he'd* been the victim . . .'

Thorne watched as Foley leaned back, *fell* back on the sofa and began to spin one of the half-dozen silver rings on the fingers of his left hand.

'Look, I don't know what Den thought, all right? He said some mad stuff at the time, but he was all over the place. They make you doubt things, don't they? That was their job in that court, to make the jury doubt, and they did a bloody good job. I mean, you're *supposed* to trust the police, aren't you, to believe them . . .?'

Foley looked up and across at Holland, then turned to look at Thorne. For the first time he looked his age. Thorne looked at the cracks across Peter Foley's face, saw hard drugs in his past and perhaps even in his present.

'Something snapped,' Foley said, quietly.

For no good reason that he could think of, Thorne took a step across the room and bent to pick up the beer can from the floor. He put it down on a dusty, chrome and glass shelving unit next to the TV, then turned back to Foley.

'What happened to the children?'

'Sorry . . .?'

'Mark and Sarah. Your nephew and niece. What happened to them afterwards?'

'Straight afterwards, you mean? After they found . . .?'

'Later on. Where did they go?'

'Into care. The police took them away and then the social services got involved. There was some counselling went on, I think. More so for the boy as I remember, he'd have been eight or nine . . .'

'He was seven. His sister was five.'

'Yeah, that sounds right.'

'So . . .?'

'So, eventually, they were fostered.'

'I see.'

'Look, there was only Jane's mum and she was already knocking on. No other way, really. I said I'd have the kids, me and my girlfriend, but nobody was very keen. I was only twenty-two . . .'

'And of course, your brother *had* just bashed their mother's brains out with a table lamp . . .'

'I said I'd have them. I *wanted* to have them . . .'

'So you stayed in touch with the kids?'

'Course . . .'

'Did you see much of them?'

'For a while, but they moved around. It wasn't always easy.'

'You've got the names and addresses?'

'Which . . .?'

'The foster parents'. You said the kids moved around. Were there many?'

'A few.'

'You've got all the details?'

'Not any more. I mean, I did then, yeah. There were Christmas cards, birthdays . . .'

'And then you just lost touch?'

'Well, you do, don't you?'

'So you'd have no idea at all where Sarah and Mark are living now?'

Foley blinked, laughed humourlessly. 'What, you mean you lot *haven't*?'

'We've traced every Mark Foley in the country. Every Sarah Foley or Sarah Whatever *née* Foley, and none of them remembers wandering into the hall and seeing their father dangling from a tow rope. Nobody recalls popping upstairs to find Mum lying in a pool of blood with her skull caved in. Call me old fashioned, but I don't think that sort of thing would slip your mind.'

Foley shook his head. 'I can't help you, mate. Even if I could, it would go against the bloody grain . . .'

Thorne looked at Holland. Time to go. As they stood up, Foley swung his legs up on to the sofa, reached down beside it for another can of lager.

'Before everything happened, before it all went tits up, Jane and Den were normal, you know? Just a normal couple with two kids and an OK house and all the rest of it. They were a good team, they were doing all right, and I reckon they'd have got over what that arsehole did to Jane. I mean, couples do, don't they, eventually, and Den would have helped her, because he loved her. But what came after, what happened to them in that trial, and the stuff later on . . . you don't get over that, ever. And that's down to *you*.'

Foley was talking about something that had happened a long time ago. He was talking about mistakes that it was too late to put right, and about a police officer long-since retired.

But he was pointing at Thorne.

EIGHTEEN

Thorne enjoyed expensive wine, but rather more often, cheap lager. This particular brand, which had caught his eye in the off-licence, was the same one Peter Foley had been drinking . . .

Another Saturday when he hadn't got home until gone ten o'clock. Eve would probably still have been up, he could have called, but he hadn't bothered. He had only managed to see her once in the last fortnight, and though they'd talked often on the phone, he'd sensed a tension starting to creep in. He was starting to use his workload as an excuse.

Thorne knew very well that when it came to relationships, he was basically bone idle. He'd been that way with the girls he'd copped off with in the fifth form, he'd been that way with his first serious girlfriends and he'd been that way with Jan. Happy to sink into a rut, wary of changing direction. Eventually, of course, Jan had changed direction herself. Got creative with her creative-writing lecturer . . .

All because he was comfortable being stuck in the mud, and now he could feel it going the same way with Eve.

There was the bed thing, for a kick-off. As he lay with his feet up on the sofa which would soon become his bed for another night, he thought about the whole, stupid business of his failure to buy a new mattress. The trip they'd arranged the week before had been cancelled for obvious reasons. He'd joked with Eve about burglars and murderers conspiring to keep them from shagging, but in reality, the delays had been . . . convenient. There *was* a part of him, a nasty part he was reluctant to acknowledge, that worried about how interested in Eve he would really be once he'd got her into bed, but that wasn't really the problem. At the end of the day, he was just plain, bloody lazy . . .

From his brand-new speakers came the mournful tones of Johnny Cash, singing his sublime version of Springsteen's 'Highway Patrolman'. As Cash sang about nothing feeling better than blood on blood, Thorne thought that if any voice could capture the love and agony, the hatred and the joy, of family ties, it was his. It helped if you'd lived it, of course.

On the floor, the cat was yowling, begging to be picked up. Thorne leaned down, put his can on the carpet and pulled her up on to his lap.

So often it came down to families . . .

He thought about Mark and Sarah Foley, whose family was torn apart in front of them, leaving each with no one save the other. A generation down the line and they were nowhere to be found. It could only be because they wanted it that way.

Mark Foley, now a man in his mid-thirties, once a terrified little boy in need of professional counselling. Had he grown up, the horror turning to hatred and festering inside him? Had he waited twenty years and then killed the man who'd raped his mother, the man he held responsible for her death and the suicide of his father? Right now, Mark Foley was as good a suspect as they had, but what had happened since 1996, between Alan Franklin's death and this new spate of killings? What had sparked off the cultivating and murdering of these completely unconnected rapists . . .?

Thorne had always known, somehow, that rape was key to the case. Hadn't he tried to explain it to Hendricks? The rape element in the killings of Remfry and Welch, and now of Howard Southern, had always felt significant. *More* significant than the killings themselves. Now, Thorne knew why. If he didn't fully understand it, he at least understood that it had a history . . .

And still that ambivalence on the part of so many involved in the investigation. A third victim and another convicted rapist. Older, yes, and a lot longer out of prison, but still a sex offender. Still a nonce. One for whom very few people, least of all those trying to catch his killer, seemed to be mourning.

And still that ambivalence, if Thorne was honest, on *his* part as well . . .

'*Seems to me that whoever killed Remfry did everyone a favour . . .*'

'*There will be people asking whether or not we should be grateful . . .*'

'*It's not like he's chopping up old ladies, is it?*'

Thorne found it hard to argue with the sentiments, but as someone who'd spent his entire adult life if not always catching killers, then at least believing that what they did was wrong, he had to try and stay out of it.

With some cases it was easy. Hate the killer, love the victim. Thorne would never forget the months he'd spent hunting a man who killed women while *trying* to put them into comas, into a state of living death. Or his last big one: tracking down a pair of killers, one a manipulative psychopath, the other who killed because he was told to . . .

Then there were the cases where it wasn't quite so clear-cut, where sympathies were not so easily divvied up: the wife, driven to murder an abusive husband; the armed robber, knocked off for grassing on his workmates; the drug-dealer, carved up by a rival . . .

Then there was this case.

When Thorne swung his legs on to the floor and stood up, Elvis jumped off and skulked away, grumbling, towards the kitchen. Thorne followed her. He dropped his empties into the bin, and for half a minute he stared into the fridge for no particular reason.

He walked into the bedroom, gathered up his duvet and pillow from the bottom of the wardrobe.

Thorne despised rapists. He also despised murderers. To go into which he despised more or less was not going to help anybody.

Eve and Denise had done for the best part of a bottle of red wine each. The laughter had been getting louder, and the language a good deal more earthy ever since the pizzas had been finished and the second bottle of red opened . . .

'Fuck him if he's not interested,' Denise said.

Eve swirled the wine around in her glass, stared through it. 'That's the thing though. He *is* interested, definitely.'

'Oh, you can tell, can you?'

'It wasn't hard . . .'

Denise gave a lascivious grin. 'Well, *that* usually means they aren't interested at all.'

Eve almost spat her wine across the table. When she'd finished laughing, she stood and began gathering up the pizza boxes. 'I don't know what he's up to. I'm not sure *he* knows what he's up to . . .'

Denise reached over, grabbed a last piece of cold pizza crust before the box got taken away. 'Maybe he's a schizo, like some of these nutters he tries to catch.'

'Maybe . . .'

'Does he talk about his work much? About the cases he's working on?'

Eve was folding the pizza boxes in half, crushing them down into the bin. She shrugged. 'Not really.'

'Oh come on, he must say something, surely?'

'We got into it a couple of weeks ago, this weird murder case.' Eve stepped across to the sink and began washing her hands. 'We ended up sort of arguing about it and he hasn't really mentioned it since.'

'Right. Except when he's using it as an excuse?'

'Maybe I'm being paranoid about that . . .'

Denise poured what was left in the bottle into her glass. She held the empty bottle aloft triumphantly. The bell rang.

'That'll be Ben,' Denise said. 'He had to stay late, get an edit finished.' She took a hearty mouthful of wine and all but skipped from the room.

Eve listened to her flatmate's feet as they hammered

down the stairs. She heard the squeal when the door was opened, the low moans as Ben stepped in and they embraced on the doorstep . . .

She made a quick decision to get off to bed before Ben came up. She would read for a while and try not to think too much about Tom Thorne, about whether he might ring the next day. She moved out into the hall, shouting down the stairs to Denise and Ben as she opened her bedroom door.

'I'm going to turn in, I think. See you in the morning . . .'

The last thing she wanted to watch was those two, all over each other.

The sun was streaming in through two vast windows at the far end of the narrow room, and yet the light was somehow cold, as if it were bouncing off the refrigerated doors and steel instruments of an autopsy suite.

Blinding white light, but Thorne knew very well that it was the middle of the night.

He wore pyjamas, with his brown leather jacket over the top. He moved quickly around the room, his steps jaunty, bouncing in time to a tune he could hear but not quite place.

The three beds were equidistant from one another, lined up precisely. The metal bedsteads made them look a little like hospital cots, but they were bigger, more comfortable. They were identical, each with thick pillows, a clean white cotton sheet and a body.

Thorne moved to the end of the first bed, wrapped his hands around the metal rail, and peered down at Douglas

Remfry. The arse poking into the air, the face buried in the sheet. He began to shake the bed, rattling the frame, shouting over the noise of it. He shook and shook and shouted, filled with contempt for who this man had once been, for what he had done.

'Come on then, up you get, you idle bastard. There's women out there begging for it. Up and at 'em . . .'

And, as the body shook on the bed, the skin began to slip off, until it lay on the sheet, gathered about the bare bones like dirty tights, rolled down around a pair of ankles.

Thorne laughed and pointed at what remained, at the rapist's skin and skeleton, sloughed away and contorted. 'For heaven's sake, Lazybones, are you ever going to get up out of that bed?'

He trotted across to the second bed, shook the flesh from Ian Welch's bones. All the time taking the piss. Feeling nothing for these dead men. For these lumps . . .

At Howard Southern's bed, Thorne paused and watched as the bed began to vibrate, something passing noisily beneath the floor. A shadow arced across the vast windows and Thorne looked up. He watched the movement, back and forth, until the smell hit him.

He laughed when he looked back at the beds, and saw what the bodies had become. What they had actually been all the time. Thorne could only presume that each had been expertly shat down on to the centre of their beds, by the body dangling at the end of a rope, high above them.

As soon as Thorne awoke, the dream began to slide away from him, the images sucked back into the darkness, until only the feelings remained. Scorn and anger and shame.

It was a little after two-thirty in the morning.

When even the feelings had faded, there were only thoughts of the woman whose defilement and death long before had, it seemed, caused everything. Now she moved through his case as surely as if she were still corporeal and Thorne was ready to embrace her.

She was nearly thirty years dead, and so was her killer, but that didn't matter.

In Jane Foley, Thorne had finally got a victim he could care about.

NINETEEN

It was Monday morning. Seven weeks to the day since the body of Douglas Remfry had been found. More than twenty-five years since Jane Foley had been raped and subsequently battered to death. Thorne was still trying to work out the connection between the two murders. He hoped that the woman sitting opposite him might be able to help . . .

Despite its somewhat dodgy reputation, and the tired old jokes about the IQs and sexual habits of its womenfolk, Essex was full of surprises. As the oldest recorded town in the country and the capital of Roman Britain, Colchester had more history than most places. Still, the last thing Thorne expected from a council building in the middle of town was what looked like a small stately home in its own grounds.

The area office for the Adoption and Fostering Service was somewhat run-down, admittedly, but amazing nonetheless. Thorne had thought that all the period or *faux*-period properties in the area had been snapped up by footballers and armed robbers a long time ago. The surprise was evidently clear in his face as he and Holland were greeted by the Service Manager, and shown into a large office with dark oak panelling all around, and heavy wooden beams criss-crossing an ornate ceiling above.

'This was originally the coach-house. I know it looks nice, but trust me, it's a bastard to work in . . .' Joanne Lesser was a light-skinned black woman in her mid-thirties, tall and – so Thorne thought – a little on the thin side. Her hair was straight and lacquered, the brows heavy, framing a face that was severe until it broke into a smile. Then, it was all too easy to picture her laughing at a dirty joke in spite of herself, or tipsy at the Christmas party.

'The place is falling to pieces, basically,' she said. 'We can only put so much weight on the floors, the filing cabinets have to go against certain walls and nothing's level. You can find your chair rolling from one side of the office to the other, if you're not careful . . .'

Thorne and Holland smiled politely, unsure as to whether or not she'd finished. After a few seconds, she shrugged and raised an eyebrow to indicate that *she* was waiting for *them*.

The only sound in the room came from a noisy, metal fan which looked like it might have been an antique itself. At the other end of the desk, an entire army of gonks, action figures and soft toys was lined up across the top edge of a grimy, beige computer.

'You spoke to DCI Brigstocke on the phone,' Thorne said. He raised his voice a little to make himself clearly heard above the fan. 'Mark and Sarah Foley?'

Lesser reached for a piece of paper on her desk and studied it.

'1976,' Holland added, trying to move things along.

'Right, well, I'm sure you weren't expecting it to be straightforward . . .' She looked up and across at them, smiling. Thorne couldn't quite manage one in return. 'All I can really tell you with any certainty is that they were never fostered by anybody who is still registered with us as an active carer.'

Holland shrugged. 'I suppose it *would* have been too much to hope for . . .'

'Right,' Thorne said. He had been hoping nevertheless.

'We're talking over twenty-five years ago,' Lesser said. 'It's possible that the people who fostered them *are* still active, but have moved to another area.'

'How do we check that?' Thorne said.

She shook her head. 'Not a clue. It's pretty unlikely anyway, I'm just thinking aloud, really . . .'

Thorne could feel a headache starting to build. He shuffled his chair a little closer to the desk, pointed to the fan. 'I'm sorry, could we . . .?'

She leaned across and switched the fan off.

'Thanks,' Thorne said. 'We'll try to get through this as fast as we can. Why was what you told us the only thing you could tell us *with any certainty*?'

'Because the only files I have access to here are current. Those are the ones concerned with active carers.'

'That's the stuff on computer?'

She snorted. 'It wasn't until ten years ago that things even started being *typed*, and even now there's still a load of stuff that's handwritten. It's not just the building that's past it . . .'

Thorne blinked slowly. It was just his luck to need help from an organisation whose systems were even more fucked up than the ones he worked with every day.

303

'But there *are* records, in one form or another, that go back further . . .'

'In one form or another, I suppose so. God knows what state they'll be in if you manage to lay your hands on them, a few scribbled pages nearly thirty years old. Hang on, some are on microfiche, I think . . .'

Thorne tried not to sound too impatient. 'There are records though?'

'Dead files . . .'

'Right, and the dead files, the files that would have the records from the mid-seventies, will be stored somewhere?'

'Yeah, they should be in Chelmsford, at County Hall. The law says we have to keep them.'

Holland muttered. 'Data Protection Act . . .'

'That's it. Everybody who's received a service from us has a right to see their records, to have access. Some people wait years. They come back in their forties or fifties, looking for details on people who fostered them when they were kids.'

'How come it takes them so long?' Holland said.

'Maybe it's the distance that makes them appreciate it. At the time, when they're kids, it can be a bit traumatic . . .'

Thorne thought about Mark and Sarah Foley. Anything they went through as foster children could not possibly have been more traumatic than what had happened before. 'What do you tell them?' he asked. 'These people that come looking.'

'Good luck.' She leaned back on her chair, took the material of her blouse between thumb and forefinger and pulled it from her skin. She flapped it back and forth, blew down on to her chest. 'We've got the records, but I couldn't really tell you where. Like I said, they *should* be over at County Hall, but laying your hands on them is another matter.'

Joanne Lesser smiled a *nothing I can do* smile and Thorne remembered a similar moment: he and Holland sitting in almost identical positions in Tracy Lenahan's office at Derby Prison. It seemed like a long time back. A few deaths ago . . .

Thorne rolled his head around on his neck. 'I know that we're talking about stuff that dates back a long way and you've made it clear that the system's not all it should be, but surely there's some sort of central storage place . . .?'

'Sorry, I thought I'd explained. We only have the active files because each time you move, each time the office relocates, you leave the dead files behind. Now, in theory, they should get taken back to County Hall and, like you say, stored somewhere. In reality, stuff just gets chucked in boxes. It goes missing . . .'

'Why would you move?'

'Council buildings are interchangeable. Somebody could decide tomorrow that this should be the new headquarters for the DSS or Refuse Collection. Unless the council renews the lease, this place might be a hotel in a couple of years.'

'Right. So, have you moved often?'

'I've only been doing this ten years and we've moved three – no, four – times since I started.' Thorne had to fight quite hard to stop himself swearing, or kicking a hole in the front of the desk. 'It gets worse. I know that some stuff got destroyed a couple of years ago when part of the archive was flooded . . .'

Thorne and Holland exchanged a glance. They were catching every red light . . .

'What about school records?' Lesser said. 'You might have more luck . . .'

Holland glanced down at his notebook. 'They attended local primary and secondary schools until 1984, after which there's no record of them.'

She considered this. 'Are you sure they're still alive?'

'We're not really sure about anything,' Thorne said. In truth, the idea that Mark and Sarah Foley might be dead was something that had been only briefly considered. It had even been suggested that the suicide of Dennis Foley might be a second murder made to *look* like a suicide. That whoever had been responsible might have wanted the children dead too. Half an hour spent looking at the files on the original case, at the post-mortem report on Dennis Foley, had soon put paid to that clever theory.

'This is probably clutching at straws,' Holland said, 'but I don't suppose there's anybody still working here, in your department, who was around back in 1976?'

'Sorry. Staff tend to move around as often as the offices do.'

'A bit like footballers,' Holland said.

'I wish we got paid as much.' Thorne thought the smile she gave Holland was of an altogether different sort from the one she'd given him.

Thorne shifted on his chair. It was enough to drag Holland's eye from Joanne Lesser back to him. Time to go.

'Right, well, thanks . . .'

'It's a long way back,' she said.

306

Holland reached for his jacket. 'There shouldn't be too much traffic at this time of the day . . .'

'No, I meant you're going back a long way. To look for these people, for Mark and Sarah Foley. I mean, what about National Insurance? DVLA? Sorry, I don't want to teach my grandmother to suck eggs, but . . .'

'It's OK,' Thorne said.

She leaned forward in her chair. 'Why do you want to find them?'

Holland stuffed his notebook away. 'I'm sorry, but we can't really . . .'

Thorne cut him off. What did it matter? 'They were fostered after their parents died. Their father killed their mother and then himself. The children discovered the bodies.' Lesser's lower jaw sagged a little. 'We think that what happened back then is connected with a series of murders that we're investigating now.'

'A *series*?' She spoke it like it was a magic word.

'Yes.'

'They're connected to it, you mean? Mark and Sarah Foley?'

Thorne could see a flush developing at the top of her chest. Her voice was suddenly a little higher. She was excited.

Thorne stood up and began pulling on his leather jacket. 'Listen, Joanne, we'll be sending someone down to County Hall to start looking for these records. I'm sure you're busy, but we'd be very grateful if you could give him as much help as you can . . .'

She rolled her chair back and stood too. 'You don't need to send anyone. I'd be happy to do it for you. I mean, yes,

I *am* pretty busy, but I can find the time.' The flush had moved up to the base of her throat. 'I'll probably be quicker on my own, to be honest. You know, without somebody else getting in the way . . .'

Thorne thought about her offer. It sounded like such a wild-goose chase that he'd probably only be wasting an officer anyway. He nodded. 'Thanks.'

At the door, while Holland took down Lesser's phone number and handed her a card, Thorne stared at the posters on the wall next to the door. One image in particular caught his eye: a girl and a boy, hand in hand, staring straight at the camera, their moist, round eyes begging. They were much younger than Mark and Sarah Foley would have been, no bigger than toddlers, and they were almost certainly actors. Still, their faces held Thorne's attention . . .

He tensed a little when he felt Lesser's hand on his arm.

'It's funny,' she said, 'to think that people can just slip through the net like that, isn't it?'

Thorne nodded, thinking that some people were a lot more slippery than others.

Driving back through the town centre, Holland talked about Joanne Lesser. He joked about the sort of woman who looked like she wouldn't say boo to a goose and then went home and lay in the bath, one hand holding some gruesome true-crime book, while the other . . .

Thorne wasn't paying too much attention. He felt as though someone had poured concrete in through his ears. The thoughts floundered in his head, sticky and dismal, while his face, as always, was easy to read.

'Like she said, we *were* going a long way back,' Holland said. 'Probably wasting our time. We'll find them somewhere else . . .'

Thorne grunted. Holland was right, but all the same, he had been counting on something a bit more positive.

Holland made for the motorway, heading out of town along the line of the Roman wall. From here at St Mary's of the Wall, during the English Civil War, a vast Royalist cannon named Humpty Dumpty was said to have fallen, later to be immortalised in the children's nursery rhyme. They passed the ancient entrance to the town, through which Claudius, the invading Emperor, had once ridden into Colchester on the back of an elephant. Thorne found it strange that two thousand years later, whether by accident or design, the far more recent history of ordinary people could be so impenetrable.

'I'm betting Miss Marple back there's already rootling through her dead files,' Holland said. He laughed, and Thorne dredged up something that might have been a smile, if one half of his face had been paralysed. 'What d'you reckon?'

Thorne reckoned that he'd been right about chasing leads. This one had sounded solid, like it wasn't going anywhere. Now it had put on a burst of speed and Thorne felt as if he could do nothing but watch it disappear into the distance.

The slice of white bread in Peter Foley's hand was blackened with dabs of newsprint from his fingers. He looked at his hands. There were still scabs on a couple of the knuckles, and oil beneath his fingernails from where he'd spent the morning tinkering with his motorbike. He used the bread to mop up the last of his gravy, then picked up his mug of tea and leaned back against the red, plastic banquette.

He stared out of the café window and watched the cars drift by. He thought about his family. The dead and the disappeared.

Bumming around . . .

That's what he'd told those fuckers, when they'd asked what he was doing back when it had happened, and it was pretty much all he'd done since as well. Holding down a job, once he'd got back into the swing of things, had become difficult. He'd developed a tendency to take things the wrong way, to react badly to a tasteless comment or a funny look. He couldn't say for sure that what had happened was responsible. He might always have been destined to be a shiftless loser with a tendency towards casual violence, but what the fuck, it was comforting to have something to blame.

To have some*body* to blame.

He should have moved away from the area. There was always some old dear with an opinion, or a pair of young mums whispering and shielding their children. Always some interfering fucker, willing to tell any woman he got close to all about his happy family. People had good memories. Not as good as his, though . . .

He remembered the argument he'd had with Den a couple of days before it had happened. He'd wanted to come round, had asked Den why nobody had seen Jane for a while, if everything was all right. Den had lost it and told him to mind his own business, said that he knew very well what was going on. He remembered his brother's face, the trembling around the mouth as he'd accused him of fancying Jane, all but suggesting they'd been screwing behind his back. He remembered the guilt he'd felt, then and afterwards, because he *did* fancy Jane and always had.

And he remembered the faces of the children, the last time he'd seen them, before that cow from the social services had driven them away. Sarah had been quiet, she'd probably not really understood what was going on, but the boy's face, *Mark's* face, pressed against the back window of that car, had been streaked with snot and tears.

He slid out of the booth, grabbed his paper, and strolled across to the counter to pay for his lunch.

He thought about his nephew and his niece and hoped that they were together somewhere a long way away. A place where nobody could ever find them and fuck their new lives up.

The afternoon stretched ahead. He would go back and lie down and wait for it to get dark. Then he would put some metal on, and drink. He would empty can after can, until the noise inside his head was quieter than the screech and the smash of the music that would be filling his bedroom.

When they got back to Becke House, Thorne filled Kitson and Brigstocke in on how things had gone in Colchester. They conferred about progress on the other flank of the operation. The Southern killing had plenty in common with those that had gone before: the cause of death; the layout of the murder scene; the wreath ordered in person from an out-of-hours floristry service – this time delivered as far as the hotel-room doorway, then hurriedly dropped after one look at the state of its recipient.

But there were plenty of differences too. There were new avenues which had to be explored . . .

Southern had been released from prison more than ten years previously. He hadn't been selected in the same way as the previous victims, and he was certainly approached differently. Unlike Remfry or Welch, he had a whole life that had to be sifted through if they were going to find out just how the killer had made himself part of it. Interviews, running into many hundreds, were still being conducted with anyone who had contact with Southern: the people he worked with; the friends he drank with; the members of the gym he worked out at; the girlfriend he'd recently broken up with . . .

These people who had been part of his new life, would, for the most part, have had no idea that Howard Southern had once served time in prison. Even if he'd told any of them – and with some people it *might* have gained him kudos, or a round of drinks – chances are he wouldn't have told them what for.

Unfortunately for him, someone had found out *exactly* what Howard Southern had once done, and had killed him for it.

In his office, Thorne went through his mail. As always, it was mostly junk. Pointless memos, press releases, crime statistics, new initiative outlines. He glanced through the monthly Police Federation newsletter, at a story about a local force recording themselves whistling the theme tunes to a host of well-known police TV shows. These recordings were being broadcast in some of the rougher estates and shopping centres in an effort to deter street criminals.

When Thorne had finished laughing, he checked his messages. There'd already been a call from Joanne Lesser to say that she'd start checking the records the following morning, and that some files had apparently been moved from County Hall to a new storage facility on an industrial estate just outside Chelmsford. The next one was from Chris Barratt at Kentish Town. There was nothing from Eve . . .

Thorne picked up the phone, wondering at the sharp twinge of disappointment he felt. He marvelled, as he dialled, at his seemingly endless capacity for indecision, for fucking about . . .

'About bloody time too,' he said.

'Calm down,' Barratt said. 'We haven't got him yet. But we know exactly who he is. We'll pull him first thing tomorrow morning.'

'How did you find him?'

'Are you listening? This is funny as fuck . . .'

'Go on . . .'

'He'd got rid of the stereo, right? Probably shifted it the same day, got himself off his tits on the proceeds. Then, he has a problem . . .'

'Which is?'

'Your taste in music.'

'Eh?'

'The poor sod's had to make himself a bit conspicuous in the end. We got the nod eventually because by all accounts he's spent the last four weeks trying to get rid of your bloody CD collection.'

'What?' Thorne's relief was all but cancelled out by his outrage . . .

By now, Barratt was making no attempt to hide his enjoyment. 'Couldn't *pay* anybody to take 'em off his hands, by all accounts. Been dragging them round every market and second-hand place in London . . .'

'Enjoy yourself, Chris. As long as I get them all back.'

'Listen, if I was you, when you *do* get them back, why don't you stick a few by the window, where people can see them. You know, as a deterrent . . .'

'I'm not listening. Just call me when you've nicked him, all right?'

'Fine . . .'

'And I'll want five minutes.'

'No problem. I'm here all day . . .'

'Not with you, smartarse. With *him* . . .'

TWENTY

He'd seen comedians on TV talking about how women could hold a hundred thoughts in their heads at one time and juggle an assortment of tasks, while men were incapable of doing even two things at once. Wanking and manoeuvring a mouse was about as much as a man could manage.

Even though he knew it was nonsense, he still found the joke funny. Even as he sat working *and* planning the next killing . . .

Multi-tasking was something of a speciality, had to be, and even though the slightly more socially unacceptable stuff he did was the more exciting, he actually enjoyed the day job too. He took pride in what he did. Of course, he couldn't have done the other things without it.

The next killing . . .

He didn't know for certain yet if the next would also be the last, but in a lot of ways it made sense. It would round things off very nicely. This one would be different in many ways of course, more symbolic than the others, but certainly no less enjoyable for it.

A date had yet to be set, but that was the final detail. The victim had been selected weeks ago. In fact, he'd pretty much selected himself.

Talk about being in the wrong place at the wrong time . . .

Thorne thought about the Restorative Justice Conference he'd sat through weeks earlier. He remembered Darren Ellis and the squeak of his shiny, white training shoes. He pictured the face of the old man who'd been sitting more or less where he was now . . .

Opposite him, in the Interview Room at Kentish Town station, sat a boy who Thorne knew to be seventeen, but, apart from the unexcited eyes, the rest of him might have belonged to any skinny-arsed fourth-former. Noel Mullen was stealing cars to order while others his age had been nicking pens and pick 'n' mix from Woolworth's. By the time his contemporaries were sneaking into pubs and feeling up girls, Noel had already acquired a decent-sized drugs habit and a growing reputation with the police in North-west London. There was a room that should have had his name on the door, in the young offenders' institute that at one time had welcomed both his elder brothers.

He still looked as if his mum should be washing his underpants and pouring the milk on his Rice Krispies . . .

'Why did you shit in my bed?' Thorne said.

The boy did a pretty good job of looking unutterably bored, but there was a jerkiness to the seemingly casual roll of the head, a tremor at the ends of the fingers. Thorne wondered how long it had been since he'd had a fix. Maybe not since he'd failed to sell Thorne's CDs, to turn Cash into cash and score with it . . .

'Come on, Noel . . .'

'What's the fucking point? You going to put in a good word for me, are you? Speak up for me in court?'

'No chance.'

'So why should I bother talking to you?'

Thorne leaned back and folded his arms. 'Listen, break into places, Noel, by all means. It's your job, after all. Break in and trash them a bit if you have to, while you're looking for the decent stuff, the gear that's going to score you the best deal. I can understand that, I really can.

'Not just the posh places, either. Don't just do the rich bastards who you might, *might* have a legitimate reason to enjoy turning over. No, why not rob from your own? Dump on your doorstep. Do the ordinary, working idiots who live on your own estate, on the poxy estate that you've already done your best to make that little bit worse than it would have been anyway, by pissing in the lift and leaving dirty needles all over what passes for a playground. Smash your neighbour's door in and see how high a black and white TV can get you. Or some cheap jewellery. Fuck it, any *good* stuff, the widescreens and the DVDs, will have been rented anyway, so who cares? Stupid fuckers aren't insured, that's not your fault, is it . . .?'

'Jesus, have you finished?'

'Do it and feel nothing. See something and take it, because all that matters is what you might be able to get for it. Feel fuck all . . .'

'You're wasting your . . .'

'*Feel fuck all.* Then see how you feel when one day one of your mates needs some cash and puts his foot through your mother's window. Size-nine Nikes tramping around your mum's living room, and going through her drawers.

317

And maybe your mate's a little bit wired, a little bit over the edge, and maybe your mother's lying there in bed at the time . . .'

'It's because you're a copper.'

Thorne stopped, took a breath and waited.

'That's why I took a shit on your bed, all right?'

It made sense. Thorne wasn't so poor a detective that he hadn't considered the possibility that his flat had been targeted. That was the problem with Neighbourhood Watch. You didn't always know which neighbours were watching . . .

'How did you know?' Thorne asked.

'I didn't, not before I got in there. There was a photo that had fallen down behind one of your speakers. You, in your fucking PC Plod outfit . . .'

Mullen leaned back and folded his arms as Thorne had done. He looked at him, as he might look at a stereo or a VCR, evaluating it, working out whether it was worth taking.

'Your hair was darker then,' Mullen said. 'And you weren't such a fat cunt.'

Thorne nodded. He remembered the photo, had wondered where it had gone. It wasn't a picture he was hugely fond of, but still, Mullen's response when he'd seen it a few weeks earlier had been a bit harsh.

'So, you take one look at an old photo and decide to use my bed as a crapper, that about right?'

Mullen grinned, starting to enjoy himself. His teeth were browning where they met the gums. 'Yeah, more or less . . .'

'You cocky little strip of piss . . .'

Thorne's movement, and the scrape of his chair across

the floor, caused Mullen to jerk back and stiffen, momentarily defensive. He appeared to recover his confidence just as quickly.

'Look, it was nothing personal.'

'And it won't be personal when I come round there, knock you over and shit in your mouth, fair enough? I'm a copper and you're a burglar. Right, Noel? Clearly there's certain things we *have* to do . . .'

Mullen's expression was closer to pity than boredom. 'You're not going to do anything.'

Other than strike a few poses to try to make himself feel better, there was nothing that Thorne *could* do. He wondered if the old man he'd seen sitting opposite Darren Ellis had felt as useless.

'Are you sorry, Noel?'

'Am I what?'

'Sorry. Are you sorry?'

'Yeah. I'm sorry I got fucking caught.'

Thorne's smile was genuine. A certain warped faith had been restored by Mullen's honesty. Perhaps, faced with a few years' hard time, he would learn a trick or two, learn how to turn it on in the same way that Darren Ellis had. For now, there was something heartening about Mullen's answer. Something reassuring about the fact that he really and truly didn't give a toss.

There was a moment when Thorne almost liked him.

The moment passed, and for a minute and more, Thorne stared into Mullen's unexcited eyes until the boy jumped up, moved quickly across the room and began banging on the door.

★

Stone took the call, held the receiver out towards Holland. 'For you . . .'

As Holland walked across their small office, Stone put his hand over the receiver. 'She sounds sexy as well.'

Holland said nothing and took the phone. He'd pretty much learned to put up with Stone's arrogance, but he still got impatient with the smirks and the shrugs and the knowing looks that actually knew fuck all.

Mind you, these days, he got impatient with a lot of things.

'DC Holland.'

'This is Joanne Lesser . . .'

'Oh, hello, Joanne.' Holland looked up to see Stone rolling his eyes and mouthing her name. Holland casually stuck up a finger.

'No luck on the actual files yet,' she said. 'I did leave a message yesterday. About some of them being moved?'

'OK. I didn't see that, but . . .'

'Don't worry, I'm still working on it. I found out something else, though.'

'Right . . .' Holland picked up a pen, began to doodle as he listened.

'A colleague on the team here reckons that the old index cards, from years back, are all piled up down in our cellar. I'll try and dig them out, presuming they haven't all gone rotten . . .'

'Do you think the cards for Mark and Sarah Foley will be down there?'

'That's why I rang. I don't see why not. There's probably not much information, they're just small cards, you know? The proper files are probably six inches thick . . .'

'What's on them?' Holland glanced up to see Stone staring across at him, interested.

'Usually just the basic stuff,' Lesser said. 'Case number, DOBs, placement dates and names of carers . . .'

Holland stopped doodling, wrote down 'names & dates'. 'That sounds great, Joanne. Really helpful . . .'

'I'll call you when I've got the information then, shall I?'

'Can you e-mail it? Probably safer . . .'

When he thanked her again for her trouble, he could almost *hear* the blushing.

'Sounded good,' Stone said, after Holland had hung up.

'Reckons she can get us a list of all the kids' foster parents,' Holland explained. 'The dates they were placed in care . . .'

Stone looked thoughtful. 'Is she going to carry on looking for the full files?'

'Probably no stopping her, but I reckon these names and dates are as much as we're going to need.'

'Let me know when you get them,' Stone said. 'I'll give you a hand on it.'

Holland leaned back, stretched. 'Shouldn't be much to do. I think I can manage it on my own . . .'

'Please yourself.' Stone looked back to his computer screen, began to type.

Holland knew that it had been a fairly petty moment of self-assertion. More so, considering that he didn't really consider it to be a worthwhile line of inquiry in the first place. Thorne had got a bee in his bonnet about it, so Holland would do what needed doing, but he couldn't help thinking that they were almost certainly wasting their time.

He didn't see how knowing where Mark and Sarah

Foley had been twenty-five years ago was going to help them find out where they were now.

Thorne stepped out of the tube station on to Kentish Town Road. He turned for home, walking down in the direction of Camden, and the police station in which he'd encountered Noel Mullen nearly twelve hours before.

He thought about what the boy had said . . .

'*I'm sorry I got fucking caught*'

. . . and wondered if he'd ever make the killer of Remfry, Welch, Southern and Charlie Dodd sorry. He had a feeling that if he *did* catch him, it would be just about the only thing the killer *would* be sorry about.

Thorne was vacillating, standing on the pavement outside the Bengal Lancer, when his phone beeped. He listened to the message, then pressed the hash button to call Eve straight back.

The apology wasn't the first thing he said but it was pretty close.

'I'm sorry . . .'

'For what?'

'Lots of things. Not calling, for starters.'

'I know you've been busy.'

The owner of the restaurant, a man who knew Thorne very well, saw him through the window. He started waving, beckoning him inside. Thorne waved back, mouthing and pointing at the phone.

'Where are you?' Eve asked.

'Just heading home, trying to decide what to do about dinner.'

'Stressful day?'

Maybe she'd heard it in his voice. He laughed. 'I'm thinking about chucking it all in, becoming a florist.'

'Bloom and Thorne sounds good . . .'

'Actually, no, I don't think I could stand the early mornings.'

'You lazy bastard . . .'

And the sights, the sounds, the *smells* of Thorne's dream came straight back to him. He shivered, though it was warm enough to be walking around with his jacket thrown across his arm . . .

'Tom?'

'Sorry . . .' He blinked the pictures away. 'You said something about Saturday. In your message . . .'

'I know you're probably working late.'

'No, I'm not, for once. I'm signed out for most of the day. Unless something comes up.' *An urgent meeting, a new lead, another body.* 'So, should be fine . . .'

'It's not a big deal, but it's Denise's birthday, so her and me and Ben are going to be in the pub Saturday night. That's it, really. Just come along if you fancy it.'

'What, a double date?'

'No. I just thought you might prefer it. No pressure . . .'

'Pressure?'

'Well, you have been sort of . . . blowing hot and cold . . .'

'Sorry . . .'

There was a pause. Thorne caught sight of the owner again, throwing up his hands. He heard Eve move the receiver from one ear to the other.

'Look, I'm sorry too,' she said. 'I didn't want to get into this on the phone. Let's just have a drink on Saturday. Take it from there.'

'That sounds good. I'll have something to show you as well.'

Thorne enjoyed listening to the laugh that he hadn't heard in a while. He pictured the gap in the teeth. 'Cut out the dirty talk,' she said. 'And go and get something to eat . . .'

A few minutes later, ten minutes since he'd first arrived outside the restaurant, and Thorne was still trying to decide what to do. There was stuff in the fridge he could eat. *Should* eat . . .

He pushed open the door, the smell of the Indian food just too good to resist. His friend, the owner, had already opened a bottle of Kingfisher.

TWENTY-ONE

'Who are you rooting for this afternoon then, Dave?'

Holland looked up from his desk to see DS Sam Karim beaming down at him. 'Sorry . . .?'

'The Charity Shield. Who d'you want to win it?'

Holland nodded. The traditional game on the eve of the season proper. Last year's FA Cup winners versus the Premiership champions.

'Whichever team isn't Manchester United,' Holland said.

'Suit yourself, mate, we'll still walk it. I fancy us for the league again as well.'

'I don't understand, Sam. You're from Hounslow, aren't you?'

Karim wandered away, still smiling. 'You're just jealous . . .'

Holland picked up the phone again and dialled. He didn't actually care one way or the other about football. Virtually everything he knew or understood about the game had been encapsulated in that fifteen-second conversation.

The line was still engaged. He hung up and looked back at his notes. Since Joanne Lesser had e-mailed the information across the day before, Holland had been working through the list of names pretty solidly. He was getting there, but it had been frustrating. Despite his bravado with Andy Stone, simply getting hold of people was sometimes tricky, even if the people themselves had no reason whatsoever to make it difficult.

The Foley children had spent the six months after the death of their parents in short-term foster care. Then, in January 1977, they'd begun the first of half a dozen long-term placements. There were still two sets of foster parents Holland had yet to speak to, but from the conversations he'd already had, a pattern had emerged. In almost every instance, the children had appeared to settle quite quickly, but had gradually become sullen and disruptive, especially in families where there were existing children. Those Holland spoke to admitted that it had been difficult, but also thought that it was understandable, considering what the children had been through. Mark and Sarah were basically nice kids, but had withdrawn, spending more and more time alone, trying to shut out everybody around them . . .

It was all interesting enough, but Holland was still not convinced that any of it would prove to be of any use. He had not yet spoken to the most recent set of foster parents and that might at least turn up *something* they could work with. Brigstocke was mooting the idea of getting photos of the Foley children, digitally ageing them, and circulating the resulting images. It seemed a decent enough idea. The Nobles, who had cared for the children up to the beginning of 1984, were due back from Majorca later that day, and were likely to have the most recent pictures . . .

Holland reached for the phone. The number for the

Lloyds, the third set of foster parents, was still busy. The instant he put the phone down, it began to ring.

It was Thorne.

'Fancy a drink tonight?' he said.

'Why not?' As soon as the words came out of his mouth, Holland knew *exactly* why not, as he felt instantly guilty. He knew, on a Saturday night especially, he should talk to Sophie first. He also knew very well that she would smile and say she didn't mind. 'Where are we going?'

'Bar in Hackney,' Thorne said.

Holland could picture himself picking up his jacket and turning for the door, catching a glimpse as the film of tears formed in a moment across Sophie's eyes. He could already hear the bang of the door as he pulled it shut behind him, and feel each heavy step down towards the street like a low punch.

'What time?' Holland said.

'About half eight. Why don't I pick you up?'

'Eh? Kentish Town to the Elephant and then back up to Hackney? That's miles out of your way . . .'

'I don't mind.'

'I'll just get the tube up to Bethnal Green and walk.'

'No, it's fine, really . . .'

'What's this bar called? I'll meet you there.'

Thorne's tone of voice told him that there was little point in arguing. 'I'll be round at eight-thirty, Dave . . .'

Thorne had rung the bell then walked back to strike the appropriate pose. By the time Holland emerged from his flat, Thorne was leaning on the car, grinning, like some sixties motorshow model gone very much to seed.

'Right,' Holland said. 'So the insurance money came through, then?'

'Not yet, but it *will*. I borrowed a bit from the bank.' Holland stood, hands in pockets, looking extremely unsure. 'It's a BMW,' Thorne added, just in case Holland was in any doubt.

'It's a very *old* BMW . . .'

'It's a classic. This is a three-litre CSi. These are vintage cars, mate.'

'It's yellow.'

'It's *pulsar* yellow.'

'Pardon me.' Holland began a slow walk around the car. To Thorne, he looked like he was examining a freshly discovered corpse.

Thorne pointed in through the car window. 'It's got leather seats . . .'

Holland was at the back of the car. He looked at the registration plate. 'P? When's that . . .?'

'There's a CD player mounted in the boot. Holds ten CDs . . .'

'What year is it?'

Thorne knew there was no way to make it sound good. '1975 . . .'

Holland laughed. 'Christ, it's almost as old as I am.'

'There's only fifty-eight thousand miles on it . . .'

'You've gone mental. Did you have it checked for rust?'

'Yeah, I had a look. Seems fine . . .'

'Underneath, I mean. Did you get it jacked up?'

'It was restored four years ago and the bloke told me it's only done ten thousand miles since the engine was rebuilt.'

'How much did you pay for it?'

'The clutch is virtually brand new . . . or it might be the gearbox. One of them's new, anyway . . .'

'Five grand?' Thorne said nothing. 'More? Bloody hell, there's no way you'll get anywhere near that for the Mondeo . . .'

'It's a present, all right? I've got fuck all else to spend money on.'

'You don't know anything about old cars. You could have got something nearly new for the same money, something nice like that hire car you had. This'll cost you a fortune in the long run . . .'

'It's gorgeous, though, don't you think?' Thorne took a tissue from his pocket and began polishing the badge on the car's bonnet.

Holland shrugged, opened the car door. 'Doesn't matter when you're sitting on the hard shoulder, does it?'

Thorne stomped sulkily round to the driver's side of the car. 'I've a good mind to make you *walk* to fucking Hackney now. Miserable sod . . .'

'I'm just trying to be practical. What happens when the big end goes on the way to a murder scene?'

Thorne dropped down into the leather seat, turned to Holland who was sinking into his. 'Next time, I'll ask Trevor Jesmond if he fancies a drink . . .'

An hour later, Thorne's mood had improved significantly. Once the introductions had been made, Eve and the others had rushed straight out to look at the car and everyone agreed that it was gorgeous. It didn't stop Holland looking for an ally a little later on, while the girls were getting a round in.

'Come on, Ben, wouldn't you have gone for something a bit newer?'

'Sorry, I think it's great,' Jameson said. 'I've got a BMW myself . . .'

Thorne held his bottle up in salute, threw Holland a sarcastic smile. 'See?'

'Tom says you make films.'

'Corporate videos, mostly.'

'Well, you must be doing pretty well. BMW . . .'

'It's OK, but I'm trying to get something of my own off the ground. Something I've written . . .'

Holland nodded. 'That's hard, I suppose?'

'It's just a question of money. I need to do a bit more top-end work for Sony or Deutsche Bank and make a few less crappy training videos.'

'What are you doing at the moment?' Thorne said.

Jameson took a swig from a bottle of Budvar. 'Oh, it's riveting stuff right now. An ongoing local authority gig and some adverts for QVC.'

Thorne grabbed some crisps from an open bag in front of him. 'Oh, so they're your fault, are they?'

'Sorry,' Jameson said, smiling, holding up his hands.

Holland smirked at Thorne. 'I didn't have you down as a fan of the shopping channel.'

'I have Sky for the football, obviously.' Thorne shoved the crisps into his mouth, wiped his fingers. 'But when I've got nothing better to do late at night, I like to watch some failed actor with an orange face try and sell me cleaning equipment, yes.'

The three sat in silence for a while. Thorne looked out of the window and across to where he'd parked the car.

Holland sipped his pint, nodded his head to the low-level Coldplay track, while Jameson looked eagerly across to where Denise and Eve were standing at the bar.

The car was safe and still looking good. Thorne turned back and stared around. It was a newish but already quietly trendy gastro-pub. Eve had said there was a decent restaurant in a room out the back but Thorne was happy enough where they were, with Belgian lager on draft and olives in bowls on the bar. They sat in a corner, around a scarred, refectory-type table on an assortment of chairs. Thorne had bagged a battered but comfortable leather armchair, and was doing his best to keep a similar one next to him free for Eve.

Though the place was popular, the bar itself was not crowded. Most people seemed eager to take advantage of the warm night and had gathered around the few tables on the pavement outside. The bar wasn't air-conditioned, but fans were spinning around overhead and the beer – as much as Thorne was allowing himself to drink – was cold.

The car was partly responsible for his mood, but Thorne was feeling as genuinely relaxed as he had for quite some while.

Eve and Denise came back with more beers and a bottle of wine, and having clearly geed themselves up at the bar, gently took the piss out of Holland, Thorne and Jameson, for no better reason than that they were blokes. The men, for all their protestations and denials, enjoyed every minute of it, Thorne especially relishing the sort of attention he hadn't enjoyed for a very long time.

They talked about football and television and house prices. And inevitably, work.

'Come on then, Dave,' Denise said. 'Tell us about this nutter you're after, the one who was on Eve's answering machine . . .'

Eve tried to interrupt. 'Den . . .!' She turned to Thorne. 'Sorry . . .'

Thorne shrugged, not caring. 'It's fine.'

'Well, yes, he's a nutter,' Holland said. 'And yes, we're after him. *Still* after him.'

'He sounds twisted,' Jameson said. 'Fascinating, though . . .'

Denise leaned forward towards Holland. 'You know there's people like that around, course you do. When you've got a connection with one of them, though, however tenuous, it's freaky.'

'Don't worry,' Holland said. 'You're not his type.'

'I know. He hunts men, doesn't he? Men who've hurt women . . .'

There was a short but noticeably uncomfortable silence, which Denise broke as if it had never happened.

'People are always going to be fascinated by this sort of stuff though, aren't they? It's a bit ghoulish, I suppose, but it's a damn sight more interesting than computers . . .'

Thorne took this as the cue to retell, for Holland's benefit, his joke about what a PC 'going down' meant in their line of work. The others laughed graciously, and Denise and Ben carried on chatting to Holland about the job. Whether they liked him or were just trying to make sure he didn't feel like a gooseberry, it gave Thorne the chance to talk to Eve.

He bumped his chair up close to hers and leaned across.

'This was a good idea,' he said.

332

'You weren't sure though, were you?' She nodded towards Holland. 'So you brought reinforcements along . . .'

'Are you pissed off?'

'I was an hour ago, yes. It's fine though.'

Thorne reached for his drink. 'I just wanted to show him the car . . .'

Eve gave him a long look. It was clear that she didn't quite believe him. 'So, apart from your case getting a bit more complicated, what happened between the night you came round for dinner and now?' Thorne glanced down, swilled the beer around in his glass, said nothing. 'I thought you were really keen. You said as much.'

'I was . . .'

'Even that night when you walked me back after we'd been in the pub you were a bit weird. Ever since you went to that wedding, in fact . . .'

Thorne bent his head and lowered his voice. 'Look, I just go a bit mental when it looks like things might get serious. I don't know what I want, and I start to get . . .'

'Serious? We haven't even slept together yet . . .'

'That's exactly what I mean. It looked like we were going to. You know, it was on the cards, so maybe I just started backing away a bit.'

'All that bollocks with the new bed . . .'

'I suppose so.'

Eve turned to look at him. She waited a second or two until he raised his head and met her stare. 'So, what do you want now, Tom?'

A smile spread slowly across Thorne's face. He leaned over, his arm dropping down into the well of Eve's chair and slipping behind her waist. 'I want to go to a hotel . . .'

For a moment Eve looked shocked, but then she began to smile too. 'What, tonight?'

'Why not? Shop's shut tomorrow, isn't it? I've got a nice car outside . . .'

Eve looked across to where Denise and Jameson were still deep in conversation with Holland. 'God, it's a fantastic idea, but it's a bit awkward. It's Den's birthday . . .'

'Pretend it's mine.'

'I don't know, I can't just bugger off.'

'She won't mind.'

Eve grabbed Thorne's hand and squeezed. 'Let me see what I can do . . .'

An hour later, as they hovered outside, saying goodbyes, Eve took Thorne's arm and spun him around. 'I don't think tonight's a good idea.'

'Did you have a word with Denise?' He looked across to where Eve's flatmate was kissing Holland on both cheeks. Behind them, Jameson stood waiting, hands thrust into his pockets. Denise caught Thorne's eye and gave him an odd smile . . .

'Not that I'm exactly in any fit state,' Eve said. 'I'd already had a bottle of red wine before you propositioned me . . .'

Thorne grinned. 'Trust me, the more pissed you are, the better it'll seem.'

'What about next weekend? We could check into a nice hotel on the coast for a couple of nights.' She looked up at him and nodded slowly. It must have been clear from his expression. 'Right, I know . . .'

'Sorry. Until this case is over, I can't commit to anything

like . . . Shit, a whole weekend away . . . it just isn't going to happen.'

'It was a stupid idea . . .'

'It was a *great* idea. Let's go out one night next week. Saturday, or before . . .'

'Next Saturday's good.'

'Right . . .' They took a few steps along the pavement, away from the bar. 'Come on, it's still not too late. I'll swing for a really nice hotel, honestly. West End somewhere, full English breakfast . . .'

She put her hands around his neck and pulled him towards her. She whispered it in his ear before she kissed him softly on the cheek. 'Saturday . . .'

As they separated, Thorne glanced across at the others standing by the bar entrance, and saw a look of something like disgust pass across Ben Jameson's face. Turning, Thorne saw that Jameson was watching Keith come hurrying towards the group, cradling a plastic bag.

Unable to hear quite what was said, Thorne watched as Keith delved into the bag and handed Denise something wrapped in red paper. Denise tore the package open and seemed delighted with what looked like a small, decorative box. She threw her arms round Keith's neck, then turned to show the present to Holland and Jameson.

Keith turned, red-faced, and looked across at where Eve was still standing, hand in hand with Thorne. She waved, and started to walk towards him. Holland sauntered the other way, towards Thorne, smiling at Eve as they passed. He seemed a little startled when Thorne dropped a hand on to his shoulder.

'I'll run you home, Dave.'

Holland looked confused. He glanced over his shoulder, watched Eve join her friends. 'It's fine, really, I can get a cab . . .'

'There's no need.'

Thorne drove down Whitechapel Road, heading south towards Tower Bridge. He took it slowly, still getting used to the steering and the clutch but also enjoying it, wanting the journey to last. They were listening to Merle Haggard as they moved slowly into the one-way system around Aldgate.

'What was going on back there, then?' Holland said.

'Keith works in Eve's shop sometimes. I think he's a bit . . .'

'No, I mean bringing me along on your night out, like a spare prick at a wedding.'

Thorne checked the rear-view mirror. 'I wanted to show you the car.' He didn't believe it himself, any more than when he'd told Eve the same thing earlier.

'Things all right with you and Eve?'

Thorne hesitated. Discussions like this one was shaping up to be weren't common between them, and where it might be going was impossible to predict. If Holland hadn't had a couple over the odds, he'd probably be saying nothing. Even socially, the difference in their ranks was rarely forgotten. The unspoken acceptance of the need to keep a certain distance was usually knocking about some-where, moderating.

Tonight, they were just two friends driving back from a bar, and Thorne decided to go with it.

'I've been fucking her around to be honest, Dave.'

'What?'

336

'No, not like that. We haven't even . . .'

'Oh . . .'

'It's a long story, but basically she thinks I'm pissing her about, and I am. One minute I'm up for it, the next I'm relieved when it isn't happening.'

For ten seconds or so before he spoke, Holland appeared to think about what Thorne had said. 'What's all that about, then?'

'I don't know . . .'

The truth was that Thorne *didn't* know, and if *he* was confused, then he could only wonder at what the hell might have been going through Eve's mind. The whole relationship felt somehow teenage. The ups and downs, the mixed messages . . .

There was nothing teenage, nothing confusing, about the short film that began to run suddenly in Thorne's head. He watched himself and Eve in the lift that carried them up towards their nice hotel room. They were all over each other, their mouths hungrily exploring necks and shoulders and their hands probing the areas beneath buckles and straps.

Thorne gripped the wheel tighter, hearing the gulps for breath that came when the kissing stopped, and the moans when it began again. The bell as the lift door opened, and the rustle of Eve's legs moving beneath her skirt as they all but ran towards their room.

He saw himself push the card into the door, watched as the two of them stepped through and fumbled, giggling, for the light switch.

There was a body on their bed. Prostrate and bleeding. The blue necklace, cheap and dreadful, biting deep into the neck . . .

Thorne hit the brakes hard, squealing to a stop at a red light. Holland held his hand out, braced himself against the dashboard.

'Sorry,' Thorne said. 'Still getting the measure of it . . .'

They said nothing for a while, until the Tower of London loomed, spotlit ahead of them, and they moved slowly past it on to the bridge.

Thorne nudged Holland's arm and nodded upriver. 'It's fucking great, isn't it?'

He loved crossing the Thames at night, never tiring of the spectacular views up and down the black river after dark. South to north across Waterloo Bridge was his favourite – to the left, the London Eye, and the dome of St Paul's away in the City to the east – but crossing virtually any bridge, in any direction, at this time was usually enough to lift Thorne's spirits. Tonight, Butler's Wharf squatted to their left, while down below to the right of them, HMS *Belfast* seemed set in sullied amber, the river around it coloured by the lights that ran along each bank.

Foul and fucked up and shitty as the place could be, it was a journey like this that Thorne would urge on anyone thinking about moving out of London . . .

'What about you and Sophie?' Thorne said. 'All geared up for it?'

Holland turned, smiling, but looking like he might throw up. 'I'm shitting myself, if you really want to know.'

'Fair enough, it's a scary business. I've not had one, but . . .'

'It's not just the baby. It's what the baby's going to mean.'

'Workwise, you mean?'

'It just feels like I'm being swept along, you know? Like

I'm not in control of what I'm doing any more.' Thorne shook his head, opened his mouth to say something, but Holland ploughed on, growing louder and more animated as he spoke. 'Sophie says it's up to me what happens afterwards, but she's going to stay at home with the baby and I'll be the only one earning . . .'

'She'd rather you were doing something else?'

'Yeah, but she was like that *before* she was pregnant. I mean, she'd be delighted if I got out of the job, no question, but there's no pressure. I'm worried that *I* might be the one to start thinking I should find something else. Something a bit better paid, you know?'

'Something safer?'

Holland turned and looked at Thorne hard. 'Right.' He turned away again, stared out of the window at the flaking hoardings and car showrooms on the New Kent Road, moving past at almost exactly thirty miles per hour.

'I'm worried that I'll resent the baby,' Holland said. His head fell sideways against the window. 'For the choices it might force me to make . . .'

Thorne said nothing. He pressed a button on the sound system's control panel, searching through the CD until he found the track he was looking for. When the song began, he nudged up the volume. 'You should listen to this,' he said.

'What is it?'

'It's called "Mama Tried". It's about a man in prison . . .'

'That's what they're all about, isn't it?'

'It's really about growing up and accepting responsibility. It's about making the right choices . . .'

For a minute, Holland listened, or pretended to. By then they were coming up to the roundabout at the Elephant &

Castle, his street just a little way beyond it. He shook his head suddenly, and laughed.

'Growing up? *I'm* not the one with the mid-life-crisis car . . .'

Thorne was starving by the time he got in. He stuck three pieces of bread under the grill while the video was rewinding. He'd managed to go the whole day without hearing the result of the match and was looking forward to watching it.

Half an hour in to a fairly dull game, and Thorne was wondering why he'd made the effort . . .

It had been more than a decade since Spurs had been involved in a Charity Shield, but Thorne and his father had been to the last few. They'd seen the goalless draw against Arsenal in '91, and the consecutive games in '81 and '82, after Cup Final wins on the bounce.

The first big game he'd ever gone to had been the Charity Shield in 1967. The trip to Wembley, an extra seventh-birthday present after Spurs had beaten Chelsea 2–1 and won the FA Cup. Thorne could still remember the roar, and his amazement at the sight of all that green, as his old man had led him up the steps towards their seats. He always loved that first sight of the grass, all the years they went to matches together after that, emerging into the noise and the light as they climbed up into the stand at White Hart Lane.

He wondered if his father had watched today's game. He'd doubtless have an opinion on it if he had.

Thorne made the call, and listened to twenty minutes of jokes without punchlines.

TWENTY-TWO

Carol Chamberlain put down the newspaper when Thorne came back to the table with the coffees.

'It's not great,' she said.

Thorne glanced at the latest lurid headline, spooned the froth from his coffee. 'It's not my problem.'

Despite the best efforts of Trevor Jesmond and those above him, the media had got hold of the story a fortnight or so earlier, after the Southern killing. It hadn't quite been the tabloid frenzy that Brigstocke had predicted, but it was pretty basic stuff. One paper had printed pictures of zippered rapist masks with red crosses through them, underneath the headline 'Three Down'. Another had gathered testimony from half a dozen rape victims and run it alongside quotes like 'Give This Man A Medal' and 'The Only Good Rapist Is A Dead One' . . .

Monday morning's batch of stories involved complaints from those campaigning for the rights and integration of ex-prisoners. There were demands that more be done to catch the killer, accusations that the Met was dragging its feet. Only the night before, Thorne had watched a heated debate on *London Live* between representatives of rape-crisis organisations, their counterparts from prisoners'-rights pressure groups, and senior police officers. The Assistant Commissioner, flanked by a scary female Commander and a sweating Trevor Jesmond, had reminded one lobby that the murder victims had themselves been raped, while assuring the other that everything possible was being done.

Thorne had turned the programme off around the time Jesmond began to look like a rabbit caught in the head-lights, blathering about two wrongs not making a right . . .

'Your superiors might decide to *make* it your problem,' Chamberlain said.

Thorne smiled. 'Is that what you used to do?'

'Of course. I did "Passing the Buck" seminars at Hendon . . .'

They were sitting at a table in the shade, outside the small vegetarian café in the middle of Highgate Woods. It was all a bit organic and right-on for Thorne's taste, but Carol had wanted to eat outside somewhere and it had seemed as good a place as any.

The poncy bread was hideously overpriced, but it was all on expenses . . .

Carol Chamberlain's cold case had been taken away from her as soon as it had become hot again. She'd had no choice in the matter and was already working hard on something else. Still, Thorne knew how much they owed her and considered it the least he could do to keep her up to speed. More than that, he actually enjoyed their discus-sions, finding Chamberlain to be an incredibly useful sounding-board. They'd met up or talked on the phone a few times now, since she'd first barged into his office. They gossiped, and bitched and bounced ideas around . . .

'At least they haven't made the connection with the Foley killing,' she said. 'They don't know about Mark and Sarah yet . . .'

Thorne reached across for the paper and flipped it over. He scanned the football stories on the back page. 'It's only a matter of time.'

'It could be good, of course.'

'How?'

'It might be the way to find them.'

'Or frighten them away for good . . .'

Once coffee was finished and pudding decided against, Chamberlain stood, and began piling up their plates. 'Let's take the long way back to the cars.' She rubbed her stomach. 'Walk some of this off . . .'

'She was asking for you, Dave . . .'

Having fetched him from his office, and pointed to the woman in question, Karim left Holland in the doorway of the Incident Room. Stone appeared silently at Holland's shoulder, and they stared across at where Joanne Lesser sat in a chair by the window.

'Mmmm,' Stone groaned. 'Soul food . . .'

Holland nodded, turned to him. 'Racist *and* sexist in two words. That's bloody good going even for you, Andy . . .'

'Fuck off.'

'Blimey, you're on cracking form, mate . . .'

'Seriously, she's bloody tasty, though. You're a right jammy sod.' Holland looked at him. 'Well she's obviously up for it. First she's on the phone, now she's come in to see you personally . . .'

Holland led the way across the Incident Room, Lesser

standing eagerly as he and Stone approached. He was sure that what Stone had been suggesting was only in his own, sexually skewed imagination. Still, for more than just the obvious reasons, he hoped that Joanne Lesser had something important to say.

Five minutes later, they sat, the three points of a small triangle, in Holland and Stone's office. Plastic cups of tea on the edges of desks . . .

'The dates have been bothering me,' Lesser said.

'The dates of the foster placements?' Holland began sheafing through the notes on his lap.

'It's slightly different now, but back then we'd have ceased to monitor a placement once the child had turned sixteen. From then on, they were no longer deemed to be the responsibility of social services . . .'

'Right.' Holland was still searching.

'I double-checked the information on the index cards – you know, the information that I sent to you – and it doesn't quite make sense.'

'What doesn't?' Stone said.

'The last recorded monitoring date was February 1984. That would have been a home visit, most probably. At least a phone call . . .'

Holland had found the page he was looking for. He ran his finger down the list, stopped at the date Lesser had mentioned. 'Mr and Mrs Noble'. The Nobles should have been back from their holidays by now. He'd left a message, but they hadn't got back to him . . .

Lesser leaned forward on her chair, looking from Stone to Holland as she spoke. 'I checked the children's dates of birth, just to be on the safe side, but there's still a problem.'

344

Holland looked at the dates. He turned the page, looking for something else, and when he'd found it, he saw the anomaly. 'They weren't old enough,' he said.

Lesser nodded, the blush beginning around her throat. Holland could almost have blushed himself. This was something he should have seen, *would* have seen if he'd been giving it the proper attention. He'd been half-arsed, hadn't considered it important enough. He should have let Stone give him a hand when it had been offered. Now, Stone was the one sitting there, probably enjoying every minute of it, as simple, *evident* facts were spelt out for Holland by a member of the public . . .

'1984?' Stone said. 'So, the kids would have been . . .'

'Fifteen and thirteen,' Lesser said. 'Mark was almost sixteen, fair enough. If it had just been him I wouldn't have been concerned, but the little girl was nowhere near old enough for monitoring to stop. You can see why I thought it might be important . . .'

'What are the reasons you might stop monitoring a case?' Holland said.

'There's only two that I can think of. If a family moves away it would be handed over to a different area, or even a completely different county.'

'I reckon that's it,' Holland said. He began turning pages again until he found the current address for the Nobles. 'Romford far enough?'

Lesser nodded. 'Doesn't come under us.'

'Does it say how long they've been living there, though?' Stone asked.

'No, I'll have to check. Last record in any local school is 1984, so there's every chance that's when they moved.' He turned back to Lesser. 'What's the other reason, Joanne? You said one reason was moving . . .'

'Adoption.' Holland and Stone both looked back at her blankly. 'Again, things are a bit more rigorous now, but then, once the adoption order had been signed, that was it. Not our responsibility any more.'

'I get the feeling you've already checked this . . .'

She shrugged. 'I know someone in Adoption, so I gave her a ring. Their records are a bit more organised than ours. Have you got a pen?'

Holland couldn't help smiling. He stretched across and grabbed a pen from his desk. 'Go ahead . . .'

'Irene and Roger Noble formally adopted Mark and Sarah Foley on 12 February, 1984. They may well have moved shortly after that, but that was certainly the last contact the children had with Essex social services . . .'

Holland scribbled down the information. From everything they knew, it seemed that it was the last contact Mark and Sarah Foley had had with anybody.

They walked slowly around the edge of the cricket field towards the children's playground; moving along the path of shadow cast by a line of overhanging oaks and hornbeams. Deep into the school holidays, there were plenty of people around. The temperature was starting to drop as the sky clouded over, but here and there were glimpses of a dark blue, like bruises fading on puffy flesh.

'Mark Foley still sounds like a good bet to me.'

'Yeah, I think so too,' Thorne said. 'Just wish I could cash it in.'

'It'll happen. He can't stay hidden for ever.'

'I've still got a problem with motive, though.'

Chamberlain threw Thorne a look of theatrical surprise. 'I thought you were the type who didn't care about *why* . . .'

'Ultimately, it's not my job, is it? But if it's going to help me catch him . . .'

'Go on . . .'

'I can see the motive for killing Alan Franklin . . .'

'It's about as good as it gets. Franklin caused everything, might just as well have killed his parents. Took him long enough to get revenge, though.'

'I think I can understand the waiting,' Thorne said.

Chamberlain grinned. 'Maybe he's just a lazy sod.'

Thorne thought he was pretty well qualified to give an opinion on that one. 'I don't think so . . .'

They came slowly to a halt.

'He was growing up,' Thorne said. 'Letting his body grow strong, letting the hatred grow stronger. Then he waits until Franklin's old, until he feels safe, before he puts an end to it in that car park.'

'Only that isn't an end to it . . .'

'No, it isn't. It should have been though, shouldn't it? Mark settles it, gets clean away with it, gets on with his life.'

'Whatever *that* is . . .'

'So why the hell does he pop up again now? Why these others? Why kill Remfry, Welch and Southern?'

'Maybe he enjoys it.'

'I'm damn sure he's enjoying it *now*, but that's not why he started. Not why he started again, I mean. Something else happened . . .'

'The rape element is crucial though, you've always said that. Maybe he was raped himself.'

'Maybe.' Thorne felt like they were going over old ground. They'd considered this back when they thought the killer might have been an ex-prisoner, looking to settle an old score. It was possible, certainly, but it felt stale to him, and unhelpful.

Chamberlain jumped at a sudden, sharp *crack* from behind them. Half a dozen boys were messing about in the cricket nets, and for a minute or two, the pair of them stood and watched. When she finally spoke, Chamberlain had to lean in close to make herself heard over the noise the kids were making.

'Something I remember from a poem at school,' she said. Thorne kept his eye on the action, inclining his head towards her to listen. '"Childhood is the kingdom where nobody dies . . ."'

'What's that from?' Thorne asked as they began walking again.

'One of those anthologies we had to read. I don't know . . .'

As they reached their cars, parked on the main road, Chamberlain stopped and put a hand on Thorne's arm. 'It's good, knocking ideas around like this, Tom, it's useful. But don't forget that if the answer's there, if it's *anywhere*, it's in the details. It's in the facts that make up the pattern of a case.'

Thorne nodded, opening the door of the BMW. He knew that there were answers. He knew too that he already had them somewhere, misfiled and, thus far, irretrievable. Lost among the tens of thousands of facts, relevant or otherwise, to the case. The ever-expanding headful of shit that he carried around with him all the time: names and places and dates and snippets of statements; words and numbers and small gestures; access codes and times of death; the look on a relative's face; the scuff-mark on a hotel guest's shoe; the weight of a dead man's liver . . .

Thorne knew that the answer was buried in there somewhere and it bothered him. Something else bothered him and he thought twice before mentioning it.

'What you were saying about patterns . . .'

'What?'

'The second and third victims. He changed the pattern of killing between Welch and Southern.'

'Of course he did. Because he presumed that once you'd connected the killings, you'd contact the prisons and warn them. He had to do the next one differently.'

'What if he *knew*, rather than presumed?' Thorne said. 'What if he knew because he's close to the investigation? We always talked about him having access of some kind. Then other stuff came along and the idea got blurred. What if I was wrong to dismiss the idea that the killer's one of us . . .?'

When Thorne got back to Becke House, he was directed straight to Brigstocke's office. Holland was telling Brigstocke and Kitson about what Joanne Lesser had said, and his subsequent phone conversation with Mrs Irene Noble. Thorne made Holland back-pedal, asked him to go over Lesser's visit again until he was up to speed.

'It's interesting that the dates of the adoption and the move look to be so close together,' Brigstocke said.

'It gets a lot more interesting. When I finally got hold of Irene Noble, told her I wanted to talk about Mark and

Sarah Foley, the first thing she did was to ask me if we'd found them.'

Thorne looked across at Brigstocke. 'How would she know we were looking?'

'No, sir, that's not what she meant,' Holland said. He flipped over a page in his notebook, read from it. '"Have you finally found them?" That's what she actually said. She's talking about twenty years ago.' Holland looked up and across at Thorne. 'She claims that the kids disappeared back in 1984 . . .'

'Just after the Nobles adopted them,' Thorne said.

'Right.' Brigstocke got up, walked around his desk. 'And around the time they moved away from Colchester.'

Holland stuck his notebook away and leaned back against a chair. 'Now it gets even better. Mrs Noble reckons that there was an official investigation at the time. The children were reported as missing, she says. The police spent weeks looking for them . . .'

'You've checked?' Brigstocke asked.

'It's rubbish. I went back to 1983, just in case she was getting the dates confused, and there's bugger all. No records of any search, no records of missing persons reports. There was nothing national, nothing local. It never happened . . .'

'What impression did you get when you spoke to her?' Thorne asked.

'She sounded like she meant it. She was upset . . .'

'Turning it on, d'you reckon?'

'No, I don't think so. Sounded genuine enough . . .'

'Where's the husband?'

'Roger Noble died in 1990. Heart attack . . .'

Thorne thought about this for a second or two, then turned to Brigstocke. 'Well, I reckon we'd better have a word with *her* then.' Brigstocke nodded. 'Where is she, Dave?'

'She lives in Romford, but she's coming into town tomorrow. Likes to do her shopping in the West End, she says . . .'

Thorne pulled a face. 'Oh *does* she . . .?'

'I've arranged to meet her at ten-thirty.'

Brigstocke took off his glasses, pulled a crumpled tissue from his trouser pocket and wiped the sweat from the frames. 'Well done, Dave. You'd better go over all this with DS Karim as soon as you can. He'll need to reassign, issue fresh actions . . .'

'Sir . . .' Holland opened the door and stepped out.

'Yvonne, can you get across this as well? We might have a bit more luck finding Mark Foley and his sister, now we know that they changed their names . . .'

Kitson, who had said nothing, nodded and took a step towards the door.

'This is looking good, you know?' Brigstocke said. 'Be great to give the Detective Chief Superintendent some positive news . . .'

Thorne couldn't help himself. 'Tell him I thought he looked smashing on the telly the other night . . .'

Brigstocke clearly couldn't be arsed to pull him on it. 'Right, a pint later to celebrate?'

'Fuck all to celebrate,' Thorne said. 'I'll be there anyway, though . . .'

'Yvonne?'

Kitson shook her head. 'Too much to do.' She turned

and stepped through the door, barking back at Brigstocke as she walked away towards the Incident Room, 'Got to change a million and one data searches from "Foley" to "Noble" . . .'

Brigstocke looked over at Thorne. 'What's got up *her* arse?'

'Don't ask me . . .'

'Maybe you should have a word . . .'

Thorne's mobile rang. He glanced at the screen and saw who was calling. He told Brigstocke he'd check back with him later and stepped out into the corridor, pulling the door closed behind him.

'Are we still on for Saturday?' Eve said.

'I hope so.'

'Right. Dinner somewhere and back to your place.'

'Sounds good. Fuck, you know what I still haven't done?'

'Who cares? You've got a sofa, haven't you?'

He had work to do, professionally and for his other, more personal project. Not that he considered the killing to be personal, not in terms of the self.

No, not really, and not to *him* anyway.

What he did to those animals in those hotel rooms wasn't actually about him, or for him. He'd always denied that, when it had come up, and he would continue to deny it. He was happy to do it, more than happy to put the line around their necks and pull, but if it had only been about him, it wouldn't be happening.

He was just a weapon . . .

Strangely, he felt that he put more of himself into his

day job. More of him had passed into what he did, by the time he'd finished working on something, than it had watching any of those fuckers plead then die. True, paying the mortgage meant being responsible to people, and what he did, even when he did it well, was rarely of any benefit to him personally, but he always felt part of it afterwards. The work usually had his fingerprints on it somewhere.

He laughed at that, and carried on working. His job was hotting up suddenly: stuff was coming in and he was really earning his money. He had less time now to get the other things organised, but actually there was very little that had to be done, and certainly no need to panic. It was all pretty much sorted.

Bar a few 't's to cross and the odd 'i' to dot, the final killing had been arranged.

TWENTY-THREE

Thorne looked unconvinced. 'I've never interviewed anybody in the same place I buy my pants.'

'There's a first time for everything,' Holland said.

They carried the coffees across to where Irene Noble was sitting waiting for them, flanked already – though the place had been open only half an hour or so – by large Marks & Spencer shopping bags. The café was a relatively new addition to the large store on Oxford Street, wedged into a corner of the ladies' clothing section and half filled with shoppers who'd obviously made as early a start as Irene Noble.

As Thorne squeezed behind the table next to Holland, he glanced around at the dozen or so women getting their breath, ready to start again. Scattered around were one or two bored-looking men, grateful for the chance to sit down and not be asked their opinion for a few minutes.

Irene Noble took a small, plastic container of sweeteners from her bag. She pressed the top, dropped a tiny tablet into her latté, and raised her eyebrows at Dave Holland. 'They probably think I'm your mother,' she said.

She was pretty well preserved for a woman who had to

be sixty or so, though Thorne thought that she was trying a bit too hard. The hair was a little too blond and brittle, the fire-engine-red lipstick applied a touch too thickly. To Thorne, it seemed that this stage was probably the one that came right before giving up altogether. Before mentioning your age to strangers, and always wearing an overcoat, and not giving a toss any more . . .

'Tell us about Mark and Sarah, Mrs Noble.'

She thought for a moment, smiling briefly before taking a sip of coffee. 'Roger used to joke about it and say that we lost them in the move. You know, like a tea-chest going missing.' She saw the reaction on Thorne's face and shook her head. 'It wasn't a nasty joke, it was affectionate. That was just his way. Something to make me laugh if I was crying, you understand? I did a lot of crying after it happened . . .'

'This was just after you adopted the children?' Holland said.

'The beginning of 1984. We'd had them four years or so by then. We had a few problems, course we did, but then things got on an even keel.'

It was clear to Thorne that her voice was affected somewhat. A 'telephone' voice. Thorne remembered that his mother had used to do the same thing. Airs and graces for the benefit of doctors, teachers, policemen . . .

'There were problems before, weren't there?' Holland said. 'With the previous sets of foster parents.'

'Right, and they gave up on the children straight away. It was only Roger and I who stuck with it. We knew that it was just something we had to get through. They were very disturbed children and, God only knows, they had every right to be.'

'What sort of problems?' Thorne said.

She paused for a few seconds before answering. 'Behavioural problems. Adjusting, you know? Roger and I thought we'd got it under control. Obviously we were wrong.' She reached for a teaspoon and stared down into her coffee cup as she stirred. 'Behavioural.' She said the word again, as if it were a medical term. Thorne glanced sideways at Holland who gave him a small shrug in return.

'So you decided to adopt them?' Holland asked. Mrs Noble nodded. 'How did the kids feel about that?'

She looked at Holland as though he'd asked a very silly question. 'They'd lost their real parents and been let down by every set of foster parents they'd had since. They were delighted that we were going to be a real family, and so were we. Roger and I had always wanted children. We might have missed out on nappies with those two, but we had plenty of sleepless nights, I can tell you . . .'

'I can believe it,' Thorne said.

'And plenty after they disappeared. Plenty . . .'

'How did they disappear?'

She pushed her cup to one side, laid one liver-spotted hand across the other. 'We moved on the Saturday morning and it was the usual chaos, you know? Boxes everywhere and removal men sliding about because there was snow on the ground. We told the kids they could sort their own stuff out, so they just got on with it. Shut themselves away upstairs . . .'

'Fighting over who was going to get the biggest room, I suppose?'

She looked quickly up at Thorne. 'No. We'd sorted out their bedrooms early on, before we moved . . .'

'What happened?' Thorne said.

'They needed to have their own space, you understand?'

'What happened, Mrs Noble?'

'Nobody heard them go, nobody saw a thing. They crept out like ghosts . . .'

'When did anybody find out they'd gone?'

'We were all over the place, you can imagine, trying to get everything together. Trying to find the tea bags and the bloody kettle or what have you.' She began to pick at a fingernail. 'It was around dinnertime, I think. Can't remember exactly. It was after dark . . .'

'So what did you think?'

'We didn't really think anything at first. They always went out a lot. They were very independent, always off somewhere together. Mark always looked after Sarah, though. He always took care of his sister.'

Thorne glanced sideways at Holland. 'When were the police called?' Holland asked.

'The next morning. Obviously we knew there was something wrong when they hadn't come back. When their beds hadn't been slept in . . .'

Thorne leaned forward. He took one of the fancy Italian biscuits that came with the coffee and broke it in half, asking the question casually. 'Who called the police?'

There was no hesitation. 'Roger. Well, actually, he went down to the station himself. He thought things might get handled faster if he went there personally, and he was right. He said they got straight on it. Two of them came to the house while I was out searching in the park and round the local streets.'

'Roger told you they came round?'

She nodded. 'They had a look in the kids' bedrooms, you know? Asked all the normal questions. Took some photos away with them . . .'

Thorne looked at Holland. A reminder about getting photos of Mark and Sarah for Brigstocke's digital ageing plan. Holland picked up on it, nodded and made a note. Thorne popped the rest of the biscuit into his mouth, chewed for a few seconds before speaking again.

'Did the police presume the children had run away right from the start?'

'Well, that was the problem, wasn't it? Everything was in boxes, all over the show. It was hard to work out straight away if they'd taken anything with them . . .'

'Eventually, though,' Thorne said. 'That was what they must have thought.'

'Yes, after a day or two I worked out which clothes were missing. There was some money gone as well, but it took me a while to realise. I thought maybe I'd mislaid it somewhere in all the moving. Once the police knew about the children, about what they'd been through, Roger said they started treating it as a runaway thing more than anything else . . .'

'What did they do?'

'Very thorough, they were. Up and down the country. Appeals for information, searches at all the stations, that sort of thing. Roger got updates from them all the time. They were taking it very seriously, Roger said, for the first week or two, anyway.'

'Roger said . . .'

'That's right. He went down and nagged them every day. Twice a day, sometimes, demanding to know what they were doing.'

'For the first week or two, you said. After that . . .?'

'Well, they told Roger, a chief inspector actually, told Roger that he was sure the children were safe. They were certain that if, you know, any harm *had* come to Mark or Sarah, they would have found out. I suppose they meant found a body . . .'

Thorne saw that the skin below Irene Noble's fingernail had torn and begun to bleed slightly where she'd been picking at it. He watched as she pressed a napkin to her tongue and dabbed at the pinpricks of blood. When she spoke again, it struck him that the telephone voice had gone, and that the Essex accent was coming through strongly. Whether she was unable to keep it up for long or had simply ceased bothering, it was impossible to tell.

'Never having had any of my own,' she said, 'I can't say for sure if I felt anything less because Mark and Sarah weren't mine, weren't my flesh and blood. D'you understand what I'm getting at?' Thorne nodded. 'After the police told Roger they thought the children were safe, it wasn't so bad, you know? We weren't so scared. We just missed them. We got used to missing them eventually . . .'

'Did you ever see a police officer?' Thorne said. 'In all the time they were looking for Mark and Sarah, did you yourself ever speak to a police officer?'

Thorne had been expecting a pause, perhaps a paling, but instead he got a smile. After a few seconds it wilted a little, and she seemed suddenly sad. Then, as she spoke, her face filled with an affectionate remembrance . . .

'Roger wanted to shield me from any of it. He did everything, handled it all. Perhaps it was his way of dealing with what had happened, throwing himself into it like he did, taking the responsibility, but I knew he was trying to protect me. He dealt with all the official side of things. The strain of it, of everything that happened and that school business on top of it, drove my husband to an early grave.'

Thorne blinked, took a breath or two. A suspicion, a *sense*, began to distil into something more potent. 'What school business was that?' he asked.

'Roger worked over at St Joseph's. It was the school where Mark and Sarah would have gone.' She said it casually, like the children had done no more than fail an entrance exam. 'It was just part-time, casual work, but he did all the bits and bobs that needed doing around the place. One day this man comes round, one of the parents, hammering on the door. Says his son's been involved in some kind of incident and mentioned Roger's name. Utter rubbish, of course, the man was on something I think, but it really upset Roger. This lunatic wouldn't leave it and went to the headmaster. The school was keen to keep it low key, which was right, *obviously*, since it was so stupid, but Roger wanted to do the right thing. He left quietly in the end, rather than upset the children. That was typical of him. It was scandalous, disgraceful that anybody could even *suggest* . . . There were always kids round here after school and in the holidays. Always kids in our house . . .'

'Roger liked children . . .'

She looked up, her face softening, grateful for Thorne's insight. For his understanding. 'That's right. He would never have admitted it, but I think, deep down, he was always trying to make up for not having Mark and Sarah any more. Being around other kids had been his own way of coping with what happened. Later on, after that unpleasantness, everything started to get on top of him. His heart just packed up in the end . . .'

'What was *your* way of coping, Irene?' Thorne said.

'I just prayed the kids were safe,' she said. 'That wherever Mark and Sarah went after they left us, they were out of harm's way . . .'

It was that sentence which stayed with Thorne, which he thought about as they struggled out of the West End through traffic, inching around Marble Arch, car and passengers overheating more than slightly.

'It was very convenient for Roger Noble,' Holland said. 'The kids going missing when they were between schools. They vanish from all education records . . .'

'It was certainly handy,' Thorne said.

'They *did* go missing, didn't they? I'm just thinking out loud . . .'

Thorne shook his head. 'Noble was responsible for them going, which is why he never reported it, but I don't think it was worse than that. If he killed them, who the hell are we looking for?'

'What are we going to do?' Holland asked. 'Shouldn't we report it? That fucker could have abused loads of other kids.'

'There's no point. He's long dead. He can't hurt any more kids now.'

'What about *her*? Do you think she knew?'

Thorne thought about what Irene Noble had said. About praying the kids were out of harm's way. He shook his head. If she *had* known, she could surely not have said that and kept a straight face.

★

In the Grafton Arms, spitting distance from his flat, Thorne shared several pints and half a dozen games of pool with Phil Hendricks. The beer seemed to have little effect, and he lost five games out of the six.

'I'm not enjoying thrashing you as much as I normally would,' Hendricks said. 'You're so obviously preoccupied with all this other shit.' Thorne, leaning back against the bar, said nothing. He watched as Hendricks potted the last couple of stripes before putting the black down without any difficulty. 'What about if we start putting money on it? That might focus your thoughts a bit more . . .'

'Let's leave it,' Thorne said. 'I'll finish this pint, and I'm off home . . .'

Hendricks took his Guinness from the top of the cigarette machine and walked across to join Thorne at the bar. 'I still don't really see it,' he said. 'How could they not know? How could they not know *something* . . .?'

Thorne shook his head, his glass at his lips. Among other things, they had been talking about Irene Noble and Sheila Franklin. About two women of more or less the same age, married to men who they loved dearly, and who, now that they were widows, they remembered with tenderness and affection. Two men whose memories lived on, fondly preserved as precious things. Two men beloved . . .

One a rapist and the other a child molester.

Thorne swallowed. 'Maybe it's an age thing. You know, a different generation.'

'That's crap,' Hendricks said. 'What about my mum and dad?' Thorne had met them once, they ran a guest house in Salford. 'My old man couldn't so much as fart without my mum knowing about it . . .'

Thorne nodded. It was a fair point. 'Same with mine . . .'

'She knew what he was *thinking*, never mind doing.'

Hendricks reached into the top pocket of his denim jacket, took a Silk Cut from a packet of ten. Thorne was irritated, in the way that only an ex-smoker *could* be. Irritated by the fact that his friend could smoke one or two, then put the pack away for a week or more, until he fancied another one as a bit of a treat. Smoke, and enjoy it, and not need another one. A packet of *ten*, for crying out loud . . .

'Are they going to be told?' Hendricks asked. 'Those women? Is someone going to break the bad news about their dead hubbies?'

'No point yet. If we get a result they'll find out soon enough . . .'

Hendricks nodded and lit his cigarette. The curls of blue smoke drifted across to where a man and a woman were now playing pool. It hung in the light above the table.

'Maybe we only *think* we know what was going on with our parents,' Thorne said. 'Maybe we only know as much or as little as they did.'

'I suppose . . .'

'There's an old country song called "Behind Closed Doors"' . . .

'Bloody hell, here we go . . .'

'It's true though, isn't it? So much family stuff is mythology. Shit that just gets handed down, and you never know for sure what really happened and what's made up. Nobody ever thinks to sit you down and pass it on. The truth of it. Before you know it, your history becomes hearsay.' Thorne took a drink. He knew that at some point, he should have talked to his father. Found out more about his parents, and *their* parents. He knew that there wasn't much point now . . .

'Fuck me,' Hendricks said. 'All that's in one song?'

'You are *such* an arsehole . . .'

They stepped away from the bar to make room for a group of lads, finished their drinks standing by the door.

'Where does all this leave you with Mark Foley?' Hendricks said.

'He's still our prime suspect.'

'Whoever he might be . . .'

'Right, and *wherever*. But he's not making my life very easy.'

'He'll slip up. We'll nail him when he does . . .'

'I'm not talking about catching him.' Thorne was finding it hard to think about his murderer without picturing him as a fifteen-year-old child. He saw a boy protecting his sister, spiriting her away from a place where one, or perhaps both, of them was being abused. 'I'm still trying to decide exactly what he *is*.' Thorne turned to look at Hendricks. 'This whole thing's all arse-about-face, d'you know that, Phil? Mark Foley or Noble or whoever the fuck he is now is a killer *and* he's a victim.'

Hendricks shrugged. 'So?'

'So, there's a part of him that part of *me* doesn't really want to catch . . .'

Thorne walked Hendricks back towards the tube. Hendricks asked Thorne about Eve, joked when he heard about their hot date on Saturday, and moaned about his own eventful but ultimately bleak love-life.

Thorne wasn't paying an awful lot of attention. He was tired, imagining himself floating gently down on to his hillside, the bracken waving a welcome as he drew nearer to it. Jane Foley was suddenly there beside him, drifting to earth, and though he could not see her face clearly, he imagined the pain etched across it, for herself and for her children.

Thorne knew that when he and Jane Foley hit the ground, their bodies would travel right through the bracken and beyond. He knew that the hillside would collapse beneath their weight and that they would sink down, deep through earth and water and the rotten wood of old coffins. Down through powdery bone and further, into the blackness where there was no sound and the soil was packed tight around them.

TWENTY-FOUR

The telephone voice was even more pronounced on Irene Noble's answering-machine message. Holland waited for the beep, then spoke. 'This is Detective Constable Holland from the Serious Crime Group. Yesterday, when myself and DI Thorne interviewed you, we forgot to ask about photographs of the children. We'd appreciate it if you might be able to lend us some pictures, which we will of course return whenever we finish with them. So, if you could get back to me as soon as possible on any of those numbers on the card we left you, I'd be very grateful. Many thanks . . .'

Holland put down the phone and looked up. From behind his desk on the other side of the office, Andy Stone was staring across at him.

'Photos of the Foley children?' Stone said.

'The DCI's still keen on getting them on the computer, ageing them up.'

Stone shook his head. 'Waste of time. Never looks anything like the kids when they eventually turn up.'

'If she's got photos from just before the children ran away, they'll be fifteen and thirteen. They can't have changed too much.'

'You'd be amazed, mate. Have you never bumped into someone you haven't seen for a few years and not recognised them? That's after a few years . . .'

Holland thought about it and admitted that he had. He also knew, from the twin murder case he'd worked on with Thorne the year before, that if people wanted to change the way they looked, it wasn't actually that hard. Still, he reckoned that if the technology was there, there was no harm in using it.

Stone remained unconvinced. 'It's a pretty basic software program which digitally ages the photographs. At the end of the day, it's all guesswork and a lot of assumptions. How can you know if someone's hair's going to fall out, or if they're going to put on loads of weight or whatever?'

'I've seen some that looked pretty close,' Holland said.

Stone shrugged, went back to what he was doing. 'Do we know she's got any photos at all?' he said, without looking up.

'Not for certain, no. Be a bit strange if she didn't, though. She was very fond of them . . .'

'You going to get somebody to go and pick them up?' Stone asked. 'Or shoot over there yourself?'

'Hadn't really thought about it. I'll see what she says when she gets back to me, see when's a good time. You want to come along?'

'No . . .'

'She's single, but probably a bit old, even for you . . .'

'I'll give that one a miss, I think.'

'Suit yourself.' Holland noted down the time he'd made the call. Wednesday the 7th, 10.40 a.m. He'd give Irene Noble until the end of the day and call again. When Stone

367

next started to speak, Holland looked across. Stone was leaning back in his chair, staring into space through narrowed eyes.

'*Very* fond of them? I think you're being a bit bloody generous . . .'

'I think she was more than very fond of them,' Holland said. 'But yes, she was also naive. Call it stupid, if you like . . .'

Stone snapped his gaze towards Holland. 'If love is blind, she must have been fucking besotted . . .'

Whoever thought that computers would do away with paperwork was sadly mistaken. There was as much paper piled up on desks as there ever had been. The only difference was that now, most of it was printed out by computer . . .

Thorne sat and read through the stories of four murders.

Those same scraps of information that clogged his brain had also been recorded somewhere on paper. On laser-printed sheets of A4, on faded and curling reams of fax paper, on Post-It notes and pre-printed memo sheets torn from a pad. The entire case was laid out like this before him. Ream after dog-eared ream, piled in stubby blocks of yellow and white and buff. Banded by elastic or bound with laminate sheets or stapled and stuffed into cardboard folders . . .

Thorne went over every piece of paper, of the jigsaw. Looking for the answer he knew to be there. Sifting through the shit, like a squawking gull flapping around a vast dump. Black, beady eye searching for that morsel of interest . . .

Hearing the trace of that Yorkshire accent in Carol Chamberlain's voice. The good sense in every flat vowel of it.

'*If it's* anywhere, *it's in the details.*'

Opposite him, Yvonne Kitson sat typing, her face all but obscured by a paper mountain range of her own. She was still working on the Foley/Noble search, sorting through tens of thousands of addresses and car registrations and NI numbers, as well as dealing with, collecting and collating, the information that was still coming in on the Southern killing.

Thorne looked across at her. He toyed with lobbing a ball of paper over to get her attention. He flicked briefly through the piles on his desk, looking for something he could screw up, then thought better of it . . .

'Apart from anything else,' Thorne said, 'murderers aren't doing the rainforests a whole lot of good.'

Kitson looked up and across at him. 'Sorry?'

He picked up a sheaf of post-mortem reports and waved them. She nodded her understanding.

'How's it going, Yvonne?'

'We won't have any more luck finding him as Noble than we did as Foley. He was only Mark *Noble* for five minutes, anyway . . .'

'Which he'd have hated. That man's name . . .'

'Too bloody right. If I was him I'd've changed my name, or at least stopped using *that* one, as soon as I got the hell out of there.'

Thorne could find nothing in what Kitson had said to argue with. He'd have gone to Brigstocke straight away, suggested they concentrate their resources somewhere else. But he didn't have the faintest idea where . . .

'Let's just plough through it,' he said.

The whole adoption/abuse/runaway lead was shaping

up to be another one of those which came to nothing horribly quickly. It was hard enough trying to work out what might have happened to someone who'd run away from home six months before. To piece together the theoretical movements of a pair of teenagers who'd vanished from a house in Romford nearly twenty years earlier was almost certainly impossible.

They had little choice but to try, and while Holland, Stone and the rest of the team did what they could, Thorne was going back over everything they already had. Sure that they already had enough.

By lunchtime, he'd found nothing, and felt as though he'd read about every murder that had ever taken place. He'd watched the hands of the pathologist rooting about in every chest cavity and down into the cold, wet depths of every gut. He'd listened to the less than helpful words of everybody who'd so much as stood at the same bus stop as one of the victims.

He'd had a belly full . . .

'What's on your sarnies today, then?'

Kitson shook her head without looking up from her computer screen. 'Didn't have time today. The kids were playing up, and everything got a bit . . .' The rest of the sentence hung there until Thorne spoke.

'You can't keep all the balls in the air all the time, Yvonne. You're allowed to drop one occasionally, you know.' Kitson glanced up, gave him a thin smile. 'Is everything all right, Yvonne?'

'Has somebody said something?' It came a little too quickly.

'No. You've just seemed a bit . . . out of it.'

Kitson's smile thickened, until she looked, to Thorne, much more like herself. Much more the type he could lob a ball of paper at.

'I'm just tired,' she said.

This next killing had to be the last one, at least for a while. It made a pretty picture, and it also made bloody good sense. Afterwards, the police investigation was bound to be stepped up, and the risk of getting caught, just statistically, would increase.

If he were to be caught, to be tried for his crimes, the next killing would be a very bad one to get done for. He would certainly be crucified with little argument. Now, though, with just the others under his belt, it would be something of a different matter. Standing trial for the murders of Remfry and Welch and Southern, he would fancy his chances . . .

If the papers were excited at the manhunt, they would be wetting themselves at a court case. The tabloids would back him, he was sure of it. He could probably even persuade one or other of the red-tops to stump up for his defence, pay to hire a top lawyer. He had decided already that should it ever come to it, he would speak in his own defence, would stand up and tell them exactly what he'd done and why. He was pretty confident that only a very brave judge would put him away for too long after that.

There would be an outcry from certain sections for sure, from the misguided and the bleeding hearts. From those who believed he should pay his debt to society, in the same way that those fine, upstanding citizens he'd killed had once done.

That would be all right with him. Let the silly bastards protest. Let them take the words 'perversion' and 'justice', and put them together like they owned them, even though they hadn't got the least fucking idea what either of them could really mean.

Perversion and justice. The degradation and the dashed hope. The hideous comedy that had started everything . . .

It was all a fantasy, of course, unless the police came knocking on his door in the next couple of days. After that, after the final killing, nothing he could say would save him. The loyalties of the gutter press would switch very bloody quickly, along with everybody else's, once the final victim had been discovered.

Rapists were one thing, but this was, after all, very much another.

Thorne was in the corner of the Major Incident Room, feeding coins into the coffee machine, when Karim approached him.

'Miss Bloom on line three, sir . . .'

Momentarily confused, Thorne reached for his back pocket, understanding when he found it empty. His mobile was on his desk in the office. Eve would have tried that first and then, having got no reply, would have called the office number . . .

Thorne crossed to a desk and picked up the phone. He held it to his chest until Karim had wandered far enough away.

'It's me. What's up?'

'Nothing serious. Keith's let me down, so I just need to change the time a bit on Saturday. I told him I was going out and he said that he'd lock up for me. Now he turns round and says that *he* needs to leave early as well, so I'm a bit stuffed . . .'

'It doesn't matter. Get over when you can.'

'I know, I just wanted to get to your place early, drop some stuff off before we go out to eat.'

'Sounds interesting . . .'

'It'll probably be nearer seven now, by the time I've sorted out the shop and put my face on.'

'I can't see myself getting home a lot sooner than that anyway . . .'

'Sorry to screw our arrangements around, but it's not my fault. Keith's usually pretty reliable. Tom . . .?'

Eve's voice had faded away. Thorne was no longer listening.

Our arrangements . . .

Zoom in close and hold.

The certainty of it came as swiftly, and snapped into place as tightly, as a ligature. Like the blue blur of the line as it whips past the face and down, only becoming clear when it begins to bite, Thorne knew in a second *exactly* what it was that he'd missed. What had lain shadowed and just out of reach. Now he saw it, brightly lit . . .

Something he'd read and something he hadn't . . .

They'd found all Jane Foley's letters to Remfry, the ones sent to him in prison and the couple that had been sent to his home address after his release. Nothing indicated that there were any letters missing, and why would there be?

Something *had* been missing though.

Thorne had read those letters a dozen times, probably more, and nowhere had Jane Foley discussed the plans for her meeting with Douglas Remfry. The rendezvous itself was never talked about specifically. Not the time, or the date. Not even the name of the hotel . . .

So how the hell had anything been arranged?

Something Thorne *could* remember reading had been written by Dave Holland. His report on that first visit to collect Remfry's stuff, the day he went round there with Andy Stone and pulled those letters out from under Remfry's bed. Mary Remfry had been keen to stress her son's success with women. She'd made a point of mentioning the women that were sniffing around after Dougie had been released. The women that were calling up . . .

Remfry, Welch and Southern had not just walked into those hotels thinking they were going to meet Jane Foley. They'd *known* they were going to meet her.

They'd spoken to her.

TWENTY-FIVE

'Not just spoken on the phone either,' Holland said. 'I'm not sure about the others, but I think Southern might have *met* her.'

They were gathered in Brigstocke's office, prior to a hastily arranged team briefing. Eighteen hectic hours since Thorne had put it together. Since he'd worked out that there *was* a her . . .

'Go on, Dave,' Brigstocke said.

'I interviewed Southern's ex-girlfriend . . .'

Thorne remembered reading the statement. 'Right. They split up not long before he was killed, didn't they?'

'That's just it. She said that the main reason she dumped him was that she'd heard about some other woman, thought he'd been two-timing her. Somebody told her that Southern had been bragging about it in the pub. Telling his mates he'd picked up this fantastic bit of stuff. Actually . . .'

'What?'

'I need to look at the statement, but I think Southern supposedly told his mates that she had more or less picked *him* up.'

Thorne looked past Holland, down to Brigstocke's desk, at the series of black and white photographs laid out in two lines across it. 'Jane Foley,' he said.

'Who *is* she, really?' Kitson said.

'Could be anybody,' Thorne said. 'We can't discount any possibility. A model he hired, or a hooker. The killer could have used her for the pictures, paid her to make the calls to Remfry and Welch. Bunged her a bit extra to pick up Howard Southern . . .'

Brigstocke was gathering his notes together. He didn't believe what Thorne was suggesting any more than Thorne himself did. 'No, it's Sarah. The sister. Got to be . . .'

'Using her mother's name,' Thorne said.

'This is all about the mother,' Holland said. 'It's all about Jane.'

Thorne moved towards the desk, correcting Holland as he passed him. 'It's all about a *family* . . .'

'Which means nothing's straightforward,' Brigstocke said. 'Which means it's a damn sight more fucked up and impossible to fathom than we can even begin to imagine.'

Thorne was thinking out loud as much as anything. 'I'm beginning to imagine it,' he said. 'Families can do damage.'

'Are we about done?' Kitson asked, suddenly. She moved towards the door without waiting for an answer. 'I've got a couple of things to do before the briefing starts.'

'I think so. Everybody clear?' Brigstocke looked at his watch and then at Thorne. The face of the watch was a whole lot easier to read. 'Right, we'll start in five minutes then . . .'

★

The 'missed-call' message had been scribbled on a memo sheet and left on Holland's desk. He screwed the paper up into his fist as he began to dial the number.

'Mrs Noble? This is Detective Constable Holland. Thanks very much for getting back to me.' He'd meant to chase her up at the end of the day yesterday, but after Thorne's moment of revelation, things had gone haywire . . .

'I'm afraid I didn't get your message until quite late,' she said. 'And I didn't know whether or not to call you at home.'

'It would have been fine,' Holland said. He probably wouldn't have heard the phone anyway over the sound of the argument he'd been having with Sophie.

'I will get these photos back, won't I?'

'Definitely. We'll take care of them, I promise.'

'You'll need to give me a little bit of time to put my hands on them. They're in the cellar, I think. Actually, it might be the loft, but I'll find them . . .'

Holland looked over his shoulder. The Incident Room was filling up. There were doubtless still a dozen or more smokers outside somewhere, getting their last lungfuls of nicotine for an hour or two, but most available seats and areas of bare desktop were already taken.

'So what do you think? A day or two?'

'Oh yes, I should think so. I've picked up such a lot of old rubbish over the years, mind you . . .'

'Once you've got the photos, when can we come and pick them up?'

'I beg your pardon?'

Holland asked the question again, raising his voice above the growing level of hubbub around him.

'Any time you like,' she answered. 'I'm not going anywhere.'

Thorne was alone in Brigstocke's office. There were only five minutes until the briefing was due to begin. Brigstocke, who would kick things off, was already in the Incident Room. After he'd said his piece, it would be down to Thorne.

He stood before the gallery of pictures on Brigstocke's desk. A series of images carefully designed to tempt and tease. To offer while at the same time giving absolutely nothing away . . .

Thorne could not be sure if the woman in the photographs was Sarah Foley. It didn't really matter. She was there and yet she was absent. In most of the shots she was kneeling, her head bowed, or else artfully shadowed. Thorne picked each picture up in turn, studied it, waited in vain for it to tell him something that it had managed, thus far, to keep to itself.

Aside from the powerful, disconcerting message the photos sent to his groin, Thorne saw nothing new.

Even physically, though the promise of submission was constant, little was revealed. In some of the photos the woman looked to have dark hair, while in others it seemed more fair. In two of them the hair definitely looked blond, but it could easily have been a wig. The body itself appeared to change, depending on how it was posed and lit. It was alternately lissom and muscular, its position making it impossible to accurately judge the height, or even the build, of the woman to whom it belonged.

Sarah Foley, if it *was* her, had not been captured.

Thorne looked at his watch. Another minute and he'd need to get out there. His job was to gee them up, to give the team enough to carry it into the home straight.

The next few days they'd work their arses off, and none more so than him. They'd be going back, as always, checking what they had in light of the new lead, but all the time there was forward momentum. He could already sense it, the hunger that increases when it smells the meal, a collective ticking in the blood. The investigation was picking up speed quickly, starting to race. From this point on, Thorne would make bloody sure nothing else got away from him.

Still, barring an actual arrest, by the weekend he'd be ready for a break. Saturday night with Eve and Sunday with his old man. He allowed himself a smile. If everything went well on Saturday night, he'd probably be making something of a late start the following morning.

Thorne was guessing that by knocking-off time on Saturday, he'd *need* something to divert him. There were other parts of him, *better* parts, that needed exercising, and he wasn't just talking about sex. It would be good to feel the fizz of it with Eve, the flush and the promise of it. The scary thrill and the wonderful release. He was also looking forward to spending a few hours with his father. He needed to feel that lurch, that welling up of whatever it was his old man could suck into Thorne's chest without trying . . .

Karim appeared in the doorway, gave him a look.

'On my way, Sam,' Thorne said.

He would speak with real passion to the officers who were waiting for him. He wanted to catch this killer more than ever now, and he wanted to spread that desire around like a disease. He wanted to engineer that heady feeling of desperation and confidence that could sometimes make things happen all by itself.

But he would take care to hold the other feeling inside, the one that had begun to come and go, and cause something to jump and scuttle behind his ribs . . .

Yes, they were moving quickly. They were suddenly tearing along, they were up for it. But Thorne couldn't help but feel as if something was moving, equally as fast and with just as much determination, towards *them*. There was going to be a collision, but he didn't know when, or from which direction.

He wouldn't see it coming.

Thorne gathered up the photos from the desk, slipped them into a folder and walked towards the Incident Room.

TWENTY-SIX

They spoke to each other slowly, in whispers.

'Did I wake you?'

'What time is it?'

'Late. Go back to sleep . . .'

'It's OK . . .'

'I'm sorry.'

'Were you dreaming about it again?'

'Every bloody night at the moment. Jesus . . .'

'You never used to have dreams before, did you? I had them all the time, always did, but never you . . .'

'Well I'm having them now. With a vengeance.'

'That's an appropriate word.'

'Will they stop, do you think? Afterwards?'

'What?'

'The dreams. Will they stop once it's all over?'

'We'll know soon enough . . .'

'I'm nervous about this one.'

'No need to be.'

'We're less in control of it than with the others. You know? With them we knew what to expect, we knew everything that might happen. That was the advantage of the hotels, they were predictable . . .'

'It'll be fine . . .'

'You're right, course it will, I know. I wake up like this and I'm still thinking about the stuff in the dream and my head's all fucked up.'

'Is that the only reason you're nervous? Something going wrong?'

'What else would it be?'

'That's all right, then.'

'You'd better be there on time, though . . .'

'Don't be silly . . .'

'You'd better fucking be there, all right? Think about the traffic.'

'I never have any problems with the traffic, and I've *always* been there.'

'I know you have. Sorry . . .'

'What about Thorne?'

'Thorne won't be a problem.'

'Good . . .'

'I'm so tired. I have to try and get back to sleep now.'

He reached for her, slid an arm across her belly.

'Come here and I'll help you . . .'

TWENTY-SEVEN

Not a very long time before, on a freezing night when weather and loneliness had seemed meant for each other, Thorne had dialled a number he had copied from a post-card in a newsagent's window. He'd driven round to a basement flat in Tufnell Park, handed over a few notes, and watched a fat, pink hand toss him off. He'd heard the woman's less-than-convincing groans and entreaties, the jangle of the charm bracelet that bounced on her wrist as she worked. He'd heard his own breath, and the low, des-perate grunt as he finished.

Then he'd driven home and gone to bed, where he'd done it again himself for twenty-five quid less . . .

Now, Thorne moved around his office, willing away the last knockings of a muggy Saturday and remembering his hands-on adventure in vice with even less pleasure than he'd felt at the time. It was a measure of how low he had felt then. Of how much he was looking forward to his evening with Eve Bloom.

He would leave Becke House feeling as positive as he had in a long time. Things had moved quickly. The few days since the woman – who might or might not be Sarah

Foley – had elbowed her way to the right part of Thorne's brain and to the forefront of his investigation had yielded encouraging results.

They'd reinterviewed Howard Southern's ex-girlfriend, confirmed her story about the other woman, and quickly managed to turn up several characters claiming to have seen Southern with a woman in the days leading up to his murder. Descriptions were predictably vague and contradictory, 'slim' and 'fair-haired' being the only adjectives that turned up more than once. A barmaid told how she'd seen the woman drag Southern away into a dark corner, where she was 'all over him, but like she wanted him all to herself'. An e-fit had been produced, but it was flatter and even more anonymous than such things normally were. The woman was no more there – on flyers and posters and front pages – than she was in the photos she had sent the men who were to be killed.

Still, it was progress . . .

Another line of inquiry involved the possibility that the woman did more than just woo the victims and lure them to their deaths. Though Thorne himself was dubious, it had at least to be considered that she had been present when they were killed.

They had gone back to the hotels in Slough and Roehampton, to the doss-house in Paddington, and asked questions. Nothing exciting had turned up when CCTV footage was looked at again, but that was hardly surprising. If Mark Foley had known where the cameras were, then so would she. A woman who'd been working on reception at the Greenwood Hotel on the night Ian Welch was killed *did* remember seeing a blond woman hanging around. She'd thought the woman must have been with the party in the bar, but didn't see her talking to anyone. The receptionist thought she was 'funny looking' . . .

Thorne was not sure *what* role the woman had played. He wondered exactly what they would charge her with when they did find her. 'Conspiracy to commit' was probably favourite. Yes, she might have turned up at the hotels, may even have answered the hotel-room doors to the victims, while Mark Foley stood hidden, tightening the length of washing line around his fingers . . .

Beyond that . . .?

If this woman *was* Sarah Foley, Thorne could not imagine her watching. He could not imagine her brother *being* watched, as he brutally raped another man . . .

It was dark, unnatural thoughts such as this one which Thorne determined, at least for a night, to dismiss from his mind, as he moved through the Incident Room, saying his goodbyes.

The doors opened as he reached the lift. Without breaking stride, Thorne walked in and turned to press the button. After a few seconds he watched the room, the desks, the *case* disappear before his eyes as the doors closed . . .

Thorne stepped from the lift and headed towards the car park, all the time thinking about what he was going to wear later on. He reckoned he'd have about half an hour after he got home before Eve was due. Maybe a bit more, if the traffic was as light as it should be.

The BMW cruised up to the barrier, then, fifteen seconds later, moved under it and out on to the road. A Carter

Family compilation was selected, and the volume turned up. He wondered what music he should put on later. Would Eve run screaming from the place as soon as she knew about the country stuff?

He was such a daft old sod. Why had he buggered about? Why the fuck had he even *subconsciously* been putting this off?

Thorne was still ludicrously excited by the car, by the shape and the feel and the sound of it. He put his foot down, enjoying the noise of the engine, smiling for several reasons as he accelerated towards the North Circular, and home.

Picking up speed . . .

Holland drove across Lambeth Bridge, no more than ten minutes from home. He remembered crossing the river further east, on Saturday night exactly a week before. Pissed and talking nonsense in Thorne's new car.

He thought about the look on Sophie's face when she'd found him later on the bathroom floor. He'd raised his head from the cool porcelain of the toilet and seen nothing he felt comfortable with. What he'd seen on her face was worry, carved in deep, and with the strange clarity that only alcohol can bring, Holland knew that it wasn't for him. For the first time, he saw that she was concerned for herself, and for the baby she was carrying. Concerned that in choosing *him* as the father of her child, she'd fucked up big time . . .

The hangover had worn off a damn sight faster than the guilt.

Holland decided that he'd do his bit to make tonight a

good one. He'd stop off and pick up a nice bottle of wine for them to have with dinner, to finish off afterwards, spread out in front of the TV. Sophie still enjoyed the odd glass of wine. It was supposed to be good for her, though before the pregnancy, she would certainly not have stopped at just the one glass. She'd have happily put away a bottle, while Holland watched as her cheeks began to flush, and waited, never knowing whether she'd become soppy or spiky. Either was fine by him. She'd take the piss and start to tease, or else she'd wrap herself around him and talk about the future, and either way they'd usually end up making love.

Before the pregnancy . . .

There was a row of shops just past the Imperial War Museum: a Turkish grocer's, a paper shop and an off-licence. As Holland pulled over to the kerb, he began to ache with the realisation that it was getting hard to remember what things were like before Sophie became pregnant.

The good things, anyway.

It never took him very long to get ready.

He didn't dress up in anything special. There were no pointless rituals, no periods of intense mental preparation, none of that rubbish. He thought about what he was doing, of course he did. He was sensible, he went over it all, but that took no more time than it did to pack his bag.

There wasn't very much to carry. Nothing that wouldn't fit into a small rucksack. Previously, with the ones in the hotel rooms, he'd taken something bigger, a bag he could stuff the sheets and bedclothes into. That wouldn't be necessary this time.

The gloves, the hood, the weapons . . .

He'd already sharpened the knife, then used it to cut off a length from the reel of washing line. He coiled it up and stuffed it into a pocket at the front of the black, leather rucksack.

It was funny, the things people carried around with them in bags. Who knew what secrets, what glimpses into people's lives, might come tumbling out if you could empty their backpacks and briefcases, their plastic sports bags and canvas holdalls? For sure, you'd need to sift through a mountain of files and folders, of newspapers, and sandwiches in cling-film, before you found anything of interest. A ransom note or a blackmail demand. Perhaps the odd dirty mag or pair of handcuffs. Then, if you were lucky, you might find the one bag in ten thousand or a thousand or less that contained a gun, or a bloodstained hammer or a severed finger . . .

You'd almost certainly be surprised if it was a woman's handbag.

He smiled as the last thing went in, and he fastened the strap. Anybody rooting through the bag he was packing would probably just be very embarrassed.

Thorne stood staring at himself in the full-length mirror on the back of his wardrobe door. He was trying to decide whether to stick with the plain white shirt or go back to the blue denim when the doorbell made his mind up for him.

On the way to the door, he nudged the volume of the music down just a little. He'd decided, after much soul-searching, that George Jones would suit any mood that might be required. He had some of the quirky, fifties songs lined up for now, but was ready to bring out the Billy Sherill stuff from two decades later when the time came. There was surely no more romantic song ever recorded than 'He Stopped Loving Her Today' . . .

Eve marched into the centre of the room, cast a quick eye over the place, then over Thorne. 'You look very summery,' she said.

She was wearing a simple, brown cotton dress that buttoned up the front. 'So do you,' Thorne said. He looked down at his white shirt. 'I thought about wearing a tie . . .'

She took a step towards him. 'God, we're not going anywhere posh, are we?'

'No . . .'

'Good. I like the shirt open-necked anyway . . .'

They kissed, their hands growing busier with every few seconds that passed. As Thorne's fingers engaged with the second button on her dress, Eve broke off and stepped away, smiling. 'Now, I don't necessarily think that wild, gymnastic shagging on a full stomach is a good idea,' she said. 'But I could eat *something*, and I'd definitely like a drink . . .'

Thorne laughed. 'Right, is it a bit warm to eat curry?'

'Curry's good any time.'

'There's a fantastic Indian round the corner.'

'Sounds perfect.'

'Or there's any number of great places in Islington or Camden. Loads of nice restaurants in Crouch End. You haven't been in my new car yet . . .'

Eve walked across to the window, fastening her buttons. 'Let's go local. It won't be fair if only one of us has had a drink.'

'No argument from me. Let me grab a jacket . . .'

'Don't bother, we're not going anywhere just yet.'

'No?'

Eve turned from the window, raising her hands to adjust the clips in her hair. Her breasts pushed against the front of her dress, and Thorne could see the redness where she'd shaved under her arms. 'I've got something in the van,' she said. 'I'll need a hand bringing it in.'

It wasn't until Holland looked at the clock on the dash that he realised it had been ten minutes since he'd pulled up outside the flat.

It was just after seven o'clock.

Ten minutes and more of sitting, clutching the plastic bag with the wine inside it, unable to get out of the car.

It was a few minutes after that, when Holland stared, confused for a moment at the small, dark patches appearing on his trousers, and realised that he was crying. He lifted his head and squeezed his eyes shut, the next breath a sigh which caught in his throat and became a sob.

Then a series of them, like punches to the heart.

For want of anything else, he wrapped his forearms around the bag, the wine bottle between his face and the steering wheel as his head dropped slowly forward. He felt the pressure of the bottle through the bag, cold against his cheek, and then, within a few minutes, the bag began to grow warm and slippery with tears, each desperate gasp between sobs sucking the clammy plastic into his mouth . . .

Like the puking wretch he'd been seven days before, Holland could do nothing but let it come, and wait for it to finish.

He cried for himself, and for Sophie, and for the child that would be theirs in five weeks. He wept, guilty and sorry and stupid and scared. The tears whose sting was sharpest though, that were squeezed out faster and bigger than most, were those he shed in anger at the spineless, selfish tosser he knew he had become.

When it was over, Holland lifted his sticky face up just enough to slide a sleeve across it, like a child. He sat, sniffing and staring up at the flat. Before, a general confusion and some pathetic, nameless fear had been twin hands pressing him down into his seat, preventing him from going inside. Now, although there was nothing vague about the shame he was feeling, like a welt across his gut, it was equally effective.

He couldn't go inside, not yet.

Holland looked down at his briefcase in the passenger footwell. He knew that even if he took work upstairs, tried to get straight into it, the first smile from Sophie would be enough to set him off again.

Maybe he could just drive around . . .

He reached down and grabbed the case, rummaged inside until he found the sheet of paper he was looking for. He cleared his throat as he took out his phone and dialled the number. Even so, when it was answered, the first word or two he spoke sounded choked and heavy.

'Mrs Noble, it's Dave Holland here again. I know it's an odd time, but I was wondering if now might be a good time to pop over and pick up those photos . . .?'

TWENTY-EIGHT

Holland made it to Romford in a notch under forty minutes, and stepped out of the car to find Irene Noble waiting on her doorstep. She marched down the path towards him. 'You did that pretty quickly. It usually comes down to the traffic in the Blackwall Tunnel. This is probably the best time, actually . . .'

She was wearing a cream trouser-suit and full make-up. Holland saw her glance towards the houses on either side. He guessed that she was hoping to see the twitch of a net curtain, a sign that one of the neighbours might be watching the young man walking towards her door.

'It was fairly easy,' Holland said. 'There wasn't much traffic at all . . .'

He followed her inside, where he was enthusiastically greeted by a small, off-white dog. Its fur was matted and smelly, but Holland tried his best to make a fuss of it, as it yapped and licked and scrabbled at his shins.

Mrs Noble shooed the dog into the kitchen. 'Candy's knocking on a bit now,' she said. 'Actually, she was Roger's dog, once upon a time. She was still only a puppy when he passed away.'

Holland smiled sympathetically as they stepped through into the living room. A blue three-piece suite sat on a carpet of pink and purple swirls, and a glass-topped coffee table stood square on to the fireplace. A squashed corduroy cushion, covered in tufts of white dog-hair, was the only thing in the room that didn't look spotless.

Holland took a step towards a beechwood cabinet that ran along the back wall. Its doors were mirrored, and its top covered in framed photographs of children.

Mrs Noble walked across and picked up a picture. 'Mark and Sarah aren't here,' she said. 'I couldn't bear looking at them and not knowing. I put them away once I felt sure they weren't coming back. Put them away and bloody well forgot where.' She must have seen concern pass across Holland's face, and reached out a hand to touch his arm. 'Don't worry, you haven't had a wasted journey. I finally found pictures of them tucked away inside our old wedding album . . .'

Holland nodded his understanding. She turned the photo she was holding, so that he could see the picture. 'David's a stockbroker, doing really well.' She put the frame back and began pointing to others. 'Susan's a nurse up at the Royal Free, Gary went into the army and now he's training to become a printer, Claire's about to have her third baby . . .'

'There's a lot of them,' Holland said.

'We fostered long-term mostly, which was the way I wanted it. I couldn't stand to see them go, you know, just when they were starting to belong. Still, we had more than twenty kids, before and after Mark and Sarah. I know what *most* of them are doing . . .'

393

She smiled, sadly, not needing to say any more. Holland smiled back, thinking of those twenty other kids, and the man who was once their foster father, and wondering . . .

'I didn't know whether you'd have eaten,' she said. 'So after you phoned I took a lasagne out of the freezer. It won't be five minutes . . .'

'Oh, right . . .'

'I presume you can have a drink?'

In spite of what he'd previously thought of her, Holland was suddenly filled with something like affection for this woman. He thought about all the children she'd lost in one way or another, and her simple belief in a man whose heart was too full of darkness to go on beating any longer. He felt comfortable . . .

'Let's both have a drink,' he said. 'I've got a nice bottle of wine in the car.'

'You have to let me pay you for the mattress,' Thorne said.

'It's fine, really. You can get dinner . . .'

'How much was it?'

'It's a late birthday present,' Eve said. 'To replace the first one.' She smiled. 'I don't remember seeing the plant anywhere at the flat, so I presume you've managed to kill it.'

'Oh, right. I was going to tell you about that,' Thorne said.

A waiter brought over their wine, and at the same time the manager came across to the table and laid down a platter of poppadoms. 'On the house,' he said. He put a hand on Thorne's shoulder and winked at Eve. 'One of my very best customers,' he said. 'But tonight is the first time he has been here with a young lady . . .'

When the manager had moved away, Eve poured herself and Thorne a large glass of wine each. 'I'm not sure how to take that,' she said. 'Does he mean that you normally come here with young *men*?'

Thorne nodded, guiltily. 'That was another thing I was going to tell you . . .'

She laughed. 'So you come in here on your own a lot then?'

'Not a *lot*.' He nodded towards the manager. 'He's talking about the number of takeaways . . .'

'I've got this image of you now, sitting in here on your own like Billy No-Mates, eating chicken tikka massala . . .'

'Hang on.' Thorne tried to look hurt. 'I do have one or two friends.'

Eve chopped the pile of poppadoms into pieces. She picked up a big bit, ladled onions and chutney on to it. 'Tell me about them. What do they do?'

Thorne shrugged. 'They're all connected to work in one way or another, I suppose.' He reached for a piece of poppadom, took a bite. 'Phil's a pathologist . . .'

She nodded, like it meant something.

'What?' Thorne said.

'You never really switch off, do you?'

'Actually, me and Phil talk about football most of the time . . .'

'Seriously.'

Thorne took a gulp of wine, feeling it swill the bits from the surface of his teeth, thinking about what Eve was saying. 'I don't believe that anybody ever leaves what they do behind completely,' he said. 'We all talk shop, don't we? Everyone gets . . . reminded of things.' She stared back at him, rubbing the rim of her wineglass across her chin. 'Come on, if you're out somewhere and you see some amazing display of flowers . . .'

'Flowers aren't bodies, are they?'

Thorne was disturbed to feel himself growing slightly irritated. He fought to keep it out of his voice as he picked up the bottle and topped up both their glasses. 'Well, some people might say that they're dying from the moment they're picked.'

Eve nodded slowly. 'Everything's dying,' she said. 'What's the bloody point of anything at all? We may as well just ask the waiter to put ground glass in the biryani.'

Thorne looked at her, saw her eyes widen and the corners of her mouth begin to twitch. They began to laugh at almost the same moment.

'I never know when you're winding me up,' he said.

She slid her hand across the table, took hold of his. 'Can you leave it behind just for a while, Tom?' she said. 'Tonight, I want you to switch off . . .'

'Kids are a bloody handful,' Irene Noble said. 'They change things beyond all recognition.' She stared across at Holland. 'But you'll still be glad you did it . . .'

Holland had supposed that if they talked at all, they might well talk about kids. He never imagined that they might end up talking about *his*.

'I just feel so guilty,' he said. 'For resenting what might happen to me. For even *thinking* about walking away from it.'

'You'll feel stuff that's a whole lot stranger and more painful than that. You'll feel like you would die for them and the next minute you'd happily murder them. You'll worry about where they are and then you'll wish you could have a second to yourself. Every emotion is unconditional . . .'

'You're talking about afterwards, when the baby's there. What about feeling like this *now*?'

'It's normal. It's not just the woman's emotions that get messed around with. Mind you, *you* can't use hormones as an excuse . . .'

Holland laughed, the two glasses of wine he'd put away helping him to feel relaxed. An hour or so earlier, he'd felt far less sure of himself. He'd thought, when they'd started to eat and he'd suddenly begun pouring it all out, that there might be more waterworks on the way, but Irene had helped him stay calm, convinced him that everything would work out for the best . . .

'I'll take these out.' She stood up, lifting the tray from the empty seat on the sofa next to her.

Holland passed over his empty plate. 'Thanks, that was great.' He was talking about more than just a lasagne that had been cold in the middle.

He sat back down and listened as she pottered around in the kitchen. He could hear her talking softly to the dog, loading the plates into the dishwasher.

It had been a conversation that Holland would never have had with his mother. Irene Noble, give or take a year or two, was the same age as his mother – a woman who'd been buying baby clothes for the last six months. A woman who refused to admit that anything could go wrong *ever*, and remained blissfully unaware that things were less than hunky-dory between her eldest son and his pregnant girlfriend.

Irene came back in brandishing choc-ices. 'I always keep

397

a stock of these in the freezer. Bloody marvellous in this weather . . .'

For a minute they said nothing. They sat and ate their ice creams, and listened to the noise of the dog's claws skittering across the lino as she scrabbled about in the kitchen.

As Irene Noble started to speak, pulling her feet up on to the sofa like a teenager, Holland watched her face shift and settle, until every one of her years was clearly visible on it.

'Whatever problems you have, I hope you work them out together, all three of you. But they won't be in the same league as some of the things that kids have brought with them through my front door. You pass them on, you know. Hand them down, like baldness or diabetes or the colour of your eyes . . .'

'You're talking about Mark and Sarah . . .'

'The other day I was very harsh about the two sets of carers who had the children before we did. About their inability to cope. The truth is that we weren't really coping any better than they had.'

'You adopted them.'

'I think it was our last effort at making them feel part of something bigger. Two parents and two children. We wanted them to come out of themselves, to engage with the rest of the world a bit more.'

'It's understandable though,' Holland said. 'That they'd be tight-knit. That the two of them would be very close, after what happened.' He looked away from her, down to the floor, thinking, *And what was still happening* . . .

'They were *too* close,' she said. 'That was the problem. When they disappeared, Sarah was pregnant, and the baby she was carrying was Mark's.'

TWENTY-NINE

They walked slowly back down Kentish Town Road towards Thorne's flat. At not much after nine o'clock, it was just starting to darken but was still warm enough to walk without a jacket. The road was as busy and noisy as ever. Cars moved past them constantly, those which could had their tops down, most had sidelights on.

Despite what Eve had said earlier, they had both tucked a fair amount of food away, though Thorne put the feeling in his stomach down to something else entirely. Before they'd left the flat, Eve had helped him make the bed, laying a clean white sheet across the new mattress she'd brought with her. Thorne knew very well that when they got back there, she was going to help him unmake it again.

There were some things in his life which he counted as certainties: there was always another body, somewhere; you could never get rid of blood completely; people who killed without motive tended to do it again. But *this* was the sort of promise that Thorne hadn't been on for a very long time . . .

Eve grabbed his hand suddenly, and raised it up,

bringing their bare forearms together. 'You'd look a lot better with a decent tan,' she said.

'Is that an invitation?'

'When was the last time you had a proper holiday?'

Even after thinking about it for a minute, Thorne couldn't provide anything as specific as a year. Lack of time was not so much the problem as lack of inclination and anybody to go away with. 'It's been a while,' he said.

'Are you a lying-on-the-beach kind of guy, or do you prefer to do stuff?'

'Both, really. Or neither. I think lying on the beach gets a bit boring, but probably not *quite* as boring as walking round a museum . . .'

'Not easily pleased, are you?'

'Sorry . . .'

'All right, where would you like to go, if you could go anywhere?'

'I've always fancied Nashville.'

She nodded. 'Right. The country-and-western thing . . .'

'Another one of my dark secrets . . .'

'I quite liked it.'

'Really?'

'You're not going to get kinky later on though, are you? Dress up in leather chaps? Bring out the bullwhip and spurs . . .?'

They turned right on to Prince of Wales Road, the sound of live jazz coming from the Pizza Express on the corner. Thorne wondered if a pizza might not have been a better idea. The combination of curry and humidity meant that beads of perspiration were popping all over him.

Still hand in hand, Thorne could feel the moisture

between their palms. He wasn't sure whether it was her sweat or his own.

The bike weaved effortlessly through the traffic. Occasionally, where it got really heavy, or the road narrowed, he would have to sit and wait. Idling, in line among the despatch riders and trainee cabbies on mopeds. Soon enough, there would be a gap and he would be away, the rucksack bouncing against his back as he drove across sleeping policemen and holes in the road . . .

He pulled up at traffic lights and checked his watch. He was probably going to get there a bit early, but it wouldn't matter. He would park up, stroll off somewhere and wait. Keeping out of sight, until it was time.

Next to him, a big Kawasaki revved up, ready for the off. A girl in cut-off jeans rode pillion, squeezing her boyfriend tighter with each growl he twisted from the engine. On amber, the Jap bike was gone, and he watched it go, easing his own machine slowly away from the lights.

Picking up no more speed than was necessary . . .

He had plenty of time, and the last thing he wanted was to be pulled over.

It wasn't so much a question of the ticket, or the points on his licence. He was so excited, so full of what he was about to do, that were some copper to pull him over and ask where he was going, he might just have to tell him.

Holland looked at his watch and was gobsmacked to see that he'd been there for an hour and a half.

'I need to be getting back,' he said. 'Could I have those photographs?'

Irene Noble climbed a little wearily from the sofa, slipped her shoes back on. 'I'll go and fetch them . . .'

While he was waiting, Holland sat, going over their conversation and marvelling at the capacity people had for self-deception. Irene Noble was far from being a stupid woman. He found it hard to understand why, even though she claimed that they, and previous carers, had caught the children in bed together, she had so readily presumed that Sarah Foley had been made pregnant by her brother. Had no other explanation occurred to her?

He heard her coming down the stairs, shouting to him. 'It doesn't seem five minutes since these were taken.'

Probably no other explanation she could live with . . .

She walked into the room holding out a small bundle of photos, half a dozen Polaroids and a couple of slightly bigger standard prints. Holland took them from her. She stepped back and perched on the arm of the sofa, pointing to the pictures as he began to look through them.

'Those are the two I had in frames on the sideboard. They're the ones that were taken at school the year before they disappeared. The others are from a birthday party we had for Sarah. Her eleventh, it would have been. Roger had just bought this instant camera . . .'

From the moment he'd looked down at the first photograph, Holland had stopped hearing anything but the sound of his own breathing. A girl in a blue-patterned dress, her hair tied back, smiling as though at something only she found funny. Holland lifted the picture of Sarah up, revealing its companion, the portrait of her brother.

'Jesus,' he said.

Irene stood up. 'What's the matter?'

Holland flicked through the other photos to make sure, stopping at one in particular and staring at it, elated and terrified. He couldn't hear as Irene Noble continued to ask him what was wrong, didn't see her moving across the room towards him.

Sarah Foley sat at the table, the knife in her hand poised above a cake, the girls either side of her looking far more excited than she did. Just visible in the top right of the picture, Mark stood in the corner of the room. His fingers were curled around the edge of the door, as if he were preparing to throw it open and run through it, or else push away from it, launching himself towards the camera, and whoever lay beyond it.

Her face was thinner then, and his perhaps a little fuller. The eyes were wider and the skin smoother, but that was understandable. These were the faces of children, which had yet to weather, but Holland was familiar with their expressions.

He was looking at pictures of people he recognised.

THIRTY

Thorne lay in bed, listening hard, trying to ascertain exactly what might be happening from the sounds he could hear coming from the bathroom . . .

For the want of anything more original to say, he'd offered Eve a coffee as soon as they'd got back to the flat, hoping she'd turn it down and delighted when she did. She'd gone to the toilet then, and he'd moved around the flat, opening windows, grinning at himself in the mirror like a schoolboy, as he passed the mantelpiece on the way to the stereo. With the first few bars of 'Good Year for the Roses' filling the room, Thorne had turned to find her standing only inches away . . .

They'd half danced, half stumbled through to the bedroom, and collapsed on to the new mattress. The laughter gave way quickly to more passionate noises as their hands and mouths went to work on each other, the wine and the wait making their movements hungrier, more desperate than they'd been earlier, before they'd left for the restaurant . . .

Then suddenly, Eve had stopped, and begun to laugh again. She'd pushed herself off the bed, grinned, and announced that she needed another visit to the bathroom. As soon as she'd closed the door behind her, Thorne had stripped quickly and slid beneath the duvet, grateful to have avoided that awkward moment when the love-handles were revealed, but feeling, all the same, that a certain spontaneity had gone . . .

Now, he could hear nothing through the wall between bedroom and bathroom. Thinking about it, the impetus might have been lost, but no more so than it would have been when the moment came for him to fiddle clumsily around with a condom. He thought about the packet he'd bought the day before, from the machine in the toilets at the Royal Oak. It lay, nestled in the drawer of his bedside cabinet, alongside the athlete's foot cream and indigestion tablets.

He decided that it might save time and trouble if he took a condom out of the packet and laid it ready. As he reached across to open the drawer, a thought struck him. Perhaps she was in the bathroom, fiddling clumsily around with a diaphragm . . .

Thorne heard water running. He sat up a little higher in bed, leaned his head back against the wall and turned his ear to it.

She was probably brushing her teeth . . .

He wondered whether he should slip out of bed, put on his dressing gown and join her. How would it feel if her teeth were clean, while his mouth still tasted of curry? Would it seem strange, the two of them spitting into the sink together before they'd so much as felt each other up?

The door opened, and Eve walked back in. She stopped next to the bed and looked down at him. Her clothes were straightened and smooth, as though it were already the following morning and she had come to kiss him goodbye. She looked sexier than anything he could remember, looked as if she found *him* more attractive than ever, and yet, for a second, Thorne wondered if she was about to turn and leave.

Before he could say anything, she laid her handbag gently down by the side of the bed, took a step back, and began to undress.

The home number was engaged, so Holland tried Thorne's mobile. The phone sat on a table in a tiny alcove beneath the stairs, where Holland fought for space with coats, umbrellas and plastic bags filled with boots and shoes.

Irene Noble hovered behind him. 'Who are you calling? Are you allowed to tell me?'

'Detective Inspector Thorne. You met him the other day . . .'

'Oh yes. Perhaps he's got a mobile.'

'I'm trying it now . . .' Holland turned away, suddenly uncomfortable with her so close. In his hurry to make the call, to pass on what he'd discovered, it hadn't occurred to him that he should really be doing it privately. He'd been relaxed, enjoying himself. Now he was on duty again, and he knew there were things he had to tell Thorne which Irene Noble shouldn't hear. 'I'm sorry, but you'll have to . . .'

Holland heard Thorne's voice telling him how sorry he was that he couldn't talk to him, asking him to leave a message. Holland pressed a button to end the call. This was a message that he wanted to deliver personally.

Still clutching the photographs of Mark and Sarah Foley, Holland was out of there in less than a minute.

He thanked Irene Noble as he backed away down the path towards his car, all the time wondering if there was a quicker way back towards North London, telling himself that there was no need to go mad, that their suspects had no way of knowing they'd been identified and would not be going anywhere.

The last thing Holland told Irene Noble, shouting through his open window just before he pulled away, was that he'd take good care of her photos. In truth, he didn't know when she was likely to see them again. Holland would show them to Thorne. He would show them to Brigstocke. They would use them to secure a warrant . . .

Holland could not know for sure how it would proceed from there, what the timescale would be, how much would be passed on to the media. Every case ended differently. Still, there was a chance, if they wanted to stem the flow of damaging publicity, and made the arrests over the weekend, that the next time Irene Noble saw the pictures would be on the front pages of the papers on Monday morning.

'You're gorgeous,' Thorne said, staring down, wanting her. 'I can't believe it's taken so bloody long to get here.'

'Whose fault is that?'

'Mine, I know.'

'Glad you're here now though?'

'God, yeah.' Thorne grinned. 'I'm thinking about what would have happened if I hadn't answered the phone in that hotel room, when we found the first body. You might

have called an hour later. It could easily have been somebody else who answered that phone . . .'

She shrugged. 'Then it could very easily have been
somebody else who was here now.'

Her body felt warm and smooth against his. He was
sure, rusty and as inept a reader of signs as he was, that he
saw desire in her eyes. Yet a minute before, when he'd
placed a hand for the first time against the naked flesh of
her breast, he'd felt a tension. There was a reserve suddenly, which seemed slightly at odds with what Thorne
had been led to expect. She'd made all the running,
cracked those dirty jokes about the bed, about being up for
it. Now, at the last moment, she was revealing herself to be
not quite as forward as she pretended to be.

Thorne felt a barrier go up. Fragile and perhaps only a
touch away from collapse, and unbearably sexy . . .

She wanted him to do the work, to be a man. It was as
though she longed to submit to him, to herself, but needed
a little help. Thorne was massively excited. He could sense
what might be waiting, if she allowed herself to go over the
edge. More than anything, he wanted to nudge her towards
it . . .

'You're *so* gorgeous,' he said, and dropped his mouth
down on to hers.

As if on cue, Thorne could hear a song beginning in
the other room. This was the one he'd thought would be
so perfect. The story of a man whose love for a woman
only ended on the day they carried him out of his front
door in a box. Thorne let the familiar richness of George
Jones's voice roll over him, as he ran his hands across
Eve's body.

He was dimly aware of another familiar sound. The bedroom door creaked open, hissing as it moved across the carpet. It was a noise which often disturbed him in the early hours, and one which, tonight of all nights, he could well do without.

Thorne stopped what he was doing and smiled at Eve, waiting to feel the unwelcome weight of the cat landing on the end of the bed . . .

Holland took the Romford Road as far as Forest Gate, then cut over towards Wanstead Flats. This was not an area of London he knew well. With one hand on the steering wheel and the other holding open the *A–Z*, he was making up his route as he went.

He'd called Sophie as soon as he'd left Irene Noble's house, to explain why he hadn't come home. He'd told her that something important had come up, grateful that it was no longer a lie. She had told him that she was tired, that she would be getting an early night, but he could hear in her voice that she was less than thrilled. He managed to tell her that he loved her before she put the phone down.

Holland tried phoning Thorne's home number. It was still engaged. He dialled the mobile again, hung up as soon as he heard Thorne's recorded message . . .

He was doing fifty on the long, straight road that cut across Hackney Marshes. It was another area in this strange part of the city that was green enough on the page of the *A–Z*, but seemed grim and far from welcoming after dark. He'd feel happier once he picked up the A107 at Clapton. He could see it at the bottom of the page, only a fingernail away from where he was now. Then it was pretty much a straight line up through Stamford Hill and on to the Seven Sisters Road. Ten minutes more, past Finsbury Park and across the Holloway Road, and he would be at Thorne's place.

Once again, he thought about doing the simple thing, and calling Brigstocke. It was probably the *correct* thing to do, but his first loyalty, as always, was to Thorne. He recalled an American cop show he and Sophie had watched one evening: *NYPD Blue* maybe, or *Homicide*. An officer had talked about giving his partner a 'heads up' on something, when really he should have taken the matter higher. Thorne wasn't his partner, of course, but it was still more or less how Holland felt.

Thorne would be grateful for a heads up on this one . . .

Surer now of his bearings, Holland laid the *A–Z* down on the passenger seat and dialled Thorne's flat again. He listened to the monotonous beep of the engaged signal, wondering why he wasn't hearing the usual, irritating 'call-waiting' message.

Holland had a good idea who Thorne would be talking to. He remembered a night in the Royal Oak when Thorne had been talking about himself and his father, and their 'forty-five-minute conversations about fuck all'. Tonight it was likely to be fuck all *and* a Spurs win in the opening game of the season. Holland could picture Thorne sitting there listening, a can of supermarket lager on the go, desperately trying to get his old man off the line so that they could both settle down and watch the goals on TV.

Two–one against Chelsea at Stamford Bridge. Thorne should at least be in a good mood.

Holland reached across and retrieved the photographs from beneath the *A–Z*. He wondered what sort of mood Thorne would be in, twenty minutes or so from now, after he'd taken a look at *them* . . .

Thorne froze, in confusion as much as anything, when he turned and saw the man taking off his crash helmet.

'How the fuck did *you* get in?' Thorne said. For a few dizzy and bewildering seconds, all he could think of was that this was some sort of jealous-boyfriend situation he'd unwittingly got caught up in, and that he was about to get involved in a very embarrassing fist-fight. It was the look on the man's face, as much as the knife he was pulling from his rucksack, that told Thorne something altogether different was happening.

Thorne turned to Eve, whipping his head around fast, and straight into the knife that *she* held, pointed towards him. The blade sliced a clean line across his chin, the point sinking itself half an inch or so into the soft flesh beneath his jaw.

He cried out, threw himself sideways and began to bleed on to the pillow.

The man took a step towards the bed.

One small part of Thorne's brain continued to function rationally, to formulate a thought. *The knife was in her bag.* The rest of it began to give shape to something dark, to a fear he'd felt before only as something fleeting and skittish, but which was now borne inside him, heavy and hooked beneath his breastbone. He pictured it, alive and feeding in his chest. He felt its strong, thin fingers wrapped around his ribs, hanging from them, pulling him down.

411

Thorne lifted his head up and pressed a hand to the gash across his chin. He tried not to let the terror sound in his voice when he spoke.

'Mark and Sarah . . .'

At the mention of his real name, a shadow fell across the man's face. 'Move away from my sister, now.'

Thorne shuffled across the mattress, oddly uncomfortable with his nakedness. He watched the woman step, nude and smiling, from the other side of the bed and gather up her clothes.

'Eve, this is so stupid . . .'

Ben Jameson's eyes moved quickly, from his sister's body back to Thorne. 'Get on to the fucking floor . . .'

THIRTY-ONE

While they were preparing him, Thorne tried to take the growing fear, the blood, the pain and keep them somewhere separate. Somewhere he could store them up, stoke them into a rage he might be able to use. The rest of his brain was focusing, coming up with answers, putting it together. Adrenaline causing the engine to race . . .

The two of them worked together quickly and efficiently. Before Thorne could even think about how he might move against them, against the two knives, it became an impossibility. Eve slipped the belt from Thorne's chinos, wrapped it around his wrists until it hurt. Ben manipulated his body, pushing the head down towards the carpet, hoiking up the knees, spreading the calves. They operated as a team, movement and stillness in sync, one busy while the other held a knife close. Thorne was never more than a few inches away from a blade. Any move, other than those he was instructed to make, was out of the question.

Now his body mirrored those he'd seen before. Distorted and discoloured. In hotel rooms and in dreams . . .

Thorne lay naked, face down on the floor, knees pulled up beneath him and hindquarters raised. His head and hands pointed towards the bedroom door. Blood from the knife-wound soaked into the carpet and grew sticky beneath his cheek.

'It didn't matter in the rest of the room,' Thorne said. 'In those hotels, traces just got lost among everybody else's. But you had to get rid of the *bedding*, didn't you, Eve? That would have been clean, that would just have had traces of you and the victim . . .'

Though Thorne couldn't see it, Eve smiled. 'Once I got them into bed, they were helpless. Same as you.'

'I never raped anybody, Eve . . .'

'It's a bit late, don't you think,' Jameson said. 'To be slotting pieces into your little puzzle? It's rather fucking pointless, considering where you are.'

'Who wants to die ignorant?'

'You can't do much about that,' Jameson said, '*however* many answers you get . . .'

'Is this the pet project you talked about? These killings? The thing of your own you wanted to get off the ground . . .'

Jameson laughed. 'That's quite funny. Be a damn sight more interesting than local authority training videos, that's for sure. There you go, there's one more piece of your puzzle. One more thing to make you a bit less ignorant . . .'

Thorne was already trying to work it out. 'It's how you got into the Register, isn't it? Not sure where the connection is. Social services?'

Eve provided the answer. 'The National Probation Directorate. Specifically the Sex Offenders and Corrections Unit . . .'

'*Towards a National Information Strategy* isn't *Citizen Kane*,' Jameson said. 'But they were more than happy for

414

me to do all the research I needed and their security *was* very sloppy. They were somewhat lax about unattended computers, access to databases, that sort of thing. Mind you, that *was* exactly why they wanted the video made in the first place . . .'

It suddenly struck Thorne that Jameson had probably been on the list that was compiled of contact numbers for Charlie Dodd. A video production company would not have seemed suspicious, bearing in mind the nature of Dodd's business. Never having known it, Thorne would not have recognised the name of Jameson's company anyway. It didn't matter a great deal now . . .

'That was fortunate for you,' Thorne said.

'We all need a bit of luck now and again,' Eve said. 'Some of us more than others . . .'

Thorne lifted his face from the carpet, feeling fibres and tiny pieces of grit sticking to the dried blood on his chin. He took the weight on his forehead and looked back through the gap underneath his arm. Jameson was delving into the rucksack he'd placed on the end of the bed. Eve stood by his side, her eyes never leaving Thorne.

'We should get this done,' she said.

Thorne saw a flash of blue as Jameson pulled out the length of washing line, then one of black, which he presumed was the hood. He felt the fear that was the creature in his chest grow heavier. He closed his eyes and saw it climbing, using the slats of his ribcage like a ladder, heaving itself upwards little by little.

As was so often the way, it was the last part of the journey that was proving the most frustrating. It had taken ages to get across the Holloway Road at the Nag's Head and up to Tufnell Park. Now the ridiculous number of traffic lights and pedestrian crossings on the Kentish Town Road was providing a last-minute annoyance.

Holland thought about calling again. He decided that even if Thorne was off the phone or had turned the mobile back on, he was more or less there now anyway, so there wasn't much point . . .

Holland drove down the inside lane, swerving back out right when he came up against a bus and deftly cutting up a black cab in the process. At the next set of lights the taxi came up *his* inside and the driver wound down his window to give him an earful. Holland held up his warrant card, told the fat cabbie to fuck off and watched, smiling, as he did.

When the lights changed, Holland swung into Prince of Wales Road. Thorne's street was the third on the right. He indicated and slowed to a stop, glancing down at the photos while he was waiting for a break in the traffic.

When one finally came, he turned, wondering if they'd even allow Thorne to be there when they made the arrests.

'It *is* the most fantastic story though,' Jameson said. 'Maybe I should write it, change all the names of course, to protect the innocent . . .'

'Whoever *they* are,' Thorne said.

'It would be in three parts. Three *acts*, if you like, same as any classic screenplay . . .'

'You live and learn.'

'Not for much longer.'

The black thing inside Thorne climbed another rib . . .

'For the first part we have to go back in time. Flared trousers and shit hair and a piece of scum who probably has both. A man who drags a woman into a storeroom and rapes her.'

'Your mother . . .'

Thorne felt the vibrations as feet moved quickly across the carpet towards him, then the pain of a heel pressing down on to the side of his face. 'Let him tell it,' Eve said.

'The rapist, thanks largely to the police, is found not guilty. The woman suffers a breakdown. Her husband goes mad.' Jameson emptied the facts from his mouth like he was spitting out dirt. 'He kills her and then himself and their bodies are discovered by their two young children who are subsequently taken into foster care. It's a dramatic start, don't you reckon?'

'That's why I'm here, isn't it?' Thorne said. The shoe came back down across the side of his face and ear. Jameson said something he couldn't make out and the foot was lifted. Thorne turned his head and saw Eve moving back across the room towards her brother. '"Thanks largely to the police", that's what you said. So, I have to die because of the way some fuckwit handled a rape case nearly thirty years ago.' He received no answer. 'Yes? Is that about right?'

'There's no point bleating about life being unfair,' Eve said. 'We're the last people you'll get any sympathy from there . . .'

'I understand why. I just want to know why *me*?'

'Because you answered the phone.'

And Thorne saw that it really was that simple. The message left by the killer on Eve Bloom's answering machine had always bothered him, and finally he understood why. It had been 'left' so that Eve had an excuse to call the hotel – a call to a murder scene that would be answered by a police officer. The wreaths had been ordered after the subsequent killings purely to make it look like part of a pattern.

They had selected their rapists with care. Their final victim, Thorne himself, had been chosen completely at random. He remembered what he'd said to Eve, what she'd said to him, twenty minutes earlier in bed:

'*It could easily have been somebody else who answered that phone . . .*'

'*Then it could very easily have been somebody else who was here now.*'

He could still see the look on her face as she'd said it. He imagined the look on his father's, as he received the news of Thorne's death.

'I've got a great title as well,' Jameson said. 'For this sordid little horror story. What do you think of "Out of the Frying Pan into the Fire"?'

'We know about Roger Noble . . .'

'Oh you do?' For the first time, though Jameson did not raise his voice, Thorne could hear emotion behind it, white-hot and lethal. 'You might know what he did, but you can't know how it felt.'

'Bad enough so that you had to leave.'

'Well done . . .'

'To protect your sister . . .'

'Noble didn't want to hurt me,' Eve said. 'He wanted to hurt my baby.'

'He made you pregnant?'

Jameson laughed. 'We're back to ignorance. We should

have a little bell to ring, or a buzzer, for when you get it wrong or say something stupid. Noble liked *boys*. The baby was mine.'

'Ours,' Eve said. 'So we left when they tried to make me get rid of it.'

Thorne realised that it had been shame he'd heard in Irene Noble's voice when she'd stared into her M & S coffee and talked about 'behavioural' problems. It had probably been her idea to move in the first place, to get the abortion performed in a different area, to avoid the scandal . . .

'What happened to the child?' Thorne asked.

Jameson answered matter-of-factly. 'We lost it. Who knows, when all this is over, we might try again.'

For perhaps half a minute, nobody spoke. Thorne lay in agony, a breeze from somewhere passing across his bare skin. The feeling had gone from his hands, and the thumping of his heart was lifting his chest clear off the carpet.

When all this is over . . .

He imagined the look that was passing between the two people who planned to kill him. He pictured something tender, an expression of the love between a man and a woman, who talked about having a baby together once he had been raped and strangled to death.

Thorne moaned in pain as he twisted his head across to the other side. 'I'm guessing that the final part of this story involves the murders,' he said. 'Remfry and Welch and Dodd and Southern. Me as the symbolic climax. It's the middle bit that's still a mystery, after you disappeared. What happened between Franklin and the men in prison? Why did you start killing again?'

419

'Lightning struck twice,' Eve said.

Then the doorbell rang . . .

Thorne tensed and raised his head, but their speed, their *commitment*, was overpowering. In a heartbeat they were on him, a knife pressed into each side of his throat, cutting off the breath he'd need before he had a chance to cry out . . .

Hendricks picked up almost immediately.

'Listen,' Holland said, 'I'm outside DI Thorne's place and I can't get any reply, but his phone's engaged . . .'

'He probably left it off the hook, while he's busy giving Eliza Doolittle a good seeing to.'

Holland felt ice at his neck. 'Sorry?'

'He had a hot date with his sexy florist. I'm not surprised he doesn't want to answer the door . . .'

'Oh, Jesus . . .'

'What is it?'

Holland told Hendricks about the pictures, about Mark and Sarah Foley. Hendricks announced that he was coming straight over. The panic Holland heard in the pathologist's voice stemmed the rising tide of it he felt in himself.

Then, looking across the road, he saw the motorbike . . .

'Dave . . .?'

Holland felt the engine that was ticking over within him moving up a gear. 'Listen, Phil, before you leave, get on the phone. Call Brigstocke and fill him in. Get some back-up round here, now. And an ambulance . . .'

'What are you going to do?'

Holland was walking along the pavement, away from Thorne's place. He was thinking about the alleyway that he remembered running along the side of a house three or four doors up. 'I'm not sure . . .'

He was seeing a face through a crash helmet. Seeing the face of a killer, smiling at the lie within the truth.

'*I've got a BMW myself . . .*'

Smiling, because BMW make bikes as well as cars . . .

THIRTY-TWO

'Why don't you just get out now while you still can?' Thorne said. 'You'll spend the rest of your lives in prison. You'll never see each other again . . .'

Jameson sounded unconcerned. 'Don't get worked up. Whoever that was at your door, they've gone.'

Thorne twisted his head, aimed his voice towards Eve. 'People know you were coming over here, for fuck's sake. There'll be fibres, bits of skin everywhere. In the bed . . .'

'Of course there will,' Eve said. 'I'm your girlfriend. Which is why *I'll* be the one calling the police.'

Thorne was stunned, but he saw immediately that they would get away with it. It was very simple. With Thorne dead, Jameson would kiss his sister goodbye for a while and slip away. On his way out, he would kick in the door that she'd previously left open for him, make sure there were signs of a forced entry.

Then she would dial 999 . . .

He had no doubt that Eve would play the part of the traumatised witness and, later, the grieving girlfriend perfectly. He knew all too well how good she was, how convincingly she would pick up the pieces of her life. He could see the officers falling a little bit in love with her as they took her shocking statement.

The idea that they would not be made to pay for his death caused a surge of fury to rush through Thorne. He did not need it, but he felt a jolt of added determination to cling on fiercely to every second.

'Tell me about the lightning, Eve.'

She said nothing, but Jameson took the bait. 'Franklin was always going to pay for what he did. It just took me a while to get round to it . . .'

Jameson had moved to stand between Thorne and the door. Eve had crossed back to the bed. He presumed that Jameson was still holding the hood, and the washing line, but he could not be certain. Thorne guessed that Roger Noble had been fortunate, dropping dead when he did. Something in Jameson's voice suggested that, had he still been alive, Jameson would have 'got round' to him as well . . .

'So why not leave it there?' Thorne asked.

'We did,' Eve said. 'Carried on with the lives we'd made, that we'd *re*made, for ourselves, until I had one too many slow dances at a party. Until some piece of shit thought that "no" meant "yes", and followed me home . . .'

Face down on the carpet, Thorne knew full well the expression on her face. He'd seen it before, the night they'd walked across London Fields and he'd told her about the case. Told her things she already knew far better than he did . . .

'*Just think of this bloke as cutting re-offending rates . . .*'

'It would be stupid to ask if you reported the rape to the police,' Thorne said.

Jameson took a step towards him, his black boots moving

into Thorne's field of vision. 'Very fucking stupid. We dealt with that one ourselves . . .'

Thorne remembered the *other* case Holland and Stone had pulled off CRIMINT. A man found raped and strangled in the boot of a car. The ligature had been removed, but Thorne could now be pretty certain that it had been washing line.

He'd solved another murder in the last few moments before his own . . .

'Which all brings us bang up to date,' Jameson said.

To me, Thorne thought. He knew he was the last in a line of dead men, connected by the strongest, strangest thread of all. The family tie which refused to break, even when it had become twisted beyond all recognition.

'You kill the man you blame for the death of your mother and father, and for your abuse at the hands of the foster parent who replaces them. You kill the man who attacked your sister. You develop a taste for it . . .'

'Not a taste for *killing*, no.'

'My mistake. A taste for some perverted idea of justice . . .'

'Listen to yourself . . .'

'Tell me you don't enjoy it . . .'

Eve's voice was flat, barely above a whisper. 'I want to do this, now,' she said.

Thorne could feel her walking towards him. At the same time Jameson moved quickly, one step bringing him next to Thorne, another lifting a boot up and across Thorne's back, until he was straddling him.

Thorne knew what was coming, but refused to submit to it. He reacted instinctively, thrusting his legs backwards and pushing his groin down towards the carpet. Hands

424

grabbed his legs, clawed at his thighs as they struggled to lift them, fought to bring his rear end upright, to make it accessible . . .

Pain and numbness had left the top half of Thorne's body as good as useless. It was no more than a dead thing, with only the dark mass that clung to his ribs still flourishing. Swinging inside him, wet and weighty, clattering off the wall of his chest as he kicked and thrashed.

'Stop it,' Jameson said.

Thorne cried out, the terror suddenly far greater than the rage. His voice sounded high and weak, and was quickly replaced by the deafening roar and squeal of agony as Jameson's gloved fist pounded into the side of his head, again and again, until Thorne could do nothing but let go, and be still, and wait for it to stop.

Seconds stretched and passed, and though Thorne had lost track of who was where, he was aware of movement, of arms and legs, of pressure . . .

He was aware of Eve's voice as the scream in his head died down a little, and he heard her saying, 'Hold him.'

He was aware that he had started to cry, and was grateful that he hadn't lost control of bladder or bowels.

Thorne raised his head an inch off the floor. The wetness slipped beneath his chin and into the gash, stinging. 'One thing,' he said, looking for Jameson, his voice somewhere between a gasp and a rattle, 'just for my own satisfaction. Are you going to rape me before or after I'm dead? We never *could* work that out . . .'

Jameson was sitting across the top of Thorne's back. He leaned down close to his ear. 'Ding, ding. Stupid again. *I've* never raped anyone . . .'

Thorne felt his head being lifted up by the hair and twisted around. He quickly forgot about the searing pain in his neck and shoulders when he saw what Eve was holding. It was dull, and dark, and thick as his fist. A warped simulation of a sex-organ, designed only for the pleasure of one who sought to invade and to injure.

A weapon, pure and simple.

'No need to bother with the condom, this time,' Eve said.

Thorne thought about the traces found at the first postmortem. The natural assumption that the victim had been penetrated by flesh and blood. That the rapist wore a condom. That the rapist was a man . . .

In wholly different circumstances, Thorne might even have laughed, but he knew very well what the thing Eve held in her hand would do, condom or not, when she rammed it into him . . .

'To answer your question though,' Jameson said, 'we find that doing both things at the same time works pretty well for us.'

Holland thought he heard a cry as he dropped down on to the kitchen floor. He froze, listening. There was music playing in the living room. Thorne's usual country crap. From somewhere, there was a series of dull thuds, and then silence.

He moved slowly and quietly through into the living room, in much the same way as the burglar who'd come in through the same window six weeks earlier. From the table on the far side of the room a red light caught his eye, flashing from the handset that had been taken off the hook.

Thorne's mobile was next to it. Holland didn't need to go any closer to know that it had been switched off . . .

The song faded out, and in the gap before the next one started, Holland heard the low murmur of voices. He turned towards the sound as the music began again.

They were in the bedroom. Jameson, and the girl, and . . .

Though he couldn't make out what was being said, relief flooded through him as he recognised one of the voices as Thorne's.

The relief turned into something that tasted bitter in his mouth, as Holland realised that he needed to act quickly, that he would have no idea what to expect on the other side of the bedroom door. He thought about Sophie as he stood, rooted to the spot, looking around the room for something he might use as a weapon.

Thorne felt the pain shoot through his neck and shoulders as Jameson shifted his weight. He watched a hand pass in front of his face. The washing line was looped around the fingers . . .

'Strange how a man's mind works,' Jameson said. 'Even close to death, they were all far more afraid of what was happening at the back end than the front . . .'

Thorne winced as Eve's hand pressed down on to the small of his back. He tensed and sucked in a breath at the touch of cold plastic brushing against his thigh.

'On that scale of one to ten,' she said, 'how keen are you *now*?'

Thorne clenched, and drove his pelvis down towards the floor, but he was unable to flatten himself. He felt only the gentle resistance of the pillows that had been placed beneath him, raising his backside just enough, however much he tried to move away . . .

Jameson grabbed a handful of Thorne's hair, lifted up his head. 'Some advice, for what it's worth.' Thorne grunted, shook his head. 'It's best not to fight the line when you feel it round your neck . . .'

Thorne channelled every last ounce of strength he had left into his neck, driving his head back down towards the floor.

He could feel his hair being torn away by the roots . . .

He could feel the thick tip of the phallus pushing at the crack of his buttocks . . .

He pushed his face towards the carpet, knowing that Jameson just needed enough room, enough space to get the hood on. The line would quickly follow and then it would all be over . . .

'Take it or leave it,' Jameson said. 'Seriously though, if you let me get on with it and let the line do its job, you'll be unconscious long before she's finished . . .'

Thorne screamed, and at the same moment, Jameson stopped pulling and smashed Thorne's head forward on to the floor. Thorne lay still, momentarily stunned, for the few seconds that Jameson needed to slip the hood over his head.

Even as he writhed and jerked, Thorne felt a bizarre calm, which grew deeper as the ligature tightened around his neck. He felt the fear inside him shrivel to nothing. He saw faces burst and scatter as flashes of light. He drifted through a black space so thick that he knew it had more to do with death than darkness.

The crash of the door and the shouting are like distant sound-effects which echo and grow suddenly deafening as the pressure around his neck is released . . .

Thorne sucked air into his lungs and reared up, snarling and snapping his head back into something, feeling it give and soften. The weight fell or was lifted from him, and he pitched forward, rolling over on to his back. He lifted his hands, numbed by the belt, and began scrabbling with dead fingers to remove the hood.

A scream, and then a crack, and the piercing squeal of castors as the bed moves at speed across the floor . . .

He stared up at the ceiling, heard grunts of effort and pain, and the crash of bodies impacting with something solid. Dropping his head to the side, Thorne saw Jameson and Holland in a heap by the wardrobe. He saw the wardrobe door swing slowly open and, in the mirror on the back, he saw Eve coming at him.

Spinning quickly from the reflection to the real thing . . .

With her knife raised, she launched herself, or stumbled or fell, towards him, and Thorne could do little but turn his face away and kick up hard at her. As she opened her mouth, grimacing with the effort or with the hatred, Thorne's foot crashed into the underside of her jaw, knocking her head back and sending a thick string of blood arcing high above them both. The last drops were still raining down long moments after she'd fallen to the floor like a side of meat . . .

Thorne climbed gingerly to his feet and moved slowly across to where Holland was standing, doubled-over and white-faced, panting. Jameson lay moaning on the floor, one arm bent awkwardly behind him and the other stretched towards a knife that he was never going to reach. He looked up, his expression impossible to read through the pulpy red mess that Thorne's head had made of his face.

A bottle of wine lay on its side, half rolled beneath the wardrobe. Thorne nudged it out with his foot as Holland began untying the belt around his wrists.

'It was all I could find,' Holland said between gulps of air. 'I think I broke the fucker's arm with it . . .'

Hands free, Thorne turned and walked back to where Eve was sprawled near the bedroom door. She still had the knife in her hand, but barely noticed as Thorne took it away from her. She was busy scanning the bloodstained carpet for half of her tongue, bitten off as cleanly as her father's had been, when he'd dropped from a banister all those years before.

Thorne sank down to the floor, leaned back against the bed. He felt the pain start to return. In his head, in his arms, everywhere.

From the other room he could hear George Jones singing like nothing had happened.

He stared at himself in the mirror on the back of the wardrobe door. Naked and covered in blood, he looked like some kind of ravening savage. He watched himself slowly move a hand to cover his genitals.

'I phoned Hendricks,' Holland said. 'There's back-up on the way.'

Thorne nodded. 'That's good. That's very good, Dave. Pass me my fucking underpants first though, would you . . .?'

PART FOUR

THE KINGDOM
WHERE NOBODY DIES

THIRTY-THREE

Yvonne Kitson rang him on his way to St Albans.

'Tom, how are you doing?'

'I'm good. What about you?'

'I'm fine. Listen . . .'

Thorne knew very well that Kitson was far from fine. Her husband had taken the kids after discovering her affair with a senior officer and now her career looked likely to fall apart as comprehensively as her family. It had been her husband who had made the call to her superiors, told them exactly what his wife had been up to, and with whom . . .

'Listen,' she said, 'I thought you'd like to know straight away. We've got a provisional date for the trial.'

It had been six weeks since the arrests of Eve Bloom and Ben Jameson. Since Thorne had been led from his own flat, a hand on his arm and a blanket around his shoulders, like so many victims he'd watched in the past, shuffling towards police cars and ambulances, saucer-eyed and colourless.

Now they would need to go through it all again. The case was already being put together, but now, with a date set, the pace would really pick up. The documentation had to be disclosed to the Crown Prosecution Service, and the

witnesses properly prepared. Everything had to be carefully gathered and shaped, so that professionals could take
it into a courtroom and use it to get a conviction.

Thorne of course would be spared the donkey work. His
moment would come later, in the witness box.

Not that Thorne had ever *stopped* going through it . . .

In stark contrast to real life, Eve Bloom was always disturbingly honest in the Restorative Justice Conferences
Thorne imagined with her daily. Of course, there had
never been the slightest interest in him sexually. If she'd
wanted to, she could easily have slept with him at her place.
What *wouldn't* have been so easy with a flatmate around
was what she and her brother had been planning to do all
along.

That she hadn't had the opportunity to do it sooner, to
get Thorne where she wanted him at *his* place, was down to
a seventeen-year-old smack-head who'd burgled Thorne's
flat and, without knowing it, saved his life.

It was down to something else too, of course . . .

Thorne had called it laziness. A fear of things going
further. A reluctance to move a relationship along. Could
it really have been something else altogether? Some inde-
finable instinct for self-preservation? Whatever it was,
Thorne was grateful for it. He hoped, God forbid it should
ever be needed, that he would recognise it next time
around . . .

Thorne ended the call with Kitson and turned *Nixon*
back up. He'd given Lambchop another chance, and was
pleased that he had. Their sound, somehow lush and
stripped down at the same time, was hypnotic. He listened
to the singer's strange whisperings, and thought about the

trial. He thought about wounds opening and scars healing, about others whose lives had been nudged, or knocked or smashed forever out of kilter . . .

Sheila Franklin and Irene Noble and Peter Foley . . .

Denise Hollins, who'd lived with one murderer and shared her bed with another. Thorne had stayed in touch with her, but their conversations were rarely easy. She could not even start to put together the intricate jigsaw of her shattered life, when so many of the tiny pieces had yet to be found.

Dave Holland, father of a three-day-old baby. Thorne was sure he would do his best to make the history of his own, brand-new family a simple one . . .

Thorne's exit was coming up and he tried to focus on some of the more mundane elements of the court case.

He indicated and moved across to the inside lane, thinking about shaving off the beard he'd grown to cover the scar, and about getting his suit dry-cleaned. Thinking about reminding Phil Hendricks to take all his earrings out before giving evidence . . .

Thorne's father had the bits of two or three different radios spread out on the table in front of him. Every so often he'd slam a piece down, or swear loudly in frustration. Then he'd look across at Thorne, sitting on the sofa, and grin like a child who's been caught misbehaving.

Thorne was looking at a picture of his father from maybe thirty years before. The majority of the old photo albums were foxed and falling apart; none had been taken out of the sideboard since his mother had died. She had been the photographer, the one who always remembered to take along the Instamatic, who bought the albums from Boots and spent evenings pasting in the pictures . . .

Thorne looked from the photo to the real thing, from the young man to the old. His father looked up at him. Thorne noticed, as he always did, the hair that like his own, was greyer on one side than the other.

'Do you want some tea?' his father said.

Thorne understood the code. 'I'll make you some in a minute . . .'

He turned a stiff, faded page and stared at a picture of a young couple, their arms around a child of six or seven. The three of them sat, squinting against the sunlight, a deep green sea of bracken rising up behind them.

Thorne smiled at the can of beer in his father's hand, at the expression on his mother's face having talked some hapless passer-by into taking the picture. He stared down at the boy, gurning happily at the camera. The brown eyes round and bright, the shadows yet to fall across his face.

Long before anybody died.

THE
BURNING
GIRL

'And now I know how Joan of Arc felt,
Now I know how Joan of Arc felt,
As the flames rose to her Roman nose,
And her Walkman started to melt . . .'

'Bigmouth Strikes Again' – The Smiths

PROLOGUE

NEARLY HALF OF ALL NEW BUSINESSES FAIL WITHIN THE FIRST THREE YEARS!

'DON'T BE ONE OF THE UNLUCKY ONES!'

Dear Local Businessman

As businessmen ourselves, we know only too well the risks involved in getting a new venture off the ground. We know too that as your business has already begun to establish itself, you must certainly be determined to succeed. We can make sure that happens.

We are a company specialising in protecting the small businessman. We can take care of everything, so that you need never worry about anything again. We can offer **guaranteed** peace of mind for a reasonable monthly premium.

Our rates begin at £400 per month, but if you should find yourself in short-term difficulty for any reason, payments may be offset at a cost to be negotiated. Compare our terms with any you might find elsewhere, but make sure that you **talk to some of our other clients first**. We're sure you will decide that ours is a service you cannot afford to be without.

Our reputation ensures that from the moment you go into business with us, you will be free to run your shop, restaurant or company, secure in the knowledge that we are there to handle any problem that may arise.

We can be contacted **24 HOURS A DAY** on the mobile phone number you will be given today by our representative.

Call us right now and buy yourself some peace of mind!

FEBRUARY

THE PRICE OF
BEING HUMAN

Later, Carol Chamberlain would convince herself that she had actually been dreaming about Jessica Clarke when she got the first call. That the noise of the phone ringing had dragged her awake; away from the sound and the smell of it. The fuzzy picture of a girl running, the colours climbing up her back, exploding and flying at her neck like scarves of gold and crimson.

Whether the dream was imagined or not, she'd begun to see it all again the moment she'd put down the phone. Sitting on the edge of the bed, shivering; Jack, who had stirred only momentarily, dead to the world behind her.

She saw it all.

The colours were as bright, and the sound as clear and crisp as it had been that morning twenty years before. She was certain of it. Though Carol had not been there, had not seen any of it with her own eyes, she had spoken to everyone, *everyone* who had. Now she believed that when she ran over it in her mind, when she imagined it, she was seeing it all exactly as it had happened . . .

The sound – of the man's feet on the grass as he climbed the slope, of his tuneless humming – was drowned out by the noise from the playground. Beneath the high-pitched peaks of shouts and screams was a low throb of chatter and gossip, a wave of conversation that rolled across the playground and away down the hillside, towards the main road.

The man listened to it as he got nearer, unable to make out anything clearly. It would almost certainly be talk about boys and music. Who was in and who was out. He could hear another sound, too: the buzz of a lawnmower from the far side of the school where a team of gardeners was working. They wore green boiler-suits, and so did he. His was only missing the embroidered council logo.

Hands in his pockets, cap pulled down low on his head, he walked around the perimeter of the playground to where the girl and a bunch of her friends were gathered. A few of them were leaning back on the metal, cross-hatched fence, bouncing gently against it, relaxed.

The man removed the secateurs from his belt and squatted, inches away from the girls on the other side of the fence. With one hand, he began snipping at the weeds that sprouted around the base of a concrete fence post. With the other, he reached into his pocket for the can of lighter fluid.

It had always been the smell, more than anything, that had worried him. He'd made sure the can was full and there was not the faintest hiss or gurgle as he squeezed, as the jet of fluid shot from the plastic nozzle through the gap in the fence. His concern was that some hint of it, a whiff as it soaked into the material of the blue, knee-length skirt, might drift up on the breeze and alert the girl or one of her friends.

He needn't have worried. By the time he'd laid the can down on the grass and reached for the lighter, he'd used half the fuel at least, and the girls had been too busy chattering to notice anything. It surprised him that for fifteen seconds or more the girl's skirt smouldered quietly before finally catching. He was also surprised by the fact that she wasn't the one who screamed first . . .

Jessica had only one ear on Ali's story about the party she'd been to and Manda's tale of the latest tiff with her boyfriend. She was still thinking about the stupid row with her mum that had gone on the whole weekend, and the talking-to she'd been

8

*given by her father before he'd left for work that morning. When
Ali pulled a face and the others laughed, Jessica joined in without really appreciating the joke.*

*It felt like a small tug at first, and then a tickle, and she
leaned forward to smooth down the back of her skirt. She saw
Manda's face change then, watched her mouth widen, but she
never heard the sound that came out of it. Jessica was already
feeling the agony lick at the tops of her legs as she lurched away
from the fence and started to run . . .*

Long distant from it now, Carol Chamberlain imagined
the panic and the pain – as shocked as she always was at
the unbearable events unfolding in her mind's eye.

Horribly quickly. Dreadfully slowly . . .

An hour before dawn, it was dark inside the bedroom,
but the searing light of something unnatural blazed behind
her eyes. With hindsight, with *knowledge*, she was everywhere, able to see and hear it all.

She saw girls' mouths gape like those of old women,
their eyes big and glassy as their feet carried them away
from the flames. Away from their friend.

She saw Jessica carve a ragged path across the playground, her arms flailing. She heard the screams, the
thump of shoes against asphalt, the sizzle as the hair
caught. She watched what she knew to be a child move like
a thrown firework, skittering across a pavement. Slowing
down, fizzing . . .

And she saw the face of a man, of *Rooker*, as he turned
and jogged away down the slope. His legs moving faster
and faster. Almost, but not quite, falling as he careered
down the hill towards his car.

Carol Chamberlain turned and stared at the phone. She thought about the anonymous call she had received twenty minutes earlier. The simple message from a man who could not possibly have been Gordon Rooker.

'I burned her . . .'

ONE

The train was stationary, somewhere between Golders Green and Hampstead, when the woman stepped into the carriage.

Just gone seven on a Monday night. The passengers a pretty fair cross-section of Londoners heading home late, or into the West End to make a night of it. Suits and *Evening Standards*. The office two-piece and a dog-eared thriller. All human life, in replica football kits and Oxfam chic and Ciro Citterio casuals. Heads bouncing against windows and lolling in sleep, or nodding in time to Coldplay or Craig David or DJ Shadow.

For no good reason other than it was on the Northern Line, the train lurched forward suddenly, then stopped again a few seconds later. People looked at the feet of those opposite, or read the adverts above their heads. The silence, save for the tinny basslines bleeding from headphones, exaggerated the lack of connection.

At one end of the carriage, two black boys sat together. One looked fifteen or sixteen but was probably younger. He wore a red bandanna, an oversized American football

11

jersey and baggy jeans. He was laden with rings and necklaces. Next to him was a much smaller boy, his younger brother perhaps, dressed almost identically.

To the man sitting opposite them, the clothes, the jewellery, the *attitude* seemed ridiculous on a child whose expensive trainers didn't even reach the floor. The man was stocky, in his early forties, and wore a battered brown leather jacket. He looked away when the bigger boy caught him staring, and ran a hand through hair that was greyer on one side than the other. It looked, to Tom Thorne, as if the two boys had blown their pocket money in a shop called 'Mr Tiny Gangsta'.

Within a second or two of the woman coming through the door, the atmosphere in the carriage had changed. From buttoned-up to fully locked-down. English, *in extremis* . . .

Thorne looked at her just long enough to take in the headscarf and the thick, dark eyebrows and the baby cradled beneath one arm. Then he looked away. He didn't quite duck behind a newspaper, like many of those around him, but he was ashamed to admit to himself that this was only because he didn't have one.

Thorne stared at his shoes, but was aware of the hand that was thrust out as the woman stood over him. He could see the polystyrene cup, the top of it picked at, or perhaps chewed away. He could hear the woman speak softly in a language he didn't understand and didn't need to.

She shook the cup in front of his face and Thorne heard nothing rattle.

Then it became a routine: the cup held out, the question asked, the plea ignored and on to the next. Thorne looked

12

up as she moved away down the carriage, feeling an ache building in his gut as he stared at the curve of her back beneath a dark cardigan, the stillness of the arm that supported her baby. He turned away as the ache sharpened into a stab of sorrow for her, and for himself.

He turned in time to watch the older boy lean across to his brother. Sucking his teeth before he spoke. A hiss, like cats in a bag.

'I really hate them people . . .'

Thorne was still depressed twenty minutes later when he walked out of the tube station on to Kentish Town Road. He wasn't feeling much better by the time he kicked the door of his flat shut behind him. But his mood would not stay black for long.

From the living room, a voice was suddenly raised, sullen and wounded, above the noise of the television: 'What bloody time d'you call this?'

Thorne dropped his bag, took four steps down the hall and turned to see Phil Hendricks stretched out on the sofa. The pathologist was taller, skinnier and, at thirty-three, ten years younger than Thorne. He was wearing black, as always – jeans and a V-neck sweater – with the usual assortment of rings, spikes and studs through most of the available space on and around his face. There were other piercings elsewhere, but Thorne wanted to know as little about those as possible.

Hendricks pointed the remote and flicked off the television. 'Dinner will be utterly ruined.' He was normally about as camp as an armoured car, so the joky attempt at being queeny in his flat Mancunian accent made Thorne smile all the more.

'Right,' Thorne said. 'Like you can even boil an egg.'

'Well, it *would* have been ruined.'

'What are we having, anyway?'

Hendricks swung his feet down to the floor and rubbed a hand back and forth across his closely shaved skull. 'Menu's next to the phone.' He waved a hand towards the small table in the corner. 'I'm having the usual, plus an extra mushroom bhaji.'

Thorne shrugged off his jacket and carried it back out into the hall. He came back in, bent to turn down the radiator, carried a dirty mug through to the kitchen. He picked up Hendricks' biker boots from in front of the sofa and carried them out into the hall.

Then he picked up the phone and called the Bengal Lancer . . .

Hendricks had been sleeping on Thorne's sofa-bed since just after Christmas, when the collection of mushrooms growing in his own place had reached monstrous proportions. The builders and damp-proofers were supposed to be there for less than a week, but as with all such estimates the reality hadn't quite matched up. Thorne was still unsure why Hendricks hadn't just moved in with his current boyfriend, Brendan – he still spent a couple of nights a week there as it was. Thorne's best guess was that, with a relationship as on and off as theirs, even a temporary move would have been somewhat risky.

He and Hendricks were a little cramped in Thorne's small flat, but Thorne had to admit that he enjoyed the company. They discussed, fully and frankly, the relative merits of Spurs and Arsenal. They argued about Thorne's consuming love of country music. They bickered about

14

Thorne's sudden and uncharacteristic passion for tidiness.

While they were waiting for the curry to arrive, Thorne put on a Lucinda Williams album. He and Hendricks argued about it for a while, and then they began to talk about other things . . .

'Mickey Clayton died as a result of gunshot wounds to the head,' Hendricks said.

Thorne peered across at him over the top of his beer can. 'I'm guessing that wasn't one of your trickier ones. What with most of his head plastered all over the walls when we found him.'

Hendricks pulled a face. 'The full report should be on your desk tomorrow afternoon.'

'Thanks, Phil.' He enjoyed taking the piss, but, aside from being just about his closest friend, Hendricks was the best pathologist Thorne had ever worked with. Contrary to appearances, and despite the sarcasm and the off-colour jokes, there was no one better at understanding the dead. Hendricks listened as they whispered their secrets, translating them from the mysterious language of the slab.

'Did you get the bullet?' Thorne asked. The killer had used a nine-millimetre weapon; what was left of the bullets had been found near the previous victims, or still inside what was left of their skulls . . .

'You won't need a match to tell you it's the same killer.'

'The X?' It had been obvious when the body had been discovered the previous morning. The nylon shirt hoiked up to the back of the neck, the blood-trails running from two deep, diagonal cuts – left shoulder to right hip and vice versa.

'Still not sure about the blade, though. I thought it might

15

be a Stanley knife, but I reckon it could be a machete, something like that.'

Thorne nodded. A machete was the weapon of choice with a number of gangland enforcers. 'Yardies or Yakuza, maybe . . .'

'Well, whoever's paying him, he's enjoying the work. He shoots them pretty quickly afterwards, so I can't be a hundred per cent sure, but I think he does his bit of creative carving while they're still alive.'

The man responsible for the death of Mickey Clayton, and three men before him in the previous six weeks, was like no contract killer Thorne had ever come across or heard about. To these shadowy figures – men who were willing to kill for anything upwards of a few thousand pounds – anonymity was everything. This one was different. He liked to leave his mark. 'X marks the spot,' Thorne said.

'Or X as in "crossed out".' Hendricks drained his can. 'So, what about you? Good day at the office, dear?'

Thorne grunted as he stood up. He took Hendricks' empty can and went through to the kitchen to get them both fresh ones. Staring aimlessly into the fridge, Thorne tried in vain to remember his last good day at the office . . .

His team – of which Hendricks was the civilian member – at the Serious Crime Group (West) had been seconded to help out the Projects Team at SO7 – the Serious and Organised Crime Unit. It had quickly become apparent that *organised* was one thing this particular operation was not. The resources of SO7 were stretched paper thin – or at least that was their story. There *was* a major turf war between two old family firms south of the river, and an

16

escalation in a series of ongoing disputes among Triad gangs that had seen three shootings in one week and a pitched battle on Gerrard Street. All the same, Thorne suspected that he and his team were basically there to cover other people's arses.

There was nothing in it for him. If arrests were ever made, the credit would go elsewhere, and anyway, there was precious little satisfaction in chasing down those responsible for getting rid of pondlife like Mickey Clayton.

The series of fatal 'X' shootings – of which Clayton's was the fourth – was a major assault on the operations of one of north London's biggest gangland families, but the simple fact was that the Projects Team hadn't the first idea who was doing the assaulting. All the obvious rivals had been approached and discounted. All the usual underground sources had been paid and pumped for information, none of which had proved useful. It became clear that a major new operation had established itself and was keen to make a splash. Thorne and his team were on board to find out who they were. Who was paying a contract killer, quickly dubbed the X-Man, to hurt the Ryan family?

'He's making life hard for himself, though, isn't he?' Thorne started talking from the kitchen and continued as he brought the beers into the living room. 'This X thing, this signature or whatever it is, it limits what he can do, where he can do it. He can't just ride up on a motorbike or wait for them outside a pub. He needs a bit of time and space.'

Hendricks took a can. 'He obviously puts a lot of effort into his work. Plans it. I bet he's bloody expensive.'

Thorne thought Hendricks was probably right. 'It's still cheap though, isn't it? When you think about it. To kill someone, I mean. Twenty, twenty-five grand's about top whack. That's a damn sight less than the people putting out the contracts pay for their Jeeps and top-of-the-range Mercs.'

'What d'you reckon I can get for a couple of hundred quid?' Hendricks asked. 'There's this mortuary assistant at Westminster who's getting on my tits.'

Thorne thought about it for a second. 'Chinese burn?'

The laugh was the first decent one that Thorne could remember sharing with anyone for a few days . . .

'How can it be the Yardies?' Hendricks said when he'd stopped giggling. 'Or Yakuza? We know our hitman's not black or Japanese . . .'

A witness claimed to have seen the killer leaving the scene of the third murder and had given a vague description of a white male in his thirties. The witness, Marcus Moloney, was an 'associate' of the Ryan family, and not what you'd call an upright citizen, but he seemed pretty sure about what he'd seen.

'It's not that simple,' Thorne said. 'It might have been, ten years ago, when people stuck to their own, but now they don't care so much and the freelancers just go where the work is. The Triads use Yardies. Yardies work with the Russians. They nicked a gang of Yakuza last year for recruiting outside schools. They were as good as giving out application forms; signing up Greek lads, Asians, Turks, whoever.'

Hendricks smiled. 'It's nice to see that they're all equal-opportunities employers . . .'

Thorne grunted, and the two of them settled back into saying nothing for a few minutes. Thorne closed his eyes and picked at the goatee he'd grown towards the end of the previous year. The beard created the illusion of a jawline and covered up the scar from a knife wound.

The puckered line that ran diagonally across Thorne's chin was the only visible reminder of a night six months before when he'd both begged for his life and prayed for death to come quickly. There were other scars, easier to disguise, but far more troublesome. Thorne would reach into his gut in the darkness and finger them until they reopened into wounds. He could imagine the scab forming then, blood black across the tender flesh. The crust that would itch and crumble beneath his fingernails, exquisite and agonising, for him to poke and pick at . . .

Lucinda Williams sang softly about an all-consuming lust, her voice sweet and saw-toothed at the same time, rising like smoke above a single acoustic guitar.

Thorne and Hendricks both started slightly when the phone rang.

'Tom?' A woman's voice.

Thorne sank back into his armchair with the phone. He shouted across to Hendricks deliberately loud enough for the caller to hear, 'Oh Christ, it's that mad old woman who keeps phoning me up . . .'

Hendricks grinned and shouted back, 'Tell her I can smell the cat food from here!'

'Come on then, Carol,' Thorne said. 'Tell me what's been happening in glamorous Worthing. Any "cat stuck up tree" incidents or Zimmer-frame pile-ups I should know about?'

The woman on the other end of the line was in no mood for the usual banter. 'I need to talk to you, Tom. I need you to listen . . .'

So, Thorne listened. The curry arrived and went cold, but he didn't even think about it. He could tell as soon as she started to talk that something was seriously wrong.

In all the time he'd known Carol Chamberlain, Thorne had never heard her cry before.

TWO

'I presume you tried 1471 . . .?'

She raised her eyebrows. Asked if he thought she was a complete idiot.

Thorne shrugged an apology.

When he had first met Carol Chamberlain the previous year, he had taken her for a frumpy, middle-aged woman with too much time on her hands; a frumpy, middle-aged woman he had mistakenly assumed to be the mother of one of his constables.

She still claimed not to have forgiven him.

Ex-DCI Carol Chamberlain had arrived in Thorne's office on a humid July morning seven months earlier, and turned the hunt for a sadistic rapist and killer on its head. She was a member of what had become known as the Crinkly Squad – a unit made up of former officers brought out of retirement to work on cold cases. Chamberlain hadn't needed a great deal of persuading to come back. Having done her thirty years, she'd been forced out of the Met – to her way of thinking at least – prematurely, and felt, at fifty-five, that she still had a good deal to offer. The first case she'd worked on had thrown up information that had changed the course of Thorne's investigation, and it would turn out later, his life. The cold case – now anything *but* cold – had quickly been taken away from her, but Thorne had kept in touch and he and Chamberlain had quickly grown close.

Thorne wasn't sure precisely *what* Carol Chamberlain got from her relationship with him, but he was happy to give whatever it was in exchange for her directness, her sound advice and a bullshit detector that seemed to get sharper with age.

Looking at her now across the table, remembering that first impression of her, Thorne wondered how he could have made so gross a misjudgement . . .

Chamberlain held up the dirty cream envelope for Thorne to see, and then tipped it, emptying the ashes on to the table. 'These arrived yesterday morning.'

Thorne picked up a fork and nudged the tines through the blackened scraps of material. He was careful not to touch any of it with his bare hands, but he didn't know why he was bothering. He wasn't sure yet if he was going to do anything about this. The pieces crumbled even as the fork touched them, but he could see that one or two fragments still retained their original blue colour.

'I'll hang on to these.' He picked up a menu and used the edge of it to scrape the ashes back into their envelope.

Chamberlain nodded. 'It's serge, I think. Or heavy cotton. Same material that Jessica Clarke's skirt was made out of . . .'

Thorne thought about what she was saying, what she'd begun to tell him the previous night on the phone. He

22

remembered a little of the case, remembered the outrage, but most of the details were new to him. He asked himself if he'd ever heard such a horrific story.

If he had, he couldn't remember when.

'What sort of sick sod does that to a kid?' Thorne said. He glanced around, anxious not to alarm those at the nearby tables.

Chamberlain waited until he turned back, looked him in the eye. 'One who's getting paid for it.'

'*What?*'

'We thought it was some sort of headcase; everybody did. Us and the schools and the papers, all getting jittery, waiting for him to do it again. Then we found out that Jessica Clarke was the wrong girl . . .'

'How d'you mean, "wrong"?'

'The girl standing next to her in the playground that day was called Alison Kelly. She was one of Jessica's best friends. Same height, same colour hair. She was also the youngest daughter of Kevin Kelly.' She looked at Thorne as though expecting a reaction. She didn't get one.

Thorne shook his head. 'Should I . . .?'

'Let me run you quickly through how it was in 1984. You'd have been about what . . .?'

Thorne did the mental calculation. 'I'd've been about to come out of uniform,' he said. 'About to get married. Sowing the last of my wild oats, probably. Going to clubs, going to gigs . . .'

'You lived in north London, right?'

Thorne nodded.

'Well, chances are that any club you went to was owned by one of the big firms, and the Kellys were the biggest.

23

There were others taking control of the south-east, and there were a few independents knocking about, but the Kellys had a stake in most things north of the river . . .'

As Thorne listened, it struck him that her normal, measured tone had become hesitant; the neutral accent had slipped, allowing her native Yorkshire to emerge. He'd heard it before, when she was angry or excited. When she was fired up about something. If he hadn't already known, he'd have guessed that something had shaken her badly.

'The Kellys were based in and around Camden Town. There were other firms, other families in Shepherd's Bush and Hackney, and they sorted things out between them most of the time. There was the occasional bit of silliness – a couple of shootings a year – but it was no worse than it had ever been. Then, in 1983, someone took a pop at Kevin Kelly . . .'

'Put out a contract?'

'Right, but for one reason or another they didn't get him. Whatever message they were trying to send wasn't understood. So, they went after his daughter.'

'And didn't get her either. Jesus . . .'

'Kelly got the message this time though. A dozen people died in the three weeks after the Jessica Clarke incident. Three brothers from one family were shot in the same pub one night. Kevin Kelly more or less wiped the opposition out.'

Thorne picked up his cup. The coffee was stone cold. 'Leaving Mr Kelly and his friends with most of north London to themselves . . .'

'His friends, yes, but not Kelly. It was like the attempt on his daughter knocked the guts out of him. Once the competition was out of the way, he retired. Upped sticks, just like that. He took his wife, his daughter and a couple of million, and walked away from it.'

'Sounds like a good move . . .'

Chamberlain shrugged. 'He dropped dead five years later. Just gone fifty.'

'So, who ran things once Kelly joined the pipe-and-slippers brigade?'

'Well, it was really just a family in name only. Kelly had no brothers or sons. He handed his entire operation over to one of those friends we were talking about: a particularly nasty piece of work called William Ryan. He was Kelly's number two, and . . .' Chamberlain saw the look on Thorne's face and stopped. 'What?'

'When you've finished the history lesson, I'll bring you up to date.'

'Fair enough.' Chamberlain put down the teaspoon she'd been fiddling with for the past ten minutes.

Thorne pushed back his chair. 'I'm going to get another cup of coffee. Do you want anything?'

They'd met in a small, Greek café near Victoria Station. Chamberlain had caught the train from Worthing first thing that morning, and was planning to get back as quickly as she could.

Standing at the counter, waiting to order, Thorne glanced over at her. He thought that she'd lost a little weight. Ordinarily, he knew that she'd have been delighted, but things seemed far from ordinary. The lines across her face were undisguised. They showed when she looked up and smiled across at him. An old woman suddenly . . . and frightened.

Thorne carried a tray back to the table: two coffees, and a baklava for them to share. He got stuck in straight away and, between mouthfuls, told Chamberlain about the SO7 operation. About the present-day organised-crime set-up in north London. About the as-yet-unidentified challenge to a powerful gangland boss named Billy Ryan . . .

'It's lovely to hear that Billy's done so well for himself,' Chamberlain said.

Thorne was delighted at the sarcasm and the smile. That was more like the Carol Chamberlain he knew. 'Oh, he's done *very* well. And Ryan's certainly *is* a family firm: brothers and cousins all over the shop, plus a son and heir, Stephen.'

'Stephen. I remember him. He'd have been five or six when all this happened . . .'

'Well he's a big boy now. A winning individual by all accounts.'

Chamberlain had picked up the spoon again. She tapped it against her palm. 'Billy married Alison Kelly later on.'

'Kevin Kelly's daughter? The one who . . .?'

She nodded. 'The one who Gordon Rooker *meant* to set fire to. The one he mistook Jessica Clarke for. Her and Billy Ryan got married just before Kelly died, if I remember rightly. It made the old man happy, but it was never going to last. She was a lot younger than he was. Just turned eighteen, I think. He'd have been mid-thirties, with a kid already . . .'

'Not exactly made in heaven then.'

'I think it lasted a year or two. Once everything went

26

pear-shaped, Billy got back together with whichever tart he'd had Stephen with. Married her as soon as the divorce from Alison came through.'

Thorne pointed his spoon towards the last piece of baklava. 'I'm eating all of this. Don't you . . .?' She shook her head and he helped himself. 'Tell me about Rooker,' he said.

'There's not a huge amount to tell. He confessed.'

'That always helps.'

By now, the smile was long gone. 'Seriously, Tom, it was about as simple a case as I ever worked on. I was the DI. I took his first statement.'

'And what did you think?'

'It seemed to fit. Rooker wasn't unknown. What he did at that school, to that girl, was well out of the ordinary, admittedly, but he was someone who'd do pretty much anything, or any*body*, if the price was right.'

Thorne had come across far too many people like that. He was coming across more of them all the time. 'Did he say who was paying it?'

'He never went as far as to name anyone, but he didn't have to. We knew that he'd worked for a few of the smaller firms before. He may even have been involved in the failed contract on Kevin Kelly. Also, we knew that Rooker *liked* to burn people. It hadn't been proved, but he was in the frame for a contract job in 1982. Someone, probably Gordon Rooker, tied the boss of a security firm to a chair and emptied a can of lighter fluid into his hair . . .'

'What a charmer.'

'Actually, he was. Or *thought* he was. Bastard was flirting with me in that interview room.' She stopped, swallowed, as if trying to take away a sour taste. 'Like I said, it was simple. Rooker pleaded guilty. He got life. And, as of yesterday, when I called to check, he was still in Park Royal Prison.'

Thorne stretched out a hand and placed it over hers for a few seconds. 'He was still there about three hours ago. When *I* called.'

The smile returned for a moment, but it looked a little forced. 'Thanks, Tom.'

'What about Jessica?'

Chamberlain's eyes flicked away from Thorne's face and she stared past him, out of the café's front window. 'The burns were major. It was a year before she could go back to school.'

'What about now? What does she . . .?'

She shook her head, her voice barely above a whisper. 'You didn't really expect a happy ending, did you, Tom?'

'One would be nice,' Thorne said after a few moments. 'Just occasionally . . .'

She turned back to him and her face softened, as if he were a child asking for something that she couldn't possibly afford.

'She threw herself off a multi-storey car park on her sixteenth birthday . . .'

Muslum Izzigil had been swearing pretty solidly for ten minutes when the two boys walked into his shop.

He was working his way through an enormous pile of tapes, all returned the night before and each one needing to be rewound. People returning videos without bothering to rewind them were the bane of his life. He took a tape out of

28

the machine, slammed it into a box, reached for another. 'Lazy bastards . . .'

He glanced across at the two boys who were flicking through the boxes in the 'used/for sale' bins near the door. He held up one of the tapes and pulled a face. 'How hard is it to rewind? Huh?' One boy looked blankly back at Izzigil, while his friend whispered something and began to laugh. Izzigil hit the rewind button for the umpteenth time and leaned back against the counter. He looked up at the screen, watched a minute or two of an Austin Powers movie, then turned his attention back to the boys.

'New releases over this side,' he said, pointing. 'We haven't got it, film is free next time. Same as Blockbuster.'

The two boys were pulling display boxes from racks in the adult section, leering at the pictures on the back. One boy rubbed a box against his crotch, stuck out his tongue and licked his lips.

'Hey . . .' Izzigil began to gesture. 'Don't mess.'

The boys quickly pulled a couple more boxes from the rack, carried an armful across to the counter and dropped them down. One was almost a foot taller than his mate, but they were both stocky. They wore baseball caps and puffa jackets, the same as Izzigil saw the black kids wearing, hanging around Shopping City on a Saturday afternoon . . .

'Got anything with Turkish birds in?' the taller boy asked.

The other boy leaned on the counter. 'He likes women who are really hairy . . .'

Izzigil felt himself redden. He said nothing, began to gather up the display boxes that the two boys had dropped and piled them up.

'Whatever you've got, I hope it's a damn sight better than this.' The shorter boy reached into his jacket, produced a plain black video box, and slammed it down hard on the counter. 'I rented this from you the other day.'

Izzigil looked at the box, then shook his head. 'Not from here. My boxes are different, look . . .'

'You trying to stitch me up?' the boy said.

'We want our fucking money back, mate . . .'

The smell reached Izzigil then. He almost retched, and let his hand drop below the level of the counter. 'You should go before I call the police . . .'

The taller boy picked up the box, opened it and shook the turd out on to the counter.

Izzigil stepped back. '*Christ!*'

The taller boy began to laugh. His friend pulled a mock-serious face. 'That film's shit, mate . . .'

'Get the fuck out of my shop!' Izzigil reached beneath the counter, but before he could lay his hand on the pool cue the shorter boy had leaned across and a knife was suddenly inches from the shopkeeper's face.

'You were given a letter . . .'

'What letter? I don't know about a letter.'

'Some friends of ours gave you a fucking letter. You were offered the chance to behave like a businessman and you didn't take it. So, now we won't be wasting any more money on fucking notepaper. Clear enough for you?'

Izzigil nodded.

'Now we stop messing about. Next time we might stop by when you're upstairs giving your hairy old lady one, and your son's down here, minding the shop . . .'

Izzigil nodded again, watched over the boy's shoulder as

his friend moved slowly around the shop, tipping display cases on to the floor, casually pulling over bins. He saw a customer put one hand on the door, then freeze and move quickly away when he glimpsed what was happening inside.

The boy with the knife took a slow step backwards. He cocked his head and slipped the knife into the back pocket of his jeans. 'Someone will pop round in the next week or two to go over things,' he said.

Izzigil's hand tightened around the pool cue then. He knew it was much too late to be of any use, but he squeezed it as he watched the two boys leave.

On the screen above him, Austin Powers was dancing to a Madonna song as Izzigil came slowly around the counter and walked towards the front of the shop. He pressed himself against the window and looked both ways along the street.

'Muslum . . .?'

Izzigil turned at his wife's voice and took a step back into the shop. He saw her eyes suddenly widen and her mouth drop open, and he turned back just as the black shape rushed towards the window. Just as the world seemed to explode with noise and pain and a terrible waterfall of glass.

They walked slowly back along Buckingham Palace Road, towards the station. It was the middle of the lunch hour, and people were queuing out of the doors of delis and coffee-shops. February was starting to bite and Thorne's jacket was zipped up to the top, his hands thrust right down into the pockets.

'How's Jack doing?'

Chamberlain stopped for a second to let a girl dart across the pavement in front of her. 'He's the same.' They moved off again. 'He tries to be supportive, but he didn't really want me to go back to it. I know he worries that I'm taking on too much, but I was going mental stuck in the house.' She looked at herself in a shop window, ran fingers through her hair. 'I couldn't give a shit about gardening . . .'

'I meant about these phone calls. That letter.'

'He doesn't know about the letter and he slept through all but one of the calls. I told him it was a wrong number.' She pulled the scarf she was wearing tighter around her throat. 'Now I'm more or less hovering over the bloody phone all night long. It's almost worse on the nights when he *doesn't* ring.'

'You're not sleeping at all? It's been going on for a bloody fortnight, Carol . . .'

'I catch up in the day. I never slept much in the first place.'

'What's he sound like?' Thorne asked.

She answered quickly and simply. Thorne guessed that she'd known the questions he would ask, because they were the ones *she* would have asked.

'He's very calm. Like he's telling me things that are obvious. Like he's reminding me of things I've forgotten . . .'

'Accent?'

She shook her head.

'Any thoughts as to his age?'

She carried on shaking it.

'Look, I know this is going to sound strange, but I'm not sure why you didn't just call the police.'

32

She started to speak, but Thorne stopped her.

'I mean the local lads. This is just some nutter, Carol. It's a kid pissing you about. It's someone who's read some poxy true-crime book and hasn't got anything better to do.'

'He knows things, Tom. Things that never came out. He knows about the lighter that was dropped at the scene, which brand of fuel was used . . .'

'It's someone Rooker spent time with inside, then. Rooker's told him to wind you up when he's got out.'

She shook her head. 'There's no reason for Rooker to send anyone after me. He confessed, remember. Anyway, Rooker bloody well *liked* me.'

'He had a relationship with you. You were the one who interviewed him. Which is why *you're* the one being targeted now, and not whoever the SIO was.'

'I think it's just because I'm next in line. The DCI on the case left the force well before I did. He emigrated to New Zealand ten years ago. He'd be a damn sight harder to track down than I was.'

It made sense, but Thorne had one other suggestion. 'Or maybe, whoever it is knows that you were . . . *affected* by what happened to Jessica.'

She looked up at him, concerned. 'How would anyone know that? How do *you* know . . .?'

They walked on in silence for fifty yards or so before Thorne spoke again. 'Are you worried that you put the wrong man away, Carol? Is that what this is about?'

'No, it isn't. Gordon Rooker burned Jessica Clarke. I know he did.'

They didn't speak again until they reached the station.

Halfway across the concourse she stopped and turned to him. 'There's no need to bother waiting. I've got quarter of an hour until the next train back.'

'It's fine. I don't mind.'

'Get back to work. I like to potter about a bit anyway. I'll buy a magazine, get myself sorted. I'm a fussy old bat like that.'

'You're not fussy.'

She leaned forward to kiss him on the cheek. 'Cheeky sod.'

Thorne sighed and broke their embrace. 'I don't quite know what you expect me to do about this, Carol. There's nothing *I* can do officially that anybody else couldn't.'

'I don't want you to do *anything* officially.'

He saw then, despite the light-hearted tone and the banter of a few moments before, just how rattled she really was. The very last thing she wanted was to let the powers-that-be see it, too. He couldn't believe that they'd take her off the Cold Case Unit, but there were plenty who thought the Met should not be using people who'd be better off queuing up in the post office.

'Right,' Thorne said eventually. 'But it's OK for me to waste *my* time.'

Chamberlain pulled a large handbag on to her small shoulder and turned on her heels. 'Something like that . . .'

Thorne watched her disappear inside WH Smith.

Walking back towards the underground, he thought about scars that you hid, and those that you showed off. Scars bad enough to make you jump off a car-park.

THREE

These rooms always had one thing in common. The size might vary, the style was usually governed by age, and the decor was dependent on the whim of budgets or the inclination of the top brass. But they invariably had the same smell. Chrome and tinted glass or flaking orange plasterboard. Freezing or overheated. Intimate or anything but. Whatever the place was like, that smell would tell you where you were with a sack over your head. Thorne could sniff it up and name its constituent parts like a connoisseur: stale cigarette smoke, sweat and desperation.

He looked around. This one had a bit of everything – a fresh coat of magnolia, the fumes charged up by the heat coming off radiators a foot thick. There was a snazzy new system of coloured chairs. Blue for visitors, red for inmates . . .

Most chairs were occupied, but a few red ones remained vacant. A black woman in the next row but one glanced across at him. The seat opposite her was empty. She smiled nervously, her eyes crinkling behind thick glasses, and then looked away before Thorne had a chance to smile back. He watched the woman beam as a young man – her son, Thorne guessed – swaggered towards her. The man grinned, then checked himself slightly, looked around to see if anyone had noticed him drop his guard.

Thorne checked his watch: just before ten. He needed to get this over with as quickly as possible and get back to the office. He'd called DC Dave Holland earlier, on his way west across London, towards HMP Park Royal . . . 'I need you to cover for me,' he'd said. 'Tell Tughan I'm off seeing a snout, or that I'm following up a hunch, or whatever. You know, some "copper" bollocks . . .'

'Do I get to know what you're really doing?'

'I'm doing someone a favour. I should be back by lunchtime if the traffic's all right, so . . .'

'Are you *driving*? When did you get the car back?'

Thorne knew what was coming. He was stupid to have let it slip. 'I got it back late yesterday,' he'd said.

The car in question, a pulsar-yellow BMW, was thirty years old, and Thorne had parted with a good deal of money for it the year before. Thorne thought it was a classic. Others preferred the term 'antique'. Holland, in particular, never missed an opportunity to take the piss, having maintained from the moment he'd seen it that the car was a big mistake. He'd gone to town when it had spectacularly failed its MOT and disappeared into the garage a fortnight earlier.

'How much?' Holland had asked, gleeful.

Thorne had cursed as he'd caught a red light. He'd yanked up the handbrake. 'It's an old car, all right? The parts are expensive.' Not only were they expensive, but there seemed to be a great many of them. Thorne couldn't remember them all, but he could recall the growing feeling of despair as they were cheerfully reeled off to him. For all Thorne knew about what was going on under the bonnet, the mechanic might just as well have been speaking Serbo–Croat.

'Five hundred?' Holland had said. 'More?'

'Listen, she's old, but she's still gorgeous. Like one of those actresses that's knocking on, but still tasty, you know?' As the car was a BMW, Thorne had tried to come up with a German actress who would fit the bill. He had failed. Felicity Kendal, he'd said as he pulled away from the lights. Yeah, that'll do.

'She?' Holland had sounded hugely amused.

'*She's* like Felicity Kendal.'

'People who call their car "she" are one step away from a pair of string-back driving gloves and a pipe . . .'

At the noise of the chair opposite him being scraped backwards, Thorne looked up and saw Gordon Rooker dropping on to the red seat. Thorne had never seen a picture, or been given a description, but there was no mistaking him.

'Anyone sitting here?' asked Rooker, a gold tooth evident as he smiled.

He was sixty, give or take a year or two, and tall. His face was thin and freshly shaved. The skin hung, leathery and loose, from his neck, and a full head of white hair had yellowed above the forehead with a lifetime's fags.

Thorne nodded towards the green bib that Rooker wore, that *all* the prisoners wore on top of the regulation blue sweatshirts. 'Very fetching,' he said.

'We've all got to wear these now,' Rooker said. 'A few places have had them for ages, but a lot of governors, including the one here, thought they were demeaning to the prisoners, which is all very splendid and progressive of them. Then a lifer in Gartree swaps places with his twin brother when nobody's looking and walks out through the front door. So, now it has to be obvious who's the prisoner and who isn't, and we all have to dress like prize prats when we have visitors. You think I'm making this up, don't you?'

The voice was expressive and lively. The voice of a pub philosopher or comedian, nicely weathered by decades on forty roll-ups a day. While Rooker was speaking, Thorne had taken out his warrant card. He slid it across the table. Rooker didn't bother to look at it.

'What do you want, Mr Thorne?' He held up a hand. 'No, don't bother, let's just have a natter. I'm sure you'll get round to it eventually.'

'I'm a friend of Carol Chamberlain.'

Rooker narrowed his eyes.

'She'd've been Carol Manley when you knew her . . .'

The gold tooth came slowly into view again. 'Did that woman ever make commissioner? I always reckoned she had it in her.'

Thorne shook his head. 'She was a DCI when she retired. That was seven or eight years ago.'

'She was a decent sort, you know?' Rooker looked away, remembering something. His eyes slid back to Thorne. 'I'm not surprised she got married; she was a good-looking woman. Still fit, is she? Is she a game old bird?' He leaned across the table. 'Do you like 'em a bit older?'

Whether the suggestive comments were an attempt to unsettle or to bond, Thorne ignored them. 'She's being *bothered*. Some lunatic is sending letters and making calls . . .'

'I'm sorry to hear that.'

'Whoever he is, he claims to be the person responsible for the attempted murder of Jessica Clarke.' Thorne looked hard at Rooker, studied his face for a reaction. 'He reckons he was the one who burned her, Gordon.'

There was a reaction, no question, but Thorne had no idea what Rooker was so amused about.

'Funny?' Thorne asked.

'Pretty funny, yeah. Like I said, I'm sorry about Miss Manley, or whatever she's called now, being bothered, but it's a laugh when you get your own personal nutter, isn't it? It's taken him long enough, mind you, whoever he is . . .'

'You're telling me you don't know who this person is?'

Rooker turned up his palms, tucked them behind his bib. 'Not a fucking clue.'

If he'd been asked at that instant to put money on whether Rooker was telling the truth, Thorne would happily have stumped up a few quid.

'I've had plenty of letters over the years,' Rooker continued, grinning. 'You know, the ones in green ink where they've pressed so hard that the pen's gone through the paper. People who want me to tell them stuff, so they can have a wank over it or whatever. I've had a few mad women and what have you, writing steamy letters, saying they want to marry me . . .'

A case the year before – when Thorne had first encountered Carol Chamberlain – had begun with just that sort of letter. It had not been genuine, but plenty were, and Thorne never ceased to be amazed, and sickened, by them. 'Well, Gordon, you're obviously quite a catch.'

39

'But this is different, right? This is sort of like a stalker in reverse. He can't stalk *me*, so he's stalking somebody else, somebody who was involved in it all, and he's *pretending* to be me. Pretending he did what I did . . .'

Thorne decided it was time to stop pissing about. 'So he *is* pretending then, is he? Because that's basically why I'm here. To make sure.'

The cockiness, the *ease*, melted slowly back into the lines of Rooker's face. The shoulders drooped forward. The voice was low and level. *Matter of fact . . .*

'You can be sure. I set fire to that girl. That's basically why *I'm* here.'

For half a minute, Thorne watched Rooker stare down at the tabletop. His scalp was visible, pink and flaking beneath the white hair. 'Like you said, though. He's waited a long time, this nutter. Why *have* you been here so long, Gordon?'

The animation returned. 'Ask the fucking judge. Miserable arsehole's dead by now, if there's any justice.' He laughed, humourlessly, at his own joke. 'Like he'd know justice if it bit him in the bollocks.'

'It was a high-profile case,' Thorne said. 'You were always going to get sent down for a long one.'

'Listen, I wasn't expecting a slap on the wrists, all right? Look at what some of these bastards get away with now, though. Blokes who've carved up their wives are getting out after ten years. Less sometimes . . .'

Without an ounce of sympathy, knowing that he deserved every second he spent banged up, Thorne could nevertheless understand the point that Rooker was making. The twenty-year tariff – or 'relevant part of the sentence' –

he'd been handed was more than twice many so-called 'life sentences' Thorne had seen doled out.

'There's no fairness to it,' Rooker said. 'Twenty years. Twenty years on fucking VP wings . . .'

Thorne tried not to smirk: Vulnerable Prisoners. 'Are you still *vulnerable* then, Gordon?'

Rooker blinked, said nothing.

'Still dangerous, though, apparently. Twenty years and still a Cat. B? You can't have been a very good boy.'

'There have been a few incidents . . .'

'Never mind, eh? Almost done, aren't you?'

'Three months left until the twenty's up . . .'

Thorne leaned back, glanced to his right. The black woman caught his eye as she fished a crumpled tissue out of her handbag. He turned back to Rooker. 'It's a coincidence, don't you reckon? This bloke turning up now, claiming responsibility.'

Rooker shook his head. 'I doubt it. This is the best possible time to get the attention, isn't it? When I'm coming up for release. For *possible* release. Mind you, if he thinks they're going to let me out, he's dafter than I thought.'

'What is it, a DLP?'

Rooker nodded. Once the tariff was completed, the Discretionary Lifer Panel of the Parole Board could recommend release to the Home Secretary. The panel comprised a judge, a psychiatrist and one other professional connected to the case, a criminologist or a probation officer. The review, unlike normal parole procedure, involved an oral hearing, and the prisoner could bring along a lawyer, or a friend, to represent him.

'I've got no sodding chance,' Rooker said. 'I've already

41

had a couple of knockbacks in as many years.' He looked at Thorne, as if expecting some sort of explanation or reassurance. He received neither. 'What have I got to do? I've been to counselling, I've gone on Christ knows how many courses . . .'

'Remorse is important, Gordon.' The word seemed almost to knock Rooker back in his seat. Thorne leaned forward. 'These people are big on that, for some mysterious reason. They like to see some victim empathy, you know? Some shred of understanding about what it is that you actually *did* to your victim, to her family. Maybe they don't think you're sorry enough, Gordon. What do you reckon? Maybe that's the question they want answering. Where's the remorse?'

'I held up my hand to it, didn't I? I confessed.'

'It's not the same thing.'

The scrape of Rooker's chair as he pushed himself back from the table was enough to make Thorne wince. 'Are we done?' Rooker asked.

Thorne eased his own chair back and looked again to his right, where the black woman was now sobbing, the tissue pressed against her mouth. He caught the eye of the man sitting opposite her.

The man looked back at Thorne like he wanted to rip his head off.

As promised, Tom Thorne had rung as soon as he'd left the prison. He'd told her briefly about his meeting with Rooker. She'd heard everything she'd hoped to hear, and yet the relief which Carol Chamberlain had expected was slow in coming.

She sat at her desk, in the makeshift office she and Jack had rigged up in the spare room the year before. It was less cluttered than it had been then, a lot of junk transferred to the top of the wardrobe and stuffed beneath the spare bed, box-files piled on top of what used to be a dressing-table. It was now used as a bedroom only once or twice a year when Jack's daughter from his first marriage made the effort to visit.

Jack shouted up to her from downstairs. 'I'm making some tea, love. D'you want some?'

'Please.'

Chamberlain could never understand those colleagues – *ex*-colleagues – who insisted that they couldn't remember certain cases. She was bemused by those who struggled to recall the names and faces of certain rapists and murderers; or their victims. Yes, you forgot a file number, or the colour of a particular vehicle, of course you did, but the *people* stayed with you. They stayed with *her* at any rate.

And she knew that they stayed with Tom Thorne, too. She recalled him telling her once that the faces he could *never* forget were those he'd never seen. The ones belonging to the killers he had never caught. The smug faces he imagined on those that had got away with it.

Perhaps those who claimed *not* to remember had developed some technique for forgetting; some trick of the trade. If so, she wished that she'd been a bit closer to some of them, spent a few more nights in curry houses or out on the piss. If she had, they might have passed the secret on to her.

For reasons she wasn't ready to admit to herself, she hadn't wanted to pull the Jessica Clarke files officially, to draw any attention to herself or to the case. Instead, she'd called in a favour, gone down to the General Registry in Victoria, and taken a quick look while an old friend's back was turned. Within a few seconds of opening the first battered brown folder, she could see that she'd remembered Gordon Rooker perfectly. The face in the faded black-and-white ID photo was exactly as she'd been picturing it since the night when she'd received that first phone call . . .

'*I burned her . . .*'

It was *still* the face she pictured now, despite the two decades that had passed. She'd tried, since speaking to Thorne, to age the image mentally, to give it the white hair and lines that Thorne had described, but without any success.

She guessed this was the way memory worked . . .

A colleague on the Cold Case Unit, now a man in his early sixties, had worked on the Moors Murders case. He told her that when he thought about Hindley and Brady, he still saw those infamous pictures of them, smug and sunken-eyed. He could never imagine the raddled old man and the smiling, mumsy brunette.

Bizarrely, Carol Chamberlain *needed* to remember Rooker's face. She equated this total recall of him with the confidence she had in his guilt. It was an illogical, ridiculous collision of ideas, and yet, to her, it made perfect sense. His face, the one she knew every inch of, was the face of the man she saw kneeling by the fence. His face, the one she remembered smiling across an interview room, was the face of the man she saw running away, exhilarated, down the hill, away from the school.

She clung to that memory now, her grip stronger since

the call from Thorne. Of course, there had been doubt, and she knew, from his question about Rooker at the station, that Thorne had sensed it. It had sprouted in the dark and pushed as she'd sat shivering. It had grown like a weed, forcing its way up through the cracks in a slab as she'd lain awake.

'*I burned her . . .*'

Now, thankfully, that doubt was dying. It had begun to shrivel from the moment she'd picked up the phone and made that call to Thorne. Now Thorne had been to see Rooker and heard him confirm it. Heard him *confess* it, *again . . .*

There was relief, but it could never be complete, for while the remembrance of Rooker's face was oddly comforting, there was also the face of Jessica Clarke to consider.

Chamberlain had seen photos; snaps of a smiling teenager, pale skin and dark hair down past her shoulders. She could still see the hands of the parents trembling as they lifted wooden picture frames from a sideboard, but the girl's face – the smooth, *perfect* face she'd had before – had been all too easy to forget.

She could hear Jack coming upstairs with the tea. She tried to blink the image away.

She always remembered Gordon Rooker exactly as he had been the first time she'd laid eyes on him. She was cursed to remember Jessica Clarke the same way.

At the end of the day, Thorne climbed into the BMW with a damn sight more enthusiasm than he'd had when getting into it eleven hours before. He pulled out of the car park of the Peel Centre, and for the next few minutes drove on autopilot. Most of his attention was focused on the far more important task of choosing the right music. The car had a six-disc CD multichanger mounted in the boot, and Thorne relished the time he spent once a week rotating the discs, making sure his selections gave him a good choice, but also a decent balance. There'd generally be something from the early years of country music and something more contemporary – Hank Williams and Lyle Lovett were the bookends at the moment. Sandwiched between them would be a couple of compilations, sometimes a soundtrack, and usually an alt country outfit he was getting into – Lambchop maybe, or Calexico. And there was *always* a Cash album.

He scanned through the choices available. It was important that he make the right one, to carry him through the thirty-minute drive and deliver him home in a different mood. He needed to drift a little, to lose himself in the music and let at least some of the tension bleed away.

The problem was Tughan . . .

Half a mile shy of Hendon, Thorne had settled for *Unchained*. By the time Cash's vocal came in on 'Sea of Heartbreak' and he was smacking his palms against the steering wheel, Thorne was starting to feel much better. As well as it was possible to feel, given the current procedural set-up. The current personnel . . .

He drove east for a while, then cut south, crossing the North Circular and heading towards Golders Green.

Thorne had clashed with Nick Tughan on a case four years previously, and he'd thanked all the deities he didn't believe in when their paths had finally separated. While

Thorne had been part of the new team established at the Serious Crime Group, Tughan had found other tits to get on at SO7. Now he was back as part of the investigation into the Ryan killings, the investigation with which Thorne and his team were supposed to cooperate. He was back giving Thorne grief. Worst of all, the slimy fucker was back as a DCI.

Though they hadn't set eyes on each other for four years, their relationship had picked up exactly where it had left off. It had been neatly encapsulated in their first, terse exchange in the Major Incident Room at Becke House:

'Thorne . . .'

'Tughan . . .'

'I'll settle for "Sir" or "Guv" . . .'

'What about "twat"?'

If an officer were to get physical, to throw a punch, for example, at another officer of equal or subordinate rank, things could get a tad sticky. If he were to throw that punch – and break a nose, or maybe a cheekbone – even if he just handed out a good, hard slap, to a *superior* officer – a DCI, say – he would be in a world of very deep shit. Thorne was thinking about just how unfair this was when his mobile began to ring.

He took a deep breath when he saw the name on the caller ID.

'Tom . . .?' Auntie Eileen, his father's younger sister. 'Listen, there's no need to panic . . .'

Thorne listened, glancing in the rear-view mirror, swerving across the road and pulling up in a bus lane. He listened as buses and cabs drove around him, deaf to the swearing of the irate drivers, to the bark and bleat of their

47

horns. He listened, feeling sick, then scared, and finally fucked off beyond belief.

He ended the call, dragged the car through a U-turn, and accelerated north, back the way he'd come.

The scorch mark rose up the wall behind the cooker and licked a foot or so across the ceiling. The patterned wallpaper had bubbled, then blistered, where the grease that had accumulated over the years had begun to cook the dried paste and plaster beneath. The windows in the kitchen were open, had been for several hours, but still the stench was disgusting.

'No more fucking chip pans,' Thorne said. 'We get rid of *all* the pans, *all* the oil in the place.'

Eileen looked rather shocked. Thorne thought it was his language but then realised when she spoke that it was more than that.

'We should disconnect the *cooker*,' she said. 'Better still, we should get someone to come and take the bloody thing away . . .'

'I'll get it organised,' Thorne said.

'Why don't you let me?'

'I'll sort it.'

Eileen shrugged and sighed. 'He *knows* he's not supposed to come in here.'

'Maybe we should put a lock on the door in the meantime.' Thorne began walking around the room, opening cupboards. 'He was probably hungry . . .'

She nodded. 'He might well have missed his lunch. I think he's been swearing at the Meals on Wheels woman.'

'They don't call it Meals on Wheels any more, Eileen.'

'He called her a "fucking cow". Told her to "stick her hot-pot up her fat arse".' She was trying not to laugh, but once she saw Thorne giving in to it, she stopped bothering to try.

With the tension relieved, they both leaned back against worktops. Eileen folded her arms tight across her chest.

'Who called the fire brigade?' Thorne asked.

'*He* did, eventually. Once he worked out that it was the smoke alarm going off, he hit the panic button. For a while, I don't think he could remember what the noise was.'

Thorne let his head drop back, looked up at the ceiling. There was a spider's web of smoke-stained cracks around the light fitting. He knew very well that, some mornings, his father had trouble remembering what his shoes were for.

'We really need to think about doing something. Tom?'

Thorne looked across at her. For years, Eileen and his father had not been close, but since the Alzheimer's diagnosis two years earlier, she had been a tower of strength. She'd organised virtually everything, and though she lived in Brighton, she still managed to get up to his father's place in St Albans more often than Thorne did from north London.

Thorne felt tired and a little light-headed, exhausted as always by the combination punches of gratitude and guilt.

'How come they called *you*?' he asked.

'Your father gave one of the firemen my number, I think . . .'

Thorne raised his arms and his voice in mock-bewilderment. 'My number's on all the contact sheets.' He started looking in cupboards again. 'Home *and* mobile.'

'He can always remember my number, for some reason. It must be quite an easy one . . .'

'And why did it take *you* so long to ring? I could have got here well before you.'

Eileen walked across to him, let a hand drop on to his forearm. 'He didn't want to worry you.'

'He knew I'd be bloody furious with him, you mean.'

'He didn't want to worry you, and then *I* didn't want to worry you. The fire was already out by the time they called, anyway. I just thought I'd better get here first, tidy up a bit.'

Thorne tried to shut the cupboard door, but it was wonky and refused to close properly, however hard he slammed it.

'Thanks for doing that,' he said, finally.

'We should at least *talk* about it,' she said. 'We could consider the options.' She pointed towards the cooker. 'We've been lucky, but maybe now's the time to think about your dad going somewhere. We could get this place valued, at the very least . . .'

'No.'

'I'm worried he might start going off; you know, getting lost. There was a thing on the radio about tagging. We could get one of those tags put on him and then at least if he *did* forget where he was . . .'

'That's what they do to juvenile offenders, Eileen. It's what they put on bloody muggers.' He moved past her and into the narrow hall. He glared at himself briefly in the hall mirror, then leaned on the door to the living room and stepped inside.

Jim Thorne sat forward on a brown and battered arm-chair. He was hunched over a low coffee-table, strewn with

50

the pieces of various radios he'd taken apart and was failing to put together again. He spoke without looking up.

'I fancied chips,' he said. He had more of an accent than Thorne. The voice was higher, and prone to a rattle.

'There's a perfectly good chippy at the end of the road, for Christ's sake . . .'

'It's not the same.'

'You *love* the chips from that chippy.'

'I wanted to *cook* 'em.' He raised his head, gestured angrily with a thick piece of plastic. 'I wanted to make my own fucking chips, all right?'

Thorne bit his tongue. He walked slowly across to the armchair next to the fire and dropped into it.

He wondered whether this was the point at which the disease moved officially from 'mid' to 'late' stage. Maybe it wasn't defined by anything clinical at all. Maybe it was just the first time that the person with the disease almost killed themselves . . .

'Bollocks,' his father said to nobody in particular.

It had been a struggle up to now, no question, but they'd been managing. The practical difficulties with keys and with mail and with money; the disorientation over time and place; the obsession with trivia; the complete lack of judgement about what to wear, and when to wear it; the drugs for depression, for mood swings, for the verbally abusive behaviour. Still, his father hadn't wandered away and fallen into a ditch yet. He hadn't started knocking back bleach like it was lemonade. He hadn't *endangered* himself. Until now . . .

'You know you're supposed to stay out of the kitchen,' Thorne said.

Then came the two words the old man seemed to say most often these days. His 'catchphrase' he called it, in his better moods. Two words spat out or dribbled, sobbed or screamed, but mostly mumbled, through teeth grinding together in frustration: 'I forgot.'

'I know, and you forgot to turn the cooker off. The rules are there for a good reason, you know? What happens if you forget that knives are sharp? Or that toasters and water aren't meant to go together . . .?'

His father looked up suddenly, excitement spreading across his face as he latched on to a thought. 'More people die in their own homes than anywhere else,' he said. 'Nearly five thousand people a year die because of accidents in the home and garden. I read it. More in the living room than in the kitchen, as a matter of fact, which I thought was surprising.'

'Dad . . .' Thorne watched as concentration etched itself into his father's features and he began to count off on his fingers and thumbs.

'Falls are top of the list, if I remember rightly. "Impact accidents", they're called. Electrocution's another good one. Fire, obviously. Choking, suffocation, DIY incidents . . .'

'Why didn't you give them my number to call?'

His father continued to count off, but began mouthing the words silently. After half a minute or so he stopped, and went back to poking about among the coils and circuits scattered across the table.

Thorne watched him for a while. 'I'll stay the night,' he said.

The old man grinned and got to his feet. He reached into his pocket and produced a crumpled five-pound note.

He held it out, waved it at Thorne. 'Here you go. Here's some . . . bugger . . .' He closed his eyes, struggling to find the word. 'A piece of the stuff people buy things with . . .'

'What do I want money for?'

'*Money!*'

'What do I want it for?'

'To nip down the road and get us some chips. I still haven't had my fucking dinner yet . . .'

He lay awake in the dark, thinking about the burning girl.

He'd never really *stopped* thinking about her, for one reason or another, not for any significant length of time, but lately, for obvious reasons, she'd been on his mind a great deal. The colours and the smells, which had understandably faded over the years, were suddenly more vivid, more pungent than they had been at any time since it had all happened. Not that he'd had much more than a second or two back then to take it all in. Once the flames had taken hold, he'd had to be away sharpish, down that hill towards the spot where he'd parked the car. He'd moved almost as quickly as the girl herself.

The rest of it – the girl's face and what have you – had been filled in afterwards. He'd seen it, swathed in bandages, splashed across every front page and every television screen. Later, he'd seen what she looked like with the bandages off; it was impossible to tell how her face had been before.

It was funny, he thought. *Ironic.* If he *had* seen her face that day at the playground, he would have realised she wasn't the one. Afterwards, of course, nobody would mistake her for anyone else ever again.

He drifted, eventually, towards sleep. Thoughts giving way to fuzzy pictures and feelings . . .

He remembered her arms flailing in the instant before she began to run, as though it were nothing more serious than a wasp. He remembered the sound of her shoes on the playground as he turned away. He remembered feeling like such a fucking idiot when he realised she was entirely the wrong girl.

Thorne spent most of the night writhing across nylon sheets, sinking into the ludicrously soft mattress in his father's spare room and dragging back the duvet which had slid away from him down the natural slope of the bed. He felt like he'd only just got off to sleep when his phone rang. He checked his watch and saw that it was already gone nine-thirty. At the same instant that he began to panic, he remembered that he'd called Brigstocke the night before to tell him what was going on. They wouldn't be expecting him at the office.

He reached down towards where the phone lay chirping on top of his clothes. His neck ached and his arms were freezing.

It was Holland. 'I'm in a video shop in Wood Green,' he said. 'We've got two bodies, still warm. And that's not the title of one of the videos . . .'

FOUR

The uniformed constable who'd been first on the scene was sitting at a small table in a back room, next to a teenage boy whom Thorne guessed was Muslum Izzigil's son. Thorne stared across at them from the doorway. He couldn't decide which of the two looked the younger, or the most upset.

Holland stood at Thorne's shoulder. 'The boy ran out into the street when he found them. Constable Terry was having breakfast in the caff opposite. He heard the boy screaming.'

Thorne nodded and closed the door quietly. He turned and moved back into the shop, where screens had been hastily erected around the bodies. The scene of crime team moved with a practised efficiency, but it seemed to Thorne that the usual banter – the dark humour, the *craic* – was a little muted. Thorne had hunted serial killers; he had known the atmosphere at crime scenes to be charged with respect, even fear, at the presentation, the *offering up*, of the latest victim. This was not what they were looking at now. This was almost certainly a contract killing. Still, there was an odd feeling in the room. Perhaps it was the fact that there were two bodies. That they had been husband and wife.

'Where was the boy when it happened?'

'Upstairs,' Holland said. 'Getting ready for school. He didn't hear anything.'

Thorne nodded. The killer had used a silencer. 'This one's a little less showy than the X-Man,' he said.

Muslum Izzigil was sitting against the wall between a display of children's videos and a life-sized cardboard cut-out of Lara Croft. His head was cocked to one side, his eyes half-open and popping. A thin line of blood ran from the back of his head, along freshly shaved jowls, soaking pink into the collar of a white nylon shirt. The body of his wife lay, face downwards, across his legs. There was very little blood, and only the small, blackened hole behind her ear told the story of what had happened. Or at least, some of it . . .

Which one had he killed first? Did he make the husband watch while his wife was executed? Did the wife die only because she had tried to save her husband?

Thorne looked up from the bodies. He noticed the small camera in the corner of the shop. 'Too much to hope for, I suppose?'

'*Far* too much,' Holland said. 'The recorder's not exactly hard to find. It's over there underneath the counter. The shooter took the tape with him.'

'One to show the grandchildren . . .'

Holland knelt and pointed with a biro to the back of the dead woman's neck. 'Twenty-two, d'you reckon?'

Thorne could see where the blood was gathering then.

It encircled her neck like a delicate necklace, but it was pooling, sticky between her chin and the industrial grey carpet. 'Looks like it,' he said. He was already moving across the shop towards the back room. Towards what was going to be a difficult conversation . . .

Constable Terry got to his feet when Thorne came through the door. Thorne waved him back on to his chair. 'What's the boy's name?'

The boy answered the question himself: 'Yusuf Izzigil.'

Thorne put him at about seventeen. Probably taking A levels. He'd gelled his short, black hair into spikes and was making a decent enough job of growing a moustache. The hysteria which Holland had mentioned, which had first alerted the police, had given way to a stillness. He was quiet now, and seemingly composed, but the tears were still coming just as quickly, each one pushed firmly away with the heel of a hand the instant it brimmed and began to fall.

He started to speak again, without being asked. 'I was getting ready upstairs. My father always came down just after eight o'clock, to deal with the tapes that had been returned in the overnight box. My mother came down to help him get things set up once she'd put the breakfast things away.' He spoke well, and slowly, with no trace of an accent. Thorne realised suddenly that the maroon sweater and grey trousers were a uniform, and guessed that the boy went to a private school.

'So you heard nothing?' Thorne asked. 'No raised voices?'

The boy shook his head. 'I heard the bell go on the door when someone opened it, but that isn't unusual.'

'It was a bit early, though, wasn't it?'

'We often have customers who come in on their way to work, to pick up a film that's been returned the night before.'

'Anything else . . .?'

'I was in the bathroom after that. There was water running. If not, I might have heard something.' His hand went to his face, pressed and wiped. 'They had silencers on their guns, didn't they?'

It was an odd thing to say. Thorne wondered if perhaps the boy knew more than he was telling, but decided it was probably down to seeing far too many of the shitty British gangster movies his father kept on the shelves.

'What makes you think there was more than one of them, Yusuf?'

'A week ago two boys came in. About the same age as me, my father said. They tried to scare him.'

'What did they do?'

'Pathetic stuff, threats. Dog mess in a video case. Throwing a litter bin through the window.' He pointed towards the shopfront, where a thick black curtain now ran across the plate-glass window and front door, rigged up to hide the activity within from the eyes of passers-by. 'There was a letter first. My father ignored it.'

'Did he keep the letter?'

'My mother will have filed it somewhere. She never throws anything away.'

The boy realised what he'd said, and blinked slowly. The hand that went to his face stayed there a little longer this time. Thorne remembered the sign he'd seen stuck to the front of the till: *You are being recorded.* 'Did your father get it on tape? The incident with the two boys?'

'I should think so. He recorded everything, but it won't be there any more.'

Thorne asked the question with a look.

'Because he used the same few tapes over and over again,'Yusuf said. 'Changed them half a dozen times every day, and recorded over them. He was always trying to save money, but this business with the videotapes was really stupid, considering that we *sold* the bloody things. Always trying to save money . . .'

The boy's head dropped. The tears that came were left to run their course, the hands that had been wiping them away now clutching the countertop.

'You're not a child, Yusuf,' Thorne said. 'You're far too clever to buy any of my bullshit, so I won't give you any, all right?' He glanced back towards the screens, towards what lay behind them. 'This is not about an argument, or an affair, or an unpaid bill. I'm not going to tell you that I can catch whoever did this, because I don't know if I can. I *do* know I'm going to have a bloody good try, though.'

Thorne waited, but the boy did not look up. He gave a small nod to Terry, who stood and put an arm on Yusuf's shoulder. The constable said something, a few murmured words of comfort, as Thorne closed the door behind him.

He arrived back in the shop in time to see the black curtain swept aside and DCI Nick Tughan stepping through it like a bad actor.

'Right. What have we got?' Tughan was a stick-thin Irishman with less than generous lips. His short, sandy hair was always clean, and the collars crisp beneath a variety of expensive suits. 'Who's filling me in . . .?'

Thorne smiled and shrugged: Me, given half a chance,

59

you tosser. He was happy to see Holland walking across to do the honours, clearly not relishing the task, but knowing that he'd earn himself a drink later. A pint sounded like a good idea, even at eleven o'clock in the morning. Including the Izzigils, there were a dozen people inside the small shop, which, combined with the heat coming off the SOC lights, had turned the place into a sauna very quickly. Keen to get some air, Thorne stepped towards the front door, just as another person pushed through the curtain. This one was dressed from head to foot in black himself.

'What happened to you last night?' Hendricks asked.

Thorne sighed. He'd completely forgotten to call and tell Hendricks he'd be stopping over at his old man's. 'I'll tell you later . . .'

'Is everything all right?'

'Yeah, fine . . . just my dad.'

'Is he OK?'

'He's a pain in the arse . . .'

'I stayed up. You should have called.'

'Oh, that's sweet.' It was Tughan's voice. The DCI was standing over the bodies of Muslum and Hanya Izzigil, a mock-sweet smile on his face. 'No, really, it's very touching that he's worried about you . . .'

Thorne was still spitting blood ten minutes later when Holland joined him on the pavement outside the shop.

'If ever there was an incentive to solve a case . . .'

'Right,' Thorne said. 'Get shot of the slippery bugger.'

'Mind you, he had a point. It *was* touching . . .'

Thorne turned, ready to let off some steam, but the broad grin on Holland's face softened the scowl on his own. He let out a long, slow breath and leaned back against the shop window. 'You look rough, Dave . . .'

Thorne had seen DC Dave Holland do a lot of growing up in recent years, no more so than since his daughter had been born. The floppy blond hair had been cut shorter recently, which put a couple of years on him, and the lines around his eyes had added a few more. Thorne knew that very few coppers stayed fresh-faced for long. Those that did were lucky or lazy, and Holland was neither of those things. He'd saved Thorne's life the year before, and the circumstances – the dark, depraved intimacies which the pair of them had witnessed and experienced – had rarely been talked about since the resulting court case.

'I'm utterly knackered,' Holland said.

Thorne looked at the gingerish stubble dotted across the pale and slightly sunken cheeks. Maybe the change in him was due to responsibility as much as experience. A few years ago, and particularly during his girlfriend's pregnancy, Holland hadn't shown a great deal of either.

'Is it the baby?'

'Actually, it's Sophie,' Holland said. 'It's probably hormones or something, but she's at me three or four times a night demanding sex.'

'*What?*'

'Of *course* it's the baby! Have you had a sense-of-humour bypass?'

'I didn't get a lot of sleep myself. I was staying at my dad's place.'

'Sorry, I forgot. How's he doing?'

'I reckon he'll be the death of me before he manages to kill himself.'

On the other side of the road, a small crowd had gathered to stare at the comings and goings at Izzigil's video shop. The café from which Constable Terry had run to see what all the screaming was about had now become a convenient vantage-point. The owner was cheerfully scurrying around, serving coffee and pastries to those who wanted to sit outside and gawp.

Holland took out a packet of ten Silk Cut. He scrounged a light from a woman walking past with a pushchair.

'How long's that been going on?' Thorne asked, nodding towards the cigarette. He hadn't smoked in a long time, but would still happily have killed for one.

'Since the baby, I suppose. It was fags or heroin.'

'Well, you're in the right place for that . . .'

North of Finsbury Park, Green Lanes straightened into a strut of what had become known as the Harringay Ladder. Looking at the bustle around its shops and businesses at that moment, it was easy to see the area for what it was: one of the busiest and certainly one of the most racially diverse areas of the city. Of course, that did not explain the presence of armed police on its streets. A fierce gun-battle in those same streets six months earlier had left three men dead, and shown the other side of the area only too clearly. Harringay was home to a number of gangs operating within the Turkish community. According to figures from the National Criminal Intelligence Service, they were in control of over three-quarters of the seventy tonnes of heroin that passed through London every year. They protected their investments fiercely.

'Does Tughan think it's about smack?'

Holland wasn't listening. 'Sorry . . .?'

Thorne pointed back to the shop. 'The Izzigils. Does our gangland expert in there think this is a turf war?'

'Actually, he thinks it's the Ryans.'

'Eh?'

'He seems to think that this is a message from Billy Ryan to whoever's been knocking his boys off. A "declaration", he reckons.'

'That's a bit of a leap, isn't it?' Thorne said. 'What's he base that on?'

'No idea. He seems pretty convinced, though.'

Thorne closed his eyes as smoke from Holland's cigarette drifted across his face. 'It makes sense on one level, I suppose.'

'What?'

'The Ryans were always going to work out who was after them long before we did.'

Thorne watched as two officers carrying body-bags moved towards the front door. Hendricks had obviously finished his preliminary examination. Thorne moved to follow the officers back inside, murmuring to Holland as he passed: 'Listen, the fact that Hendricks is staying at my place . . . Are people making cracks about it?'

Holland was enjoying a long drag. He laughed so much that he began to choke.

Thorne had spent the last three years based at the Peel Centre in Hendon, and his familiarity with it, with Becke House in particular, had bred a good deal of contempt. The building – a dun-coloured, three-storey blot on an already drab landscape – had once housed dormitories for recruits. The beds had given way to open-plan incident rooms and suites of poky offices, but there were still plenty of fresh faces to be spotted around the place, with the Metropolitan Police cadets now housed in another building within the same compound.

It always struck Thorne as strange that the Serious Crime Group should be based where it was, hand in glove with a cadet-training centre. He remembered arriving back late one afternoon, a year or so earlier, and bumping into a uniformed cadet as he turned from locking his car. He'd spent the previous few hours trying to explain to an old woman why her son-in-law had taken an axe to her daughter and grandchildren. The look on Thorne's face that day had stopped the cadet dead in his tracks, hacking off his cheery greeting mid-sentence and sending the blood rushing from his smooth cheeks . . .

The meeting was taking place in the office that Russell Brigstocke was reluctantly sharing with Nick Tughan. The SO7 Projects Team was based in a collection of Portakabins at Barkingside, where Tughan and his team still spent a fair amount of time, but since the joint operation had begun, there'd been something of a shake-up on the third floor of Becke House. Holland and DC Andrew Stone now shared *their* office part time with two DCs from Serious and Organised Crime, leaving the third office to Thorne and DI Yvonne Kitson. The latter spent most of her time in the Incident Room, collating information alongside office manager DS Samir Karim and their opposite numbers from SO7. So, more often than not, Thorne had his office, such as it was, to himself.

'Right,' said Tughan. 'Game on. I think we've got ourselves a war . . .'

Tughan's Irish accent could switch between syrupy and strident. Today, it went right through Thorne. He remembered the scrape of Gordon Rooker's chair across the floor of the visiting room at the Royal.

Tughan leaned against the desk in a vain effort to make his superiority appear casual. He held up a piece of paper inside a transparent plastic jacket. 'This was found among the dead man's paperwork. There are photocopies for each of you.'

Brigstocke and Kitson already had their copies. Holland, Stone and Thorne moved forward and took theirs from the desk.

'This letter isn't dated,' continued Tughan, 'but, according to the son, it was delivered by hand five or six weeks ago.'

'Late Christmas present . . .' Stone said, looking for the laugh, a little too full of himself, as usual.

Tughan ignored him, pressed on. 'It's nothing we haven't seen before. Subtler than some I've come across – lots of stuff about the dangers facing new businesses. But basically it's a simple protection scheme. Only problem is they were moving in on someone who was already protected.'

'"They"', Thorne said, 'being Billy Ryan.'

'To the best of my knowledge, yes.'

'The "best of your knowledge"?'

Tughan smiled thinly and turned away from Thorne. 'We're moving forward on the basis that this letter originated from the Ryan family, or from criminals closely associated with them.'

Thorne let it go, but it still bothered him. It wasn't like

threatening letters were sent out on headed notepaper. How could Tughan be so sure that this one came from the Ryan family?

Thorne caught Brigstocke's eye, but the DCI did not allow him to hold it for very long. Brigstocke's attitude to the entire SO7 operation basically involved keeping his head down until they disappeared. Thorne had a lot of time for the man – he was hard and principled, caught far too often between those above and below him – but he still had an irritating predilection for hedging his bets. At the same time, of course, Thorne was well aware that his own refusal to do the same thing had often landed him in plenty of trouble . . .

Yvonne Kitson was less afraid than some to speak her mind. 'It doesn't make a lot of sense,' she said. 'They send a threatening letter. They send the bully boys round to chuck a bin through the window. Then they have the owners *killed*?'

Holland looked up from the letter. 'Right, that's quite an escalation, sir.'

'It's not complicated,' Tughan said. His smile took him way over the line that separated informative from patronising. 'This was a straightforward campaign of intimidation. It might well have got nasty eventually, but it wouldn't have gone as far as killing. Then the Ryans discovered that the video shop was protected by the same people responsible for the murder of Mickey Clayton and the others. The same people that are paying the X-Man.'

'A bit coincidental, isn't it?' Holland asked.

Tughan had been waiting for this. 'I don't think so . . .'

'It was the letter,' Thorne said. 'That's what started everything.'

'It was *probably* the letter.' Tughan couldn't keep the irritation off his face at having his thunder stolen. 'It doesn't really matter now how it started . . .'

Thorne took Tughan's expression as his cue to get stuck in. 'Whoever was protecting Izzigil's business took major offence at the Ryans trying to move in.'

'Major offence?' Holland said. 'That's putting it bloody mildly. They've had four of Billy Ryan's top men killed.'

Brigstocke agreed: 'Whatever happened to breaking somebody's legs?'

'It's about a lot more than territory now,' Thorne said. 'It probably always was. We're presuming they're Turks, right? Whoever's been hitting the Ryans . . .'

'We can't presume anything,' Tughan said. 'The fact that the video business was Turkish needn't be significant.'

'It *needn't* be, no. But I still think it is.'

'We've heard nothing from the NCIS . . .'

'They're not infallible. We're probably talking about somebody relatively new here. Maybe an offshoot of an existing gang.'

'Granted, it's a Turkish area, but other groups might still try their luck.'

'They'd be idiots if they did . . .'

'The Ryans did.'

'Right,' Thorne said. 'And look what they got for their trouble.'

Tughan seemed to decide suddenly that a physical barrier between himself and Thorne might be a good idea. He moved behind the desk and slid into the chair. He looked at his computer, affecting an air of thoughtfulness, but, to Thorne, it seemed more like regrouping.

'We're assuming that on one side we've got the Ryans, right?' Thorne continued quickly before Tughan had a chance to pull him up: 'If we assume that on the other side we've got an as yet unknown Turkish operation, it all starts to add up. If you're a newish gang, looking to establish yourself, you don't go up against the big Turkish gangs that have already got the area sewn up. Not if you want to be around in six months' time. You so much as start sniffing around one of those big heroin operations and they'll wipe you out, right?'

If anybody disagreed, they were keeping quiet about it.

'What makes more sense, if you're looking to make a splash, is to go up against somebody else completely. Somebody unconnected with local business or local territory. When that letter dropped on to the doormat in that video shop, somebody saw an opportunity to expand in a different direction altogether; to send out a message to the gangs around them without getting anybody's back up. This lot, whoever the hell they are, probably see the Ryans as a soft target.'

Tughan had been typing something. He raised his eyes from his computer screen and smiled. 'Somebody should tell Billy Ryan that.'

There wasn't a trace of a smile from Yvonne Kitson. 'And the Izzigils . . .'

'So who are they?' Stone asked. 'If we want to stop a war, we'll need to know who's up against who.'

Tughan stabbed at a key, leaned back in his chair. 'I think DI Thorne might well be right when he suggests that we're dealing with a Turkish – or possibly Kurdish – group here. I'm liaising with the NCIS, specifically the Heroin Intelligence Unit . . .'

Thorne shook his head. 'I told you, I can't see that this is about heroin. This is about not shitting on your own doorstep.'

'Is that a technical term?' Brigstocke asked. 'I must have missed that seminar.'

Thorne smiled. 'I've seen a couple of Guy Ritchie films.'

Tughan raised his voice a little, bridling slightly, as always, at any exchange that rose above the funereal. 'I'm confident that we will establish the identity of this gang quickly. We will find something connecting them to the video rental business, or we might get a lead from Turkish community leaders in the area . . .'

'Only the ones with a death wish,' Brigstocke said.

'One way or another, things are much clearer now than they were.' Tughan brandished the letter whose implied threats had probably been the catalyst for at least six deaths. 'We've made a real breakthrough today.'

Thorne's mood blackened in an instant. He remembered the film of tears across a pair of dark eyes, red around the rims.

A real breakthrough . . .

He doubted that Yusuf Izzigil would see things in quite the same way.

They drove back from the restaurant in virtual silence.

As always, Jack stayed well within the speed limit as he steered the Volvo through streets that were still slick after an early evening downpour. The short journey was one that they tried to make at least once a month – sometimes more if there was a birthday or anniversary to be celebrated. Jack always drove, always stuck to half a bitter while they waited for the table, and a glass of wine with the meal.

'Are you cross with me?' Carol said, eventually.

'Don't be silly. I was just worried.'

'It's like I spoiled your evening.'

'You couldn't help it. What happened, I mean. You didn't spoil my evening.'

Carol turned away from him and stared out of the window. She could still taste the vomit at the back of her throat. Instinctively, she looked again to make sure there was none on her blouse.

'You must be coming down with something,' Jack said. 'I'll call the quack first thing.'

Carol nodded without shifting her gaze from a scratch on the car window, from the darkness moving past it.

It had come over her from nowhere as she was digging into her spaghetti – a heat that had prickled and spread quickly – until she'd had to throw down her fork and rush to the toilet. She'd emerged ten minutes later, pale and with a weak smile that had fooled nobody: not the manager, who offered to call a doctor and assured her that the meal was on the house, and least of all her husband. Jack had shrugged at the waiters and smiled. He'd taken her arm: 'Come on, love. You're white as a sheet. We'd best make a move . . .'

Carol knew full well what the trouble was. This was the first physical symptom of a virus that had been lurking inside her, waiting for the chance to blossom since the day she'd handed over her warrant card. She'd tried to ignore it

on other occasions, when an unfamiliar reaction to something had forced her to ask the question.

Have I stopped being a copper *inside*?

She knew what the answer was. The cold-case stuff was
Mickey Mouse; it was just playing at what she used to do
for real. Now, she could feel doubt, worry, pain, anger.
And fear. She felt them all in a way she never had for those
thirty years she'd spent watching other people feel the
same things. She felt like a *civilian*. And she hated it.

She knew that this was all about Gordon Rooker. The
reassurance that had come from Thorne's visit to the Royal
had lasted no more than a couple of hours. God, it was all
so bloody stupid. After all, the facts were pretty obvious:
Rooker was locked up; Rooker was guilty; whoever had
been phoning her and sending the letters was some nutcase
who, by the look of it, had probably stopped now anyway.

It hadn't been facts, though, that had made her throw
up. She needed to deal with the feelings. She needed to
deal with the *panic*.

She needed to start behaving like a real copper again.

'It's definitely not the food,' Jack said as he slowed to
turn into their quiet crescent. 'How many times have we
eaten in that place over the years . . .?'

Hendricks was already asleep by the time Thorne got in,
just after eleven. As Thorne crept past the sofa-bed towards
the kitchen, Elvis, his psychotic cat, jumped down from
where she'd been curled up on Hendricks' feet and followed him. While he waited for the kettle to boil, Thorne
poured some cat munchies into a grubby plastic bowl and
told Elvis one or two things about his day. He'd rather have

71

talked to his friend, who was a marginally better conversationalist, but the snoring from the next room made it clear just how well away Hendricks was. Thorne didn't want to wake him. He knew that Hendricks had probably had a fairly tough day himself.

Up to his elbows in the cadavers of Muslum and Hanya Izzigil.

Drinking his tea at the kitchen table, Thorne thought about those who would spend the coming night sleepless. Those with money worries or difficulties at work, or relationship problems. It was odd what could keep some people awake, while a man who dealt in death – usually one that had been anything but peaceful – could sleep like a baby. He thought about Dave Holland, bleary-eyed at 4 a.m., who would tell him just how ludicrous *that* expression was.

Of course, he didn't know what went on in Phil Hendricks' *dreams* . . .

Thorne hadn't slept brilliantly himself since the night he'd come so close to death the year before. There had been nightmares, of course, but now it was just as if his body had adapted and required less sleep. Most nights he'd get by on four or five hours and then collapse into something approaching a coma when he took a day off.

Having removed his shoes, Thorne carried them, and what was left of his tea, towards the bedroom. On the way through the darkened living room he picked up his CD Walkman and a George Jones album. He held the bedroom door open for Elvis, and watched as she hopped back up on to Phil Hendricks' legs.

'Sod you, then,' Thorne said.

He padded into his bedroom with his tea, his shoes and his music, and closed the door behind him.

It was a sudden change in the light, no more than that.

Carol Chamberlain saw it reflected in the dressing-table mirror as she sat taking her make-up off. She'd washed most of it off earlier, rubbing cold water into her face in the toilets at the Italian restaurant. Trying to stop the dizziness and to bring back a little colour to her cheeks.

Jack was moving around downstairs. Locking up, pulling out plugs. Keeping them safe . . .

She sat in her nightdress and stared hard at herself. It was time to sort her hair out, and maybe shift a few pounds though, at fifty-six, that was a damn sight harder than it used to be. She could try to get back to how she was when they'd taken the job away from her: her 'fighting weight', Jack called it.

Leaning closer towards the mirror, cream smeared across her fingers, she saw the light change. A glow – pink at first, then orange – that crept through a gap in the curtains and lit up the room behind her. She opened her mouth to call out Jack's name, then closed it and pushed back her chair. As she walked towards the window, she saw the glow reaching up and illuminating the bare branches of the copper beech at the end of the drive. She knew more or less what she was going to see when she reached the far side of the room and looked out. She wondered if he'd be there. She hoped that he would be . . .

He was already looking up when she pulled back the curtains, standing motionless next to the car, the can of lighter fluid white against his gloved hand.

Waiting for her.

For a few long, still seconds they stared at each other. The flames were not spectacular, and the light danced only across the dark material of the man's anorak. The blaze never threatened to break up the shadow, blue-black beneath the hood that was pulled tight around his head.

The fire was already beginning to spread across the Volvo's bonnet. It drifted down around its edges, into its mouldings, where the lighter fluid had run and dripped. Still, the words, sprayed in fuel and spelled out now in flame, were clear enough.

I burned her.

Carol heard locks being thrown back downstairs, and saw the man's head turn suddenly towards the front door. He took a step away from the car, then looked up at Carol for another moment or two before he turned and ran. She had seen nothing, *could* see nothing of his face, but she knew very well that he had been smiling at her.

A few seconds later, Jack burst out of the front door in his vest. He ran, arms raised and mouth gaping, on to the front lawn. Carol half-saw him turn to look up, at the same moment she moved away from the window and back into the heart of the room.

FIVE

Thorne had never conducted an interview alongside Carol Chamberlain before and, although this was in no sense official, he still felt slightly odd, sitting there next to her, waiting for Rooker to be brought in. He looked around the small, square room and imagined himself, for no good reason he could think of, as a father, sitting with his wife. He remembered the sobbing black woman he'd seen on his last visit. He pictured himself and Chamberlain as anxious parents waiting for their son to be marched in.

The door opened and an officer led Rooker into the room. He looked angry about something until he saw Chamberlain; then, a broad smile appeared.

'Hello, sexpot,' he said.

Thorne opened his mouth to speak, but Chamberlain beat him to it. There was an edge to her voice that Thorne could not recall hearing before.

'One more out-of-order remark and I'll come round this table and tear off what little you've got left between your legs that hasn't already withered away. Fair enough, Gordon?'

Rooker's smile wobbled a little, but it was back in place

as he pulled back his chair and plonked himself down at the table. The officer moved towards the door. 'Give us a shout when you've finished,' he said.

'Thanks,' Thorne said, looking up. 'I thought you'd retired, Bill.'

The officer opened the door, turned back to Thorne. 'Got a year or two left yet.' He nodded towards Rooker. 'Feels like I've been in here as long as this cunt.' He quickly looked across to Chamberlain, reddening slightly. 'Sorry, I didn't . . .'

Chamberlain held up a hand. 'Don't apologise. That sounds about right to me . . .'

Rooker cackled. The officer stepped out of the room, letting the door swing shut, hard, behind him.

'This is getting to be a habit,' Rooker said. He produced a tobacco tin from behind the green bib and removed the lid. 'Twice in a week, Mr Thorne. I don't have family who come as often as that.' He teased out the strands of tobacco, laid them carefully into a Rizla and rolled it pin-thin. 'Nothing *like* as often as that . . .'

In fact, it had been just over a week since Thorne had first encountered Gordon Rooker. And seven days since Carol Chamberlain had stared down from her bedroom window at the man who was claiming Gordon Rooker's crime as his own.

Rooker lit his roll-up. He picked a piece of tobacco from his tongue and looked across at Chamberlain. 'I thought *you'd* retired,' he said.

'That's right.'

'Living out in the sticks with a houseful of cats, listening to *The Archers* . . .'

'What do you know about where I live?'

Rooker turned to Thorne. 'If she's not on the job any more, what are we doing here?'

By 'here', Rooker meant the Legal Visits Room. It was normally reserved for confidential interviews, for meetings with police officers or solicitors, for official business. Thorne was content to keep things *unofficial* . . . for now. He had seen no real reason to go to Brigstocke and certainly not to Tughan. The connection between Rooker and Billy Ryan was twenty years old and tenuous at best to the SO7 inquiry, *and* he'd promised Carol Chamberlain that he'd try to sort things out on his own time. He'd discreetly pulled a few strings and called in a favour or two to ensure that he, Chamberlain and Gordon Rooker could discuss one or two things in private.

'What we talked about a week ago,' Thorne said, 'it's escalated.'

Rooker looked, or *tried* to look, serious. 'That's a shame.'

'Yes, it is.'

'I told you last time . . .'

'I'll forget the rubbish you told me last time and pretend we're starting from scratch, OK? This has to be down to some fuckwit you've done time with, or somebody who's written to you. You told me all about some of the letters you get, right?'

'Right.'

'So, any bright ideas, Gordon?'

Rooker took three quick drags. He held the smoke in and let it out very slowly on a sigh. 'I've got to have some sort of protection,' he said.

Thorne laughed. '*What?*'

'Word got around after you were here last time . . .'

Thorne shrugged. He'd obviously opted for privacy a little too late. 'You've not exactly been popular for quite a while now, Gordon. Talking to a copper isn't going to make much difference.'

'You'd be surprised . . .'

Chamberlain's voice was quieter than when she'd spoken before, but the edge had sharpened. 'If you've got something to say, Rooker, you'd best say it.'

Another drag. 'I want this parole. I really need it to go my way this time.'

'And?' Thorne stared blankly across the table at Rooker. 'Not a lot we can do about *that*.'

'Bollocks. It's down to the Home Office. You can get it done if you want to.'

'Why would we want to?'

'I need a guarantee that I'm getting out . . .'

'Don't want much, do you?'

'It'll be worth it.'

'Unless you're telling us who Jack the Ripper was and where Lord Lucan and Shergar are holed up, I doubt we'd be interested.'

Rooker didn't seem to find that funny.

'What about these letters?' asked Chamberlain. 'The phone calls. That's what we're here to talk about.'

Rooker stared down at the ashtray.

'Whoever's doing this has been to my *house* . . .'

'I want protection.' Rooker looked up at Thorne. 'After I'm out.'

'Protection from who?' Chamberlain said.

'New identity, national insurance number, the lot . . .'

'Billy Ryan,' Thorne said.

'Maybe . . .'

'Is Billy Ryan going to come after you?'

'Not for the reason you think.'

'So why should we give a toss?'

'I can give him to you.'

Thorne blinked. This was interesting. This was far from tenuous. He avoided eye contact with Chamberlain, refused to show Rooker anything, kept his voice casual. 'You're going to grass up Billy Ryan?'

Rooker nodded.

'Grass up the Ryans,' Chamberlain said, 'and you really *will* be a target.'

'That's why I want protection.'

It was a straightforward piece of gangland logic, and Thorne could see the sense of it. 'Get Ryan before he gets you. That it?'

'Don't make out like you wouldn't like to put him away. He's a piece of shit and you know it.'

'And you're a fucking saint, are you, Gordon?'

'It's him or me, isn't it? What would you do?'

'After what you did at that school, what you did to that girl . . . I'm inclined to let Billy Ryan have you.'

Rooker's head dropped and stayed down as he stubbed out what was left of his cigarette. He ground the butt into the ashtray until there appeared to be nothing left of it at all. For a moment, Thorne wondered if he'd palmed it, like a magician. When Rooker finally looked up, the cockiness had gone. The lines in his face had deepened. He seemed suddenly tense. He looked like a frightened old man.

'I didn't burn the girl,' he said. 'It wasn't me.'

Thorne saw Chamberlain's hands clench into fists on the table, white across her knuckles as she spoke. 'Don't piss me about. Don't you bloody dare piss me about . . .'

Rooker licked his lips and repeated himself.

And Thorne believed him. It really was that simple. All that struck him as odd was that Rooker seemed so reluctant, so hesitant about his denial. Surely things were arse about face. Thorne remembered how, a week before, the man sitting opposite him had admitted to setting a fourteen-year-old girl on fire as easily as he might own up to nicking lead off a roof. Now, he was taking it back, denying he'd had anything to do with it, and it was as if it were the hardest thing in the world.

It was like he was confessing his innocence.

Dave Holland and Andy Stone got along, but no more than that. A year or so ago, when they'd first begun working together, Holland had resented Stone's easy charm, and bridled at his place as the young pretender – pretender to *what* he was never sure – feeling threatened. They'd kicked along well enough since then, though there were still times when the ease with which his fellow DC told a joke or wore a suit made him want to spit.

'I feel like shit warmed up,' Stone said.

Holland looked up from the computer screen and smiled. 'Caning it again last night, were you?'

'Still sweating Carlsberg and Sea Breezes.'

Holland raised an eyebrow. 'Cocktails?'

'I was with a very classy lady, mate . . .'

Holland was at least self-aware enough to admit that

now, with a baby to think about, his resentment had distilled into plain, old-fashioned jealousy.

'I bet I still had more sleep than you, though,' Stone said.

'Right . . .'

Holland had more or less grown used to the physical fatigue. He could happily nod off at pretty much any time, and was not beyond catnapping in the Gents after a really bad night. It was mentally that he was still finding things tough. There was a fuzziness about his thinking these days, a reluctance to go in any direction other than the path of least resistance. There was a time, back before the baby and the rough patch they went through even before that, when Sophie would badger him about being the kind of straightforward, head-down, career copper that his old man had been. She didn't have to bother these days, and she knew it. Holland didn't have the mental energy to do a great deal else.

And there was the way the baby made him feel: the sheer, fucking size of the love and the terror. Looking down at her sometimes, he could feel his heart swell and his sphincter tighten at the same time.

Holland closed his eyes for a few seconds. He could remember so vividly the first time he'd walked into a CID suite. He could recall virtually every moment of that first case he'd worked on with Tom Thorne. He saw in perfect detail the clothes he'd been wearing on a particular occasion in Thorne's car, or in the office when they got a break in the case. It was only the excitement of it, which he knew had been intense, that seemed suddenly distant and hard to imagine . . .

'Where's that plum from SO7, anyway?' asked Stone. 'He's never here when he's needed, is he?'

They were going through the paperwork and computer data relating to what had quickly emerged as the less than legitimate business activities of Muslum Izzigil's video shop. When one or two members of Brigstocke's team had expressed surprise that video piracy was still big business, they had been subjected to Tughan at his most patronising: 'Five thousand copies from one stolen master tape, knocked out at a couple of quid a pop. You might be looking at half a million per year per film. It's not quite up there with heroin, but there's a damn sight less risk and you don't tend to get put away for so long.'

Some, notably Thorne, had remained sceptical. Then again, Thorne was sceptical about *everything* that came out of Tughan's mouth, and there was certainly evidence that pointed towards a sophisticated smuggling operation. There was no such evidence leading them to whoever was running it; whoever Muslum Izzigil – among many others in all likelihood – had been fronting for; whoever had reacted so aggressively when Billy Ryan had tried to muscle in on their territory.

Whoever was paying the X-Man . . .

There was a DC from SO7 who, theoretically at least, was supposed to be working with Holland and Stone, but whenever there were paper-trails to slog through, urgent meetings would materialise back at Barkingside, or mysterious sources would suddenly need chasing up on the other side of London.

'They're taking the piss, aren't they?'

Holland found it hard to disagree with Stone's

assessment. He was about to chip in with a comment of his own when something on the screen caught his eye. He stared at it for a few seconds, scrolled back to check something else, then held up a hand, beckoning Stone from the other side of the room. 'Come and look at this, Andy.'

'What?'

'A name.' He highlighted two words on the screen for Stone to look at, moved to a different page and highlighted the same words again. Stone stared down at the screen from behind his shoulder. 'Just a name,' Holland said. 'Nothing to tie it to anything dodgy, as yet.'

'There wouldn't be. These fuckers are too clever for that.'

'Maybe . . .'

'Definitely. We won't catch 'em with Windows 2000, I can tell you that.'

Holland grunted. 'Well, whoever they are, their name just keeps cropping up . . .'

'I was a dead man,' Rooker said.

Chamberlain leaned back in her chair, waiting. Thorne moved in the opposite direction. 'Don't get existential on us, Gordon. Keep it simple and keep it honest. All right?'

'I was fucked, all right? That simple enough? Whoever did the girl made it look like me. I was known for stuff like that, wasn't I? For using lighter fuel . . .'

'"Whoever did the girl". I take it you can't tell us who that was?'

'I can tell you who paid for it. I can tell you whose idea it was to kill a kid.'

'We knew that. We knew it was one of the other firms who . . .'

'You knew fuck all.'

Next to him, Chamberlain sat stock still, but Thorne could feel the tension radiating off her. He asked the question slowly: 'So, who was it then?'

This was Rooker's big moment. 'It was Billy Ryan. That's why I can give him to you. Billy Ryan put the contract out on Kevin Kelly's little girl.'

A pause, but nothing too dramatic before Thorne asked the obvious question: 'Why?'

'It wasn't complicated. He was ambitious. He wanted to take on the smaller firms, but Kelly wouldn't have it. He thought things were fine as they were. Billy reckoned Kevin was losing his edge.'

'So he tried to take over?'

'Billy wanted what Kevin had. *More* than Kevin had. He'd tried to get him out of the way earlier but fucked it up.'

Thorne remembered Chamberlain's gangland history lesson: the failed attempt on Kevin Kelly's life a few months before the incident at the school. 'Were you anything to do with that, Gordon?'

'I'm not getting into anything else. Point is, the Kelly family *thought* I was.'

'So, Billy targets his boss's daughter, but whoever he's paying tries to kill the wrong girl.'

'Yeah, that got fucked up as well, but it still worked. Kevin Kelly goes mental, wipes out anybody who's so much as looked at him funny, then hands the whole fucking business over to Billy Ryan and walks away. It couldn't have gone better.'

Thorne saw Rooker flinch slightly when Chamberlain

spoke. 'I'm not sure Jessica Clarke or her family would have seen things in quite the same way.'

'How come you know any of this?' Thorne asked.

'Because Billy Ryan asked me to do it, didn't he? I was the perfect person to ask. I'd done a bit of freelance stuff for one or two people, a few frighteners and what have you . . .'

'You're telling us that Ryan offered you money to kill Kevin Kelly's daughter.'

'*A lot* of money . . .'

'And you turned the job down.'

'Fuck, yes. I don't hurt kids.'

Chamberlain groaned. 'Jesus, this stuff makes me sick. It always comes down to this "noble gangster" bollocks. "We only hurt our own", and "it was only business", and "anybody who touches kids should be strung up". He'll be telling us how much he loves his mum in a minute . . .'

Rooker laughed, winked at her.

The room wasn't warm, and up to this point Thorne had kept his leather jacket on. Now he stood and dropped it across the back of his chair. Chamberlain stayed where she was. Thorne guessed that her smart, grey business suit was new. He thought she might have had her hair done as well, cut a little shorter and highlighted, but he'd said nothing.

'I hope this isn't an obvious question,' Thorne said. 'But why did you confess?'

'Billy Ryan made sure that every face in London thought I'd done it. I was well stitched up. That lighter they found by the fence was left there deliberately.' He looked at Chamberlain. 'You saw what Kevin Kelly did to the people he *guessed* were responsible. Imagine what he'd have done to me. I had Kelly after me for what he thought I'd tried to do to his Alison, *and* Billy after my blood because I was the only person who knew who'd really set it all up.' He turned back to Thorne. 'I was a marked man.'

'So, prison was a preferable option, was it?'

Rooker took the lid off his tobacco tin. He put the cigarette together without looking down, and spoke as if he were trying to explain the mysteries of calculus. 'I thought about running, pissing off to Spain or further, but the idea of spending years looking over my shoulder, shitting myself every time the doorbell went . . .'

Chamberlain shook her head. She glanced at Thorne and then looked back to Rooker. 'I'm not buying this. You'd be just as much of a marked man in prison.'

Rooker put down his half-finished roll-up. 'Do you think I didn't know that?' He reached down and gathered up the bottom of the bib and the sweatshirt underneath, then hoisted them up above sagging, hairy nipples to reveal a jagged scar running across his ribs. 'See? I was a marked man from the moment I walked into Gartree, and Belmarsh, and this place . . .'

'So why not just take your chances outside?'

'It's on my terms in here. I'm not scared of it.' He pulled down the sweatshirt, smoothed the bib across his belly. 'On the outside it could be anyone who's on a big pay-day to take you out. It's the bloke who wants to know the time. The bloke taking a piss next to you, asking you for a light, whatever. In here, I know who it's going to be. I can see it coming and I can protect myself. I've had a couple of scrapes, but I'm still breathing. That's how I know I did the right thing.'

Thorne watched Rooker's yellow tongue snake out and moisten the edge of the Rizla. He rolled the cigarette, slid it between his lips and lit up. 'You did the right thing by Billy Ryan as well. You never grassed him up.'

'I wasn't a *complete* fucking idiot.'

Chamberlain drummed her fingers on the table. 'That "honour among thieves" shite again.'

'So why now?' Thorne asked.

'Listen, it was you who came to see me, remember. Started me thinking about this. Started people round here whispering.'

'*Why now, Rooker?*'

Rooker removed the cigarette from his mouth, held it between a nicotine-stained finger and thumb. 'I've had enough. I'm breathing, but the air tastes of stale sweat and other men's shit. I'm arguing with rapists and perverts about whose turn it is to change channel or play fucking pool next. I've got a grandson who's signing forms with West Ham in a few weeks. I'd like to see him play.' He blinked slowly, took a drag, flicked away the ash. 'It's time.'

Chamberlain stood up and moved towards the door. 'That's all very moving, and I'm sure it's just the kind of stuff the parole board loves to hear.'

Rooker stretched. 'Not so far, it isn't. That's why I need a bit of help . . .'

'I still don't see why you confessed to the attempted murder of Jessica Clarke. You could have got yourself safely banged up by putting yourself in the frame for any number of things. That security manager you tied to a chair and set light to, for instance. Why claim that you tried to kill a fourteen-year-old girl?'

Thorne had the answer. 'Because you're less of a marked man on a VP wing. Right, Gordon? You're harder to get at.'

Rooker stared, and smoked.

There was a knock, and the prison officer put his head round the door, offered tea. Thorne accepted gracefully and Chamberlain declined. The officer bristled a little at Rooker's request for a cup but disappeared quietly enough at the nod from Thorne.

'So, who was it?' Chamberlain said.

Thorne knew that she was thinking about the letters, about the calls, about the man she'd thought was smiling up at her from her front garden.

'If it wasn't you who took Billy Ryan's money, you must have some idea who did.'

Rooker shook his head. 'Look, I haven't got a clue who this nutter is who's been pestering you . . .'

'Who burned Jessica Clarke?' Chamberlain asked.

'I haven't got the faintest, and that's the truth. I don't know anyone who *would* have done it. Who *could* have. Over the years, I've started to wonder if maybe it was Billy himself . . .'

They sat in the car for a minute, saying nothing. When Thorne leaned forward to turn the key, Chamberlain suddenly spoke.

'What did you make of all that?'

Thorne glanced at her, exhaled loudly. 'Where do you want to start?'

'How about with Rooker getting himself put away for something he didn't do?'

'I've heard similar stories once or twice,' Thorne said. 'I suppose if you've got a headcase like Billy Ryan on your back . . .'

'Twenty years, though?'

'Yeah, well, he didn't bank on that, did he?'

Chamberlain turned her head, stared out across the car park.

'You not convinced?' Thorne asked.

She spoke quietly, without looking at him. 'I haven't got the foggiest bloody idea. I'm not far away from a free bus pass, and, to be honest, I'm no better at working out what goes on in the heads of people like Gordon Rooker than I was when I first pulled on a uniform.'

Thorne started the car. As he pulled out of the car park his mind drifted back to how their interview with Rooker had ended. Thorne had almost gasped when he'd suddenly remembered something else from Chamberlain's history lesson. 'Hang on, didn't Ryan *marry* Alison Kelly a few years after all this happened?' Chamberlain had nodded. 'He tries to kill her, pays someone to set fire to her, maybe even does it himself . . . and then marches her down the aisle as soon as she's old enough?'

'That was the perfect fucking touch,' Rooker had said. 'That was good business, wasn't it? The heir marrying the daughter, like he was cementing alliances.' He had chuckled at the sight of Thorne shaking his head in disbelief, then nodded towards Carol Chamberlain. 'She'll tell you about Billy Ryan. She knows him. She knows what he's like.'

Chamberlain had remained silent.

Rooker stared at Thorne through a sheet of blue smoke. 'Billy Ryan's *cold* . . .'

SIX

On Monday morning, just after ten-thirty, Tughan stuck his head round the door, scanned the bodies in the Major Incident Room, and backed out again, his face like a smacked arse.

Holland checked his watch.

Samir Karim shuffled his sizeable backside along the edge of a desk and leaned in close to him. 'Someone's in trouble,' he said.

Holland nodded. He knew who Karim was talking about. Behind an adjacent desk, DI Yvonne Kitson had her head buried in a thick, bound manuscript. 'What you reading, Guv?' he asked.

Kitson looked over the top of a page and held up the latest edition of the *Murder Investigation Manual*. A weighty set of strategies, models and protocols produced by the National Crime Faculty. It was, in theory at least, required reading for all senior investigative officers, and covered everything from crime-scene assessment and media management to offender profiling and family liaison.

If there was a 'book' by which homicide detectives were supposed to do things, this was it.

'Having trouble sleeping?' Holland asked.

Kitson smiled. 'It's not exactly holiday reading, but it doesn't hurt to keep up with the latest guidelines, Dave.'

'Trouble with guidelines for solving murders is that they're only really any use if the murderers are following some of their own.'

'You know who you sound like, don't you?' Kitson said.

Holland knew very well, and thought that maybe there was still hope for him, after all. It struck him as odd that people had taken to talking about Tom Thorne without using his name . . .

As if on cue, the man himself walked through the door looking almost as angry as Tughan had been a few moments before . . . and still was, judging by his expression as he loomed at Thorne's shoulder.

'You've kept a lot of people waiting, DI Thorne.'

Thorne spoke to the room, without so much as a glance towards Nick Tughan. 'I'm sorry. The car wouldn't start . . .' He caught the beginnings of a smirk on the most likely face. 'And neither should you, Holland. I'm not in the mood.'

'OK, we've wasted enough time,' Tughan said. 'Core-team briefing in my office. Five minutes . . .'

While Tughan spoke, Thorne let his mind drift. He was taking it all in, but he was thinking about other things . . .

Thinking about Yvonne Kitson for one. He'd seen the copy of the *Murder Manual* that she was cradling as he'd walked into the Incident Room. It was like her to stay on top

91

of things; she was someone who Thorne had always admired for her ability to juggle her responsibilities at work and at home. Those responsibilities had shifted somewhat since the previous summer, when her husband had found out about the affair she'd been having with a senior officer and walked out with the three kids. She had the kids back at home now, but she was a changed person. Before, she'd been moving effortlessly upwards. Now, she was clinging on. Thorne could see the difference in her face. She seemed to be hanging on every one of Tughan's words, but Thorne was pretty sure he wasn't the only one thinking about other things . . .

His mind drifted on to his father. He needed to talk to him, to see how everything was going. Perhaps it would be easier if he just called Eileen.

Then, he started thinking about why, nearly three days after he and Chamberlain had been to Park Royal prison, he still hadn't told Tughan what Gordon Rooker had told them.

All over the weekend Hendricks had kept bringing it up, looking at him as if he were an idiot, nagging him about it while they slobbed out in front of *The Premiership* . . .

'You want to get Billy Ryan yourself, don't you?' Hendricks had said. 'You want to catch whoever set fire to that girl. Whoever as good as killed her . . .'

'Heskey is such a bloody donkey. Look at that . . .'

'You're an idiot, Tom.'

'I do *not* want to get him myself.'

'So why haven't you told anybody about Rooker?'

Thorne knew no more than that it was because of his relationship with Chamberlain, and, OK, to a degree because of the one he had with Tughan. He had also virtually convinced himself that Rooker's information, his *offer*, related to a case that was twenty years old. It was not *strictly* relevant to the investigation into the killings of Mickey Clayton, the Izzigils and the others. He would, of course, have fucking *loved* to nail Billy Ryan on his own, but he didn't have the first idea how . . .

Tughan was talking about Dave Holland and Andy Stone. He commended them on the work that had thrown up the all-important name. Thorne focused on what Tughan was saying, but noticed how pissed off Holland looked at having to share any credit with Andy Stone.

'The NCIS have been working on this for us over the last forty-eight hours,' Tughan said, 'and we now have a decent bit of background on the Zarif family.'

Tughan was leaning against the front of the desk. Brigstocke stood to the left of it, arms folded. There were maybe a dozen people facing them, crammed into the small office: the senior officers from Team 3 at the Serious Crime Group (West), together with their opposite numbers from SO7.

'The Zarif family would appear to be model citizens,' Tughan said. 'Each property they own or have a stake in, every business interest we've been able to establish – mini-cabs, a chain of video outlets, haulage, van hire – are all completely legal. Not even a parking ticket.'

'Par for the course, right?' Brigstocke said.

Tughan nodded towards one of his DCs, a squat, bearded Welshman named Richards. Thorne's heart sank as Richards started to address them. He'd been stuck in the corner of a pub with him a day or two into things and been less than riveted.

'Think of it as three concentric circles,' Richards said.

Not caring if it was spotted or not, Thorne closed his eyes. The tedious little tit had given him the 'concentric circles' speech in the pub. Cornering him next to the fruit machine, he'd explained – in ten minutes when it could easily have been covered in two – the basic way a gangland firm, or family, operated. There were the street gangs: the robbers and the car-jackers and those who'd shove a handgun in a child's face for the latest mobile phone or an MP3 player. Then came the institutionalised villains: those controlling loan-sharking operations, illegal gambling, arms-smuggling, credit-card fraud. Finally, there were the tycoons: the seemingly legitimate businessmen who ran huge drug-trafficking empires and money-laundering networks, and who behaved as if they were respectable captains of industry.

'Think of three concentric circles,' Richards had said, an untouched half of lager-top in his fist. 'They all touch and bleed into one another, but the points where they actually meet are always shifting, impossible to pin down.' He'd smiled and leaned in close. 'I like to think of them as concentric circles on a target . . .'

Thorne had nodded, like he thought that was a great idea. He preferred to visualise the circles as ripples moving out across dirty water. Like when a turd hits the bottom of a sewer-pipe.

He was jolted back from dull remembrance to even duller reality by Richards talking about 'footsoldiers'. Thorne rubbed his eyes, let his hand fall over his mouth to cover the aside to Sam Karim: 'Jesus, he thinks he's in an episode of *The Sopranos* . . .'

'The Izzigil video shop is a good example of how it works,' Richards said. 'The name Zarif appears on the deeds of the property, and on the paperwork at Companies House; and the vehicles that theoretically distribute the perfectly legal videotapes are leased from their company. But there's nothing tying them to anything illegal going on in those premises and they can't be held responsible for what the people who hire their vans and lorries get up to.'

Tughan cleared his throat, took over: 'There are three brothers. We'll distribute photos as soon as we have them.' He glanced down at his notes. 'Also a sister, and probably plenty of cousins and what have you knocking about. At this stage, even the NCIS don't know a great deal about them. They're Turkish Kurds, been here a couple of years, kept their heads down.' He looked up from his clipboard. 'Getting their feet under the table. Main business premises and homes in the area you'd expect, between Manor House and Turnpike Lane.'

A voice from the back of the room: 'Little fucking Istanbul . . .'

Tughan smiled for about half a second. 'Now they've got themselves established, it seems like they're looking to expand. And poor old Billy Ryan's on the receiving end.'

'Let's bring a bit of pressure to bear,' Brigstocke said. 'See just how well established they are.'

Tughan pushed himself upright, tugged at the sharp creases in the trousers of his suit, dropped his clipboard down on to the desktop. 'Right, DS Karim, DC Richards, let's get some Actions organised and allocated . . .'

As the briefing broke up, Thorne was amazed when

Tughan stepped over and spoke almost as if the two of them didn't hate the sight of each other.

'Fancy coming to see Billy Ryan?' Tughan asked.

'What about the Zarifs?'

'We'll give that a day or two. Get ourselves a bit of ammunition first.'

'Right.'

'At the moment, the Ryans are four–two down. Let's go and see how they're coping with getting spanked, shall we?'

Thorne nodded, thinking that the surprises were coming thick and fast. *Four–two down*. It was tasteless, but still, *any* joke from Nick Tughan was firmly in *X-Files* territory . . .

They said virtually nothing as they sat in Tughan's Rover, heading towards Camden Town, the music from the stereo conveniently too loud to allow casual conversation. They took what was more or less Thorne's usual route home, south through Hampstead and Belsize Park, through one of the most expensive areas of the city towards what was arguably still the trendiest, though the combat-wearing media brigade in Hoxton or Shoreditch might have welcomed the argument. They drove past the development on the site of Jack Straw's Castle, the coaching inn on Hampstead Heath named after one of the leaders of the Peasants' Revolt and once a favourite haunt of Dickens and Thackeray. Now, on certain nights of the week, gay men who liked their sex casual, and perhaps even dangerous, would gather there in darkened corners before disappearing on to the Heath with strangers.

'Dick-ins of a completely different sort,' Phil Hendricks had said.

They parked in front of a snooker hall behind Camden Road Station, a few streets away from Billy Ryan's office. Thorne was hugely relieved to escape from Tughan's car, deciding that, although his own taste in music had irritated a few people in its time, he wouldn't wish Phil Collins on his worst enemy. The man was perhaps second only to Sting in terms of smugness and his capacity to make you pray for hearing loss. As they walked towards Ryan's place, Thorne couldn't help wondering if gangland enforcers ever considered using a Phil Collins album as an alternative to pulling people's teeth out and drilling through their kneecaps . . .

Getting in to see the managing director of Ryan Properties was much like getting in to see any other successful businessman, save for the fact that the receptionist had tattoos on his neck.

'Wait there,' he said. Then, 'Not yet.' And finally, 'Go in.'

Thorne wondered whether he spoke only in two-word phrases. When he and Tughan eventually strolled into Billy Ryan's office, Thorne gave the receptionist a pithy, two-word phrase of his own. He watched as Billy Ryan stood and greeted Tughan like a respected business rival. Tughan shook Ryan's hand, which Thorne thought was distinctly fucking unnecessary, and when he himself was introduced he did no such thing, which Ryan seemed to find amusing.

Thorne recognised the two other men present from photos. Marcus Moloney had risen quickly through the ranks and was known to be one of Ryan's most trusted associates. The younger man was Ryan's son, Stephen.

'Shall we crack on, then?' Ryan said.

As the five men sat – Tughan and Thorne on a small sofa and the others on armchairs – and while drinks were offered and refused, Thorne took the place and the people in. They were in one of the two rooms above an office furniture showroom from which Ryan ran his multi-million-pound empire. It was spacious enough, but the decor and furnishings were shabby – ironic, considering what they knocked out from the premises downstairs, which, of course, Ryan also owned. Thorne wondered whether the man was just tight or genuinely didn't care about high-quality leather and chrome.

In his twenty-five years on the job, and never living more than a mile or two away from where he now sat, Thorne had come across the name William John Ryan with depressing frequency. But, up to this point, he had miraculously avoided any direct dealings with him. Staring at him in the flesh for the first time, across a low table strewn with a variety of newspapers and magazines – the *Daily Star*, *House & Garden*, the *Racing Post*, *World of Interiors* – Thorne was grudgingly impressed by the way the man presented himself.

Ryan's complexion was ruddy, but the mouth was small and sensitive. When he spoke, his teeth remained hidden. The red cheeks were closely shaved and looked as if they might have been freshly boiled. The scent of expensive after-shave hung around him, and something else – hairspray, maybe, judging by the way the sandy hair, turning to white in places, curled across the collar of his blazer. Thorne thought he looked a little like a well-preserved Van Morrison.

'I presume you've made no progress in catching this maniac,' Ryan said.

Ryan's Dublin accent had faded a little over the years

but was still strong enough. Tughan turned his own up a notch or two in response. Thorne couldn't tell if it was deliberate or not.

'We're following up a number of promising leads,' Tughan said.

'I hope so. There needs to be a result on this, you know.'

'There will be . . .'

'This man has butchered friends of mine. I have to assume that, until he's caught, members of my own family might well be at risk.'

'That's probably a fair assumption.'

Moloney spoke for the first time. 'So do something about it.' His voice was low and reasonable, the face blank and puffy below thinning, dirty-blond hair. 'It's fucking outrageous that you aren't offering Mr Ryan's family any protection.'

Ryan spotted the look on Thorne's face. 'Something funny?' he asked.

Thorne shrugged. 'Not laugh-out-loud funny.' He looked at Moloney. 'More ironic, seeing as it's Mr Ryan's family that's normally *offering* the protection. Then again, "offering" isn't really the right word . . .'

Now it was Stephen Ryan's turn to chip in: 'Cheeky cunt!' The son was thought by many to have become the muscle of the Ryan operation. Though he had his old man's features, as yet unsoftened, the voice was very different, and not just in tone. Thorne knew very well that Stephen had been sent to an exclusive private school. His accent was pure Mockney.

Thorne smiled at Stephen's father. 'Nice to see that the expensive education was well worth it.'

Ryan returned what in some lights could be mistaken for a smile. He looked at Tughan, nodded at Thorne: 'Where did you find this one?'

Tughan glanced at Thorne as if he were wondering the same thing himself. 'We'll make this quick, Mr Ryan,' he said. 'We just wanted to check that nothing else has cropped up at your end since we last spoke.'

'Cropped up?'

'Any other thoughts, you know? Theories about who might be . . . attacking your business.'

'I told you last time, and every time before that . . .'

'You might have thought of something since then. Heard something on the grapevine, maybe.'

Ryan leaned back in his chair, spread his arms wide across the back of it. Thorne could see that his shoulders were powerful beneath the cashmere blazer, but, looking down, he was amazed at the daintiness of the feet. Ryan was supposed to have been a fair amateur boxer in his younger days but also, bizarrely, had something of a reputation as a ballroom dancer. Thorne stared at the small, highly polished loafers, at the oddly girlish, silk socks . . .

'I don't know who's doing this. I wish I did . . .'

Thorne had to admit that Ryan lied quite brilliantly. He even managed to plaster a sheen of emotion – something like sadness – on to his face, masking what was clearly nothing more noble than anger, and a desire for brutal vengeance. Thorne glanced at Moloney and Stephen Ryan. Both had their heads down.

'I have no bloody idea who it is,' Ryan repeated. 'That's what you're supposed to be finding out.'

Tughan tugged at the material of his trousers, crossed one leg over the other. 'Has anybody else remembered anything? An employee, maybe . . .?'

It was 'employee' that made Thorne smile this time. If Ryan spotted it, he didn't react. He shook his head, and for fifteen seconds they sat in silence.

'What about these leads you mentioned?' Stephen Ryan looked at Thorne like he was a shit-stain trodden into a white shagpile.

'Thank you,' Thorne said. 'We'd almost forgotten. Does the name Izzigil mean anything at all?'

Shaking heads and upturned palms. Stephen Ryan ran a hand across his closely cropped black hair.

'Are you sure?'

'Is this now a formal interview?' Moloney asked. 'We should get the brief in here, Mr Ryan.'

Ryan raised a hand. 'You did say this was just a chat, Mr Tughan.'

'Nothing sinister,' Tughan said.

Thorne nodded, paused. 'So, that's a definite "no" on Izzigil, then?' He nodded to Tughan, who reached into his briefcase and took out a couple of ten-by-eights.

'What about these?' Tughan asked.

Thorne pushed aside the papers and magazines, took the pictures from Tughan and dropped them on to the table. 'Does anybody recognise these two?'

Sighs from Stephen Ryan and Marcus Moloney as they leaned forward. Billy Ryan picked up one of the pictures, a still from CCTV footage on Green Lanes, taken nearly three weeks earlier: a fuzzy shot of two boys running; two boys they presumed to have been running away from Muslum Izzigil's video shop, having just hurled a four-foot metal bin through the window.

'Look like any pair of herberts up to no good,' Ryan said. 'Ten a fucking penny. Marcus?'

Moloney shook his head.

Stephen Ryan looked over at Thorne, eyes wide. 'Is it Ant and Dec?' He cackled at his joke, turning to share it with Moloney.

Tughan gathered up the pictures and pushed himself up from the sofa. 'We'll get out of your way, then . . .'

Moloney and Stephen Ryan stayed where they were as Billy Ryan showed Tughan and Thorne out. The receptionist gave Thorne a hard look as he passed. Thorne winked at him.

Ryan stopped at the door. 'What this arsehole's doing, the cutting, you know? It's not on. I've been in business a long time, I've seen some shocking stuff.'

'I bet you have,' Thorne said.

Ryan didn't hear the dig, or chose to ignore it. He shook his head, looking thoroughly disgusted. 'Fucking "X-Man" . . .'

It didn't surprise Thorne that Ryan knew exactly what it was that the killer did to his victims. Two of them had been found by Ryan's own men, after all. The nickname, though, was something else – something that, as far as Thorne was aware, had been confined to Becke House. Obviously, Ryan was a man with plenty of contacts, and Thorne was not naïve enough to believe that they wouldn't include a few who were eager to top up a Metropolitan Police salary.

Thorne asked the question as if it were an afterthought.

'What does the name Gordon Rooker mean to you, Mr Ryan?'

There was a reaction, no question. Fleeting and impossible to define. Anger, fear, shock, amazement? It could have been any one of them.

'Another arsehole,' Ryan said, eventually. 'And one who I haven't had to think about for a very long time.'

The three of them stood, saying nothing, the smell of aftershave overpowering close-up, until Ryan turned and walked quickly back towards his office.

The light had been dimming when they'd arrived. Now it had gone altogether. Turning the corner into the unlit sidestreet, Thorne was disappointed to see that the Rover didn't at least have a window broken.

'Who's Gordon Rooker?' Tughan asked.

'Just a name that came up. I was barking up the wrong tree . . .'

Tughan gave him a long look. He pressed a button on his keyring to unlock the car, walked round to open the driver's door. 'Listen, it's almost five and I signed us both out for the rest of the day anyway. I'll drop you at home.'

Thorne glanced through the window and saw the empty cassette box between the seats. The idea of a balding millionaire bleating about the homeless for another second was simply unbearable.

'I'll walk,' he said.

SEVEN

Thorne cut up Royal College Street, where a faded plaque on a flaking patch of brickwork identified a house where Verlaine and Rimbaud had once lived. By the time he came out on to Kentish Town Road it had begun to drizzle, but he was still glad he'd refused Tughan's offer of a lift.

As Thorne walked past some of the tattier businesses that fringed the main road, his thoughts returned to Billy Ryan. He wondered how many of the people who ran these pubs, saunas and internet cafés were connected to Ryan in some way or another. Most probably wouldn't even recognise the name, but the working lives of many, honest or not, would certainly be touched by Ryan at some stage.

He thought of those who looked up to Ryan. Those in the outer circles who would be looking to move towards the centre. Did those likely lads, keen to trade in their Timberland and Tommy Hilfiger for Armani, have a clue what they might be expected to do in return? Could they begin to guess at what the softly spoken ballroom dancer had once been – might still be – capable of?

'I've seen some shocking stuff . . .'

Just before the turning into Prince of Wales Road, Thorne nipped into a small supermarket. He needed milk and wine, and wanted a paper to see what the Monday night match was on Sky Sports. Queuing at the till, he became aware of raised voices near the entrance and walked over. A uniformed security guard was guiding a woman of forty or so towards the doors, trying to move her out of the shop. He was not taking any nonsense, but there was still some warmth in his voice: 'How often do we have to do this, love?'

'I'm sorry, I can't help it,' the woman said.

The security guard saw Thorne coming over and his eyes widened. We've got a right one here . . .

'Do you want a hand?' Even as Thorne said it, he hadn't quite decided who he was offering the help to.

Though the woman had three or four fat, plastic bags swinging from each hand, she was well dressed. 'It's something I feel compelled to do,' she said, revealing herself to be equally well spoken.

'What?' Thorne asked.

The security guard still had a hand squarely in the middle of the woman's back and was moving her ever closer to the door. 'She pesters the other customers,' he said.

'I tell them about Jesus.' The woman beamed at Thorne. 'They really don't seem to mind. Nobody gets annoyed.'

Thorne slowly followed the two of them, watching as they drifted towards the pavement.

'People just want to do their shopping,' the security guard said. 'You're holding them up.'

'I have to tell them about Him. It's my job.'

'And this is mine.'

'I know. It's fine, really. I'm so sorry to have caused any trouble.'

'Don't come back for a while this time, OK?'

With a shrug and a smile, the woman hoisted up her bags and turned towards the street. Thorne moved to the exit and watched her walking away.

The security guard caught his eye. 'I suppose there are worse crimes . . .'

Thorne said nothing.

He'd arrived home to a note from Hendricks saying that he was spending the night at Brendan's. Thorne had put the frozen pizza he'd picked up from the supermarket in the oven. He flicked through the *Standard*, watched *Channel Four News* while it was cooking . . .

Now, five minutes into the second half, Newcastle United and Southampton appeared to have settled for a draw. It was chucking it down on Tyneside and the St James' Park pitch was slippery, so there were at least the odd hideously mistimed tackle and some handbags at ten paces, but that was as exciting as it got.

Thorne snatched up the phone gratefully when it rang. 'Tom . . .?'

'You not watching the football, Dad?' Time was, the TV coverage of a match would be swiftly followed by ten minutes of amateur punditry over the phone with the two of them arguing about every dodgy decision, every key move. That all seemed a lifetime ago.

'Too busy,' his dad said. 'Different game I'm concerned about, anyway. You got your thinking cap on?'

'Not at this very moment, no . . .'

'All the ways you can be dismissed at cricket, if you please. I've made a list. There's ten of them, so come on.'

Thorne picked up the remote, knocked the volume on the TV down a little. 'Can't you just read them out to me?'

'Don't be such a cock, you big fucker.' He said it like it was a term of endearment.

'Dad . . .'

'Stumped and hit wicket, I'll give you them to start . . .'

Thorne sighed, began to list them: 'Bowled, LBW, caught, run out. What d'you call it . . . hitting the ball twice? Touching the ball . . .?'

'No. *Handling* the ball.'

'Right. Handling the ball. Listen, I can't remember the other two . . .'

His father laughed. Thorne could hear his chest rattling. 'Timed out and obstructing the field. They're the two that people can never remember. Same as Horst Bucholz and Brad Dexter.'

'*What?*'

'They're the two in *The Magnificent Seven* that nobody can ever remember. So, come on then. Yul Brynner, I'll give you him to start . . .'

Southampton scrambled a late winner five minutes from the final whistle, just about the time when Thorne's dad began to run out of steam. Not long after, he put down the handset, needing to fetch a book, to check a crucial fact. A minute or two into the silence that followed, Thorne realised that his father had forgotten all about the call and wasn't coming back. He'd maybe even gone upstairs to bed.

Thorne thought about shouting down the phone, but decided to hang up instead.

EIGHT

An attractive young woman placed menus on the table in front of them.

'Just two coffees, please,' Thorne said.

Holland looked a little disappointed, as if he'd been hoping to put a spot of breakfast on expenses. After the waitress had gone, Holland scanned the menu: 'Some of this stuff sounds nice. You know, the Turkish stuff.'

Thorne glanced around, caught the eye of a dour, dark-eyed individual sitting at a table near the door. 'I can't see us eating here too regularly, can you?'

When the coffees arrived, Thorne asked, 'Is the owner around?' The waitress looked confused. 'Is Mr Zarif available?'

'Which?'

'The boss. We'd like to speak to him . . .'

She picked up the menus and turned away without a word. Thorne watched her drop them on to the counter and stamp away down the stairs at the back of the room.

'She can say goodbye to her tip,' Holland said.

The café was at the Manor House end of Green Lanes,

opposite Finsbury Park, and not a million miles away from where Thorne had once been beaten up by a pair of Arsenal fans. It was small – maybe six tables and a couple of booths – and the blinds on the front door and windows made it a little gloomier than it might have been. The ceiling was the only well-lit part of the room, the varnished pine coloured gold by the glow from dozens of ornate lanterns – glass, bronze and ceramic – dangling from the wooden slats and swinging slightly every time the front door opened or closed.

Holland took a sip of coffee. 'Maybe he's got a thing about lamps.'

Thorne noticed the slightly incongruous choice of background music and nodded towards the stereo on a shelf behind the counter. 'And Madonna,' he said.

They both looked up at the sound of heavy footsteps on the stairs. The man who emerged around the corner and walked towards their booth was big – bulky as much as fat – and round-shouldered. A blue-and-white-striped apron was stretched across his belly, and his hands were tangled in a grubby-looking tea-towel as he struggled to dry them.

'Can I help you?'

Thorne took out his warrant card and made the introductions. 'We'd like to have a word with the owner.'

The man edged behind the table, squeezed himself in next to Holland and sat down. 'I am Arkan Zarif.'

Thorne was happy for Holland to kick off and listened as he told Zarif that they were investigating a number of murders, including that of Muslum Izzigil, and that they needed to ask him some questions regarding his various business interests. Zarif listened intently, nodding almost constantly.

When Holland had finished, Zarif thought for a few seconds before suddenly breaking into a smile and holding out his hands: 'You need proper coffee. *Turkish* coffee.'

Holland raised a hand to refuse, but Zarif was already shouting across to the waitress in Turkish.

'Mr Izzigil was murdered just up the road from here,' Holland said.

Zarif shook his head. 'Terrible. Many murders here. Lots of guns.'

He had a strong Mediterranean accent, his face folding into concentration as he spoke. Though olive-skinned, Thorne could see that the rest of his colouring was unusual. His eyes were a light green beneath his heavy brows. His hair was dark with oil, and the stubble across his jowls was white, but Thorne could see from the thick moustache, and the wisps around his ears, that his natural colour was a light, almost orangey brown.

'You have to speak with my son,' he said.

'About Mr Izzigil's murder?'

'These business interests. My sons are the businessmen. They are *great* businessmen. Just two years after we come here and they buy this place for me. How's that?' He held out his arms, his smile almost as wide as they were.

'So who is the owner of this place?' Holland asked. 'Of all the other businesses?'

Zarif leaned forward. 'OK, here it is. See, I have three sons.' He held up his fingers, as if Thorne and Holland would find it as hard to understand some of the words as he did to find them. 'Memet is the eldest. Then Hassan and Tan.' He nodded towards the waitress who was watching from behind the counter, smoking. 'Also my daughter, Sema.'

Thorne caught movement near the door and turned to see the man who had clocked him earlier rising to leave. It didn't look like he'd settled his bill. Zarif gave him a wave as he went.

'Memet runs things here,' Zarif said. 'Deliveries and everything else.'

Holland scribbled in his notebook. He'd never quite lost the habit. 'But it's in your name?'

'The café was a present from my sons.' He leaned back against the red plastic of the booth as his daughter put three small cups of steaming coffee on the table. She said something to Zarif in Turkish and he nodded. 'I love to cook, so I spend my time in the kitchen. My wife helps, and Sema. Chopping and peeling. *I* do all the cooking, though.' He poked himself in the chest. '*I* pick out the meat . . .'

'Is Memet here?' Thorne asked.

Zarif shook his head. 'Gone out for the day.' He picked up his coffee cup, pointed with it towards the street. 'Next door is Hassan's minicab office, if you want. My other two sons are usually in there. I'm certain they just play cards all day.' He took a slurp of the coffee and with a grin gestured for Thorne and Holland to do the same. 'Good?'

'Strong,' Thorne said. 'Zarif Brothers owns a number of video shops, is that right?'

Another proud smile. 'Six or seven, I think. More, maybe. They get me all the latest films, the new James Bond . . .'

'Muslum Izzigil was the manager of one of those shops a quarter of a mile up the road. He and his wife were shot in the head.'

Zarif's eyes widened as he swallowed his coffee.

'Did your sons not mention that to you, Mr Zarif?'

The daughter began talking loudly to him in Turkish from behind the counter. Zarif held up his hands, spoke sharply to her, then turned at the noise of the door opening. The irritation instantly left his face: 'Hassan . . .'

The door closed. Several of the lanterns clinked against one another. Thorne turned to see two young men moving purposefully across the room. He was in little doubt they'd been summoned from next door by the customer who'd just left. One of the men stopped at the counter and began talking in a low voice to Sema. The other marched across to the end of the booth.

'My old man's English isn't so good,' he said.

Thorne looked at him. 'It's fine.'

Another stream of Turkish, this time from the son to the father.

Thorne held up a hand, put the other on Arkan Zarif's beefy forearm. 'What's he saying?'

Zarif rolled his eyes and began to slide out of the booth. 'I'm being sent back to the kitchen,' he said.

Holland caught Thorne's eye, disturbed at losing control of the interview. 'Hang on . . .'

Zarif turned back to the table. 'You want more coffee?'

'It's fine,' Thorne said, answering Zarif and Holland at the same time.

As Arkan disappeared down the stairs, Hassan slid into his place. With a wave, he beckoned to his sister for his own cup of coffee. He leaned back and stuck out his chin.

Rooker lay on his bunk, glued to the TV that was bolted to the wall in the corner, swearing at *Trisha*. Mid-morning was virtually written in stone. If the subject was a very good one,

112

he *might* defect to *Kilroy*, but it was always a lot more polite and BBC. The people on *Trisha* were usually not too bright and a damn sight more likely to swear and row.

This morning's was especially good: 'Problems with Intimacy' . . .

There was some poof banging on about how he'd never been able to tell his kids that he loved them and a woman who couldn't bear her husband putting his arm around her in the street. Rooker decided that they ought to try crapping next to a child molester or showering with rapists.

He'd spent well over a third of his life in prison but had never got used to the proximity of some of those he'd been locked up with. He remembered reading about how all animals needed a certain amount of territory – even rats or rabbits or whatever – a bit of space that was all theirs, or they'd start to go mad, attacking each other. Fucking rabbits going mental! Plenty of people inside *did* lose it, of course, plenty of them *big time*, but he was surprised it didn't happen more often. He was amazed that a lot more prison officers didn't die every year.

Thinking about it – and he'd had plenty of time to think about it – he'd been wary of getting close to others at school. Changing rooms made him uncomfortable. He'd go home dirty after games rather than jump in the showers with the rest of them. He often wondered if this distance he felt from other kids was why he had ended up in his particular line of work . . .

On the show, Trisha asked the woman if she loved her husband, even though she hated him touching her in public. 'Yeah, I love him sometimes,' she said. 'Other times, I could kill him.'

113

Rooker laughed along with the studio audience. He knew that the difference between him and most people who said things like 'I could kill him' was that he really could do it. He could remember what it was like to put a gun to someone's head, to pull a knife across a throat, to pour lighter fuel into some poor bastard's hair . . .

The programme finished and he stepped out on to the landing. He could smell lunch coming as he walked down to the floor. You could always smell the food going in one direction or the other.

'DLP going for it this time, d'you reckon? Rooker?' Alun Fisher had served three years of a five-year tariff for causing death by dangerous driving. He had a history of drug abuse and mental illness. His refusal to eat properly meant that he spent as much time on the prison's health-care wing as he did in the VP Unit. 'Bound to approve you, this time. You'll be counting the days, yeah?'

Rooker grunted, stared across at the card school in the corner. He *was* feeling confident this time. They were bound to go for the deal, considering what he was offering. He could probably afford to pick up one of the pool cues and bash Fisher's head in and they'd *still* send a police limo to pick him up.

'You're going to have it sweet on the outside,' Fisher said. 'That's what everybody reckons. You'll be looked after 'cos you never grassed.'

Rooker stared at him.

Fisher nodded and grinned, the teeth blackened and rotten from years of drug use. 'Never fucking grassed . . .'

★

114

'The business was Mr Izzigil's. Our company owns the building which is looked after by a letting agency. I didn't actually know him.' Hassan Zarif had the same accent as his father, but the grammar and vocabulary were virtually faultless. Two years here and already their native language had become their second. It was clear that, in all sorts of ways, the Zarif boys were quick learners. 'My brother popped in occasionally, I think, and perhaps Izzigil would give him a film or two as gifts. Disney films for his children . . .'

'Right,' Thorne said.

'Zarif Brothers owns the property, but the video business was Mr Izzigil's.'

Holland failed to keep the sarcasm from his voice. 'You said that.'

Zarif cocked his head, put a finger into the empty metal ashtray, and slowly began to spin it on the tabletop. He was in his early twenties – tall, with a mop of thick, black hair which sat high on his head. A pronounced chin marred the brooding looks and was emphasised by the polo neck he wore under a heavy, brown leather jacket with a fur collar. He sighed slightly at having to state the obvious again. 'He rented out movies.'

'That's not what paid for his son's school,' Thorne said. 'Or the nice new Audi in his garage.'

Zarif shook his head, spun the ashtray.

'He had over thirty thousand pounds in a building society "wealth management" service,' Holland said.

'Some people have no vices . . .'

Thorne leaned across, gently nudged the ashtray to one side. 'So, you've no idea at all why anybody would want to put a bullet in his head? And put one in his wife's head for good measure.'

Zarif clicked his tongue against the roof of his mouth, as if he were trying to decide exactly how to answer.

Thorne knew that this meeting was as important for the young man sitting opposite him as it was for them. Hassan Zarif knew he was safe, at least for the time being. This was about making impressions. He wouldn't want to appear obstructive, but he had a natural cockiness, and a place in the world he thought he'd earned the hard way. It was a tricky balance to strike, but while he played the part of concerned local businessman, he also had a message to send. He wanted to let them know, nicely, of course, that neither he nor the rest of them were to be pissed around.

'Maybe he fucked the wrong man's girlfriend,' Zarif said.

From behind the counter, Zarif's sister began to laugh. Thorne glared at her, none too keen on the joke, but saw that she was actually laughing at something Zarif's friend was saying to her. He turned back to Zarif. 'As we told your father, we're investigating a number of recent murders.'

'It's a dangerous city.'

'Only for some people,' Thorne said.

Zarif smiled, held up his hands. 'Listen, I've got stuff to do, so . . .'

Thorne asked his questions, played the game. He had his own message to send and wasn't overly concerned with subtlety.

'Do you have any information that might assist us in investigating the death of Mickey Clayton?'

116

Zarif shook his head.

'Or Sean Anderson?'

'No.'

The X-Man's victims. 'Anthony Wright? John Gildea?'

'No and no.'

Thorne reached into his jacket, pulled out some change. He dropped a couple of pound coins on to the table. 'That's for the coffee.'

Outside, it was raining. They walked quickly back towards Thorne's BMW.

'Seems to me,' Holland said, 'that we spend a lot of time going to see these fuckers, asking them questions, listening to them tell us they don't know anything, and then leaving again.'

Thorne looked into the park as they walked alongside it. The trees were shiny and skeletal. 'Same as it ever was . . .'

'He was so full of shit,' Holland said. '"Disney films for the kids?" They'd have been involved somewhere in supply, delivery, all of it. They'd have taken a massive cut of Izzigil's earnings, *on top* of what they got out of the piracy, out of the smuggling operation . . .'

Finsbury Park wasn't Thorne's favourite green space. He'd been to a few gigs there over the years, though – the Fleadh to see Emmylou Harris, Madstock once with a WPC he fancied. When the Sex Pistols reformed and played there, back when he was still living with his wife, he'd been able to hear every word from their back garden in Highbury, which was over a mile away . . .

Holland was grimacing. 'That coffee was shit as well,' he said. 'It tasted like something you'd find in a Gro-Bag.'

Thorne laughed. 'It's an acquired taste.'

'Listen, d'you fancy having a pint later? The Oak, if you like, or we could go into town . . .'

'Sophie letting you out for the night, is she?'

'Happy to see the back of me, mate. I'm getting on her nerves a bit, I think. Fuck it, I'm getting on my *own* nerves . . .'

They'd reached the car. Thorne unlocked it and climbed in before leaning across to unlock Holland's door. 'Can we do it another night? I'm busy later.'

Holland dropped into the passenger seat. The rain had left dark streaks across the shoulders of his grey jacket and at the tops of his trousers. The suit was starting to look a little tired, and Thorne knew that Holland would go into M&S at some point soon to buy another one that was exactly the same.

'Hot date?' Holland asked.

Thorne smiled when the engine turned over first time. 'Not remotely . . .'

NINE

Leicester Square after dark was right up there with the M25 at rush hour or the Millwall ground, in terms of places that Thorne thought were best avoided.

The buskers and the occasional B-list film premiere made little difference. For every few smiling tourists, there was someone lounging against the wall outside one of the cinemas, or hanging around in the corner of the green, with a far darker reason for being there. For every American family or pair of Scandinavian backpackers there was a mugger, or a pickpocket, or just a pissed-up idiot looking for trouble, and the crappy funfair only seemed to bring out the vultures in greater numbers.

'I pity the uniformed lads working round here tonight,' Chamberlain said.

There were plenty of places in the city that were alive with the promise of something. Here, there was only a threat. If it wasn't for the stench of piss and cheap burgers, you'd probably be able to *smell* it.

'The only good thing about this place,' Thorne said, 'is the rent you can get for it on a sodding Monopoly board . . .'

A quarter to seven on a Tuesday night, and the place was heaving. Aside from those milling around, taking pictures or taking cameras, there were those moving through the square on their way to somewhere more pleasant. West towards Piccadilly and Regent Street beyond. South towards the theatres on the Strand. East towards Covent Garden, where the street entertainment was a little artier, and the average burger was anything but cheap.

Thorne and Chamberlain moved through the square on their way to a brightly lit and busy games arcade, slap-bang between Chinatown and Soho. They passed partially steamed-up windows displaying racks of Day-Glo, honey-glazed chickens and leathery squid which drooped from metal hooks like innards.

'How sure are you that he's going to be there?' Chamberlain asked.

Thorne ushered her to the left, avoiding the queue outside the Capital Club. 'Billy was under investigation well before things turned nasty. We know near enough everything he gets up to. We know all his routines.'

Chamberlain quickened her pace just a little to keep up. 'If Ryan's half the character I think he is, I wouldn't be surprised if he knows quite a lot about you, too.'

Thorne shivered ever so slightly, but gave her a grin. 'I'm so glad you came along to cheer me up . . .'

They cut off the square and walked to a Starbucks on the other side of the street from the arcade. They didn't have to wait long before Ryan appeared. Halfway through their coffees, they watched as one of the heavy glass doors was opened for him, and Ryan moved slowly down the short flight of steps towards the street. Marcus Moloney was at his shoulder. A few paces behind were a pair of Central Casting thugs who looked as though they might enjoy shiny objects and the sound of small bones breaking.

As Thorne approached from across the street – heavyset and with his hands thrust into the pockets of his leather jacket – Ryan took half a step back and reached out an arm towards one of the gorillas behind him. He recovered himself when he recognised Thorne: 'What do you want?'

Thorne nodded past Ryan towards the arcade. It was packed with teenagers, queuing to ram their pound coins into the machines. 'I was just a bit bored, and I'm a big fan of the shoot-'em-ups. This one of your places, is it?'

Moloney looked up and down the street. 'Looking for a discount, Thorne?'

'Is that how you try to get coppers on the payroll these days? A few free games of Streetfighter?'

Ryan had recognised Thorne, but had failed to recognise the woman with him. 'Grab-a-Granny night, is it?' He looked Chamberlain up and down. 'Don't tell me she's on the job. I thought coppers were supposed to look *younger* these days . . .'

'You're a cheeky fucker, Ryan,' Chamberlain said.

Then Ryan *did* recognise her. Thorne watched him grit his teeth as he remembered exactly what had been happening the last time their paths had crossed.

'You looked a bit jumpy a minute ago,' Thorne said. He nodded towards the two bodyguards. 'These two look a touch nervous as well. Worried that whoever did Mickey Clayton and the others might come after you, are you, Mr Ryan?'

Ryan said nothing.

A group of young lads burst out through the arcade doors, the noise from inside spilling momentarily on to the street with them: the spatter and squeal of guns and lasers, the rumble of engines, the beat of hypnotic techno . . .

Moloney answered Thorne's question: 'They can fucking well *try* . . .'

'I wonder what I might find,' Thorne said, 'if I were to put you up against that wall over there and pat you down.'

Moloney looked unconcerned. 'Nothing worth the trouble.'

'Trouble?'

Moloney sighed heavily and stepped past him. Thorne watched him walk a few yards up the street. He took out a mobile phone and began to stab angrily at the keypad. Thorne turned back to see the pair of heavies stepping up close to their employer, who was looking into the distance. Ryan was trying hard *not* to look at Carol Chamberlain.

'You remember Carol?' Thorne said. 'DI Manley, as she'd have been when you last saw her.'

'It took you a moment, though, didn't it?' Chamberlain took a step to her left, placed herself in Ryan's line of vision.

'That would have been the Jessica Clarke case, wouldn't it, Mr Ryan?'

'I don't think it's quite come back to him,' Chamberlain said. 'The girl who was set on fire? These things can slip your mind, I understand that.'

'It was Gordon Rooker who got sent down for that, wasn't it? I think we were talking about him a few days ago, weren't we, Mr Ryan?'

The wind was rushing up the narrow street. It lifted the

hair from the collar of Ryan's overcoat as he spun around. 'I'll say the same thing I said then, in case *your* memory's playing up. I haven't had the displeasure of thinking about that piece of shite for a long time.'

'That's funny,' Thorne said. 'Because he's been thinking about you. He specifically asked me to say "hello" . . .'

Ryan's mouth tightened and his eyes narrowed. Thorne reckoned it was more than just the wind that was slapping him around the face.

'So . . . hello,' Thorne said.

Thorne saw the relief flood suddenly into Ryan's face. He watched him step quickly past him the instant he heard the noise of the engine. Thorne turned to see a black people-carrier roar up to the kerb and screech to a halt. The door was already open and Stephen Ryan jumped out.

Thorne gave Ryan's son a wave and received a cold stare in return.

Stephen shrugged as his father barged past him. 'Sorry . . .'

'Where the *fuck* have you been?'

Billy Ryan climbed into the car without looking back. He was quickly followed by his son and the two heavies, who pushed past Thorne and Chamberlain without any delicacy. As Moloney marched up, the driver's window slid down. Thorne recognised the receptionist he'd exchanged pleasantries with at Ryan's office.

'Sorry, Marcus. Traffic's fucked all over the West End.'

Moloney ignored him and moved to the rear door. With one foot already inside the car, he looked at Thorne. 'Careful you don't get shot . . .'

Thorne opened his mouth, took a step towards the car.

Moloney pointed over Thorne's shoulder towards the arcade: 'The shoot-'em-ups . . .' He pulled the door shut and the car moved quickly away from the kerb.

'What was all that "hello" business?' Chamberlain asked.

Thorne watched Ryan's car turn the corner and disappear. 'Politeness costs nothing. What time's your train?'

'Last one's just before eleven.'

'Let's get some food . . .'

Marcus Moloney downed almost half his Guinness in one go. He set the glass down on the bar and leaned back in his chair.

'Tough day, mate?' said the man next to him.

Moloney grunted, picked up the glass again. It wasn't so much the day as the last few hours. First the business outside the arcade, and then the fallout: all the way back to Ryan's place in Finchley, Moloney had been given an earful. Whatever it was that Thorne and the woman had been going on about, it had got his boss very wound up. As if things weren't tense enough already, with everything that was going on. Still, Ryan was safe at home now, taking it all out on his wife. She'd be doing what had to be done. She'd be making all the right noises, massaging his ego and anything else he fancied, and thanking Christ that he still hadn't found out about the landscape gardener who was giving her one three times a week.

Moloney downed some more of the Guinness. His pager was on, as always, but his time was his own for a few precious hours and he was keen to unwind a little.

He had known plenty of coppers like Thorne before . . . With the bent ones, it was easy. You knew what made them tick, what got them off. Not that Thorne was necessarily incorruptible; everybody had their price. Moloney saw it offered and accepted every day. Problem was, Thorne was the sort who would take the dirty money, do what was asked of him for a while and then blow up in everyone's face. Do something stupid because he hated himself. It didn't matter if he was bent or not – and it was easy enough to find out. Thorne had to be watched. He was definitely going to cause them trouble.

Moloney drained his glass, waved it to get the barman's attention, and nodded for another. The man on the chair next to him got up and asked where he could find the Gents. Moloney pointed the way and asked if the man wanted a drink. The offer was graciously accepted. While he waited for the beers, Moloney looked around the crowded bar: plenty of faces. He drank in here pretty often, and one or two of the regulars who knew him had already said hello, or offered to buy him a drink, or held up a glass and waved from the other side of the room.

A lot of people wanted to know him.

The fact that none of them did, that so few people *really* knew him, was becoming harder to deal with lately. He was definitely drinking more, flying off the handle at the slightest thing, on the job and at home. It was all down to this war. Things had ratcheted up once the murders had started. What the Zarifs were doing, what Ryan was going to do in return, was the real test . . .

The man came back from the Gents and took his seat at the bar. Moloney handed him his pint of lager. When his

125

Guinness had settled and been topped up, he raised the glass.

'Good health,' Moloney said.

Thorne and Chamberlain had shared a bottle and a half of red wine with their dinner, and the thickening head may have had something to do with his reaction, his *over-reaction*, when he'd walked into the living room. The smell had hit him the second he'd opened the outer door.

'Fucking hell, Phil. Not in my flat . . .'

'It's only a bit of weed. I'm not shooting up. Jesus . . .'

'Do it round at Brendan's.'

Hendricks had needed to make a real effort not to laugh, and not just because he was stoned. 'Take a day off, why don't you?'

Thorne stalked off towards the kitchen. 'I fucking wish . . .'

Waiting for the kettle to boil, Thorne had calmed down and tried to decide whether to apologise or just pretend the argument had never happened. He'd recently discovered that, within the City of London, a pregnant woman in need of the toilet was still legally allowed to piss in a policeman's helmet. That dope should still be against the law was, he knew, only marginally sillier.

'Make us a piece of toast while you're in there,' Hendricks had shouted.

'*What!?*'

'I'm kidding.' Then, Hendricks hadn't been able to stop himself laughing any more.

If he was honest, it was the associations that went with dope-smoking that riled Thorne. He'd tried it a couple of times at school and, even then, passing an increasingly soggy joint around and talking about how great the shit was and how they all had the munchies seemed ridiculous to him. The drugs being taken in the corners of playgrounds these days were more dangerous, but there was none of that palaver. The kids just dropped a pill and got on with it.

There was also the fact that his ex-wife had liked the occasional joint, provided, so it turned out, by the creative-writing lecturer she'd later left him for. Thorne had smelled it on him, the day he'd walked up his own stairs and dragged the skinny sod out of his own bed. Why he hadn't punched him or put in an anonymous call to the Drugs Squad was still something Thorne occasionally woke up wondering about.

Thorne had mumbled something approaching an apology as he'd carried his tea into the living room. Hendricks had smiled and shaken his head.

They sat listening to the first Gram Parsons album. Thorne was wide awake and watched as Hendricks grew drowsier, then perked up, then began to wilt again . . .

'The shit we have to deal with is the price we pay for being human,' Hendricks announced, out of the blue.

Thorne slurped his tea. 'Right . . .'

'The difference between us and dogs or dolphins or whatever.' Hendricks took a drag of his joint. He was starting to sound a little like someone stoned on a sketch-show. 'We're the only animal that has an imagination . . .'

'As far as we know . . .' Thorne said.

'As far as we know, yeah. And all the dark, dark shit that gets done to people, the killing and the torture, started off as pictures in some weirdo's head. It all has to be *imagined*.'

Thorne thought about what Hendricks was saying. It made sense, though how some of the horrors they'd both encountered over the years had ever been imagined by *anybody* was beyond him. 'So?'

'So . . . that's the flipside of all the beautiful stuff. We get people who imagine great works of art and books and gardens and music, but the same imagination that creates *that* can also imagine the Holocaust, or setting fire to kids, or whatever.'

'All right, Phil . . .'

'You want one, you have to live with the other.'

They sat in silence for a while.

Finally, Hendricks leaned forward to stub out what was left of the joint, and to sum up: 'Basically . . . you want Shakespeare, you also get Shipman.'

Dark as the conversation had become, Thorne suddenly found the concept strangely funny. 'Right.' He nodded towards the stereo. 'Serial killers are the price we pay for country music.'

A massive grin spread slowly across Hendricks' face. 'I think . . . *that* . . . is a very tough choice . . .'

Moloney had decided to make a night of it. He strutted out into the freezing car park at closing time, full of Guinness and full of himself. 'Don't worry, I know a few places where we can still get a drink.' Moloney chuckled and threw an arm around the shoulder of his new best friend. 'Actually,' he said, 'I know *plenty* of fucking places.'

His drinking partner expressed surprise that Moloney

was planning to drive. He asked him if he was worried about being pulled over.

Moloney unlocked the Jag. 'I've been stopped a few times.' He winked. 'It's not normally a problem . . .'

'After you've been drinking?'

'They tend to look the other way . . .'

'Nice to have a bit of influence,' said his friend.

'Better than nice. Get in . . .'

They drove south through Islington, crossing the Essex Road and heading towards the City. The traffic was light and Moloney put his foot down at every opportunity. 'This place I'm taking us, behind the Barbican, there's usually a bit of spare knocking about as well. We lay out a few quid, they'll give us a good night. Up for that?'

It was as the Jag was moving far too fast towards the roundabout at Old Street that the man in the passenger seat placed the muzzle of the Glock against Moloney's waist.

'Go left and head for Bethnal Green . . .'

'What? Fuck . . .'

The gun was rammed into Moloney hard enough to crack a rib, to push him against the driver's side door. He cried out and struggled to keep his feet on the pedals.

Moloney drove, following the instructions he was given, body seizing up and mind racing. He knew that there was no way he could reach his own gun. He knew that nobody had a clue where he was. He knew, now, that he was not a brave man. Every breath was an effort. Any attempt to speak resulted in another jolt of agony as the gun was jammed hard against the broken rib.

The traffic and the lights melted away behind them as

Moloney steered the Jag off a quiet road and on to a narrow, rutted path. They crossed slowly over a stretch of black water, still, like motor oil, on either side of a graffiti-covered bridge.

'Pull up over there.'

As soon as the car was stationary, the man raised the gun and pressed it against Moloney's ear. He leaned across to the dashboard and turned off the headlights.

Moloney closed his eyes. 'Please . . .'

He felt the man's hand reach inside his jacket, move slowly around until it had located, and removed, the gun. He opened his eyes when he heard the door open, craned his head round to watch as the man moved behind the car.

The gunman tapped on the driver's side window with the gun. He took a step away from the car as Moloney opened the door. 'Move over to the other side,' he said.

Moloney did as he was told, gasping in pain as he lifted himself up and over the gearstick. 'Why?'

The man slid into the driver's seat. He closed the car door behind him. 'Because I'm right-handed,' he said.

Then Moloney felt his guts go, and everything began to happen very quickly.

The gun was in his ear again, and a hand was twisting him over on to his front, pushing his head across the back of the seat. The hand was reaching down, scrabbling for something, and the seat suddenly dropped back until it was almost flat. The hand began gathering up Moloney's jacket and the shirt beneath and pushing it up his back.

'You're making such a fucking mistake . . .' Moloney said.

Then, in a rush, the breath was sucked up into him, as the man with the gun began to cut.

Thorne woke with a start, disorientated. He could hear music, and Hendricks was looming above the bed in his boxer shorts, holding something out to him and mouthing angrily.

As he tried to sit up, Thorne realised that he'd fallen asleep with his headphones on. He turned off his Walkman, blinked slowly and moaned: 'What time is it?'

'Just gone three. It's Holland, for you . . .'

Thorne reached out for his mobile, the ringing of which he'd been unable to hear, but which had clearly woken Hendricks up.

'Thanks,' Thorne said.

Hendricks grunted and sloped out of the bedroom.

'Dave?'

Holland began to speak, but Thorne knew without being told that there was another body. Holland just needed to tell him which side it belonged to.

Thorne had no way of knowing it, but as he steered the BMW through the deserted streets towards the murder scene, he was following almost exactly the same route as the dead man had done a few hours earlier. Down to King's Cross and then east. Along the City Road and further, through Shoreditch and into what, forty years before, had been Kray territory. The streets of east London were much safer then, if some people were to be believed.

Marcus Moloney might well have agreed with them.

The car was parked on an area of waste ground, no

more than a hundred yards from the Roman Road. Here, the Grand Union Canal ran alongside a rundown piece of parkland called Meath Gardens and the railway line divided Globe Town from Mile End.

A man, asleep on a narrowboat moored further up the canal, had heard the gunshots. He'd come along five minutes later with his dog to investigate.

Thorne parked the car, walked across to do some investigating of his own.

The silver Jag was brightly lit by a pair of powerful arc-lights that had been set up on either side of it. Its doors were open. Thorne didn't know whether that's the way they had been found.

'Sir . . .'

Thorne nodded as he passed a DC from SO7 walking quickly in the opposite direction. As he got nearer to the car, he could make out the shape of the body, folded across the front seat, like a suit carrier. Every few seconds, the white hood of a SOCO bobbed into vision through the rear wind-screen. Stepping to the side, Thorne could see Holland and Stone huddled near the front wing. Holland glanced up, threw him a look he couldn't read, but which definitely didn't bode well. There were more SOCOs working in the footwells and on the back seats. There were stills and video cameramen. There were three or four other officers with their backs to him, talking on the edge of the canal bank.

The lights showed up every scratch, every mark on the car windows, every speck and gobbet of brain matter glued to the glass with blood.

Thorne grabbed a bodysuit from a uniform who was handing them out like free gifts. 'Dave . . .'

Holland made to come over, then stopped and nodded towards the group of officers who were now walking back in the direction of the car. There were three men in suits of varying quality: Brigstocke, Tughan and a senior press officer called Munteen. It was the man in uniform who Thorne was most surprised, and horrified, to see there. He couldn't recall the last time he'd encountered Detective Chief Superintendent Trevor Jesmond at a crime scene.

Jesmond pulled his blue overcoat tighter around him. 'Tom.'

'Sir.'

Thorne broke the short but awkward silence that followed. He nodded towards the car. 'The Zarifs have really upped the stakes now. Marcus Moloney's in a different league from Mickey Clayton and the others. It's going to get a bit tasty from here . . .'

He looked at Russell Brigstocke, and received the same look he'd got from Holland.

'The stakes have certainly been upped,' Jesmond said, 'but not for the reasons you're assuming . . .'

'Oh?' Thorne glanced at Tughan, who was studying the gravel.

Jesmond looked as drawn, as defeated, as Thorne had ever seen him. 'Marcus Moloney was an undercover police officer,' he said.

TEN

Thorne left the Moloney murder scene as the sun was coming up and drove through streets that were showing the first faltering signs of life. He spent a couple of hours at home – showered, changed and had some breakfast – but he was still getting through on what little sleep he'd managed before being woken by Hendricks with the phone call.

Driving towards Hendon, he couldn't decide whether the *heaviness* he felt was due to the lack of sleep, the wine from the night before or the memory of the atmosphere on that canal bank. The change in those who hadn't known the truth about Moloney was clear to see as soon as word had got around. The volume had fallen; the movements in and around the Jag had become a fraction more delicate. Bodies were always accorded a measure of respect, but that measure tended to vary. Dead or not, a gangland villain was treated by the police a little bit differently to a fellow officer.

Thorne hated that 'one of our own' nonsense, but he understood it. The life of a police officer was clearly worth no more or less than that of a doctor or a teacher or a shop assistant. But it wasn't doctors, teachers and shop assistants who had to pick up the bodies, inform the next of kin and try to catch those responsible. Yes, sometimes the self-righteous anger when a policeman died could make his skin crawl, and the speeches made by senior officers could sound horribly false, but Thorne told himself he could see it all for what it really was. There was nothing false about the relief and the fear, nor about anger at feeling both of those things.

Nothing false about 'there but for the grace of God' . . .

It was early, but Thorne knew Carol Chamberlain would be up and about. She needed to know that *everything* had changed. He called her as he hit the North Circular and told her about Marcus Moloney.

'Well, he certainly had me fooled,' she said.

'Me too,' Thorne admitted. And neither of them was stupid.

Moloney was clearly a committed and brilliant under-cover officer, but still, it bothered Thorne that he hadn't sensed something. *Anything.* There was a lot of crap talked about 'instinct', but if there was one thing Thorne was certain of, it was that instinct was unreliable. He certainly possessed it himself, but it came and went, failing him at all the wrong moments, as inexplicable as a striker's goal drought or a writer's block. And it had landed him in the shit plenty of times over the years . . .

Occasionally, Thorne felt like he could look into a killer's eyes and see exactly what was on his mind. See all those dark imaginings that Hendricks had been talking about the night before. Sometimes, Thorne thought he could spot a villain by the way he smoked a cigarette. Other times, he wouldn't know the enemy if he was wearing a ski-mask and carrying a sawn-off shotgun.

'How come you *didn't* know?' Chamberlain asked. 'About Moloney?'

Thorne didn't have an answer, and by the time he hung up on Chamberlain and pulled into the compound at Becke House, he was extremely pissed off about it. Why *hadn't* Tughan told him? It was a fucking good question.

The answer wasn't particularly satisfactory: 'It wasn't deemed necessary, or prudent . . .'

'Talk English,' Thorne said. He turned to Brigstocke. He and Tughan had both stood up when Thorne had come marching into the office without knocking. 'Russell, did you know?'

Brigstocke nodded. 'It wasn't to go below DCI level,' he said. 'That was the decision.'

Tughan sat back down again. Thorne could see a copy of the *Murder Investigation Manual* on the desk in front of him. 'Moloney's role as an undercover officer was strictly on a "need to know" basis,' he said, as if he'd just read the phrase in the book.

Thorne sighed, leaned back against the door. 'Did he have a wife? Kids?'

Brigstocke nodded again, just once.

'Have they been told he was carved up and shot in the head? Or is that on a "need to know" basis, too?'

'Close the door on the way out,' Tughan said, looking away.

'A few things suddenly make a lot more sense, though,'

Thorne said. 'I wondered how you could be so certain that the Izzigil murders were down to Ryan. How you knew where that threatening letter had come from. Obviously you had a hotline . . .'

Tughan slammed a piece of paper on to the desktop. 'Why the hell is everything always about you, Thorne? An officer has been killed. You just said it: "*carved up and shot in the head*". The fact that you hadn't been told that he was a police officer is pretty fucking unimportant, wouldn't you say?'

Brigstocke was no great admirer of Tughan himself, but his expression told Thorne that he thought the DCI had a point . . .

And as Thorne calmed down, he could see Tughan's point too. He felt a little ashamed of the outburst, of the sarcasm. He walked across the office, dragged a spare chair over to the desk and dropped into it. He was relieved to see that Tughan didn't object.

'How long had Moloney been in there?'

'Two years, more or less,' Tughan said.

Thorne was amazed it had been so short a time. 'He got where he was in the organisation pretty bloody quickly.'

Tughan nodded. 'He was bright, and Billy Ryan liked him. Stephen Ryan treated him like an older brother . . .'

'He was doing a pretty good job,' Brigstocke said.

Tughan corrected him: 'He was doing a *very* good job and, with him dead, it's all been worse than useless.'

'Hang on,' Thorne said. 'In two years he must have put together a fair bit of evidence against Ryan.'

'More than a "fair bit", but Moloney was the key witness. He would have been the one standing up in court. All the evidence was based on conversations *he'd* had, things *he'd* seen, or been told. We've got sod all that'll stand up without him.'

'What about the Izzigil killings? He knew about that, right? There must be something . . .'

Tughan picked at something on his chin. He was freshly shaved, rash-red from the razor, but Thorne could see a small patch of sandy stubble that he'd missed to the left of his Adam's apple. 'He knew about it *afterwards*. He knew something was being planned a few days before it happened but couldn't find out who was being hit or who'd been given the contract.'

'It was true Ryan liked to have Moloney around,' Brigstocke said. 'But there were others he trusted to get the really dirty work done.'

'Stephen?' Thorne suggested.

'Yeah, Stephen,' Tughan said, 'and others.'

Thorne thought about how hard it must have been for DS Marcus Moloney. Once the killings had started, he'd been caught in an impossible position. He'd have wanted to dig around, to try to find out the names of the people Ryan was planning to have killed so that he could tell his colleagues at SO7. He'd also have known full well that if he *did* go sniffing around after information he wasn't meant to have, he ran the risk of exposing himself and ruining everything.

And later – after Muslum and Hanya Izzigil had been killed – had he felt somehow responsible?

'We can still get Ryan,' Thorne said.

The other two men in the room looked at him with renewed interest. This was what Thorne had been putting off, but now was the perfect moment. He'd told Chamberlain on the way in that he was going to have to come clean about what they'd been up to. He hadn't realised it was going to be quite this important.

'How?' Tughan asked.

'I've got a witness.'

Tughan smiled. It was the perfect moment for him, too. 'Is this where you tell me about Gordon Rooker?'

Thorne just about stopped his jaw dropping. '*What?*'

'You must think I'm fucking stupid, Thorne. All that crap when we saw Billy Ryan about "barking up the wrong tree". *You* have been, but only by treating me like a mug.'

'Hang on . . .'

'I did some homework, none of it particularly taxing. I know all about your trips to Park Royal, both alone and with ex-DCI Chamberlain.'

Thorne glanced at Brigstocke, got a look back that said he'd known about *this* as well.

'It had nothing to do with this case,' Thorne said. 'There was no connection.'

'There is now, though, right?'

'That's what I'm trying to tell you . . .'

'Which is why you were hassling Billy Ryan outside one of his arcades last night?' Tughan seemed to enjoy watching the puzzlement that Thorne knew was spreading across his face. 'I knew about it while it was happening.'

Thorne cast his mind back to the previous evening. He remembered Moloney walking away from them, talking angrily on his mobile. Thorne had thought he'd been calling for the car . . .

'Right, let's hear it . . .'

So Thorne told them the whole story, ancient and modern. He told them about the calls to Carol Chamberlain and about his visits to Gordon Rooker. He told them about Jessica Clarke and about Rooker's revelation regarding her attacker. He told them about Rooker's offer . . .

'Why's he waited twenty years?' Brigstocke asked.

It was the first of many questions – all of the obvious ones which Thorne had asked himself, and Gordon Rooker. He gave the answers he'd been given: tried to explain why Rooker had confessed to such a heinous crime; why a man like him was able to survive better inside than on the street; why he had decided that he had to make sure Billy Ryan would not be waiting for him on the outside.

'So, we get him out, offer him witness protection, and he will testify against Billy Ryan for the attempted murder of Jessica Clarke?'

'Rooker knows all sorts of stuff,' Thorne said. 'He'll tell us everything, and he'll tell the court everything.'

Rain was starting to come down outside. The drops were heavy but not yet concentrated. For a few moments the noise of their sporadic tapping against the window was the only sound in the room.

'Who's making these calls to ex-DCI Chamberlain and getting creative with lighter fuel in her front garden?' Tughan sounded sceptical. 'We're presuming he's the man who really set fire to the girl, are we?'

'I don't know,' Thorne admitted.

'It's a bit bloody coincidental, don't you think?'

'Rooker denies all knowledge of it.'

'There's a shock.' Tughan looked to Brigstocke. 'Russell?'

'Some crony of Rooker's? An ex-con, maybe? Someone he's been in contact with . . .?'

Thorne tried not to sound impatient. 'We've got time to check all of this,' he said. 'Look, Billy Ryan as good as killed that girl, and we've got a chance to nail him for it. Christ knows, he's done plenty of other things, but we can *get him* for this. It's got to be worth considering.'

Thorne stopped himself adding: *We should do it for Marcus Moloney.* But only just . . .

The rain was falling harder now, beating out a tattoo against the glass.

'Obviously, people a damn sight higher than me are going to be doing the considering,' Tughan said. 'A damn sight higher than Jesmond even . . .' He took a breath and reached for the phone.

As he and Brigstocke got up and headed towards the door, Thorne thought about what Brigstocke had known and had chosen not to pass on. He wondered if he should have a chat with him about whose side they were supposed to be on. He decided it was probably not the right time.

By lunchtime in the Royal Oak, the mood of the team had lightened a little, though it might just have been the power of beer.

The Oak was the team's regular, but for no other reason than proximity. No one could remember a time when it hadn't been full of coppers, so no one could swear that they were the reason for the atmosphere, or the lack of it. It wasn't that Trevor, the cadaverous landlord, hadn't made an effort. He'd decorated the front of the lacquered-pine bar with Polaroids of various female regulars, all hoisting up their T-shirts to reveal bras or bare breasts. Elsewhere, he'd gone for a Spanish theme, with a good deal of fake wrought iron, a couple of sombreros gathering dust on a shelf above the bar, and two days a week when he cut up pork pies and Scotch eggs into small pieces and called it a tapas menu.

There was no Tughan, Kitson or Brigstocke in the pub, but most of the others were there. They raised a glass to Marcus Moloney. His death had eased a little of the tension between the Serious Crime Group mob and their counterparts from SO7. They were understandably united in their resolve to bring to justice those responsible for his death. For *all* the recent deaths.

Thorne applauded the sentiment, even if that's all it was. He hoped that the cracks wouldn't begin to show again too soon. He pushed away a half-eaten plate of chicken and chips as Holland slid in next to him with a tray of drinks. By now, everyone had moved on to Coke, mineral water or orange juice. Thorne, feeling himself starting to wilt a little, poured out his can of Red Bull. He glanced up at Holland and remembered the invitation he'd turned down. 'Did you go for that beer last night? Sounded like you were set on a major session?'

'Just had a couple in here with Andy.' He nodded towards the other side of the bar where Andy Stone, Sam Karim and a female DC from SO7 were deep in conversation. 'Good job I didn't, really. Bearing in mind what time we were called out.'

'I wasn't exactly stone-cold sober myself at four o'clock

this morning,' Thorne said. 'Given what was down by that canal, it was probably a good thing . . .'

'Found out something brilliant in here last night, though.' Holland grinned and inched his chair a little closer to Thorne's. 'You know Andy Stone reckons he has quite a bit of success with the women . . .?'

Thorne followed Holland's gaze: Stone and the female DC seemed to be getting on extremely well. '*Yes* . . .?' Thorne stretched the word out.

'He told me one of his tricks. He'd had a bit more to drink than me . . .'

'I'm listening,' Thorne said.

'He keeps a book on philosophy in his car.' Holland laughed as Thorne's eyes widened. 'Seriously. On the passenger seat, or down by the tapes, or wherever. Girl gets in . . . "*Oh what's this?*" . . . Picks it up, has a look, she's convinced Stone's a deep thinker.' There was a pause, then Thorne almost snorted Red Bull down his nose. 'This is the worst bit,' Holland said, 'it fucking works.'

Thorne laughed even harder, wiped the drink from his jacket. He looked up when he heard a familiar Mancunian accent.

Hendricks was pointing at the can of Red Bull. 'That stuff won't wake you up if you apply it externally,' he said.

'What are you doing up here? I thought you had Moloney's PM to do.'

Hendricks glanced at his watch. 'Starting in a couple of hours. There's a queue of corpses out the bloody doors down at Westminster Morgue.'

Holland got up to make room for Hendricks and headed for the Gents.

'Tughan wanted to see me over the road.' Hendricks dropped into the chair Holland had vacated. 'He wanted a preliminary report.'

'Well? Do I get to hear it?'

Hendricks looked confused. 'What d'you think I came here for?'

'Go on, then . . .'

'Moloney died from gunshot wounds to the head. Almost certainly a nine mil. No bullets found in the car, so I'll have to dig them out to be certain.'

'Same pattern of knife wounds?'

'Yeah . . .'

Thorne had heard Hendricks sound *more* certain. 'Not sure?'

'I'm still not convinced I know what sort of blade he's using. It could be a filleting knife. Also, the cuts weren't quite as neat as they were on Clayton and the others.'

'Perhaps he had less time.'

'Right. And maybe Moloney struggled a bit more than some of the other victims.'

'This is the first time he's done it in a car, remember. He had less room to manoeuvre than he did with the others . . .'

Hendricks nodded. It all made perfectly good sense.

'You'd say it *was* the same killer, though,' Thorne said. 'The X-Man.'

It was a few seconds before Hendricks gave a nod that said '*probably*'. Enough time for Thorne to find himself wondering if they hadn't got things arse about face. They were assuming that the Zarifs had targeted the Ryans again and killed Marcus Moloney, unaware that he was a police officer. But there was an equally plausible possibility . . .

'What if the killer knew *exactly* what Moloney was?'

'Sir?' It was Holland, back from the Gents.

The more Thorne articulated it, the more convinced he became. He thought back to the previous night, in the street outside the games arcade: Moloney on the phone, not to Billy Ryan's driver, as Thorne had thought, but to Nick Tughan. Making the last call he was ever going to make. Unaware that his cover had been blown . . .

'I think they found out he was a copper,' Thorne said. 'With what was going on, with what had happened to the others, they had a perfect way to get rid of him, didn't they? I think Billy Ryan killed Moloney.'

Thorne reached for his mobile to make the call to Tughan. Before he could start dialling, it began to ring.

It was Russell Brigstocke.

'Tom? We've just had a call from the Central Middlesex Hospital . . .'

Thorne didn't quite take it all in. He just heard the key word and immediately thought: Dad.

'Up by Park Royal.'

The initial relief quickly gave way to mild panic. 'What's happened?' Thorne guessed what the answer would be before Brigstocke gave it.

'Somebody tried to kill Gordon Rooker.'

ELEVEN

Thorne could think of better places to be on a sunny morning. He hated hospitals for all the obvious reasons, as well as for a few others unique to the job he did – to some of the cases he'd worked . . .

He shuffled his chair a little closer to the bed. Holland was sitting next to him. On the other side of the bed, a prison officer relaxed in a tatty brown armchair.

'You're a lucky bastard, Gordon,' Thorne said.

Rooker had been attacked two days earlier, an hour or so after Thorne and Chamberlain had confronted Ryan in the street, and four hours before Marcus Moloney had been murdered. Thorne had presumed it had been the confrontation with Ryan which had prompted him to do something about Rooker, but now he realised that it could not have been organised in the time. It had to have been Thorne's earlier meeting with Ryan in his office, when he'd first mentioned Rooker's name, that had sparked things off.

He'd certainly touched a raw nerve . . .

Thorne tried to picture Ryan as he'd stood in the street

outside his arcade, the wind whipping across his face. Ryan had stood there and smiled when Thorne had offered the greeting from Rooker, safe in the knowledge that a special greeting of his own had already been arranged. Rooker in the evening; Moloney later that night. Two problems solved within hours of each other.

What was it Rooker had said? *Billy Ryan's cold . . .*

Rooker tried to lift himself up the bed a little. He grimaced in pain. 'Define lucky,' he said.

The improvised shiv – actually a sharpened paintbrush – which Alun Fisher had stuck into his belly during an art class had somehow missed every vital organ in Rooker's body. He'd lost a lot of blood, but the surgery had been about patching him up rather than saving his life.

Rooker settled back. 'Lucky that I'm alive, but it's hardly fortunate that certain parties have got wind of things, is it?'

Thorne decided that it wouldn't do Rooker any good to know who was responsible for mentioning his name to Billy Ryan.

'Told you I'd be marked, though, didn't I?' Rooker said. 'Now I've got even more reason to make sure the fucker gets put away.'

Rooker's hair was lank and his skin was the colour of a week-old bruise. The gold tooth still glinted in his mouth, but half of the top set was missing, the bridge sitting in a glass on the bedside cabinet. A drip ran into his left arm and an oxymeter peg was attached to the index finger. His right wrist was connected, rather less delicately, to a prison officer, one of two on a rotating bedwatch. The officer, skull and chin neatly shaved, sat with his head in a paperback.

Rooker raised the handcuffs, lifting his and the officer's arm. 'Fucking ridiculous, isn't it?' The prison officer didn't even look up. 'Like I'm going to do a runner. Like somebody's going to spring me. Like who?'

Holland smiled. 'Got no friends, Gordon?'

'See any flowers?'

'Friends, acquaintances . . . we'll have to check all of that,' Thorne said. 'One or two people are still bothered by this bloke turning up out of the blue and claiming responsibility for what happened to Jessica Clarke.'

'Check what you like,' Rooker said. 'I can't help you. I tell you what, though: if it *is* the bloke who did it, who *really* did it, we both know who can give you his name.'

The small room was strangely half lit. The curtains had been drawn against the dazzling sunshine, filtering it through thin, brown and orange nylon. A dirty amber light moved across the pale walls, softening the metallic gleam of the dressing-trolley and the drip-stand.

'Tell me about Alun Fisher,' Thorne said.

With what few teeth were left in his upper jaw, Rooker bit down hard on his bottom lip. 'He's nothing. A fucking little tosspot . . .'

Thorne heard the prison officer chuckle quietly and glanced across. It wasn't clear whether it was Rooker or his book that he was finding so funny.

'A little tosspot with a smack habit . . .'

Thorne could see where it was going. 'And a drug debt, right?'

'A fucking big one. Three guesses who he owes the money to . . .'

'So Fisher just walks up to you in the middle of a class?'

Holland said. 'Stabs you, just like that, while you're doing your Rolf Harris bit?'

'I thought you could see it coming,' Thorne said. 'That's what you told me last time. If someone was going to have a pop at you, you'd know about it . . .'

Rooker sniffed, cast his eyes to the right. 'Well, *somebody* looked the other fucking way, didn't they? Took their eye off the ball. These teachers in the Education Department don't get paid much, do they? Or maybe a screw fancied a new car, a holiday for the wife and kids . . .'

If the prison officer was upset, he wasn't showing it. Park Royal was already carrying out an inquiry into exactly what had gone wrong, while Alun Fisher sat in a segregation cell waiting to see what they were going to do with him. Having fucked up and left Gordon Rooker breathing, he was probably more worried about what Billy Ryan was going to do. He might suddenly find that his debt had increased in all sorts of ways.

'So are you going to press charges?' Holland asked.

'Not much point, is there? They'll move Fisher to another prison. Might as well try to get through the rest of the time without any hassle.'

'Up to you,' Thorne said.

Rooker moved his hand and began scratching the top of his leg. The prison officer raised his head, waited a few seconds, then yanked the hand back down to the mattress.

'What you were saying about checking my friends,' Rooker said. 'How long is all this going to take? The sooner they get everything sorted out, you know, and arranged, the quicker we can start talking. Right? This has been going on too long already . . .'

Thorne knew what Rooker meant, realised that he was reluctant to talk specifically about protection, and evidence, and *Ryan*, with the prison officer in the room.

'It won't be a quick decision,' Thorne said. 'They've only been considering the position seriously for the last couple of days.'

Rooker shook his head. 'Right. That's typical. Maybe, if they'd considered it a bit earlier, I might not have had a fucking paintbrush jammed in my guts . . .'

Thorne knew that was probably his fault. He looked at the indignant expression plastered across Rooker's yellowish chops. He could remember feeling guiltier. From the corner of his eye, he saw the prison officer look up when Holland's mobile rang. The DC checked the caller ID, stood up and took the phone out of earshot to answer it.

'You're supposed to turn those off in here,' Rooker said. 'They can interfere with medical equipment, you know. Fuck up the machines . . .'

The prison officer spoke for the first time: 'Shame you're not wired up to a couple then. Might have done us all a favour.'

Thorne couldn't help smiling. 'How long's he going to be here for?'

'We'll get him shifted back to the healthcare wing tomorrow, with a bit of luck,' the officer said. 'It's a level-three unit. They've got all the facilities, all the medication for any infection or what have you . . .'

Rooker looked less than delighted, but it made sense. The prison would want him back as soon as possible. The officers would be wanted back where they could be of more use, and the hospital would be glad to get shot of any patient who needed guards.

Thorne heard the single, short tone as Holland ended the call and turned to ask him. 'What?'

'That was DCI Tughan. He wants me to give you a message. You're not going to like it . . .'

'Fuck . . .'

Thorne could guess what the message would be. They must have turned down Rooker's offer. There hadn't been enough time for it to get up as high as it needed to go. It must have been blocked at a lower level. It would be interesting to find out exactly *where* . . .

Thorne stood and pulled on his jacket. 'It's not looking too promising, Gordon.'

He saw the prison officer smirk, and return to his book.

Thorne managed to make it through to the end of the day without having it out with Nick Tughan. He lost himself in a pile of unread memos, Police Federation junk mail and case updates from investigations he'd been working on before this one.

He then spent an evening in front of the TV without calling Tughan at home.

By lunchtime on Friday, just when he thought he'd given up on the idea, he found himself cornering Tughan in the Incident Room, spoiling for a fight. Sam Karim, who had been talking to Tughan when Thorne had marched over, made himself scarce pretty bloody quickly. Tughan leaned across a desk, flicking through the *Murder Investigation Manual* that seemed to have become his Bible.

'Answer in there, is it?' Thorne asked.

Tughan glanced up. 'What do you want, Tom?'

Thorne wasn't 100 per cent sure. 'Why didn't they go for it?'

'All the obvious reasons.'

'Such as?'

'Oh, come on. Russell and I raised a number of concerns when you first brought it to our attention. When you *eventually* brought it to our attention . . .'

It was clear to Thorne that Tughan was as riled up as ever. 'This was a genuine chance to get Ryan for something and make it stick.'

'Right. On the word of a man who confessed to it twenty years ago, and who suddenly decides to change his story . . .'

'Ryan is panicking. He's seriously fucking rattled. Why else would he try to get Gordon Rooker out of the way after all this time?'

Tughan went back to the manual. He licked a finger and began to flick through the pages. He was trying to slow things down, to put a foot on the ball. 'Securing the release of a potentially dangerous prisoner is not something to be undertaken if there is any room for doubt.'

'He'd be released into our custody, for fuck's sake.'

'The last thing we need is a compensation case for wrongful imprisonment.'

'How could Rooker claim compensation for that? He *confessed*.'

Tughan looked at him as if he were an idiot. 'If a decent lawyer gets a sniff of what's going on, that confession might suddenly turn out to have been all but beaten out of him . . .'

'These are just excuses.'

Tughan turned over another page.

'You're just pissed off because *I* came up with a way to nail Billy Ryan.'

'I think you should get back to work . . .'

'Same thing with the idea that it was Ryan who killed Moloney. Is anybody actually *pursuing* that line of inquiry?'

The colour began to rise above Tughan's button-down collar. 'What's that supposed to mean?'

'Ryan had the perfect cover. He knew exactly what the X-Man did to his other victims. His men found two of the bodies, for fuck's sake.'

'I know all this . . .'

'All he had to do was make sure that whoever killed Moloney used the same type of gun and carved the X. It was a piece of piss . . .'

'We're looking into it.'

Thorne snorted. 'Right, but not too hard. Because it came from me.'

Tughan slammed the manual shut. It sounded as though he was trying hard to keep his voice down. '*Me* again. There's over fifty officers working on this case . . .'

'Don't give me that fucking "team player" speech.' Thorne leaned forward, gripped the edge of the desk. 'It's all well and good as long as *you're* the captain of the team. That's the truth.'

'I'm not going to stand here and listen to this.' Tughan picked up the manual and waved it angrily at Thorne. 'Who do you think you're talking to?'

Thorne stepped back from the desk, laughing in spite of his anger. 'What? Are you going to throw the book at me?'

For a few seconds, Tughan glared. Then, he dropped his eyes, gave a smile some room on his face. He opened the manual again and leafed through it until he found the page he was looking for. 'Maybe just a bit of it,' he said. Tughan snatched up a pen, dragged it hard across the page, and tore it out. He hesitated for just a second before stepping forward and pressing it hard against Thorne's chest. 'Something to think about.'

Thorne grabbed at the torn-out sheet while Tughan stamped out of the room. Tughan had underscored one section hard enough to go through the paper . . .

'The modern-day approach to murder recognises the fact that there is no longer the place for the "lone entrepreneur" investigating officer.'

Hendricks was working late. For the second night in a row, Thorne sat alone in front of the TV, trying to regain some equilibrium. It rankled that Tughan was choosing to ignore perfectly sound ideas, but, more than anything, Thorne couldn't cope with the idea that Ryan was going to get away with it. Yes, Tughan might nail him one day for drugs offences, or fraud, or bloody tax evasion. Who knew, perhaps even the Zarifs would get him?

But he wouldn't have paid for Jessica Clarke . . .

Thorne brooded for most of the evening, then shouted at a TV chef for a while until the sourness began to dissipate and he started to feel better. Fuck it, February was almost over and spring was around the corner. He was thinking about maybe picking up his dad, driving down to Eileen's place in Brighton for the weekend, when the phone rang.

'Are you watching ITV?' Chamberlain asked.

'I was going to call you. The Rooker thing's a non-starter . . .'

'Put it on,' she demanded.

Thorne reached for the remote, changed the channel and turned up the volume.

A female reporter was talking straight to camera. Thorne watched, not clear what he was supposed to be seeing, until the camera cut away from the reporter and the story was told in a series of related shots . . .

An empty playground. A group of schoolgirls gathered at a bus stop. A can of lighter fluid.

Thorne felt his guts jump.

'He tried to do it again,' Carol Chamberlain said. 'He tried to burn another girl.'

MARCH

THE WEIGHT OF
THE SOUL

TWELVE

Thorne pulled up outside the house and sat for five minutes. It felt like the longest pause for breath he'd taken in a while. The time had passed in a flurry of activity, mindless and otherwise: seven days between the attempt to kill one young girl, and this, a visit to the father of another who had died almost twenty years earlier.

Seven days during which the powers-that-be had quickly changed their minds about Gordon Rooker's offer . . .

Thorne waited until the engine had ticked down to silence and it had begun to get cold in the car before he got out and walked towards the house. It was in the centre of a simple Victorian terrace on the south side of Wandsworth Common, not far from the prison. Thorne rang the bell and took a couple of steps back down the path. There were lights on in most of the houses: people settling down to eat, or getting ready for a Friday night out. The place would probably fetch around half a million. It was certainly worth much more now than it had been fifteen years ago, when the Clarkes had moved back here from Amersham. Back from where Jessica had gone to school.

The man who answered the door nodded knowingly while Thorne was still reaching into a pocket for his warrant card. 'Don't bother,' he said, stepping away from the door. His voice was thin, and a little nasal. 'What else would you be?'

Ian Clarke had been on the phone within an hour of that first news report. He'd sounded angry and confused. He'd insisted on being told the details, had demanded to know exactly what was being done. Thorne sensed that he'd calmed down a little during the week that had followed.

'Thanks for coming. There might be some tea on the way, with a bit of luck . . .'

'That'd be great . . .'

'We've got some Earl Grey, I think . . .'

'Monkey tea's fine.'

The tea delivered, Mrs Clarke announced that she had work to do. She smiled nervously as she stepped out of the room. She was wearing what, to Thorne, seemed like the look people gave to seriously ill patients before closing doors behind them in hospitals.

'Emma runs her own catering business,' Clarke said. He pointed towards the ceiling. 'She's got a small office at the top of the house.'

'Right. What about your daughter?'

There was the shortest of awkward pauses before Clarke responded. 'Isobel?'

Thorne nodded. The *second* daughter.

'Oh, she's around somewhere.'

Clarke had split from his first wife in 1989, three years after Jessica's death and almost immediately after they'd moved back to London from Buckinghamshire.

Thorne had seen it plenty of times with bereaved parents. It was often impossible to deal with the guilt and the anger and the blame. Impossible to look into the eyes of a husband or wife and not see the face of a lost child.

'No more news, then?' Clarke asked. He ran a hand across his skull. He'd lost a fair amount of hair and cut the remaining grey brutally short. It emphasised the chiselled features and lively, blue eyes that belied his age. Thorne knew that he had to be in his early fifties at least, but he looked maybe ten years younger.

Thorne shook his head. 'Only the same stuff rehashed to sell a few more papers. None of it's coming from us, I'm afraid.'

'Witnesses? Descriptions? It was a busy street, for God's sake.'

'Nothing's changed since I last spoke to you on the phone. I'm sorry.'

'I know I don't really have a right to be told anything at all. I'm grateful . . .'

Thorne waved away the thanks and the implicit apology. For a few seconds they drank their tea and stared into the flame-effect gas fire. On the mantelpiece, Thorne could see postcards, cigarettes, a party invitation in a child's handwriting. The large wooden mirror above reflected a watercolour on the wall behind him.

Clarke caught Thorne studying it. 'That was Jessica's mother's,' he said. 'One of the few things I got to keep.'

Clarke was sitting on a lived-in leather armchair. Thorne was adjacent, on the matching sofa. They were both leaning forwards, mugs of tea on their knees.

161

'It's like the old joke, then?' Clarke said, suddenly changing tack. 'About the police having their toilets stolen.'

Thorne smiled. 'Right . . .'

Though Thorne obviously understood, Clarke trotted out the tawdry punchline anyway: 'You've got nothing to go on.'

'We need a bit of luck,' Thorne said. 'We *always* need a bit of luck.'

Clarke put down his mug and stood up. 'And if he tries to do it to another girl, would that count as a bit of luck?' He smiled and walked past Thorne to draw the curtains.

Thorne was struck again by how good Clarke looked for his age, though the fleecy blue tracksuit top may have been helping to create the illusion. He was grateful for finding something with which to break the slightly awkward silence. 'You look pretty fit,' he said. He patted his belly. 'I could do with shifting this.'

Clarke walked round the sofa, dropped back into his armchair. 'I manage a leisure centre,' he explained.

Thorne nodded, thinking that actually, it explained nothing. Most hairdressers had terrible hair, and he'd known plenty of dishonest coppers. 'Listen, we're making an assumption,' he said. 'We're assuming that this recent incident is connected, in some way, to the attack on your daughter.'

Clarke pulled at his lip with a finger and thumb. 'Obviously. It's the same . . . *kind* of attack. Whoever this lunatic is, he must be aware of what happened to Jess. He must have read about it . . . . yes?'

'Yes. Or there could be other connections.'

'Could there?'

'I said we're making an assumption.'

'Other connections, right.' Quickly: 'Such as?'

Clarke had been correct when he'd said that he had no right to be told anything, but Thorne knew bloody well that there was no other reason for him to be sitting in the man's living room. He'd *come* to tell him.

'It's possible that the man found guilty of attempting to murder your daughter in 1984 was not in fact the man responsible.'

Clarke gave a short bark of a laugh. '*What?* Because some psycho's gone out and bought himself a can of lighter fluid?'

'No . . .'

'That's bloody ridiculous.'

'Hang on, Mr Clarke.'

'So, if a prostitute gets cut up in Leeds tomorrow night that means Peter Sutcliffe's innocent, does it?'

'We had good reason to believe that Gordon Rooker was innocent *before* the attack last week.'

The skin tightened across Clarke's jaw at the mention of Rooker's name. 'I presume that "good reason" is some bloody police euphemism, yes? Like when doctors say "as well as can be expected" when somebody's on their deathbed. Yes? Am I right? Because, don't forget, we're talking about the man who confessed to setting my daughter on fire.'

'Yes, I know.'

'The man who *confessed*.'

'He's withdrawn that confession.'

'Well, he's a bit *fucking* late . . .' Clarke slapped both palms hard against his legs, and grinned as if he'd been half joking, but there'd been no mistaking the venom in his voice. He reached behind the armchair. 'Hang on,' he said. He found a switch, and flicked on an uplighter. 'Best to lift the gloom a bit.'

Thorne looked up at the soft circle of light on the ceiling. 'You're right. Of course you are. It's *very* fucking late . . .'

'So, you think the man who attacked the girl last week is the man who really attacked Jess?'

'We've got to consider the possibility.'

'Where's he been for the last twenty years, then?'

It was, of course, the obvious question and Thorne had only obvious answers. 'Living abroad, maybe. In prison for something else . . .'

'And he's doing this now, because . . .?'

'Because he's worried that Rooker's about to come out. He's trying to make us look stupid, tell us we got it wrong. Or he's trying to claim credit that should rightfully be his. I don't honestly know, Mr Clarke.'

'The toilet joke again . . .'

'Pretty much, yeah.'

For want of anything else to do, Thorne brought the mug to his lips and tipped it back, though he knew full well that the tea was finished. 'Listen, we don't know who this man is, or if he *is* the man who attempted to murder your daughter, and neither, so he says, does Gordon Rooker.'

'So, you don't believe *everything* he says?'

'What he *does* say is that he knows who is responsible for what happened to Jessica. He knows who paid the money, and he's going to tell us.'

'It was some gangster.' Clarke said it as if it were in inverted commas. 'I was told, unofficially, that no one could be one hundred per cent sure which one, but that he was probably killed shortly after what he did to Jess. Right?'

Thorne saw Clarke's expression start to darken when he didn't answer him instantly. He knew that the water was suddenly getting deep and that he shouldn't wade in any further. 'I'm sorry, but I can't really go into . . .'

Clarke held up his hands. He understood.

'I just wanted you to be clear about something,' Thorne continued. 'If Rooker comes out of prison, it's only so that the man who was behind what happened to your daughter can go *in*.'

Clarke pondered this for a minute. He turned his chair towards the fire, held his hands towards it. Thorne thought that it had suddenly become a lot colder. He also thought: How can he stand to look into a fire? What does he see when he stares into the flames?

'You should have a picture of Jess,' Clarke said, suddenly.

The smallest of shivers crept across the nape of Thorne's neck. He felt as if the man opposite him had somehow known what he was thinking. He watched as Clarke got up and walked across to a pine chest in the corner of the room. Photos in assorted metal frames were scattered across the top.

'Right . . .'

'A reminder.'

Clarke picked up a small frame, began removing the clips that held the picture in place. 'This is a good one.' He removed the glass and took out the photograph. He waved it at him.

Thorne stood and moved across the room to take the picture from Clarke's outstretched hand. Clarke handed it over and stepped towards the door. 'That's the "before". You need the "after" as well. I don't keep any out down here because they upset Isobel. That's the *only* reason.'

He left the room. Thorne heard him running up the stairs, heard a door open and close.

You should have a picture of Jess . . .

Thorne thought about how Clarke had said it. As though it were a simple piece of good advice that would aid his well-being. *You should check your cholesterol. You should keep up your pension payments. You should have a photo of my dead daughter.*

Thorne knew that Clarke was well aware that this visit was not procedural. This was not part of any inquiry, and nor was the offer of the photograph. This was something Ian Clarke wanted *Thorne* to have. Thought he *should* have . . .

When he heard a door close upstairs, Thorne stepped out into the hallway and waited near the front door. Now seemed as good a time as any to be making a move.

Clarke jogged quickly down the stairs and pressed a small black book into Thorne's hands. 'I thought you might want to look at her diary. It doesn't matter if you don't. Let me have it back either way when you've finished with it.'

'Right, of course . . .'

Clarke handed over the photo with a small nod. Thorne took it with barely a glance, afraid of staring. Of being *seen* to stare. When he looked back at Clarke, it was clear from the man's expression that this was a reaction he'd seen a hundred times before.

166

'There were gangsters at her funeral,' he said. 'Murderers and drug barons and men who get paid to hurt people. They came to show their respects after she'd killed herself.' He spoke calmly, though the anger was clear enough, like something moving behind a muslin curtain. 'It was a gorgeous day when we buried her, a really stunning day. We all said how that was Jess's doing, because she loved the good weather so much, and then that lot turned up in dark suits and sunglasses like something out of *Reservoir Dogs* and ruined everything. Kevin Kelly and his tarty wife, and that other one who'd taken over . . . Ryan. A bunch of them. All standing there, sweating, with huge wreaths. One of them spelled out her name, for pity's sake. Hovering with tasteless fucking wreaths for my little girl, who'd died because her friend happened to be a gangster's daughter . . .'

Thorne was finding it hard to look at him. Rubbing his thumbs across the shiny surface of the photo in his hands. Nodding when it felt as though he should.

'We worked our arses off to send Jess to that school, to raise the money for the fees. What did Kelly have to do? How many people did he have to kill or rob to send that little . . . to send his little girl to that school?'

Thorne saw a figure appear on the landing at the top of the stairs: a teenage girl with long, ash-blond hair.

Clarke turned when he saw Thorne raise his eyes. 'Isobel . . .'

Thorne was unsure whether Clarke was talking to the girl or introducing her. He couldn't help but wonder how much she looked like her half-sister. He wanted to look at the photo to check, but the picture on top was of Jessica after her attack, and Thorne felt unable to move it, to slide the photo of her *unscarred* to the front . . .

'Hello,' he said.

The girl tugged at a corner of her sweater, muttered a sullen greeting in return. Clarke gave Thorne a weary, parental shrug. 'She's thirteen,' he said by way of explanation. Then his face changed. 'She'll be fourteen in a couple of weeks . . .' He reached past Thorne to open the front door.

Thorne toyed with some cod response about kids growing up too fast, but before he had a chance to make it, Clarke stepped in close and lowered his voice. 'This man, whoever he is, attempted to murder Jess. You said that. You said it a couple of times, actually.'

'Sorry, I don't . . .'

'He didn't *attempt* to murder her, Mr Thorne. He murdered her.' Clarke looked Thorne in the eyes as he spoke.

Thorne instinctively looked away, but then, ashamed, forced himself to meet Clarke's eyes again.

'It took a couple of years for her to die, but he murdered her.'

There was little to say except 'goodbye', so they both said it, and let the front door close between them.

Thorne glanced back. Through the frosted squares of red, blue and green glass in the front door, he could make out the shape of Ian Clarke climbing slowly up the stairs towards his daughter.

The crowd at the bus stop is just that at first: a crowd; massed, indistinguishable, and not just because of the quality of the film. A tight knot of people bunched on the pavement, bundled up against the cold weather or, in the case of the girls, huddled into a gang, a million things to talk about while they wait for the bus.

There is no sound, but it isn't hard to imagine the screams, the shouts of anger and incomprehension.

The knot unravels in a moment, people wheeling or jumping away, revealing the man for the first time. An old woman points at him, pulls at the sleeve of the woman with the pushchair standing next to her. Girls cling to one another, to blazers and bags, as the man, his face hidden inside the hood of a dark anorak, turns and jogs casually away up the street . . .

Hendricks appeared from the kitchen. 'The food'll be ready in a couple of minutes,' he said.

Thorne got off the sofa and ejected the tape from the VCR. While he was up, he grabbed the bottle of wine from the mantelpiece and refilled Carol Chamberlain's glass.

'Nothing from any other angles?' she said.

Thorne shook his head as he swallowed from his own glass. 'These are the best pictures we could get.' CCTV footage seemed to play an increasingly large part in most investigations these days. Often, the cameras were no more than a deterrent, and a pretty unsuccessful one at that. The crack dealers on Coldharbour Lane and the heroin mules around Manor House knew exactly where they were and treated them with the same disdain they might accord a traffic warden. Most of the time, they would happily go about their business in full view of the camera, knowing just when to turn a head or angle a shoulder to avoid the incriminating shot, then wink at the lens when the deal was done. Once in a while, though,

Thorne would find himself staring at more significant footage: grainy, black-and-white pictures of armed robbers, of killers, or, more disturbingly, of those about to become their victims.

In this case, a potential victim who got lucky.

'It doesn't make sense,' Chamberlain said. 'How did he ever think he'd get away with it? If, God forbid, he hadn't been rumbled. If that girl hadn't seen what he was doing with the lighter fluid and he'd managed to set her alight . . .'

'Even if he had, he might still have got away,' Thorne said. 'People would have been far more concerned with helping the girl. You know as well as I do that by and large people are afraid to do anything. They don't want to be the have-a-go hero who gets shot, or gets a knife stuck in him.'

Chamberlain stared into her glass. 'Why a bus stop, though? Why the different MO?'

'There's a lot more security around schools now,' Hendricks said. 'He'd've been lucky to find a school like Jessica Clarke's, where he could just march up to the playground.'

She shook her head. 'The middle of Swiss Cottage at four o'clock in the afternoon? It's stupid. The place was heaving.'

Hendricks leaned his head back into the kitchen to check on something for a second. 'He obviously wanted to make a splash.'

'Do you think it's the same bloke?' Thorne stared hard at Chamberlain.

'Yes, I'm fairly certain. It looked like the same anorak . . .'

Thorne shook his head. 'No, I don't mean that. Do you

think it's the same man who set fire to Jessica Clarke twenty years ago?'

There was no quick answer. 'He didn't look . . . old,' she said. 'I know you couldn't see his face. It was more the way he held himself, I suppose.'

'You're thinking about Rooker, about somebody like he is,' Thorne said.

'I know . . .'

'Suppose this man was in his early twenties back then. He'd only be in his early forties now.'

'It was seeing him run away. It seemed wrong, somehow, for the man I was imagining.'

'He *jogged* away,' Thorne said. 'Even if he was in his fifties, or sixties even, that's not out of the question, is it?'

Hendricks carried his glass across the room and topped it up. 'Just jogging away, casually, like he did, makes a lot of sense. It's the right thing to do if you don't want to draw attention to yourself, if you don't want to look like you're legging it away from something . . .' From the kitchen, the timer on Thorne's cooker suddenly buzzed. Hendricks put down his wineglass and went to do whatever was necessary.

'If it *is* him,' Chamberlain said, 'is Billy Ryan behind what he's doing now?'

'God knows, but, if he is, I haven't got the first idea why.'

Hendricks swore loudly. Either dinner was ruined or he'd burned himself.

'You all right in there, Delia?' Thorne shouted.

There was another bout of slightly more subdued swearing.

171

Chamberlain laughed. 'It smells good, whatever it is.' She drained her glass, glancing at her watch in the process.

'Listen, why don't you stay the night?' Thorne asked. 'We can sort out a bed . . .'

'No, I'm going to get the last train. If you can give me a taxi number . . .'

'It's no trouble, really. I'm sure Jack can make his own breakfast.'

She shook her head and took a step towards the kitchen.

Thorne put a hand on her shoulder. 'When we get Ryan, he's going to tell us who took his money twenty years ago and burned Jessica. He's going to give me a name.' He pointed towards the VCR. 'If it was this bloke, I'll get him. If it wasn't this bloke, and whoever it was is still alive, I'll get *him*. Then, I'll get this bloke as well. That's a promise, Carol . . .'

When Chamberlain looked at him, her expression a mixture of gratitude and amusement, Thorne realised that his hand had moved from her shoulder. In his effort to reassure her, he'd been gently rubbing her back in small circles. She raised her eyebrows comically. 'So, this offer to stay the night,' she said. 'What exactly did you have in mind?'

Ian Clarke sat on the sofa, his arm around his wife. He stared across the room in the direction of the television.

He cried once a year on his first daughter's birthday. The day that was also the anniversary of her death. For the rest of the time, everything was kept inside, squashed and pressed inside, his ribs, like the bars of a cage, holding in the thoughts and feelings and dark desires.

He sat still, going over the details of Thorne's visit, the things that were said, feeling as if his ribs might crack and splinter at any moment.

His wife laughed softly at something on the television and nestled her head into his chest. His hand moved automatically to her hair. He stared at a small square of white wall a foot or so above the screen. From time to time, he could hear a gentle thud on the ceiling as his second daughter moved around upstairs.

Thorne lay awake in bed, wondering if it was simply indigestion he was suffering from, or something a little harder to get rid of.

Enjoyable as the evening had been, he'd been happy to see Carol call for a cab. And he'd been relieved when, later, Hendricks had decided to leave the clearing up until the morning and get an early night.

The uncertainty that surrounded every aspect of the Billy Ryan/Jessica Clarke case had squatted next to him all evening, like an unwanted dinner guest. Now he felt it pressing him down into the mattress as he stared up at the Ikea light fitting he hated so much.

Not knowing was the worst thing of all.

In the course of some of the cases he'd investigated over the years, Thorne had learned things, seen things, understood things that, given the choice, he'd have preferred to avoid. Still, in spite of all the horrible truths he'd been forced to confront, he preferred knowledge to ignorance, though the dreadful weight of each was very different.

Beneath the duvet, his hand drifted down to his groin.

He fiddled around half-heartedly for a few minutes, then gave up, unable to concentrate.

He began to think about the photos of Jessica Clarke, out in the hallway inside his leather jacket. He pictured the image of her blasted and puckered face pressing against the silk lining of the pocket. He thought about the diary in his bag, waiting for him.

It was reading he'd postpone until another night . . .

Reaching across for his Walkman, he pulled on the headphones and pressed play: *The Mountain*, Steve Earle's 1999 collaboration with the Del McCoury Band. He rubbed at the tightness in his chest, deciding that it almost certainly *was* indigestion.

It was impossible to stay down for too long, listening to bluegrass.

THIRTEEN

'You're looking a bit better, Gordon,' Holland said.

Rooker grunted. 'It's all relative, isn't it?'

'OK then,' Stone said. 'You look better than a bag of shit, but not quite as good as Tom Cruise. How's that?'

The prison officer who had been standing behind them took a step forward, leaned down. 'Can we hurry this up?'

They were gathered around a table in the small office-cum-cubicle in a corner of the visits area. A TV and VCR had been set up. Holland was stabbing at a button, trying to cue up the tape.

Without looking at him, Stone waved a piece of paper towards the prison officer. 'Don't worry, it's not a long list.' The paper was waved in Rooker's direction. 'He isn't exactly your most popular guest, is he?'

This was part of the checking-up that Thorne had spoken about to Tughan when the doubts about Rooker were first raised. While Stone and Holland had headed into HMP Park Royal, others on the team were looking at those who had recently moved in the opposite direction; those who might have associated closely enough with

Gordon Rooker to do him a favour on the outside . . .

The list Stone was brandishing contained the names of all those who had been to the prison to see Rooker in the last six months. If the man who had made the calls to Carol Chamberlain, and perhaps been responsible for the attack in Swiss Cottage, had cooked up something with Rooker, chances were the plans would have been hatched in the visiting area. Something *could* have been organised via the telephone, but it was highly unlikely. As a Category B prisoner, any calls made by Gordon Rooker would, at the very least, be randomly monitored. If Rooker had an accomplice, Thorne felt sure that his name would be on the visitors list.

'It's easy to check names and addresses,' Thorne had told Holland, 'but I want you to go through them with Rooker in person, get any extra information you can from him. See how he reacts when you show him the pictures. Let's make absolutely sure we're not being pissed about . . .'

Copies of the visiting area's security tapes had been requested from the prison, sifted through and edited until the team was left with a sequence no more than a few minutes long. This was the tape which Holland, Stone and Rooker were about to watch . . .

'Here we go,' Holland said, leaning back from the video recorder.

Stone patted Rooker on the shoulder. 'This is very much a highlights package, Gordon. And we want you to provide the commentary, all right?'

Rooker picked up a pair of glasses from the table and inched his chair a little closer to the screen.

Out of the screen-snow came a series of clumsily cut-together shots, the images jumping disconcertingly from one to the next: half a dozen individuals walking into the visiting area, depositing bags and coats on or beneath chairs and sitting down. Each a different size in frame, sliding or slumping behind the narrow tables – not a single one of them looking particularly pleased to be there . . .

'Cath, my eldest daughter.' Rooker pointed and spoke while Holland scribbled. On the screen, a dark-haired woman in her late thirties sat down. She wore jeans and a sweatshirt. If she'd been wearing a bib, she might have been a prisoner. 'Her son's being taken on by West Ham . . .'

A jump-cut replaced the woman on the screen with another. In her early seventies, probably. A buttoned-up green overcoat. Handbag clutched in front of her on the table. 'My mother's youngest sister, Iris. Pops by every now and again to tell me who's died . . .'

A man, around the same age as Rooker. Arms moving animatedly as he spoke. Dirty grey suit and hair the same colour. 'Tony Sollinger, an old drinking mate. He got in touch with Lizzie out of the blue, told her he wanted to come in. Insisted on telling me he had cancer, for some fucking reason . . .'

A woman, anywhere between fifty and seventy. Hair hidden beneath a patterned headscarf. Saying little. 'Speak of the devil. The wife . . . the *ex*-wife, as near as dammit, on her annual visit . . .'

From somewhere on the wing behind them came a sudden howl of what might have been rage, or pain, or neither. Holland and Stone both turned. The prison officer didn't so much as raise his head.

'You can see why people aren't queuing up to visit, though,' Stone said. 'It's hardly fucking Alton Towers.'

The prison officer looked like he was laughing, but he did it without making any noise.

'Wayne Brookhouse,' Rooker continued. 'He used to go out with my youngest.' A man in his early twenties. Dark, curly hair and glasses. Lighting a cigarette from the nub-end of another. 'My daughter never bothers, so he comes in, tells me what she's been up to. Supposed to be a mechanic, probably just a cut-and-shut merchant. Ducks and dives, but he's a decent lad . . .'

A black man, fortyish. Very tall and smartly dressed. A short-sleeved white shirt and dark tie. 'Simons, or Simmonds, or something. Fucking prison visitor. I reckon deep down they're all after some sort of thrill, but he's harmless enough. It's better than talking to some of the beasts in here . . .'

And finally, the most recent visitor. A broad-shouldered man, a little shorter than average. Hair greying at the sides. Sitting very still and staring at the top of Gordon Rooker's bowed head.

Stone laughed, turned from the image of Tom Thorne and looked at Holland. 'Christ, this one really looks like a nasty piece of work.'

Then white noise, until the tape ended and began to rewind.

Holland put away his notebook. Stone leaned back in his chair and turned to Rooker. 'Five real visitors in six months. Looks to me like you've been all but forgotten, mate.'

Rooker stood up. 'That's what I'm hoping . . .'

He turned and walked out of the door. The prison officer calmly stood and followed, picking the dirt from beneath his fingernails with the edge of a laminated ID badge.

'It's gone very quiet around here,' Kitson said.

Thorne had to agree. He knew that she wasn't just talking about the fact that many of the team had taken lunch early and gone over to the Oak. 'I think, as far as the Swiss Cottage thing goes, it's going to get a lot bloody quieter,' he said. 'Things *might* pick up, if somebody makes a decision about Billy Ryan . . .'

Since they'd changed their minds about Gordon Rooker, the joint operation had divided itself, somewhat less than perfectly, into two distinct strands. There was, understandably, a major emphasis being placed on catching the man who'd tried to set light to the girl in Swiss Cottage, but that investigation hadn't turned up anything within the all-important first twenty-four hours. In spite of the time and location of the attack, there wasn't a single useful description. The man's face had been hidden beneath the hood of his anorak, while witness accounts of height and build had varied as much as might be expected, bearing in mind the thick, cold-weather clothing and hunched posture of the attacker.

The girl herself was already back at school, while her mother was cashing in, discussing her daughter's lucky escape and the shocking ineptitude of the police on any TV or radio show that would have her. Her daughter had been selected, as far as anyone could ascertain, completely at random. Another brick wall. It wasn't that the leads weren't going anywhere. There simply weren't any in the first place.

Meanwhile, whether he was connected to what had happened in Swiss Cottage or not, there was still Billy Ryan. While a case against him was being built behind prison walls, there was uncertainty about how those on the ground should proceed.

Nick Tughan was all for the softly-softly approach. There was still the dispute with the Zarif brothers to be dealt with, and Tughan didn't think there was anything to be gained by confronting Ryan directly about Rooker, or about Jessica Clarke. For once, Thorne had been largely a spectator when things had come to a head in the middle of the previous week.

'We're working with Rooker,' Tughan had said. 'We're putting the evidence against Ryan together, but while that's happening there's still the minor matter of a gang war going on. My first responsibility is to make sure there's no more killing.'

Brigstocke had gone in studs-up. 'Come on, Nick. This is hardly about saving innocent lives, is it?'

Tughan reacted angrily. 'Tell me Hanya Izzigil wasn't innocent. Tell me Marcus Moloney wasn't.'

Brigstocke had looked at his feet, then sidelong at Thorne. He hadn't got off to a very good start . . .

'We don't know what Ryan's going to do next.' Tughan had wandered to the window then and looked out across the North Circular. 'He tried to sort Rooker out and he screwed it up. He's going to have to respond to Moloney's murder sooner or later. It's been nearly a fortnight . . .' He turned and held up a hand before Thorne could say anything. 'Even if it *was* him who had Moloney killed, it's going to look bloody funny if he doesn't retaliate, isn't it?'

'Why don't we press him on Moloney, then?' Brigstocke had asked. 'Why don't we press the fucker on a lot of things?'

'This isn't just about Ryan, by the way. Whatever happens, I want the Zarifs as well.'

'Obviously, but we're talking about Billy Ryan, and right now there's a lot of sitting about on our arses. We should be trying to disrupt his operations.'

The commanding view of cars and concrete was obviously too much for Tughan to resist. After a few moments' thinking, or pretending to think, he turned back to the window. 'Let's just wait . . .'

Brigstocke had let out a weary sigh. 'Rooker might not be enough, Nick. I think we should get everything we can.'

There was only ever going to be one side Thorne was on, and he couldn't resist chipping in for very long. 'You were the one who said Rooker was unreliable.' He had taken a step to his left so that he could at least see the side of Tughan's face. 'Don't you think a jury might agree with you? However good the evidence is, Rooker just might not be a credible witness. Ryan's legal team are going to be doing their best to make him look anything *but* credible. It can't hurt to go after something else to back him up, can it?'

Brigstocke had held up his hands. 'I don't see how it can.'

'Let's just remind Ryan that we haven't forgotten him,' Thorne had suggested. 'Stir things up a bit . . .'

Now, days later, sitting in his office with Yvonne Kitson, Thorne was still smiling about what Tughan had said next: 'That's what you're good at, isn't it, Tom? Stirring things up. You're a spoon on legs.'

Kitson spun her chair around to face him. 'Is Brigstocke winning the argument, d'you reckon?'

'Russell gives as good as he gets,' Thorne said, 'but he needs a prod every now and again. I reminded him that *he* was a DCI as well, and he got a bit shirty.' Kitson laughed. 'I think he might just go over Tughan's head . . .'

Thorne looked across at Kitson and suddenly remembered a moment sitting in the same office with her the year before. He'd been watching her eat her lunch, staring as she took her sandwiches from the Tupperware container and unwrapped the foil. He'd thought she had everything under control . . .

Thorne's stomach growled. Karim was bringing him back a cheese roll from the pub. Surely even the Oak's culinary wizard couldn't fuck *that* up.

'What are you doing for lunch, Yvonne . . .?'

Before she could answer, there was a knock, and Holland put his head round the door. He came in, followed by Andy Stone, and together they gave Thorne a rundown on the morning's session at Park Royal.

Thorne looked at the pictures – stills from the tape they'd shown Rooker – laid out on his desk in front of him. 'Well, I think we can safely discount the wife, the daughter and the auntie,' he said.

Holland pulled a face. 'I'm not being funny, but couldn't any one of them have been passing messages between Rooker and somebody else?'

Thorne was not known as the belt-and-braces type. In this case, though, it was better to play it safe. 'Right, sod it,' he said. 'With the exception of the old lady, have a word with all of them.'

As he and Holland were leaving, Stone turned back with a grin. 'Are you sure you don't want us to check the old woman out? She looks pretty dodgy to me.'

Thorne nodded. 'Right. The gap between perception and reality.' He looked innocently at Stone. 'I'm sure some of the great philosophers have got plenty to say on the subject, Andy.'

Holland fought back a laugh as he quickly stepped out of the room. Stone looked blank as he turned and followed him, leaving Thorne unsure as to whether or not he'd cottoned on.

'What was all that about?' Kitson asked.

Thorne was still grinning, highly pleased with himself. 'Just something Holland told me about Andy Stone and his winning ways with the opposite sex.'

'Right. He's a bit of a shagger, isn't he?'

'Apparently. I never seem to meet any, but if some people are to be believed, women are falling over themselves to jump into bed with coppers all of a sudden . . .'

It took Thorne a second to realise what he'd said, and who he'd said it to. When he looked across at Kitson, the colour had already reached her face.

'Sorry, Yvonne . . .'

'Don't be stupid.'

He nodded. Stupid was exactly how he felt. 'How is everything?'

'Oh, you know. Shitty . . .' She smiled and spun her chair towards her desk.

'How're the kids doing?'

The chair came slowly back around again. She obviously wanted to talk. 'The eldest's been playing up a bit at school. It's hard to know whether it's anything to do with what's been happening, but I still manage to convince myself that it is. I try and tell myself not to be so bloody stupid and guilty *all* the time. Then one of them bangs their head, or twists an ankle playing football, and it feels like it's my fault . . .'

The phone on Thorne's desk rang, and Kitson stopped talking.

It was the security officer at the gatehouse. He told Thorne that somebody had driven up to the barrier and was asking to see him.

In point of fact, the woman – so the duty officer had explained – had not come to see him specifically. He just happened to be the highest-ranking member of Team 3 in the building at the time. It was a piece of luck, both good and bad, that Thorne would reflect on for a long time afterwards.

The woman stood as he came down the stairs into the small reception area. Thorne nodded to the officer on the desk and walked across to her. She was in her mid-thirties, he guessed, and tallish, certainly as tall as he was. Her hair was the colour of the cork pin-board on the wall behind his desk, her complexion as pale as the wall itself. She wore smart grey trousers with a matching jacket, and, for no good reason, Thorne wondered if she might be a tax inspector.

'Did you find a parking space?' he asked. On second

thoughts, he never imagined civil servants to be quite so attractive . . .

She nodded and held out a hand, which Thorne took. 'I'm Alison Kelly,' she said.

Perhaps the stunned expression on Thorne's face looked a lot like ignorance. She repeated her name, then explained exactly who she was. 'Jessica Clarke was my best friend. I was the one she got mistaken for.'

Thorne released her hand, slightly embarrassed at having held on to it for so long. She didn't seem overly bothered. 'Sorry, I know who you are. I just wasn't expecting you to walk in, or to . . . I just wasn't expecting you.'

'I probably should have called.'

They looked at each other for a second or two. Thorne could feel the eyes of the duty officer on them.

'Right, then.' *What do you want?* This would perhaps have been a little brusque, but it was all Thorne was thinking. Rather than ask the question, though, he looked around, as if searching for a place where they could talk in private. 'I'm sure I can find us somewhere where we can chat, or whatever.' He pointed to the exit. 'Unless you'd rather go for a walk or something . . .?'

She shook her head. 'It's bloody freezing out there.'

'Spring's not far away . . .'

'Thank God.'

Becke House was an operational HQ, as opposed to a fully functioning station, and, as such, it had no permanent interview suite. There was a small room to the right of the reception desk that was occasionally used in emergencies, or to store booze whenever a party was thrown. A table and chairs, a couple of rickety cupboards. Thorne opened the door, checked that the room was unoccupied and beckoned Alison Kelly inside.

'I'll see if I can organise some tea,' he said.

She moved past him and sat down, then began speaking before he'd closed the door. 'Here's what I know,' she said. Her voice was deep and unaccented. Just the right side of posh. 'You're not getting anywhere trying to find the man who squirted lighter fluid all over that girl in Swiss Cottage ten days ago.' She paused.

Thorne walked across to the table and sat down. 'I'm not quite sure what you're expecting me to say to that . . .'

'Three days before *that* happened, somebody tried to kill the man who's in prison for burning Jess, by stabbing him in the gut with a sharpened paintbrush. It's pretty obvious that there's a connection. Something's going on.'

'Do you mind me asking how you know all these things?'

She gave a small shake of her head. More as if she couldn't be bothered to answer than as if she was actually refusing. Then she continued to demonstrate just how much she *did* know. 'Even if you weren't aware that the man who did the stabbing owed Billy Ryan a load of money, you'd have to be an idiot not to work out who was behind it.' She tucked a few loose strands of hair behind her ear. 'Ryan was *clearly* responsible.'

'Clearly,' echoed Thorne.

'He wanted Rooker killed for the obvious reasons.'

The obvious reasons. Thorne was relieved to discover that she didn't know *absolutely* everything . . .

'Though why he should choose now to get revenge for what Rooker did twenty years ago is anybody's guess.'

Thorne was disturbed and excited by the bizarre and abrupt conversation. He felt oddly afraid of this woman. Her attitude fascinated him, and pissed him off.

'You said, "the man who's in prison for burning Jess". That's a bit odd, don't you think? You didn't say, "the man who burned Jess". It just seems a strange way of putting it.'

She looked blankly at him.

'Have you got any reason to think that Gordon Rooker *isn't* the man responsible?' Thorne asked.

She couldn't conceal the half smile. 'There *is* something going on, isn't there?'

Thorne felt pretty sure he'd just walked into an elaborate verbal trap. There was clearly even more going on behind Alison Kelly's green eyes than he'd begun to suspect.

Now she wasn't even trying to hide the smile. 'That's the other thing I know,' she said. 'That you're not going to tell me anything.'

The time for politeness had long since passed. 'What is it you want, Miss Kelly?' Thorne immediately saw the front for what it was, but only because he noticed it crack and slip a little: there was a softening around the jaw, and in the set of her shoulders.

'You aren't the only one who wasn't expecting me to walk in here,' she said. 'I needed a bloody big glass of wine before I drove up. I've been sitting in the pub opposite, surrounded by coppers, getting some Dutch courage.' The smile suddenly seemed nervous. The voice had lost any pretence at confidence or authority.

'I want to know what that girl did,' she said. 'What her *friends* did at that bus stop that saved her. I want to know what it was that alerted them. What it was that *we* didn't see, that we didn't do.'

'I really don't think there's much point . . .'

'The first thing I knew was when Jess ran at me, and I stepped out of the way. Do you understand that? All I could do was watch it, then.' Her voice was barely above a murmur, but it seemed to echo off the shiny white walls. 'I heard the crackle when it reached her hair. Then I smelled it. Have you ever smelled it? I mean, have you ever smelled anything *like* that?

'I wasn't actually sick. I felt like I was going to, like I was going to heave, but I didn't. Not then. Now, just the thought of it . . . just the smell of a match being struck . . .'

She looked, and sounded, disorientated. She was an adult in a playground. A child in a police station.

'That could have been my hair. *Should* have been my hair . . .'

Thorne opened his mouth, but nothing came quickly enough.

'I want to know why Jess wasn't all right, like that other girl was. Why wasn't she? I want you to tell me what we could have done to save her.'

Thorne turned *Eastenders* up just enough to drown out the noise of Hendricks singing in the bathroom. He pulled Elvis on to his lap, flicked through the sports pages of the *Standard* folded across the arm of the sofa. He couldn't stop thinking about what Alison Kelly had said. He wasn't the only one who couldn't cope with ignorance . . .

Alison Kelly's need for certainty sprang from something a little deeper seated than his own, though. There'd been plenty of things he would have done differently, given half a chance, but not too many bad things for which he felt *responsible*. She'd had twenty years of blame and guilt. Each had fed off – yet perversely fattened – the other, until they'd become the twin parasites that defined her.

Thorne asked himself how much better off Alison Kelly really was, than the girl who'd been mistaken for her.

Elvis jumped away, grumbling, as Thorne stood up and walked across to the front door. He opened his bag and took out the small black book that had remained unopened since Ian Clarke had handed it to him.

The dirge from the bathroom seemed, thankfully, to have abated. Thorne carried the diary back across to the sofa. He picked up the remote and muted the volume of the TV as he sat down again.

When the pins and needles started, Chamberlain moved from the edge of the bath to the toilet seat. She turned her head so that she couldn't see herself in the mirror. It was half an hour since she'd come upstairs, and she wondered how much longer she was going to have to sit there before she stopped feeling like a silly old woman.

She'd spent the weekend going over the cold case she was supposed to be working on for AMRU: a bookmaker, stabbed to death in a pub car park in 1993. A dead man and a family who deserved justice as much as anybody else, but Chamberlain was in no fit state to help them get it.

She was finding it hard to care about anything . . . about anything else . . .

The Jessica Clarke case had been one she'd been close to. As close as she had ever been to any case.

And she'd got it wrong.

Three nights earlier, on the last train home after the evening round at Tom Thorne's, she'd almost convinced herself that she was being stupid. What could she have done differently? Rooker had confessed, for heaven's sake. There was no earthly reason why they should ever have looked for anyone else . . .

Sitting on that all-but-deserted train, she'd *almost* convinced herself, but wrong was wrong, and it still hurt. She felt the pain of professional failure, and another, much worse pain, that comes from knowing you've let down someone very important.

Another train had begun rushing past, and she'd turned to watch. Her reflection had danced across the windows of the train as it flashed by. After it had gone, she'd stared at her face, floating in the darkness on the other side of the glass, and noticed that she was crying.

The most painful thing, of course, was feeling useless. Being surplus to requirements. It was knowing that she'd got it wrong, and that she would play no part in putting it right again.

She'd heard the swish of the carriage door as it slid back, and watched the man moving towards her, reflected in the window. Watched as he'd weaved slowly back towards his seat with a bag from the buffet. Watched as he'd stopped at her table . . .

'Are you all right, love?'

In the bathroom, Chamberlain raised her head as she heard footsteps on the stairs. They stopped, and she heard Jack call out her name.

There'd been a few days, a couple of weeks earlier, when

she'd begun to feel like a copper again; when she went in with Thorne to see Gordon Rooker; when the two of them had confronted Billy Ryan outside his arcade. Then, once they'd begun to deal with Rooker, she'd been eased gently aside, and it had felt as bad as when she'd handed in her warrant card seven years before. It was only to be expected, of course. Friday night round at the flat in Kentish Town – Thorne showing her the CCTV footage – had been a favour and nothing else. She knew that there weren't likely to be any more . . .

She dropped slowly to her knees and reached into the cupboard under the sink for the cleanser and a cloth.

If anybody else was going to sort things out for Jessica Clarke, she'd be happy for it to be Tom Thorne. But she didn't want *anybody else* to do it . . .

The footsteps on the stairs started again, and grew closer. She held the dry cloth under the tap for a few seconds, told herself to start worrying about dead bookies and stop being so bloody ridiculous.

The knock came, softly, as she squeezed a thick line of pale yellow cleanser around the rim of the bath.

'Are you all right, love?'

14 March 1986

Taking over a year out of school is really starting to cause a few problems. Now that Ali and Manda and the rest have moved up, I'm stuck with people who are younger than me that I didn't really know before. I can talk to most of the girls in my own year about everything. About the ops and the grafts and all the rest of it. But I only see them in the playground at lunchtime, and some of them are already a bit distant because they're one year higher up the school and are acting like they're one year older or something.

The girls in my class are trying too hard. I think that's basically the problem. I know bloody well they've been spoken to about what to say and what not to say. I also happen to know that someone from the hospital came to the school to see the teachers the week before I came back, and some of them are better at appearing natural about it than others.

My new class teacher is pretty cool, though.

There are a <u>couple</u> of girls I think are OK in the new class, but a lot of the time I can't stand most of them. Maybe I'm being unfair because I know it's a bit awkward. I remember feeling a bit strange around a girl in junior school who had a harelip. I can remember trying <u>not</u> to ignore her, then gabbling when I spoke to her and going red. Actually, with some of the girls it's really hard to tell the difference between fear and shyness. There's a few, though, who are just going way over the top in trying to be my new best friend and a couple are just ignorant bitches.

Maybe things will settle down a bit in time.

Shit Moment of the Day

Hearing it go quiet when I took my shirt off before PE.

Magic Moment of the Day.

Mum thinking she was being subtle when an advert for the Nightmare on Elm Street *video came on, and she stood in front of the TV so I wouldn't see Freddy Krueger's face.*

FOURTEEN

The elegant row of substantial Victorian houses would not have been out of place in Holland Park or Notting Hill, when, in point of fact, it was part of a conservation area in the middle of Finchley. The sunlight could easily have belonged to a warm August day, but the temperature was in single figures, and the first day of spring was still a fortnight away. The man on the green enjoying the afternoon with his dog might have been a pillar of the community. As it was, he was anything but.

Walking towards him, watching him smile as the Jack Russell ran and slid and jumped at his knees, Thorne doubted that Billy Ryan enjoyed as uncomplicated and loving a relationship with any other living creature.

'I'm surprised,' Thorne said. 'I'd've thought a Rottweiler or a Dobermann. Maybe a pit-bull . . .'

Ryan didn't look overly concerned to see him. 'I've got nothing to prove. I don't have an undersized cock to compensate for. And I like small dogs.'

Thorne watched Ryan shake his head and wave to someone behind him. He turned to see his friend the receptionist climbing *back* into a Jeep parked at the other side of the green. Thorne gave the man a jaunty salute but got nothing very friendly back.

'Afternoon off, Mr Ryan?'

'Perk of being the boss.' He smiled, adjusting the frames of his lightly tinted sunglasses. 'I reckon I've earned it.'

'Right . . .'

Ryan bent to take a slobber-covered ball from the dog, who growled and wrestled until it was torn from his mouth. Ryan faked throwing the ball in one direction, then threw it in the other. Once the dog had started chasing it, Ryan walked slowly after him.

Thorne moved alongside him, nodding towards the car. 'Is he all you've got?'

'How d'you mean?'

'I'm sure he's tooled up and all that, but even so. Surely you must think you're a target *now*, Billy.'

Ryan was wearing a long black cashmere coat over a red wool scarf. He pulled the scarf a little tighter to his neck. 'Now?' he said.

'After Moloney.'

Ryan gave him a sideways look, but turned away again before Thorne could even begin to read anything into it. 'That was a shame,' he said.

'A shame how he died? A shame that he was killed? Or a shame that he was a copper?'

'Pick one.'

'You didn't send a wreath,' Thorne said. Moloney had been buried quietly the weekend before. His wife had refused the full Police Service funeral that had been offered.

Ryan shrugged, expressionless. 'Shitty way to go, I'll grant you. Not exactly a hero's death. But he did rather put himself in the firing line, wouldn't you say?'

'Who did the firing, do you reckon?'

'I'm not doing your job for you . . .'

The dog had returned with the ball. Ryan hurled it away again and carried on walking.

'Puts you in a tricky position though,' Thorne said. 'There's obviously a need to strike back, or at least be seen to strike back . . .'

'Strike back against who?'

'. . .when, actually, retaliation would be pretty bloody ironic.'

'Let's pretend you're not talking bollocks for a second.'

'Yes, let's.'

'Why would it be ironic?' The soft brogue had hardened suddenly. The end of the word bitten off and spat, as Ryan stopped and turned.

Reflected in the lenses of Ryan's aviators, Thorne could see the expanse of green at his back, and the tiny figure of the dog racing towards them. *Because it was you who had him killed, you murdering prick.* 'Because he was a police officer, obviously,' Thorne said.

This time, Ryan snatched the ball from the dog and stuffed it into his pocket. The terrier yapped a couple of times and then wandered off, its nose to the ground. He wasn't the only one on the scent of something.

'You didn't answer my question,' Thorne said.

'Which one?'

'About you being a target for the Zarif brothers.'

'The *who* brothers . . .?'

'You seem very relaxed, which is strange, considering you were bleating about protection the other day.'

'I've never bleated in my fucking life, and I was talking about my family.'

'My mistake . . .'

Ryan took off his sunglasses. As the sun had certainly not gone anywhere, Thorne could only assume that it was some kind of gesture. Maybe Ryan wanted Thorne to see his eyes.

'You don't get to the top in business by walking away when that business is threatened. You stand your ground or somebody takes it.'

'Kevin Kelly walked away,' Thorne said.

The sunglasses went back on. 'Before your time, son. You know nothing about it . . .'

Thorne smiled. 'I know people who were there.'

'Aye, right, course you do. Where *is* Miss Marple today, anyway?'

'Kevin Kelly walked away and handed the whole she-bang over to you. Pretty lucky, considering you hadn't done much to deserve it. The way I understand it, there were others in the firm who might have had a greater claim. Faces who'd done a bit of time, got a decent reputation, you know? Still, it's up to the boss, and when he decides he's had enough, he gives it all to you. You must have done some serious brown-nosing to get the nod, Billy . . .'

Ryan said nothing. The sun highlighted the sheen of lacquer on his hair.

'So, Kevin Kelly buggers off to the country, thankful that *his* little girl isn't the one who looks like the Phantom of the Opera, and the Kelly family becomes the Ryan family.'

'The old woman's memory must be going,' Ryan said. 'I remember different . . .'

'What happened at that school, terrible as it was, *disgusting* as it was . . . did you a bit of a favour, I'd say.'

Somewhere in the trees at the edge of the green, a dog was barking, but Ryan didn't take his eyes from Thorne. He nodded knowingly. 'I wondered when you were going to bring up Gordon Rooker again.'

Thorne looked equally knowing. 'I didn't,' Thorne said.

He didn't need to see Ryan's eyes to know that they had darkened. Ryan began walking towards the trees, quicker this time.

Thorne stayed a pace or two behind, raising his voice as he followed: 'I don't know whether you heard what happened to Mr Rooker. You know, seeing as you mention him. He was attacked in prison apparently. Stabbed in the stomach. While he was *painting*, of all things. He's all right now, in case you were worried. He's *safe* now . . .'

Ryan stopped. He was trying to smile, but his lips were pursed, his teeth well out of sight. 'Is this official?'

Thorne considered the question. He noticed that Ryan was shuffling his feet and remembered that he'd done the same thing outside the arcade, waiting for his car. 'Well, I'm being *paid* for it . . .'

'Because there's really no fucking point to it, is there? Whatever it is you're expecting me to say, even if I say it, it won't get you anywhere. Not unless you're recording it and, to be honest, mate, even then, there are people getting paid by *me* who make sure that kind of shit doesn't stand up. So, I think we're done chatting . . .'

'I'm not recording anything,' Thorne said. 'Really, I'm

just interested in where you stand on a few issues, and I'm trying to be upfront about it.' He grinned, pushing his hands deep into the pockets of his leather jacket. 'Who can be arsed going round the houses? The term we use is "being lawfully audacious".'

'The term *I* use is "pushing your fucking luck".'

Ryan stuck two fingers in his mouth, and whistled as he marched off towards the car. Thorne wasn't sure whether he was whistling for his driver or for his dog.

Either way, both came running.

Outside, it was cold and dark, and the traffic on the North End Road was nose to tail. Inside the car, Thorne was warm, and in a remarkably good mood.

The rest of the day, back at Becke House, had gone pretty well, notably because Tughan and the rest of the Projects Team were spending it over at Barkingside. Thorne had begun scaling a mountain of paperwork. He'd got up to speed on some of the cases that had been nudged on to the back burner over the past few weeks.

He had also caught up on the investigation Holland and Stone had been making into the visitors on the Park Royal security tape.

'Sod all of any significance,' Holland had said. 'The wife and the daughter are what you'd expect: neither of them's Mother Teresa, but I think they're harmless enough. Philip Simmonds, the prison visitor, is definitely a bit spooky, but most of those types are, if you ask me . . .'

Stone had nodded, added his own observations: 'Wayne Brookhouse, the youngest daughter's ex-boyfriend, is a bit dodgy. No less than you'd expect from a mate of Rooker's. Nothing worse than that, though. Tony Sollinger's dead. Bowel cancer, three weeks ago.' He'd looked up from his scribbled notes. 'How did it go with Ryan, Guv?'

Thorne had been pleased with his afternoon stroll in Finchley, and so too was Brigstocke, having finally succeeded in persuading Tughan that they should at least be letting Billy Ryan know that they were still around. It was predictable that Tughan had needed talking into a slightly more forceful approach. It was also ironic, as in theory that was just what the Projects Team was supposed to have. It was the team's bad luck that its DCI thought 'pro-active' was something you took for constipation.

As it happened, most of the teams that made up the Serious and Organised Crime Unit were pro-active to some degree. The Flying Squad – TV's Sweeney – were the most well known. Using carefully nurtured intelligence sources, they could occasionally prevent armed robberies from taking place, or even catch the villains with the guns in their hands – *going across the pavement* – which was the most highly prized result of all.

For Thorne, and others on murder squads, the situation was slightly different. Those who hunted killers could only ever be *re*active. You could find out where a robbery was going to take place or which security van might be getting blagged, but you never knew where a body was going to turn up. Usually, of course, you never knew *when*, either, but, as things stood, Thorne could hazard a guess that one or more would be turning up sooner rather than later . . .

He was coming down through Belsize Park, past the overpriced delicatessens and organic greengrocers', when he suddenly decided that he was going to have an early dinner. He took a left just before Chalk Farm tube station, then cut across to Camden and pointed the BMW towards the Seven Sisters Road. He called Hendricks as he was approaching Manor House and told him that he would be eating out.

The food was delicious, and the size of the portions decidedly non-nouvelle . . .

Arkan Zarif hovered at the table, watching as Thorne took the first mouthful of his main course. Thorne had chosen a dish he'd never seen before – spiced lamb meatballs wrapped in a layer of potato. He chewed, nodding enthusiastically, and the old man beamed with delight. 'I picked out the meat,' he said. 'Of course, I cooked it also, but picking out the meat is the important part.' He watched for a few moments more, his mouth gaping, smiling as another forkful went in. 'OK, I leave you to enjoy your dinner . . .'

Thorne swallowed and pointed to the seat opposite. 'No, please. Join me. It's not often you get a chance to eat with the chef.'

Zarif nodded. 'I drink a glass of scotch with you.' He turned and spoke in Turkish to his daughter, who stood, scowling, behind the counter. She looked at Thorne, who smiled sweetly back. The old man frowned as he sat down and leaned across to whisper. 'Sema is permanently miserable,' he said. 'It is not your fault.'

Thorne watched her pouring a glass of Johnny Walker

for her father, and topping it up with mineral water from a plastic bottle. 'Are you sure? I do tend to have that effect on women.'

Zarif had a wheezy laugh. He repeatedly slapped a huge hand against his chest until it had died away.

Sema brought the drink to the table, then moved back behind the counter without a word.

'*Serefé.*' Zarif held up his glass.

Thorne was drinking beer. He raised his bottle of Efes.

'It means "to our honour".'

'To our honour,' Thorne said, as the bottle touched the glass.

In the minute or so of silence that followed, Thorne devoured most of what was on his plate. He sliced off huge chunks of the meatball, spooned up the rice, washed it down with the cold beer.

Zarif took small sips of his Scotch and water. 'You like the lady's thigh,' he said.

Thorne looked up, chewing. He grunted his confusion.

'This dish is called *kadinbudbu*. This means "lady's thigh". So, you like the lady's thigh. I joke that if you don't enjoy the *kadinbudbu*, then maybe you don't like ladies. You see?' The wheezy laugh erupted again.

'What about vegetarians?' Thorne asked.

Zarif picked up the menu, gave him a look like *that* just proved the joke was true. 'All the dishes on the menu mean something. Turkish names always have meaning. What was your starter?'

'The fried aubergine . . .'

Zarif pointed to the dish on the menu. '*Imam bayildi*. This means "the priest fainted". You see? When this dish

202

was given to the priest, he enjoyed it so much that he fainted from pleasure.'

'I'm sorry I didn't faint,' Thorne said, 'but it was very good . . .'

'*Hunkar begendi.*' Zarif stabbed at the menu again. 'This is a dish I make very well. Diced lamb in white sauce. This means "the Emperor loved it".'

'Did he love it as much as the priest?'

Zarif didn't get the joke. 'All names mean something, but some have bad translations. Funny translations, you see? We have English customers who ask why the names are always in Turkish. I tell them if they were in English, my menu would have dishes called *rubbish kebab* and *stuffed prostitute.*'

Thorne laughed.

'No, really this would put people off . . .'

'Only some people,' Thorne said. 'Others might come in specially.'

Zarif laughed loudly, slapping his chest again, the drink spilling over the edge of his glass.

Thorne suddenly thought about his father. He thought about how much he would have enjoyed this conversation. He pictured him laughing, scribbling down the names of the dishes . . .

'What about people's names?' Thorne said. 'Do they always mean something?'

Zarif nodded. 'Of course.'

Thorne had finished eating and pushed away his plate. 'What does Zarif mean?'

The old man thought for a few seconds. 'Zarif is . . . "delicate".'

Thorne blinked and saw a breath of blood across Anaglypta wallpaper. The body of Mickey Clayton bent over a kitchen chair. Gashes across his back . . .

'Delicate?' he asked.

Zarif nodded again. He waved to get his daughter's attention, and, when he had it, spoke quickly to her in Turkish. The scowl grew more pronounced as she moved across to a small refrigerated cabinet to one side of the counter.

'Now, my first name, Arkan? This is the best joke of all. It has two meanings, depending on where you are, how you say it. It means "noble blood" or "honest blood". This sounds nice, you see? But it also means "your backside". It means "arse".'

Thorne laughed, swilling the last of the beer around in the bottle. 'My name means different things to different people as well.'

'Right.' Zarif waved his fingers in the air, searching for the words. 'A thorn is small, spiky . . .'

'Irritating.' Thorne drained the bottle. 'And it can be difficult to get rid of . . .'

Sema arrived and put down a dish in front of Thorne. He looked at Zarif for explanation.

'That is *sutlac*. On the house . . .'

It was a simple rice pudding – set thick, creamy and heavily flavoured with cinnamon.

'This is gorgeous,' Thorne said.

'Thank you . . .'

Thorne saw the old man's expression change the second he heard the door open. He half turned and from the corner of his eye saw two men enter. The look on Sema's face told him that the two Zarif brothers he had yet to meet – Memet and Tan – had popped in to introduce themselves.

Arkan Zarif stood and walked over to the counter, where the men took it in turn to lean across and kiss their sister. They began talking in Turkish to their father. Thorne watched them while pretending to look around. He stared at the ornate arrangements of tiles, mounted and hanging on the walls next to Health and Safety certificates in cheap clip-frames.

Both brothers, unlike Hassan and their father, had very little hair. Memet, who Thorne put somewhere in his early forties, had a receding hairline and had chosen to wear what little he had left very short. He also had a goatee, thicker than Thorne's, but also more clearly defined, and like Thorne's, failing to hide a double chin. Tan, younger by maybe fifteen years, was shorter, and whip-thin. He wasn't losing his hair but had shaved it anyway – aping his eldest brother, Thorne guessed. He too had facial hair, but it was little more than a pencil-line running along his top lip and around the edge of his chin, in the style George Michael had worn for a while until someone pointed out that it looked ridiculous. Tan clearly fancied himself as something of a hard man and stared across at Thorne while Memet did all the talking.

Knowing that Thorne wouldn't understand, Memet Zarif made no attempt to lower his voice as he spoke to his father. He smiled a lot and patted the old man's shoulder, but Thorne could hear a seriousness in the voice.

At the mention of his name Thorne glanced up. He remembered what Carol Chamberlain had said when she'd been talking about Billy Ryan. About these people knowing as much about you as you did about them. Knowing more . . . Thorne returned Tan's thousand-yard stare for a second or two before going back to his pudding.

It was disconcerting, *exciting* even, to think that one of these men – Thorne was putting his money on Memet Zarif – had probably given the order to have Mickey Clayton and the others executed. If he, or his brothers, thought that the law was going to go easier on them because they hadn't wielded the gun or the knife themselves, they hadn't learned as much as Thorne presumed they had. And, though Thorne had his own ideas, the received wisdom was that the Zarif brothers were also responsible for the death of DS Marcus Moloney. Whatever he thought of Nick Tughan, Thorne knew that he would make Memet, Hassan and Tan pay for that.

When Thorne looked up from his *sutlac* again, Memet and Tan were at the table.

'What is it you want?' Memet Zarif asked.

Thorne took another mouthful, then loaded his spoon again. When he answered the question, it was as if he'd just that second remembered he'd been asked it. 'I *wanted* some dinner, which I'm actually still having, so maybe you should think about being polite and leaving me in peace to finish it. If you want me to get as annoyed as I *should* be and cause a scene in your father's restaurant – you know, maybe turn over a table or two – I suggest you carry on with the attitude.' He turned to the younger brother. 'And if that look is supposed to be intimidating, you'd better get a new manual, son. You just look like a retard . . .' Thorne turned away before the two men had any chance to react.

He leaned round them, caught their sister's eye, and scribbled in the air – the universally accepted gesture when asking for the bill.

Memet and Tan walked to a table in the corner, where they were quickly joined by another man, who came scuttling from the back of the room. Sema brought them coffee and biscuits dusted with sugar. They lit cigarettes and spoke a mixture of Turkish and English in hushed voices.

Arkan Zarif carried Thorne's bill across on a plate. 'You will stay for some coffee . . .?'

Thorne took a piece of Turkish delight from the plate and examined the bill. 'No, thank you. Time to go, I think.' He dug around in his wallet for some cash.

Zarif looked towards the table in the corner, then back to Thorne. 'My sons are suspicious of the police. They have bad tempers, I know that, but they stay out of trouble.'

Thorne chewed the sweet, and decided that the old man's thinking was only marginally less divorced from reality than that of his own father. He dropped a ten and a five on to the plate. 'Why the suspicion of the police?' he said.

Zarif looked uncomfortable. 'Back in Turkey, there were some problems. Nothing serious. Memet was a little wild sometimes . . .'

'Is that why you left and came here?'

Zarif waved his hands emphatically. 'No. We came for simple reasons. All Turkish people want is bread and work. We came to this country for bread and work.'

Thorne stood and picked up his jacket. He thanked the old man, praised the food, then walked towards the door, thinking that you could work for bread, or you could just take somebody else's . . .

Common sense told his feet to keep on walking past the table in the corner, but another part of his brain was still thinking about names.

Irritating. Difficult to get rid of . . .

The three men at the table fell silent and looked at him. The blue-grey smoke from their cigarettes curled up towards the ceiling, floating around the hanging lamps like the manifestation of a dozen genies.

Thorne pointed upwards at the swirls and strands of smoke, then leaned down to address Memet Zarif. 'If I was you, I should start making wishes . . .'

He was still smiling as he made his way back to the car, taking out his mobile and dialling the number as he walked.

'Dad? It's me. Listen, I've got a great one for you. Actually, we can do a whole list, if you like, but I think you should do this one as a trivia question first. Right, have you got a pen? OK, what sort of . . . No, make that: *where would you be* if you ordered a stuffed prostitute?'

FIFTEEN

Rooker had been moved earlier that week to HMP Salisbury, one of a handful of prisons in the country with a protected witness wing. He'd pronounced himself delighted with the move. Now he was rattling around with only half a dozen other cons for company and not a paint-brush in sight.

'How did Billy Ryan first approach you?' Thorne asked. 'How was the idea of killing Alison Kelly first brought up?'

The purpose-built interview suite had freshly decorated pale yellow walls, but was still a lot less glamorous than it sounded. Whoever had designed and equipped the place hadn't put in a long day: a table, chairs, recording equipment, an ashtray . . .

Rooker cleared his throat. 'I'd met Ryan a couple of times . . .'

'Like when you got the original contract on Kevin Kelly?'

'I'm not talking about that.'

'Ryan hired you for that as well, though, didn't he?'

'I thought we'd got past this . . .'

'It's amazing he came back to you after you'd messed that one up.'

Rooker sat back in his chair and folded his arms. He looked like a sulky kid.

'Listen,' Thorne said. 'This is going to get brought up in court. Ryan's brief is going to be all over you, doing as much as he can to discredit your statement. You're not exactly a model citizen, are you?'

Rooker leaned forward slowly, pulled his tobacco tin across the table and began to roll up. He was a different character from the one Thorne had first met at Park Royal a month before. It was clear that he had still not fully recovered from the stabbing, but also that his initial cockiness was far from being the whole story. Thorne knew very well that survival in prison was all about front. All about what others *thought* you were. Pretence could be every bit as useful as a phonecard or a stolen chisel.

'The point is that I was perfect,' Rooker said. 'The word was that I *had* been the one hired to do Kevin Kelly the year before . . .'

'Right. The word.'

'Like I said, that's what everyone *thought*. Which made me the ideal choice for Billy Ryan when he decided to do the daughter.'

'The perfect cover.'

'Exactly.'

Rooker's cigarette was already alight. Thorne watched the smoke rise, remembering the words he'd spoken to Memet Zarif a week before, envious now, as he had been then. As he was around anyone who still had the joy of smoking. Some of Thorne's more prosaic dreams were filled with smoke-rings and nicotine and the glorious tightening in the chest as it hits . . .

'So, how did Ryan make the approach? He couldn't risk being seen with you.'

'Not straight away, no. It was all arranged by a third party. A face called Harry Little. He's dead now . . .'

'In suspicious circumstances?'

'Not as far as I know. He was in his late fifties back then, I think.'

'Go on . . .'

'We met in a pub in Camden. It might have been the Dublin Castle, I can't remember. Anyway, Harry was all over me. Very friendly. We'd never been particularly matey, so I knew he was after something, and I knew it was something heavy because he had a reputation, you know? He starts talking about Billy Ryan, going round the houses with it. I mean, we're getting through a fair few pints, know what I mean? Eventually, he says that Billy wants a meet, and that he'd be in touch with when and where and what have you, and it was obvious even then that this was something a bit special.' He saw enough of a change in Thorne's face to qualify what he'd said. 'Special as in *different*, you know? From the normal run of things.'

Thorne nodded. *The normal run of things*. Putting a bullet in the back of somebody's head, or throwing them out of a window, or beating them to death . . .

'Where did the meet with Ryan take place?'

Rooker stubbed out his fag and pushed his chair back. 'Listen, can we take a quick break? I really need to have a piss . . .'

While Rooker was gone, Thorne stood and stretched his legs. He walked to the far wall, leaned against it and closed his eyes. The faces shifted around in his mind, jockeying for position: Billy Ryan, Memet Zarif, Marcus Moloney, Ian Clarke, Carol Chamberlain. The dead faces of Muslum and Hanya Izzigil. The face of their son, Yusuf.

The two faces of Jessica Clarke . . .

A prison officer opened the door and ushered Rooker back into the room. Thorne rejoined him at the table.

'Have you got any children, Mr Thorne?'

'No.'

Rooker sat and shrugged, as though whatever he was going to say was no longer relevant, or would not make any sense.

Thorne was curious, but keener still to crack on. To get out. He hit the red button on the twin-cassette recorder that was secured to the wall. 'Interview commencing again at . . . eleven forty-five a.m.' He looked at Rooker. The lid was already off the tobacco tin again. 'Tell me what happened when you met with Billy Ryan.'

'It was a track through Epping Forest, up near Loughton. I just got the call from Harry Little one night and drove up there . . .'

'There were just the two of you?'

Rooker nodded. 'We sat in Ryan's car and he told me what he wanted.'

'He told you that he wanted you to kill Kevin Kelly's daughter, Alison.'

Rooker looked directly into Thorne's eyes. He knew this was the important stuff. 'Yes, he did.'

'What did you think?'

Rooker seemed confused.

'Well, like you said, this was different from the normal run of things.'

'Everybody knew that Ryan was a bit mental . . .'

'But still, a *child*?'

'He wanted a *war*. He wanted to do something that would send the whole fucking lot spinning out of control, you know?'

Thorne blinked and remembered Ryan's face close to his own, the cheeks almost as red as his scarf. The eyes glassy. The faintest quiver around the small mouth as he spoke: '*I think we're done chatting . . .*'

'Was it Ryan's idea?' he asked. 'The burning?'

'Christ, yes.' Rooker ran a hand through his hair, sending a shower of tiny white flakes floating down to the table. 'He thought that since it was something I'd done before, I might be more comfortable with it.'

'*Comfortable?*'

'I told you. He was mental . . .'

'It was something you were known for, though? The fire? The lighter fluid? So, when Ryan suggested it as a method, didn't you hear any alarm bells?'

'What?' Rooker grinned. 'Fire-alarm bells, you mean?'

Thorne's face was blank. 'Look at me, Gordon. I'm pissing myself.'

'Sorry . . .'

'Weren't you even a little bit suspicious?'

Rooker took a long drag, then another, held the smoke in.

'Come on, it was obviously going to point to you, wasn't it? Are you seriously telling me that while you were busy

213

thinking how mental Ryan was, you didn't for one moment think that he might be planning to set you up?'

The smoke drifted out on a noisy sigh. 'Later I did. I realised afterwards, after it had happened and I was being fingered for it anyway. Yeah, *then* it was fucking obvious, and I knew I'd been stupid, but it was a bit late. I was in the frame and Ryan had his excuse to come after me. By then, of course, I knew damn well that he really needed me out of the way to shut me up.'

'So, what did you think when he asked you?'

'I thought, No fucking way.'

'Because it was risky?'

'Because it was a fucking kid.'

Thorne leaned towards the recorder. 'Mr Rooker slams his hand on the table. For emphasis.' He flashed Rooker an exaggerated smile. 'I'm saying that just in case anybody thinks that was the noise of me hitting you with a chair or something . . .'

Rooker grunted.

'So, what happened when you turned Ryan down?'

'He wasn't happy . . .'

'What did he say?'

'He said that he'd find somebody else to do the job. I remember him saying exactly that when I got out of his car just before he drove away: "There's always somebody else . . ."'

And Thorne could picture Ryan saying it. He could picture Ryan's face as he said it, and he felt something tighten in his stomach, because Ryan would have known that it was true. Bitter experience had taught Thorne that it was one of the few things that you could rely on. There's always somebody else willing to do what another won't. Something darker and more depraved. Something inexplicable. Unimaginable . . .

Thorne announced, for the tape, that he was formally suspending the interview.

Then he punched the red button.

'We'll carry on after lunch,' he said.

Thorne was just shy of Newbury when he turned off the M4 and pulled slowly into the car park at Chieveley Services. A car flashed its lights as he approached and Thorne parked the BMW next to it. Holland got out of a car-pool Rover, leaned against it and waited for Thorne to join him.

Thorne had received the call just after seven on the M3 as he was heading home from Salisbury. He'd turned off at the next services to pick up a sandwich and consult the road atlas. The traffic had been heavy on the A road that had taken him across to the M4, and even worse for the journey back west.

Holland offered Thorne a bulky torch. Thorne took one look at it and plumped instead for the Maglite he kept in his boot, taking his gloves out at the same time. Torches sweeping the ground ahead of them, they began to walk towards the farthest corner of the car park.

'How did we get hold of this so quickly?' Thorne asked.

'Swift and harmonious cooperation between ourselves and the lovely lads from Thames Valley.' Holland smiled at the incredulous look on Thorne's face. 'I know, hard to believe. They found the lorry this morning, ran the number plate and at the end of a very long paper-trail – half a dozen different companies – whose name should pop up? A flag on their computer system alerts the Thames Valley lot, tells them it's a name we're very interested in, and Bob's your uncle . . .'

'What, they just called us?'

'Amazing, isn't it, forces working so well together? Someone should get hold of Mulder and Scully . . .'

The lorry stood in almost total blackness. The light from the restaurant and shopping complex five hundred yards away died just short of it, leaving the two Thames Valley woodentops standing watch as little more than dark shapes. As Thorne and Holland got nearer, their torches picked out the reflective bands on the officers' uniforms, and the fence of fluttering blue crime tape that had been erected around the vehicle.

Pleasantries were exchanged with the two officers, who gratefully accepted the offer to go inside and get themselves some tea. Thorne and Holland walked slowly around the outside of the truck.

It was a white Mercedes cab, fitted with what looked like a twenty-five, or thirty-foot solid-sided body. Dirty, dark green. No company logo or markings of any sort.

Thorne climbed up to the passenger door, gingerly took hold of a handle.

'I think the Thames Valley boys have been over a lot of it already,' Holland said.

Thorne pulled open the door. 'Well, I hope they were careful. We'll need to get SOCO down here.'

'They're on their way . . .'

Thorne shone his torch around the cab's interior. There were papers scattered across the seats and in the footwells.

Whoever had gone through it hadn't been too careful. It was unclear whether that was the fault of the officers who had discovered the abandoned vehicle, or those responsible for hijacking and then dumping it.

'What was it carrying?' Thorne asked, jumping down from the cab. 'What was it *supposed* to be carrying?'

'Well, the manifest they found in the cab says DVD players. Full load, top of the range, well worth nicking.'

'Well, whatever was in there, I wouldn't bet against Billy Ryan already having his hands on it. Looks like he's decided to hit the Zarifs where it's really going to hurt them. What about the driver?'

'No sign. Not so much as a Yorkie bar . . .'

'What d'you reckon?'

'Your guess is as good as mine,' Holland said. 'Maybe the hijackers took him . . .'

Thorne was on his knees, shining his torch underneath the truck. Oil, dirt and nothing else. 'Or maybe they just beat the shit out of him and he's gone running back to the Zarif brothers. Either way, I don't fancy his chances.'

A couple of teenage lads who'd obviously seen the torchbeams came wandering down from the direction of the restaurant carrying burgers and Cokes. Thorne shone his torch towards them. They shouted and put their hands up to shield their eyes.

'Go and tell them to piss off, will you, Dave?' Thorne watched Holland walk towards them, then turned back to the lorry, thinking that, for once, the old cliché about there being 'nothing to see' was absolutely spot on. The rear doors were obviously not locked, but had been pushed together. After trying and failing to open one of the huge

217

doors with one hand, Thorne put his torch on the ground, grabbed hold with both hands and pulled.

The stench of piss hit him immediately. He bent to retrieve his torch and pointed it inside, jumping slightly as Holland stepped around from the side of the truck.

'Fuck . . .'

'Sorry,' Holland said, grinning. He added the light from his own torch to Thorne's, revealing, little by little, the interior of the empty box. 'Smells lovely, doesn't it? Tramp's been in there overnight, I reckon. Kids maybe . . .'

Thorne lifted a leg and reached up. 'Give us a hand, will you?'

Holland locked his fingers together, making a cradle for Thorne's foot. Thorne stepped into it and heaved himself up into the back of the lorry. The smell was even worse inside.

'Jesus . . .'

'Maybe somebody was very pissed,' Holland suggested. 'Thought it was a new kind of Portaloo. Makes a change from doing it in phone boxes . . .'

Thorne played the torch across the scarred metal floor. The light caught slick trails where the liquid had run, puddles where it had pooled.

Having seen quite enough, he turned, ready to jump down, when the Maglite caught something. There were markings high up on the side of the box, near the driver's cab. Thorne trained the beam on the spot and moved slowly towards it.

'Has anybody else been in here?' he shouted. He knew the answer already. Nobody could have missed this in daylight . . .

'I'm not sure,' Holland said. 'I think they just opened the door, saw that it was empty . . .'

The scratches were recent, Thorne was sure of it, the marks bright against the dull, dark metal.

Holland was leaning into the truck, fixing his torch on Thorne. 'What's the matter?'

It was a single word. The language was unfamiliar. Scored in broken lines deep into the side of the box with a knife. A nail maybe.

UMIT.

'It wasn't tramps or kids in here,' Thorne said. 'And the Zarifs aren't smuggling dodgy videos.' He turned towards the open doors and the figure of Holland standing in the darkness. 'They're smuggling people.'

'What? Illegal immigrants?'

'It could be trafficking for prostitution, but I doubt it. I'm guessing these people were perfectly willing. Paid their life savings on the strength of some gangster's promise . . .'

Holland said something else then, but Thorne couldn't make it out. He spun around slowly on the spot, the circle of light from his torch dancing lazily across the dirty walls. Miserable, remembering . . .

The woman on the tube, that first day. A baby and an empty cup.

Arkan Zarif's words.

Bread and work . . .

It was well after midnight by the time Thorne turned into Ryland Road and pulled up behind a dark blue VW Golf. He felt wiped out. He was walking past the Golf towards his flat when he noticed a man asleep in the driver's seat.

Thorne slowed his pace and leaned down to take a closer look. There was some light from a lamp-post twenty feet away, but not a great deal. The man in the car opened his eyes, smiled at Thorne and closed them again.

Thorne continued on towards his door, reached into a pocket for his keys. Perhaps he'd rattled Billy Ryan more than he'd realised . . .

Hendricks had already made up the sofa-bed and was lying there reading a paperback with an arty-looking cover.

Thorne filled him in on the day's events.

As far as work on the case went, Hendricks had not been involved practically since the post-mortem on Marcus Moloney, but it was important that he remain part of the team. Besides, Thorne was certain that his particular skills would be required again before it was all over.

'There's a message on the machine for you,' Hendricks shouted through to the kitchen. 'Sounds interesting . . .'

Thorne wandered in with his tea, pressed the button, sat on the arm of the sofa-bed to listen. The message was from Alison Kelly. She asked if he was free the following evening and left a phone number.

Hendricks put down his book. 'Was that who I think it was?'

Thorne turned off the living-room light and walked towards his bedroom. 'Hard to be sure,' he said. He was smiling as he opened the bedroom door. 'I don't know who you think it was, do I . . .?'

A few hours later, Thorne padded back into the living room, as awake as he'd been when he'd left it. He moved slowly towards the window. As he edged past the end of the sofa-bed, he banged his foot against the metal rail.

Hendricks stirred and sat up, woken by the impact, or the swearing.

'It's four o'clock in the morning . . .'

'Yes, I know.'

Though there was no one left in the room to disturb, the darkness dictated that they spoke in whispers.

'What are you doing?' Hendricks moaned.

Thorne was feeling irritable, and the throbbing pain in his foot was not helping matters. 'Right now, I'm thinking that it's getting a bit bloody crowded in here.' He stepped across to the window. 'How long can it possibly take to get rid of a bit of damp anyway?'

Hendricks said nothing.

Thorne pulled back the blind and looked out into the street. The Golf had gone.

18 May 1986

Ali and I went into town today. We just hung around really. Ali bought a bag and a couple of new tops and I got some LPs. Afterwards we got a burger and sat on a bench outside the library. A couple of lads were messing around and they were both staring. I started joking around with Ali, asking her which one of us she thought they fancied. It's only the sort of thing I would have said to her before. (Ali was always *the one lads fancied, by the way!) She looked uncomfortable and threw her burger away, and I know I should have left it, but I was just trying to make her laugh. I told her that it was obviously true what they say about how good-looking* girls always hang around with an ugly mate, and then she started to cry.

Now I feel guilty that I've upset her, but also angry because her feeling sad or guilty or whatever it is she feels seems so fucking trivial when I look into the mirror on the back of the bedroom door, and half my face still looks like the meat in her burger.

I know I'll feel differently about today by the morning and Ali and I will be best mates again before the end of school on Monday, but it's difficult not to feel a bit low when I'm writing this stuff down and it's my own fault. I always write at night, staring out of the window and listening to the Smiths or something equally miserable. Maybe I should have bought some cheerier music when I was in town. The soundtrack to tomorrow's entry will be courtesy of Cliff Richard or the Wombles or something . . .

Shit Moment of the Day
The stuff with Ali.
Magic Moment of the Day
A comedian on the TV making a joke about burn victims sticking together.

SIXTEEN

A single word was written on the whiteboard in red felt-tip pen.

UMIT.

'It means "hope",' Tughan said. 'In Turkish . . .'

Feet were shifted uncomfortably, and awkward looks exchanged. Thorne thought that if the people who'd been taken from the back of that lorry were now being handled by Billy Ryan, hope was something they would almost certainly have run out of.

It was Saturday morning, the day after the discovery of the abandoned lorry. The SO7 team was back at Becke House to work through this latest development. All that was *actually* developing was a sense of frustration . . .

'Customs and Excise are all over this now,' Tughan said. 'Not sure what they'll get out of it, but it'll probably be a damn sight more than we do . . .'

Thorne stood with Russell Brigstocke and the rest of the core team – Kitson, Stone, Holland and their SO7 counterparts – in a corner of the Incident Room. They watched as Tughan wore out a small strip of carpet in front of one of the desks. Weekend or not, there were always those who made no concessions to casual wear, but, despite the sharp and predictably well-pressed suit, Thorne thought that Tughan was starting to look and sound a little tired. Maybe not as tired as Thorne himself, but he was getting there.

'In terms of the Zarif brothers, you mean?' Thorne asked.

Holland held up his hands in a gesture of exasperation. 'Surely there must be something tying them to this? Something that will at least give us an excuse to make their lives difficult . . .'

Tughan put down his coffee and began to flick through a hastily assembled report on the hijacking. 'It's like six degrees of fucking separation,' he said. 'Between this lorry and the Zarifs there are any number of haulage companies, leasing agencies, freight contractors. They own the vehicle, *theoretically*, but if we spend a lot of time trying to tie them to whatever the vehicle was carrying, *we'll* be the ones whose lives are difficult.'

'I bet they're laughing at us,' Holland said. 'Them *and* the bloody Ryans.'

Tughan shrugged. 'Without any bodies, without the people who were inside the lorry, we've got sweet FA.'

'I can't believe they've got everything covered.' Holland looked around for support, found a little in the way of nods and murmurs.

'I've had a thought,' Brigstocke said. All eyes turned to him. 'Have we checked to see if that lorry's tax disc is up to date?'

The joke got a decent, and much needed, response, even if some of the laughter was lost in yawns.

'Do we know what was inside the lorry?' Kitson said. 'Specifically, I mean. Are we ever going to know how many?'

Tughan shook his head. 'Anywhere between a dozen and, I don't know . . . fifty?'

'There were that many found dead in the back of that lorry at Dover, weren't there?' Holland said.

'There were more,' Thorne said. He remembered the smell when he'd stepped up into that box the night before. He wondered what it must have been like for whoever had opened a pair of lorry doors a few years earlier and stared as the sunlight fell across the tangled heaps of crushed and emaciated dead. Fifty-eight Chinese immigrants, crammed like sardines into a sealed lorry, and found suffocated when it was opened on a steaming summer's afternoon. Their clothes in nice, neat piles. Their bodies in considerably less ordered ones . . .

There had, of course, been a major outcry at the time. There were demands for tougher controls, for positive action to curb this barbaric trade. Thorne knew very well that more *might* have been done had the corpses in the back of that lorry been those of donkeys or puppies or kittens . . .

'How can that many get through?' Stone asked. 'Don't these lorries get searched?'

'Sometimes,' Tughan said. 'They can hide in secret compartments or behind stacks of false cargo . . .'

Stone was shaking his head. 'You'd think they'd check the lorries a bit more thoroughly after all that business at Dover, though.'

Thorne knew that it wouldn't have taken a particularly

225

thorough search to have found those Chinese immigrants earlier. To have saved their lives. They'd tried to hide behind a few crates of tomatoes . . .

'The smugglers aren't stupid,' Tughan said. 'They'll try to avoid the ports that have got scanners, but even those that *do* have them are overrun. They can't possibly check any more than a handful or you'd have queues fifty miles long waiting to board the ferries.'

Thorne knew Tughan was right. Unable to sleep the night before, he'd booted up his rarely used computer and surfed the Net for a couple of hours. He'd gone to the NCIS site and taken a crash course in Turkish organised crime. He'd looked at the way the gangs and families operated both in the UK and in Turkey, and had followed the link from there to the NCIS pages on people-smuggling.

It had made for grim reading. It hadn't helped him sleep . . .

Customs and Excise were still more concerned with finding illicit alcohol and tobacco than they were with the smuggling of and, worse still, the *trade* in people. Though a few scanners had been installed, it was simply too big an undertaking to check anything more than a small random sample of vehicles passing through most ports. Seven thousand lorries a day came through Dover; on a good day, 5 per cent of them might be searched. It was little surprise that often no effort at all was made to conceal the people being smuggled. Those doing the smuggling knew full well that they could afford to be brazen.

Tughan talked some more about the hopelessness of trying to curb the growing trade in desperate people. He mentioned the valiant efforts being made by the police, the immigration services, the NCIS and Customs. He described an operation, yet to yield substantial results, involving MI5 and MI6 agents infiltrating the businesses of those responsible . . .

Thorne listened, wondering if he should jump in and help. After all, it wasn't often that he had the facts and figures at his fingertips. He was not usually the one who'd done his homework. He decided not to bother, figuring that it might be a bit early in the morning for some people to handle the shock.

Yvonne Kitson had brought a flask of Earl Grey in with her. She poured herself a cup. 'So, until we find these people, find out what Ryan's done with them, we won't know who they are or how they got here.'

Brigstocke pointed to the whiteboard, to the single word, scrawled in red: *Hope*. The colour of crushed tomatoes . . .

'Well, we can be pretty sure that at least some of them are Turkish,' Brigstocke said. 'Kurds, probably.'

Thorne knew the most likely route: 'From Turkey and the Middle East through the Balkans.' He ignored the look of surprise from Brigstocke, the look of amused horror from Tughan, and carried on, 'Then across the Adriatic to Italy.'

Tughan took over. 'The smugglers have a range of options. They change the routes to keep the immigration services on their toes, but there are a few key places – Moscow, Budapest, Sarajevo are all major nexus points . . .'

Thorne smiled. *Nexus points!* Nick Tughan was not a man to let himself be outdone. Thorne half expected him to march across like a teacher and write it on the whiteboard.

'But Istanbul is the big one. It's smack on the most direct route to the West from most of the major source countries.'

'Right,' Brigstocke said. 'And where the Zarif brothers have got plenty of friends and contacts.'

Holland rubbed his eyes. 'What about getting in here?'

'I already told you,' Tughan said, 'the smugglers aren't stupid.'

Neither am I, Thorne thought. 'They've got a few choices at this end as well,' he said. 'They can risk a major port or try a back-door route like the one through Ireland. There's another way in that's becoming quite popular – via Holland and Denmark, then over to the Faroe Islands, the Shetlands and across into mainland Scotland.' Thorne wasn't sure whether the short silence that followed was *considered* or simply *astonished*.

It was Yvonne Kitson who eventually spoke up. 'All right,' she said, turning to him, mock-aggressive. 'What planet are you from, and what have you done with Tom Thorne?'

DC Richards – the tedious Welshman who had so enjoyed making his 'concentric circles' speech – cut off the laughter before it had really begun. 'What are we actually going to *do*, sir? About the Zarifs and Billy Ryan?'

Tughan gave a thin smile, grateful to one of his own for passing the baton back to him. Back where it belonged. 'It's tricky, because both sides have got good reason to lie low for a while. The Zarifs know we're looking at their smuggling operation, and Ryan's got any number of immigrants to dispose of.'

'I can't see Memet Zarif and his brothers lying low for

228

very long,' Thorne said. 'They'll want to hit back at Ryan for this. Close to home, maybe . . .'

Tughan considered this for a second. 'Maybe, but I think we've got a bit of time to play with. I want a full-on policy of disruption. Let's make it hard for them to do *any* business; let's fuck them both around.' He pointed at Holland, reminding him of what he'd said earlier. 'Make their lives difficult . . .'

Thorne knew that 'disruption' essentially meant arresting, or, at the very least, hassling a variety of low-rank workers in the two organisations: drug dealers, debt collectors – those in DC Richards' outer circles. It was time-consuming, heavy on manpower and, worst of all, as far as Thorne was concerned, it had little effect on the people they should be really going after. It was a policy that could produce results in the right circumstances, but there were just too many bodies around this time. It made him feel like a glorified VAT-man, and he resented it. He wanted to hurt Billy Ryan and the Zarif boys in more than just their wallets . . .

'Not convinced, Tom?' Tughan asked. Obviously, Thorne's face was giving away as much as it usually did.

Thorne hated the eyes on him, the barely suppressed sighs from those without the bollocks or the brain power to speak up. 'It's like we're trying to catch a killer,' he said, 'and while we're waiting for him to do it again, we're busy cutting up his credit cards. Nicking a few quid out of his wage packet . . .'

Tughan's response was remarkably calm, gentle even. 'We're not dealing with everyday criminals, Tom. These men are not ordinary killers.'

Thorne traded small shrugs with Brigstocke, exchanged a 'what the hell' look with Dave Holland. He knew that Tughan was right, but it didn't make him feel any happier, or any less lost.

Thorne had never thought the day would come, but he was starting to yearn for a decent, honest-to-goodness psychopath . . .

There was a message from Phil Hendricks on Thorne's mobile: he'd be spending the night at Brendan's. Thorne texted him back: he was sorry for being a miserable sod the night before, and hoped that wasn't the reason Hendricks was staying away.

'What's Ryan going to do with them?' Kitson asked.

The pair of them were back in their own office, working their way through paperwork, while, up the corridor, Tughan and Brigstocke were still hammering out a plan for 'disruption'. Thorne put his phone down and glanced at his watch before he looked up. Another fifteen minutes and he'd head home.

'Probably exactly the same as the Zarifs would have done,' he said. 'He'll exploit them. The poor sods hand over every penny they've got, and when they arrive here they find that they owe these "businessmen" a lot more. In the time it takes them to get people smuggled into the UK they might be working with criminal organisations in half a dozen different countries. It might take months, even years, and the smugglers are incurring extra costs on the way. Palms need to be greased all along the route, and the cost of that gets passed on to the people in the backs of the lorries.'

Kitson shook her head. 'So, even if they get here in one piece, they're up to their eyeballs in debt . . .'

'Right. But, luckily, people like that nice Mr Zarif have lots of jobs they can do to work their debts off. At one pound fifty an hour it should only take them a couple of years . . .'

'And they can't do anything about it. They can't kick up a fuss.'

'Not unless they want to get reminded, forcibly, of just who they're dealing with. I mean, there're so many of these buggers over here, aren't there? Nicking our jobs or claiming our dole money. Who's going to notice if a couple of them disappear?' Thorne's voice dropped, lost its ironic swagger. 'Or there's worse. Don't forget, back where these people have come from, the smugglers have plenty of friends who know *exactly* where their families are.'

Kitson sighed, a slow hiss of resignation. 'It's a great new life . . .'

Thorne thought about all the clichés. It was hard to think of hope as something that sprang eternal, but easy to see it being crushed and dashed. Hope died violently. It was bludgeoned and it was burned.

Hope was something that bled.

He dropped some papers he hadn't bothered looking at into a drawer, and slammed it shut. The action distracted him from the face of the woman on the tube train. The sound drowned out the noise of nothing rattling in the bottom of her chewed polystyrene cup.

Thorne had read plenty the night before about trafficking. He knew about women being kidnapped, forced into heroin addiction and the vice trade. He guessed

231

that the Zarifs were involved in that particularly lucrative area of human trading.

He knew that there were worse things than begging . . .

At the sound of raised voices outside the door, Thorne looked up. Holland knocked and stuck his head in. 'They've found the lorry driver,' he said. He pushed the door further open and stepped into the office. 'In some woods behind a lay-by on the A7.'

'How?' Thorne asked.

'Shot in the head . . .'

'Nice.'

'But not until they'd smashed half of it to pulp with a dirty great tree branch.'

'The A7,' Kitson said. 'That's the main road between Edinburgh and Carlisle. My ex had family up there . . .'

Holland had his notebook in his hand and began flipping through the pages.

Thorne had been right on the nail at the morning briefing. It looked like the lorry had been hijacked after coming into Scotland on the route he'd described. The cargo would have been loaded on to another vehicle, then the original lorry driven south and dumped at Chieveley.

Holland had found what he was looking for. 'Right,' he said. 'The lay-by was just north of Galashiels. It was the Lothian and Borders boys who found the bodies.'

'Found the *what*?' Thorne said.

'There were two other bodies. Three altogether.' Holland looked from Thorne to Kitson. 'No identification on them. Gunshot wounds to the head.'

Kitson spat out the breath in her lungs like it had suddenly become foul. She took a mouthful of fresher air. 'A couple of them put up a fight, maybe?' She looked to Thorne.

He nodded. 'Or tried to run.'

'I think that's the theory they're working on,' Holland said.

Thorne immediately pictured the two men thrashing desperately through woods in the dark. Tearing, breathless, through wet leaves and sprawling over rotting stumps. He saw them fall before the echo of the shots had died away. He knew that whatever last word passed through their heads the second before the bullet did, it had certainly not been *umit*. He had been taught a Turkish toast; maybe he should go back and learn a few Turkish prayers.

The door opened wider and Holland stepped aside as Brigstocke and Tughan marched in.

'Ten bodies now,' Tughan said. 'Double figures. This has to stop . . .'

Double figures? Tughan was making it sound as if the Ryan–Zarif turf war had now exceeded some unspoken quota of acceptable victims. Thorne had known stranger things to be true, but, for whatever reason, he had the impression that the plan to 'disrupt' had been superseded in light of the news from north of the border. Tughan certainly looked as if he now had something rather more direct in mind.

Brigstocke swept a hand through his thick, black hair, nudged his glasses with a knuckle. 'Ten bodies, and the civilian victims are starting to outnumber the soldiers.'

'Let's stop pissing around with monkeys then,' Thorne said. 'Go straight for the organ-grinders . . .'

Tughan held up a hand. 'That's exactly what we're going to do.'

'All right.' Thorne was thinking: I've got a date later, but there's still time. I needn't hang around too long. Finchley is a bit of a schlep, and trickier in terms of just dropping by, but Green Lanes isn't too far out of my way . . .

'We *will* put Billy Ryan away,' Tughan said. 'We'll get him with the Rooker case, and we'll get the Zarif brothers as well, eventually. Right now, our top priority has to be preventing any more deaths.'

'Eventually' was one word that Thorne hadn't wanted to hear.

'I'm going to the detective chief superintendent in the first instance and he may well have to take it higher. We'll make an official approach to Ryan, almost certainly through his solicitor, and we'll do the same thing to the Zarif family, probably via a community leader, or perhaps a priest.' Tughan was nodding to nobody in particular, as if he were trying to convince himself of something. 'Things have got to the point now where intervention might well do us as much good as investigation. Sitting down with these people is not something we do every day of the week, but if getting them around a table might help us put a stop to this fucking chaos, I'm happy to do it.'

Thorne looked thoughtful for a second or two before he spoke. He was thinking it was no great surprise that Tughan was not exactly proposing to kick anybody's door in.

'Do we have to provide the sandwiches?' he said.

★

'Where you going?' The man behind the simple wooden counter asked the question with only the most cursory glance up from his newspaper. The thick accent transformed the three words into one: '*Werrugoeen?*'

'I'm not going anywhere,' Thorne said, 'but you're going back there to tell your boss that somebody wants to have a quick word with him.' Thorne looked hard at the man who was now giving him his full attention. He pointed back over the man's shoulder towards the dimly lit space behind him. He knew that a second man, sitting on a tatty armchair in the corner behind and to the left of him was also studying him intently.

Thorne held up his warrant card. 'Quick as you can.'

The man slapped down his paper, snorted back phlegm and disappeared into the gloom.

The minicab office consisted of little more than a waiting room the size of a cupboard. An unpainted door to the right of the hatch led back into any number of rooms behind. Thorne guessed that the drivers themselves would be sitting nearby in their dodgy Vauxhalls and Toyotas, or perhaps waiting in the Zarifs' café next door. He turned and watched a few seconds of a film he didn't recognise on the TV bolted above the front door. The local news might be on the other side, might be showing the three goals Spurs had put past Everton earlier in the day. He let his eyes drop to the man on the armchair. The latter raised an eyebrow as if they were both just frustrated customers waiting for a lift home. He held Thorne's stare for longer than was strictly necessary before standing and walking through the side door towards the rear of the office.

A few seconds after it had closed, the door opened and

Memet Zarif stepped into the waiting room. At the same time, Thorne was aware of the man he'd first spoken to resuming his position behind the counter. A few feet further back, hovering in the shadows, stood the man who'd been sitting in the armchair.

'You want a cab, Mr Thorne?' Memet said. He wore a simple white shirt, buttoned at the collar, over black trousers and tasselled loafers.

Thorne smiled. 'No, thanks. I think I'd like to get home in one piece. Last minicab I took, the driver didn't know that a red light meant stop . . .'

'My drivers know what they're doing.'

'You sure?'

'Of course.'

'They know how to fill out insurance forms, do they?'

Memet laughed, glancing across to the men behind the counter and nodding towards Thorne. The man from the armchair moved forward and stood at the shoulder of the receptionist. He spat some Turkish in Thorne's direction.

Thorne whipped his head round and smiled. 'Same to you,' he said. He turned back to Memet, still smiling at the tremendous fun they were all having. 'So, you don't think it would be worth my while getting a few officers round here, checking that all your cars and all your fantastic drivers are fully insured?' Thorne was fighting against the sound of gunfire from the TV set. He raised his voice: 'I'd be wasting my time, would I?'

The noise from the TV suddenly dropped enough for Thorne to hear Memet sigh. 'Do you think we are stupid?'

It seemed to Thorne that everyone was awfully keen to tell him that the likes of Memet Zarif and Billy Ryan were

236

anything but stupid. He didn't doubt that they were *careful*, but he refused to buy into a myth that he and his team were up against the gangland chapter of Mensa. Thorne had caught his fair share of supposedly clever villains, and he knew equally that plenty were thick as shit and doing very nicely for themselves. He knew that, actually, the most successful villains got by on instinct, like many of those who were out to catch them.

Instinct was fallible, though, as Thorne knew only too well.

Do you think we are stupid?

Memet was certainly clever enough to load a simple question with meaning. He was no longer talking about a minicab firm . . .

Thorne moved past Memet, talking as he pushed open the wooden side door and stepped into a dimly lit corridor. 'I like what you've done with this place,' he said. Through the thin wall, he could hear the men behind the counter moving round to intercept him.

Memet was following as Thorne walked calmly along a strip of greasy linoleum. The place smelled faintly musty. Flakes of magnolia paint crackled under his shoes.

'Did you do it yourself, or did you get professionals in?'

'What do you want, Mr Thorne?'

They walked past the doorway that led to the reception hatch. The two hired hands stared at Thorne, then looked to Memet for instructions. At the end of the corridor was a small, gloomy living room. The three men sitting around the table put down their playing cards and looked up as Thorne approached. Hassan Zarif made to stand up, then relaxed as he saw his older brother looming at Thorne's shoulder.

Thorne took the scene in fast. The two other men at the table were Tan, the youngest brother, and the heavyset man he'd seen at the café with Hassan when he'd been in there with Holland. For a few seconds, the only noise was the muffled soundtrack from the TV in the waiting room and the bubbling of the air filter in a large tank of tropical fish sitting on an oak sideboard.

Thorne pointed to the table. The pile of crumpled five- and ten-pound notes in the middle was about to spill on to the carpet. 'I could make up a four for bridge if you fancy it,' he said.

Memet pushed past him and took the empty seat at the table. 'Just say what you've come to say.'

'It's funny, you talking back there about drivers. It reminds me: they found the driver of your lorry.'

Memet shrugged, looked confused. 'Our lorry . . .?'

Hassan leaned across and spoke to him in Turkish. Memet nodded.

'The police at Thames Valley called me about it yesterday morning,' Hassan said. He spoke to Memet and Tan as if he were filling them in on some minor business glitch. 'The lorry wasn't damaged, as far as they can tell, and the haulier will claim for their lost load, so I didn't think there was any need to contact our insurance company.' He looked up at Thorne. 'I haven't had the chance to talk to my brothers about it yet, but it's fairly trivial.'

'Pass on our gratitude to the officers who found it,' Memet said.

Thorne had to concede that they played it well. 'It wasn't very trivial for the driver,' Thorne said. 'They found him with half his head missing.'

The heavyset man failed to conceal a smile. He looked down and began to tidy up the notes when he saw that Thorne had caught it.

Hassan ran a hand back and forth across his prominent chin. The stubble rasped against his palm. 'Well, that clears one thing up at least,' he said. 'We can assume that the driver wasn't in league with the hijackers.'

Memet did a convincing enough job of looking shocked and saddened, though Thorne knew very well that the news would have come as something of a relief. A dead driver was a driver who wouldn't be telling the police anything. 'They killed him?' he said, turning to Hassan. 'For what? What was this lorry carrying?'

Playing it *very* well. Certainly far from stupid . . .

'I think the police said it was CD players,' Hassan said.

Thorne corrected him. '*DVD* players, actually. The good news is that they didn't get the entire load.'

The heavyset man carried on straightening banknotes, but now the three brothers looked directly at Thorne. Memet's face was a blank. Hassan was trying too hard to look no more than innocently curious. Tan was persevering with the hardman glare.

'That's right,' Thorne said. 'Apparently, a couple of the DVD players were shot, trying to run away.'

Only Memet Zarif was able to hold the look, to continue to meet Thorne's eye.

'Don't worry, I'll get straight in touch if we find any more,' Thorne said. 'Just thought you'd be interested in what we'd established so far.'

More bubbles from the fish tank. Voices from the TV along the corridor.

As Thorne turned to leave, he became aware of another figure seated in the corner to his right and a little behind him. He stared until the man leaned slowly forward and his face moved from shadow into light. Thorne recognised him as the son of Muslum and Hanya Izzigil.

Thorne took a step towards the boy. 'Yusuf . . .'

It may just have been the light, but the boy's eyes seemed changed. The previous month, with his parents dead in the next room, they had brimmed with tears, but that was not the only difference that Thorne could see. There was a challenge in their stillness, in their *dead*ness, and in the set of the boy's shoulders as he stared at the man who'd failed so miserably to provide him with any justice.

Clearly, there had been others who'd made him promises they had more chance of keeping.

'We are taking care of Yusuf now,' Hassan said.

Thorne stared at the boy for a few seconds more, looking for a sign that some part of him might not yet have become theirs. He saw only that the boy was lost. He turned, and moved slowly back the way he'd come in. 'I'll let you get back to your game . . .'

'Are you sure you don't want that cab home?' Memet asked.

Thorne said nothing, his back to them.

Tan Zarif spoke up for the first time. 'We'll do you a very good price,' he said. 'Green Lanes to Kentish Town for a fiver. How's that sound?'

Thorne felt something tighten in his gut at the revelation implicit in the simple details of the journey. He turned and looked deep into Tan's eyes, trying to swallow back the panic and sound casual. 'I thought we'd talked about this,' he said. 'Drop the "we know where you live" hardman shit or change the look.' He drew a finger from ear to ear along the line of his jaw, the same line marked out on Tan by his pencil-thin beard. 'The George Michael thing is scaring nobody . . .'

Thorne took a deep breath and held it as he walked quickly back along the corridor, through the empty reception area and out on to the street. He let the breath out and turned to see Arkan Zarif staring at him from the doorway of the café.

The old man raised his hand as Thorne came towards him, brought it up to his mouth. 'You come inside for coffee? For *sutlac*, maybe . . .?'

Thorne slowed his pace, but kept on heading towards his car. 'I can't. I've got to be somewhere . . .'

It was true that he had less than an hour to get home, shower and change, but that wasn't the only reason why he'd refused the old man's invitation. Even if he'd had the time, Thorne knew that the coffee would have tasted even more bitter than usual.

When he thought about the burning girl, he often thought about the others, too. About her friends.

They'd been the first to see it, of course, to spot the flames. The one who had been standing closest, the one who really was Alison Kelly, screamed like it had been her who was on fire. He'd jumped slightly, perhaps even cried out as the scream had moved through him like a blade. He'd turned his head towards the noise then, and seen the flames reflected in the girl's eyes. They were dark brown and very wide, and the flames that were growing, that were climbing up the girl who was actually burning, seemed tiny, dancing in her friend's eyes in that second before he'd turned and run. He still remembered how small they had seemed, flickering against the dark brown. How far away.

As he'd rushed away down that steep hill, careering towards the car, that scream had followed him. He could feel the echo of it at his back, rolling down the hillside after him, all but knocking him off his feet as he went. Then the screams had grown, of course, louder and more hysterical, pushing him downhill even faster.

He'd stood still for just a second or two before jumping into the car, and he remembered that moment now vividly. Remembered the shortness of breath and the picture on the backs of his eyelids. He'd closed his eyes and the shape of the flames had still been there, imprinted. Gold and red edges bleeding into the blackness.

A snapshot of the flames. The ones he'd seen jumping in the eyes of the girl he'd been sent there to kill.

SEVENTEEN

'How did you get my number, anyway?' Thorne asked.

Alison Kelly put down her glass, tucked a strand of hair behind her ear. 'On your card?'

Thorne smiled and shook his head. Like everyone else on the job, he had a generic Metropolitan Police business card. It gave the address of Becke House, together with the phone and fax numbers at the office. It bore the legend 'Working for a safer London', printed in blue as a jaunty scribble. It left a space to write in mobile, pager or other numbers.

'I never write down my home phone number,' Thorne said. 'You didn't get it out of the phone book, either . . .'

She still wasn't giving anything away.

'You got my number the same way you found out everything else, right?'

They were sitting in a corner of the Spice of Life at Cambridge Circus. Alison nursed a large gin and tonic. Thorne was on the Guinness, and enjoying it. The lounge contained acres of red velvet, far too many brass rails and, inexplicably, was crammed with annoyingly healthy-looking Scandinavian tourists.

Thorne tore open a packet of crisps, grabbed a handful. 'I'm not going to get a straight answer, am I?'

'I was a gangster's daughter until I was fourteen,' she said. 'Then everything changed. *Everything*. Dad walked away from it all and took us and a great big bag of his tasteless "new" money with him. Spent the rest of his life playing golf and doing crosswords in his conservatory. A couple of years later, Billy and I were together, but once that marriage was over, I was completely out of it. I was out of the life, and that's how I wanted it. Gangland was just something Mum and I saw on the TV, and I was just a lowly legal secretary with a private-school accent and a pony. Now, I'm a slightly better-paid legal secretary with less of an accent and no pony. And I'm *still* out of it. But . . .'

'*But?*'

She grinned, picked up her drink. 'I've still got a few friends who are very much *in* it.' She drained her glass. 'We'll have a girls' night out a couple of times a year. You know the kind of thing – family-run restaurant, shed-loads of booze on the house, I complain about work and they complain about how long their husbands and boyfriends are getting sent down for.'

'Sounds like a fun evening . . .'

'One or two of them may or may not know certain police officers pretty well and can call in a favour if they're asked nicely. Getting a copper's phone number is hardly rocket science.'

'I *should* be shocked,' Thorne said, 'but I'm too busy thinking about another round.'

She picked up Thorne's empty glass and pushed back her chair. 'Another one of those . . .?'

For the next hour or so they talked about the difficulties of doing, or not doing, what was expected of you. It was soon obvious that this was something they both knew a great deal about.

Thorne told her that if he were the sort to do what was expected, or at the very least encouraged, he wouldn't be there drinking with her.

Alison told Thorne about her reluctance to do bugger all and sit on her arse spending her old man's money. She told him about upsetting her mother by refusing the offer to set her up in a business.

'Sounds like you were trying to distance yourself,' Thorne said. 'From the money. From everything that *made* the money. Like you blamed it for what happened to Jessica.'

Her pale complexion flushed a little. 'If my dad hadn't been who he was, *what* he was, then it wouldn't have happened. That's not a delusion . . .'

They both took a drink to fill the short pause that followed. By now, she'd moved on to white wine. Thorne had moved on to his next Guinness.

'Why did you marry Billy Ryan?' he asked.

She thought about it for a few seconds. Just rising above the buzz and burble of pub chat, the voices of the latest boy-band drifted through from the jukebox in the bar next door.

'It sounds like I'm joking,' she said, 'but it really did seem like a good idea at the time.'

'He must have been . . . what? Mid-thirties?'

'Older. And I was only eighteen.'

'So who the hell thought that was a "good idea"?'

She smiled. 'Not my mum, for a start. She thought the age difference was too big. I mean, Billy's son was only ten years younger than I was, for God's sake. But Dad was all for it. I think there were a few people who thought it was a good thing, you know, some of the old boys who'd been around a bit. Even though Dad had been out of it a few years by then, and Billy was running the show, some people thought it was a good way of . . . building bridges, or something. The old guard and the new guard.'

'You make it sound like it was arranged.'

She shook her head. 'I wish I had that as an excuse. I'd like to say I married him to make everybody else happy. And I knew that I *was*, to some extent. But the simple fact is that I loved him.' She paused, but looked as if she needed to say something else. She searched for the right words. 'He was impressive, back then.'

Thorne thought about the Billy Ryan he'd so recently encountered. There would be some who might still describe him as impressive, but lovable was not a word that sprang to mind. 'What went wrong?'

She took a good-sized slurp of wine. 'Nothing . . . for a while. I mean, I never really hit it off with Stephen, who was a right little sod even then, but he wasn't really the problem. His old man was. There were two sides to Billy.'

Thorne nodded. He didn't know many people without at least a couple . . .

'There was part of him', she said, 'that just wanted to have fun. He liked to have friends over or go out to parties. He used to take me into all the clubs. He wanted to dress up and show off and hang around with actors and pop stars. People writing books. He loved all that . . .'

'I bet the actors and pop stars loved it as well.'

'When it was just the two of us, though, he could be a whole lot different. If it was just him and me and a bottle of something, he became somebody else, and I was on the receiving end. Maybe he was still having fun, I don't know . . .'

Thorne saw her eyes darken and knew what she meant. He remembered the feet, dainty inside highly polished shoes, but also Ryan's shoulders, powerful beneath the expensive blazer.

Two sides. The dancer and the boxer.

'It's a pretty good reason to leave someone,' he said.

'He was the one who left.'

'Right . . .'

'He said he couldn't cope with the problems I had. All the stuff with Jess I was still trying to deal with.'

Thorne had to fight to stop his mouth dropping open. *Problems? Stuff?* All of them, all of it, the result of what her husband had done.

Alison saw the look on Thorne's face, took it as no more than mild surprise. 'I did have some bloody awful mood swings, I know I did. Billy wasn't exactly what you'd call supportive, though. He kept saying I was neurotic . . . that I needed help. He kept telling me that I hated myself, that I was impossible to live with, that I needed to get over what had happened when I was in that playground.'

When a man paid by Billy Ryan had come to her school to kill her. When flames had devoured her best friend in front of her eyes.

'No,' Thorne said. 'Not exactly supportive.'

She swirled around the last of her wine in the bottom of the glass. 'He was right about me needing help, of course, but I needed a damn sight more after a couple of years with Billy. I got through a bit of that money my mum had been offering then.. Pissed a lot of it away paying strangers to listen. Any number of the buggers at fifty quid an hour.'

Thorne stared at her.

Her eyes widened when they met his. 'I'm all right now, though,' she said.

'That's good . . .'

As she downed her drink, she contorted her face into a series of deliberately comical twitches and tics. It wasn't particularly funny, but Thorne laughed anyway.

She put down the glass and reached for her handbag. 'Let's go and get something to eat . . .'

Rooker stared at a spider on the ceiling, wishing things were noisier. It was always noisy in prison, always. Even asleep, five hundred men could make a shitload of noise. During the day, it could be unbearable. The pounding of feet in corridors and on stairs, the clank of metal – buckets and keys, the slash and smash of voices echoing from cell to cell, from landing to landing. Even a tiny noise – a fork on a plate, a groan in the night – was magnified somehow and charged. It was like the anger floating around the place had done something to the air itself, made it easier for sound to move through it and carry. Distorted, deafening. It was something you got used to. It was something *Rooker* had got used to.

Here, though, it was like the bloody grave.

Even the relative peace of the VP wings he'd been on was like a cacophony compared to this. There, the shuffling nonces made noises all of their own. Same thing went for the old fuckers they got lumbered with. They always stuck the very old fellas on the VP wings. The stroke victims and the doolally ones, and the ones who had problems getting around. They were no trouble, most of them, but, Christ, once the lights went out, the hawking and the coughing would start, and he'd want to put pillows over all their pasty, lopsided faces.

He missed it now though. The silence was keeping him awake.

He allowed himself a smile. There would be plenty of noise in a few weeks when he was out – when it was all over and he was home, wherever that would be. There would be silence when *he* wanted it, and noises he hadn't heard in a very long time. Traffic, pubs, football crowds.

When it was all over . . .

The sessions with Thorne and the rest were wearing him out. Thorne especially had a way of digging at him, of pushing and pushing, until the effort of remembering and repeating it over and over again was like shovelling shit uphill. He knew it had to be done, that it would be worth it, but he'd forgotten quite how much he hated them. Even when you were supposed to be helping them, when you were supposed to be on the same side, the police were a pack of mongrels.

He felt a familiar flutter in his gut that was coming often now, whenever he thought about life on the outside. It was like a bubbling panic. He'd imagined being out for so long and now that it was within his reach he realised that it scared the living shit out of him. He'd known plenty of cons who'd done a lot less time than him and couldn't hack it on the outside. Most were fucked up on booze and drugs within a year. Others all but begged to be sent back to prison, and, eventually, they made sure they got what they wanted.

It wasn't going to be easy, he knew that, but at least with Ryan out of the way he would have a chance. He would have the time to adjust.

If he ever felt a moment's doubt, wondered about changing his mind and telling Thorne and the rest to stuff it, he just had to remember that night in Epping Forest, one of the last times he'd ever clapped eyes on Ryan. He just had to remember the look on Ryan's face.

Getting out scared him, but Billy Ryan scared him more.

Rooker turned on to his side to face the wall, wincing at the jolt of pain in his belly. It was still sore. On balance, he preferred the pain to the panic, but still, he decided that once he'd got out and away, once he'd let the dust settle, he'd do some ringing round. He'd call in a favour or two and get that shitbag Fisher sorted out.

Thorne looked across at the clock on his bedside table. 5.10 a.m. Only ten minutes later than the last time he'd looked.

He turned and watched Alison Kelly sleep.

She was dead to the world, and had barely stirred since she'd finally drifted off for the second time. Thorne knew he would have no such luck. He had scarcely blinked since being woken nearly three hours before by the sobbing.

He watched her sleep and thought about what he'd told her . . .

For a while, he'd been unable to get a word out of her. Every attempt at speech caught in her throat, was strangled by the heave of her chest that seemed to shake every inch of her. He'd held her until she'd calmed a little, then listened as it began to grow light outside, and the tears and snot dried on his arms and on his neck.

She'd asked some of the questions he'd already heard, and others he'd seen in her eyes when she'd spoken about her past. The whispers and the sobs had added a desperation he'd heard before only in the voices of the recently bereaved, or from the parents of missing children.

What could she have done differently?

Why did Jessica burn?

When was she ever going to stop feeling like she was burning herself?

So, Thorne had held on hard to her, and finally given her the only answer he had, hoping that it might serve as the answer for all of her questions.

The tears had stopped quickly after that, and she'd seemed to grow suddenly so tired that she couldn't even hold up her head. She'd dropped slowly down on to the pillow, her face turned away from him, and Thorne had no idea how long she'd lain staring at his bedroom wall. He'd known it would be wrong to ask, even in a whisper, if she was still awake . . .

Now, staring up at his cheap lampshade, he wasn't sure why he'd told her. Maybe it was what she'd said in the pub about Ryan. Maybe it was a simple desire in him to give something. Maybe it was a belief in the plain goodness of

251

fact, in its power to smother the flames of doubt and guilt. Whatever the reason, it was done. Thorne knew he'd moved into strange territory and he wasn't at all sure how he felt about it.

Knowing that he would not get back to sleep, he eased himself to his feet and moved towards the door. Standing on Alison's side of the bed, he looked down at her face. He saw half of it, pale in a wedge of milky light bleeding into the room through a crack in the curtains. The other half was in darkness, where shadow lay across it like a scar.

6 June 1986

We all drove out to a country pub today. The weather was nice enough to sit outside, which was probably a good idea. It was crowded in the pub anyway and I didn't want to put anyone off their ploughman's lunch. I don't think I'm ever really going to be great with lots of people around.

Mum and Dad let me have half a lager, which was another very good reason to be outside!

There were lots of wasps buzzing around the food, which was pissing everyone off. I kept perfectly still, hoping that one might settle on me, settle on the scar. I wanted to know what it felt like, or even if I could feel it at all. But Dad was flapping his arms around and swearing and none of them came near me.

Dad had brought his new camera along and insisted on taking loads of pictures. We both smiled like always, like it was perfectly normal and I pretended that I was fine about it so Dad wouldn't be upset. Afterwards I made a joke about the woman at Boots getting a nasty shock when she developed the photos and Mum went a bit funny for a while.

Ali rang later to tell me she's got to dress up and help out at some swanky dinner party her parents are having. She says she's dreading it. She says there's probably going to be several hardened criminals sitting around trying to make polite conversation and eating Twiglets. That made me laugh and I wanted to tell someone, but Mum and especially Dad have still got a real problem with Ali and her family. I don't even tell them when me and Ali are meeting up outside school.

Shit Moment of the Day

In the pub garden, there was a family a few feet away from us, on one of those wooden tables with a bench attached on either side. They had a teenage boy with them, and a girl of four or five, and she stared at me for ages. I pulled faces at her. I rolled my eyes and stuck my tongue down behind my bottom lip. I kept trying to make her laugh, but she just looked frightened.

Magic Moment of the Day

I was in the kitchen after tea and we had the radio on. Mum was out in the garden having a fag, and Dad was drying up. The new Smiths single came on, and I was singing along. I was waving my arms around like Morrissey, wailing in a stupid high voice and messing around. When I got to the bit

253

about knowing how Joan of Arc felt, Dad looked across at me with a tea towel in his hand. There was a pause and then we both just pissed ourselves laughing.

EIGHTEEN

If Thorne were to make a list of the places he least liked to be beside, the seaside would come fairly near the top. Admittedly, British seaside resorts were marginally less attractive than those slightly more glamorous ones in Australia say, or Florida, but even then, Thorne was far from keen. The sea might be warmer, bluer, *cleaner*, but it had its own drawbacks.

Margate or Miami? Rhyl or Rio? As far as Thorne was concerned it pretty much came down to a choice between shit and sharks . . .

Having said that, what he'd seen of Brighton so far that morning hadn't been too unpleasant. A ten-minute taxi ride from the station to Eileen's house. A five-minute walk from there to the pub.

Thorne's father, and his father's best friend Victor, had travelled down together from St Albans the day before. Victor had rung while Thorne was getting ready to go out and meet Alison Kelly. They'd arrived in one piece, Victor had told him. His father was excited, but fairly well behaved. He was looking forward to a weekend away.

Thorne had wanted to catch an earlier train, but getting himself together and out of the flat that morning had been complicated. Alison had caught him looking at his watch as they'd shared breakfast in the kitchen, and it had only heightened the awkwardness that hung between them, heavy as the smell of burned toast.

What had been said in the early hours . . .

That was far harder to deal with, and certainly to talk about, than what they'd been doing to each other a few hours earlier. The sex had been snatched at and sweaty, the two of them equally needy, physically at least.

The morning did its job on them, muggy, thick-headed and cruel. It shone a fresh, harsh light on what was now unsayable.

Thorne belched, tasting last night's Guinness. Victor laughed. Eileen tried to look disapproving. His dad appeared not to have noticed.

'Sorry,' Thorne said. He knew that he was looking slightly rough, knew that Eileen could see it. 'I had a bit of a night . . .'

She sipped her tomato juice. 'That explains why you got here so late.'

By the time Thorne had reached his aunt's house and got a cup of tea down him, there'd been nothing left to do except head off for a quick drink before Sunday lunch.

'It won't be easy to get into a decent restaurant,' Eileen said. 'They'll all be full if we don't get a move on.'

Thorne said nothing. Eileen had been a life-saver since his dad's illness had kicked in, but she could be a bit prissy when she felt like it. He hoped she wasn't in that sort of mood.

'Beer or birds?' Jim Thorne said suddenly.

Thorne stared at his father. 'What?'

'Your "bit of a night". On the beer or on the birds?'

Thorne wasn't sure which was throwing him more, the question or the way it was couched.

'Maybe both,' Victor said. He grinned at Thorne's father and the two of them began to laugh.

Victor was probably the only friend that Thorne's father had left. He was certainly the only one Thorne ever saw. He was taller and thicker-set than his father, especially now, as Jim Thorne was losing weight. He had much less hair, and false teeth that fitted badly, and the two old men together often reminded Thorne of some bizarre, over-the-hill double act.

'Maybe,' Thorne said.

His father leaned towards him. 'Always a good idea, I reckon. Get a few pints down you and even the ugly ones start to look . . . wossname . . . the opposite of ugly?'

Victor supplied the word his friend was searching for. 'Pretty? Attractive?'

Jim Thorne nodded. 'Even the ugly ones start to look attractive.'

Thorne smiled. A bizarre double act: the straight man occasionally needing to provide a bit of help with the punchlines. He glanced across the table at Eileen, who shook her head and rolled her eyes. There wasn't too much wrong with her mood.

Victor raised his glass, as if proposing a toast. 'Beer goggles,' he said.

'The same goes for women, you know,' Eileen said. 'We can wear wine goggles.' She pointed towards Thorne's father. 'I reckon Maureen probably had a pair on the night she got together with you.'

Thorne watched his father. They hadn't talked much about his mother since her death. Almost never since the Alzheimer's. He wondered how the old man would react.

Jim Thorne nodded, enjoying it. 'I think you're probably right, love,' he said. 'Bloody strong ones an' all.' He raised his glass until it covered the bottom half of his face. 'I was stone-cold sober . . .'

Once the drink had been supped and the glass lowered, Thorne tried and failed to catch his father's eye. The old man's gaze was darting around all over the place.

The pub was old fashioned in the worst sense and half empty, probably as a result. They sat in a tiny bar – the sort of room that might once have been called a snug – around a rickety metal table near the door. The absence of anything like atmosphere was mostly due to the strip lighting. It buzzed above their heads, washing everything out. It made the place feel like a waiting room that smelled of beer.

Thorne knew why they'd chosen this particular pub: his father liked places that were brightly lit. He was forever wandering around his house turning all the lights on, even in the middle of the day. It might have been forgetfulness, but Thorne thought that the old man was simply trying to keep the darkness away, knowing it was creeping up on him and struggling to stay in the light, where he could see. Where he could still be seen . . .

'Who's for another one?' Victor asked.

Eileen shook her head, slid her empty glass away from her. 'If we want to get proper Sunday lunch some-where . . .'

They began to gather their things together – bags, coats, hats. As Eileen, Victor and his father moved slowly, one by one towards the door, Thorne checked under the table to make sure no one had left anything behind.

He was wishing he was somewhere else. He was thinking about the case; about Rooker and Ryan and two men running for their lives through a dark wood. He was picturing Alison Kelly and Jessica Clarke; faces on his pillow and in a drawer beside his bed.

Beneath her chair, Thorne found Eileen's umbrella. He grabbed it and followed her to the door. Now he thought about it, perhaps a day out was a good idea. Feeling like a youngster being dragged around by three, slightly strange, grown-ups, might be just what he needed.

They walked towards the seafront. Thorne dragged his heels and stared at things he wasn't really interested in to avoid getting too far ahead of his father and the others.

Spring was a few days old but hadn't found its feet yet. It was grey – the type of day Thorne associated with the seaside. He couldn't help thinking that the picture would be complete if Eileen had a reason to put up her umbrella. This was, he knew, a little unfair on the city of Brighton. Expensive and deeply fashionable, with a thriving music scene and a reputation as the gay capital of Britain, it was hardly the typical coastal resort. Still, prejudice was prejudice, and, as far as Thorne was concerned, if you could buy rock with the name of a place running through it, he was happy to stay away.

As if to confirm his preconceptions, there were people 'sunbathing' on the beach. Several families were encamped on the pebbles, windbreaks flapping around them, the goosepimples visible from a hundred yards. Stubbornness, optimism, stupidity – you could call it what you liked. It seemed to Thorne as perfect an embodiment of Englishness as he'd seen in a while.

'Look at those daft sods,' Eileen said. 'In this weather!'

Thorne smiled. There were other things, of course, that were even more English . . .

'It's getting bloody cold, if you ask me.' Eileen pulled her coat tight to her chest. 'Ten or twelve degrees at most, I should think. Colder, with the wind-chill factor.'

The wind-chill factor. A concept oddly beloved of forecasters in recent years. Thorne wondered where it had come from, and if they used it in places where the wind-chill might actually *be* a factor . . .

'*Well, here in Spitzbergen it's minus forty degrees, but with the* wind-chill factor, *it's officially cold enough to freeze the bollocks off a zoo-full of brass monkeys . . .*'

They moved on, Thorne listening to his father witter on about how many years, how many workmen and how many thousand gallons of gold paint it had taken to complete the Royal Pavilion, until they reached the restaurant. Eileen put on her poshest voice to ask the waiter for a table. When they sat down, Thorne, who had already decided that he was going to pay for lunch, checked the prices. They all went for the three-course Sunday afternoon special. It wouldn't break the bank.

'This is nice,' Victor said.

Eileen nodded. 'I normally cook a big lunch for everyone on a Sunday, but Trevor and his wife are away and Bob's off playing golf, so I decided not to bother. Besides, it's a treat to go out, isn't it?'

Thorne grunted, thinking that, at less than a tenner a head, 'treat' might be putting it a bit strongly. 'Shame we won't see Trevor and Bob,' he said. Trevor was Eileen's son, and Thorne guessed that he probably hadn't gone anywhere. Lunch with barmy Uncle Jim wasn't exactly a tantalising prospect. It almost certainly explained husband Bob's game of golf, hastily arranged once he'd found out that the dotty brother-in-law and dotty brother-in-law's mate were coming down for the weekend . . .

'I know,' Eileen said. 'They both said how much they were looking forward to seeing you.'

Thorne suddenly felt enormously sorry for Eileen. For having to lie. For the shit she had to put up with from his father. For doing all that she did and getting nothing in return. Thorne couldn't remember if he'd ever really thanked her for anything. 'Maybe next time,' he said.

Eileen nodded towards Thorne's father. He was staring at the table, tapping the blunt end of a knife against his teeth. 'I think your dad's having a good time,' she said.

Victor reached across for the water jug. 'He's having a brilliant time, definitely.'

'Did we thank you for bringing him down?' she asked.

Victor beamed. 'It's fine, really. It's fun for us both to go on a bit of a jaunt.'

'Thank you anyway, though. I couldn't get up to fetch him down and he wouldn't have been able to get here without you . . . you know, keeping him company.'

'He's no trouble, honestly.'

Thorne knew that both of these people loved his father, that they sacrificed a great deal for him, but it still set his

261

teeth on edge to hear them talk about him as if he were not there.

'He's trouble when he wants to be,' Eileen said.

Victor laughed and poured Jim Thorne a glass of water.

Thorne tuned out the conversation and looked away, searching to see if there was any sign of their first course. He felt a hand on his arm and saw that it belonged to his father.

'You look like you've got a lot on your mind, son,' the old man said.

Thorne nodded. In his mind a young girl's arms were thrashing, as she whirled across a playground, as she danced around a kitchen, as she tumbled through the air from the roof of a multi-storey car park . . .

Jim Thorne leaned in close and whispered, 'Sometimes, I think you've got it worse than I have.' He jabbed a finger into the side of his head. The hair at his temple was white, whereas his son's was grey. 'You want to try this, Tom. Can't recommend it highly enough. However bad you feel, however much it hurts to think about something, half an hour later and you can't remember fuck all. Just like that, *whoosh*, it's gone. Excellent. Goldfish brain . . .'

Thorne stared at his dad for a few seconds. He couldn't think of a single thing to say. He was rescued by a waitress who materialised at their table with four bowls of watery-looking soup.

'Four and three, forty-three . . .'

When Eileen had suggested bingo, Thorne had felt almost suicidal, and the enthusiasm of Victor and his father had done nothing to change his mood. They walked past what little was left of the West Pier, now all but derelict having caught fire with suspicious regularity. They carried on to Brighton Pier, formerly the Palace, but now renamed as it was the only functioning pier the city had left. Thorne sulked all the way there.

Bingo. It was right up there with karaoke and poking red-hot needles into your eyes . . .

'Two little ducks, twenty-two . . .'

Now that he was *playing*, though, the excitement of the game was getting to him. Even though the prizes on offer – an oversized teddy-bear and a giant, inflatable hammer – hardly justified his increased heart rate.

'On its own, number seven . . .'

'*Bingo!*'

The call came from an old woman sitting a few feet away. Thorne swore under his breath and sat back hard in his chair at the same time as everybody else. He slid back the blue plastic squares that had been covering all but two of his numbers.

He was sitting next but one to his father.

The old man leaned across Eileen and grinned. 'If you've got a hundred old women, how d'you make ninety-nine of 'em shout "fuck"?'

Thorne shook his head. 'Don't know.'

'Get the other one to shout "Bingo".'

Thorne had heard the joke before, but laughed anyway like he always did.

'How many numbers did you need?' Eileen asked.

'Just the two,' Thorne said.

'Imagine what it's like in a big hall. Tens of thousands of

pounds they play for sometimes. More on a national game . . .'

Thorne decided immediately that he'd best not venture into one of those places. If the excitement was relative to the money up for grabs, he'd probably drop dead on the spot.

Where they were, in an arcade at the end of the pier, couldn't have been much different to one of the grand bingo halls that were still dotted around London. Most were former cinemas, but several still retained the grandeur of the Victorian music halls from which they'd been converted. Thorne and the others sat on uncomfortable moulded chairs around a small podium with the plastic grids in front of them, and slots into which to shove their pound coins. It was quick and easy. There was no cash to be won. It was bingo-lite.

'Your next full house in just one minute . . .' The caller's voice echoed through the cheap sound system.

Thorne looked up at him. He was stick-thin and balding. The huge microphone that was pressed against his mouth masked the bottom half of his face. The oversized sunglasses hid the rest of it. Shoddy as the set-up was, the concession to form in the shape of a frilly shirt and wilting bow-tie was something to be admired.

Thorne put his coin into the slot for the next game.

'Come along now, ladies and gents, only a few places left . . .'

Thorne looked around. There were no more than half a dozen people in the whole place. The bloke had more front than Brighton.

'Eyes down for your first number . . .'

Thorne leaned forward, fingers hovering, ready to flip back the plastic squares. A few feet to his right, he could hear that his father was still laughing at his 'bingo' joke. He saw Eileen lean over and whisper, then pick up a coin and push it into the slot for him.

'Five and six, fifty-six . . .'

Thorne's father began to laugh louder. The old woman who'd won the previous game shushed them and shook her head. There were increasingly loud mutterings and murmurs from Thorne's right. He turned at the same moment as Eileen reached for his hand and implored him for some help.

'Two and four,' his father shouted suddenly, 'your mother's a whore!'

Victor giggled, and Thorne saw the colour drain from Eileen's face. He reached across and took hold of his father's arm. 'Dad . . .'

'Three and six, cocks and pricks!'

Thorne stood up and stepped around the back of Eileen towards his father. He heard sniggering, then a voice of encouragement from somewhere behind him. 'Go on, mate, why don't you get up there and have a go?'

Thorne lowered his head until it was close to his father's. The look of excitement, of *glee*, that he saw on the old man's face made him catch his breath.

'Two fat ladies,' his father announced, 'I wouldn't fuck either of them!'

There was a whistle of feedback as the caller put down his microphone. Thorne was shocked to see that the man had no teeth and was at least twenty years older than he'd taken him for. From the corner of his eye, Thorne could see a man in a dark suit – the manager, he guessed – marching towards them with a walkie-talkie in his hand. Thorne knew he should compose himself, should prepare the usual excuses and explanations, but he was far too busy laughing.

The coffee he'd bought at Brighton station had gone cold. Thorne stared out of the carriage window into the blackness as the train moved far too slowly back towards London. He let his head drop back and closed his eyes, wondering why it was that he so rarely felt this tired in bed, when he should sleep.

He pictured his father and Victor, lying in twin beds in Eileen's spare room and talking about the day they'd had. Laughing about what had happened on the pier. In truth, he had no idea whether his father knew what he was doing at moments like that. Were they events he could objectively look back on and enjoy? Thorne hoped that they were, and imagined his father struggling to hold on to the memory of his bingo-calling exploits before it slipped away from him.

Whoosh, it's gone. Excellent. Goldfish brain . . .

Earlier in the day, Thorne had imagined himself as a child with a gaggle of eccentric adults. He knew of course that this was a momentary illusion, that in reality the reverse was true – that trying to look after his father was as close as he'd come, as close as he might *ever* come, to being a parent.

He didn't bother stifling an enormous yawn. When he'd finished, he caught the eye of a woman sitting opposite and smiled. She looked equally knackered and smiled back.

He'd heard plenty about parenting. From seasoned campaigners like Russell Brigstocke and Yvonne Kitson.

From Dave Holland, who still had milky sick-stains on his lapels. Everything they'd told him seemed suddenly relevant to his situation . . .

Nobody could prepare you for it.

You never stopped learning.

There was no right way and no wrong way.

Thorne knew from talking to these people, from listening to their conversations, that there were times when you needed to come down hard. And times when you did, only to feel shitty later, when you realised that you'd got it wrong. Now, Thorne understood what they meant. Sometimes, though they might not like what their children were doing, or the effect that their behaviour was having on other people, it was important to accept that the child was simply having fun. He pictured the look on his father's face as he was shouting out obscenities . . .

Thorne wondered if it was too late to call Alison Kelly. He decided it probably was. Then he reached for his phone and dialled anyway.

'Hi, it's Tom. Hello . . .?'

'Hi . . .'

'Sorry if it's late. I was wondering how you were.'

'I'm tired.'

'Me too. It was quite a night.'

She laughed. 'Yes, it was, wasn't it?'

Thorne pictured her naked. Pictured her crying. Pictured her turned away from him, trying to take in what he'd said. 'I was wondering how you were about what I told you.'

Static crackled on the line. Thorne thought he'd lost the signal, looked at the screen on his phone.

'I'm fine about it,' she said finally. 'I'm . . .grateful.'

'I shouldn't have said anything.'

'You told me the truth . . .'

'You were upset . . .'

'I needed the truth. I *need* the truth.'

Thorne noticed the woman opposite turning her head away. He lowered his voice. 'Some truths are harder to handle than others.'

There was silence.

'Alison . . .?'

'I'm a big girl,' she said. Another laugh, humourless. 'At least *I* got to *be* a big girl . . .'

'Do you want to do it again? Go out?'

He heard a breath let out slowly. 'Why do I think you're just being nice?'

'No, really . . .'

'Let's give it a few days, shall we?' she said. 'See how we feel . . .'

Because of the darkness on the other side of the window, it took Thorne a few seconds to realise that they'd entered a tunnel. He checked the phone. This time he had lost the signal. He stared into space for a few minutes, then reached across the aisle for a newspaper that had been discarded on a table. He turned it over and began to read.

He was asleep before he'd finished the back page.

NINETEEN

The waitress slid a plate of perfectly arranged biscuits into the middle of the table. She picked up the empty tray and moved back, stopping at the door to cast a somewhat perplexed glance back towards the group of men and women gathered in the conference room.

It was certainly an odd collection . . .

Detective Chief Superintendent Trevor Jesmond cleared his throat noisily and waited for silence. 'Shall we get started, ladies and gentlemen . . .?' Tea and coffee were poured as Jesmond made the introductions.

There were seven people around the long, rectangular table. Jesmond was at the head, with a Turkish-speaking uniformed WPC adjacent to his right. Further down the same side of the table sat Memet Zarif, who was next to an elderly man, described as a well-respected Turkish community leader. Opposite them sat Stephen Ryan and a smartly dressed woman named Helen Brimson, introduced by Jesmond as the solicitor representing Ryan Properties. The last person to be introduced sat sweating beneath his leather jacket, a pen in his hand and a sheaf of paper in front of him.

269

'DI Thorne will be taking notes. Keeping minutes of the meeting . . .'

Helen Brimson sat forward and cut in: 'I presume these proceedings will be subject to a valid Public Interest Immunity Certificate?'

Jesmond nodded, and kept on nodding as she continued.

'I want it confirmed that any notes taken will form the basis of an internal police document *only*, that they will not be disclosed in open court should any action arise at a later date . . .'

Thorne scribbled without thinking, hoping that there wouldn't be too much more of this legal bullshit to wade through.

'This meeting is purely part of an ongoing process of community consultation,' Jesmond said. He held out his arms. 'I'm grateful that everyone has agreed to take part, and to come here this morning . . .'

'Here' was a bland and anonymous hotel just outside Maidenhead. A businessman's hotel, like any one of a hundred others around the M25. Easy enough to reach and far enough away from the spotlight.

This was what Tughan had been talking about a little over a week before – getting them around the table, trying to put an end to it.

Zarif placed a hand on the shoulder of the man next to him, the 'well-respected community leader'. The pair of them wore smart suits and tidy smiles. 'My brothers and I have been asked, through our good friend here, to assist the police in any way we can,' he said. 'I would like to think that we were already doing everything in our power to aid these investigations, but if there is anything else we can do, of course we shall be happy to do it.'

Jesmond nodded. Thorne scribbled. There was clearly going to be a *lot* of bullshit flying around.

'The same goes for myself,' Stephen Ryan said. A thick gold chain hung at his throat. A pricey suede jacket over the open-necked shirt. 'It goes for my father and for everyone connected with Ryan Properties. An important business meeting has meant that my father can't be here today, but he wanted me to stress his disgust at these killings . . .'

Thorne could barely believe his ears. He thought about Alison Kelly. It had been just over a week since their phone conversation on the train. There had been no contact between them since . . .

'. . . and his desire to prevent any further bloodshed.' Ryan looked along the table at Thorne. 'Are you going to write that down?'

Thorne thought, I'd like to take this pen and write something across your face, you smug little shitehawk.

He wrote: Ryan. Disgust. Desire.

Jesmond snapped a biscuit in half, careful to shake the crumbs on to the plate. 'I don't need to tell any of you that this is what we want to hear. But we need *action* if anything's going to change. If this bloodshed you refer to is really going to stop.'

'Of course,' Zarif said.

Ryan held up his hands: *Goes without saying*.

Jesmond put on his glasses, reached for a piece of paper and started to read the names printed on it. 'Anthony Wright. John Gildea. Sean Anderson. Michael

271

Clayton. Muslum Izzigil. Hanya Izzigil. Detective Sergeant Marcus Moloney.' Jesmond paused there, looked around the table. 'Most recently, Francis Cullen, a long-distance lorry-driver and two as yet unidentified bodies found along with his.'

Thorne looked at Ryan, then at Zarif. Both wore serious expressions, suitably sombre in response to the roll-call of victims. Those they had lost. Those they had murdered.

'These are the deaths we know about,' Jesmond said. 'These are the murders we are currently investigating, all of which, to some degree, have involved your families or your businesses . . .'

Ryan's solicitor tried to cut in.

Jesmond held up a hand. 'Have, at the very least, *affected* your families or your businesses. Miss Brimson?'

'I have advised my client that, for the purposes of this meeting, he should say nothing in relation to any specific case on which you might ask him to comment.'

'Who's being specific?' Thorne asked.

He received an icy smile. '"Might", I said. *Might*.'

'I'll make sure I underline it,' Thorne said.

Zarif poured himself a second cup of coffee. 'It's a shame that this is your attitude, Mr Ryan. It is people's refusal to speak about these things, to get involved, that is so dangerous. It's what makes these murders possible.'

The old man next to him tugged at his beard, nodding enthusiastically.

'There are some in my community who are afraid to speak up,' Zarif said. He looked towards Jesmond. 'We had thought that those in Mr Ryan's . . . circle might be a little less fearful.'

Zarif was pressing all the right buttons. Ryan's anger was controlled but obvious.

For a long ten seconds no one spoke. Thorne listened to the sound of the cars on the nearby motorway, the rattle of a fan above one of the ceiling vents. The weather had taken a turn for the better in recent days and the room felt arid and airless.

'These killings, whoever and whatever the victims might have been, are simply unacceptable,' Jesmond said eventually. 'They hurt people across a wide range of communities. They hurt people and they hurt businesses . . .'

Thorne wrote, thinking, They hurt your chances of promotion . . .

Ryan smiled thinly. 'Sometimes they're the same thing.'

'I'm sorry?' Jesmond said.

'People and business.' Ryan leaned forward, looked hard at Zarif across the table. 'Sometimes, your business might actually *be* people. You know what I mean?'

Now it was Zarif's turn to exercise some control. He knew that Ryan was talking about the people smuggling, about the hijack. He turned to the old man next to him and muttered something in Turkish.

When Zarif had finished, the Turkish-speaking officer translated for Jesmond. 'There was some swearing,' she began.

Thorne looked at Zarif's face. He wasn't surprised . . .

'Mr Zarif said that some people should think a little about what they were saying before they opened their mouths . . . opened their *stupid* mouths.'

Thorne looked from Ryan to Zarif, in the vain hope that the two of them might clamber on to the table and get stuck into each other. Go on, he thought, Let's end it here and now . . .

Jesmond thanked the WPC. Thorne looked across and caught her eye. He'd forgotten her name. He knew that she was there to ensure that any incriminating statement could be noted, however inadmissible it would later prove to be. He knew there was fat chance of *anything* much that mattered being said by *anybody*. This was politics and pussyfooting. The whole seemingly pointless exercise was about what was *not* being said.

'We need to be united in our efforts,' Jesmond said. He looked around the table until he was satisfied that tempers were being held in check.

'There seems little point in continuing', Brimson said, 'if my client has to sit here and be insulted.'

Thorne glanced at her and Ryan. Their arms were touching, and he idly began to wonder if they might be sleeping together. He knew Brimson was only doing her job, but surely there had to be some other reason why the bile wasn't rising into her mouth. 'Would Mr Ryan prefer to sit *here* and be insulted?' he said.

Ryan didn't bother looking up. 'Fuck you, Thorne.'

Thorne turned innocently to Jesmond. 'Should I write that down . . .?'

'I want to get two messages across to you this morning,' Jesmond said. 'The first, and I want there to be no mistake about this, is that, as far as the murders I have already mentioned are concerned, we are *in no way* scaling down any of those investigations.'

'No way,' Thorne repeated.

Jesmond glanced at him, nodded. 'Some of you will already know this, but DI Thorne is one of the officers actively involved in seeking those responsible.'

Thorne was tempted to give a little wave.

'The second message is by way of a direct appeal.' Jesmond removed his glasses, slid them into his top pocket. 'We want this level of consultation to continue, for everyone's benefit. On behalf of the Commissioner, I'm appealing to you directly. We want you to use your influence. As businessmen. As important members of your communities. We want you to do whatever you can to prevent further loss of life.'

Thorne's pen moved across the paper. He was struggling to keep up with Jesmond's speech. He sat there, hot and headachey, fighting the urge to doodle.

Fifteen minutes later, the waitress knocked and entered. She asked if the biscuits needed replenishing, but the meeting was already starting to break up. Ryan and Zarif left a minute or two apart, each chatting animatedly with his adviser.

Jesmond gathered up his papers. 'How would you say that went, Tom?' He didn't wait for the answer, perhaps guessing that it would be a long time coming. 'I know. These kind of meetings are buggers to get right.' He snapped his briefcase shut. 'Let's just hope we get something out of it.'

With the possible exception of writer's cramp, Thorne doubted it . . .

Methodical in this, as she was in everything – up one aisle then down another, missing none of them out – Carol Chamberlain steered her way past a small logjam near the checkouts, and turned towards detergents, kitchen towels and toilet roll.

Jack appeared, grinning at the side of the trolley, and dropped large handfuls of shopping into it. 'Do we need dog food?' he asked.

Chamberlain nodded, then watched her husband head up the aisle and disappear round the corner. She moved on slowly, picking things off the shelves. Reach, drop, push. Methodical, but miles away . . .

'When we get Ryan, he's going to tell us who took his money twenty years ago and burned Jessica. He's going to give me a name.'

Thorne had made her a promise. He'd told her he was going to find the man who'd been responsible for what had happened twenty years before. He'd told her that he was going to put right her mistake.

He'd told her what he thought she wanted to hear.

That had been more than a fortnight ago, round at his flat, and she hadn't seen Thorne since. She hadn't spoken to him on the phone for almost as long. She knew he was busy, of course, knew that he had far better things to do than keep *her* up to date.

Reach, drop, push . . .

Her cold case from 1993, the murdered bookie, was going nowhere. There was nothing in it to get the blood fizzing in her veins. Nothing to distract her.

Naturally, it was how Jack preferred it. He relished the calm at the end of the day, the fact that she had nothing, of any shape or form, to bring home. He was happier now that she rarely needed to be away from home *at all*. She loved him fiercely, knew that he felt as he did only because he loved her just as much. She'd have been lost without him, helpless without the anchor of his concern. But, feeling as she felt now, as she'd felt since this had all begun, that anchor was starting to pull her down.

She wanted this to be over.

Reach, drop, push . . .

Tom Thorne was the man in whom she'd placed her hopes. She'd had no choice but to do so. Much as Chamberlain liked and respected him, she hated feeling beholden. Hated the fact that it was out of her hands.

Hated it.

She wanted to load up her trolley, pile it high with heavy bottles and tins, and charge, shouting, down the aisle. She wanted to watch the families and the shelf-stackers scatter as she ran at them. She wanted to hear the rattle of the trolley and the squawking of two-way radios as she burst past the tills and flattened the guards, and rushed at the plate-glass windows . . .

Jack came hurrying towards her, clutching cans of dog food to his chest. As soon as they'd tumbled noisily into the trolley, she reached out and slid her arm around his. They moved together towards the next aisle.

23 August 1986

The new Smiths album is awesome. It's got 'Bigmouth Strikes Again' on it and Dad still puts his head round the door if he hears it, and laughs when it gets to the 'Joan of Arc' line.

Ali's got a boyfriend! She met him at some club. I don't know when she went clubbing, or who she went with, but apparently this bloke just walked up to her and asked if she wanted a drink. I met him the other day and he seems nice enough, but when he said hello to me, like everything was normal, he kept looking at Ali, so she could see how 'sensitive' he was being, like he was checking to see what she thought of him.

I don't know if they've really <u>done anything</u> yet.

There's another bloke who she says she's got a big crush on as well. Ali has a crush on somebody different every week. This one's much older than she is, which is why she's so keen, if you ask me. Also, he used to work with her dad, which means that he's probably got a nickname like Ron 'The Butcher' or something. Ali always used to joke about trying it on with one of those blokes, one of her dad's friends. You know, flirting with them and saying, 'Is that a gun in your pocket, or are you just pleased to see me? Oh, it's a gun . . .'

There's another song on the album called 'I Know It's Over'.

I was listening to it on my headphones and there's a bit where Morrissey is singing about feeling soil falling over his head. Like that's how it feels when this relationship he's been in has finished, when he's been dumped or whatever. I was trying to imagine it. Like I'd been with someone and he'd finished with me. I was lying there with it on loud and my eyes closed, putting myself in that position. For a while, it made me feel deep and romantic, like some poet or something. Then, suddenly, I started feeling angry and stupid and I couldn't stand to listen to it again. I always skip that track now. The words and the melody were making me cry, making me _want_ to cry, but the feelings weren't real. The emotion behind it was fake. I'd thought that pity from other people was painful enough, but when I start pitying myself, that's just about as bad as it gets.

I'm not likely to have a fucking relationship, that's the simple truth, and if by some miracle I did, you wouldn't need to be Mastermind to figure out why it might not work. Unless I got it together with some other Melt-Job, of course. You know, our eyes meet across a crowded plastic surgeon's waiting room . . .

No chance of that. Just because I look like I do, doesn't mean I have to fancy other people who look the same, does it?

Being dumped wouldn't make me sad. It would make me want to kill whoever I'd been having the relationship with for being such a wanker. Such a cowardly shithead.

I don't want to have a relationship anyway.

Reading all that back, it sounds _so_ pathetic. Like I'm some brat and I'm pretending that I want to be on my own because I'm really feeling so sorry for myself. I can't help how it sounds. I know what I think.

Shit Moment of the Day

Decided not to bother with this any more because it's stupid.

Magic Moment of the Day

Ditto.

TWENTY

'Tell me again about the meeting with Ryan. Tell me what he said that night in Epping Forest . . .'

Rooker was wreathed in cigarette smoke. His sigh blew a tunnel of boredom through the fug. 'Is there nothing else you could be doing?' he asked. 'It's not as though I'm suddenly going to remember something I haven't already told you, is it?'

Thorne stared at the tapes in the twin-cassette deck. Watched the red spools spinning. 'I don't know . . .'

'Not after twenty years. Do you not think I've had enough time to remember?'

'Or enough time to forget.'

'Oh for fuck's sake . . .'

It had been nearly a month now since the attack on the girl in Swiss Cottage. Nearly a month since the Powers That Be had agreed to take Gordon Rooker up on his offer to give evidence against Billy Ryan. Tughan had told Thorne the day before – the day of the round-table session in Maidenhead – that, all being well, Ryan was likely to be charged within a week or so.

The case was being carefully built on a number of fronts; many of the people connected with Rooker and Ryan back in 1984 had been sought out and questioned. Some were still in the game. Some had long since sloped off to the suburbs. Others had gone even further, to countries with better weather and more attractive tax systems. A few had talked, but not enough for Tughan and his team to feel confident.

Omerta, the Mafia called it: the code of silence. The foreign language and associations made it sound honourable, dignified even, but there was no honour or dignity in the lives of these people, hiding out in villas, mock-Spanish and otherwise, shitting themselves. Thorne would have liked to spend some time with a few of these old fuckers, these fossilised hardmen in Braintree and Benidorm. He wanted to slap their stupid, perma-tanned faces and press a picture of Jessica Clarke up close . . .

'Like I told you before,' Rooker said, 'I got the call from Harry Little and drove up to meet Ryan in Epping Forest. A track near Loughton . . .'

One way and another, Rooker's testimony was going to be key, and, as with all evidence from convicted criminals, it would not be hard to discredit. If it was given any credit in the first place.

Whatever happened, they had to be sure it was nailed down tight . . .

'You got into his car . . .' Thorne said.

'I got into his car.'

'What kind of car was it?'

Rooker looked up, stared at Thorne like he was mad. 'How the fuck should I know? It was dark. It was twenty years ago.'

Thorne sat back, like he'd proved a point. 'Details are important, Gordon. Ryan's defence team are going to slaughter you if you give them a chance. If you can't remember the car, maybe you can't really remember *exactly* what Ryan said. Maybe you were confused. Maybe you thought he was asking you to do something when he wasn't. You with me?'

'It might have been a Merc. One of those old ones with the big radiators.'

'Do you understand what I'm saying? This is why we have to do this.'

Rooker nodded, reluctantly. 'I wasn't confused,' he said.

The door opened and Thorne muttered his thanks as a guard stepped in with drinks. Tea for him. A can of cheap cola for Rooker. The guard closed the door behind him. The drinks were taken.

'This is warm,' Rooker said.

'When you got into his car, did Ryan come straight out and say what he wanted or did you talk about other stuff first?'

'He wasn't really the type to chat about the weather, you know? We might have talked about this and that for a couple of minutes, I suppose. People we both knew . . .'

'Harry Little?'

'Yeah, Harry. Other faces, what have you. I don't remember him beating around the bush for very long, though.'

'So, he asked if you'd be willing to kill Kevin Kelly's daughter, Alison?'

Rooker puffed out his cheeks, prepared to trot out the answers one more time. Thorne asked the question again . . .

'Yes.'

'In exchange for money that he would give you.'

'Yes.'

'How much? How much was he proposing to pay you to kill Alison Kelly?'

Rooker looked up quickly, stared at Thorne. A charge ran between them, flashed across the metal tabletop. Thorne realised, shocked, that this had not come up before.

Rooker seemed equally taken aback. 'I think it was about twelve grand . . .'

'You *think*? *About*?'

'It *was* twelve grand. Twelve thousand pounds.' He said something else, something about what that sort of money might be worth now.

Thorne had stopped listening. Now he knew what Alison Kelly's life had been worth. He was wondering whether he would have told her – the exact amount – had he known it on the night he'd started whispering truths to her in the dark. Thinking that he probably shouldn't have said anything at all . . .

'Did Ryan say why he wanted you to do this?'

'He was trying to get at Kevin Kelly, wasn't he?' Rooker said. 'He wanted him to take on the other firms. He wanted to take over . . .'

'I know all that. I'm not talking about that. Did he say why he was trying to do it by killing a child? You said yourself that it was extreme. That it was out of the ordinary.'

'Right. Which is why I walked away. But, beyond what I've already told you, I don't know anything else. Same with all the jobs I did back then. *Why* was never my business.'

Thorne took a slurp of tea. He opened his mouth to ask something else, but Rooker cut him off.

'How many more times do we have to do this?'

'This is probably the last time,' Thorne said. 'The last time *we* need to go over it, at any rate. I'm not saying there won't be further interviews with other officers . . .'

'Tell me about afterwards.'

'The trial?'

'*After* the trial. Tell me about what happens to me.'

It was Thorne's turn to sigh. This was an area which Rooker seemed keen to keep going over . . .

'I've told you,' Thorne said. 'I don't have any say in what happens, where you end up, any of that. There's a special department that takes care of that stuff.'

'I know, but you must have some idea. They'll presumably move me a good way away, right? Don't you reckon? A whole new identity, all that.'

'There are different . . . *levels* of witness protection. I think it's safe to say you'll probably be top level. To start with, at least . . .'

Rooker seemed pleased with what Thorne had told him. Then he thought of something else. 'Can I pick the name?' he asked.

'What?'

'My new name, my new identity. Can I choose it?'

'Got something special in mind, have you?'

'Not really.' He laughed, reached into his tobacco tin. 'Don't want to go through all this then end up with some twat's name, do I?'

Thorne felt something start to tighten in his chest. The cockiness that he'd first seen in Park Royal was back.

Rooker was talking to him as if he were a mate, as if he were someone he liked and trusted. It made Thorne want to reach across the table and squeeze his flabby neck.

Thorne looked at his watch, bent his head to the recorder. 'Interview terminated at two-thirty-five p.m.' He jabbed at the button.

'Are we done, then?' Rooker asked.

Thorne nodded towards the recorder. 'We're done with *that*.' He leaned forward. 'What did it feel like, Gordon?'

'Come again . . .'

'When you killed someone for money. When you carried out a contract. I want you to tell me how it felt.'

Rooker continued to roll the cigarette, but slower, the yellowed fingers suddenly less dextrous than before. 'What's this got to do with anything?' he asked.

'We already know that *why* wasn't your business, so I was just wondering what *was*. Did you get job satisfaction? Did you take pride in your work?'

Rooker made no response.

'Did you *enjoy* it?'

Rooker looked up then, shook his head firmly. 'You enjoy getting the job done clean, that's all. Getting the money. If you start to enjoy the *doing*, if you start to get some sort of kick out of it, you're fucked.'

Thorne had to disagree. The X-Man clearly relished what he did, and he hadn't made too many mistakes yet.

'So what, then?' Thorne said. 'You just turn off? Go on to some sort of automatic pilot . . .?'

'You focus. Your mind goes blank . . . No, not blank exactly. It's like it's fuzzy, and there, right in the middle, is a point of light. It's really sharp and clear. Cold. You relax

285

and stay calm and move towards that. That's the target, and you don't let anything take you away from it . . .'

'Like guilt or fear or remorse?'

'You asked me, so I'm telling you,' Rooker said. 'It's the job . . .'

'You talk about it in the present tense.'

Rooker put the completed cigarette into the tin. He snapped the lid back on. 'I'm still living with it.'

'A lot of people are still living with it,' Thorne said.

Phil Hendricks was doing some teaching at the Royal Free, and Thorne had arranged to meet him after work. He'd caught the train to Hampstead and they'd eaten at a Chinese place a stone's throw from the hospital. Afterwards, they'd crossed the road to the nearest pub and sunk a couple of pints each inside fifteen minutes. Neither had said a great deal until the edges had been taken off . . .

'Don't let Rooker wind you up,' Hendricks said. 'He's trying to make it sound like some fucking Zen mind-control thing. He just killed people. There's no more to it than that.'

'I wasn't in the mood for him, that's all.' Thorne smiled, raised his glass. 'Just one of those days . . .'

One of those days that seemed to roll around every month or so. When, for no good reason, Thorne stopped and caught himself. When he saw what he did, looked at the people he was dealing with every hour of his life. When, after ticking along for weeks, doing the job without thinking, he was suddenly struck by the stench and blackness of it all. It was like waking up briefly only to find that real life was far worse than the nightmare.

Thorne decided that in some ways, when things became extreme, his own life was similar to his father's. There were times when he heard himself saying things – to killers, and to their victims – that were every bit as bizarre, in their way, as anything that his father ever said.

'Six and nine,' Thorne said, grinning at Hendricks. 'Your face or mine?'

It had become a running joke between them since Thorne had told him about what had happened in Brighton: they had been exchanging filthy bingo calls by phone and text message all week.

Hendricks got up to fetch another round. He grabbed his crotch, sniffed his hand as he turned towards the bar. 'All the threes, I smell cheese . . .'

Thorne looked around. The place was busy, considering that it was only a Tuesday night. It's proximity to the hospital meant that the place was probably full of medics. Thorne knew very well that many of them would have their own edges to take off . . .

He was trying, and failing, to think up another bingo call when a fresh pint was plonked on the table in front of him.

'You know that the body loses weight after death?' Hendricks said.

'This sounds good . . .'

Hendricks sat down, drew his chair closer to the table. 'Seriously. You weigh a bit less dead than you did when you were alive and kicking.'

Thorne picked up his glass. 'It's a bit drastic, don't you think? As diets go . . .'

'Shut up and you might learn something. You can lose

anything from a fraction of a gram upwards. Sixteen grams or thereabouts is the average.' Hendricks shook his head, took a sip of lager. 'The students I was talking to today looked about as interested as you do.'

'Go on then, what causes it?'

'No one's a hundred per cent sure. The air in the lungs, probably. But, this is the good bit . . .'

'Oh, there's a good bit, is there?'

'People used to think it was the weight of the soul.'

The phrase rang in Thorne's head. He nodded. Waited to hear more.

'In the eighteenth century they constructed elaborate scales, designed to weigh terminally ill patients in the moments just before and just after death.' Hendricks let the words sink in, relishing his tale. 'It was a big deal back then – trying to measure the soul's weight as it left the body. Trying to isolate it. They were still doing similar things in America in the early 1900s, and there was a famous experiment in Germany just twenty-five years ago . . .'

Thorne was amazed. A century or more ago and it was easy to put such a theory down to lunatics in fancy dress, to mumbo-jumbo masquerading as science. But *twenty-five* years ago?

'But it's just the air in the lungs, right?'

'That's the best guess,' Hendricks said. 'Unless you go for the soul theory . . .'

Thorne smiled across the head of his beer. 'Did you start drinking before you finished work, or what?'

They drank in silence for a minute or more. Thorne was beginning to feel light-headed. He'd only had a couple of drinks and knew it was tiredness more than anything.

There were pictures forming, dissolving and forming again in Thorne's head. Bodies and scales. Men in wigs and duster coats loading vast weights on to wooden beams. Monitoring the death throes of the wheezing, whey-faced dying, and scratching figures into notebooks. Eyes wide, raised up from inky calculations and then higher, far beyond their primitive laboratories . . .

Thorne looked across at Hendricks. It was clear from the grin, and the faraway expression, that his friend had gone back to thinking about numbers, and rhymes and dirty jokes.

Hampstead Heath was only a couple of stops on the overground from Kentish Town West. They were walking towards the station when Thorne's mobile rang.

'Tom . . .?'

Thorne looked at Hendricks, raised his eyebrows. 'Bloody hell, Carol, it's a bit late for you, isn't it?'

'I know, sorry. I couldn't sleep.'

'You haven't had any more calls, have you?'

'No, nothing like that . . .'

A huge lorry roared past and Thorne lost whatever Chamberlain said next. There was a pause while each of them waited for the other to say something.

'I just called to see how you were getting on.'

'I'm OK, Carol . . .'

'That's good . . .'

'*Everything's* OK. The case is more or less where it was the last time I spoke to you, but it's coming together.' He'd known straight away of course, that this was what she really wanted to know. 'I'm sorry,' he said. 'I meant to call.'

'Don't be daft. I know you must be busy. Listen, I'll leave you to it . . .'

'How's Jack?'

'He's fine. It's fine, Tom . . .'

Hendricks pointed to his watch: the last train was due in a few minutes.

Thorne nodded, picked up speed. 'Why don't we meet up next week?' he said. 'Come down and we'll go for lunch. I'll whack it on expenses.'

'Sounds great. I'll speak to you next week, then . . .'

'Take care, Carol. Phil says hello . . .'

She'd already gone.

At the station, they sat on a bench, waiting for the west-bound train. On the other side of the tracks, three teenage boys drifted aimlessly up and down the platform.

'Sixteen grams on average, you said?'

Hendricks looked blank for a moment or two, then nodded. 'Yeah . . .'

'That's for what? A man of medium height and weight?'

'Right. A woman of medium build would be around twelve grams, I suppose.'

So, a child would be less, Thorne thought. Three quarters as much, maybe eight or nine grams. That didn't make sense, though, did it? Thorne's head was starting to spin. Surely the soul of a child would weigh *more*. It's only as we grow older that we become corrupted, soulless . . .

Eight or nine grams.

Their train rumbled into the station. Thorne spoke over the noise of it, to himself as much as Hendricks.

'A handful of rice,' he said. 'Christ, no . . . *less*. A few grains . . .'

TWENTY-ONE

3 November 1986

If another person leers at me and winks or says something moronic like 'soon be legal', I might have to do something drastic. It's like they're really saying 'as soon as you're sixteen, you can have sex, you know, which is absolutely normal'. I feel like grabbing them by the wrists and saying, 'Thanks a million, I hadn't realised that. All I need now is to find someone who's desperate enough and a big fucking bag to go over my head.'

Why do people presume I'm <u>interested</u>?

Why do people <u>always</u> presume?

I've been frantic for days, wondering how to tell M & D that I'd rather die than go to this party they've been so busy planning for tomorrow. First birthday since the recovery, since the final op. It's like it's such a big deal and I know they just want me to have a good time and do normal things and I can't make them understand.

I don't want a party. I don't want the attention.

The falseness of all that.

When I get angry they just fucking smile at me. They indulge me <u>all the time</u> and it makes me want to scream and smash something. While Ali and the others would be getting grounded or whatever, I get treated with kid gloves.

Like <u>all</u> of me's scarred. Like <u>none</u> of me can be touched.

I want to be shouted at and punished. I want to tell them to stick their party up their arses just to see them lose their tempers for once and tell me that the whole thing's off. Whenever I <u>do</u> start being a bitch, they just stare at each other and they have this <u>look</u> that kills me, as if they're thinking that this behaviour's acceptable and should be forgiven. You know, black clothes and black moods, like it's all perfectly normal for your average, horribly disfigured teenage girl.

When I try to tell them how I feel about this birthday, I know they think it's just some trauma I'm having, some understandable reaction after everything I've been through, and that I don't really mean it.

I <u>do</u> really mean it.

This party, just the thought of it, makes me sweat and makes me ache. Nobody has a clue. Even Ali doesn't seem to get what I'm talking about. She keeps telling me that it'll be a laugh, that I'm just being a stroppy cow, and asking me if there's going to be any tasty men there.

I know M & D have probably spent a fortune on hiring the hall and the disco and everything, and I love them to death for doing it. If I thought for a second that I could get through it, I wouldn't be making a fuss. Watching my mates dance and drink and get off with people sounds great, but I know bloody well what would happen.

I know that, eventually, someone would want to say something.

I've imagined it for weeks now, ever since they told me. Ever since they announced that they wanted to throw a party and looked a bit upset when I told them to throw it as far away from me as possible. Sometimes I imagine it's Dad and other times it's one of my friends, usually Ali. The music stops and there's this howl from the speakers as they grab the DJ's microphone. They start to make this speech. They say something about bravery and make some crap jokes and people pretend to find them funny. Then there's that awkward few seconds of silence that you get after a speech. Then they all start to clap and everyone stares.

Everyone. Stares.

And the pale half of my face, the smooth half, reddens until the blush becomes the colour of the scar. Both halves matching as I burn all over again.

Singing 'Happy Birthday', and Mum and Dad are hugging each other and a few of my mates are crying, and they're all watching me standing in a circle of light in the centre of the room, with looks on their faces like I'm six years old.

Like I'm special . . .

★

Thorne closed the diary, lay back and pressed it to his chest. He opened it again, took out the photograph he'd been using as a bookmark. Pictured her slipping away into the darkness on a bleak November night.

The music, a Wham track, fading behind her as she walks away from the hall, from the party, moving towards the lights of the town centre.

Unmissed still. Her friends dancing, shouting to one another above the music while she climbs.

The smell of exhaust fumes and the sound of her shoes echoing off the grey concrete stairwells.

A voice of concern, the first few worried looks from her friends as, half a mile from them, she steps out into the cold. Into fresh air. The desperate rush of the black towards her. The night kissing both sides of her face as she tumbles through it . . .

Thorne jumped slightly when the phone rang, the sudden movement sending Elvis careering from the end of the bed. Thorne looked at the clock: 4.35.

Brigstocke wasted no time on pleasantries. 'We're getting reports of an incident at an address in Finchley . . .'

Thorne was already out of bed. 'Ryan's place?' he said.

'Right. Uniform are on the scene, but there's some confusion. At least one person injured, by all accounts, but beyond that we don't know much.'

'Zarif sent the X-Man after Ryan, you think?'

'You know as much as I do, mate . . .'

Thorne was moving quickly around the bedroom, snatching up socks and underpants, grabbing at a shirt. 'Are you on your way up there?'

'Tughan's got it,' Brigstocke said, 'but you live a lot

nearer than he does, so I reckon you'll probably beat him to it.'

'Cheers, Russell. I'll call you when I get there . . .'

Thorne moved into the living room to find that Hendricks was already sitting up in bed. Thorne told him what was happening.

'Want me to come along?' Hendricks asked.

Thorne had gone into the kitchen. He came out shaking his head, gulping down a glass of water.

'You sure? I can be dressed in one minute . . .'

Thorne picked up his jacket, felt in the pockets for his keys. 'No point. We don't know exactly what's happened yet,' he said. 'But I wouldn't bother going back to sleep, if I was you . . .'

The streets were all but deserted as Thorne drove up towards the Archway roundabout and turned north. He knew he might be over the limit to drive, but he felt clear-headed and focused. He was seeing the tail-lights early, anticipating the few cars that were coming at him from side-streets. Thinking a long way ahead.

He chose the route through Highgate, avoiding the road that ran parallel, that would have taken him under Suicide Bridge. The iron footbridge that had long since replaced John Nash's viaduct – the original 'Archway' – was the preferred jumping-off point for many of the city's depressed. Thorne did his best to avoid it when he could, unable to drive beneath it without unconsciously bracing himself for the impact of a body on the roof of the car.

Tonight, he was in a hurry, but with the pages of a dog-eared diary still dancing in front of his eyes, he would have done almost anything to avoid the bridge.

His mobile rang again as the car flashed across a red light and on to the North Circular. Thorne checked the display, saw 'Holland Mob' flashing . . .

'I know,' he said. 'I'm on my way to Ryan's place now.'

Holland laughed. 'I'll see you there . . .'

If the Zarifs had hit Ryan, there was no way of knowing how things would pan out. Thorne guessed that Stephen would take up the reins, and he didn't seem the sort to forgive and forget. Then again, from what Thorne had seen, there might be nothing to Billy's son and heir *except* a temper. He might go to pieces, leaving Ryan Properties to implode and the Zarifs with new possibilities for expansion. The whole messy business might have started out as a reaction to Ryan's firm moving into their territory, but Thorne couldn't believe that Memet and his brothers would have gone to all the trouble they had without wanting something substantial out of it. Whichever way things went, there were likely to be big changes ahead. *Messy* changes . . .

Thorne reached the Finchley conservation area within fifteen minutes. He swung the BMW hard around the green and recalled his encounter there with Billy Ryan a fortnight before. He didn't know what he was going to find when he reached Ryan's house, but something told him that somebody else was going to be walking the dog for a while.

It was a three-storey detached house at one corner of the green. There were two squad cars parked outside, but no sign of an ambulance. Thorne showed his warrant card to the PC at the door and stepped inside. He was looking at the trail of blood that snaked along the hall carpet when a second uniformed officer appeared in front of him.

'I'm DI Thorne. Where's the ambulance?'

'It came and went away empty, sir. The victim was already dead when they arrived. Dead when they were called, if you ask me . . .'

Thorne wondered if Hendricks had got himself dressed yet. 'Where?'

The officer pointed to a doorway down the hall.

Thorne moved towards it, wishing he'd taken some gloves from his boot. 'Any ID?'

'Yes, sir. According to Mrs Ryan, the dead man is her husband, William John Ryan.'

Thorne stepped carefully around the bloodstains that grew bigger as he neared the doorway. The door was ajar. He nudged it all the way open with his shoe.

Ryan was on the kitchen floor, curled close into a corner, one hairy forearm streaked with red and propped up oddly against a cupboard. His white shirt was sopping – dark patches soaking through the silk at the shoulder and beneath the arm. The good-sized gash in his neck still wept a little blood, the lines of grout running red between the terracotta floor-tiles.

You didn't need a medical degree . . .

Thorne was aware that the uniform had joined him at the door. He glanced at him, then looked back to Billy Ryan. 'So, what's the story?' he asked.

'The story's a bloody odd one. She just walked in and stuck a knife in him, by all accounts. Over and over again.'

Thorne swung around, stunned. 'His *wife* killed him?'

'No, sir. Not his wife.' The uniform turned, nodded towards the doorway from which he'd first appeared. 'The other woman . . .'

Thorne pushed past him, moved down the corridor without a word. He could feel the breath rushing from his lungs, could hear a noise that grew louder in his head, like wasps trapped beneath a cup. He knew what he was going to see . . .

The two officers sitting on the sofa stood up, their faces grim-set, when Thorne entered the living room. The woman, handcuffed to one of them at the wrist, had little choice but to rise with him. A WPC on the other side of her stared at Thorne, waiting, her hand clasped tight around Alison Kelly's elbow.

Thorne opened his mouth to speak, then closed it. There was nothing he could think of to say. Alison looked at him for a second or two.

He was sure she gave him a small nod before she lowered her head.

APRIL

IMMORTAL SKIN

TWENTY-TWO

A couple of years before, while driving to work early one morning, Thorne had been shaken by the sight of a horse-drawn hearse coming at him out of the mist. He'd pulled over and stared as the thing had rattled by. The breath of the horses had hung in front of their soft mouths like smoke before drifting back through the black feathers of their plumes.

The genuine spookiness of that moment came back to Thorne now as he watched the undertakers slide the coffin from an almost identical glass-sided carriage. If there was one person he would not wish to be haunted by, it was Billy Ryan.

St Pancras Cemetery was the largest in London. While not as well known as Highgate or Kensal Green, and with fewer grand monuments or famous residents, it was nevertheless an impressive and atmospheric place. Thorne watched as the pall-bearers hefted the coffin on to their shoulders and began to move slowly away from the main avenue. The vast acreage, shared with Islington Cemetery, stood on the site of the notorious Finchley Common, once the killing ground of highwaymen Dick Turpin and Jack Sheppard. It was an appropriate place, too, Thorne decided, for Billy Ryan to go into the ground and rot.

The hearse could go no further. The beautifully tended beds near the cemetery entrance had given way quickly to overgrown woodland that in places was virtually impenetrable. The elegant displays of daffodils, tulips and pansies had been replaced by nettles, brambles and a jungle of ivy that crept across the doorways of burial chambers and grasped the stone wings of smiling angels.

'Pardon me, sir . . .'

Thorne stepped aside to let one of the funeral directors pass. He and three others beside him were hurrying to catch up with their colleagues. They each carried vast floral tributes: crosses, wreaths, arrangements that spelled out 'DAD' and 'BILLY'. Dozens more were already being lined up at the roadside. A great day for Interflora . . .

Thorne had glanced at the noticeboard near the entrance as the procession had swung in through the main gates. There were half a dozen other funerals taking place that morning. Three were listed as being for babies, with the words 'No Mourners' handwritten beneath their typed entries on the timetable.

The Ryan bash was definitely the main event.

Times had certainly changed for the Ryan family and those like them. There was still a profit in vice and gambling, but the big money was in drugs. It was a dirty business in every sense and had only got dirtier since Johnny Foreigner had moved in and dared to stake a claim. The rule-book had been well and truly torn up, but, though the good old gorblimey days when you could leave your door open in the East End and villains 'only killed their own' were long gone, some things remained the same.

They still loved their mums and they still loved an honest-to-goodness, old-fashioned funeral: curly sandwiches and warm beer and well-worn tales of plod, porridge and pulling teeth for fun and profit.

The brown moss was damp and springy underfoot as the cortège made its way towards the centre of the cemetery. The crowd had thinned out. Only close family, friends and certain police officers would be present at graveside. Thorne looked at these people with whom he had spent the best part of the day: sniffing through the moving tributes in the church; processing slowly through Finchley; muttering about how pleased Billy would have been with the turnout.

Thorne had watched from inside the dark, unmarked Rover at the back of the line. He'd stared as pedestrians had bowed their heads or tipped their hats, unaware to whom they were showing respect. Thorne had found it funny. Respect was, after all, very important to a certain type of businessman . . .

Those carrying Billy Ryan's body moved awkwardly along the narrow grove, struggling to retain the necessary degrees of dignity and balance as they stepped across gnarled roots and around leaning headstones. One of their number walked two steps ahead of the coffin to push aside overhanging branches. The mourners followed gingerly, in single file.

Thorne was not the only police officer present. Tughan was a little way ahead of him, and a fair number of SO7 boys were knocking around somewhere. Thorne recognised plenty of other faces, too. These were a little harder, the eyes that bit colder. He wondered how many mourners were carrying weapons; how many years the pall-bearers had done between them. He wondered whether the killer of Muslum and Hanya Izzigil might be the man next to him.

It occurred to Thorne that, with the exception of the vicar and the blokes in the black hats, there were probably no men there without either a warrant card or a criminal record. Come to think of it, even the vicar looked dodgy . . .

They rounded a corner and the track widened out towards a freshly prepared grave. A green cloth lay all around the hole, garish against the clay. It was a decent-sized plot, expensive, with room for a fitting memorial. More flowers were already laid out, waiting. There were a few recently filled graves here, among many that were far older, the gleaming black headstones and brightly coloured marble chippings incongruous next to the weathered stones. The epitaphs were gold-edged and vulgar alongside the faded names that belonged to another age: Maud, Florence, Septimus . . .

The vicar spoke to begin the service:

'Oh God . . .'

It pretty much summed up the way Thorne felt.

On the far side of the grave Stephen Ryan was clutching his mother's arm. His eyes were bloodshot; whether from cocaine or grief, it was hard for Thorne to tell. The eyes flashed Thorne a look, intense and loaded, but impossible to read.

Thank you for coming . . .

What am I supposed to do now . . .?

What the fuck do you think you're doing here . . .?

Get ready . . .

Thorne looked from the son to the mother. Ryan's wife stared, unblinking, at the coffin. Thorne had not had the pleasure. He remembered something Tughan had told him, and if the rumours were to be believed, any number of gardeners and personal trainers certainly *had*. The botox and plastic tits had clearly been doing the trick, and now she'd have much more money to spend on keeping herself desirable. When she raised her eyes towards him and then higher to the trees beyond, Thorne could see that they were dark and dry beneath the heavy make-up.

The vicar droned on, the occasional word lost to the caw of a crow or the rumble of a passing plane.

Thorne wondered if Billy Ryan had kept those old boxing skills sharp by practising them on the second wife as well as the first. It was, he decided, highly probable. Either way, the fucker had finally been made to pay for everything he'd done to Alison Kelly.

But had he *really* paid for Jessica Clarke?

Thorne stared at the widow and the heir as the coffin was lowered into the grave. He couldn't be sure, but Ryan's wife looked like she just wanted to be certain he was never coming out. Stephen began to sob, and Thorne realised that *he'd* been holding on to his mother for support, not vice versa.

When various armed robbers began stepping forward to sprinkle dirt on to the coffin lid, Thorne decided it was about time to move in the opposite direction. He turned and walked slowly back along the rough, narrow track towards the main avenue. As he did, he read the head-stones, in the same way that it was impossible not to look through a lighted window as you wandered along a street. Many of those resident beneath his feet seemed to have 'fallen asleep', which struck him now as always as childish and silly. But it was perhaps understandable that there were nearly as many euphemisms here as there were bodies. 'Passed into rest' and 'gone to a better place' were, even Thorne had to admit, marginally more acceptable than 'hit by a truck' or 'fallen down a lift shaft'. Certainly better than 'knifed several times in his hallway, then again in his kitchen'.

Thorne emerged on to the wide road that ran down to the cemetery gates. He stopped by the hearse to rub the muzzle of one of the horses. A shiver ran down the animal's flank before it whinnied, and released a series of turds which splattered on to the tarmac.

One bad memory well and truly exorcised . . .

Moving along the line of cars, Thorne walked past a number of serious-looking characters in long black coats, many of whom he knew to have written best-selling true-crime memoirs. They were doubtless greatly honoured to be policing Billy's service. Security, along with a healthy smattering of soap stars and minor sporting figures, was a prerequisite of the traditional gangland funeral.

Thorne stopped next to a large, metal litter-bin. It was overflowing with plastic bags, plant pots and dead flowers. Leaning against it was someone he hadn't expected to see. 'Is there really any point you being here?' Thorne asked.

Ian Clarke was clutching a large wreath of white lilies. He was wearing jeans and a dark blue jacket over a brown polo shirt. He clearly found Thorne's question highly amusing. 'No point whatsoever,' he said. 'I went to Kevin Kelly's funeral, too. It was the least I could do . . .'

Thorne found himself wondering if Clarke could possibly know about Ryan's part in what had happened to his daughter. He dismissed the thought, wondered instead if he should tell him. That idea was sent packing even quicker. If he hadn't opened his mouth once already, they wouldn't be standing in a cemetery at all.

He looked over towards the gatehouse. A gardener was moving slowly around the edge of a flower bed. One hand manoeuvred a strimmer, the other pressed a mobile phone to his ear.

When Ian Clarke began to speak, it was so quietly, and with such an absence of emotion, that it took Thorne a few seconds before he realised that he wasn't talking to himself. Once he'd begun to listen, Thorne could tell that he might just as well have been.

'It's the few days just after the burn that are the worst. Not just . . . emotionally, but that's when all the real damage gets done, the *peak* damage. The progression of the injury can be ten times worse than the burn itself. Did you know that? That's what really causes the scarring . . .

'She couldn't open her eyes or her mouth after it happened. She couldn't bite. The screaming came out through her teeth, like a sound I'd never heard before. Like a noise that was bleeding out through what was left of her skin. There was a lot of screaming in those first few days.

'She had to wear a mask, a clear mask to keep a steady pressure on the damaged skin. It's basically to reduce the final height of the scars. To keep them supple. Over a year she wore that hideous bloody thing. Over a year, she wore

307

it and hated it for twenty-three hours a day. Pointless in the end, though, because it hadn't been fitted properly and the damage had already been done. She had to keep still, you see, utterly still, absolutely fucking motionless while they put Vaseline across her face, and then this jelly stuff. She couldn't move a muscle while it set . . .

'I could have let them anaesthetise her. *Should* have done. I didn't want her to have another operation, though. You understand? She'd already had six skin grafts and twenty-five blood transfusions by then. Some of the junior doctors used to joke, you know? They used to say she spent more time in the bloody hospital than *they* did.

'That mask I was talking about, the pressure mask, they do it all with lasers now, you know. They scan the face with these lasers and it's always a perfect fit. No doctors or parents to mess it up. The treatment of burns is so much better now than it was then. Everything's moved on. Now they use hyperbaric oxygen therapy to reduce the scarring in the early days. Amazing things, new techniques, new discoveries all the time: microdermabrasion, laser skin resurfacing, chemical peeling, you name it. There are sites I've got bookmarked on the computer at home, you know? Medical newsgroups, chatrooms you can join. You can find just about anything on the Internet if you're interested enough, or nerdy enough, depending on how you want to look at it, and you've got the time. I'm quite the expert on all the new developments.

'These are good days to get burned . . .

'The grafts are amazing now, really amazing. Single-sheet grafts, that's what's really made the difference. Back in our day, they only did split-skin grafts. You understand what I'm saying? They took shavings from different areas and it was virtually impossible to stop it contracting. To stop the scar tissue tightening. Now, they've got artificial skin which they can use for temporary grafting. It's amazing stuff, you know? Made from shark skin and silicon. Back then . . . God, listen to me, talking as if it was a hundred bloody years ago . . . *Back then*, they used cadaver grafts. Just the name makes you go a bit funny, doesn't it? Skin harvested from the dead.

'Skin from corpses. On my girl's neck. Lying across her face . . .

'They can even grow skin in labs now. They can *grow* it. Skin that's as near as damn it the same as the stuff we were born with. It's as thick as human skin, that's the real step forward. They call it "immortal skin". "Immortal" because the cells never stop growing. *Ever*. Did you know that there's only one naturally occurring human cell in which immortality is considered normal? Do you want to guess? It's the cancer cell . . .

'Now, they've got immortal skin . . .'

Finally, he paused.

Thorne took half a step towards him. 'Ian . . .'

'Bad guys have scars. Monsters and murderers in films and on TV. The Phantom of the fucking Opera and the Joker and Freddie Krueger.'

'Maybe we've moved on from that kind of rubbish, too,' Thorne said.

If Clarke heard what Thorne had said, he chose to ignore it. 'It's like wearing a mask you can never take off,' he said. 'Jess wrote that in her diary.'

'I read it . . .'

Clarke looked up, his eyes bright, his voice suddenly cracked and raw. 'What she said about the party? You remember what she wrote that last day, about the speech someone was going to make on her birthday? It was exactly what I was planning to do. *Exactly*. Even down to the crap jokes . . .'

Thorne found it hard to meet the man's gaze, as he had that day in the house off Wandsworth Common. He dropped his eyes slowly to the ground. Down past the fists that had tightened around the edge of the wreath, the knuckles white as the petals that had fallen at Ian Clarke's feet.

TWENTY-THREE

'I think you're an idiot, Tom.'

'Cheers. Thanks for that . . .'

'I think you're a *fucking* idiot.'

'Jesus, Carol . . .'

The shock of hearing Chamberlain swear – not an everyday occurrence – somehow softened the blow of the comment itself.

Chamberlain's pithy character assassination simultaneously managed to kill the conversation stone dead; to thicken the space between them. After half a minute spent tearing up beer mats and avoiding eye contact, Thorne held up his empty glass. Without fully shifting her gaze from the back of a stranger's head, Chamberlain nodded. She slid her empty wineglass across the table.

Thorne walked across to the bar, ordered a pint of Guinness and a glass of red.

They were in the Angel on St Giles High Street. The pub, pleasantly tatty and old fashioned, stood on or around the site of a tavern which, several hundred years before, had been on the route from Newgate Prison to the gallows at Tyburn. The condemned man's final journey, which took him along what was now Oxford Street, involved stopping at the tavern for a last drink. The drink was given free, the joke being that the customer would pay for it 'on his way back'.

Thorne handed over his ten-pound note, knowing that he wouldn't receive a great deal of change. The concept of free drinks certainly belonged in a bygone age, like small-pox or press-gangs. These days, you could crawl into a pub on your hands and knees with two minutes to live and you'd be lucky to find so much as a complimentary bowl of peanuts on the bar.

Those who knew the history of the pub also knew that the custom for which it had once been famous had spawned the phrase so beloved of publicans and pissheads alike. Thorne walked back to the table, put down the drinks. 'One for the road,' he said.

Chamberlain understood the reference. Her smile managed indulgence and disapproval at the same time. 'Right, and we all know who's likely to be the one swinging, don't we?'

Thorne's face, save for the moustache of froth, was a picture of innocence. 'Do we? I can't see why.'

He could see perfectly well why, but felt like arguing about it. He was less certain about why he'd told Carol Chamberlain what he'd said to Alison Kelly in the first place. He'd actually decided to tell Chamberlain, to *confide* in her, well before this evening. Well before Alison had killed Billy Ryan even. So he could hardly blame the beer . . .

'The sex part I understand,' she said.

'Oh, good . . .'

'After all, you *are* a bloke.'

'Right. I'm a mindless brute in helpless thrall to my knob.'

Chamberlain reddened slightly. 'You said it.'

The blush made Thorne smile. 'I didn't tell her because I slept with her,' he said.

'So why, then?' She answered the question herself. 'Because you're an idiot.'

'Let's not start that again . . .'

She shook her head, exasperated, and took a slug of red wine.

Thorne wondered if the things she'd seen, that she surely must have heard, had made Chamberlain blush back when she was on the force. Perhaps it was simply a reaction that suppressed itself in certain situations, like a bookmaker's pity or a whore's gag reflex. She was certainly a damn sight less worldly than she often pretended.

'You're pissed off because it wasn't *you*,' Thorne said. 'Because you had nothing to do with it.'

'I'm pissed off because of a lot of things.'

It didn't sound like an invitation to pry, or a willingness to share. Thorne held his tongue and waited to see where she wanted to go.

'You're right, though,' she said. 'I knew I could never play a part in bringing Ryan down. However much you indulged me . . .'

'Carol, I never . . .'

She silenced the protestation with the smallest movement of her hand. 'Still, knowing I wasn't going to be involved didn't stop me imagining certain . . . scenarios.'

313

'Ryan dead, you mean?'

'Not just dead. I thought about killing him myself. I thought about it a lot.'

Thorne raised an eyebrow. 'How was it?'

'It was great.'

'The way you killed him or the way it made you feel?'

'Both.'

'And the reality isn't quite as good as you'd imagined it . . .'

She pulled a tissue from her sleeve, dabbed at a ring of wine left on the table. 'It's not the right result, Ryan being dead.'

Thorne had turned the same thing over and over in his head, looked at it from every angle, examined it in every conceivable light. 'Do you not think he's paid for what he did?'

Chamberlain said nothing.

'Look, the law could have taken its course, and Tughan, or somebody like him, might have got lucky and maybe, five years from now, Billy Ryan would have been cock of the walk in Belmarsh or Parkhurst. I'm not necessarily saying that what happened was right or that he got what was coming to him. How the hell could I, knowing . . . what I had to do with it? I just can't find it in myself to feel the slightest bit gutted that he's dead.'

The flash that had been in Chamberlain's eyes when she'd talked about killing Billy Ryan had gone. It had been replaced by something warmer, more muted. 'I'm not exactly heartbroken myself,' she said.

Thorne lifted his glass. 'Let's not overlook the substantial saving of taxpayers' money. Of *our* money. Or

314

the fact that overpaid solicitors might have to wait that bit longer for flash cars and luxury holidays . . .'

Chamberlain did not come close to returning his smile. 'It's not the right result, because with Ryan dead we'll never get him, will we? How will we ever know who Ryan gave that money to? How will we ever know who burned Jessica?'

The beer was suddenly vile in Thorne's mouth. He swallowed it quickly, tasting it thick and brackish as it moved down his throat. He felt it settle in his stomach, black and heavy, like doubt. Like guilt.

'Why did you tell her, Tom?' Chamberlain asked. 'If it wasn't just a post-coital thing?'

Thorne shook his head. 'I honestly have no idea.' And he honestly didn't. 'Not beyond a simple, strong feeling that she needed to know.'

'"She needed to know", or you needed to tell her? They might have seemed like the same thing at the time.'

'It felt good to tell her. I won't pretend it didn't.'

'What about now?'

Now felt like a world away from *then*, though it was less than three weeks since he and Alison Kelly had slept together. Ten days since she'd stuck a blade into Billy Ryan. *Now* seemed infinitely confused and uncertain. *Then*, it had all seemed straightforward. Then, there had only been light and shadow, and a simple choice between a hot, hard knowing and an ignorance that looked and sounded anything but blissful.

Thorne blinked before answering Chamberlain's question, remembered the inscription on a headstone he'd walked past at Billy Ryan's funeral a few hours before.

In life, in death, in dark, in light. We are all in God's care . . .

It was supposed to be simple. Life was light and death was darkness. But for some souls, the situation was always going to be more complex. There could be little doubt that Ryan's had been a life lived in darkness. Through it and for it. Right now, Thorne was not so certain where *he* stood . . .

'Now? I wish to God I'd kept my mouth shut,' he said. 'Not for Ryan's sake . . .'

'For hers.'

'She'll spend a long time in prison.'

'There's a lot for the court to take into account . . .'

Thorne shook his head. 'A *long* time. And she's not hard, you know? She must *think* she is. She made a decision to do what she did. She *chose* prison.'

'Same as our friend Gordon Rooker,' Chamberlain said. 'Maybe we're not making these places scary enough.'

'Right.' It was an automatic response, meaning nothing. Alison Kelly would find it tough enough.

Chamberlain put down her glass, leaned forward. '"She *chose* prison." You said it yourself. You didn't put the weapon in her hand, Tom . . .'

'In a way, I did.' He took a sip of Guinness. It wasn't really tasting any better. 'Didn't somebody say that knowledge is a dangerous thing?' Feeling his brain start to fuzz up just a little. Breathing a bit more heavily.

Thinking: knowledge is a knife . . .

'Probably,' Chamberlain said. 'Some smart-arse.'

The dour look on her face, the way her soft Yorkshire accent suited the word so perfectly, made Thorne laugh. A hole was punched through the murk that had been settling

316

about their heads and sucking away the joy that was normally there between them.

'How's your cold case going, anyway? The case of the punctured publican . . .'

'It wasn't a publican, it was in a pub car park and "cold" doesn't come close. There's icicles hanging off the bloody thing. Mind you, I've not exactly been giving it my undivided attention.'

'Maybe now you'll be able to focus a bit more.'

'Maybe . . .'

Thorne touched his glass to her hand. 'Billy Ryan. Jessica Clarke. You need to let it go now.'

Slowly, her eyes widened. '"Let it go". Right. And the names Bishop, Palmer and Foley mean nothing to you . . .'

Thorne's hand moved to his scrubby beard and his thoughts to the cases Chamberlain was talking about. Cases that had left their mark on him. Carved deep, but never less than fresh, never less than tender. How had one fifteen-year-old put it? 'Like a mask you could never take off.'

'I think', he said after a few moments, 'that I preferred it when you were insulting me . . .'

Tottenham Court Road tube station was pretty handy for both of them. Thorne would take the Northern Line up to Kentish Town. Chamberlain could change at Oxford Circus, just two stops away from Victoria Station and the last train back to Worthing.

They walked past the church of St Giles in the Field. It had been founded at the start of the twelfth century as a leper hospital, and its parish records contained the names

317

of Milton, Marvell and Garrick. The burial grounds that lay behind the spiked metal fence contained many of those who'd met their end at Tyburn tree and whose final taste of alcohol had cost considerably less than Thorne and Chamberlain had just spent.

They crossed the road at Denmark Street and turned towards the Charing Cross Road. To the north of them, the skyline was dominated by Centre Point. The office block – once thought smart, and even stranger, tall – had stood totally empty for some time after it was first erected, and a charity for the homeless, as an ironic gesture, had taken its name. The building rose above an area that a hundred and fifty years before had been the city's most notorious and overcrowded slum. The Rookery had been a maze of filthy alleyways, rat-runs and courts where the poor had lived in squalor, and where crime had been as endemic as the disease. A sprawling network of so-called 'thieves kitchens' and 'flash houses' had made it a virtual no-go area for the police officers of the time.

Thorne outlined the history of the place as they walked. It had flourished, if that was an appropriate word, for over a century, before being demolished to make way for what was now New Oxford Street some time in the mid-nineteenth century. Thorne couldn't remember the exact date.

'You and I seem to talk about history a lot,' Chamberlain said.

Thorne laughed. 'Some of it not quite so dim and distant.'

'Why do you think that is?'

Thorne considered the question for a moment. 'Maybe because we think we can learn from it.'

'Can we?'

'We *can*. I'm not sure we *have*. I'm not convinced anything's changed very much.'

Chamberlain said something, but her words were lost beneath the wail of a siren as a police van rushed past them towards Leicester Square. Thorne shook his head. Chamberlain waited for the noise to die down before she repeated herself. 'Perhaps that's reassuring.'

Gazing through the windows of Internet cafés and computer stores, Thorne couldn't help but picture the gutters running with sewage, families packed into cellars. Men and women driven to prostitution and theft to maintain a standard of living that could only be described as inhuman.

'Have you read *Oliver Twist*?' Thorne asked. It was the iniquity of life in the Rookery, and places like it, that Dickens had described, perhaps a touch romantically, in his creation of Bill Sikes, Fagin and his gang of under-age rogues . . .

Chamberlain shook her head. 'I've only seen the musical. Shameful, isn't it?'

Thorne had taken a few steps before he decided to make his confession. 'I was in a production of *Oliver!* at school. I was the Artful Dodger . . .'

Chamberlain took his arm. 'Now *that* I would have paid good money to see.'

'You'd have felt very ripped off . . .'

Thorne had actually enjoyed himself. He'd done his turn, shown off and clowned around, blissfully unaware that the real people on which the characters were based did somewhat worse than pick a pocket or two.

'Can you remember any of the songs?' Chamberlain

asked. She began to hum 'Consider Yourself', but Thorne didn't join in.

'I remember I had a battered top hat that you could squash, and then it would pop up again. I remember my nan waving at me on the first night when I walked on. I remember spending the whole time trying to cop off with a girl from the sixth form who was playing Nancy.'

They turned into the entrance to the tube station. Walked down the stairs towards the turnstiles.

'Right,' Chamberlain said. 'So you were in helpless thrall to your knob even then . . .'

Back at the flat, Thorne sat at the kitchen table waiting for the kettle to boil. He called his father but the line was permanently engaged . . .

He was still getting used to having the place to himself again. Hendricks had moved back into his flat the week before, and, if he was being honest, Thorne missed having him around. It *was* good to have some peace and quiet, though, and he certainly didn't miss the discarded trainers dotted about the place or the disparaging comments about his record collection.

After five minutes he rang the operator, asked them to check his father's line. His dad's phone had been left off the hook.

It was nice to have some privacy back too. Although Hendricks had shown no such inhibitions, Thorne had felt somewhat uncomfortable about being less than fully clothed in front of his friend. He knew he was being stupid, or worse, but the journey from bathroom to bedroom had occasionally been a little awkward.

Thorne carried his tea through to the living room. He put some music on and, while he was up, took a well-thumbed encyclopedia of London from the shelves.

The Rookery of St Giles had been demolished in 1847.

He drank tea and listened to Laura Cantrell, and to the hum of distant traffic between the tracks. He sat and read . . .

While various King Georges had come and gone, while science and revolution were changing the world beyond recognition, the deprivation and crime in the worst areas of the capital had reached incredible levels. The poor and the sick had robbed and murdered one another, and sold their children to buy gin, while the law had more or less left them to get on with it.

Two centuries on, the drugs were different. The gun had replaced the cudgel and the cut-throat razor. The Rookeries were called housing estates.

Thorne remembered what Chamberlain had said when the siren had stopped screaming.

'*Reassuring*' was definitely *not* the word . . .

TWENTY-FOUR

'So, come on,' Rooker said. 'What level of protection do I get?'

He looked from Thorne to Holland and back again, searching their faces for some hint. The two detectives looked at each other, milking the moment.

To say that the SO7 case – specifically the part involving the testimony of Gordon Rooker – had been thrown into confusion would be an understatement. The concept of witness protection did, after all, become a little pointless when the individual from whom you were providing protection had been carved up by an ex-wife. As Thorne had explained to Rooker before, there were different levels of protection, each appropriate to the perceived threat. Rooker had clearly grasped the concept, and, with the prison jungle drums going mental, had been on the phone before Ryan's death had so much as made it into the papers. He'd ranted and raved and demanded to know where he stood. It had been explained to him through appropriate channels that, in the immediate aftermath of Billy Ryan's murder, *his* peace of mind was pretty low on everybody's list of priorities.

Now, face to face with Thorne for the first time since Ryan's death, Rooker was still looking for an answer. '*Well? What level do I get?*'

Thorne sniffed, nodded thoughtfully. 'I think maybe a more basic method of disguise, as opposed to a completely new identity, and perhaps some means of raising the alarm should you feel threatened.'

'Come again?'

Holland smirked. 'A wig and a whistle.'

'Oh, fuck off and behave yourselves . . .'

On a practical level, no one had so much as decided where Rooker should even go. He was still on the protected witness wing in Salisbury, which did seem pretty stupid. He could be transferred back to the VP wing at Park Royal or even, it had been suggested, back into the general prison population elsewhere, now that he was obviously in no danger from Billy Ryan. This idea had thrown Rooker into such a furious panic that the solicitor who'd passed on the information had briefly feared for his physical safety. In the end, unable to make a quick decision, they'd decided to leave him where he was. It was where he wanted to be, but Rooker still seemed far from content . . .

'I don't understand,' Holland said. 'I thought you'd be delighted that Billy Ryan was six feet under.'

Rooker sucked his teeth. 'Ten feet would be better. Yeah, if I had one, I'd've raised a glass to Alison Kelly for sticking a knife in the cunt, course I would. Shame it wasn't a paintbrush . . .'

'So, why are we here?' Thorne asked. 'Frankly, we've got better things to do.'

323

'How d'you know I'm not still a target?'

Thorne pretended to rack his brains. 'Oh, I don't know. Maybe because Billy Ryan's pushing up daisies in St Pancras Cemetery . . .'

'What about Stephen?'

'What about him?' Holland said.

'Nobody knows what he's likely to do.'

Thorne glanced at Holland. He had to admit that Rooker had a point. Since his father's murder, a great deal of time had been spent fruitlessly speculating as to exactly how Stephen Ryan was going to react.

'He might decide to play the big man,' Rooker said. 'Come after me because of his father.'

Holland picked at a fingernail. 'Can't see it, Gordon. I know Steve's not the sharpest tool in the box, but even he knows you didn't top his old man.'

Rooker's eyes narrowed. 'You know perfectly fucking well what I mean.'

Holland's mood changed in an instant. 'Watch your mouth.'

'Sorry. Look, I just think that now might be a good time to tie up a few loose ends, you know? And I think they'll use someone a bit more reliable than Alun Fisher next time.'

'I really don't think so,' Thorne said. 'We aren't the only ones with better things to do. Stephen Ryan's got quite enough to worry about at the moment . . .'

The man on the motorbike pulled over to the pavement and waited. He sat letting the traffic move past him, revving the bike for no good reason. Letting his breathing grow shallower.

It was a hot day and he'd have been sweating under his gear anyway, but in those places where the leather met flesh, the two skins slid across each other on a sheen of perspiration.

He raised the dark visor just a little and took a few gulps of air that was anything but fresh. He swallowed petrol fumes and hot tar. He could taste the flavoured grease from the seemingly endless parade of fast-food outlets on this stretch of the Seven Sisters Road.

The bike, which had been his only since that morning, had cut easily through the traffic, and he was well ahead of schedule. He thought about parking up and grabbing a Coke but knew that he'd be taking a stupid risk. He had a bottle of water in the box on the back, along with a few other bits and pieces. There'd be somewhere better to stop up ahead. Maybe he could take a stroll around Finsbury Park, kill some time before delivering the message.

This was a big job, his biggest yet. He'd told his wife to pack for a spring break. All the swimming things and plenty of high-factor sun cream for the kids. He'd told her that it was a surprise, knowing that she'd be thrilled to bits with the amazing place he'd booked for them all in the Maldives. Four weeks, fully catered, would make a big hole in what he was getting for the job, but there'd still be a decent amount left for other things. They'd been talking about shelling out to send their eldest private. The secondary schools in his part of Islington were a disgrace, and going private was a damn sight cheaper than upping sticks and moving. They'd have enough to cover three or four years at least, and still have some left over to tart up the house a bit. A conservatory maybe, or a loft conversion. He knew a few builders, people who'd give him a good price and still do a top-notch job.

Doing a good job without charging silly money. It was simple really. He thought that he could build a decent reputation for himself by doing the same thing. He knew there were others, a few foreigners especially, who asked for more, but he believed that pitching yourself somewhere in the middle was the best policy long term.

He flicked on his indicator, edged the bike's front wheel towards the road.

Not the cheapest, but one of the best: that was what he wanted people to think. All anyone really wanted was to believe they were getting value for money, wasn't it? Everyone loved a bargain.

A lorry's horn blared as it rumbled by him. He pulled out into the stream of traffic, accelerated, and overtook it within seconds.

Rooker was standing. Maybe he thought it gave him some authority. 'We had an agreement,' he said.

Thorne leaned back in his chair. He knew exactly how much authority *he* had. 'I'm a police officer, and, unless I'm much mistaken, you're a convicted felon. This is a prison, not a gentleman's club, and the only part of you I'd ever consider *shaking* is your neck. Are we clear?'

Rooker ground his teeth.

'Any agreement you might have thought you had is worth precisely less than fuck all,' Holland said.

Thorne shrugged. 'Sorry.'

Rooker sloped across the room, dragged back his chair and sank on to it. He pushed a palm back and forth across white stubble, the loose skin beneath his chin shaking gently. 'There's stuff I know,' he said. 'Stuff about plenty of people. I told some of it to DCI Tughan's boys, but there's other bits and pieces. There's a few things I kept back.'

'Why was that, then?' Thorne asked.

'Because I wasn't sure you lot were being completely straight with me . . .'

Holland laughed. 'Straight with *you*?'

'I was right as well, wasn't I?' Rooker smiled thinly. His tongue flicked the spit away from his gold tooth.

Thorne could well believe that Rooker hadn't told them everything. He could equally well believe that Tughan had kept a few pieces of information back from the team himself. Thorne didn't really give a toss on either score.

'Whatever you may, or may not, have told SO7, the deal was based on you helping to put Billy Ryan away . . .'

Holland took over. 'Now that he's been put away for good, you're not a great deal of use.'

'I want to talk to Tughan.'

'You can talk to whoever you like,' Thorne said. 'I'm sick of listening to you . . .' He reached behind for the leather jacket that was draped across the back of the chair.

Rooker slid a hand forward, slapped a palm down on the scarred metal tabletop. It was a gesture of frustration as much as anger. 'I need to get out. I was *supposed* to get out.'

'You'll be out soon enough,' Holland said.

Rooker spoke as if his mouth were filled with something sour, with something burned. 'No. *Not* soon enough.'

'Unfortunate turn of phrase, Holland.' Thorne pulled on his jacket.

'Without your say-so I'll never get through the DLP next week. Those evil bastards'll make sure I die inside.'

'You'll get out eventually,' Holland said. 'Think how much more enjoyable it'll be. Things are always better when you've looked forward to them for a while.'

Thorne tried to catch Rooker's eye. The irises, green against off-white, darted around like cornered rats. 'Especially now you don't have to worry about Billy Ryan paying someone to put a bullet in your spine.'

'Well *you* certainly won't be worrying about it,' Rooker said.

Holland stood, tucked in his chair. 'I reckon you've probably still got time to do something useful,' he said. 'Why not squeeze in a quick degree? Come out with a few letters after your name . . .?'

Rooker muttered curses.

Thorne watched as he snatched the lid from his tobacco tin, dug into it. 'Why are you so *very* keen to get out, Rooker? Got a little something stashed away?'

Rooker spat back the answer without so much as raising his head. 'I told you before.'

'Right. Some desperately moving crap about fresh air and wanting to watch your grandson play football.'

'Fuck you, Thorne.'

'You never know, Gordon. If the pair of you avoid injury, you might be out in time to watch him score the winning goal in the FA Cup Final. Although, with him playing for West Ham . . .'

The motorcyclist idled the bike, steady against the kerb, waiting out the final minute.

Trying to focus. Deciding to go half a minute early, to take into account the probable wait for a gap in the late afternoon traffic. Trying to clear his head. Trivial thoughts intruding, sullying the pure white horizon of his mind in the final few moments. They'd need to set aside enough for school uniforms. They weren't cheap when you needed to buy four or five of everything. Did the all-inclusive package in the Maldives include booze? He'd need to check. That could make a big difference . . .

He let one car pass, two cars, a pushbike, before accelerating away hard from the kerb and swinging the machine across both lanes in a wide U-turn. He pulled up outside a dry cleaner's, two doors along from the address he would be visiting. Then, within fifteen seconds, the moves he'd gone over in his mind a hundred times or more in the last few hours.

He flicked the bike on to its stand, left the engine running.

He walked quickly to the box on the back. It had been left unlocked.

He reached inside, withdrew his hand as soon as it had closed around the rubberised grip of the gun, and turned away from the street.

The arm swung loose at his side as he walked, quickly but not *too* quickly from kerb to shopfront. Without breaking stride, he turned right into the open doorway of the minicab office.

He was two large paces towards the counter before the man behind it looked up and by then the gun was being levelled at him. A man in an armchair in the corner lowered his newspaper and executed a near-perfect double-take before crying out. Hassan Zarif cried out too as a bullet passed through him. The spray of blood that fell across the calendar behind him was somewhat overdramatic in comparison with the gentle hiss from the weapon that had caused it.

The motorcyclist fired again and Zarif fell back, dropping behind the wooden counter. The gun bucked in his hand, but only slightly. No more than it might recoil had it brushed the surface of something hot to test the temperature.

As he strode forward, his target having disappeared from sight, the door to the right of the counter burst open, and the motorcyclist turned just as the gun in Tan Zarif's hand began to do its work. The bullet smashed through the plastic of the darkened visor. By the time the first passer-by had spilled his shopping, and others – who knew very well that a car was not backfiring close by – were starting to run, the man in the leathers had dropped, with very little noise, on to the grubby linoleum.

For a few seconds inside the tiny office, there was only the ringing report of the unsilenced gunshot. The high-pitched hum of it rose above the deep rumble of a bus, passing by outside on its way towards Turnpike Lane.

Tan Zarif shouted to the man in the armchair, who jumped up and ran past him through the doorway that led to the rear of the office. Zarif stepped smartly across to the body. And it *was* a body, that much was obvious: the ragged hole in the visor and the blood that poured along the cushioned neck of the helmet and down, made it clear that the man on the floor would not be getting up again.

It didn't seem to matter . . .

The man who had been sitting in the armchair, the man who was now behind the counter bending over the bloodied figure of Hassan Zarif, clapped his hairy hands across his ears as Hassan's younger brother emptied his gun into a dead man's chest.

The first part of the drive back had been pleasant enough. They'd moved through the Wiltshire and Hampshire countryside quickly, but with enough time to enjoy the scenery, to laugh at the signs to Barton Stacey and Nether Wallop. Once they'd joined the M3, however, things had quickly become frustrating. It was one of those journeys where drivers had decided to sit there, beetling along at seventy or below in *all three lanes*. As usual, Thorne sat in the outside lane, grumbling a good deal and damning those ahead of him for the selfish morons they were. He never for a moment entertained the possibility that he might be one of them.

A couple of weeks into spring, and summer weather seemed to have come early. The BMW's fans were chucking out all the cold air they could, but even in shirtsleeves it was stifling inside the car.

Holland took a long swig from a bottle of water. 'Still pleased you bought this?'

Thorne was singing quietly to himself. He reached across, turned down the volume of the first Highwaymen album. 'Say again?'

'The car.' Holland fanned himself theatrically. 'Still think it was a good move?'

Thorne shrugged, as if the fact that they were all but melted to the leather seats was unimportant. 'When they made these, cars didn't have air conditioning. It's the price you pay for a classic.'

'I'm surprised they had the wheel when this thing was made . . .'

'Good one, Dave.'

'And what you pay to keep this on the road for a year would buy you a car with A/C.'

Thorne drew close to the back of a Transit van and flashed his lights. He slammed his palm against the wheel and eased his foot off the accelerator when the signal was ignored.

'Rooker's not easy to like, is he?' Holland said.

'Probably the right reaction, considering you're one of the Met's finest and he kills people for a living. Not that I haven't met plenty of murderers I could sink a pint or two with . . . and more than a few coppers I'd happily have beaten to death.'

'Right, but Rooker's an arsehole, whichever way you look at it.'

'You do know that bit about "the Met's finest" was ironic, don't you . . .?'

Holland opened his window an inch, turned his face towards it. 'Absolutely.'

'Rooker was a touch more likeable when I had something he wanted,' Thorne said. 'And he'd probably say the same thing about me.'

He pulled across into the middle lane but was still unable to get ahead of the Transit van. It had a sticker on the back that read: 'How am I driving?' Thorne thought about calling the phone number that was given and swearing at whoever was at the other end for a while . . .

'Tell me about some of them,' Holland said. 'The murderers you got on with.'

Thorne glanced into his rear-view mirror. He saw the line of cars snaking away behind him. He saw the tension, real or imagined, around his eyes.

He thought about a man named Martin Palmer; a man who, in the final analysis, had killed because he was terrified *not to*. Palmer had strangled and stabbed, and his final, clumsy attempt at something like redemption had been made at a tragic price. He had changed Tom Thorne's thinking, not to mention his face, for ever. Thorne had not 'got on' with Martin Palmer. He had despised and abused him. But there had been pity, too, and sadness at glimpsing the man a murderer could so easily have been. Thorne had been disturbed, was still disturbed, by feelings that had asserted themselves; and by others that had been altogether absent when he'd sat and swapped oxygen with Martin Palmer.

Then there was last year: the Foley case . . .

The murderers you got on with . . .

'I don't really know where to start,' Thorne said. 'Dennis Nielsen was all right if you got to know him, and Fred West was quite a good laugh, till he topped himself. Talking of which, I remember one night, I was playing darts with Harold Shipman. Harry, I used to call him . . .'

Holland let out a loud, long-suffering sigh. 'If you're going to try to be funny, can you turn up the music again?'

They drove on, the car barely getting into top gear for more than a few minutes at a time. The monotony yielded only briefly to drama when Thorne spent too long watching a kestrel hovering above the hard shoulder, and came within inches of rear-ending an Audi.

'How's Sophie and the baby?' he asked.

'They're good.'

'What is she now?'

'Nearly seven months. It feels like we're getting our lives back a bit, you know?'

Thorne shook his head. He had no idea at all.

'There's not so much panic,' Holland explained. 'I mean, it's still bloody scary, and we're knackered all the time, but we know more or less what we're doing.' He paused, glanced across at Thorne. 'Well, Sophie always did, but now *I* know, more or less what I'm doing. You should come round and see her . . .'

'So, you're fine with it all, then? The dad bit. I know you had some worries.' Thorne remembered a conversation they'd had the previous summer. Bizarrely, it had been on the very day he'd bought the BMW. Holland had been drunk, had confessed to feeling terrified. He'd told Thorne he was worried that he might resent the baby when it came, that Sophie might make him choose between the baby and the job.

'I was being stupid,' Holland said. He turned to Thorne, grinning. 'Chloe's brilliant. She's into everything, but she's fucking brilliant . . .'

'I'm glad it's working out,' Thorne said.

'Tell you the truth, the last couple of weeks have been great. A chance to recharge the batteries, you know? The only problem is that Sophie's starting to get used to having me around again . . .'

The officers on the investigation had all been spending more time with loved ones in the fortnight or so since the Ryan murder. The job had recently involved a lot of paperwork, much of it from other cases, and a good deal of time sitting on arses waiting for somebody – Stephen Ryan in particular – to get off theirs. To make a move. The investigation had wound itself down, or spiralled into chaos, depending on your point of view.

'D'you reckon Stephen Ryan is going to do anything?' Holland asked.

Thorne grunted, but only with pleasure as the Transit van finally indicated and moved inside. Thorne swerved back into the fast lane and powered past it, gaining a pointless thirty feet but enjoying it nonetheless.

He had no idea that, twenty miles ahead of him, uniformed officers were taping off the area around a minicab office on Green Lanes. Others were gathering witnesses and starting to take statements. Phil Hendricks was already on his way to the crime scene, while an ambulance was moving in the opposite direction, its services clearly not required.

Stephen Ryan had made a move.

TWENTY-FIVE

Wednesday morning in the Major Incident Room. Two days after the fatal shooting at the Zarifs' minicab office. A team back on its feet, but yet to get the feeling back in its arse . . .

'We've had word from Immigration,' Brigstocke said. 'They think a few more from the lorry might have turned up. I say "think" because the individuals concerned aren't telling anybody very much.'

'Where?' Thorne asked.

Brigstocke glanced at the sheet of paper he was holding. 'A car wash in Hackney. One of those places where there's half a dozen of them on your car at once, you know? With sponges and chamois leathers, inside with vacuums . . .'

Stone nodded. 'There's one near me. Inside and out for a tenner. Plus a tip . . .'

'The owner's being questioned,' Brigstocke said. 'So far, surprise, surprise, he's pleading ignorance. There'll be a connection to the Ryans somewhere down the line, but I don't think it'll be much different from the others . . .'

A man and a woman, suspected of being from the

hijacked lorry, had been detained the previous week in Tottenham, having been discovered working in a restaurant kitchen. Two men had been seized a few days before that from a shopfitting wholesalers in Manor House. In both cases an astonishing bout of amnesia seemed to have struck all concerned. Arrests had been made, but none would lead to anything other than deportation orders for the illegals and fines for their employers. There would be enough red tape to stretch back to where the people in the lorry had originated and nothing to incriminate those who mattered in the Ryan *or* the Zarif organisations.

Tughan took over from Brigstocke. 'Let's move on to the shooting in Green Lanes. What about the witnesses, Sam? Any luck?'

Karim shook his head. 'Hard to believe, I know, but we still can't find *anybody* who saw *anything* that contradicts Memet Zarif's story. We've even got a couple who conveniently noticed a man in a balaclava carrying a gun and running away after the gunshots had finished.'

'Yeah, right,' Thorne said.

Holland let out a grunt of laughter. 'That's one couple who won't go short at Christmas, then . . .'

According to Memet Zarif and the others in the minicab office at the time, the man in the leathers who had shot and wounded Hassan Zarif had *himself* been shot dead by a mysterious second gunman who'd followed him inside and fled once he'd killed him. The police knew it was cock and bull. They guessed that the 'second' gunman was Memet or Tan Zarif, but with no murder weapon or corroborating witness, there was little anyone could do to prove it.

'We are sure about one thing, though,' Tughan said. There was a certain amount of laughter, which he acknowledged with uncharacteristic good humour. 'I know, I've already alerted the media. We have a name for the victim: the *dead* one, that is. He was Donal Jackson, thirty-three. A known associate of Stephen Ryan.'

This last fact came as no surprise to anyone.

'Is he the bloke who did the Izzigils, do we think?' Stone asked. 'Same gun . . . ?'

Tughan opened his mouth but Thorne was quicker. 'No chance,' he said. 'It's the same *type* of gun, that's all. Whoever was hired to kill the Izzigils was good. Clinical, you know? This idiot got himself killed and didn't even manage to take anybody with him . . .' He trailed off, his mind focusing suddenly on the failed attempt to kill an innocent fourteen-year-old girl. Now, twenty years later, the son of the man behind that had fucked up a hit of his own.

'DI Thorne's probably right,' Tughan said. 'Word is that Jackson was pretty new to contract stuff. Picked up the job because he was Stephen Ryan's mate, because Ryan wanted to go a different way from his old man. Also, according to the people we've spoken to, Jackson was pretty cheap.'

Stone snorted. 'Pay peanuts, you get monkeys.'

'You'd've thought shelling out for a decent hitman was pretty basic,' Kitson said.

Others picked up on her sarcasm, mumbled their agreement.

'Haven't these people heard of a false economy?'

'You just can't get the staff.'

'He'll pay for it in the end,' Thorne said. 'What he did, what he *failed* to do, is going to cost him.'

'Think it's all going to kick off?' Holland asked.

'I think Ryan should have dug into his pocket and hired a trio of hitmen.' Thorne was only half joking. 'One for each brother. He should have done it properly and killed all three of them.'

'This might be a good time to announce that in terms of the joint operation, we're going to be scaling things down a bit,' Tughan said.

Thorne stared at him. Surely he was joking. 'You what?'

'We've had results, some good ones, but the fact is that the Job can't see us getting too much more out of this. We're wrapping it up.'

Thorne looked across at Brigstocke, eyes wide. The look he got back told him that there was nothing worth arguing about. This was for information, not discussion.

'Billy Ryan, one of our main targets, is no longer a worry, even if, sadly, we can't claim credit for that. In point of fact, from now on, there's not going to be much in the way of results that we won't have to share with Immigration or the Customs and Excise mob. There are one or two loose ends that we've yet to tie up and there'll be a few more arrests, but the pro-active end of it just isn't justified in terms of resources . . .'

'How can we pull out of this now?' Thorne asked. 'After what just happened?'

Tughan was already putting papers into a briefcase. 'It was Stephen Ryan's last hurrah. He messed it up. It's a war he's going to lose, and then hopefully things will settle down again . . .'

'*Hopefully?*'

'Things *will* settle down again.'

'Meanwhile, we just look the other way. We do some paperwork and nick a few nobodies and let them kill each other . . .?'

Tughan turned to Brigstocke. 'I want to thank Russell and his team for their cooperation and for their hospitality. We've done some good things together. We've achieved a lot, really, we have, and I think I'll be borne out on that in the weeks and months to come. Anyway, I'm sure you'll be looking forward to getting back to work on your own cases. To getting your offices back, at least.'

There was a smattering of unenthusiastic laughter.

'We'll have a pint or two later, of course, and say our goodbyes. Obviously, we won't be vanishing right away. Like I said, there are a few loose ends . . .' And he was moving away towards the door.

Brigstocke cleared his throat, walked a few paces after Tughan, then turned. He looked to Thorne, Kitson and the rest of his officers. 'I'll be getting together with DS Karim later. Re-assigning the casework.' His parting words were spoken like a third-rate manager trying to gee up a team who were six–nil down at half time. 'There's still plenty of *disorganised* criminals out there who need catching . . .'

For a few seconds after Brigstocke had left the room, nobody moved or spoke. One of those uneasy silences that follows a speech. Gradually, the volume increased, though not much, and the bodies changed position, so that in a few subtle turns, half paces and casual shifts of the shoulder, the single team became two very separate ones. The officers from each unit began to huddle and look to their own, their conversations far from secret, but no longer to be shared.

The members of Team 3 at the Serious Crime Group (West) stayed silent a little longer than their SO7 counterparts. It was Yvonne Kitson who sought to break the silence and change the mood at the same time. 'How's the philosophy going, Andy? Nietzsche is it this week, or Jean-Paul Sartre?'

Stone tried to look blank, but the blush betrayed him. 'Eh?'

'It's all right, Andy,' she said. 'All blokes have tricks. All women too, come to that.'

Stone shrugged, the smile spreading. 'It works . . .'

'Obviously you have to use whatever you've got.' Holland lounged against a desk. 'Only some of us prefer to rely on old-fashioned charm and good looks.'

'Money goes down quite well,' Karim said, grinning. 'Failing that, begging usually works for me.'

'Begging's excellent,' Kitson said.

Holland looked to Thorne. He was six feet or so distant from them, the incomprehension still smeared across his face like a stain.

'What about you, sir?' Holland asked. 'Any tricks you want to share with the group?'

Stone was laughing at his joke before he even started speaking. 'I'm sure Dr Hendricks could get his hands on some Rohypnol if you're desperate . . .'

But Thorne was already moving towards the door.

'Can't you be predictable just once in your life,' Tughan said. 'I thought you'd be glad to see the back of me.'

Tughan stood in the doorway to his office. Brigstocke was nowhere to be seen.

'Look, we can't stand each other,' Thorne said. 'Fair enough. Neither of us loses a great deal of sleep about that, I'm sure, and once or twice, yes, I've said things just to piss you off. Right? But *this*' – he gestured back towards the Incident Room, towards what Tughan had said in there – 'is *seriously* stupid. I know you're not personally responsible for the decision . . .'

'No, I'm not. But I stand by it.'

'"Ours is not to reason why". That it?'

'Not if we want to get anywhere.'

'Career-wise, you mean? Or are we back to results again?'

'Take your pick . . .'

Thorne leaned against the door jamb. He and Tughan stood on either side of the doorway, staring across the corridor at the wall opposite. At a pinboard festooned with Police Federation newsletters and dog-eared photocopies of meaningless graphs. At an AIDS-awareness leaflet, a handwritten list of last season's fixtures for Metropolitan Police rugby teams, a torn-out headline from the *Standard* that said, 'Capital gun crime out of control', at postcards advertising various items for sale: a Paul Smith suit; a scooter; a second-hand PlayStation . . .

'It's the timing I don't understand,' Thorne said. 'Now, I mean, after . . .'

'I think this decision was made *before* the shooting in the minicab office.'

'And that didn't cause anybody to rethink it?'

'Apparently not.'

Richards, the concentric-circles man, came along the corridor with a file that was, by all accounts, terribly important. Tughan took it with barely a word. Thorne waited until the Welshman had gone.

'When we found that lorry driver dead and those two in the woods with bullets in the backs of their heads, you were fired up. "This has got to stop," you said. You were angry about the Izzigils, about Marcus Moloney. You were up for it. There's no point pretending you weren't . . .'

Tughan said nothing, clutched the file he was holding that little bit tighter to his chest.

'How do these people decide what *we're* going to do?' Thorne asked. 'Who we target and who we ignore? Which lucky punters have a chance when it comes to us catching the men responsible for killing their husband or their father, and which poor sods might just as well ask a traffic warden to sort it out? How do these people formulate *policy*? Do they roll a fucking dice every morning? Pick a card . . .?'

Tughan spoke to the pinboard, scratched at a small mark on the lapel of his brown suit. 'They divvy up the men and they dole out the money as they see fit. It goes where they think it's most needed, and where they think it might get a return. It's not rocket science, Thorne . . .'

'So, which deserving cause came out of the hat this time?'

'We're shifting direction slightly, looking towards vice. The Job wants to crack down on the foreign gangs moving into the game: Russians, Albanians, Lithuanians. It's getting nasty, and when one of these gangs wants to hit

343

another operation they tend to go for the soft targets. They kill the girls . . .'

Thorne shrugged. 'So, Memet Zarif and Stephen Ryan just go about their business?'

'Nobody's giving them "Get out of Jail Free" cards.'

'Talking of which . . .'

'Gordon Rooker will be released by the beginning of next week.'

Thorne had figured as much. 'Right. He's one of those loose ends you were talking about.'

'Rooker can give us names, a few decent ones, and we're going to take them.'

'Define "decent".'

'Look, there'll be better results, but there'll be plenty of worse ones. Right now, this is what we've decided to settle for.' Even Thorne's sarcastic grunt failed to set Tughan off. He'd remained remarkably calm throughout the entire exchange. 'You're a footie fan, right? How would you feel if your team played beautiful stuff all bloody season and won fuck all?'

If Thorne had felt like lightening the atmosphere, he might have asked Tughan if he'd ever seen Spurs play. But he didn't. 'You won't be offended if I don't hang around for the emotional goodbye later on?' he said.

'I'd be amazed if you did . . .'

Thorne pushed himself away from the door, took half a step.

'I'm the same as you,' Tughan said. 'Really. I want to get them all, but sometimes . . . no, *most* of the bloody time, you've got to be content with just some of them. Not always the right ones, either – nowhere near, in fact – but what can you do?'

344

Thorne completed the step, carried on taking them.
Thinking: *No, not the same as me.*

He'd found nothing suitable in Kentish Town and fared little better in Highgate Village, where there seemed to be a great many antique shops and precious little else. He'd carried on up to Hampstead and spent half an hour failing to find a parking space. Now, he was trying his luck in Archway, where it was easy enough to park, but where he wasn't exactly spoiled for choice in other ways.

Having decided – with no idea what else to get for a seven-month-old baby – to buy clothes, Thorne couldn't really explain why he was wandering aimlessly around a chemist's. As it went, it was no ordinary chemist's and had quickly become Thorne's favourite shop after he'd discovered it a few months earlier. Yes, you could buy shampoo and get a prescription filled, but it also sold, for no reason Thorne could fathom, catering-sized packs of peanuts past their sell-by date, motor oil, crisps, and other stuff not seen before or since in a place you normally went for pills and pile cream. It was also ridiculously cheap, as if the chemist were just trying to turn a quick profit on items that had been delivered there by mistake. Thorne might have wondered if somewhere there wasn't a grocers with several unwanted boxes of condoms and corn-plasters, if it weren't for the fact that there were a number of such multi-purpose outlets springing up in the area.

Maybe small places could no longer afford to specialise. Maybe shopkeepers just wanted to keep life interesting. Whatever the reason, Thorne knew a number of places where the astute shopper could kill several birds with one stone, even if it might not otherwise have occurred to him to do so. One of his favourites was a shop that sold fruit and vegetables . . . and wool. Another boldly announced itself as 'currency exchange and delicatessen'. Thorne could never quite picture anyone asking for 'fifty quid's worth of escudos and a slice of carrot cake' and was sure the place was a front for some dodgy scheme or other. He remembered a small shop near the Nag's Head which had seemed to sell nothing much of anything during its odd opening hours. The owners, a couple of cheery Irish guys, appeared uninterested in any conventional definition of 'stock', and no one was hugely surprised when the place closed down the day after the IRA ceasefire.

It was easy for Thorne to imagine places and people as other than they seemed. It was in his nature and borne of experience. It was also, for better or worse, his job.

In the chemist's, Thorne finally realised that, though disposable nappies would be useful, they were really no kind of a present. He looked at his watch: the shops would be shutting soon. After a few words with the woman behind the counter, who he was seriously starting to fancy, Thorne stepped out on to the street.

He stood for a minute, and then another, letting people move past him as the day began to wind down. It wasn't that he had any grand moral notions about *serving* these people. He didn't imagine for one second that he, or the thousands like him, could really *protect* them.

But he had to side with those of them who drew a line . . .

He knew from bitter experience that some of them might one day be his to hunt down. Some would think nothing of hurting a child. Some would wound, rape or kill to get whatever it was they needed.

That was a fact, plain and terrible.

Most, though, would know where to stop. They would draw a line at round about the same place he did. Most would stop at cheating the tax man or driving home after a few drinks too many. Most would go no further than a raised voice or a bit of push and shove to blow away the cobwebs. Most had a threshold of acceptable behaviour, of pain and fury, of disgust at cruelty that was close to his own.

These were the people Thorne would stand with.

The lives of these people, to a greater or lesser extent were being affected every minute of every day by the Ryans and the Zarifs of the world. By those who crossed the line for profit. Some would never even know it, handing over a cab fare or the money for a burger without any idea whose pockets they were lining. Whose execution they might unwittingly be funding. Some would be hurt, directly or through a loved one, their existence bumped out of alignment in the time it took to lose a child to drugs. Twisted by those few moments spent signing the credit agreement. Smashed out of existence in the second it took to be in the wrong place at the wrong time.

They worked in banks and offices and on buses. They had children, and got cancer, and believed in God or television. They were wonderful, and shit, and they did not deserve to have their lives sullied while Thorne and others like him were being told to step away.

Thorne thought about the woman he fancied in the chemist's and the bloke who lived in the flat upstairs, and the man passing him at that very second yanking a dog behind himself. He remembered the Jesus woman and the reluctant security guard who'd thrown her out of the supermarket.

I suppose there are worse crimes.

The lives of these people were being marked in too many places by dirty fingers . . .

He turned as the chemist stepped out of his shop and pressed a button. They both watched as a reinforced metal grille rolled noisily down over the door and window. Thorne looked at his watch again and remembered that the Woolworth's across the road sold a few kids' clothes. He couldn't remember whether it closed at five-thirty or six.

TWENTY-SIX

Chamberlain stood in the doorway watching Jack at the cooker. She loved her husband for his attention to detail and routine. He wore the same blue-striped apron whether he was making a casserole or knocking up cheese on toast. His movements were precise, the wooden spoon scraping out a rhythm against the bottom of the pan.

He caught her looking at him and smiled. 'About twenty minutes. All right, love?'

She nodded and walked slowly back into the living room.

The paper on the walls came from English Heritage – a reproduction of a Georgian design they'd had to save up to afford. The carpet was deep and spotless, the colour of red wine. She let herself drop back on to the perfectly plumped cushions and tried to remember that this was the sort of room she'd always dreamed of; the sort of room she'd imagined when she'd been sitting in dirty, smoke-filled boxes trying to drag the truth out of murderers.

She stared at the watercolour above the fireplace, the over-elaborate frame suitably distressed. She'd pictured it –

or something very like it – years before, while she'd stared at the photos of a victim; of the body parts from a variety of angles.

She pulled her stockinged feet under her and told herself that these walls she'd once coveted so much weren't closing in quite as quickly as they had been.

What had Thorne said?

'*Billy Ryan. Jessica Clarke. You've got to let it go.*'

She was trying, but her hands were sticky . . .

As it went, she knew that Ryan would quickly become little more than the name on a headstone.

She could keep on trying, but Jessica would always be with her.

And the man who'd stood looking up at her bedroom window – the flames dancing across the darkness of his face – would become, if he were not *actually* the man who had burned Jessica, a man who they were never going to catch. In her mind, he was already the one who had touched the flame to a blue cotton skirt, all those years before.

In the absence of cold, hard fact, imagination expanded to fill the spaces. It created truths all of its own.

Jack called through from the kitchen, 'Shall we open a bottle of wine, love?'

Fuck it, Chamberlain thought.

'Sod it,' she said. 'Let's go mad . . .'

Thorne stared at the screen, his eyes itchy after an hour spent trawling the Net for useless rubbish. He wrote down the name of an actor he'd never heard of and reached for his coffee . . .

His father had called while Thorne was still in Woolworth's, struggling to make a decision.

'I'm in trouble,' Jim Thorne had said.

'What?'

Thorne must have sounded worried. The impatience on the face of the girl behind the till had been replaced, for a few seconds, by curiosity.

'Some items for lists I'm putting together, maybe for a . . . *thing*. Bollocks. Thing people read, get in fucking libraries. A *book*. Other stuff, trivia questions driving me mental . . .'

'Dad, can I talk to you about this in a few—?'

'I was awake until three this morning trying to get some of these names. I've got a pen by the bed, you know, to jot things down. You saw it when you were here. Remember?'

Thorne had noticed that the girl on the till was staring at her watch. It was already five minutes after closing time and there were no other customers in the shop. He was still holding two different outfits in his arms, unable to decide between them.

He had smiled at the girl. 'Sorry . . .'

'Do you remember seeing the pen or not?' His father had started to shout.

The girl had nodded curtly towards the baby clothes Thorne was carrying. Her eyes had flicked across to an angry-looking individual standing by the doors, waiting to lock up.

'I'd better take both of them,' Thorne had said. He'd handed over the clothes, returned to his father. 'Yes, I remember the pen. It's a nice one . . .'

His father had spat down the phone. 'Last night the

351

bloody thing was useless. Needs a . . . new pen. Needs a new bit putting in. Fuck, you know, the thin bit with fresh ink you put in . . . when the fucker runs out . . .'

'Refill . . .'

'I need to go to a stationer's. There's a Ryman in the town.'

The girl had held out a hand. Thorne had put a twenty-pound note into it. 'I'll call you when I get home, Dad, all right? I can go online later and get all the answers.'

'Where are you now?'

'Woolworth's . . .'

'Like the killer . . .' his father had said.

'*What?*'

'It was the Woolworth's Killer who did Sutcliffe in Broadmoor. Remember? He'd killed the manager of a Woolworth's somewhere, which is how he got the name, and then, when him and the Ripper were inside together, he stabbed the evil fucker in the eye. With a pen, funnily enough. A fucking pen!'

'Dad . . .'

'We got your bike from Woolworth's in 1973. Can't remember who did the Christmas advert that year. Always big stars doing the Woolies Christmas ads, you know – TV stars, comedians, what have you. Always the same slogan. "That's the wonder of Woolworth's!" Fucking annoying tune went with it, an' all. I'll bet Peter bastard Sutcliffe wasn't singing *that* when the pen was going in and out of his eye.'

Then his father had started to sing. '"That's the wonder of Woolworth's . . ."'

The girl behind the counter had all but thrown Thorne's

change at him. The security guard by the door had held the door wide and glared.

"'. . . that's the wonder of good old Woolies . . .'"

Thorne had just listened . . .

He'd bought the computer cheaply the year before, stuck it on a table underneath the window in the living room. One of the old-model iMacs, it was 'snow' white when he'd bought it, but was now distinctly grubby. Thorne listened to the low hum from the monitor and thought about the inside of his father's head.

Did the words get lost somewhere between the brain and the mouth? If they made it out of the brain, did they just take a wrong turn? If his father could *hear* the word he wanted inside his head, if he could *see* it perfectly well, then the frustration must have been unbearable. He imagined his father as a tiny, impotent figure, raging inside his own skull. He imagined him standing next to a pair of enormous speakers that blared out the word he was unable to speak. Dwarfed by its illuminated letters, fifty feet high.

Swearing and shouting and a certain amount of public embarrassment – under the circumstances, they were the very least you could expect. Jesus, Thorne was amazed his father hadn't smashed his own brains out against a wall. Bent down to finger the grey goo as it leaked from his head, and tried to pick those elusive words out of the soup . . .

A new page was downloading. Thorne waited for a list to appear on the screen, then scribbled down the names of the ten tallest buildings in the world. He'd call his father in the morning, give him all the useless information he'd asked for.

'The Job can't see us getting too much more out of this . . .'

Thorne leaned back in his chair, cradled his coffee cup and thought about the team celebrating that night in the Oak. Tughan would have made a speech, rather more fulsome than the one he'd given in the office. They'd have drunk toasts to their results. Arms thrown around shoulders as they lifted glasses of lager and malt whisky, and drunk to lies. To what they'd been told to settle for.

He pictured other glasses being raised elsewhere, by those who *really* had something to celebrate. Those who would be extremely happy if they knew – and there was every reason to think that they would know – that for the time being the police were off their backs.

Thorne had only a mug of lukewarm coffee, but he raised it anyway.

To *some* of the police . . .

He reached forward to turn the computer off but then paused. He typed 'immortal skin' into the search engine and waited. Eventually, a site appeared that gave all the details Ian Clarke had told him about. The page was dense with information, closely typed, difficult to read.

Thorne's eyes closed and he dreamed for a few minutes, no more than that, of holes in flesh that healed. Of scars fading like the words written in sand, and of lines etched into skin that vanished; the X replaced by smooth, fresh flesh that smelled of babies . . .

When he jolted awake, the screen had frozen. He swore at the computer for a few seconds, then pulled out the plug.

And went to bed.

TWENTY-SEVEN

The car containing Memet and Hassan Zarif pulled away from the traffic lights at Stoke Newington station and accelerated across the Stamford Hill Road.

Sitting three cars behind them, Thorne was still unsure where the brothers were heading. They were driving in the general direction of the restaurant and minicab office, but it wasn't the route Thorne would have chosen. They were a little too far south.

Thorne made it through the lights with a few seconds to spare. He turned up the soundtrack to *O Brother, Where Art Thou?* and sat back. Wherever the Zarifs were going, he was along for the ride.

He'd tried the minicab office first, but none of the brothers had been around. The same surly individual he'd encountered on his first visit there had shaken his head and invited Thorne to search the premises. The man had shrugged and drawn phlegm into his mouth when Thorne had turned to walk back out of the door.

Outside, Thorne had stood for a moment, considering where to go next. A smart black Omega had pulled up and one of Zarif's drivers had asked if he needed a lift. Thorne had shaken his head without giving the driver a second glance. His decision made, he'd marched towards his car. Looking through the windows of the restaurant as he'd passed, Thorne had seen Arkan Zarif and his wife moving about in the half light, setting up the tables for lunch.

The cars crossed the Seven Sisters Road at the bottom end of Finsbury Park, heading north again.

Memet Zarif's BMW was somewhat newer than Thorne's, and now, sitting no more than fifty feet behind it, he wondered if its occupants were aware that they were being followed. His car was fairly distinctive – both in shape and colour – and if they knew where he lived, the chances were they also knew what he drove.

Thorne decided that it didn't really make a fat lot of difference. They'd be stopping somewhere eventually and he only needed a quick word . . .

After leaving the minicab office, he'd driven a mile or two east, to Memet Zarif's home address. It was an ordinary-looking, semi-detached house in Clapton, with a view across the River Lea to the Walthamstow Marshes beyond. There were plenty of pricier places around, but Thorne guessed that, somewhere, Zarif had other property they were as yet unaware of.

Thorne had spent forty minutes loitering with a newspaper, then watched as the front door eventually opened, and Hassan Zarif had emerged. His arm was in a sling, the only visible sign of the bullet that had shattered his collarbone. As Hassan had waited on the drive near the car, his elder brother had appeared, a wife and child next to him on the doorstep. Memet had kissed his family goodbye, and Thorne had walked back towards the side-street where he'd parked up.

When the dark blue BMW had moved past him a few minutes later, Thorne had eased his car slowly out and fallen into the stream of vehicles behind it.

They moved through heavy traffic into Stroud Green and then dropped down towards the somewhat better-preserved environment of Crouch End. This was an area popular with creative types who were not quite in the Highgate and Hampstead league. Despite the lack of a tube station, property prices had gone through the roof in recent years, and the place was crammed with trendy restaurants and bars. The majority of its better-than-averagely heeled shoppers tended to ignore the handful of less salubrious establishments: the adult magazine shop; the working men's caff; the massage parlour . . .

The main road divided either side of the clock tower, and Thorne watched as Zarif took the right-hand fork, then pulled sharply across and parked on a double-yellow line. Thorne cruised past as the brothers stepped out of the car, and swung into a side-street as they crossed the pavement towards a door.

The sign in the window flashed red after dark. At half-past eleven in the morning, the letters spelled out 'sauna' in grime. The girl on reception probably looked a little better herself once the daylight had disappeared; a little less pasty and pissed off. The smile she'd slapped on when Thorne came through the door became a scowl as soon as he produced his warrant card.

'Oh, for fuck's sake,' she said.

'Nothing like that going on here, is there?' Thorne

walked towards the door in the far corner, tipping his head from one side to the other. 'Neck's a little bit painful,' he said. 'Got anybody through here who can do something about stiffness . . .?'

'Sorry if I don't piss myself.'

Thorne reached for the handle. The girl was either too lazy, or too scared or too engrossed in her magazine to try and stop him.

The room on the other side of the door was clearly designed to be a lounge, but it had not been expensively decorated. Thorne guessed that this wouldn't bother most customers, as the eye would quickly be drawn from the multicoloured carpet to whatever hardcore activities were taking place on the big-screen TV. Right now, a blonde in pop-socks was engaged in an enthusiastic bout of fellatio. The permed stallion on the receiving end, eyes tight shut in cutaway, looked suitably grateful . . .

Hassan Zarif was sitting, side on to the door, in a velour armchair. A red towelling robe gaped open across his chest and he was using his one good arm to flick through the pages of a *Daily Mirror*. He let out a sound somewhere between a grunt and a moan when he looked up and saw that he had company.

'That's a shame . . .' Thorne said, nodding towards the sling. 'You could have a wank *and* read the paper if you hadn't gone and got yourself shot . . .'

Hassan shifted uncomfortably in his chair, caught between a desire to stand and the need to hide his erection.

'Don't get up,' Thorne said.

It didn't take too long for Hassan to recover his composure. He crossed his legs, pulled the robe across his chest. 'If you've come here for a freebie, I'll see what I can do,' he said. 'I'm pretty sure a number of police officers get VIP treatment in here . . .'

Thorne walked slowly across the room. He picked up a remote from a glass-topped table, flicked off the TV. 'Sorry, but the slurping makes it really hard to concentrate.'

'I presume you do *want* something . . .'

'This one of yours, is it?'

'I'm sorry?'

Thorne held out his arms. 'This place part of the Zarif Brothers empire?'

Hassan smiled. 'No. This business is owned by an acquaintance, but we may, in fact, be looking to invest in similar premises . . .'

'Right. So this is . . . what? Research?'

'This is exactly what it looks like. I'm not certain you can *arrest* me for it, but go ahead and try if you like. I'm happy to let you make a fool of yourself.'

Thorne nodded. 'How happy would you be if I stepped over there and snapped your other arm? How *happy* would you be with somebody else wiping your arse for a while . . .?'

Hassan stuck out his prominent chin and pointed towards the ceiling. Thorne looked up at the tiny camera mounted high above a flap of peeling Anaglypta.

'You'd be amazed at how easily a videotape can go missing in an evidence room,' Thorne said. He moved towards the archway on the far side of the room, leaned against a plastic pillar and stuck his head through. To his left, a number of rooms – 'suites', as they were advertised on a poster in reception – ran off a carpeted corridor.

Thorne turned back into the lounge, looked across at Hassan. He thought he'd got the three brothers fairly well worked out: Tan, the youngest, was the hard man – the one with a short fuse; Hassan was the one that made business plans and worked out where to hide the money. Neither was the one Thorne needed to speak to.

He gestured back towards the archway. 'Big brother through there, is he?'

'I presume you followed us here, so you know he is.'

'You're sitting here waiting for sloppy seconds, that about right?'

Hassan said nothing, but his jawbone moved beneath the skin where the teeth were clenching.

'You *presume*?' Thorne said. 'So you didn't see me? That's good news. It's been a while since I've tailed someone and I thought I might have lost the knack.'

Before he stepped through the archway, Thorne picked up the remote and turned the movie back on. The blonde woman resumed her performance.

'This one's a classic,' Thorne said. 'Don't worry, I won't tell you what happens at the end, in case you haven't seen it . . .'

Rooker turned the phonecard over and over in his hand as he waited for his turn to make a call. He had a fair amount of credit left that he'd never get the chance to use up now. Phonecards were always in demand in prison, were as good as hard currency to those with people to talk to. He'd swap this one for a few fags before he left.

He'd made more calls than usual in the last couple of months, but before that there hadn't really been many people he'd wanted to speak to. Fewer still who had wanted to speak to him.

The man in front of him swore and slammed down the phone. Rooker avoided making eye contact as he stepped forward to take his turn. He slotted in the card and dialled the number.

When the call was eventually answered, the response was curt, businesslike.

'It's me,' Rooker said.

'I'm busy. Be quick.'

'You know I'm coming out in a couple of days . . .?'

The man on the other end of the line said nothing, waited for Rooker to elaborate.

'I'm just checking, you know, confirming that we still have an agreement . . .'

There was a grunt of laughter. 'Things have changed a little.'

'Right, and whose doing well out of that? You're quids in now, right?'

'Let's hope so.'

'Course you are. Competition's out of the way, aren't they?' Rooker cleared his throat, did his best to sound casual, matey. 'Listen, I'll be relocated. I don't know where yet, but I'll let you know as soon as I do.'

There was a long pause. Rooker could hear voices in the background. The man he was talking to spoke to somebody else, then came back to the phone. 'That's fine. I hope it all works out, all right?'

'Hang on, I want to know that you're guaranteeing me protection.'

'From who?'

'From whoever . . .' Rooker was trying to control his temper. This was the same conversation he'd had with Thorne, for Christ's sake. Unbelievable . . .

'Don't worry. We had an agreement, as you say.'

'Good. Great.' Rooker saw his own grin; a lopsided reflection in the battered metal plate above the phone. 'So you were joking just now, right?'

'Just joking . . .'

'I mean, anything could happen, couldn't it? The deal was that you'd look after me. That you'd take steps . . .'

'You have that guarantee.'

Steel crept into Rooker's voice. 'If anything happens to me . . .'

It was there too in the voice of the man on the other end of the line. In the words he repeated before ending the call: 'You have that guarantee.'

What had been described in reception as the 'VIP Suite' was little more than a large bathroom with a sofa in one corner. The walls were panelled in glossy, orange pine that ran with moisture. Red bathrobes hung on hooks, and a pink, plastic jacuzzi took up most of the available space. The wall-mounted TV, probably set up to show the same film that was playing in the lounge, was switched off. Memet Zarif had no need of such visual stimulation. The real thing was being eagerly supplied by the woman sharing his bathwater, though, in the absence of an aqualung, she was providing manual rather than oral relief.

The woman, whose enhanced breasts bobbed in the water like buoys, stopped what she was doing the second she saw Thorne.

Memet reached for her wrist, dragged her arm back beneath the water. He spoke to her, but his eyes never strayed from Thorne's. 'Carry on.'

For a few tepid seconds nobody did much, then, finally, with a splash, the woman yanked her hand away and climbed out. Dripping, she walked behind Memet and pulled on a bathrobe, her lack of shyness as obvious as the scars and stretch-marks. She slipped her feet into sandals and turned back to Zarif. 'Do I need to fetch someone?'

Memet shook his head, unconcerned.

The woman sized Thorne up like she was working out how big a stick she'd need to scrape him off the bottom of her sandal.

'Am I a copper or a hired thug?' Thorne asked. 'Or both? I know you're finding it hard to decide.' He nodded towards Memet. 'Your friend in there's helping me with my inquiries, so why don't you go somewhere and wash your hands . . .'

The woman slipped the scrunchie from her hair, shaking it loose as she crossed the room. She stopped for just a second to hiss at Thorne, before stepping out into the corridor.

'Tosser . . .'

'You're a fine one to talk,' he said.

When Thorne turned back to Memet, he had disappeared under the water. Thorne waited, watched as he lifted up his balding head and shook the water from it like a dog.

'Sorry to interrupt . . .'

'She was right,' Memet said. 'You *are* a tosser.' The accent made the word sound a good deal more serious than when the woman had said it.

'I just thought you might like to know that we found a couple more of your missing DVD players,' Thorne said.

Memet smiled, but the effort was obvious. 'Well done.'

'They're turning up all over the place. This lot were working in kitchens and cleaning cars. Maybe one day we'll find out exactly where they came from. What d'you reckon?'

'Good luck . . .'

'Where's Tan, by the way?'

Memet wiped water from his eyes, grunted a lack of understanding.

'Well, Hassan's out there waiting his turn like a good boy, and I know how close the three of you are, so I was just wondering where the baby of the family had got to?'

'My brother's on holiday . . .'

'Oh, right.' So, Tan was almost certainly the one who had put six bullets into Donal Jackson. Thorne wasn't hugely surprised. 'A sudden urge to get away, was it? You can get some very good last-minute deals if you shop around.'

'He was upset after what happened. After the shooting.'

'I'm sure it was very traumatic for all of you . . .'

Memet's face darkened suddenly. 'Hassan was nearly killed. In the middle of the day, a man walks in with a gun.'

'I know. Not very sporting, was it? Thank heavens for that mysterious second gunman. You sure it *was* a gunman, by the way? It couldn't have been Batman or Wonder Woman, could it?'

Memet said nothing. He moved his arm back and forth through the water. The banter was done with.

The plastic tiles squeaked beneath Thorne's shoes as he

364

took a step towards the jacuzzi. 'So, here's the thing: I think Stephen Ryan's a shitbag, and I'm not a great deal fonder of you. In fact, if Ryan was sharing your bathwater right now, I'd be head of the queue to chuck a three-bar fire in . . .'

'Am I supposed to be upset?'

'You're supposed to *listen*. There's not going to be any retaliation for what happened in the minicab office, do you understand? It's over. You boys can all put your guns down now.'

'You don't know what you're talking about . . .'

'I don't care what the "policy" is on this. I don't give a toss about efforts being concentrated elsewhere, about resources being redistributed or even about the fact that you fuckers are doing us all a favour by killing each other. I'm just telling you this: if any more bodies turn up, if Stephen Ryan's cousin's auntie's best mate's brother-in-law so much as twists his ankle, I'll start making a major nuisance of myself. Whatever the *official* position on this might be, *I'm* not going anywhere . . .'

There was amusement in Memet's voice, but also genuine confusion and curiosity. 'Why are you taking all of this so . . . personally?'

Suddenly, Thorne felt helpless, like the tiny, impotent figure that he'd imagined his father to be. The words he wanted to say were vast and deafening. They were made to be roared or screamed. To be sucked up and spat like powerful poison. Instead, Thorne heard them departing from his mouth as little more than murmurs, half hearted and sullen. 'Because you don't stop where other people do,' he said. He looked at the floor as he spoke, sweat stinging his eyes. He stared at the strip of grubby mastic where the tiles met the base of the jacuzzi. 'Because you don't have a *line . . .'*

There was a long moment of silence, of stillness, before Memet heaved himself on to the edge of the bath. Water gathered in thick droplets on his round shoulders. It ran through the dark hair clinging to the fat on his chest and belly.

'I will talk to those with some influence in the community . . .'

'Don't start with that "pillar of the community" bollocks.' Thorne wasn't murmuring now. 'I heard enough of it at that hotel.'

'My family has done all that was asked of us . . .'

'Does Mrs Zarif know about these lunchtime hand-jobs, by the way?'

'You're starting to sound very desperate.'

'Whatever it takes . . .'

Memet sat and dripped.

'Talk to me about what you *do,*' Thorne said. 'Here and now, come on. Tell me about the killing, and the buzz or whatever it is, that you get from controlling people's lives. It can't just be about the money . . .' He paused as Memet climbed to his feet and stared at him, a defiance in his stance, some strange challenge in his nakedness. 'There's nobody worth hiding from in here, is there?' Thorne said. The water was cooling, but the room seemed to be growing hotter by the second. 'It's just the two of us. I'm not writing anything down, my memory's not what it was and I haven't got a tape recorder in my pocket, so it stays in this room. Every bit as discreet as everything else that goes on in here. Talk to me about it *honestly*. Just once . . .'

Slowly, Memet reached for the towel that was draped across the arm of the sofa and began to dry himself. 'That day in my father's café,' he said. 'You told me to make a wish, remember?'

Thorne remembered the lamps hanging from the ceiling, the cigarette smoke dancing around them like a genie. He recalled his parting shot as he'd walked out of the door. 'So, did you make one?'

'I made one, but it didn't come true . . .'

Thorne beat Memet to the punchline. He smiled, but felt the sweat turn to ice at his neck as he spoke.

'Because I'm still here.'

TWENTY-EIGHT

'I knew I should have got a toy or something.'

'Don't worry, I'm sure we can exchange them.'

'You'll be lucky. I've chucked the bloody receipt away . . .'

They spoke quietly, conscious of the baby asleep in a Moses basket beneath the window.

'We can just hang on to them, you never know . . .'

Thorne had known as soon as he'd clapped eyes on Holland's baby that all the clothes he'd bought were far too small. Holland was holding up the tiny outfits, trying and failing to find something positive to say about them.

'What, are you going to have another baby?' Thorne asked.

'Well . . .' Holland laughed and sipped from a can of lager.

Thorne, furious with himself, eventually did the same.

'Sophie's had to nip out and see a mate,' Holland said. 'She'll be sorry she missed you. Said to say "hello" . . .'

Thorne nodded, feeling himself redden slightly. He knew very well that Holland was lying, that his girlfriend would have done her level best to make herself scarce on learning that Thorne was coming round. For all he knew, she might have been hiding in the bedroom, waiting for him to leave.

They were sitting on the sofa in Holland's living room. The clutter made the first-floor flat seem even smaller than it was. Thorne looked around, thinking that if the rest of the place was as cramped, then Sophie wouldn't have had the room to hide . . .

Holland read his thoughts. 'Sophie thinks we should find a bigger flat.'

'What do you think?'

'She's right, we should. Whether we can afford to is a different matter . . .'

'Rack up that overtime, mate.'

'Well I *was*. God knows whether there'll be any on the cards now.'

Though Thorne had brought the beer, he didn't feel much like drinking. He leaned over, put his can down by the side of the sofa. 'Don't worry about it, Dave. The SO7 thing might have gone, but there'll be some nutter out there somewhere putting a bit of work our way soon.'

Holland nodded. 'Good. I hope he's a real psycho. We could do with three bedrooms . . .'

The joke was funny only because of the dark truth that fuelled it. Thorne knew all too well that in a world of uncertainties, in a city of shocking contrasts and shifting ideas, some things were horribly reliable. House prices climbed or tumbled; Spurs had bad seasons or average ones; the mayor was a visionary or an idiot.

And the murder rate went up and up and up . . .

'What d'you reckon about the operation just getting called off like that?' Holland asked. 'I know you and the DCI weren't exactly best mates, but still . . .'

Thorne didn't fancy rehashing the conversation he'd had with Tughan the day before. Instead, he told Holland how he'd spent the morning.

'I reckon they'd booked the entire massage parlour for themselves.'

'Like when they close Harrods so some film star can go shopping,' Holland said. 'Only with prostitutes . . .'

Thorne described the confrontations in the lounge and the VIP Suite, playing up the comedy in his exchanges with Hassan and Memet Zarif. He exaggerated the moments that had felt like small victories and glossed over those that were a little more ambiguous.

He left out the fear altogether . . .

'Will it do any good, d'you think?' Holland said.

'Probably not.' Thorne looked across at the baby. He watched for a few seconds, counted the breaths as her tiny back rose and fell. 'But we can't let these fuckers just . . . swan about, you know? Most of the time, they'll run rings round us, I know that, but every so often we've got to give them a decent tap on the ankles, just to let them know we're still there . . .'

Thorne lifted his eyes to the window, saw that it was rapidly darkening outside. 'I thought it would do *me* some good,' he said.

The baby began to stir, crying softly and kicking her pudgy legs in slow motion. Holland moved quickly to her and squatted down next to the basket. Thorne watched as he pulled the dummy from his daughter's mouth, gently pushed it back in, and repeated the action until she was peaceful again.

'I'm impressed,' Thorne said.

Holland returned to the sofa. He picked up his beer. 'Can I ask you something?'

'As long as it doesn't involve nappies.'

'There's a rumour going around . . .'

Thorne hadn't bothered taking his jacket off. It was warm in the flat, but he'd been unsure how long he would be staying. Suddenly, it felt as stifling as it had been standing next to that jacuzzi a few hours earlier.

'Right . . .' Thorne said.

'Did you have a thing with Alison Kelly?'

A variety of images, hastily constructed denials and straightforward lies flashed through Thorne's head in the few seconds before he spoke. Where had the rumour come from? It didn't really matter. There was only a headache to be gained from worrying about it, or trying to work it out . . .

Thorne didn't want to deceive Dave Holland. He didn't want to look him in the face and make shit up. In the end, though, he chose to tell the truth because he couldn't be arsed to lie, as much as anything else. 'I slept with her, yes.'

Holland's expression rapidly changed from shock to amusement. Then it became something different, something ugly, and that was when Thorne decided to tell him everything else. He wouldn't stand for Holland sitting there looking *impressed*.

When Thorne had finished the story, when the words had moved from the simple repetition of things said over a pub table to those that best described Billy Ryan's body, bleeding on a kitchen floor, they sat and watched Chloe Holland sleep for a minute or two.

Holland drained his can, then squeezed it very slowly out of shape. 'Are we just talking here? This is off duty, right?'

'If you mean "Can we forget about rank?" then yes.'

'Right, that's what I mean . . .'

The sick feeling that came with thinking he shouldn't have said anything was, for Thorne, becoming horribly familiar. 'Don't forget that it's only temporary, though, or that I can get pissed off very quickly, all right?' He was smiling as he spoke, but hoped that the seriousness beneath was clear enough. He knew that Holland thought he was every bit as much of a *fucking idiot* as Carol Chamberlain had, but he didn't want to hear it again . . .

Holland weighed it up and did what Thorne had repeatedly failed to do. He kept his mouth shut.

Thorne spent most of the drive back from the Elephant and Castle thinking about Alison Kelly. Bizarrely, it had not occurred to him until now, but he began to worry about whether she would say anything to anyone. He began to ask himself what might happen if she did . . .

If she were to mention to her solicitor the conversation with a certain detective inspector, they would certainly recommend that she go public with the information. After all, it could only strengthen a diminished-responsibility plea. Wasn't it reasonable to conclude that the balance of a person's mind might be disturbed after they'd just been told that their ex-husband had tried to have them burned to death when they were fourteen years old? That he'd been responsible for setting fire to her best friend? Wouldn't that make *most* people go ever so slightly round the twist?

Mutterings from the public gallery and nodding heads among the jury . . .

Why on earth should the accused have believed such an outlandish tale?

Well, Your Honour, she was told it by one of the police officers who was investigating her ex-husband. Told it, as a matter of fact, in that very police officer's bed . . .

Gasps all around the courtroom . . .

In reality, Thorne had no idea what would happen to him were the truth to get out. He certainly felt in his gut that there would be some form of action taken against him, that he should probably resign before that could happen. Another part of him was unsure exactly what rule he'd broken. Maybe there were guidelines in that manual he'd never bothered to read. He could hardly go to Russell Brigstocke and ask.

The more he thought about it, the simpler it became. Would she tell anyone? Would Alison Kelly, either alone or on the advice of others, sacrifice him in return for a lower sentence, or even a nice cushy number in a hospital?

He thought, as he drove across Waterloo Bridge, that she might well.

Going around Russell Square, he decided that she probably wouldn't.

By the time Thorne pulled up outside his flat, the only thing he knew for certain was that he would not blame her if she did.

All thoughts of Alison Kelly flew from his mind as he approached his front door, then stopped dead with his keys in his hand. He stared at the scarred paintwork and pictured the face of Memet Zarif, the water running slowly through the heavy, dark brows. He stared at the gashes in the woodwork, at the ridges and clinging splinters picked out by the glow from the nearby streetlamp. He felt again the chill at his neck, and knew that Memet had made a decision. When wishes were not enough, action needed to be taken.

Thorne stared at his front door; at the ragged 'X' carved deep into it.

TWENTY-NINE

Thorne was dragging the car around and flooring it back towards the main road within a minute, spitting his fury out loud at the windscreen as he drove. His heart was dancing like a maniac in his chest, his breathing as rapid as the baby's he'd been watching only an hour before.

It was important to try to stay calm, to get where he was going in one piece. He had to hold on to his anger, to save it up and channel it against Memet Zarif when he finally got hold of the fucker . . .

He shouted in frustration and stamped on the brake, his cry drowning out the squeal as the wheels locked and the BMW stopped at the lights with a lurch. He watched his knuckles whiten around the wheel as he waited for red to turn to green.

Watching a taxi drive past. Feeling his chest straining against the seat-belt over and over. Listening to the leather move against the nylon, the spastic thumping of his heartbeat . . .

The realisation was sharp and sudden, like a slap, and Thorne felt the stinging certainty spread and settle across him. Slowly, he leaned forward and flicked on his hazard lights, oblivious to the cars snarling round him and through the traffic lights.

A taxi . . . a minicab . . .

He recalled the face he'd barely registered that morning behind the wheel of a black Omega – the driver outside Zarif's place on Green Lanes who'd asked if he needed a cab. He remembered where he'd seen that face before.

Thorne waited until the lights had changed again, turned the car around and cruised slowly back towards his flat.

Why was this man driving a cab for Memet Zarif? Would he still be working this late in the day? It was certainly worth a try . . .

Thorne's mind was racing every bit as fast as it had been before, adrenalin fizzing through his system, but now a calmness was making its presence felt, too, flowing through him where it was needed.

The calmness of decision, of purpose.

He was dialling the number before the BMW had come to a standstill outside the flat. He listened to the call going through as he stepped out on to the pavement.

The phlegm-hawker who answered was no more polite on the phone than he had been in person.

'Car service . . .'

'I need a cab from Kentish Town as soon as you can,' Thorne said.

'What's the address?'

'Listen, I need a nice one, a good-looking motor, you know? I've got to impress someone. You got a Merc or anything like that?'

'No mate, nothing like that.'

Thorne leaned back against his car. 'You must have *something* nice. A Scorpio, an Omega, that kind of thing. I don't mind paying a bit over the odds . . .'

'We've got a couple of Omegas.' The man sounded like he resented every syllable of the conversation.

'Yeah, that's great. One of those. Which driver is it?'

'What's the difference?'

Was there a hint of suspicion in the question? Thorne decided it was probably just a natural sourness. 'I had one of your lot a couple of weeks ago and he wouldn't shut up . . .'

Thorne was told the driver's name and felt the buzz kick in. 'That's perfect,' he said.

'What's your address, mate?'

Thorne stared at the 'X' on his front door. There was no way he was going to give them an address they would clearly be all too familiar with. The very last thing he wanted was for the driver to know who he was picking up. He named a shop on the Kentish Town Road, told the dispatcher he'd be waiting outside.

'Fifteen minutes, mate . . .'

Thorne was already on his way.

The fifteen minutes was closer to twenty-five, but the time passed quickly. Thorne had plenty to think about. He couldn't be certain that when the driver had spoken to him that morning outside the minicab office, he hadn't done so knowing *exactly* who he was. Thorne could only hope that the man he was now waiting for had simply been touting for business, and that he'd just been viewed as a potential customer.

When the Omega pulled up, Thorne looked hard at the driver. He saw nothing that looked like dissemblance . . .

Thorne climbed into the back of the car, knowing full well that he'd been wrong about these things before.

'Where to?' the driver asked.

It was the one thing Thorne hadn't considered. 'Hampstead Garden Suburb,' he said. It was a couple of miles away from them, beyond Highgate. Thorne was hoping it was far enough away, that he'd have got what he needed well before they arrived . . .

The driver grunted as he steered the Omega into the traffic heading north along the Kentish Town Road.

They drove for five minutes or more in complete silence. Perhaps the dispatcher had mentioned that the customer was not fond of chit-chat. Perhaps the driver had nothing to say. Either way, it suited Thorne perfectly. It gave him a little time to gather his thoughts.

He'd recognised Wayne Brookhouse – had finally remembered his face – from the CCTV tape of Gordon Rooker's visitors. He remembered Stone and Holland laying out the black-and-white stills on his desk. Brookhouse, if that was his real name, wasn't wearing the glasses any more and his hair was longer now than it had been when he'd last visited Rooker. He was supposed to be the daughter's boyfriend, wasn't he? Or ex-boyfriend, maybe . . .

What had Stone said about Brookhouse after he'd been to interview him? '*A bit dodgy*'? Thorne had good reason to believe that the young man driving him around was rather more dodgy than anyone had thought.

The soft leather seat sighed as Thorne relaxed into it. 'Busy day, Wayne?'

Brookhouse looked over his shoulder for as long as was possible without crashing. 'Sorry, mate, do I know you?'

'Friend of a friend,' Thorne said.

'Oh . . .'

Thorne watched the eyes move back and forth from road to mirror. He could almost hear the cogs whirring as Brookhouse tried to work out who the hell he'd just picked up. Thorne decided to give him some help . . .

'How's your love life, Wayne? Still giving Gordon Rooker's daughter one? What's her name again?'

Thorne watched Brookhouse's back stiffen, felt him struggle to figure out what might be the 'right' answer, given the circumstances. Thorne was starting to doubt that Brookhouse had ever even *met* Gordon Rooker's daughter.

'Who the fuck are you?' Brookhouse said. He'd clearly decided that aggression was his safest option.

'You won't be seeing a tip with an attitude like that . . .'

'Right, that's it.' Brookhouse indicated and began to pull over to the kerb.

'Keep driving,' Thorne said. His tone of voice made it obvious that he did not respond well to aggression.

Brookhouse swerved back towards the centre of the road and they drove on past the tennis courts at the bottom of Parliament Hill.

'Who put you up for the part?' Thorne asked. 'I can't work out whether you were already one of Memet's boys and he suggested you to Rooker, or whether you did have some kind of connection with Rooker and he was the one who found you the job driving the cab.' He waited for an answer. Didn't get one.

'It's not vital information,' Thorne said. 'I'm just curious.

Either way, you were clearly just passing messages backwards and forwards. Popping in to see Rooker, playing the part of the harmless tearaway who used to shag his daughter, giving him messages from Memet . . .'

There were still a great many questions that needed answering, but Thorne had worked one thing out: whatever deal Rooker had been trying to strike with him, he had been busy setting up another with Memet Zarif. If he was going to hand over Billy Ryan, Rooker had clearly decided to play it very safe indeed.

'Rooker told us you were a car mechanic. Is that bollocks, Wayne? Would you know a big end from a Big Mac? You certainly convinced my DC when he interviewed you . . .'

'You're Thorne.'

'Spot on. And *you're* fucked . . .'

Through the gap between the seats, Thorne watched Brookhouse's hand slide across, reaching for something on the passenger seat. Thorne leaned forward, grabbed a good handful of Brookhouse's hair and pulled his head back.

'*Ow, Jesus!*'

Thorne looked and saw that Brookhouse had been reaching for a mobile.

'Look, I was just pretending to be a visitor,' he said. His voice had risen an octave or two. 'Like you said, I was just delivering a bit of information, nothing important, I swear. I know fuck all about fuck all, that's the truth.'

Thorne stared at the tiny mobile phone, small and shiny, nestled in the folds of a dark blue anorak that had been neatly laid across the seat. Wayne Brookhouse had posed as a car mechanic, and as the ex-boyfriend of Gordon

Rooker's daughter. Thorne suddenly wondered if he might not have played *another* role.

'*Now* you can pull over,' Thorne said. 'Anywhere . . .'

'What for?'

Thorne barely registered the cry as he dragged Wayne Brookhouse's head a little further back. 'I need to make a call . . .'

Chamberlain reached for the phone, both eyes still on the TV programme she was trying to lose herself in.

Thorne's voice concentrated her thoughts.

'Oh, hello, Tom . . .'

Thorne spoke quickly and quietly, and her expression changed when she heard the edge in his tone. From his armchair, Jack looked across at her, concern in every line of his face. He pointed the remote control, turned down the volume on the TV.

Thorne told her to listen.

Chamberlain smiled at her husband and shook her head. It was nothing . . .

Thorne pressed the handset hard against Brookhouse's ear until he began to moan in pain.

'Now, say it again,' Thorne said. 'Like you mean it.'

Brookhouse winced and took a deep breath. 'I burned her . . .'

Thorne yanked the phone away, his fingers still clutching Brookhouse's hair. Something in the near silence on the line, a horror in the gentle hiss, told him that Carol Chamberlain had recognised the voice.

'Carol . . .?'

'There's a train from here in less than fifteen minutes,' she said. 'I can be there in an hour and a half . . .'

Thorne felt a second or two of doubt, but no more. He had been fairly sure what Chamberlain's reaction would be as soon as he'd decided to make the call. 'Give me a ring when you're coming in,' he said. He flicked his wrist sharply to one side, smacking Brookhouse's head against the window. 'There'll be a cab there to meet you.'

THIRTY

Wayne Brookhouse's face – open and attractive beneath the mop of thick, dark hair – broke into a smile. He looked relaxed and happy. Only the redness, livid around his right ear, and the expressions on the faces of the two people sitting opposite him indicated that anything might be out of the ordinary.

'How much longer we going to carry on with this?' Brookhouse said.

It was not far short of midnight, and in the two hours since Thorne had first confronted him, in the time spent waiting for Carol Chamberlain to arrive and travelling back to Thorne's flat, Brookhouse had recovered his confidence.

'Hadn't really thought about it,' Thorne said.

'That much is fucking obvious . . .'

Chamberlain looked at Thorne. They were sitting next to each other on kitchen chairs. Brookhouse was a few feet in front of them in the middle of the sofa. 'I don't think there's any time limit, is there?' she said.

Thorne shook his head, stared for a few seconds at

Brookhouse before speaking. 'Tell us how it worked between you, Rooker and Zarif.'

Brookhouse's smile didn't falter. 'They clearly aren't paying you enough,' he said, looking around. 'This place is shit.'

'Why were you pretending to be responsible for the attack on Jessica Clarke?'

Thorne knew this was not going to be easy. In the time that Brookhouse had honed his cocky act, Thorne had put a few pieces of the puzzle in place. He was now working up to the really important questions by asking a few to which he already knew the answers.

'It smells as well,' Brookhouse said. 'It stinks of curry . . .'

Whoever had put the idea together – and right now Thorne's money was on Gordon Rooker – had been intent on putting the ball into the police's court. Drawing the police to him. And, like mugs, they'd come. Brookhouse had made the calls and sent the letters and, sure enough, eventually some idiot had gone along to have a word with Gordon Rooker and started the ball rolling. They'd pressed Rooker until, finally, he'd confessed his innocence, and told them about Billy Ryan. Then he had them . . .

Some idiot . . .

'So, Rooker was sorting out a deal with us, and at the same time making sure he had a slightly different kind of protection from Memet Zarif, right? Is that right, Wayne?'

'You came to my house.' Chamberlain crossed her legs, smoothed down her skirt.

Thorne glanced at her, imagining for a bizarre moment that the two of them were interviewing Brookhouse for a job.

'You stood in my front garden and looked up at me, didn't you?'

Brookhouse stretched out his legs, knocked the toes of his trainers together. 'This is *so* fucked up,' he said. He nodded towards Chamberlain. 'Look at her. She's not a copper. She's like my fucking auntie or something . . .'

'*I'm* a copper,' Thorne said.

'So? You wouldn't be with her if this was anything official. It's obvious you aren't going to arrest me. This is something . . . private. Right?'

Thorne shrugged. 'So what are you going to do, Wayne? You want to call the police?'

Brookhouse leaned forward, his forearms braced across his knees. 'I might call a solicitor, yeah.'

'The phone's by the front door . . .'

The man on the sofa held Thorne's stare for a few seconds, then, slowly, the smile reappeared. 'You can't do shit to me.' He started to laugh softly in short, high-pitched bursts, and Thorne could see that the amusement was real. The little fucker really found the situation funny. He genuinely believed that they could not touch him, that he was protected.

'You're absolutely right, Wayne. This is private, which means that I won't lose my job if I come over there and kick your balls up into your throat.'

Thorne's threat, or perhaps it was his expression as he made it, was enough to stop the laughter, but no more than that.

'Fine,' Brookhouse said. 'It's probably the only way this can end up, right?'

'That's up to you . . .'

385

Brookhouse sat up straight. 'It's OK with me if it means we can get this shit over with. I'll take a pasting if I have to, but I'll hurt you at the same time, man, I swear.' Another nod towards Chamberlain. 'She going to have a crack as well, is she? 'Cos I tell you, I've got no fucking problems with giving her a slap as well.'

The confidence vanished for a second as Chamberlain stood suddenly and stepped towards him, shouting: 'No fucking problems with trying to set fire to a young girl at a bus stop, either, have you?'

'No idea what you're on about . . .'

Thorne knew now that the attack in Swiss Cottage had been made to up the stakes, had been the only option left when it looked like Rooker's offer had been rejected. It had certainly done the trick, leaving the police no option but to agree to Rooker's deal.

'That was you, too, wasn't it, Wayne? At that bus stop?' Chamberlain stood, red-faced, above him. 'That's attempted murder, and you're looking at the same sentence Rooker got . . .'

Brookhouse stared at her, calmly bringing up his hand to wipe her spittle from his cheek.

'Jack of all trades, aren't you?' Thorne said. 'Are you the only one Memet's got who can do all these things? Or has the family blown all its money on hookers and expensive hitmen?'

Brookhouse said nothing . . .

Thorne leaned forward. This was an important one. 'Who put the cross on my door, Wayne?'

The answer came at the back end of a yawn. 'Piss off . . .'

386

Thorne's fingers curled into fists at the exact moment that Chamberlain turned to him, suddenly composed again.

'Have you got any handcuffs knocking about?' she asked.

Gordon Rooker was shopping.

He'd spent a lot of money already. He'd splashed out on smart new clothes and several pairs of fashionable shoes. He'd got drinks in for a bar-full of strangers who were now his closest friends. He'd bought the latest mobile phone, a nice radio and a massive flat-screen TV that he'd seen in a magazine and planned to put in the corner of his new living room. He didn't know where that living room was going to be yet, or how much money he'd have to buy all these things when he *really* got the chance, but he relished the planning. He savoured the dream of *owning* again, the joy of the notes passing through his hands.

Lying on his bunk in the dark, he tried to imagine the future. This was something he'd done countless times before, of course, when there was even a sniff of hope that he might be let out, but this time it was different. He could taste, smell and touch the freedom that was no more than a few days away.

He ate an expensive meal – three courses and a fancy bottle of wine – in a restaurant that was almost certainly no longer in business. He left a large tip and walked out of there feeling like his shit would taste of sugar . . .

Money had been mentioned back when Ryan was still alive. It had been part of the deal then, even though they'd been a bit coy about exactly how much. He was likely to cop for a bit less now than he would have done originally, but they still had to give him *something*, surely. They couldn't just dump him in a strange town or city, point him towards the nearest dole office and tell him to get on with it, could they?

He'd tried getting some straight answers out of that bastard Thorne, but it had been like trying to piss up a rope. There was still so much that was unsettled, and it was disconcerting after twenty years of routine, but he could live with it. A release date, in black and white, was all the certainty he needed.

He bought books, dozens of them: spy thrillers and biographies. He'd learned to lose himself in them and looked forward to choosing his own.

He bought a season ticket at Upton Park. Wherever he ended up, he'd sneak back now and again to watch his grandson play.

And he bought himself a woman. Inside, you developed strong wrists, but cash handed over to lie back and watch a tart doing the work could only be money well spent.

In his cell, Rooker drifted towards sleep thinking about big, soft beds, and about flesh beneath his fingers that was not his own.

THIRTY-ONE

Thorne hadn't known Wayne Brookhouse for long, of course, but this was definitely a look he'd not seen before. The eyes bulged. The face seemed stiff and yellow as old newspaper.

Thorne knew Chamberlain's features far better, but they were distorted by an expression that to him was equally as strange.

'This is *so* . . . fucking . . . out of order,' Brookhouse said. He panted out the words, his head twisting from side to side, the bed shaking as he fought against his restraints.

One wrist was cuffed to the metal bedstead, the other lashed to it with a black tie which Thorne normally only dug out for funerals. Thorne was sitting across his prisoner's legs, holding tight to the rail at the foot of the bed to avoid being pitched off as Brookhouse struggled and bucked.

Chamberlain finished unbuttoning Brookhouse's shirt and reached towards the bedside table. The appliance she picked up was plugged into a red extension reel, which in turn ran to a socket in the corner of the room. She flicked the cable aside as she took a step towards the head of the bed. 'It's funny,' she said, 'because, normally, I bloody hate ironing . . .'

Brookhouse spat out a string of curses. He was doing his very best to appear unafraid, to make the fear look like rage, and he wasn't making a bad job of it. Maybe it would have been harder to disguise if Thorne had been holding the iron. Perhaps, much as he was struggling, Brookhouse found the sight of a woman in her mid-fifties playing amateur-hour torturer faintly ridiculous.

To Thorne, the only ridiculous thing was that Brookhouse wasn't a damn sight *more* scared. Thorne could see something in Carol Chamberlain's eyes that he'd never seen before. Or maybe something that was usually there was *missing* . . .

'Tell us about the X-Man,' Thorne said.

Brookhouse screwed his eyes shut. 'I can't . . .'

Chamberlain lowered her arm. The face of the iron was no more than six inches above Brookhouse's chest. 'This is heavy,' she said.

Thorne stared at Chamberlain. They were busking this. *He* couldn't tell whether she meant it, so Brookhouse certainly couldn't. 'Come on, Wayne . . .'

Brookhouse winced. It was obvious, though the iron was not touching him, that he was starting to feel its heat. 'He's gone, he's gone.' He began to shout, to gabble his words. 'He got out of the country. All right?'

'Where?' Thorne asked.

'I don't fucking know, I swear. Serbia, maybe. I think he was a Serb . . .'

'Give me a name.'

'I don't know his name, I never met him . . .' He tensed as the iron dropped another inch. 'Look, I saw him in the café once, that's all. He was just sitting on his own in the corner, smiling. Dark hair, you know, same as they all fucking look. Smile like a film star, loads of fucking teeth, I remember that . . .'

Thorne remembered the man in the car outside his flat. He remembered that smile. He wondered how close he'd come to feeling a blade against his back; the brightness of its edge, teasing before the blackness of the bullet . . .

'When did he leave, Wayne?'

'A while ago. A few weeks after he did the last one. After the copper.'

Moloney . . .

So, Thorne had been wrong about Billy Ryan having Marcus Moloney killed. It *had* been Memet Zarif who had ordered the killing, without realising he was targeting an undercover officer. The murder of Moloney had, in Thorne's mind, been one more thing Ryan had paid for with his own death. One more thing that had justified Thorne telling Alison Kelly what he'd told her. Now, Thorne had to take Moloney's death off that list, but it didn't make much difference. There were still plenty of things Billy Ryan had needed to pay for . . .

'If he's gone,' Thorne said, 'who put the "X" on my door?'

'It could have been anyone.' The sweat left a stain on Thorne's sheets when Brookhouse turned his head. 'It was just to put the shits up you a bit, that's all.'

'Who ordered the killings?' Chamberlain asked. 'Was it Memet?'

Brookhouse shook his head.

'Is that a "no"?' Chamberlain moved the iron to her left hand, shook out the right for a few seconds, then moved it back. 'Or a "no comment" . . .?'

Thorne steadied himself as Brookhouse's knees jerked up into his backside. He rode out the struggle, thinking about the dead and about those who had taken money to arrange their deaths. Those for whom knives and guns were the tools of their trade: the butcher who had murdered Mickey Clayton, Marcus Moloney and the others; the man who had shot Muslum and Hanya Izzigil; whoever had gunned down Francis Cullen and the two still unidentified immigrants who had been dragged from the back of his lorry and had tried to run for their lives.

The men who'd got away with it.

Like a man whose tools had been a naked flame, and a can of lighter fuel . . .

Thorne looked at Brookhouse, wondering just how close he might have got to Gordon Rooker. Rooker probably trusted him a damn sight more than he'd ever trust a police officer. Thorne asked himself how much Rooker might have had to reveal, how much he'd had to give up before his arrangements with Memet Zarif were finalised. It couldn't hurt to ask.

'Who burned Jessica Clarke, Wayne?'

Thorne saw something flicker, just for a second, in Brookhouse's eyes. A spark of *something*, that he immediately did his best to hide, like a small boy caught stealing and jamming the booty far down into his pocket. Thorne glanced at Chamberlain and knew immediately that she'd seen it, too.

'You *know*, don't you?' she said.

Thorne watched as Chamberlain let the iron fall a little further. He could see the tendons stretching on the inside of her forearm as she took the weight of it, the concentration on her face as she moved it, as slowly as she could.

'You won't . . .' Brookhouse said.

Thorne watched, compelled, as Chamberlain reached down and turned the dial on the iron to its highest setting. A drop of water fell from it on to Brookhouse's chest. He flinched as if it were boiling.

'You're imagining the pain as something quick,' Chamberlain said. 'A moment of agony as I press the iron down and then release it. Just a second or two of hissing and then it's over, right? OK, I want you to think about how it would be if I let the iron go. If I just left it sitting there on your chest. Sizzling on your chest, Wayne. How long do you think it would take to start sinking in . . .?'

When Brookhouse took his eyes from the iron and looked at Chamberlain's face he started to talk. 'Jesus, how fucking thick are you people? There was no other man. There was only me, pretending to be him.'

'Pretending to be the man who really burned Jessica . . .?'

'*Him*. Rooker. Rooker *was* the man.'

And Thorne could see it: bright as a flame and certain as a scar. In the walk and in the fucking wink of him, and in the cunt's fingers moving through his greasy, yellow hair. In the tongue that slid across a gold tooth and in that sly smile before Gordon Rooker bent to snap the lid from his tobacco tin . . .

Thorne had known from the moment he'd recognised

Brookhouse that Rooker had been lying. But not about *this*. It was obvious that Brookhouse couldn't have burned Jessica, but Thorne had never presumed that the man making the calls – the man on Chamberlain's front lawn – had been the real attacker. He'd always thought that there was someone else, and that Rooker had probably known who he was . . .

'Tom . . .?'

Everything had been built upon the belief, *his* belief that Rooker had been innocent. Wasn't it him that had put the pressure on Rooker in the first place, *forced* him to admit that he wasn't the one?

Chamberlain had raised the iron and stood looking at him, waiting for something. Guidance, perhaps.

The vast, dreadful stone of his own stupidity crashed on to the floor of Thorne's gut. Its weight exactly equalled the elation of knowing, of finally getting the name. He felt hollow and bloated; cancelled out . . .

Almost every single thing that Rooker had told them was true. He'd only changed one, tiny fact. When Billy Ryan had asked him to kill Alison Kelly, he'd said yes.

'He was perfect . . .'

Chamberlain still hadn't got it. 'What?'

Rooker had almost certainly been involved in the earlier attempt to get rid of Kevin Kelly. Billy Ryan, as Kelly's number two, had a very good reason to want Rooker dead. It made him the ideal choice to carry out a contract on Kelly's daughter . . .

'Maybe Ryan offered to lift a contract he had out on Rooker,' Thorne said. 'In return for Rooker doing him one small favour.'

Chamberlain looked unconvinced, but it didn't really matter either way. What was beyond dispute was Rooker's fear of Billy Ryan, a fear based on the knowledge that Ryan did not forgive those who fucked up. It had driven Rooker to confess, to condemn himself to prison and to a life spent with only the fear itself for company. It grew with every attack, with every beating in the showers, until it dictated everything Rooker did. Fear was what drove him. It was what eventually gave shape to a scheme that might protect him when he finally came to start life again outside prison.

Which he would be doing just a few days from now . . .

Thorne decided that Brookhouse could kick as much as he wanted. He swung his legs around and slid off the bed. 'What's Rooker's arrangement with Memet Zarif?'

Again something flashed in Brookhouse's eyes. This time, there was no mistaking genuine terror.

'A lot more scared of Memet than he is of us,' Chamberlain said.

Thorne watched Brookhouse's eyes dart to meet his own. He saw the tears begin. He saw the hope that their meaning might not be understood. Thorne began to suspect that he may have been wrong about which of the Zarif brothers was pulling the strings.

'*Not* Memet?' Thorne asked.

There was a moan which seemed to come from Brookhouse's belly as he started to thrash around on the bed.

'Hassan . . .?'

Thorne repeated the name, raising his voice over the noise Brookhouse was making to blank him out. There was still no response. Thorne nodded to Chamberlain, who moved the iron back into position. 'Who is it, Wayne?'

395

As the iron descended again towards his chest, Brookhouse gradually began to grow still. The sobbing died away, his body stiffened and his eyes closed tight shut. It was clear that he was waiting for the pain, that he was prepared for it.

Something . . . some*one* frightened him a lot more.

Chamberlain held the iron an inch above his chest. Thorne watched the skin begin to redden, saw the translucent edges of blisters gaining definition.

'Looks like you're happy to let us get on with this, Wayne,' Thorne said. 'Maybe we should just go down to the station. You might be less happy about going to prison for attempted murder . . .'

Brookhouse gasped out his words on snatched breaths. 'The girl at the bus stop was just for show. So the deal would happen. I was never going to do it . . .'

'It's not much of a defence . . .'

'Doesn't matter, does it?' Brookhouse opened his eyes. He looked, glassy-eyed, at the edge of the iron, then up at Thorne. 'We're not going to the station, are we?'

Thorne stared back at him. Terrified as he was, Brookhouse knew very well that this was never going to get as far as paperwork.

'You're right, we're not.' Thorne turned to Chamberlain. 'Burn him . . .'

The flippancy with which Thorne had issued the instruction was in stark contrast to the way he felt. It was as if the blood were poised to explode from beneath every inch of his skin. The tendons in his neck felt ready to snap, and things had stirred, and begun to jump and slither in his stomach.

Burn him . . .

The pair of them had struggled to overpower Brookhouse, to drag him through to the bedroom and tie him down. Since that moment, Thorne had stood outside himself, impotent as he'd followed Carol Chamberlain further into the shadows. She'd told him to fetch the iron and he'd done it. He'd watched her weighing up ends and means in an instant of rage, and her decision had taken him with it. He'd been borne along with her, exhilarated and appalled, deferring to something far beyond a rank that had been long since taken from her.

He watched the steam drifting from beneath the iron like the breath of funeral horses. He listened to the scrape of the handcuffs against the metal rail as Brookhouse strained against his bonds.

'Get a towel under him,' Chamberlain said. 'When there's contact he'll probably piss himself . . .'

Thorne was not sure if this was a simple practicality or a last attempt to scare Brookhouse into talking. He looked into Chamberlain's eyes and knew one thing: if he *didn't* talk, she *was* going to press a hot iron on to his chest.

Brookhouse said nothing.

The iron moved towards the scarlet skin in slow motion . . .

Chamberlain had obviously reached the point where she thought she had nothing left to lose. Thorne watched her about to torture a man, and tried to decide if what *he* had was worth holding on to.

There was scarcely any air between metal and flesh . . .

Thorne knew that the sound and the smell of it could be no more than a moment away. He tried to speak, but once more he'd become as his father was. The words 'no' and 'stop' refused to come. He heard the hairs on Brookhouse's chest begin to crackle. He put out a hand.

'Carol . . .'

Brookhouse screamed hard and sucked in his chest, then screamed louder still as the mattress pushed him back up again, into the steaming base of the iron.

Chamberlain moved as if her's was the skin kissed by hot metal, and when she and Thorne had finished shouting, they could only stand still, pale and stiff as corpses, looking away while Brookhouse sobbed and spat bubbles of nonsense.

'Ba . . . ba . . .'

Thorne listened to Brookhouse's gibberish. He watched him kick a leg, slowly, as Holland's baby had done.

'Ba . . . ba . . . ba . . .'

Thorne looked across the bed at Chamberlain. He was unable to tell if the horror on her face was at what she had done with the iron or at something she could see stuck to the flat of it.

It was perhaps an hour after Wayne Brookhouse had gone. The two of them were sitting in darkness, unable to drink fast enough – when the word suddenly danced into Thorne's head.

'What are we going to do about Rooker?' Chamberlain asked. 'With what that fucker did to Jessica? We can't let him come out . . .'

Thorne wasn't paying much attention. He was trying to place a word, recalling precisely where he'd seen it on a page. *No*, on a screen . . .

Brookhouse had not been talking nonsense at all.

Thorne had seen the word a month or so before on the NCIS website. On a night when he'd been unable to sleep, when he'd sat at his computer and absorbed the miserable realities of human trafficking. That same night he'd trawled through pages of information about organised crime in the UK and in Turkey. He'd speed-read dense blocks of text about the set-up of Turkish gangs, the customs and the hierarchies of the most powerful families in Ankara and Istanbul . . .

A word that looked to English eyes as though it should mean *baby* or *child* and meant exactly the opposite.

'Tom? What about Rooker . . .?'

Baba . . .

Thorne felt it where the hairline brushed the nape of his neck. He knew that Gordon Rooker was not the only person he'd misjudged.

THIRTY-TWO

Thorne waited nearly a week before going back to Green Lanes.

He'd spent the days at work, going through the motions – pushing paper around his desk as one case wound down and others moved up a gear. All the time he was weighing up everything he'd learned about what had been done and who should pay for it, and waiting in vain for something that might change the most depressing fact of all. There was nothing he could do . . .

It was just after eleven-thirty on a warmish Thursday night. The café had not been closed very long when Thorne pressed his face against the glass in the door. He could just make out Arkan Zarif alone at a booth towards the back. He could see Zarif's daughter Sema moving back and forth behind the counter.

Thorne banged on the glass.

Zarif looked up, peered to see who it was. From outside, Thorne couldn't read the expression on the old man's face when he recognised who was at the door. Zarif nodded towards his daughter and the girl came from behind the counter, unlocked the door and held it open for Thorne without a word.

The main lights in the place had been turned off, but a number of the lanterns overhead were glowing: orange and red bleeding through coloured glass and slats in metal. There was music playing at a low level, a woman singing in Turkish. Thorne couldn't tell if she was in love or in despair.

Zarif held up his glass, shouted something to his daughter as Thorne approached his table. Thorne turned to the girl and shook his head. She moved back behind the rows of cups and glasses.

'No wine?' Zarif said. 'Coffee then . . .?'

Thorne slid into the booth without answering.

For a few moments they studied each other, then Zarif emptied his wineglass. His hand seemed huge around the stem. He reached for the bottle and poured himself another.

'*Merhaba, Baba,*' Thorne said. Hello . . .

Zarif smiled and raised his glass. '*Merhaba . . .*'

'We sat in here once and talked about what names meant, remember?'

Zarif said nothing.

'We joked about how they can mean more than one thing. Like the word *baba* . . .'

'The meaning of this word is simple,' Zarif said.

'I know what it *means*, and I also know how it's used. I know the respect that it inspires back in Turkey. And the fear.'

'*Baba* is "father", that's all.'

'Father as in "head of the family", right? Father to your

children, and to your friends, and to those who earn you money. Father to those who kill for you and father to those who you wouldn't think twice about *having* killed if it suited you.'

'I look after my wife and children . . .'

'Of course you do. You're just running a small family business while others are out with the guns and knives you put into their hands. How does it work, *Baba*? You run things until you croak or you're past it and then the boys take over?'

Zarif swilled wine around his mouth, then swallowed. 'When business no longer interests me, I will retire. Now, things are still interesting. It's a good arrangement . . .'

'It's a *great* arrangement. Memet and his brothers front it up, handle all the attention from the likes of me, while you're just the harmless old boy in the kitchen, chucking meat on the grill.'

Zarif folded his hands across his gut. He was wearing the same grubby, striped apron Thorne had seen the first time he'd come into the café. 'These days, I truly enjoy the cooking more than . . . other parts of my business. It's easy to be at the heart of things here. I'm in the kitchen, people know where I am.'

It struck Thorne suddenly that Zarif's accent was less pronounced than when they'd spoken before. There was little, if any, groping for the right word. The act had been dropped.

Sema Zarif stepped from behind the counter and walked past them. She glanced at Thorne as she moved towards the stairs, and for the first time Thorne caught the trace of a smile. As if he were no longer someone to be worried about . . .

'You must have thought I was such a fucking idiot,' Thorne said. 'Sitting at your table, eating with you . . .'

'Not at all. If you want to feel better, you must know that you are a man far from the one I took you to be.'

The white parts of Zarif's thick moustache were stained red with wine. Thorne stared at it, thinking that it looked like Zarif had been feasting on something raw; wishing that he'd said yes to a drink; wanting to know what the hell Zarif was talking about.

'A man who would torture to get what he wants,' Zarif said. 'The performance with the hot iron was . . . remarkable.'

Thorne felt something clench beneath his breastbone. 'When did you speak to Wayne Brookhouse?' he asked.

Zarif raised his glass to his mouth, answered quietly across the top of it. 'It was several days ago, I think . . .'

When Brookhouse had left Thorne's flat, in the early hours of the previous Friday morning, the goodbyes had been less than fulsome. Chamberlain had said nothing as Thorne had untied him. The two of them had stood and watched without a word as he'd rushed, swearing and stumbling, towards the door. Only at the last moment had Thorne taken Brookhouse to one side, held him against the back of the door and tried to press some good advice upon him.

'Don't go back,' he'd said. It had been hard to make himself understood, to be sure his words were being heard and taken seriously, but Thorne knew that he had to make the effort. 'Are you listening, Wayne? Go home, pack a bag and make yourself very fucking scarce . . .'

Thorne watched as Zarif took another sip of wine.

Wayne Brookhouse had not been nearly as clever as he'd thought he was. He'd made the decision to go back to Zarif and tell him what had happened, and Thorne knew that he almost certainly hadn't received the sympathy or the respect he thought he deserved. Thorne could imagine Brookhouse showing Zarif the burn on his chest, cursing those responsible and assuring his boss that he'd done what was expected, that he'd said nothing.

Thorne could imagine the artfully faked concern on the *Baba's* face, the stone-cold resolve as he'd made the only decision possible.

'Where is he now?' Thorne asked.

'I haven't seen Wayne for a day or two. He's gone away, maybe.'

'If a body turns up, you know I'll be back.'

'It won't turn up.' Zarif made no effort to hide the smile or to disguise the double-meaning. He knew that he was safe, and seeing that knowledge smeared across his fat face was like a blade sliding back and forth across Thorne's chest. He said nothing and tried again to convince himself that he'd done the right thing. If not the right thing, then the *only* thing he could have done.

He felt sure that even if he'd done the sensible thing a week earlier – if he'd asked Wayne Brookhouse to drive his taxi to the nearest police station – it would have made no difference. Brookhouse would have said nothing. Zarif's lawyers would have had him back picking up customers within a few hours. The police would have been left with nothing but a few awkward questions to throw at Gordon Rooker, and even less to link the Zarif family to anything worth talking about.

Even if Thorne were to come clean now – if he were to go to Brigstocke or Tughan or Jesmond and tell him what he knew and how he knew it – there would be little to gain. He could admit to torturing a witness and with his next breath explain that the witness had now disappeared; that the witness was, in all likelihood, dead and buried. The only person on the end of any awkward questions after *that* would be Thorne himself.

And he'd been asking himself plenty of those already.

'Mr Rooker was released yesterday, so I understand.'

'You know he was . . .'

'This was a surprise.' Zarif raised his thick grey eyebrows. 'Knowing that he told you a number of lies, you still chose to let him out of prison.'

Thorne tried hard to draw some spit up into his dry mouth. 'I chose not to take the steps that might keep him there . . .'

I chose not to reveal what I'd discovered. I chose not to tell anyone that I'd kidnapped a suspect, that I'd held him against his will and done nothing as this information was forced from him with extreme violence. I chose not to reveal the extent of Gordon Rooker's brutality, or of my own.

I chose to keep the truth quiet and to protect myself . . .

'I wonder what Rooker is doing?' Zarif asked.

'If he's got any sense, he'll be watching his back. You're not fond of leaving loose ends lying around, are you?'

Zarif looked genuinely hurt. 'You've got it wrong. Rooker has nothing to fear from me. We had an agreement, we had shared interests.'

'Right. He helps you deal with Billy Ryan and in return you look after him once he's out. What are we talking?

Money, I presume. Protection? Something above and beyond what we can provide . . .'

'An *agreement*, which I fully intend to honour.'

Thorne ran his hand along the surface of the table, scraped salt into the palm of his hand. 'Honour, right. That's important, isn't it? I remember you touching glasses with me and drinking to it. How much honour was there for Marcus Moloney? Sliced up and shot in the head in his car.' He dropped the salt on to the floor. 'Was that an honourable way to die, do you think?'

'Did he behave honourably?' Zarif asked. 'Doing what he was doing?' He flicked a fingernail against his glass. 'Have *you*?'

Another question Thorne had asked himself, and answered, a thousand times in the previous few days. 'When I came down to your level, no.'

Zarif looked up at the sound of his daughter calling to him from the top of the stairs. He answered her, watched her go, then turned back to Thorne. He emptied the last few drops of wine into his glass. 'Time for you to leave . . .'

Thorne reached across the table, grabbed the wineglass and pushed it hard into the old man's face. He felt the glass break and ground it through the soft hair of Zarif's moustache, blood springing bright to the surface and running down as Thorne twisted and pressed.

'We need to lock up.'

Thorne blinked away the fantasy and stood up. He walked to the counter, leaned back against it. 'You got the message I gave to Memet about retaliation for the shooting?' He pressed on before Zarif could answer. 'Of course you did. Hence the message of your own on my front door.'

Zarif spread his arms wide. Sweat stains darkened the white nylon of his shirt. 'I'm sorry for that, really. That was Hassan's doing.'

This was a genuine surprise. 'Hassan?'

'He is normally the most cautious of my sons, but you upset him.'

'Well now he's upset me.'

'I will be sure to tell him.'

'Do that.'

Zarif grunted, began to slide his bulk along the seat. 'Have you replaced your door?'

Thorne shook his head.

'Please' – Zarif gestured casually towards the counter – 'take some money from the till.'

He got to his feet and fixed Thorne with the same expression of vague amusement that had recently been on his daughter's face. 'Go ahead, help yourself . . .'

Thorne wondered if perhaps there was more on offer than just a few tenners to cover the cost of a new door. Zarif had already admitted that Thorne was not the man he'd thought he was. Was he pushing a little, perhaps, trying to find out just what sort of a man Thorne *really* was . . . ?

Zarif's smile was returned with bells on. 'I think I'll let you owe me,' Thorne said.

Zarif shrugged and stepped towards the door. He held out a hand in front of him, beckoning Thorne to leave. Thorne pushed away from the counter and walked slowly back the way he'd come in. He felt the faintest flutterings of pride, but at the same time knew that he was kidding himself. He guessed that the feeling would probably not last as far as the pavement.

'Blood and money,' Thorne said.

'What?'

'You told me that you came to this country for bread and work. Blood and money. I think that's closer to the mark . . .'

Zarif stepped around Thorne and opened the door. The breeze began to stir the lanterns above their heads. Diamonds and stars of colour danced gently around the walls. 'That first time, when we talked about names, about what they meant, we talked about yours also,' Zarif said. 'Thorne. Small and spiky, and difficult to get rid of.'

Thorne remembered. 'It depends on how seriously you take that kind of thing.'

'I take my business *very* seriously . . .'

'Good, because I'd rather not see your face again, unless it's in a courtroom. I don't want to come back here, however good the food is.'

Zarif nodded. 'We understand each other.'

'Fuck me, no,' Thorne said. He caught Arkan Zarif's eye, and held it. 'Never.'

Thorne turned towards the street, opening his mouth to suck down the fresh air. A few seconds later, he heard the door close behind him with a gentle click.

He'd been right about the pride not lasting very long. It was a warm night, but Thorne was shivering as he walked back towards his car.

He imagined it . . . he *felt* it, as a frenzy of metal wire, tangled and tightly wound somewhere deep inside him. Each

408

time he'd managed to work a piece of it loose, he would pull at it in desperation, succeeding only in winding the coils even tighter, making the snarl that much harder to unravel . . .

Thorne had put some music on, then turned the volume down. He'd opened a bottle of wine and left it untouched. Nothing made it easier. Nothing helped him make sense of the mess, or understand his own part in creating it. There'd been so many bodies and so much grief, and so little to show for it.

He asked himself what else he could have expected. Hadn't he always known that the likes of *Baba* Arkan Zarif were fireproof? They had complex mechanisms in place that protected them, soldiers who would sacrifice themselves and any number of men and women on the right side of the law who would keep them untarnished. Still, the knowledge that nobody was answerable, that no one would pay for a fraction of the carnage, was horribly corrosive.

A few of Ryan's people were dead and a couple of Zarif's. Business had been hit on both sides. Life moved easily on, but not for Yusuf Izzigil, who'd lost both parents. Nor for the family of Francis Cullen, nor for Marcus Moloney's widow, whose name Thorne had never even bothered to learn . . .

And there were the other deaths, those for which, for good or evil, Thorne himself would always be responsible.

Billy Ryan and Wayne Brookhouse.

Thorne felt the knots inside tighten a little further. He thought about where lines were drawn. He wondered whether his had just moved further away, or if he'd long since overstepped it and was moving on. Moving to a much darker place where people couldn't quite make out his face and the lines had disappeared.

He looked at the telephone . . .

He closed his eyes and saw the face of Gordon Rooker. It was starting to regain its colour, the smugness reddening in the fresh air. Thorne saw the gold tooth catch the light as Rooker bought fruit from a market stall. As he sat with other men around a pub table. As he smiled at something he was reading in a magazine.

And there was always the burning girl.

Her arms windmilling as she tumbled through blackness towards the street.

Her face in the photograph her father had given him; the features ravaged, the smooth skin overwritten by rough, discoloured ridges.

Her voice in the diary. Funny and furious. Deserving to be listened to . . .

He got up from the sofa and walked across to the table near the front door . . .

He dialled a Wandsworth number and exchanged a few cursory pleasantries with the man on the other end. He made arrangements to return a diary and some photographs. Then, he told him to get a pen.

Gave him an address.

Thorne turned the music up then, and poured himself a drink. He sat back down on the sofa, pulled his feet up and considered the weight of his soul. He wondered if it might be possible to exercise it, to beef up the soul, to strengthen it by working out spiritually. If so, then bad deeds would surely *cost* you weight. Those who were truly wicked would wind up with souls that weighed next to nothing.

He reached for the wine bottle.

Wondering, in light of the phone call he'd just made, if his soul had gained a little weight. Or lost it.

MAY

IGNORANCE

THIRTY-THREE

It was the day before the Cup Final – a little over a month since the man who used to be known as Gordon Rooker had been found murdered by an intruder in his own home – when Thorne received the call . . .

Three weeks into May and it was gently drizzling. Everything else was equally as predictable.

While the Zarif and Ryan investigations had become little more than a couple of dozen boxes stacked on metal shelves at the General Registry, other cases had arrived to fill the void. Other victims that cried out for attention, that demanded action. There was never a shortage of rage, or lust, or greed. Or of bodies, when the chemistry that was there to control such things turned everyday feelings into something murderous.

Disfigured them.

Tom Thorne had read the *Murder Investigation Manual* in an hour and forgotten the whole thing almost as quickly. He knew he was adept at forgetting what didn't really matter; what there simply wasn't room for. Every day there were a thousand new pieces of information that needed good, clean space – that needed the chance, however slim, to move together, around and within one another, to spark and create the idea or the ghost of an idea that might just help to catch a killer.

But many other things were far from forgotten. They just got shifted around, crammed into smaller spaces in Thorne's head and in his heart. And in that other place that there wasn't really a name for, where the coils just got wound that little bit tighter . . .

On the couple of occasions he'd seen Carol Chamberlain, or spoken to her, they'd talked happily enough about their respective cases: his ongoing and hers long unsolved. Only their immediate past was jointly understood to be off limits.

Individually, and alone, it was far harder to escape.

Alison Kelly had phoned one afternoon and they'd talked for a few minutes. Thorne had asked her how she was. The talk had been so small, so pathetically prosaic, that he'd almost asked her *where* she was. As the time passed, he thought of her face and body less than he thought of the knife in her hand, but each time she came into his mind he thought of the inscription carved into the foundation stone of Holloway Prison, where she waited for the trial that was only a matter of weeks away:

'May God . . . make this place a terror to evil-doers.'

Thorne knew there was no God-given reason for Alison Kelly to be terrified . . .

Going home time. Sheltering beneath a concrete overhang in the car park of Becke House, Thorne breathed in the smoke from Holland's cigarette and watched the rain make a mess of the car he'd cleaned only that morning.

'Why don't you come round tomorrow?' Thorne asked. 'Watch the game with me and Phil . . .'

Despite Thorne's best efforts, Holland's enthusiasm for football was still no more than lukewarm. 'I can't get excited about it,' he said.

'Excited? It's the Cup Final . . .' Thorne was conjuring a tirade of sarcastic abuse when his phone rang.

Something in Eileen's voice froze the smirk on Thorne's face. Chased the blood from it.

'Tom . . .?'

'What's happened?'

Thorne started walking towards his car, his pace quickening with every second of silence that passed before Eileen spoke again.

'There was a fire . . .'

'Jesus, again?' Thorne used a shoulder to press the phone to his ear, dug frantically in his pockets for the car keys. 'Is he all right?'

From behind him, Thorne could hear Holland shouting something. Thorne raised a hand without turning. 'Eileen? Is he all right?'

'I'm sorry, Tom.' She started to cry. 'They found him in the bedroom.' She sounded like a small girl.

Thorne leaned hard against the car. He gasped out his pain, then smothered it quickly, before it became a scream. He was instantly all too aware of how much time he would have. He told himself that, now, Eileen needed to be comforted.

He yanked open the car door and climbed in. 'Eileen,

don't.' He stabbed the key into the ignition.

A fire . . .

He thought about the cooker he'd never got around to removing from his father's house. It would only have taken a phone call. Five minutes of his time. Victor would have been happy to take care of it. Eileen could have found someone to take the thing away, had *offered* to, but Thorne had promised that he'd get it organised.

He hadn't even put a lock on the kitchen door . . .

It was down to him.

'Where is he, Eileen? Where have they taken him?' Thorne listened carefully, but his aunt's words were fractured by sobs. 'It's OK, Eileen. I'm coming . . .'

Then another thought that hit him like a wrecking-ball. It smashed him back in his seat and held him there, his hand shaking against the steering wheel.

He pictured Arkan Zarif across a table, remembered what had been said when they'd talked about the deal to protect Gordon Rooker.

'An agreement which I fully intend to honour . . .'

The agreement had certainly involved a degree of protection. Could it also have included retribution should anything happen to Rooker.

Thorne was sure the tightness across his chest was all that was preventing the contents of his stomach rising into his mouth.

An accident, or one that had been arranged? Would they be able to tell which it was? Would Thorne ever *know* . . .?

Either way. Down to him . . .

He glanced to his right and saw a figure coming towards

the car, moving fast through the drizzle. Holland raised his hands, mouthing, '*Everything OK?*'

Thorne felt like he'd forgotten how to breathe.

He nodded slowly and started the car.

ACKNOWLEDGEMENTS

In researching this novel I learned a huge amount from two books in particular: *Gangland Britain* by Tony Thompson (Hodder & Stoughton 1995) and *Gangland Today* by James Morton (Time Warner Books 2002). My gratitude is due to both these authors.

For their time and patience I am once again grateful to DI Neil Hibberd, and to DCI Jim Dickey as well as to Richard Baldwin, the cemeteries manager for the London Borough of Camden. For their joke, I owe Phil Nichol and Carey Marx one large drink between them.

Enormous thanks are due to Vedat Suruk Deniz and his brother Sedat Suruk Deniz of the Archgate Café in London N19, for the warm welcome, the good advice and of course for the wonderful *sucuk*. For his extensive knowledge of the Turkish language and for help with matters of translation I have to thank Hikmet Pala.

At Time Warner it is high time I thanked David Young, Ursula Mackenzie, David Kent, Terry Jackson, Jess Clark (coincidental), Duncan Spilling, Richard Kitson, Nicola Hill, Andy Coles, John Turnbull, Robert Manser, Simon

Sheffield, Nick Ross, Richard Barker, Andrew Halley, Gill Midgley, Miles Poynton, Emily Sugarman, Nigel Andrews, Emma Fletcher and Rooney.

And of course, a debt is owed as always to: Sarah Lutyens, Susannah Godman, Lucinda Prain, Mike Gunn, Alice Pettet, Paul Thorne, Peter Cocks and Wendy Lee.

As ever the biggest thankyou goes to my wife Claire, for support and saintly patience.

And coffee.

An extract from Mark Billingham's exciting
new thriller

LIFELESS

Available in Little, Brown hardback in June 2005

PROLOGUE

The first kick wakes him and shatters his skull at the same time.

He begins to drift back towards unconsciousness almost immediately, but is aware of the intervals between each subsequent kick – though actually no more than a second or two – warping and stretching. It gives his brain, which is itself already beginning to swell, the time for one final, random series of thoughts and instructions.

Counting the kicks. Counting each smash of boot into flesh and bone. Counting the strange and, oh God, the glorious spaces in between.

Two . . .

Cold, in the early hours of the morning and damp. And the attempt to cry out is agonising as the message from the brain dances between the fragments of bone in what had once been his jaw.

Three . . .

Warm, the face of the baby in his hands. His baby. The face of the child before it grew and learned to despise him. Reaching in vain for the letter, dog-eared and greasy, in the inside pocket of his coat. The last link to the life he had before. Groping for it, his flappy fingers useless at the end of a broken arm.

Four . . .

Turning his head, trying to turn it away from the pain towards the wall. His face moving against the floor, the stubble-rasp like the breaking of faraway waves. Feeling the blood, warm and sticky between his cheek and the cold cardboard beneath. Thinking that the shadow he'd glimpsed, where the face of his attacker should have been, looked blacker than black. Slick, like tarmac after a shower. Thinking that it was probably a trick of the light.

Five . . .

Seeming to feel the tip of the boot as it breaks through the delicate network of ribs. Aware of it in there, stamping around, distorting his organs. Kidneys – are they his kidneys? – squeezed out of shape like water-filled balloons.

Sinking fast through six, seven and eight, their impact like crashes at a distant front door, vibrating through his shoulder and his back and the tops of his legs. The grunts and growls of the man standing above him, of the man who is kicking him to death, growing quieter and further away.

And, Christ, what a jumble, such a scramble of words. Riot of colours and sounds. All slipping away from him now. Fuzzing and darkening . . .

Thinking. Thinking that this was a terrible and desperate kind of thinking, if it could still be called such a thing. Sensing that the shadow had finally turned away from him. Luxuriating then, in the bliss as the space grew, as the knowing grew that, sweet Jesus, the kicking had finally stopped.

Everything so strange now, and shapeless and bleeding away into the gutter.

He lies quite still. He knows there's little point in trying to move. He holds on tight to his name and to the name of his only child. Wraps what's left of his mind around these two names, and around the name of the Lord.

Prays that he might cling on to the shape of these few, precious words until death comes.

ONE

He woke up in a doorway opposite Planet Hollywood, with a puddle of piss at his feet that was not his own, and the sickening realisation that this was real, that there was no soft mattress beneath him. He exchanged a few words with the police officer whose heavy hand had shaken him roughly awake. Began to gather up his things.

He raised his face slowly skywards as he started to walk, hoped that the weather would stay fine. He decided that the emptiness at the centre of him, which might have been simple fear, was probably even simpler hunger.

He wondered whether Paddy Hayes was dead yet. Had the young man charged with making the decision pulled the plug?

Moving through the West End as it shook away the sleep and slowly came to life was always a revelation. Each day he saw something he had never seen before.

Piccadilly Circus was glorious. Leicester Square was better than it looked. Oxford Street was even shittier than he'd thought it was.

There were still plenty of people about, of course.

Plenty of traffic. Even at this time the streets were busier than most others in the country would be during the rush hour. He remembered a film he'd seen on DVD, set in London after most of the population had been turned into crazed zombies by some plague. There were bizarre scenes where the whole city appeared to be utterly deserted, and to this day he didn't really know how they'd managed to do it. Computer tricks, like as not. This – the hour or so when the capital showered, shaved and shat – was about as close as it ever came. Far from deserted, but quite a few zombies shuffling about.

Most of the shops would be shut for another hour or two yet. Very few opened their doors before ten these days. The caffs and sandwich bars were already up and running, though. Hoping to pull in passing trade for tea and a bacon sandwich, for coffee and croissants, in much the same way that the burger vans and kebab shops had tempted those weaving their way home only a few hours earlier.

Tea and a sandwich. Normally he'd have spent the previous night gathering enough together to get himself something to eat, but today someone would be buying him breakfast.

Halfway along Glasshouse Street, a man in a dark green suit stepped out of a doorway in front of him and tried to pass. They moved the same way across the pavement, and back again. Smiled at each other, embarrassed.

'Nice morning for a dance . . .'

The sudden knowledge that he'd clearly encountered a nutcase caused the smile to slide off the man's face. He turned sideways and dropped his head. Shuffled quickly past muttering, 'Sorry' and, 'I can't . . .'

He hoisted his backpack higher on to his shoulder and carried on walking, wondering just what it was that the man in the suit couldn't do.

Return a simple greeting? Spare any change? Give a toss?

He walked up Regent Street, then took a right, cutting through the side streets of Soho towards Tottenham Court Road. A strange yet familiar figure, stepping in unison alongside him, caught his eye. He slowed then stopped, watching the stranger do the same thing.

He took a step forward and stared into the plate glass at the reflection of the man he'd become in such a short time. His hair seemed to be growing faster than usual, the grey more pronounced against the black. The neat-ish goatee he'd been cultivating had been subsumed under the scrubby growth that sprouted from his cheeks and spilled down his throat. His red nylon backpack, though already stained and grubby, was the only flash of real colour to be seen in the picture staring back at him from the shop window. The grease-grey coat and dark jeans were as blank, as *anonymous*, as the face that floated above them. He leaned towards the glass and contorted his features; pulling back his lips, raising his eyebrows, puffing out his cheeks. The eyes, though – and it was the man's eyes that told you *everything* – stayed flat and uninvolved.

A vagrant. With the emphasis on vague . . .

He turned from the window to see someone he recognised on the other side of the road. A young man – a boy – arms around his knees, back pressed against a dirty white wall, sleeping bag wrapped around his shoulders. He'd spoken to the boy a couple of nights before. Somewhere near the Hippodrome, he thought. Maybe outside one of the big cinemas in Leicester Square. He couldn't be certain. He did remember that the boy had spoken with a thick, north-east accent: Newcastle or Sunderland. Most of what the boy had said was indecipherable, rattled through chattering teeth at machine-gun speed. Head turning this way and that. Fingers grasping at his collar as he gabbled. So completely ripped on Ecstasy that it looked as though he was trying to bite off his own face.

He waited for a taxi to pass, then stepped into the road. The boy looked up as he approached and drew his knees just a little closer to his chest.

'All right?'

The boy turned his head to the side and gathered the sleeping bag tighter around his shoulders. The moisture along one side of the bag caught the light, and grey filling spilled from a ragged tear near the zip.

'Don't think there's any rain about . . .'

'Good,' the boy said. It was as much a grunt as anything.

'Staying dry, I reckon.'

'What are you, a fucking weatherman?'

He shrugged. 'Just saying . . .'

'I've seen you, haven't I?' the boy asked.

'The other night.'

'Was you with Spike? Spike and One-Day Caroline, maybe?'

'Yeah, they were around, I think . . .'

'You're new.' The boy nodded to himself. He seemed pleased that it was coming back to him. 'I remember you were asking some fucking stupid questions . . .'

'Been knocking about a couple of weeks. Picked a fucking stupid time, didn't I? You know, with everything that's going on?'

The boy stared at him for a while. He narrowed his eyes, then let his head drop.

He stood where he was, kicking the toe of one shoe against the heel of the other until he was certain that the boy had nothing further to say. He thought about chucking in another crack about the weather, making a joke of it. Instead, he turned back towards the road. 'Be lucky,' he said. He moved away, his parting words getting nothing in return.

As he walked north, it struck him that the encounter with the boy had not been a whole lot friendlier than the one earlier with the man in the green suit who'd been so keen to avoid him. The boy's reaction had been no more than he'd come to expect in the short time he'd spent living as he was now. Why should it have been? A wariness – a suspicion, even – was the natural reaction of *most* Londoners, whatever their circumstances. Those who lived and slept on the city's streets were naturally that bit more cautious when it came to strangers. It went without saying that anyone who wasn't abusing or avoiding them was to be viewed with a healthy degree of mistrust until they'd proved themselves. One way or another . . .

It was a lot like prison. Like the way a life was defined behind bars. And he knew a fair bit about how *that* worked.

Those who slept rough in the centre of London had a lot in common, he decided, with those sleeping in white-washed cells at Her Majesty's pleasure. Both were communities with their own rules, their own hierarchies and an understandable suspicion of outsiders. If you were going to survive in prison, you had to fit in; do what was necessary. You'd try not to eat shit, of course you would, but if that's what it took to get by, you'd tuck right in. What he'd seen of life since he began sleeping rough told him that things were pretty much the same on the streets.

The café was a greasy spoon with ideas above its station. The sort of place that thought a few cheap sandwich fillings in Tupperware containers made it a delicatessen. The reaction, within a minute or two of him shambling in, sitting down and showing no obvious intention of buying anything, was predictable.

'Hey!'

He said nothing.

'You going to order something?'

He reached across for a magazine that had been left on an adjacent table and began to read.

'This is not a dosshouse, you know.'

He smiled.

'You think I'm joking . . .?'

He nodded towards a familiar figure outside the window as the fat, red-faced proprietor came around the counter towards him. With impeccable timing, the man he'd been smiling at pushed through the door, just as the café owner was leaning in menacingly.

'It's OK, he's with me . . .'

The threatening expression on the proprietor's face softened, but only marginally, when he turned from the tramp's table and looked at the Metropolitan Police warrant card that was being thrust at him.

Detective Sergeant Dave Holland pocketed his ID,

reached across and dragged back a chair. 'We'll have two teas,' he said.

The man sitting at the table spoke in earnest. '*Mugs* of tea.'

The owner shuffled back towards the counter, somehow managing to sigh and clear his throat at the same time.

'My hero,' the tramp said.

Holland put his briefcase on the floor and sat down. He glanced round at the two other customers: a smartly dressed woman and a middle-aged man in a postal uniform. Back behind his counter, the owner of the place glared at him as he took a pair of white mugs from a shelf.

'He looked like he was ready to chuck you out if I hadn't come in just then. I was tempted to stand there and watch. See what happened.'

'You'd have seen me deck the fat fucker.'

'Right. Then I'd've had to arrest you.'

'That would have been interesting . . .'

Holland shrugged and pushed dirty-blond hair back from his forehead. 'Paddy Hayes died just after eleven-thirty last night,' he said.

'How's the son doing?'

'He was pretty upset beforehand. Wrestling with it, you know? Once he'd decided, once they turned off the machines, he seemed a lot calmer.'

'Probably only *seemed*.'

'Probably . . .'

'When's he going home?'

'He's getting a train back up north this morning,' Holland said. 'He'll be getting home around the time they start the PM on his old man.'

435

'Won't be too many surprises there.'

They both leaned back in their chairs as the tea arrived with very little ceremony. The fat man plonked down two sets of cutlery, wrapped in paper serviettes. He pointedly nudged a laminated menu towards each of them before turning to empty the ashtray on the adjoining table.

'You hungry?' Holland asked.

The man opposite glanced up from the menu he was already studying. 'Not really. I had a huge plate of smoked salmon and scrambled eggs first thing.' His eyes went back to the menu. 'Of *course* I'm fucking hungry.'

'All right . . .'

'I hope you've brought your chequebook. This could get expensive.'

Holland picked up his tea. He cradled the mug against his chin and let the heat drift up to his face. He stared through the narrow curtain of steam at the dishevelled figure sitting across from him. 'I still can't get used to this,' he said.

'What?'

'This. You.'

'*You* can't get used to it? Jesus!'

'You know what I mean. I just never imagined you anything like this. You were the last person . . . You *are* the last person . . .'

Tom Thorne dropped his menu and crossed stained fingers above it. The decision made, he stared hard across the table.

'Things change,' he said.